A WELL-MADE BED

A Well-Made Bed

ABBY FRUCHT & LAURIE ALBERTS

RED HEN PRESS | PASADENA, CA

Book design and layout by Selena Trager

Library of Congress Cataloging-in-Publication Data

Names: Frucht, Abby. | Alberts, Laurie, author.
Title: A well-made bed / Abby Frucht, Laurie Alberts.
Description: First edition. | Pasadena, CA : Red Hen Press, 2016.
Identifiers: LCCN 2015036129 | ISBN 9781597093057 (softcover)
Subjects: LCSH: Female friendship—Fiction. | Drug traffic—Fiction.
| BISAC:
 FICTION / Literary. | GSAFD: Black humor (Literature)
Classification: LCC PS3556.R767 W45 2016 | DDC 813/.54—dc23
LC record available at http://lccn.loc.gov/2015036129

The Los Angeles County Arts Commission, the National Endowment
for the Arts, the Pasadena Arts & Culture Commission and the City of
Pasadena Cultural Affairs Division, Sony Pictures Entertainment, the
Los Angeles Department of Cultural Affairs, the Dwight Stuart Youth
Fund, and the Ahmanson Foundation partially support Red Hen Press.

First Edition
Published by Red Hen Press
www.redhen.org

ACKNOWLEDGMENTS

Thanks to the assorted technologies (despite their dark sides) for allowing us to write this book together while living a thousand miles apart.

A portion of this novel first appeared in *Numéro Cinq*.

For A and J and J and A and C.

—Abby Frucht

For Tom and Becky.

—Laurie Alberts

CONTENTS

PROLOGUE

Pauline, 1989 1

I

WILD LIFE

Jaycee, 2010 9

Noor, 2010 32

Jaycee & Noor, 2010 47

II

A COOL DRINK OF WATER

Hilary Emory, 1980 91

Jeff Parmenter, 1989 103

Hil, 2010 121

III

THE JUMP

Jaycee, 2010 127

Noor, 2010 141

Hil, 2010 165

IV

HUNGER MOUNTAIN

Noor, 2010 171

Jaycee, 2010 183

Noor, 2010 196

V

THINGS LIVE ON EACH OTHER

Hil, 2011 217

Jeff Parmenter, 2011 221

VI

BLISS ROAD

Noor, 2011 237

Jaycee, 2011 245

Hannah, 2011 249

Hilary Emory, 1982 254

VII

NOT YOU AND ME

Noor, Jaycee 2011 273

EPILOGUE

Noor, 2013 299

A WELL-MADE BED

Pauline, 1989

Pauline stopped to adjust her sweatpants as the other kids made their way out of dress rehearsal. Her friend Noor stalled in the cloakroom, frowning at the prospect of walking home.

"My parents wouldn't want me to walk home at night," Noor said.

"Not night, twilight," Pauline corrected, since that's what her dad called it. She knew the only reason they'd be walking was that her dad's car was in the shop again. Noor's parents had a Lexus because they were doctors but Noor's mother had driven it to her job at the hospital while Noor's father stayed home on North Street to cook supper for the girls, so walking it was.

Their matching costumes, made of brown sweatshirts and sweatpants on which had been sewn an abundance of oversized maple and oak leaves cut from four colors of felt, had been the hit of all the costumes in dress rehearsal, not because of the sewn-on leaves, so much, but for the actual tree limbs with actual dried-out leaves still barely clinging to them. The lopped-off branches were to be waved back and forth when you were on stage, as if a wind were blowing, or shaken so hard that some of the dead leaves might flutter into the faces of tomorrow night's audience. They would need to pluck fresh branches along the way to Noor's this evening, though it was getting more difficult to find branches with leaves—only the oaks still had them. That was another reason for walking—to look for fresh branches, Pauline's dad said.

Pauline watched the parents file out of the gym with their kids, on the way to their safe, warm, reliable cars. A lot of the kids were still wearing their costumes for warmth, she surmised, or maybe only for fun. "Don't be such a baby," Pauline added, as they headed up College Street.

Noor sulked and Pauline resolved to be nicer after that. Noor was younger by six months, and Pauline was mature for her age. Everyone said so.

"It will be fun walking in twilight," Pauline's dad said. "You can be walking, talking trees, and you'll be warm with those leaf hoods." He pulled his yellow stocking cap so far down you couldn't see his orange hair, which meant he was upset about something he didn't want to talk about. Pauline's hair was a streakier, darker shade of red than that of the Shattuck side of the family and so long she could sit on it. Everyone always told her how pretty it was.

"My parents are really going to be mad," Noor whispered.

She was in a grumpy mood anyway since Pauline was invited to a party Saturday night but Noor wasn't. It was a movie sleepover. Pauline had said yes at her mom's urging, even if going might be an act of disloyalty to her friend. "How many times does Noor go to movies with her parents that we can't take you to?" her mom had said in. "Besides, Noor's parents don't let her go to sleepovers."

"Don't dawdle girls," Pauline's dad said.

Both girls lifted their tree branches higher and picked up the pace, leaving the last of the street lights behind.

"We're going the wrong way," Noor kept saying.

"Don't worry about it, it's just another way home," Pauline explained. What Noor meant was they weren't going down State Street as their mothers would have gone, for Pauline's dad thought it more adventurous to go up—up past the cooking school, past a trio of half-open, dented mailboxes.

When the sidewalk disappeared, Noor took hold of Pauline's elbow, struggling not to drop her branches, resisting every step, and in fairness Pauline couldn't blame her. In the cold sky, the mountains crouched and seemed to roll nearer. The shoulder of the road was just gravel and dead weeds. Invisible horses snorted in a pasture as if they knew how Noor feared their enormous faces. The few cars that passed them swung wide to give them room.

Noor let go of Pauline's arm, lagging behind as they tackled the hill.

"The sidewalk would be even more slippery if we took the route down State Street," Pauline's dad said, making no sense, because the road wasn't in the least bit slippery, and besides, there was no sidewalk left.

"Try to keep up with us, Noor. Walk a little faster. You can do it," Pauline pleaded, supposing she might be more appropriately cast, in life, as Noor's babysitter than as her classmate, friend, or fellow tree. After all, she was getting calls to babysit already, like for the Emory girl whose mother had phoned Pauline a few months ago to ask if Pauline "might spend some time with Jacqueline Charlotte." Since then, she had been there a bunch of times. Unlike Pauline's parents, the Emorys went to cocktail parties and dinner engagements, which were plentiful if you were a famous children's book author and the famous children's book author's wife and illustrator, Mrs. Emory bragged. Pauline and Jacqueline Charlotte were in the same grade, Mrs. Emory had added, or would be if Jacqueline Charlotte were not home-schooled, so you wouldn't exactly call it babysitting.

The first night Pauline had babysat, it was clear the minute you met her that Jaycee—her name was Jaycee, not "pathetic Jacqueline Charlotte," she'd told Pauline—wasn't friendless only because she was home-schooled and held her gym class on a rickety stationary bike with an hourglass for timing, but because of her off-putting stumpy figure, her weird, old-fashioned outfits, and a habit of scrunching her eyebrows. Jaycee's living room was crowded with a floor loom and a spinning wheel smudged with fingerprints. The house smelled like moss and lanolin, and Jaycee was wearing a Little House on the Prairie skirt and top.

"Do you really spin wool and weave or is it only in your mom's pictures?" Pauline asked.

"My mom does it most. But I can teach you."

"Next time," Pauline said. She stopped herself from reaching to smooth Jaycee's mussed eyebrows.

"Didn't you bring any magazines?" Jaycee asked. "I never get to read any."

Pauline shrugged and turned the pages of one of Jaycee's dad's books, The Good Egghead, about a really dumb chicken who laid the tastiest eggs that made the best Three Egg Cake in the valley. The Emorys' picture books all had valleys in them. Pauline recognized some of the titles from elementary school, but the valleys held more wildflowers than any valleys she had seen.

"Haven't you read these a million times?" Pauline asked.

Jaycee shrugged. "We could make tea," she said, throwing down her own book but then rearranging it more properly on the coffee table. She jumped up for the kitchen. She had Home Economics class in there, she told Pauline. She'd made boiled cookies last week. With excitement she unscrewed the lid on a sourdough starter and held the surprisingly fruity concoction to Pauline's nose.

"I've never had sourdough," Pauline said. Jaycee gaped at her as if she had confessed to having never tasted bread.

"Let me make the tea," said Pauline, but Jaycee jerked away the tea kettle.

"Just because you're the baby sitter doesn't mean I can't boil water," she protested. "I do it all the time."

Pauline supposed this made sense.

Now they had a composting toilet, new last year, Jaycee explained. Until then they'd used the outhouse. And they had a stove and no longer cooked on a fireplace. But their enamel cups burned Pauline's fingers when she drank.

"Your mom told me you're eleven, right?" she asked Jaycee.

"Just about, but I skipped a grade," Jaycee said.

"How can you skip a grade if you're—" Pauline stopped herself from saying *if you're not in school.* She felt awkward to be the baby-sitter of a girl practically her own age, not to mention one who lived like her own great great-grandparents had, but Jaycee felt awkward too, she reminded herself. Who wouldn't? Imagining she might do Jaycee some good by acting more compassionately toward her, Pauline had accepted Jaycee's request to exchange locks of hair, though what she'd do with a clump of Jaycee's frizz she didn't know.

"You're a pretty girl. We could use you," Jaycee's father, Mr. Emory, had said. He meant, Pauline had come to understand, that Mrs. Emory could use her green eyes and long red hair in one or two of their picture books. Jaycee, or rather a less frumpy version of her, was in lots of their pictures. Pauline felt sad that the girl's own parents made the pictures of their daughter prettier than the real Jaycee.

The strangest thing, though flattering, was that Mrs. Emory had ended up sketching Pauline's face from memory, copying her long red hair and her green eyes and even her posture. Pauline found the picture just last week while snooping in the study. Now, walking home from play rehearsal, she resolved to ask for portrait payment next time she babysat.

"Come on," she said again to Noor.

"But if we walk right next to each other our branches get tangled," Noor objected.

"I'll walk on the road side," said Pauline's dad. "Then Pauline you take my hand and Noor, you put your branches down and hold Pauline's hand. We can get you another branch tomorrow."

"But you're walking too fast," said Noor, inventing new problems with every breath.

"We'll walk slower," Pauline encouraged. She couldn't wait to be grown, or rather grow into her grown-up self, the way a puppy grows into its paws. She put both of her branches in one hand, then used her empty hand to reach for Noor's.

"I can't hold both branches in one hand," said Noor, ignoring Pauline's dad's instructions to lay them down. "I have to hold one each."

Noor held the branches straight up, her arms higher than must have been comfortable. It was not quite totally dark out yet. Just dusk. Or maybe just past dusk.

"My parents wouldn't like me walking on the side that's close to the road," she complained, "but I don't want to walk on the other side, either, 'cause it's closer to the horses." The moon climbed higher, a sliver moon that, if Pauline held her branches in front of her eyes, appeared closer than if she didn't.

"We're almost there," Pauline soothed her friend. Pauline's dad often took her on strange excursions, like going through the Capitol Building instead of past it on the sidewalk if they were walking downtown, and even, once, along the aisle in the movie theater and out the other side into daylight again, just so she would never feel lost no matter where she found herself. Still, he wasn't like Noor's dad, smelling comfortingly of the cardamom pods he ground in their kitchen Saturday mornings. Maybe if Pauline listened hard enough she would hear him frying tonight's pakoras. She had excellent hearing. A dog barked in the distance, and someone yelled "Roscoe, get in here." In the silence that followed she caught the sound of a car pulling near on the road behind them, and soon the funnels of light came zigzagging around, careening. Everybody out of the way! Pauline thought, but then there didn't seem to be an out of the way.

"Shit!" said her dad. He never swore.

A cone of yellow light surrounded them. Noor's branches whirled like tops, then disappeared. There was no screeching of brakes. There was no screech at all.

PART I

Wild Life

CHAPTER ONE

Jaycee, 2010

"You are deceiving me, yes, that you were born in New York City?" Frida insisted.

Jaycee's seatmate on LAN flight #2513 Miami to Lima was a buoyant thirty-something who worked for a small cultural exchange operation based in Miami. Although she lived in Lima with her husband and their six-year-old son, she traveled to and from Miami once a month to touch base with the rest of the staff. She was perfect for the job. Despite the flight being a red eye—it had left Miami at 7:00 p.m. and was due to arrive in Lima after 4:00 a.m.—the wide-awake Frida seemed determined to take Jaycee under the wing of her gregarious generosity. But even though Frida's insistence that Jaycee couldn't possibly have been born in New York City was meant to be a compliment, it only pissed Jaycee off.

"Hungary? Bulgaria!" Frida guessed, laughing with mischief and delight when pressed for ideas about where Jaycee appeared to be from, as if Jaycee had been mistaken all her life about being born in New York City and moving to Vermont when her dad got famous enough to quit his day job. Jaycee was mortified, as much by her own annoyance as by Frida herself. She'd always known she looked like a serf in a kerchief with child-bearing hips thriving on a diet of hard, green potatoes from burlap sacks, but no one had ever been so rash as to say as much.

Still she only played along, saying, "Me? Bosnia-Herzegovina?" not wanting to turn her seatmate away. Not many people took to Jaycee like Frida did. It was as if Frida thought she recognized Jaycee from a previous flight on a different airplane, or, better yet, as if they knew each other by sharing a whole other plane of existence, like in addition to being airline passengers on their way to Lima, they were dolls side by side in a toy chest somewhere, their mouths pin-tucked in red embroidery thread, silenced until the here and now. Besides, Frida was pretty. Jaycee had always longed for a pretty friend, especially because, being homeschooled, she hadn't known many girls her age. The pretty ones had tended either to ignore her or be extra kind. Or worse, she remembered, thinking back to her babysitter, they died. Even the plain girls had viewed Jaycee with uncertainty, perhaps seeing their worst fears manifest in her coarse, pebbly, hand-knitted sweaters, and the ox manure stuck to the soles of her shoes.

You couldn't ever outgrow things completely, though. The old name, Jacqueline Charlotte, was still on her passport, and the wire-rimmed spectacles chosen by her father, which crisscrossed all things seen and unseen, remained her only accessory. Despite her dislike of them, she never forgot the debate she waged with her dad when she was a teen demanding her first, way overdue, pair of eyeglasses. "Most ordinary Americans didn't wear eyeglasses in the mid-nineteenth century," he'd claimed with an aggrieved air, as if, rather than showing his anger at her challenge to his parental authority in the matter of her clothing, he chose to reveal a truer, less negotiable unhappiness instead, that of his bruised, incorrigible ego. "So when you're working you'll need to do without any glasses at all, wire-rims or horn-rims, it doesn't matter. For authenticity's sake," he commanded, meaning, for the sake of his ragged stretch of pasture with six outbuildings that passed as Hillwinds Living History Books, or better yet, for his own sake. Jaycee argued that she wouldn't be able to see what she was shelving, honey or peppermint soap, much less do her homework, and that she would look less modern in granny glasses than without them.

"Without glasses, people will think she's wearing contact lenses," her mother, Hannah, agreed, taking Jaycee's side more bravely than she ever took her own side, and knowing how proud her husband was of his own contact lenses, which he claimed to wear only on book tours.

"You fly many times too?" Frida asked. In addition to her wedding band she wore a large, pronged gumball ring, which she explained her son had given her, both rings on one finger. Otherwise she was unadorned except by nature and classic taste in simple clothing: a brushed linen blazer, slacks, and trim boots.

"I've only flown three times," Jaycee answered. Once to an uncle's funeral, once with her dad to a book fair in Cleveland, and once on a half-hour flight to a conference where Hil was Guest of Honor in creepy Chautauqua. She had never seen her uncle before she faced him in his coffin, and in Cleveland she'd sat at a table selling stacks of Hil's chapter books to kids her age who looked desperate to escape their well-meaning parents and hang out at the mall, and at Chautauqua Hil's claim to being Guest of Honor was belied by there being countless other authors all teaching writing workshops in poorly air-conditioned rooms that smelled like the hot dogs for sale in the cafeteria, hot dogs that Jaycee wasn't allowed to eat.

After making this embarrassing admission, Jaycee toyed with the idea of pretending to need to go to the bathroom and finding an empty seat in the rear of the plane, maybe next to the screaming baby or the deaf man she'd stood near in line, since what was the point of having your first adventure if all you did was talk about the life you'd left behind? Since this trip really was her first adventure, marking her first time away from Hillwinds and her parents, she really didn't know if having an adventure meant you kept jumping from one place to another whenever you felt like it or bore things out a while to see what became of you wherever chance put you. She opted to see what chance had in store for her, here next to Frida on the flight to Lima. She had nothing to lose; she had only to gain. Things big and small—things good or bad—would come to her, things that had nothing to do with Vermont. It would be like her mother's tatting, a constellation of knots amid polished threads. Jaycee's parents didn't know where she was going. She'd told them only she was taking the bus to Burlington to attend a costume making class, and then she really did go to a costume shop and purchased a bonnet so as not to have been lying, but after that she got a cab to the airport and ate oatmeal at the friendly little diner-type place overlooking the runways, which was what her parents would want her to eat, especially since she was buying it on their debit card.

"You and your family have hobbies?" Frida asked. Her English was practically perfect, the sole irregularity an absence of nuance that made for unabashed truth-telling, like when she said of her husband "Arturo I trust him maybe too much. And maybe too I love him more than I like him. Why am I telling you this?"

"Trab-a-hey at park histo-ri-ca," Jaycee plodded, ashamed of herself for having failed to bone up on her miserable Spanish. It seemed rude to speak English just because Frida spoke it so well, so Jaycee hoped to appear as if she were trying to meet her halfway. Only what could be worse than to mix and match her misbegotten syllables with pidgin English and sidestep Frida's question along the way? *Did* Jaycee have hobbies? She wasn't sure. It was hard to tell hobbies from normal activities when you worked as the events planner/docent/craftsperson/storyteller/seamstress/role-player not to mention babysitter at your dad's *Park Historica* for a supposed living. Was picking wool a hobby? Was kiln firing a hobby or was it part of her job? How about running the lambs amid the dandelions with the kindergarten visitors, or avoiding the stationary bicycle by doing jumping jacks instead? Were these things recreational activities or were they only her so-called life at Hillwinds? And how about catering to her father's ego? Was that life or was it only work, work, work, she wondered, taking one of Frida's pretzels by mistake.

Did she even *have* a life? The idea that she had a family gave her the willies. She loved them, but she hated them. She resented them and she begrudged them and she wished she'd never met them but now that she was thousands of miles away from them she felt a speck of renewed forbearance of them. Still she didn't like to think of them being a family, her and her parents and the sixteen-going-on-fifty-one farm cats and the scores of dead mice and her dad's narcissism, which seemed like a whole other breed of animal even as she stroked it, groomed it, and always—like her mom, for Jaycee and her mom were in this Hillwinds thing together—appeased it.

"Do *you* have hobbies?" she asked Frida.

"Oh, yes, I have hobbies!" Frida said. She seemed surprised to be asked. Perhaps she hadn't been asking Jaycee about hobbies at all. Maybe her English was worse than it sounded. Maybe Frida had asked her, "Do you have babies?" or, "Do you fuck cabbies?"

Jaycee paused in her thinking, pleased by her own vocabulary. She never used the word "fuck." Although she'd heard the old Buddhist—or was it Taoist—saying, that no matter where you go, you're still your old boring self (or maybe it was Alcoholics Anonymous who said that, she thought, recalling her bygone fiancée, Mike, coming home from a meeting reciting lines from the "Big Book"), she intended to prove the saying wrong. She would not remain her modest, too obedient self, perfumed in Eau de Lanolin and Essence de Milk. She longed to misbehave. Would she enjoy being bad? Or would she prefer to spend the rest of her days teaching second grade field trippers how to candle eggs? There seemed to be no middle ground.

Saying she wanted to click on some photos of her husband and son, Frida bent forward to dig for her phone, the gumball ring catching on the the zipper of her carry-on.

"Oh wait," she remembered. "No phones on planes! But I wanted to show you my family. We bull fight for our hobby," she said, handing over an elegant, linen stock business card that read in gold lettering in Spanish and English: Cultural Exchange International, Frida C. Amez Carbajal, along with the impressive title, Director of Speakers Series.

"You have card?" Frida asked.

Jaycee said no. Bullfighting indeed. It tickled her to suppose that despite the countless differences between her and her comely seatmate with the broad, open brow and fresh, warm smile, Frida, like Jaycee, had learned to be wary of bulls in the pasture. The closest things to bulls at Hillwinds were two placid, draft oxen of the Randall Lineback breed, trained at the yoke since five months old. They wouldn't trample you if you crawled underneath them and poked fun at where their testicles would be if only they weren't castrated, but the gaggles of schoolchildren Jaycee led through the split rail fence to pet them (no cameras allowed) appreciated her pretense of fear.

"Yes. We don't hurt them we just tease them," said Frida, and then without another word she dropped off to sleep, her head on Jaycee's shoulder.

Jaycee didn't dare fidget, not even to get up to go to the bathroom. She was grateful she wouldn't be required to explain her own reason for traveling to Peru, which seemed flimsy now that she was on her way. Aside from being desperate to get away from Hillwinds, her plan was to visit Enrique Escobar Castillo, whom she had known for a year when they were fifteen and sixteen years old, respectively. Enrique had somehow been expected to be a girl. He had been among three exchange students in Montpelier that year, and was considered fortunate to have been matched with the unusual Emorys. Jaycee pitied him for it. The other exchange students stayed with families that sent their kids to real school.

After less than a month of Jaycee's mother's homeschooling, Enrique caught on to what he was missing. Learning English, for one thing, since Jaycee's mother insisted they struggle to communicate in Spanish. In protest, he refused to complete the cemetery lesson which had been Jaycee's favorite of her mother's annual excursions. You learned a lot about demographics simply by reading the headstones, like how many babies people needed to have to make up for how many babies died, and all the women who died in childbirth and the men who were killed in wars, and the waves of deaths from flu epidemics and whole families gone in a single day from fire, murder, measles, or food poisoning. Enrique was crushed to see the chalky little markers used for infants, since he was already counting on fathering five kids. The cemeteries in his town were in walls, not in the ground, he added via hand gestures, and it gave him the shivers to step on the graves. He longed for regular teachers and intramural sports—the one time Jaycee had been allowed to join some public school girls at Pre-Teen Basketball Night at the Rec. Center on Barre Street, there was a vast, dark gymnasium that took ten minutes for the lights to go on after the attendant flipped the switch, and then, when Jaycee got a basket, she cheered herself so hard her bonnet fell off. Enrique wanted the American school cafeteria lunches of which the other exchange students bragged when he saw them at gatherings, and what he seemed to imagine were mile-long chalkboards. Too, there would be señoritas. So although he kept living at Jaycee's house, he was spared the home-schooling and allowed to attend U 32 in East Montpelier, his dark head gleaming with excitement as if already on the lookout for the mother of his children. He and Jaycee maintained a cousin-like fondness, or what Jaycee imagined it would be like to be hot for your own cousin who hardly knew you existed. She hadn't even been allowed to accompany Enrique to Ben & Jerry's Ice Cream factory with the other high school kids. "Why pay for your cavities when you can get them at home for free?" her mom had said. "Besides, we could churn ice cream here if we wanted," she added, making Jaycee stay home and starch aprons instead. Enrique fit in better with the other Vermont kids than Jaycee did, and all of them knew it. She'd never blamed him for that. She'd enjoyed setting his plate at the rough-hewn kitchen table and crossing his path amid the baskets of spindles crowding her parents' living room.

This trip to Peru, she supposed today, was to atone for all the deeds that she and Enrique had never performed together and all the things they had never even tried and failed to say to each other. But these undone things might not come to much, she feared. Really, her parents should be the ones to atone for keeping their daughter the way they'd kept her, her hair heavily parted like Emily Dickinson's and, though they watched *Masterpiece Theater* in their bedroom, they hadn't allowed her any TV until she turned eighteen. At least they'd paid for Jaycee's airfare, albeit unknowingly, thinking they were paying her Hillwinds-related expenses in Burlington, her dad handing over his public library card for use at ATMs.

"This is a public library card, Dad," she had said. "You can use library cards in ATMs too?" She honestly didn't know. Neither did her father.

"Uhhh . . ." he said, until her mom broke in with, "Give me his wallet. Let's hope he still has his debit card."

In their shared agitation over her bus trip to Burlington, her addled parents treated her like she was first in the family going to college . . . although she never did go to college. She had never even taken her GED. She blamed this on her dad, modifying her resentment of him with the encouraging thought that, even as a child, she'd been shown the very worst of him. His foolish need for control, his outdated airs, his embarrassing clothing pinned to the clothesline alongside her own and that of her mom—he couldn't get any worse than he already was.

And finally, now, she would be seeing *the world*. And the world, or Enrique, would see her. She tried turning her neck without waking Frida, glancing along the aisle past the heads of sleeping passengers to where the airplane's oval window covers were pulled firmly shut.

In exchange for her work as Events Planner, Skits Director, and everything else at Hillwinds, Jaycee received room and board (or as her bygone fiancé, Mike, used to call it, "cot and potatoes"), the ungainly family Buick to drive to the supermarket, and, now that Hillwinds wasn't faring quite as poorly as expected in this rocky economy since a few of the tourists who might otherwise have toured castles in Ireland came there instead, she also received a paltry monthly allowance of which the value fluctuated less predictably than the numbers of visitors. There'd been several improvements to Hillwinds in the years since the motley theme park first came into being, like the opening of the gift shop, The Maple Jug Mercantile, which was managed by Mrs. Emory, who did little but chat up the customers from her perch behind the register. Hannah delegated all grunt work to Jaycee, including the Sisyphean task of getting her from the house to the shop in her wheelchair, a daily activity involving so much weight-bearing exercise that Jaycee reasoned it would prohibit her own bone loss even postmortem. Another improvement was the outfitting of the role-playing studio, but although they were finally booking tours to the optimistically scheduled opening of the set for *Mabel's Stirrups*, which like all Hil's reprints featured the Living History Books logo cross-stitched on the cover, Jaycee's purchase of the props, cue cards, soundtrack, costumes and accessories would now have to wait for her return to Burlington.

Since Jaycee was never paid actual wages, she never had to hassle with either paying, withholding, or cheating on taxes. And although she'd built up no social security and acquired no credit rating, it was true she'd never wanted. She thought of her life in just those words, *never wanted*, words she might include in the Hillwinds brochure describing the village idiot. It was foolish to want, when you had all you needed, including a tussle behind the blacksmith shop with one of the teachers chaperoning a school group, which made for disarmingly agreeable memories even though sometimes it still hurt where he'd bitten her toe. How pathetic to be getting by on memories, though, when there were more years ahead of her than there were behind. Still it wasn't the years that interested her now; it was the days, the week, her planned visit with Enrique. He was way more experienced than she was in all sorts of ways. Widowed young, he had two of his five planned kids already and managed a row of new high-rise apartments across from El Parque del Amor in Miraflores, Lima, which overlooked the cliffs dropping into the Pacific. The name meant Love Park, Jaycee knew from her guidebook, and it featured an oversize statue of two lovers engaged in a prelude to heavy petting.

Jaycee punched open the ashtray on her seat arm, as if looking for the remains of a long-departed passenger who had been lucky enough to be a smoker before they outlawed it on planes. Maybe Enrique would help put her on Facebook. She wasn't even online. She had needed to make all her plans with Enrique on one of a row of PCs at the library, and it had taken her weeks to figure out she didn't need to use the same PC each time. It had been all she could do to persuade her dad to authorize the purchase of the old, used Gateway, which didn't even have a disc drive. What did Hil want? That they hire a flock of scribes to do publicity? At least he was growing more malleable with age, she reflected, recalling the peculiar thing Hil said to her last night when she stepped outside her house. He was sitting on the stoop, spit-polishing his shoe buckles with his shirt hem. She wondered if he knew how earnest he looked while engaged in small acts of self-preservation, as if he feared that a tarnished buckle might tarnish his reputation. "Uhhh . . . I do feel that we might have considered this setback yesterday or the day before," he said.

"Considered what setback, Dad?" she asked, holding open the door with one hip while dragging out her luggage, which had no wheels, in preparation for her early morning trip to Boston.

Instead of answering, her father rose and wandered onto the Hillwinds Living History Books property, which Mike once dubbed *The Compound*. In Hannah's pictures for Hil's books—*Together the children snow-shoed to School*, a caption might read—the trees looked sturdier and more cheerful than they ever looked at Hillwinds, and the snow looked cozy and bright where it blanketed the outbuildings. But Jaycee's dad had the flu all through last winter, so it fell on Jaycee to shovel, plow, stoke the stoves, repair the snowshoes, do the sugaring, and make the shopping trips to town when her mom's legs were hurting.

"What setback, Dad?" she called again.

She meant, which setback in particular? All of the above? Or were there other setbacks she didn't know about yet?

But the old man just drifted back to the yard until eventually he bumped into the clothesline, from which hung a few sleep shirts and Jaycee's flannel nightgown. Then he backed up, paused, and aimed right for the nightgown, causing it to fall to the grass below. He'd used to joke with his daughter by clowning like this, reversing direction as if he were a car, shifting to neutral before revving recklessly forward again, but tonight the performance was more antic and sad than usual, and now that she thought of it, her dad did seem, lately even more himself than he was before. More abstract, she meant, more loopy, less in touch with the world. Finally she shouted, "Good Night, Dad! See you when I get back from Burlington!" supposing he wouldn't remember where she was going anyway.

Not until the plane touched ground at Jorge Chavez International Airport did Frida stir, lifting her damp head off Jaycee's shoulder. Amid the bustle of deplaning and catching up again briefly at baggage after rushing for a ladies room, the only thing the new friends had time for was Frida's photo. It showed Frida, Frida's good-looking husband, Arturo, and their little boy, Hugo, posing in an actual bullfighting ring waving red capes at an actual bull with bows on his horns.

"Oh my god! It's a class you take! Like ballroom dancing?"

"Yes. Only dancing is not half as good for marriage as bull fighting." Frida smiled.

After customs, Jaycee dragged her luggage over to an official-looking box that she could only hope was an ATM. She had used the ATM in Montpelier only a couple of times, and once, with the fifty bucks it gave her, plus some scrimped-up allowance, she'd succumbed to an experimental burst of vanity and had her first and, so far, only manicure, during which the manicurist gestured at Jaycee's eyebrows and asked if she would like those done as well. Jaycee hadn't understood. Did she want her eyebrows *done?* Polished? Filed? The manicurist waxed them, then gestured at Jaycee's upper lip. "Do what you think is necessary," Jaycee allowed. That was six years ago already, when she was twenty-six. At thirty-two she wished she'd made the leap again and had her whole self *done* at the airport in Miami.

Jaycee pulled out the debit card and hesitated, worried the Peruvian version of the machine might wrest the card away from her. She had enough cash to last her a day or so, but it seemed important to learn right away that she would succeed in this crucial, inelegant task. Though she had hoped that when she hit foreign soil, she might escape the running commentary of her parents' directives, so far they still cluttered up her head. *Don't put the debit card in the slot for receipts. Shield the keyboard from view when you punch in your PIN.* Jaycee glanced right and left. Aside from a handful of arriving tourists wandering around with backpacks and bleary, 4:00 a.m. expressions, the vast room was nearly empty but for a lady in a shower cap and rubber gloves pushing a trash bucket. The sad thing was Jaycee's parents hadn't even said those things. Their dictates, this time, were her own invention.

Spanish or English, the ATM asked?

She pressed the button for English.

Soles or dollars?

Her finger hovered over the button for twenty soles, the smallest sum offered, equivalent to roughly seven dollars, and then darted to the button for 500 soles before settling on a button in between. The machine appeared to think about it a minute, but in the end it dealt the money like a smooth hand of cards. All in all she was pleased. It was easier to get money from this grimy monstrosity than it was from her dad. She dragged her luggage outside to a funny little stall selling sundries in the dark, deciding to wait for Enrique's advice on some moony looking cheeses with buttery rinds the size of throw cushions. She bypassed some Cadbury bars and a packaged twist of dough incorrectly labeled *CRUELLER,* and selected a candy bar—nougat probably—whose label she couldn't decipher. With both hands, the shopkeeper snapped the bill taut and scanned it for flaws with acute perspicacity. Everybody in Peru checked both sides of all bills for counterfeit, Jaycee soon learned. Maybe even the thieves who robbed the tourist busses paused before fleeing, to vet their catch. Pairs of thieves worked the airport, according to the US State Department Travel Advisory she'd downloaded at the library. Or worse, the cabbie drove you to a devastated outskirt and threatened to leave you crouching amid the rabid feral dogs if you didn't fork over. But Enrique had been thoughtful enough to arrange for a hotel driver, who stood at some distance waving a sign with her name on it.

She pressed her face to the window of the cab, determined not to fall asleep on her first unbroken dawn in what really did look like *the world,* that is, the vast, sepulchral, but strangely bustling place she had half expected never to discover on leaving Vermont.

Peeling posters flapped on pitted walls. Hunks of concrete lined the road where it swung along cliffs overlooking a beach on which black waves swirled past a flimsy pier. Past the tall glass doors of Hotel Tiki she could see a clerk sprawled on an orange vinyl couch in a grim little lobby. Jaycee gave him her name, feeling so heavy with sleeplessness all of a sudden that she found herself eyeing the shiny couch. What was taking him so long to give over her key? Was there a problem with her reservation?

No, everything was good, the desk clerk answered. But then why did he go on standing there, fingering the key on its wooden anchor, unwilling either to hand it to her or lead her up the scary, open stairway to her room? Around them vibrated the waning pulse of the next door nightclub at closing hour. Maybe he wanted his tip in advance, seeing as her luggage had no wheels.

"Es problemo? Necessito sleepo pronto. Yo morte. If no sleep, I'll die," she insisted, noting how basic her feelings became when she needed to try to speak them in Spanish. "Domage," she tried. "Necessito domage! Et aqua aussi," confusing her two half-languages with a third invented dialect. "I desire a wet egg," she might be saying. The clerk nervously eyed his 1950s style telephone, a more contemporary style than in Jaycee's parents' house.

"I'll call the room," he said inexplicably. Why should he call her room when she wasn't in it yet? But the phone rang just once before the faintest, scratchiest memory of Enrique's voice answered. Indignation seized her. What was Enrique doing there in her room already? Were they to consummate their non-relationship before it was even daylight enough to look twice at each other? Outside, an old dog nosed the stoop. The clerk lunged for it seeming to shoo it away, then slipped it a treat from inside his pocket.

Upstairs a door opened and down came the sounds of Enrique's bare footsteps, familiar to her from when, at fifteen years old in her parents' house, she'd lain awake eavesdropping on his midnight forays to the kitchen for snacks. At once she was boldly ashamed, dilated with longing. She raked her hair with trembling fingers and leveled at the stairway the cousin-like expression she'd worn as a girl, a face that might conceal, until they were alone, her wells and spouts of sentiment and physical need. His smile was unchecked, and when he lifted her luggage with one hand, she felt sure that her reasons for making this journey were not as flimsy as she'd feared. To think they'd soon be sharing a twin bed together like the beds in the guidebook photos of this vivid city, a city far away from everywhere, made her nearly cry out in advance of their coupling. They climbed the open stairway level by level until they reached a small rooftop courtyard with rubber mat flooring and a rocking-bench with a striped canopy. The tops of neighboring buildings loomed on all sides and the nightclub went quiet from one second to the next. Now that Jaycee stood under the night sky with him, the old idea about remaining the same person no matter where you went seemed sadder, dumber and even less accurate than ever. She couldn't wait to find out who she soon would be. It was like when she was making herself come via what was so far the only method that had ever really worked for her, which was to lie on her stomach on her cot in her room in Vermont and rub her clitoris in circles against the lumpy mattress through the telltale threadbare sheet, knowing she would soon burst free of whatever struck her at that moment as being the most pathetic thing about her. Except that this time, instead of lying there afterward dreading her return to her usual self, a return that happened in stages not unlike the open stairway descending past the levels of the Hotel Tiki, she would lie in Enrique's arms and find that she was changed forever, no matter if they ended up being seriously in love or just shared a wild, adventurous week together learning how they felt about each other.

Enrique had reached door 401 and waited for her to join him before going inside. It was the only door up there.

"We have the tallest room, no?" he boasted. She recalled her urgent tangle with the teacher at Hillwinds, the toe-biting chaperone. He had acquitted her stolid figure, her nipple-heavy breasts, all the aspects of her person that despite her sheltered upbringing, she had learned to disparage. She felt the same thing due to happen again now, only sweeter and more lasting, the sky tipping overhead, the smell of car exhaust thick in what nevertheless felt like pure, dizzying oxygen. Enrique needed no key to lead her into their room. There were two twin beds, of which one was unmade. On it perched a young woman primly clothed in *petites*, buckling her shoes. She was surely too old to be one of Enrique's children. Twenty-two or twenty-three, Jaycee guessed in a flash, the knowledge thudding flatly inside her skull. The girl's name was Amanda. She had a thin brown face whose eyes fixed on Jaycee with a ringing kindness. There would be no place to hide from such a ruthless sympathy. Not even the shower, which had no curtain, and with its drain in the center of the bathroom floor, would provide refuge.

"Amanda is my new wife," Enrique grandly explained.

He lifted Jaycee's suitcase onto a slatted luggage table, gently nudging aside Amanda's extra panties, a pair of tiny, black lace boyshorts folded as neatly as driving gloves. *There is a certain age when a woman must be beautiful to be loved, and then there comes a time when she must be loved to be beautiful.* Who wrote that, Jaycee wondered, recalling, as if it had happened forever ago, her arrival on this rooftop and all the joy and pleasure she had been poised to accept in this faraway place. But even Montpelier, for all the years she'd been trapped there, was far away from somewhere.

"So you have one whole bed for yourself," Enrique reassured her, motioning to the untouched llama wool blanket, the bed flush against cinderblock painted in thick red gloss. Jaycee couldn't make sense of the reason he gave for him and Amanda being here in her room. Either the fancy apartments he managed went bust or he had been fired. His children were at their grandmother's house. Jaycee undressed herself under the covers, forgoing the babydoll nightie she'd found in a Montpelier consignment shop and had mended in secret, a task that had excited her sexually. For a moment she flashed back on her old flannel nightgown with the faded nosegays trampled in the grass after her father knocked it off the clothesline. It grieved her to think of it lying there soaking up stains. But while Enrique was in the bathroom, Amanda rose to tuck her in, caressing the blanket with genuinely soothing affection. Maybe this was one of her duties at home—tucking in the maiden aunts.

"You're pregnant?" Jaycee saw. "Gravitos?" she added, reinventing the word off the top of her head.

Amanda bobbed her head accommodatingly as Frida might, meaning as much *yes* as she might mean *no*. It was like joining a support group, coming to Peru. Or maybe it was Be-Kind-to-Fatties Month in all of South America. Jaycee shut her eyes on a first twinge of hunger, although no smell of breakfast, and just a crack of dawn, parted the curtains. When she woke a while later it was to hear the kitteny mews of Amanda and Enrique having sex. By keeping still enough she heard every suck and slide. Yes, this trip was her chance to do new things . . . but it hurt that this first outrageous experience required her lying in rigid silence with her ankles pressed together. The sex sounded important, like they were committing themselves to a long, shared project. She had to wonder how she knew this, which was more than just knowing, just as she'd known, from the smallest bite, that the nougat she had purchased at the airport stall and unwrapped in the taxi was something she had never eaten before. When they stopped and their breathing slowed, she pulled herself up to chew two Pepto-Bismol tablets and sip from the purified water Enrique had thoughtfully provided, squinting at a scrap of paper—a receipt for three soles— on which he'd stood the bottle to remind her to pay him back for it.

She'd reimburse him by paying for supper later that day at the cliffside mall in Miraflores. He would not be going with her next day on their planned tour to the rainforest, he said over their meal. He and Amanda were moving in with his mom to save money, he said. To reimburse him for the tour, which he had booked in advance, Jaycee needed to visit two more ATMs, one near the arcade and the other outside an upscale kids' clothing shop, since she owed him too much to withdraw so many soles in one transaction. In kindness to Jaycee, Amanda walked ahead of them. The girl had a finishing-school deportment of the kind you learned from nuns. She wore narrow eggplant-colored flats, of which the scuffed, dented toes, in pointing straight forward, called attention to her path being always plain before her. In contrast, Jaycee was duck-footed, as if of two or three minds as to where she should go next. It reminded her of childhood, wishing Hil wrote science fiction instead of historical. The girl lugging the maple syrup bucket would be replaced by a tomboy who zapped her parents with gamma rays.

"Only why am *I* paying for *your* cancelled trip?" she asked the shrugging Enrique, although it didn't feel like money when she handed it over. Anyhow it was her parents' money, so who cared what happened to it? She slid the few remaining soles into her pocket where she kept the Pepto-Bismols. At least she wouldn't get travelers' diarrhea, which would set her apart from the other tour-goers she met up with next day in Puerto Maldonado to travel via skiff along the Tambopata River.

↶

The guide, whose name was Carlos, had lost his prized motorcycle to a thief at an outdoor rock concert in a clearing at the border with Chile just a week before, and he was still angry enough about it that he feared he might behave in a mean way, he said, apologizing in advance to the small gathering of tour-goers waiting for their skiff to be made ready. You couldn't tell how old he was. The only thing you knew was he was younger than he looked and that, like many Peruvians', his teeth were better cared for than most Vermonters'. He carried a clunky pair of binoculars, never letting go of the strap when he passed them around to whichever of the tour-goers (that would be Jaycee) hadn't thought to bring any, and he shared his copy of *The Peterson's Guide to the Birds of South America* only by holding it arm's length away, scared somebody might drop it overboard. He treated the book like a diary, composing lengthy notes, including hand-drawn maps and sketches, in the margins of its pages. Aside from Jaycee, the only others on the tour were two overweight men in their thirties from Italy named Raphael and Antonio, who dressed all in white except for the caps of opposing soccer teams, neither team Italian.

"Do you have all your passports?" he asked again, and then, "You all have yellow fever vaccination papers?"

Jaycee was the only one who hadn't been vaccinated. There was a clinic in Puerto Maldonado, Carlos said, but since the serum didn't start protecting you until two weeks after it was injected, there was no point in going back for it now.

"Do you have cash?" Carlos asked, in case the guards at the entrance to the wildlife preserve required paying off.

"Some," said Jaycee, not revealing how little "some" was. She had only the equivalent of maybe twenty US dollars, not even enough to tip him at the end of the tour. The reason for her having so little cash was that the ATM in the glassed-in booth at the first bank she stopped at in Puerto Maldonado, a booth flanked by two cops drinking Inca Colas while watching a string of assorted parades march around the village square, wouldn't give her any money. It was the evening before the tour. She had walked from her hotel at the outskirts of town. She liked it there. The region had a dusty frontier aspect, swarming with motorcycles and miniature taxis like large yellow insects. Seeing no reason to venture further up the muddy river, she would have just as soon stayed there, admiring the three-toed sloth that lived in a tree above a chipped swimming pool, and the riverfront, where toddlers played on piles of junk. Even the junk suited her, because it was real life. If she had enough money, she would have foregone the rest of the tour, rented the room for another few nights, and walked around town partaking of the national sweet tooth, tasting all the different ice cream novelties, layer cakes, gelatins, and candies for sale on every street. There were also, she noted, several dentists, the chairs and equipment in full view of the sidewalks as if to offer drop-in service between desserts.

But the hotel took only cash and the ATM at the second Banco was the same as the first: it wouldn't give her any money no matter how many times she checked the PIN. Instead it flashed a message: *Funds Declined.* The acronym, PIN, wasn't up to the task of conveying a new personal identity, she thought to herself the next day on the skiff, imagining what PIN or code name she might conjure for herself if she ever did acquire a new identity. The misspelled *crueler* came to her, pastry and perversity. She blinked, satisfied, accepting a dollop of sunscreen from Raphael and Antonio. There was something woebegone about the men's relationship, as if their Peru trip were a last ditch experiment in remaining a couple.

Heads touching in tender collaboration, they cropped and edited countless photos on a shared new silvery digital camera.There were photos of the driver of the skiff, his bashful wife and their chirpy baby boy dwarfed by an oversized life jacket, and of the gold-digging boats with their carpeted ramps, and then the first capybaras, world's largest rodent, that they spotted on the riverbank. The photos of the boxed turkey sandwich lunches were as artfully made as the pictures the two men took of each other, as if they planned to decide later on, in private, which memories were worth keeping.

"That's a toucanet," said Carlos, pointing with his binoculars to a bird-like shape in a distant tree, then flipping to the page in the Peterson's guide so they could see what it looked like. In addition to the trip up the broad, yellow river, the tour included three nights' room and board at a lodge in the rainforest featuring a Welcome Drink, Nocturnal Hike, Dawn Visit to Clay Lick, and Swim with Caimans. The Eco-lodge grounds had a sparse, sandy, spindly appearance, as if it had been too hastily cleared. But there were mango and Brazil nut trees and a welcome meal of curried prawns steamed in a banana leaf. Afterwards, Raphael and Antonio shared a pitcher of beer on the thatched veranda, and Jaycee sat nearby until they asked her to join them. They were scared about swimming with caimans, they said. Caimans were alligators. But Jaycee was more scared of her own bathing suit, a pilly long-waisted thing with misshapen cups and a stretched out butt. If only she'd found a new one before leaving Vermont.

"Just swim where I swim," Carlos said to them all next day at the river, and then, later, in the dark of that night, "Be careful. Don't touch the tree trunks, you can't see what's on them," while probing the home of a funnel-web spider with a pencil eraser in hopes the spider would scuttle out to have its picture taken. There was a lady from California once who touched a poison dart frog and died a week later. "Only she brushed one finger against one tree trunk. Just step where I step," Carlos told Jaycee, which was how she ended up at the door to his bunk along the row of staff dormitories once the night hike was over: by following his flashlight along the cross-sectioned tree trunks that formed a footpath in the dark.

"Well then, come in," he might have offered, but instead he just sputtered his flashlight at her before stepping aside with what looked like true deference. How humiliating. Was this how women threw themselves at men? Without even knowing they were doing it? His room included all the creature comforts Jaycee's room was missing. Cascades of mosquito netting hung at the window and over the bed, the sheets tucked up tight according to either the rules of his employment or his personality. You didn't flush your toilet paper down the toilets in Peru. You stuffed it in a bin. He kept his bin neatly lined, and not too smeary with crap like in a lot of the restrooms she'd been in so far.

"All the rooms have soap and pillows. You been cheated!" he said when she told him that her room had neither, just bare mattress ticking. "You must have been delivered to the inactive bungalow."

It was he who had led her there the first day by mistake, they recalled.

She felt sandy, well-oiled, and either too old or too young to be climbing on top of him. Her breasts were too heavy, so pendulous. And she would rather lie under him than on top. She would drink his sweat. She would catch it on her tongue. Her eyes would sting from his salt. She hoped his eyes would stay open the whole time and not veer away.

"Do you have condoms?" she asked.

"How about we take maybe one and half a second to get to know each other first?" he asked with evident humor while unbuttoning his shirt. He put his face and five fingers between her thighs, and when she finally gave up trying to come, he was hard enough to plunge inside her, which meant, she realized, he hadn't been hard enough before. It wasn't her first time rolling a condom, just like the shared pitcher of beer on the terrace hadn't been her first shared pitcher of beer. She often reminded herself of these sorts of things—this isn't my first time buying Dots at the movies, this isn't the first time I read *Rolling Stone*, I've used Shower Gel before or something very much like it—in order not to feel so fusty and out of date.

"Where did you learn your English?" she asked later on. She meant: How do we all learn anything? She felt oddly alert for this time of night, but with only a few things inviting her attention—the way the scrim of the mosquito netting backlit Carlos's shoulder, the call of some animal thing on the riverbank seeming to promise Parooo, Parooo, with a deep, rolling R the way its countrymen said it. Of course she wasn't turning into another person, yet, but nor did she dread going back to her room, either. She felt all primed up, and even a little emotional. She would flip onto her belly when she was alone and fuck the bed until she covered her mouth to scream.

"*My* English?" he asked. Amused, he dug in a drawer, withdrew a comb, and started grooming her with fond concentration. "You're like all white American girls, you know. Want to sleep with dark Peruvians."

"I don't have enough money to tip you," she said.

Shocked, incensed, he pulled his hands away, leaving the comb stuck in her eyebrow.

"For the tour, I mean!" she apologized. "The ATMs weren't working in Puerto Maldonado!"

She even gave him a kiss. Never having insulted a man before, she pictured him making note of her gaff amid the notes in his bird guide, although she did wonder if what he said was true. No, she decided, it wasn't that he was Peruvian at all, she would have gladly jumped in bed with the two gay Italians if they had led her to their bungalow to look at more tarantula photos.

"Those ATMs in Puerto Maldonado they always work perfect," Carlos said. "When you get to a phone, you need to call the help number. You do it collect. Did you tell your card people you come to Peru, maybe? Cause if you don't they don't know it's you, for sure."

"Yes," she answered. Mike had said something years ago about needing to tell your credit card people if you suddenly found yourself trotting the globe (Oh sure, she'd thought, that would be me) and somehow she'd remembered.

"Did you check the machine to make sure it service your network?"

"I didn't at first, but then the hotel told me."

"Puerto Maldonado is one shipshape town," Carlos considered. "It's the new beginning. If they don't give you your money in Puerto Maldonado, then there is something the matter with your money."

Jaycee had to agree, recalling her walk along the bustling little lanes. All the storefronts wide open even at night, and the dentists and lawyers in plain view amid the bakeries, cleaners, and real estate agents, and the families eating supper in their shops with the TV on, the scrubbed kids in plaid school uniforms balancing full plates on their knees. Kids got out of school late there, way after dark, and skipped home along sidewalks lit by rolled-up storefronts. It gave her a pang to see life sweet as that, so unlike Hillwinds.

Jaycee fastened her bra, lifting each breast and then allowing it to settle into its own center of gravity. There was a mirror on the wall. Despite Carlos's care, her hair was corrupt. A hornet's nest. To be leaving his bed came almost too naturally to her. She pulled Carlos' towel from where it hung in the bathroom and tucked it over her arm to bring back to her room. She took the soap from where it sat on the edge of the sink but she left him the wrapped bar on the window sill. He had a good clean smell. It wasn't for her to take that away from him. Maybe, innately, she was of broader experience than she had ever imagined, like she was her own doppelganger, as if, in addition to dipping candles at Hillwinds, she'd been dispensing with one night stands all her life, like an everyday heartless American girl with a PIN, sunglasses, underwire bras, and passable sex appeal . . . but she had to admit she doubted it, looking down at the bunches her t-shirt made when she tucked it in. There had to be something worth giving and taking from these sorts of encounters, but the soap and the towel weren't going to be it.

"Maybe because you can't tip me and because of my motorcycle being stolen, you will do something else very nice for me," Carlos remarked as if reading her mind. "Deliver to my sister Lilianna in Lima her wedding present from me. I can give it to you when we get back to Puerto Maldonado. You fly right back to Lima after there, yes? You're not like other tourists heading for Cuzco and Machu Picchu. Our Italians suspect you are CIA. Maybe they're right."

"I'm not going to Machu Picchu," Jaycee said. "I don't like ruins. How long have you been working as a tour guide? You're really good at it."

"Only the weeks they call me for. And for another tour outfit I do it the same, paid by number of tourists. How about it? Bring my wedding present to Lilianna?"

Jaycee tilted her head to at least make a show of weighing a variety of possible answers.

"Why not?" she said.

CHAPTER TWO

Noor, 2010

In the middle of the night Dan reached over and asked, "Are you awake?"

Noor hadn't been but now she was; before Dan spoke she'd been walking on the side of a highway with lights approaching from behind. It was a relief to realize she was in her bedroom, where the only light filtered through a crack in the curtains—the moon, or had she forgotten to switch off the halogen in the barnyard? Dan's hand cradled her shoulder, his thumb rubbing the strap of her nightgown.

"What's the matter? Aren't you on call?" she said, meaning, why aren't you in the guestroom like on the nights when you might get called out? Why are you waking me now?

"Not tonight," Dan said. "Mike needed to switch off."

"Okay," Noor mumbled.

Dan slid a finger under the strap, across her collar bone, and traced a line between her breasts.

Noor sat up on her elbows. "Dan? I'm not ovulating, you know."

"Is that the only time I can make love with my wife?"

Noor heard no pique in his tone, just yearning. "No," she said. She lay back down and rolled toward him. His physical bulk, the heat from his body comforted, then stirred her as Dan pulled her lower lip gently between his teeth, then slid to her neck, and down.

"There was a time, you know, when it wasn't just about making a baby. There's got to be fun, too," Dan murmured into the saddle between her hipbones. "All work and no play . . ."

"Look who's talking," Noor said, then gasped. He was above her now, long arms supporting his weight, knees pushing her legs apart. For an instant, as she arched her pelvis, she caught a glimpse of his blue eyes with their widened pupils seeming to reach for her yet remain inward, more complicated than usual. She was supposed to be the one with the intricate inner life, the exotic whose parents spoke a foreign language and moved back to the suspect country they'd come from. What, she wondered, did he see when he looked at her black eyes? She knew she was a selfish lover. She always held herself apart, didn't really want to acknowledge the other person when she made love, even though it was her husband. She could love him sitting on the couch eating popcorn, or in a canoe on the Winooski River, but never at the supposedly closest moment. Whenever she did something for his sake alone, taking him in her mouth, it felt false to her, forced. "Where do you go?" he used to ask.

"I'm just concentrating on feeling," she'd say but they both knew it was a lie. Dan was an open door, orderly rooms, swept floors, no unexpected turns, always who he appeared to be, and she was a secret to both of them. The words, "I love you Dan," shaped themselves but they never attached to the man who was moving inside her body. And he accepted that about her, didn't insist that she be with him, which was love too. Then Noor stopped thinking altogether, as the bright buzzing grew and her lizard brain took over. She closed her eyes again, wrapping her legs and arms tighter, pulling him deeper as though she were any woman at home in her husband's love.

At 6:30 she made Dan coffee, eggs and toast and sat across from him for ten minutes while he chewed and listed the day's schedule of checkups, calf and horse castrations, tooth rasping, pre-purchase exams and x-rays before he had to run off with his pager and cell phone and mobile vet truck. Through the window the sky bloomed luridly pink beyond the half bare maples marking their southeast fence line, then paled into overcast dawn. She felt tender toward Dan and stood to kiss him at the door. It was easier to give herself over to him when they were up and about, performing their litany of small tasks.

"What time tonight?" Noor asked, reaching up to place her hands on his shoulders.

"Not past 7:00, I hope," Dan said. "But you know how it is. Got to run," he said, his eyes sliding away from hers.

That wasn't like him to look so preoccupied. Dan was a straight shooter, tall and rangy, prematurely silvering blond hair, sincere even-featured face. Noor's brother Ahmed once accused her of marrying Dan because he looked like a poster-boy American. So un-Pakistani. So unlike us, he meant, even though both Noor and Ahmed had been born and raised right there in Vermont. "You think marrying Dan will make people stop asking where you came from?" He'd hit a shared nerve. Hadn't people always thought they had the right to ask, "Where are you from?" as though she had a duty to tell them. It used to be, "Oh, a cute little Indian girl." Now it was something more freighted and suspicious. "You ain't one of them Al Qaedas are you?" a car mechanic had asked. Or, the former flatlanders, the PC Montpelier-oids, overbearing in their solicitous empathizing—"It must be so tough for you lately." And, apropos of nothing, "The invasion made me ashamed to be American," their bumper stickers reading "Coexist" spelled out in letters formed from crescents, crosses and Jewish stars.

Dan's business was booming, no wonder he was preoccupied. He was always on the run, up and out of the house sometimes three or four nights a week for emergencies—cows with prolapsed uteruses ("uteri," she imagined Dan correcting) horses with colic, sheep with the bloat, and so on. In their first years of marriage she'd gone out with him on night calls, loving the mysteries of dimly lit barns and the soft grinding of cows chewing their cud, their frozen breath hovering above their pink nostrils. Now she couldn't stand most of the dairies—they kept their cows in big coverall buildings with screens for ventilation. The cows were never pastured anymore so that every acre could be used for the corn turned into silage or hay fermenting in huge white plastic bales that gave the herd a permanent case of stinking diarrhea, all in the name of efficiency.

Many of Dan's equine clients were off-putting in other ways—the dressage queens—spoiled, often flirtatious, women in tight riding breeches who didn't have the sense not to over-grain their horses into colicking, or hand-treated them with horse cookies and organic carrots into nippy, ill-mannered beasts. She and Dan, sitting up drinking cocoa in the wee hours, used to laugh about them. Now Dan often slept in another room so he wouldn't wake her when his pager went off, and talked about switching to doctoring small animals, since house pets were where the real money was. He joked you could earn more money balancing the acidity in a guppy bowl than breeding a prize-winning Holstein. She knew it was unfair of her to judge him for wanting to make the switch when he'd already been kicked in the knee twice by recalcitrant cows and broken two ribs from a run-in with a fractious stallion. But she'd fallen in love with Dan the large animal vet, one of a dying breed, and didn't think much of the pet vets who made big money brushing the teeth of schnauzers and selling all kinds of unnecessary vaccinations against diseases the indoor dogs would never contract. It was unfair to judge Dan for anything—if they ever managed to have a child the much shorter hours of a small animal vet would allow him to spend time with their kid, and he wouldn't be crawling home at 4:00 a.m., leaving his stinking, filthy coveralls in the mudroom after performing barn surgery, too wired to sleep before heading off again in his mobile vet truck.

Clearing the table, Noor decided they needed to make more effort, do more together, remember why they'd stood on that hillside pasture eight years ago, laughing as the guests stepped over manure piles in their dainty strapped sandals and shined leather shoes, her mother in the brilliant peacock green shalwar kameez, lips pursed with doubt, Noor in a simple white gown, getting grass stains and stick-tights on the once-only lace. "I miss you," Dan had said, or she thought he'd said, last night before they both fell back to sleep. Well, she missed him too.

Later that morning, after she had finished her barn chores—hay, grain and water for everyone except no grain for Daisy, who was cresty and prone to founder, let the horses out to pasture, and mucked stalls—Noor saw an old man shuffling down the road at an unsteady gait. Perhaps he was somebody's grandfather out for a stroll. There were a lot of new houses going in and she no longer knew all her neighbors. He was wearing such a strange outfit she was sure if he lived around there she'd recognize him: a wide sleeved, blousy shirt, a blue vest, baggy trousers, and over his shaggy white hair a cloth hat shaped like an overturned bucket with a rounded, not quite pointy top. Plus, he carried not a cane but a hooked shepherd's staff like a Yorkshire farmer on "All Creatures Great and Small," which she had seen more times than she cared to remember since it was Dan's favorite. As a country vet dependent on sonograms and digital radiograph machines, he had a soft spot for Dr. Herriot stripping down and lathering up to shove a bare arm inside a cow.

Noor whistled to her old collie/shepherd cross, Jiyah, who was headed stiffly out to the end of the driveway to investigate the odd old man. Jiyah pretended for a moment not to hear Noor's whistle—or maybe she hadn't, she was getting on—and then paused and headed back to the house. Noor shrugged off the old man; it was time for her first lesson.

Half an hour later, Noor walked backward beside the aged pony Daisy, holding the lead rope as they made a dusty circle, Daisy's unshod hooves shuffling along through the sandy footing, her head hanging low in the unseasonable autumn heat. "Okay, now Ricky," Noor said, "just close your eyes and see if you can feel Daisy's body going back and forth, back and forth, rocking you in the saddle. Can you feel that?"

Ricky Bayler, a seven-year-old located somewhere on the semi-verbal end of the autism spectrum, giggled though he didn't answer. That was an improvement. Along with his behavioral peculiarities and limited speech, Ricky was physically rigid. He walked on his tiptoes with his arms pushed down by his sides. This was his fifth therapeutic riding session and they were still working on feeling the horse's movement, a path to helping him, passively, to relax his rigid muscles. Ricky's mother, Barbara, one of Noor's regular volunteers, walked on Daisy's other side, a steadying hand on Ricky's thigh. Only Barbara could touch him. If anyone else so much as brushed against him, Ricky started up a high pitched shrieking and clapped his hands over his eyes. Yet Ricky allowed Daisy to nuzzle him when he gave her a carrot after each lesson, giggling at the tickle of her rubbery, prehensile lips on his open hand. And he enjoyed running the brush over her chestnut flanks. The plan, the hope was that Ricky might, through osmosis, translate the old pony's pleasure in being brushed and stroked, as well as his own pleasure in touching her, into an acceptance of contact with human beings other than his mother. After a few serpentines through the line of orange traffic cones, meant to increase Ricky's awareness of the sway of Daisy's body as she bent around them, their time was up. A tantrum threatened when he had to dismount, then was averted when Noor asked Ricky if he'd like to give Daisy her carrot in the barn. Barbara helped Ricky clamber down, nearly getting clocked in the nose by Ricky's boot. Ricky ran ahead in his tip-toe robot rush until Noor called out, "Ricky, would you like to lead Daisy in?"

Ricky stopped, beeped like a machine in backup mode, and robot-walked backwards toward them.

"It's a good sign that he didn't want to get off," Noor told Barbara.

"Maybe," Barbara said, "but he hates changing activities, period."

Barb was afraid to hope, Noor knew, afraid to be burned again after the many and varied miracle cures, the gluten and casein free diets, the facilitated speech attempts, the auditory integration training, the secretin and Vitamin B6 injections, the DMG supplements. Noor was furious at all the charlatans who sold hope to the desperate and gullible. How did they live with themselves? Perhaps there were people who saw *her* this way, too, though she made no wild claims about therapeutic riding providing *cures*. At the very least her clients enjoyed it, which was more than you could say for any of the other treatments Ricky had endured.

"Beep," Ricky announced, then reached for and clenched Daisy's lead rope under her chin.

"That's great, Ricky," Noor said. "You know, Daisy really likes it when you hold her lead rope loosely."

Still on his tiptoes, Ricky managed to match his stride to Daisy's lolling walk, and loosened his death grip until a bit of slack appeared in the lead rope. His mother allowed herself a tiny glimmer of a smile. After Ricky had brushed Daisy's back and giggled at her nuzzling lips, then robot-ran ahead of Barbara to the car, Noor put Daisy back in the pasture and brought in Moon Pie to eat hay in a stall before his turn to work. In the house, she kicked off her barn shoes, put on a fresh pot of coffee and glanced down the driveway, hoping to see her volunteers Andrea and Donna, who had agreed to be here for Ellie Davis, a five-year-old with cerebral palsy, requiring a leader and two helpers to stabilize her. No messages on the machine.

The weird old man was still out there, on the other side of the road now, still shuffling along, head low, but not making much progress. Maybe he was lost, or not feeling well. Maybe it was progress enough for him to be outside, but shouldn't he be headed back in the direction he'd come from where someone, she hoped, knew him and looked after him? Noor poured a cup of coffee and carried it out to the front porch where Jiyah lay thumping her tail. Noor wavered. Once she acknowledged the old guy he'd become her responsibility, at least for the day, and she had things to do. Noor sighed and called out, "Hello?"

The odd old man didn't reply. Probably hard of hearing like Jiyah. Still no volunteers. If they didn't show she'd have to reschedule Ellie Davis because she couldn't safely keep that little girl on Moon Pie alone, and her mother was too afraid of horses to even get near. Ellie would be disappointed and Noor pissed. Running a business that depended on volunteers was difficult, but that's the way all therapeutic riding programs worked. There was no way she could pay two or three assistants to help out five or six hours a day. It wasn't really a money-making proposition. Dan had started dropping comments about it lately. Just last week he'd remarked that maybe the expenses of maintaining the elderly horses should be equaled by what she contributed to the family financially. Were two a family, Noor had wondered? "It's not enough to have work that is justifiable in terms of the greater social good. What about *our* greater good?" Dan had complained, checking his pockets for wallet, pager, cell phone before heading out.

"And if we had a kid with a disability, wouldn't you want it to have a place to go for help?" Noor had countered, standing one foot on top of the other in the autumn morning chill.

But Dan just sat down on the bench in the mudroom to lace up his work boots. "Let's have the kid first before we worry about it being disabled."

Having the kid was turning out to be a lot harder than they'd figured. Noor had had two miscarriages already and hadn't conceived in two years of trying. As a large animal vet you'd think Dan could make it happen—he had plenty of success with bulls and cows, mares and stallions. Maybe you had to have four legs to succeed with Dan. Where were Donna and Andrea, damnit, Noor wanted to know, bringing herself back to the immediate problem. All her volunteers had their own reasons for coming here. Some did it because they wanted to be around horses or were considering a career in occupational, physical, or mental therapy; others needed to fulfill a community service requirement for graduation, and the rest had what Dan called the do-gooder gene but didn't want to commit to doing good for more than an hour a week. Andrea and Donna fit that category while Noor, according to Dan, was just a do-gooder, period. She used to think he meant it as a compliment but now she wasn't sure. And what was with the old guy at the end of her driveway? He was looking in her mailbox now, peering into the open flap. Noor walked down the path to the mailbox. She said, "Sir, can I help you with anything?"

"Uh," he said. "Oh dear." He closed the mailbox and looked at her from under the silly hat. His eyes were the palest blue, the pupils black dots. The wool vest he wore appeared homespun and the blousy shirt could have been out of the nineteenth century. He wore buttoned trousers, mis-buttoned, Noor saw. She looked away from the gap in his fly. "Do you live near here?" she asked.

"Uh, not so far."

"Do you need a ride home?"

"Uh, no, I don't think so. Thank you." With that he turned and shuffled down the road again. Noor looked after him, worried, but just then Donna and Andrea came barreling down the gravel road in a plume of dust in Donna's Corolla, each holding a big paper coffee cup—the reason for their tardiness, no doubt—Donna driving one-handed, and behind them Ellie's mom in her Honda with Ellie in the back seat. Noor hurried back to the barn to get the black and white Moon Pie off the cross ties. She'd already curried him and picked his hooves, things that Ellie couldn't do, though with help she could brush.

"Sorry we're late," Andrea offered. "Hey, there's my girl," she said with real warmth, turning to hug Ellie who had appeared, grinning in the barn with her crutches and braced legs. Noor immediately forgave tardy Andrea. Ellie's mother flinched as gentle Moon Pie, still on the cross ties, snorted to clear his nasal passages.

"Let's get a helmet for you, Ellie," Noor said. "Do you remember which one fit last time? Was it the red one?"

Later Noor noticed that the old man was back again, resting against her mailbox. Maybe he'd only gone a few steps beyond her yard and turned back. She walked down to the road.

"Would you like to come in for a drink of water?" she asked.

"Water. Uh, yes, that might suit. A cool drink of water," he replied. He spoke in a strange, archaic fashion though he bore no accent. Noor led the old man into the kitchen where he lowered himself stiffly into a chair. She ran the tap cold and when he'd gulped down half a glass she said, "Please let me give you a ride home. It's so hot out there today. You must be tired. Where do you live?"

"Uh, that's the predicament," he said. "I'm not at all certain."

"Oh. Well, do you have a wallet with an address in it?"

"Perhaps I do." He shuffled through his pockets, pulling out a large chambray handkerchief which he fumbled. But in his back pocket he found a leather billfold, and in it Noor discovered an expired driver's license with his name—Hilary Emory. It had a rhyme-y ring, like Hickory Dickory, appropriate since she recognized it as that of the well-known local children's book writer who ran that ragged theme park/living history museum a few miles away, on Barnes Road, a place where his books were "Brought to Life!" the ads promised, as if the books were boring on their own. There she went, dissing other people's ways of making a go of things when her way of getting along seemed just as shaky. Only it didn't feel shaky to her. It felt necessary and right, despite the fact that if Dan wasn't, resentfully, picking up some of her bills, she'd be out of business by now. As it was she had stacks of bills Dan hadn't even seen. She hadn't yet paid for a thousand bales of first cut hay stacked in the loft and she was paying for grain and shavings with credit cards. The barn was going to need a new roof by spring. She put the driver's license back in Mr. Emory's wallet. "Do you still live on Barnes Road, Mr. Emory?

"You may call me Hil. Everyone does. Except for the daughter."

"Alright, Hil, is this address current?"

"I suppose it is. If you say so, my dear."

"I'll just check it. Where *is* your daughter? Can you tell me how to reach her?" But Mr. Emory didn't answer. She pulled out the local phonebook and found the number on Barnes Road, thank god, and memorized it. "Could you wait for me a minute, Mr. Emory. I'll just get my things."

In the bedroom Noor dialed. The phone rang so long she was about to hang up when an elderly female voice answered. "Yes?"

"Is this Mrs. Emory?"

"Yes it is. But we aren't going to buy anything." The voice was querulous, indignant.

"No, no, I'm not selling, my name is Noor Khan . . . I run a therapeutic riding stable on the lower end of Bliss Road. Mr. Emory showed up here this morning. He seems a bit . . . confused."

"Oh not again. I told him to stay nearby. He doesn't listen to me. He never did. I always had to listen to him. Well I can't come get him. I don't drive anymore. And our daughter is traipsing around at a costume workshop in Burlington . . . she's no help. I suppose I'll have to call the police."

"Mrs. Emory, I'd be glad to give your husband a ride home. I have errands to run anyway." She had planned to go to the feed store on Barre Street and then around the corner to the Hunger Mountain Food Co-op, if there was time. Barnes Road was in the opposite direction, but not that far away. Now she'd have to take the Forester instead of her old Ford 150 farm pickup which would be hard for Mr. Emory to climb into.

"Well, I suppose you had better," Mrs. Emory said. The phone went dead. Noor sighed. In the kitchen, Mr. Emory—Hil—appeared to be asleep. Noor gently grasped his shoulder and his eyes opened.

"I know you," he said. "You're the little Indian girl."

"Pakistani, actually." Maybe it was her tee-shirt and faded jeans that made him think her younger than she was, or perhaps to a man his age she looked like a girl. "I'm going to drive you home now."

"No, I *know* you. I know who you are."

"Alright. Now we know each other. Would you like to use the bathroom Mr. Emory—Hil—before we head out?"

It took another fifteen minutes to get him in and out of the bathroom—with his shirttail hanging out of his barely buttoned trousers with the new urine stain—and into the Forester. Noor tried not to look at the dashboard clock more than once. She backtracked up Bliss Road to Center, where Mr. Emory must have blundered across the dangerous blind curve onto Bliss instead of heading down Center Road, she supposed. She always took the shorter route into town from the other end of Bliss and so hadn't seen him out there wandering before. Just past the peeling sign for HILLWINDS LIVING HISTORY BOOKS, at the junction of Barnes and Center Roads, which was nearly three miles from her place, a pretty long walk for a man in his condition, stood a pair of old Capes with perennial gardens that needed thinning. The front door to the one with the neatly swept porch was locked, and at the other house, the larger of the two, Noor had to ring repeatedly while Hil muttered beside her. Finally the door opened. An obese woman with straggily gray hair sat in a wheelchair. Her thick, misshapen legs appeared beneath a longish sack of a dress.

"You really have become a lot of trouble," Mrs. Emory said, shaking her head at her husband. "Could you help him in?"

"I can walk," Hil said irritably. He followed his lumpy wife into the gloom of the house as Noor helplessly followed, holding Hil's shepherd crook. Though the old house contained valuable antiques, she caught a glimpse of dirty dishes crowding the counters through the kitchen door. Cobwebs filled every corner. The windows were shut tightly keeping the whole place airless and sour. These two needed help. She wondered whom she should call. Social Services? The Council on Aging?

"Does your daughter ever visit from Burlington?" Noor asked carefully.

Mrs. Emory pursed her lips. "Oh, she's only gone for two weeks. She lives next door. She knows I can't take care of him myself but off she went. Had to learn to make new hats for her dad, she said. It's always about what everyone else needs. Do you think he'd take care of me if things were reversed? I've got diabetes pain in my legs and palpitations and it's just too much." She spoke of her husband as though he weren't right in the room, slumped in a chair, his uncut hair testament to the level of care afforded him. How could the daughter have gone off and left them without help? What did they eat? The only food Noor saw was a couple of half eaten packages of Keebler cookies.

Noor snuck a glance at her watch. "I'm sorry, Mrs. Emory, but I have a riding lesson to give soon and I have errands to run." Forget the Co-op, she'd be lucky to get the grain before her 1:00 showed up. She needed those three bags of Vintage Senior. Even her horses were senior citizens. How had she allowed herself to get involved with these two? "I'm going to have to leave."

"I apologize for taking your time," the woman said sharply.

"That's no problem. Goodbye, Mr. Emory—Hil."

Noor hurried out, back into the fresh fall air. She'd like to give that daughter a piece of her mind. She'd bring them a loaf of bread and some cheese and orange juice later. That way she could ease her conscience and be done with them. Noor sat in the driver's seat for a moment, feeling guilty about abandoning the cranky old couple to their squalor, and angry because it was their daughter, not she, who had really abandoned them, before turning the key in the ignition and continuing on with her day.

⸎

Noor came back in the house after putting away the bags of feed and shavings, kicked off her boots in the mudroom and walked into the kitchen to see the message machine flashing on the counter. Dan, she thought, calling to say something sweet about last night. Noor hit the play button, let the robotic machine voice announce, "One new message." Then a female voice, soft but urgent: "Hello, Doctor Driscoll? This is Mindy Francis, in Calais? My llama is sick and I need to get in touch with you. Please call."

"Call the office like everyone else," Noor said aloud to the empty kitchen. Dan didn't give his clients his cell because then he could never escape them. He preferred they call the office that he shared with two other vets and have the receptionist page him. In fact, their home phone was under Noor's name, not his, for privacy. Mindy whatever her name was had to be unusually persistent or awfully worried about her llama to have worked that out.

The phone machine was flashing again when Noor went inside for a cup of afternoon coffee. There were two new calls.

"Hello? I'd call your cell but I accidentally erased your number. Can you call me please?" and a half hour later to the minute by the date stamp, "This is really important. Please call," both times without bothering to identify herself. Mindy with the llama. The woman had nerve, imagining he'd know it was her without saying.

Noor picked up the phone and hit the call back button. A woman answered on the second ring. Noor said, "Hi, is this Mindy? Dr. Driscoll is out on calls. Have you tried the office? They'll page him for you."

"I did, but he hasn't called back."

"Okay, maybe I can reach him. What's wrong with your llama?"

"Well . . . he's lying down a lot and he's not eating his hay."

Didn't sound like an emergency to Noor but what did she know about llamas? "Listen, I'll get in touch with him and have him call you. What's his name?"

"The llama? Jorge."

"Whore-Hay?"

"You know, with a J. It's *Span*ish," Mindy said impatiently.

"*Jorge*. Has Dan—Dr. Driscoll—seen him before?"

"Yes, he gave him shots in the spring and he trims his nails for me."

"Okay, I'll see what I can do."

"Thank you. Are you . . . his wife?"

"Yes I am." And you must know my name too, if you called here, Noor thought. Mindy wouldn't be the first of Dan's clients to harbor a crush on him, but this one surely wasn't trying very hard to hide it, if that's what it was. On the other hand, this one wouldn't be the first neurotic owner to freak out over every minor animal health issue and demand Dan's attention ASAP. He'd once had someone call him because her pet donkey's bray didn't sound familiar and someone else had called him because her horse's pee looked orange in the snow.

When Noor called Dan's cell he was driving between clients.

"Hey Hon, what's up?" He was in work mode. What did she expect, that he'd swoon at the sound of her voice?

"You've got a client calling us at home about her llama. Mindy, uh," Noor looked at her jottings, "Francis. She's called three times."

"Oh, she's just one of those Nervous Nellies."

"Nellies? You sound like your grandma. Do you need her number?"

"It's in my phone. I'll take care of it. Thanks, Hon."

"Wait, Dan?"

"Yeah?"

"You want to go out for dinner tonight? We could go to the Black Door."

"That would be great, Noorie, but I can't. Just going to grab something on the run. I already had an emergency colic and I'm behind. I won't be home until 9:00 most likely."

Noor sighed. "Okay. You better call Llama Lady."

"Right," Dan said, distracted again. "Will do." And he hung up.

Will do? Who was he talking to? Noor dipped into a jar of tamari almonds, shorthand for the lunch she hadn't had time for due to the Emorys, and chewed thoughtfully. Then a car rumbled up the driveway, her afternoon volunteers, and Noor hustled back out to get ready for her next lesson.

CHAPTER THREE

Jaycee & Noor, 2010

"Is your mamacita ella esta aqui?" Jaycee asked Hugo, surprised that Frida's cell phone would be answered by a child.

Jaycee stood on one foot at a rented phone in an internet café in a heavily trafficked outskirt of Lima, her other foot on her bags to protect them from toppling. Frida's embossed business card was in her hand. She hadn't meant for it to be. She had simply slid her hand into her pocket and there the card was, and there, too, right beside her on the busy sidewalk, was an open door leading to the internet café. There was a jumble of wooden school desks with pencil troughs carved into them like the desk on which she'd learned her alphabet at home, and people clacking away on unstable keyboards amid spools of power cords. Outside on the road marched another parade, the hats bigger than armchairs. Even though parades were like weather here, people still paused to watch and to catch the blue corn candies thrown into the crowd.

The topmost, and by far the heaviest, of Jaycee's bags was the zippered Minnie Mouse bag that Carlos had packed with his sister's wedding gifts, but which Liliana had refused to accept, *washing her hands of her brother*, she pantomimed in her doorway after Jaycee was dropped off by the cab to deliver it. Jaycee was nonplussed, since the contents of the bag had spoken so highly of Carlos's character when she'd rummaged through it on the flight from Puerto Maldonado, placing the generous array of gifts on the empty seat beside her before rewrapping them in the same crumpled newspaper. There was a miniature painting of a jungle scene with a gold painted frame, two tall, imposing, similarly painted plaster candlestick holders, and a matching vase. A substantial platter, also molded of plaster, showed a portrait of a woman who, oddly enough, resembled Frida, although, unlike Frida, who had been so cheerful the whole plane ride over from Miami to Lima, the woman on the platter appeared bereft, her round eyes spilling over with amateurishly painted tears. It was as if she had suffered some awful misfortune, or as if the portraitist was predicting somehow that Frida would come to a sad end. Finally, out of the bag of gifts came two bottles of dark Cuzqueña beer, and on top of all that, one of the tempting, traditional cheeses Jaycee had been admiring in the food stalls she'd perused, which turned out to weigh a ton. They looked like fresh baked breads, the rinds bursting with ripeness, the cheeses luxuriating in their own heat, melting back into custards and creams. The cows in the dairy where such cheeses were made had names, Carlos had told her. They were called in for milking one by one. There was Ida, Elvira, Claudia, and Odette. Black ladies in hats, Jaycee saw in her mind's eye.

Hugo put on his father. Jaycee remembered the good-looking man in the photo on Frida's cell phone, earnestly waving his bull-fighting cape.

"Esta Frida aqui?" Jaycee asked a second time.

Frida remembered Jaycee at once. "I fell asleep with my drool on your shoulder," she said. "The least we can do is give you some place to sleep."

"It'll be just for one night," Jaycee said. Her plane departed Lima for Miami late next night, and she would be in Vermont by Monday evening. She had enough for a bus to the airport, that's all. Her debit card was "es rotos," she explained.

Hugo loved having house guests, Frida replied. Jaycee would sleep in the little boy's room that night, and they would build him a special maze-style tent using all the living room furniture covered by clothes-pinned bed sheets.

After writing down the street address for Frida's house, Jaycee called the international assistance number on the back of the malfunctioning debit card and was told that the account showed "insufficient funds."

"What should I do?" she asked the operator, putting out of her mind for the time being her dad's obscure musing on her front stoop: *I do feel that we might have considered this setback yesterday or the day before.* There must be money somewhere out there or maybe even a credit card, she assumed, for paying household expenses and Hillwinds bills, the things, that is, that her dad took care of. Leave it to Hil to have gone all these years without allowing her to peek at the family ledger even while sending her off to buy role-playing props.

"Deposit more money!" the operator said. "Either that or cut the card in half, if that makes you feel better than hanging onto it."

In the kitchen at Frida's house, Frida asked Hugo to please draw Jaycee a map of their house, the little boy's specialty. The rooms were situated every which way like piles of blocks with no actual hallways, just doors that led to doorways and doorways leading past doors. There were very few windows, heavily draped. The nook was in the bathroom, Frida said.

"The nook?" Jaycee wondered, squinting through the crooked spectacles as she studied her map.

"The washing machine," Frida explained.

Jaycee gathered her ample laundry out of her bag, passing the husband, Arturo in one of the narrow archways. He wasn't quite as appealing as he'd looked in the photo—too gangly—but he was kindly and given to bashfulness. What could Frida have meant when she said that she trusted him "maybe too much?" He seemed more harmless than a fly, first showing her to the cabinet where they kept the detergent and laundry softener and then leaving her to herself in the damp pink bathroom. In a dish at the sink lay Frida's gumball ring, which Hugo had given her so lovingly for her birthday. Jaycee slipped it past her own knuckle, then slid it off and placed it back in its dish. Later she regretted not having taken a long enough moment to indulge in the silly make-believe jewel as the slosh of the clothes washer spun gently through her. It wasn't a kid she wanted but the ring itself, the silly toy, all toys, all things denied her.

For supper there were four bowls of soup, tumblers of freshly pressed mango juice, chicken cutlets with rice, and an extravagant assortment of tinned layer cakes called King Kongs.

"No cuys," Frida promised, reassuring Jaycee that they'd be eating no guinea pigs that evening. Jaycee was glad to see so much food, since it saved her having to bring out Carlos' cheese and presenting it as a gift for everyone to share. She'd thought about doing that . . . but she wanted to save the cheese for herself, so instead she brought out the big candlestick holders and placed them on the table between the bottles of beer, noting for the first time how crudely Carlos's wedding gifts to his sister were fashioned, the plaster lumpy and misshapen under the careless slathers of paint. Between the candlestick holders she propped up the heavy platter showing the crestfallen Frida look-alike, which made the real Frida burst into chimes of laughter.

Over dinner they talked about the Plaza Dos de Mayo, debating whether the buildings were blue or purple. Jaycee had been driven by it at 2:00 a.m.: mammoth purple buildings featuring rows of ornate windows surrounded a derelict square with clusters of teenagers hanging out in it. But Arturo said, BLUE, as if his life depended on it. He worried he was colorblind, he said, Frida making the translation. "Maybe it only looks purple at 4:00 a.m." Jaycee proposed.

Much later that night, when everybody had been asleep for a while, Hugo padded into his bedroom, woke Jaycee with a child-slap and told her, crying, that he wanted to sleep in his own bed. So she crept around until she found the living room, lifted a few corners of the crazy maze tent, and crawled onto a couch beneath a lean-to made of a billowing sheet. It was a nice place to sleep, and when morning came, she didn't want to get up to face her very last day before returning to Hillwinds and the absurdly named Yam Rock.

What rock *didn't* look like a yam, she often wondered, but the name had won first prize in the Name the Boulder contest, of which the entry fee paid for all the Hillwinds Christmas decorations. By the time she crawled out from under the tent, Frida was pouring coffee, little Hugo was setting the table, and Arturo was folding Jaycee's laundry. A pair of underpants was missing, she learned when she was dressing. It was by far her sexiest pair. She checked the washer, the rooftop clotheslines, her luggage, and even inside her jeans. In her mind she blamed Arturo, but since he was in the middle of taking finals at pharmacy school, she decided not to mention it. Then, no sooner had she made this generous decision she found the panties where she'd tucked them in a pocket in her luggage.

When it was time to meet her bus, she considered leaving them the cheese after all, since they had been so very generous. But even though she knew she might not get it through customs, she thrust the heavy cheese deeper into her bag and thanked Hugo for letting her sleep in his tent.

Hugo nodded, unimpressed by the jungle scene miniature she gave him from the bottom of the bag of gifts from Carlos.

"We hope very much we see you again," said Frida, although she looked relieved to see her houseguest go. Arturo blushed beet red when Jaycee shook his hand goodbye.

"Yo tambien," said Jaycee, who regretted as soon she walked out the door that the last glimpse she had of her friend, the glimpse she would likely carry forever into her memory, was of the weepy face on the platter, the tears like kernels of corn, as if they were spilling from the watery fountains depicting giant ears of maize that cooled so many public squares in Peruvian cities. Still, the leaving of the gifts made Jaycee happy, the way the giving of gifts was supposed to do, even though she hadn't been the one to buy them. She felt good, kind, and coolly unburdened, except by the cheese, on which she could hardly wait to gorge herself in what she feared might be a final ecstasy of greed before her freedom from All Things Hillwinds expired, and the vase, which, since the words *Peru Souvenir* were stenciled on it, she decided at the last minute to bring home to her mom.

⌒

Because Jaycee had no money left to pay for a bus ticket when she arrived at the airport in Burlington, she spent her last nickels calling her mom to come get her. Fortunately Hannah didn't ask why she was at the airport. It was chilly for October, so she waited inside and dozed off on a bench. Her mom's foot was too numb from the diabetes to do any driving, so she was sending a driver. It was her mom's own fault, Jaycee thought, and she dreamt the Michael Jackson amputation song dream she'd dreamt before. Foot by foot, one two three, ABC Baby, knee by knee. Not until Jaycee's name was paged did she jerk awake and run to the baggage claim area where she was supposed to have been waiting to see a slender Indian lady wearing jeans and a peacoat standing none too patiently before her.

"Uhh . . . are you the car?" Jaycee asked, and brought herself up short. It was her dad who said Uhhh all the time, not her.

The Indian lady answered no, she was not a car.

"But you're the driver," said Jaycee. She reached for the pocket in which she kept her granny glasses when she couldn't bear to wear them, still uncertain as to whether it was better to stumble around half-blind or watch even her own thoughts coming and going.

"I drove here, yes, and I've been waiting almost an hour since I got here." The driver glanced at her wristwatch, her wrist dusky with down. How did such a heavy, athletic looking wristwatch appear so regal, so womanly? But, broke, and having needed to bypass the Au Bon Pain in the Miami airport where she had bought a ham baguette a week earlier, Jaycee was way too hungry to muster a kind word for game-playing cab drivers with chips on their shoulders. She hadn't been able to eat her cheese, since it was packed in her luggage, and then she'd slept through mealtime.

"I just want to be sure that my parents have paid you. I don't have any money. I slept through breakfast and then I couldn't buy lunch."

"Your parents need to be told what's too much to ask. It's not my place to do that," the lady warned. She took hold of Jaycee's bag, but Jaycee wrested it away in time to drag it out the door. Those were some mean boots the lady was wearing. The boots kicked some blown leaves sideways, stomped on an upended coffee cup, then kick-glided toward parking. The peacoat was littered with pine shavings.

"My name is Noor Khan," she told Jaycee when they had exited the airport and were snaking toward the highway in a small red SUV. "I'm not a social worker. I'm not an elder care worker, and I'm not a driver. I own a therapeutic riding farm. You might know it; your dad sure does. You shouldn't have left your folks in their condition for someone else to feel obliged to look after them. They haven't paid their bills. There's no hot water. The electricity might be shut off any day now. We're lucky it's not January. There's food in the pantry on credit but there needs to be somebody able to cook it, not to mention wash dishes. Your mother's in a twist about having no television service. Your father's never upset by anything, is he? There are blankets for warmth and it's not my place to draw the line at candles. The woodstove is clogged. Do you have anything to eat in your bag, by the way? I missed lunch, trying to get my work finished before picking you up."

Jaycee told her how a storm in Miami had caused her plane to be rerouted to Newark, where the customs agent was apparently lax enough—or maybe it was his head cold?—to allow her to bring in the oversized cheese. "The stove is clogged?" she asked. It was Hil's pride and joy to maintain that stove. Daily he scooped out and carted the ash. Weekly he wiped inside the window, brushed the creosote from the pipe, and yearly climbed up on the roof to clear it of any creosote. His devotion to that stove was a chronic annoyance, second only to his devotion to his fame and to his daughter, or rather, her obedience to him. The heavy part in Jaycee's hair was his longest-term project, but he would gaze on it again over her dead body. Her hair hung loose now, slept upon, inadequately brushed. How was it a woman with pine shavings on her peacoat kept her hair so smartly styled, so bluntly, sleekly layered, she wondered of Noor?

Noor pulled the car up to a bakery outlet. "They have day-old loaves to go with the cheese," she said, handing over some cash and keeping the engine running for warmth. "I'll need the change," she added. "I keep waiting to win the lottery but since I never buy a ticket it never happens."

In Jaycee's haste to buy bread she knocked a plastic bag of cinnamon buns off a shelf and dropped some quarters on the floor when she was handed her change. She remembered the name, Noor Khan. She remembered throwing up in the composting toilet when she was a girl, the vomit foaming in the bowl. *Noor Khan, daughter of local doctors . . . only a broken femur* the newspaper had written, as if the paper hadn't known you could bleed out fast from a broken femur. They seemed to be chastising the hit and run accident victim for not being smashed like her friend, Pauline. There had been some uncertainty surrounding the tragedy. What was it, exactly, Jaycee tried to remember? Pauline's dad was run over, Noor and Pauline had been thrown but Pauline's head had hit a stone wall . . . *at the velocity as calculated by* . . . Something queasy like that. And why had the Indian girl survived, when the others had died? "Because she was dark," Jaycee's mother had observed illogically. "She blended in with the night."

The clerk found a plastic knife, a handful of napkins and a paper plate, which Noor spread out on the car seat between them. Already she'd fetched the cheese from Jaycee's luggage and for a minute, as if the women were friends or, at any rate, not antagonists, they sat admiring the lunar glow it cast. It was larger around than a dinner plate. On some fields beyond the windshield stood a smattering of cows. Jaycee gazed at the amicable herd of females, miffed at herself for starting off on such rotten footing with Noor.

"Good of you to come get me," Jaycee finally said, but when Noor didn't soften, Jaycee added, "How was my trip? Nice of you to ask. But you know what they say. Wherever you go, you aren't not there. And then you come home. Nobody asks you what comes next."

Noor barely blinked. With true grace wielding the clumsy knife, she tended only to the prospect of lunch, dinner, snack, whatever. At first, the cheese was as Jaycee had imagined, the press of the blade being fought back against by the bloat from within . . . but then the rind burst open and in addition to the white ooze melting forth, there came the sight of a whitish bricklike thing that stopped the knife inside the margin of a plastic bag. No sooner had the funny substance made its appearance then so did a cop car, its muffler scraping over the median.

"Holy Schist," said Jaycee, her goody two shoes vocabulary getting the better of her. She jumped out of the car and threw the cheese in a trash pail next to the door. It made a clean-sounding thunk, meaning the trash pail was otherwise empty. The scraping muffler announced the cop car's arrival in the bakery lot. Two cops got out. The male cop walked right past the trash pail into the bakery while the woman cop stood in the parking lot smoking. When the cop came out of the bakery holding a bag with grease spots on it, the other cop tossed her cigarette onto the ground. By the time the cops drove off again, the Forester was in drive, Noor's foot on the brake. They watched traffic for a while, as if some passing truck might save them, whatever they did, from doing something they'd regret. Jaycee gave the door a push with her elbow, and since she hadn't shut it properly, it swung back open. Noor didn't stop her from getting out. Noor could have stopped her, and so could Jaycee have stopped herself, but instead she stopped herself from stopping herself, and when she bent to scoop the parcel out of the trash pail, not even Noor was watching. Finally Jaycee was back in the car with the cheese in its wrapping on her lap, which was where it belonged. It was like sleeping with Carlos and suspecting Arturo of stealing your panties, until you couldn't tell the difference between the things that were done to you and the things that were done for you, the things that you took and the things you received.

"Holy Schist," she repeated, in awe of her greed and its promise of more greed, and more greed, and more.

The pretty Noor placed her hand on Jaycee's arm, as if they really were friends or at least co-conspirators, and Jaycee, startled speechless by the other woman's touch, lowered a fingertip to their cache.

"Fuck me!" Noor said.

"Holy schist!" Jaycee exclaimed again.

"What did you say?"

"Holy *Schist,*" Jaycee repeated, reddening. "You know, schist, metamorphic rock. It's something my mother taught me to say instead of shit. Okay, holy shit! I can't believe I took that through customs. Good thing I got rerouted through Newark instead of Miami like we were supposed to."

Noor couldn't believe it either. Why wasn't this reckless girl on the news right now, being shackled and led away for hiding a big chunk of suspicious substance in her suitcase?

"I can't believe you got the smelly cheese through, let alone this," Noor said. "Jesus. Do I want this stuff in my car? NO." Noor glanced through the side window and swiveled to look at the now empty parking lot. Not likely Burlington cops were on the lookout for two thirty something women in a Forester with a *Horses Help People* sticker on the rear bumper and dog hair on the seats. Dog hair and more than a pound of caked, slightly iridescent Andes Mountain High.

"Well what do you think I should *do* with it?" Jaycee wailed, wincing as though about to be spanked.

Noor glanced around for the cop car again. "What is it about you and your family? Why do you all keep involving me in your problems, expecting me to solve them? Turn it over to the cops, throw it away, snort it, do what you want. Please don't get *me* thrown in jail for the rest of my life. I have a life I'd rather not throw away. Don't you?"

"I'm really sorry," Jaycee said. "I had no idea it was in there. I don't even know what it is. And no, not really. Not including last week I don't. I don't have a life I don't want to throw away, I mean. Holy Schist."

Feeling a little guilty for her outburst, Noor licked the tip of her index finger, touched it to the crystalline chunk, and rubbed just the barest amount along her top gum as she'd seen people do in movies. She hadn't liked coke when she tried it in college—didn't like the way it jangled her nerves and made her taste metal in her mouth, though the metallic flavor might have come from whatever the coke had been cut with. And this stuff was probably pure, un-cut, a strange glistening yellow-white. Damn. Jaycee was right. It really *was* schist. Noor's gum tingled and went numb and her heart jumped. "It's cocaine," she said. She remembered a film she'd seen in high school about the terrible conditions of the Indians who grew and harvested the coca leaves in the Andes, and what a tiny percent-age of the drug's value they earned by their labors. Something about them chewing the leaves to dull the hard work. Also, something about all the chemicals that were used to cook the coca leaves and render them into pasty white crumbles—kerosene, benzene, one of those zenes and sulfuric acid or rat poison or something. She put her fingertip to her gums again, trying to rub it back away.

"People drink coca tea," Jaycee was saying, "So it couldn't be all bad, could it? They serve it to wimpy backpackers to dull altitude sickness. In hotels they serve it."

Noor pointed out, "This isn't tea," with more patience than she felt. "Besides, even the tea would be illegal to bring into this coun-try."

"You tell me," said Jaycee. "What if Carlos . . . I can't just throw it away, what if some kid finds it? Oh my god, what if Carlos—he was the guide at the rain forest park who asked me to bring it—I mean the cheese, I thought it was a cheese, to his sister in Lima—what if he comes looking for his stuff? I never would have brought it into your car if I knew what was in it, I swear. Holy Schist. He could find my address through the tour operator. Holy Schist! But wait a minute. Maybe they have Enrique's address, not mine, since he's the one who made the reservations. But wait. No, I had to give it to them at the lodge. My address. So they do. He does. Carlos knows where I live."

"What about the sister? And who's Enrique, and please don't say 'Holy Schist' again. Say 'Holy Fuck.'"

"Holy Fuck," Jaycee repeated.

Noor laughed. "Who's Enrique?"

"Just a guy. Our high school exchange student. Forget it. But Carlos' sister, Lilianna, wouldn't even let me in her door. She said she washed her hands of her own brother"—Jaycee mimed Lilianna's emphatic hand washing motion—"and now I know why. So I left them with Frida. The funny painted candlesticks and the platter and the rest of the gifts."

"I doubt very much your Carlos is going to come looking. And you could just tell him they took away the *cheese* at customs."

Frida? Carlos? Enrique? Lilianna? Noor calculated that Jaycee had made more friends over ten days of travel abroad than Noor herself had managed to keep over decades in Montpelier. But cocaine? Forgetting how hungry they both had been, they sat for a while in silence, eyeing the now empty pasture before them and wondering when the cows had filed over the hill. At least someone still pastured cows, Noor noted absently. They reached for the bread simultaneously, wrestling with a chunk of it as if it were a wishbone. Jaycee won, breaking off the larger piece. "We could sell it," Jaycee said. "God knows my family needs the money."

Whoa! Not as innocent as she seemed.

"You *could* do that," Noor said, chewing her bread hunk thoughtfully. "What do you mean '*we*'?" she added, choosing that law-abiding question over the more dangerous, more shocking question that crossed her mind: Why can't I do it? I need money too. But that was ridiculous. She wasn't a criminal. A gangster therapeutic riding instructor? It sounded like a reality show.

Jaycee grabbed another heel of bread and tried to scrape some of the smeary cheese from the back side of the wheel without ingesting any illicit stuff.

"What does that cheese taste like?" Noor asked.

"Like a barnyard." Jaycee stopped and stared at Noor. "I don't know anyone who could help me sell it. If you help me, I'll give you half the money."

"You're nuts. You ought to go flush it down your toilet or something. Except knowing your house, the water will probably be shut off by the time you get there."

"But it would be such a lost opportunity," Jaycee protested. "All my parents' stupid money cards failed on my trip. Insufficient funds. You saw what the house was like. I could get them some help. Don't look at me like that. It's true. I've never had any money of my own. Don't you think we could find someone to sell it? I'd ask my old fiancé but Mike was into alcohol, not drugs, and last I heard he'd joined the National Guard. Maybe he's in Afghanistan. I don't want to talk to him anyway. Not after he called me the escaped spinster from Sturbridge Village."

"Wrap it up," Noor said, meaning not Jaycee's lament but the cheese. "Let's get on the highway without that stuff sitting on the seat."

Jaycee dutifully repackaged the cheesy coke, slid it back inside the zippered Minnie bag, and sat drumming her hands on her knees. Noor found the exit to I-89 South and merged with traffic, thinking about what half the money could do to help with her floundering business. With more help and more cash, maybe Noor and Dan could finally afford to go on vacation and let someone else take care of the place for a week.

"You work too hard. You put your body under too much stress," the fertility doctor had scolded, adding that they might finally consider in vitro, since they'd about exhausted their chances with the fertility drugs. It could pay for that. Her share wouldn't be enough money to build an indoor riding arena. It would be enough to move one or two of her horses to a place with an enclosed teaching space this winter and keep the business running a while longer. What a shame you couldn't just put Jaycee's cheesy cache on E-bay and sell it to the highest bidder.

"This windfall is my only chance," Jaycee interrupted Noor's musings. "It just dropped into my lap. I'll never get another chance like this. You can't say no to these things. You have to accept what life offers, not turn it away. If I don't sell it I'll never get to leave Hillwinds again. I'll turn into my parents. Except they chose this life, I didn't. Don't you know *anybody*?"

Gerry Wilcox, Noor thought, despite herself. Gerry'd had a crush on her through high school. He was a kid who flunked his classes because he didn't try, talked about switching to a tech school and never did. She had been a girl on track for college and med school. She never would have given him a glance but they were in the same gym class for two years running and he used to make her laugh, mimicking thick-bodied, glowering Mr. Boswell's peculiarly high voice and bulldog lower lip. "Ladies!" Boswell would sneer at the boys, "The girls in the class can climb the ropes faster than you can," oblivious to insulting the girls, and Gerry Wilcox would stick out his lip and go falsetto. Noor had even agreed to go to a deli with Gerry once; he bought her a root beer and a petrified-looking, plastic wrapped pastry. But when he'd asked her if she'd go out with him, she'd lied and said her parents would only let her date Pakistani boys. She told him she felt bound to honor her parents' wishes for the next two years—though there weren't any other Pakistani kids in the school—so as not to hurt poor Gerry Wilcox's feelings, and then, after that, she really *hadn't* dated any other guys, as if she were as spooked as he was by the specter of her parents' disappointment in her. The term "honor bound" had done the trick, as if he feared she'd be stoned to death if she so much as ate lunch with him. But still he flirted and complimented her shiny black hair and grinned at her in the halls. Then she was off to college and occasionally saw him around town on holidays and vacations—driving a tractor, then a backhoe, then on street corners hanging out smoking cigarettes looking thin and older than his years. Through the old high school grapevine she'd heard he was a dealer. He'd know what to do. She could give Jaycee his name. But she wouldn't. She wasn't going to get involved in Jaycee's illicit activities. No way. This was just a weird story to tell Dan. He'd shake his head and suggest she report it to the cops. She wouldn't do that though. The senior Emorys were too desperate and Jaycee too pitiful to turn in . . . which meant, Noor realized, that if Jaycee were a normal person, a person with a life she didn't want to throw away, Noor *would* turn her in. There was no end to the ways Noor unnerved herself.

Noor took the Montpelier exit, crossed the bridge and turned onto State Street, past the capitol dome, through the downtown muddle of government buildings and hip little shops, turned left and continued out Main Street through town until it became suddenly rural. The road divided just past the Cutler Cemetery. She took the right up the hill on Center Road for a mile or so and a left turn onto Barnes. The Emorys' little matching capes sat close to the road, both in need of a paint job.

"Listen," Noor said as she pulled up to Jaycee's driveway. Lights off in both houses, she noticed. She knew the electricity was cut but the Emorys hadn't lit even a kerosene lamp to welcome their daughter home after two weeks away. "I don't know what you're going to do with that stuff but leave me out of it. Good luck. All power to you. If you want to sell drugs to schoolchildren so you can move out of your childhood home like most people manage to do before they're half your age, go for it. You know, some people go to college to get away from their parents. Other people get jobs or get married or just rough it for a while. And yes, it's true, some people sell drugs to schoolchildren. Whatever floats your boat, Jaycee. I mean that. I have no right to tell you how to go about your life." Refusing to meet the eye of crestfallen Jaycee, Noor stepped out and opened the rear hatch so Jaycee could drag her bag onto the grass. She forced herself to get back in the car without checking on the elderly Emorys. They were their daughter's problem now.

⟡

That Sunday morning Dan was in the shower when Noor got a phone call from Jaycee. Rather than answer, Noor waited for voice mail. The message thanked Noor again for picking her up at the airport, but then it ended with a plaintive "Call me," that sounded more like, *Please tell me you've changed your mind about going in on this deal with me since you don't just throw away a treasure chest when it falls in your lap, do you?*

No way, Noor thought, remembering she had to call Dan's mother to wish her a happy birthday. Today. Now, before she forgot. She'd neglected to send a card. She was sure his mother had called Dan yesterday or the day before—she always called a day or two before her birthday or wedding anniversary or Mother's Day, to remind them without actually reminding them, putting her tall, angular self into their minds, where her Midwestern cheerfulness would fester. Noor flipped open Dan's cell phone, sitting as it always did when he was home, beside his wallet on the end of the kitchen counter. She hit recent calls received and found Mrs. Driscoll's number embedded between several calls from an unidentified local number. She jotted down his mother's exchange on a napkin—was it willful that she could never remember her mother-in-law's number? Then, on a hunch, first listening to hear that the shower was still going, she punched "calls sent" and discovered that Dan had made quite a few calls in the past five days to that same local number. She made a record of it beneath Dan's mother's on the napkin, then snapped his phone shut. Heart racing, flushed and fearful of what she'd find, she picked up the land line receiver and hit the received calls on the caller ID. Bingo, except instead of winning, she'd lost. The number belonged to the Nervous Nellie, Mindy Francis—or someone listed in the phone book as M. Francis, a single woman, obviously—who lived in Calais and perhaps wasn't such a Nervous Nellie after all, or nervous about something other than her llama *Jorge*. Whore-Hay. Maybe it meant nothing—maybe a flurry of calls had gone back and forth discussing appointment times or llama medicines. Noor grabbed Dan's cell again and scrolled through calls sent and received; Mindy's number appeared too often and too far back to be calling about a llama who wasn't enjoying his meals. Noor put down the phone and collapsed onto a kitchen chair. He was having an affair. Maybe. Probably. Hot tears threatened to overflow and a surprisingly sharp pain pierced her sternum. This is what your husband's unfaithfulness feels like, she told herself, like a health teacher or an old public service announcement: this is your mind on drugs; this is your heart in the frying pan.

"Hey," Dan said, emerging from the steamy shower, wrapped in a towel, his shapely hairy calves fluffed with blond fur, his bony feet leaving big wet footprints on the floorboards as he passed from bathroom to hall leading to the bedroom. He never dried his feet until he was sitting on the bed. Too tall, he'd said, he'd have to hop around like a stork and most accidents happened in the bathroom, didn't she know? "Have you seen my biking tights?" he called back over a shoulder.

"In the bottom drawer," Noor said flatly. She could hear Dan whistling "Stairway to Heaven" as he pulled on clothes in the bedroom. Dan had had the hideous song stuck in his head for days. The Germans called it a brain worm. Maybe it would worm its way in and keep chomping. It would serve him right. But why had he made love to her so avidly just two nights ago if he was having an affair? It was her fault—she should have made them spend more time together sooner. No, it was his fault, the slimy deceiver with the honest face. Maybe there was another explanation. She had to confront him and ask. But if he had already deceived her he could lie about it to her face just as easily. What would be gained by asking? She had to think this through. If he admitted an affair one of them would have to move out and she'd be in an even deeper hole with the bills. That was the worst reason for people staying together—because breaking up was too expensive. And she still loved him. She did. Or she loved who she'd thought he was.

No, she had to think first before doing anything. She had to be sure. Of course there *could* be another source of income if she did change her mind and joined Jaycee in her cocaine deal and received the offered half. But what was the matter with her? She wasn't going to change her mind even if Jaycee was begging her to. Noor's husband was calling some llama lady too often and Noor was planning to get back at him by ending up in jail? Forget it. Just ask him. Ask: "Dan, are you fucking the llama lady?" Or worse, "Are you in love with Mindy Francis?" No, she wouldn't say anything. She would rather not know. She would rather play the fool. But that wasn't it. She would just rather have faith in him, believe in him more than the ache in her gut was telling her to, until she simply couldn't anymore.

Without telling Dan where she was going, she headed out to the barn to push her face into the sweet herbivore scent of Daisy's furry neck, and listen to the horse's rhythmic grinding of hay. Then, on impulse, she brushed and tacked up Luna, a small Morgan horse who had a little too much spunk for the kids now that the weather was getting colder. Noor would ride her way through the ache in her gut, over and under her seesawing thoughts: Dan. Mindy. Ask him. Pretend she didn't know. Did she? Just stop thinking! Riding always settled her, attuning to an animal via the instincts of her body rather than the twists and turns of her mind. She pretended she didn't see Dan waving to her as he backed the Forester out of the driveway, his bike loaded on the rack. Hearing Jiyah howl her outrage at being locked in the house—the dog didn't know she was too old and wheezy to accompany Noor on rides anymore—Noor felt like howling too.

A breeze riffled Luna's red/brown mane and fallen leaves made little whirlwinds; Luna pretended to be skittish. Thankfully, the mare demanded Noor's total attention. Noor held her to a walk on the shoulder of Bliss Road, then cut through a break in the stone wall that bordered the Currans' farm.

The cornfields were harvested and although the manure was piled along one side, it hadn't been spread yet. So much waste—broken ears on the ground, spilled corn kernels. She wondered if as much was lost before mechanical harvesting. Didn't the Old Testament demand the corners of fields and the gleanings be left for the poor? She was sure there was something like that in the Quran too, if only she could remember the verses. Here the only gleaners were the Canadian geese coursing southward, fueling up for their travels.

Her parents—what would they think if she and Dan broke up? They'd be scandalized. They already were scandalized that Noor had married a man who touched animals for a living, scandalized that Noor did the same. The horses were their fault, actually, or at least her father's. A year after the hit and run accident, after Noor's injuries had healed and she'd turned into a pre-teen agoraphobe, flinching at loud noises, afraid to walk on sidewalks or roads, her father, who had played polo as a young man in Pakistan, came up with the idea that she should do something physical, something to build her confidence, and decided riding lessons would be the thing. Noor had protested but finally complied, as she had always complied with her parents' wishes at that age, and it wasn't until she was brushing the enormous beast's coat at her first lesson, then sitting on its back with a silly grin, that she realized she'd forgotten to be frightened. Her parents, who had expected her to go to med school or be a university researcher, hadn't realized how little they'd like where the years of horses led her. They told their friends in Pakistan that she was a therapist, neglecting the therapeutic riding part. A divorce would do them in. She wondered if she could get away with just not telling them. That was one good thing, at least, about not being able to have children yet. There would be no reason to tell her parents the truth. It was the same with selling drugs, she supposed—since she didn't have kids, she didn't need to worry about what kind of mom she'd be.

To force herself to pay attention, to not think of Dan, her parents, or her bills, Noor let Luna break to a big extended trot down one side of the cornfield, then slowed the mare, then gathered her into a canter. There was such a thin line between controlling and harmonizing with a horse. Of course the rider gave the cues, chose the direction and the speed, but the unpredictability of all horses and their oversized-rabbit nervous systems gave riding that frisson of risk that Noor loved. Still, the ideal, the dream, was to enter a partnership, not domination, and to follow the animal's rhythm so closely that you imagined, for a moment, you were one, despite the fact that riding was, at its best, a form of benevolent subjugation of the horse, as her brother Ahmed once called it.

The mare snorted and pulled, asking to be allowed to go full out, that flattened gallop that always felt to Noor like going into overdrive. Noor let her rip until halfway down the field Luna began to fade, blowing and huffing, not fit enough to cover that much ground so quickly. Noor asked for a trot, then a walk, bringing the mare down smoothly. They exited the Curran field along a tractor road, then veered off onto a logging trail that cut into the woods. The leaves had half fallen off the deciduous trees and splattered the trail with reds and yellows that would turn brown underfoot in a few more weeks but for now carpeted the trails with reflected light. She returned the way they'd come, passing the Currans' farm equipment—a tedding rake and an empty red metal hay wagon not yet put away for the winter—and a deflated mylar balloon escaped from some child's birthday party caught in the crotch of a tree. When Noor was brushing the sweat marks out of the mare's thickening winter coat, she realized that although she still didn't know what she'd do about Dan, she had at least already made one decision, with the help of Jaycee's pesky, pleading voice on the phone that morning. She would contact Gerry Wilcox about selling Jaycee's cocaine and she wouldn't tell Dan a thing about it. The idea of keeping a secret from Dan was almost as appealing as the money itself. Secrets were the weapon of the passive-aggressive, she knew. He had his secret; now she'd have hers. And maybe, soon, a fat wad of money to pay her bills. For an instant she felt the same disgust she'd felt before—what would her clients think if they knew they were riding horses fed on drug money? She wondered if it would change how she felt about her clients, if she would become more callous as a result of Dan's betrayal and her new willingness to engage in criminal acts. Well, it was a risk they'd all have to take.

Back in the house, Noor looked in the book, found Jaycee Emory's phone number, and dialed. When there was no answer she looked up the number for Hilary Emory's little theme park.

"Hillwinds. Maple Jug Mercantile," answered Jaycee's chipper voice.

"I've changed my mind," Noor said. "I'll be in touch. If you still need me, I mean."

"Crap," said Jaycee. "I threw it away. I brought it to the dump. The bears will eat it."

Noor felt a gut wrench resembling a lesser version of what she'd felt on seeing Dan's calls to Mindy.

"April Fools!" Jaycee said, and then, hushed and excited, "No, I need you."

Noor hung up before Jaycee could reveal any more childishness.

⌘

Before Noor went looking for Gerry Wilcox she went online. A kilo or so of cocaine from Peru was apparently worth about ninety thousand dollars on the street. And that was *on the street*, after whoever would sell it had taken his percentage and she'd divided the remains with Jaycee. Most likely what they had was half a kilo of what was known as *fishscale*, a compressed, iridescent cake formed before final processing. Who knew how pure, but it would be cut to 20–40 percent pure before it was sold by the dealer, who would use any number of benign white powders: lactose, laxatives to stretch the drug or baking soda to make it into crack—a thought Noor preferred not to entertain. She could live with selling recreational coke, that's all—the kind of stuff rich people sucked up their noses using straws made of rolled-up hundred dollar bills. She would make that perfectly clear to Gerry. Hell, even Jaycee had probably been high herself a bunch of times without knowing it just from handling the coke-dusted bills in the cash register at the end of a hard day at Hillwinds. Except they probably didn't allow a cash register at Hillwinds. Maybe an abacus. At least it wasn't heroin.

And of course whatever price they came up with had to leave Gerry, or whomever they finally settled on, a chance to get a payoff. Gerry was the only one she'd trust not to take advantage of her ignorance, though who knew how he'd changed over the years. And how to get in touch? She'd heard cell phones were traceable and could be hacked into, that you should never say anything on a cell that you wouldn't want to see posted online; she couldn't call him, unless she got one of those "burner" temporary cell phones like the drug dealers on TV used and tossed. But did he even have a phone number? Maybe he was in jail by now.

She'd last run into Gerry two years ago, when she'd just parked her car in the center of Montpelier, in the lot near the train trestle over the Winooski River. Gerry was standing by the train tracks, smoking a cigarette and talking to an unsavory looking guy in a fatigue jacket. Noor waved hello and Gerry had called out to her— "Hey Noor, what's new-er?" a silly thing he used to say to her in high school, just to make her frown. His conversation partner nodded his head at her and walked off. Noor asked Gerry how he'd been.

"Can't complain," Gerry said. "Look at you. You gone off to law school or something since the last time I seen you?" When he grinned his face took on familiar, sexy lines, nearly dimpled. The endearing Gerry Wilcox grin.

"Nah, just an appointment with a lawyer." Noor felt unaccountably embarrassed to have Gerry see her dressed in crisp black slacks and a blazer with a carefully knotted scarf, instead of her usual jeans and barn boots; the law school dig was due, no doubt, to her toting the leather briefcase her grandparents had given her father when he got into medical school at Dartmouth, a case in which he used to carry anatomy and physiology texts and tiffin tins of her mother's aloo gosht stew.

"You getting divorced from the Ken doll so you can marry me, huh?" She'd thought it a ridiculous question then, just Gerry's teasing. Maybe he'd been prescient. Without the marrying Gerry part, of course. Gerry had laughed a scratchy smoker's laugh, revealing an incisor gone missing since their one and only accidental high school kiss. "If he's Ken, that makes me Barbie but I'm more of a Midge," she said, accepting his little dig about the fact that she hadn't married an Asian or a Muslim man, after all. "I don't think they've done a Paki Midge yet, do you?"

"Dunno," Gerry said, throwing his cigarette onto the railroad cinders by the tracks. "I'll have to ask Taylor. I think they got a Michelle Obarbie in the works."

Noor laughed. "Who's Taylor?"

Gerry's six-year-old daughter, it turned out; she lived with her mother in Burlington. He did some "business" up in Burlington and so saw his daughter pretty regularly.

"Are you divorced?" Noor asked. "I didn't know you'd been married, Gerry."

"I ain't been. What about you? Got any rug rats of your own?"

"Just horses and a dog," Noor said. "I've got a therapeutic riding farm for disabled kids."

"Yeah, I'm pretty sure I heard something about that. Made me proud. Good for you, good for you."

"What are *you* up to these days, Gerry?"

"A little this, little that. Got a little lawn-mowing/landscaping business and I'm going to get a plow rig someday to keep going in the winter. Sell the odd joint now and then to help pay the bills." He grinned again. "We ought to get a burger sometime, sit down and ketchup, you know?"

"Call me," Noor said, knowing he wouldn't and if he did she wouldn't go. And then she'd hurried off to an appointment with the lawyer who was helping her incorporate her nonprofit business, as Dan had insisted.

She started with the phone book, running a finger down the Wilcoxes, and was surprised to see that Gerry not only had a land-line but an address on Barre Street, most likely in the old factory housing near the granite factory. Some of these houses had been painted up with unusual combinations of gray and chartreuse or maroon and mustard, mimicking the exotic colors of the finely de-tailed Victorians on the better streets of Montpelier. But the junk in the tiny, crowded yards, the sagging porches with clotheslines, the two sets of doors and the multiple metal mailboxes gave them away as hard up.

Noor called Gerry on Monday at 11:00 a.m. He'd always liked to sleep in, she remembered, kicking herself when it was clear the call woke him. She needed him clear-headed, not with a morning hard-on. She cringed at the image—she wasn't in the habit of imagining men's bodies—not even Dan's—in compromising poses. She'd nev-er even managed a decent sexual fantasy. Oh, the unshakeable legacy of the ABCD: American Born Confused Desi. Her brother hated the term Desi, imagining that its original reference to the Indian subcontinent somehow diminished Pakistani pride.

"You want to see *me*?" Gerry mumbled.

God, why was she taking on this fool's errand? For money, that's why. And because Dan was doing who knows what with Mindy Francis. If Noor did end up in jail it would be his fault.

"No, no, that's okay, I mean ..." Gerry said. She heard scrabbling noises and imagined him sitting up in bed, knocking a clock or a water glass off a bedside table as he tried to get his bearings. "Okay, I'm just, you know, surprised to hear your voice."

They agreed to meet at the stone tower in Hubbard Park in half an hour. Noor hoped no one she knew would be in the park at 11:30 a.m.—just the usual dog walkers with their good citizen dog poop baggies in hand. She drove straight to the park, left her Forester in the lower lot and walked the shortest trail up from the frog pond to the tower, an empty stone garrison about ten feet square with zigzagging stairs climbing to an open viewing stage with crenellated walls about chest height. From there she could see Camel's Hump to the west, the distant trail cuts of the ski areas, the chapel tower at Vermont College to the east, and the roads leading to Berlin and Barre to the South. The view to the north was half blocked by trees. The foliage was past peak, more browns than reds, especially on the higher hillsides—and the air held a chill. She wanted to be there first so she could see Gerry coming and so, if anyone else showed up, it would look like an accidental meeting. She needn't have worried. Gerry was ten minutes late, huffing up the trail with a lit cigarette in hand which he tossed before heaving himself up the many stairs, metal treads ringing under his boots. His hair was still damp from the shower, his jeans were holey, and his cough rough.

"So what's the big deal?" he asked between sputters.

"You need to quit smoking," Noor advised.

"Uh-oh, my old high school honey drags me out to the wilderness to lecture me on my health."

"No, but it wouldn't be a bad idea." She decided against reminding him she'd never been his honey, even if that one time in eleventh grade she'd let him kiss her. It was unintentional—he went to peck her cheek after the deli "date" and she'd turned her head the wrong way. It had scared her because his lips had felt just right—cushy *and* forceful—and for an instant she'd wanted him to kiss her for real but then she'd said "Whoops!" and went on as though it never happened. She knew now what she hadn't been able to identify then: Gerry was both sexy and unsuitable, which made him more sexy, which made him more unsuitable, and so on.

Gerry recovered his wind and looked about at the view of city, fields, forests, and distant peaks spread out in a near-360-degree panorama. "I ain't been up here since high school," Gerry said. "I forgot how nice it is. So?"

Noor glanced around furtively, searching for approaching hikers on the spokes of trails emanating from the tower.

"Oh, hush-hush, eh? Hey, ANYBODY WANT A JAY?" he shouted into the woods. She slapped him on the arm and he laughed, his eyes crinkling into the deep folds of a hard-living man.

"I've got a business proposition for you," Noor said.

"Oh yeah? I like the idea of a proposition. Too bad it's business."

Noor ignored the flirtation. "Well, this friend of mine"—funny to think of Jaycee as a friend—"just got back from a trip to South America and she discovered that somehow she'd gotten a . . . well, a wrong package in her luggage. It looks to be about a half a kilo or so of Peruvian cocaine."

Gerry shook his head and whistled. "Half a kilo uncut?" Now he was whispering too. "And you don't think whoever lost this package won't come looking to get it back?"

"I don't think so. She asked me if I could help her sell it and you're the only one I could think of who might know where to start."

"Big endorsement of my character. You think I got the cash to buy that much coke off anyone?"

"No . . . I just thought you might, you know, know someone. You'd get a cut, of course."

"And you would too, right?"

"Well, that's sort of the point, isn't it?"

"Little Noor Khan with the homework always done and the Ken doll husband is selling coke." Gerry shook his head. She couldn't tell if he were mourning her downfall or enjoying it. Either way it made her shiver out there on the tower, watching something moving among the trees. Squirrel? No, it was a gray fox, a flash of pewter trimmed with pale rust around the neck like a faded version of its redder cousin. The fox stood stock still a moment before darting out of sight again. Maybe she'd dreamt it. This whole experience was surreal.

"It's just a one-time thing. There won't be any more of it," Noor said, as though that made her less culpable. A one-time thing, like the only time she'd ever stolen anything, a lacy napkin monogrammed "N K" in a Victorian style tea shop in the Na'ima Karachi hotel because it bore her initials, and Na'ima meant tranquility, of which she needed more. She'd shocked herself with the theft then, which was nothing compared to selling coke. She wasn't really a drug dealer if she only did it once, right? Yeah, like you weren't really a murderer if you only killed one person.

She ignored the urge to ask Gerry how much she'd get for her share after everyone else got their cut when—if—it was all said and done. They hadn't even weighed it yet. Still, she ought to know what the reward was going to be for taking this big of a risk. She could see the headlines: "Do-Gooder Gone Bad" or maybe, "From Horses to Horse." Except horse was slang for heroin, not cocaine. She was a drug naïf.

"*Course* it's a one-time thing," Gerry said. "You wouldn't want people thinking you're a low-down sleazy dealer like me, right?" The Gerry grin, only mocking now.

"I'm sorry, Gerry. This was a big mistake. I knew it was from the start but that damn Jaycee kept bugging me. I said I'd try and I've tried. I'll tell her no. I didn't mean to insult you." She was half-relieved to have it out of her hands now. She couldn't sell the stuff for Jaycee. Fine. The fox was gone, the woods were empty, and she hadn't made a deal. Maybe she'd leave here with her integrity intact after all.

"Wait a minute, wait a minute. Let me think." Gerry lit another cigarette, held it between thumb and forefinger, and gazed toward the distant Camel's Hump. "How much does your friend expect to get for this . . . *product*? And just how much did she pressure you, Noor? I still remember that one time I asked you out for coffee and you acted like I sent the bounty hunter to kick in your door."

Noor's face went hot, and she bypassed the question, saying, instead, "She still has to weigh it." She'd seen an old fashioned metric scale that made her think of the scales of justice in the Emorys' house, unsuccessfully wiped of sunflower husks. Never mind; she could pick up a postage or kitchen scale and keep the elder Emorys out of it.

"Here's the deal, little Noor Khan. I'd never have the cash to buy it off you . . ."

"Maybe you could sell it and pay us after you got it sold?" Noor interrupted, desperation allowing her to ignore the fact that she hadn't gotten the okay from Jaycee to let anyone sell their coke on spec.

"Nah," Gerry said. "That's not my thing, selling coke. I'm strictly small time weed. And I don't even want to be doing that forever. I don't want to be sixty years old and hanging out on the corner of the schoolyard with a bag of tricks. I don't even want to be near schoolyards. I sell strictly to guys I know from jobs and such. But I might know someone who could find a market for that coke of yours. He's a dealer up in Burlington. He might want to get his hands on some good quality blow to sell. I'd have to get back to you."

"Gerry, how would I know that this guy wouldn't, you know—" she was going to say, how do you know he wouldn't sell it to schoolchildren, but instead she said, "How do you know he wouldn't just take the *product* and run off with it?"

Unspoken between them—how do I know *you* won't?

"You'll just have to trust me, won't you?"

Strangely, she did. If the cocaine got stolen she'd be back where she was before meeting Jaycee. She'd leave it in the hands of fate, which she'd been taught was sacrilege. Her parents believed in Divine Destiny, not Fate. Divine Destiny required that you live a moral life although everything was ultimately in the hands of Allah. Fate, which was so much simpler, happened whether or not you lived a moral life. The deal would go through or not. She would end up behind bars or not. She was just a little cog in a big, indifferent wheel that might or might not turn. If it did turn, there was no way that some creepy dealer was going to have scruples about selling only to lawyers and doctors and CEOs. No way for Noor to stay clean.

Gerry shook his head. "Damn, I never expected to see you trying to set up a deal. I mean, I thought you was better than that."

"It's for fertility treatments," she improvised. "We've been trying for years. You know how much that costs?" Why did it matter to her that Gerry didn't think as well of her as he had ten minutes ago?

Gerry shrugged. "Yeah. That's a good reason, I guess. How come everyone who don't want a kid's got 'em already, and the ones that want them can't get them? Taylor was an accident but now I got her I love her. Won't Ken doll pay for the docs?"

Noor sighed. "Dan went into debt for his equipment—mobile digital radiography machines ain't cheap." Ain't? She was copying Gerry's idiom, trying to make herself fit in with him, or maybe trying to suppress the snobbery that never let her take him seriously when they were kids. "And he's still paying off vet school."

"You could adopt."

"That costs a ton too." Noor wanted to get out of this conversation before she told him her other, real secret, which was that even before she'd found out about Dan's calls to Mindy, she wasn't sure if she wanted kids anymore. She'd never been the type to look longingly at babies, carriages, baby clothes. It had just seemed like the time, partly because Dan wanted it. And now it wasn't anymore. Maybe she only liked kids as her clients, in one-hour increments, when she could be sure she had something to offer. Though neither of the miscarriages had been her fault, it seemed to her as though they had. Dan thought that was nonsense—instead of grieving over lost babies he hardened himself, referring to them as *fetuses* (feti, she imagined herself foolishly correcting him*)*, like they were something a cow had dropped in a field. And she'd hardened herself against Dan, without meaning to. Another in the little steps leading up to Mindy.

Gerry sighed. "Okay, I'll see what I can do. I'll call you when I got something."

Noor grabbed a piece of paper with her temporary number written on it and pushed it toward Gerry. "Don't call my landline about this, please."

He looked her up and down, not lasciviously, but taking her measure in a way that made Noor avert her eyes, then folded the paper and tucked it into his back pocket. "You been watching your cop shows, eh Little Noor Khan? And you ain't told your husband. If I didn't know better I'd think he done something to make you mad."

Noor pursed her lips. "I've got kids coming for riding sessions soon. I've got to get going. But thanks, really."

"Always on the run."

Noor smiled apologetically and started down the zigzag steel staircase.

"Wait," Gerry called to her. "Wait. I got to have a sample, enough for me to check it out before I call the guy, and then if he's interested, I got to give him a taste."

Voices were coming closer. Two women, calling their wayward dogs.

"Call me and tell me where to meet you," Noor replied. "I'll have to go to my friend's first to get the stuff." She hurried down the rest of the stairs, setting up a hollow ringing. The women—a lesbian couple, maybe, as one woman had a butch cut—were using those plastic ball thrower sticks, shooting tennis balls into the woods and across the dried weeds in the clearing by the tower. A border collie named Ellen—the women were shouting encouragement—in a blur of black and white whipped past a lumbering golden retriever named Portia. A placid scene, while she'd just made—she hoped—the first and last drug deal of her life. That's all it took, a couple of minutes of conversation, to step over the line from being a clean nosed good citizen to being a felon. Anyone could do it. Anyone could step onto a seesaw not knowing which end was going to finish up. Except, Noor thought, you didn't ordinarily step onto a seesaw at all, did you, and if you did, it wasn't by accident.

Hurrying back through the woods to the frog pond, Noor forced herself to be honest about the situation. She was using Gerry. Even if he stood to make money, he'd be taking a risk, and she was leveraging his old (and maybe even current) crush on her to get what she wanted. As for Dan, if he knew, he'd think she'd gone crazy. Maybe she had, but it was partly—mostly—his fault.

◦

Noor got no answer when she called Jaycee from her parked car in the lower Hubbard Park lot, just a recording saying Jaycee's phone was no longer in service. She pushed down a moment of panic when she wondered if Jaycee had disappeared with the cocaine to sell it on her own and take off somewhere, leaving Noor as virtuous and as poor as she had been before. Fate, after all. But of course, it was the unpaid phone bill again.

After her teaching sessions, barn chores and a quick meal of leftover pot roast heated in the microwave—she stuck the remainders back in the fridge without a note to Dan—he could get his own dinner—she headed over to Jaycee's on Barnes Road, passing the peeling old-fashioned placard advertising Hillwinds Living History Books. The driveway leading to both Emory houses was empty. Noor considered leaving a note on Jaycee's door but steeled herself and knocked on the Emorys'. She could hear a thumping within and, as expected, Mr. Emory turned the knob. He asked cheerfully, "It isn't trick or treat time again, is it? I'm sorry. I don't have any candy." With a circle of yellowed tatting in hand, he looked past her at the car.

"It's me, Noor, Mr. Emory," she said.

"Ah, you're that Indian girl. I know who you are. You're a dusky princess. I could use you in—"

"Don't be stupid, Hil," Mrs. Emory shouted from somewhere unseen. "Let the girl in."

"I'm just looking for Jaycee," Noor said, unwilling to enter and get caught fixing cans of beef stew again.

"She's at the Maple Jug," Mrs. Emory shouted. "She's closing up."

"The Maple Jug?" said Noor.

"Up in Hillwinds. The shop," Mrs. Emory said. "You just passed it, the driveway before ours."

"Thanks, thanks a lot," Noor said. "Nice to see you, Mr., Mrs. Emory." She backed away and made her escape, but not before he followed her out with that scraggly tatting and dirtied it by swabbing just one of Noor's headlights with it. Why one, she wondered? Why not both headlights, or neither? But there was no sense trying to make sense of Hilary Emory.

Up the hill to Hillwinds then. She'd never been there before. She'd been home with the flu the day her seventh grade class visited. Or so her parents had thought, since what looked like flu was actually the result of sitting up in Hubbard Park tower the evening before, with a couple of girls and a bottle of peppermint schnapps a friend had stolen from her parents' liquor cabinet—Noor's parents, good Muslims, didn't drink. So she'd never been to Hillwinds Living History Books before. Poor sucker Jaycee—she not only lived a few yards from her parents' door but apparently she also ran their business in their backyard.

Noor reversed onto Barnes Road and followed the drive up the hill. Jaycee must still be here, if her parents actually knew where she was. There was the Emorys' ugly beige Buick and one broken down yellow school bus in an otherwise empty parking lot. Why hadn't Jaycee just driven herself to the airport and parked there while she was traveling in Peru since her parents didn't drive, Noor wondered. Who knows? Maybe she couldn't afford the parking. Or never got her driver's license and didn't drive on highways. Except for a gigantic boulder—a glacial erratic, she remembered from some long ago geology class—hanging over the parking lot, Hillwinds was pretty in a hokey sort of way: fields, cross rail fences, a couple of oxen grazing, and the dim glow—kerosene?—coming from a little store front bearing a sign: Maple Jug Mercantile. The porch was pasted with old fashioned advertising from the mid-nineteenth century. Jaycee, dressed in a long gingham frock, an apron, and a silly-looking bonnet could be seen within, fussing with something on a shelf.

Noor knocked on the glass. Jaycee startled, as if it were inconceivable that anyone would show up at the Maple Jug Mercantile. When she saw Noor, Jaycee smiled broadly and beckoned her in like a long lost sorority sister and not a mere acquaintance attempting to help her sell a shit-load of coke. The door jingled with out-of-season sleigh bells arrayed over the transom to announce customers. Jaycee was wearing little round metal framed spectacles, part of her costume, Noor supposed. She was sure that Jaycee hadn't worn them the day Noor picked her up in Burlington.

"Hey!" Jaycee enthused. "I'm almost done here."

Inside, the store was meagerly stocked: glass pint and quart jugs of maple syrup shared shelf space with faceless corn cob dolls, toy rolling hoops, and men's suspenders. Little jars of ointments and tonics on the windowsills caught the late afternoon light. Noor stood next to a small, brightly chromed potbelly stove from which emanated moderate heat while Jaycee closed an old fashioned ringing till—so they did have a cash register, of sorts—and turned down the kerosene lamp. Out it sputtered. Jaycee struggled out of the bonnet and apron and frock, revealing maroon velour leggings that sagged in the nap-worn knees and tightened over her wide, child-bearing hips, and a shrunken mock turtleneck that showed how little elastic remained in her bra. Noor wasn't sure which outfit looked worse. Jaycee hung her Hillwinds duds on a hook inside the shop door, but continued to wear the little wire rim granny glasses, not part of her costume after all. Noor suddenly wished she were on a school trip to Hillwinds and not about to become forever entangled in a criminal bond with this odd duck. Jaycee shut the damper on the stove, bundled herself into what must have been her father's hand-me-down wooly sweater coat, and ushered Noor out the door, padlocking it behind them with an important air as though the store contained valuables. Past the broken-down bus, which gave Noor goosebumps, they walked side by side toward their cars. Maybe there were school kids still up on the property, abandoned like their bus, forced to stamp pats of butter to earn their keep.

"Hillwinds looks a little quiet, or is it just late in the day?" Noor wondered aloud.

"Both," Jaycee said, glancing across the dirt road that separated the few outbuildings and the barns and field from the Maple Jug and the parking lot.

Jaycee continued, "It probably costs more to keep it open than it brings in once foliage season peaks, though I did sell that marble-making kit today. Finally. Make your own marbles. In case you keep losing yours. My mom came up with that joke. She used to work the cash register but it's hard to get her up to the store these days," Jaycee added almost wistfully. Maybe she missed the company.

"We could get one of those marble kits for your dad," Noor said.

Jaycee sighed, as if she'd already thought of that herself. "I really should stay another hour but what's the point? Did you talk to what's his name?"

"I did. Gerry. He doesn't have the money to buy it himself but he knows someone who might. He needs a sample. He said the guy has to have 'a taste.'"

"I've got it at home," Jaycee said. "C'mon."

Noor waited on the driveway while Jaycee got out to lock the double gates behind their cars. Jaycee pulled one gate shut, then, when she reached for the other, the first gate swung open again. Noor started to get out to help but, finally, Jaycee succeeded at a task that she must have done every day, and Noor followed the beige Buick back to the Emory houses. Jaycee would do better to walk it, she thought. It certainly wouldn't hurt the girl to get a little exercise.

They entered Jaycee's little frame house, a smaller, sparer version of the ancient cape her parents inhabited. She struggled out of her lace-up boots and put on pilled fleece moose slippers, leftovers from the Maple Jug Mercantile five Christmases ago, Noor guessed.

"Would you like some tea?" Jaycee asked. "I have homemade or store bought. *Whatever floats your boat,*" she added slyly, having learned the phrase from Noor just a few days earlier.

But this wasn't a social call, for god's sakes, just business. Nevertheless Noor said yes to the tea, unable to deny Jaycee a once in a lifetime chance to be hospitable, an opportunity to make up for the ride home from the airport and her parents' demands while Jaycee was in Peru. And, Noor knew she *was* getting an awful big share of the proceeds just for making the connection. If the deal worked out. She quashed a stab of disappointment, imagining it might not. So much for accepting fate. It had to work out. Even if she wasn't going to use the money to purchase her own fertility, as she'd told Gerry, her purpose for the money, keeping disabled kids on ponies, was just as valid. Maybe more valid, since the world didn't need another child, but it did need someone to help kids who were here already.

The electricity bill apparently still hadn't been paid. Jaycee's living room was dim in the late afternoon. It held a tired-looking off-white canvas couch, a couple of saggy armchairs, some now redundant standing lamps, shelves of books, and a steamer trunk serving as a coffee table holding a blackened kerosene lamp, all in a space about the size of a horse stall.

"That was my mom's steamer trunk," Jaycee said. "From when she was in her twenties. It has costumes in it, really neat stuff. Someday I'll have to show them to you."

Noor ignored this remark. "We have to weigh it," she called when Jaycee disappeared into the kitchen. "I brought a postal scale."

Noor sat down on the couch while Jaycee bustled in the kitchen. She heard the water run, the clatter of a tea kettle. She got up to peruse the bookshelves. Numerous Hilary Emory kid books took up one long shelf. She drew out a book because of its equine title. The cover of *Mabel's Stirrups* showed a young red-haired girl in profile, patting the nose of a pinto horse leaning over a pasture gate. She checked out the horsey content, then stopped at a full-face illustration of Mabel, who wasn't Mabel at all but Pauline. The same luscious russet hair, the green gold eyes, the lovely curved lips of Noor's long dead friend. Noor's heart sped up and she felt shaky. Like cocaine, without the feel-good part of it. Jaycee appeared bearing a tray holding two cups with saucers and a honey jug with a wooden dipper. A couple of dubiously rough-hewn cookies, like dog biscuits, sat on another saucer. "I'll fetch you a spoon," Jaycee said, "then I'll get our gold mine out of its hiding place so—"

"I knew this girl," Noor interrupted.

Jaycee leaned over her shoulder to look at the book. She smelled of liniment and horehound drops.

"It's Pauline," Noor said, as matter-of-factly as if Pauline were sitting right in the room with them, waiting for her tea.

"Yes," Jaycee said. "My parents used to pay her to be my friend." She laughed ruefully. "Babysit, in other words."

Noor set the book down on the coffee table and took a seat on the couch. "That was *you* then. I knew she got paid to babysit a girl our age." How could she have forgotten that name, Jaycee? Pauline had pronounced it J.C., like Jesus Christ, with the emphasis on the second initial, not JAYcee, the way this one and her parents said it. But Noor had worked hard to forget everything that Pauline had said, to forget Pauline herself. She hadn't, though. She hadn't forgotten. Even if she'd forgotten in her head, her shaky body remembered.

"I thought she was so cool," Jaycee said, sitting beside Noor and running a hand over the book cover. "And so pretty. My father took a picture of the two of us, then cut me out, for my mother to use Pauline for her Mabel illustrations. That was you in the accident," Jaycee said. "I realized that already but I didn't want to bring it up. You were the little Indian girl that survived."

"Pakistani," Noor said. "Yeah, it was me." Noor felt a great deadening come over her, recognizing, in Jaycee's remark that Noor was "the little Indian Girl," the same words Jaycee's dad had used to describe her. That meant that the whole Emory family, no, more likely the whole town, had sat around talking about the little Indian girl at their dinner tables, the little Indian girl who was hit by the car, the little Indian girl who didn't die, the little Indian girl please pass the potatoes. "But I don't remember any of it, just walking with Pauline and her father after play rehearsal and a car coming fast up the road behind us. I *do* remember it was the day after Halloween, because Pauline had taken my candy home with her the day before, and when we got to her house we were going to sort through our bags to trade our favorites. I liked Kitkats and she liked Reese's Peanut Butter Cups."

She didn't need to tell Jaycee any of this. And she was lying. She remembered every bit of the accident.

"My father wished I looked like her. No, probably he wished I *was* her," said Jaycee.

Noor shrugged. If she had Jaycee for a daughter she'd probably wish the girl looked like Pauline too. But she pitied Jaycee, disregarded by her own father in favor of her far more appealing babysitter. Noor's mother once told her that she and Pauline had a different sort of beauty. Pauline was the all-American girl, only sultry for one so young, and she, Noor, would be small-boned and exotic among the clumsy Americans. Noor had felt that her mother was trying to console her, but Noor hadn't envied Pauline's beauty; she'd reveled in it, been proud of her friend, and prouder still to *be* her friend. Pauline was the pretty one; Noor was the smart one. Jaycee was the no one. Noor wondered if Pauline had ever learned that her face had been appropriated by the Emorys in one of their picture books. At least Hannah had done justice to Pauline's uncommon sensuality and beautiful auburn hair.

"She sure was pretty. I wonder if—" Jaycee said, stopping with a laden sugar spoon hovering over her cup.

"You wonder if what?

"I've always wondered if my dad liked Pauline better than he liked me. But sometimes I wonder if he liked her the wrong way."

"Eeew, creepy," Noor said. "We were only eleven years old."

"Not that he did anything," Jaycee said quickly. She got up quickly from the couch, knocking her baggy velour knees into the steamer trunk and sloshing tea into the saucers. "Oops. I'll go dig out the cocaine. I've got it hidden in my basement in a pickle crock."

Noor waited, sipping at her cooling tea—chamomile, not her favorite—while Jaycee slap-footed down the stairs. Pauline used to talk about the weird girl she had to "babysit," a girl their own age, maybe older, who lived in a house full of spindles and looms and half-finished woolen bedspreads, with a composting toilet. A girl with no television, no crushes on boys, a girl who'd never heard of Michael Jackson or U2 or Elton John or even tape players, didn't know anything about music except what you could tootle out of a tin fife.

Noor had wanted to go over there with Pauline one night but Pauline's mom had nixed it, intuiting perhaps that the two of them would have made a third wheel of Jaycee, rolling their eyes and cracking poorly veiled jokes at the girl's expense. Pauline had a secret mean streak that had thrilled Noor. How fitting that Emory had used her face for *Mabel's Stirrup*—Pauline had loved horses, and had made fun of Noor for being so afraid of them that she cringed at the mention of the book *Black Beauty*. A psychiatrist might have insisted that the teenaged Noor was identifying with her dead friend via her newfound connection to horses but did it matter? They were her life now and Pauline was long gone.

Noor got up and retrieved from her car the postal scale and the ream of printer paper she'd purchased, separately, in a fit of paranoia, at two different discount stores in Berlin. It was quiet at the Emory seniors' house. She ducked back into Jaycee's and pulled the curtains, caught off guard by how clean the curtains were, how free of dusty cobwebs, unlike the ones in the house across the yard.

"Maybe we should lock the door in case your parents show up," Noor cautioned. "Your dad, I mean," knowing that Jaycee's mother hardly ever left her chair.

"Good idea." Jaycee was waiting with the caked drug, which appeared more yellow than white under the room's poor lighting. The cheesy crust had been peeled away, and the perforated plastic bag replaced with another bag, which sat securely inside a Tupperware container. Jaycee was proving more adept than Noor had expected.

"Please don't tell me you fed that cheese to your parents," Noor said.

"Buried it in my compost pile. I tried really hard not to lose any of the coke. There will probably be some pretty happy earthworms though. Not to mention the cats."

"Did you try any of the coke?"

"No."

The package weighed out at one and a quarter pounds, more or less. Noor made a mental note to look up the conversion into grams to estimate what it would be worth, then solicited Jaycee's help in making two tiny paper envelopes no larger than postage stamps, as Gerry had instructed, to hold samples for him and the dealer guy. Using a razor blade they scraped a pinch of coke into each of the paper packets, being careful to seal them properly by folding down the tops. After Gerry's and the seller's cuts, Jaycee and she might each end up with something between fifteen and twenty thousand dollars if Noor's research was correct.

"What will you do with your share?" Noor asked Jaycee. "I mean, if the sale goes through." It was the first real question she'd ever asked Jaycee, she realized. It was getting dark. Jaycee used a tissue to wipe the soot from the blackened chimney of the kerosene lamp, lit the wick and did the same for another lamp on a small sideboard near the kitchen. She seemed to do this all as unmindfully as switching on lights, though she dropped the match on one occasion and on other, smudged her face with soot. The electricity was probably shut off at the Emory's often.

"I don't know. Pay bills? I don't really know what I want to do with it," Jaycee said.

"Have you ever lived away from your parents? You could rent a place or put down a down payment." Don't get involved, Noor chided herself, but she couldn't help asking.

"No. I should've made my escape before they got so decrepit. Now it's too late. They need me, as you know. Hey, I lied a minute ago. I did try some. I stayed up all last night. It was fun and then it wasn't."

Noor smiled. "That's kind of how I felt about coke when I tried it in college."

"I wish I'd gone to college," Jaycee said.

"You still could."

Jaycee shrugged. They sat another moment looking at their future sealed in a tupperware container on the antique steamer trunk. Fifty years from now, who knew? Maybe coke would be one of the active ingredients in the drug that cured Alzheimer's. Sure, put a good spin on it, Noor thought to herself. She picked up the two tiny envelopes, like bite-size fortune cookies for Gerry and the dealer, ready to go home.

Jaycee said, "Do you want to go with me to visit Pauline's grave? It's been too long since I've paid my respects. Did your parents let you go to the funeral? Mine didn't. I don't know why. They thought it would upset me too much, I guess."

Noor took a deep breath. She'd never been able to face the grave herself. She'd missed the funeral because she was in the hospital with her own injuries and later it was just too hard to ask her parents to drive her there. Pauline's mother had moved away somewhere with Pauline's little brother soon after the accident. Noor thought about tracking them down, but what could she say, I'm sorry your daughter and husband died twenty years ago and I'm still standing here knocking at your door, can I have a glass of water and then I'll go home? She'd tucked Pauline away into a closed dark place not unlike Jaycee's trunk, a vault in which she'd stashed her thoughts about her parents in Pakistan, fallen back into their pre-American lives with their cook, their maids to clean and bring them tea on a silver tray, her brother's search for the perfect Pakistani wife, her relatives, that whole other side of her life. It was the same vault in which she'd packed away the two miscarriages, the repeatedly failed attempts to get pregnant after them. Of course she opened the vault from time to time to mourn the losses.

She'd never forgotten the glare of the headlights running up on top of them, the great smack—not a thud like you'd think, but a smack of metal and flesh and being thrown through air to land in fiery pain, the squeal of the receding car as it zigzagged away, the silence of Mr. Shattuck lying face down on the other side of Pauline, the three of them flung into each other like dominoes, with Noor the furthest from the road. Not knowing yet that she had a smashed femur and broken arm, a concussion, and would soon have something else as well that hurt horribly, some other pain that she might never be able to identify, she had pulled herself, whimpering, over the dried weeds and brush at the fence line toward Pauline who was on her back, head against a stone, making mewling baby noises as black fluid ran from her mouth and ears. There was a smell, coppery and weird. Pauline's hand flexed and opened, flexed and opened, just like Mrs. Harvey's three-week-old infant whom Noor had seen a few days earlier. Noor looked down at her friend in the near dark, a piece of skull buckled above an ear and the red gold hair black now from the blood seeping, examining her like some unprepared-for specimen from science class, some lab quiz you couldn't study for. She touched the center of Pauline's starfish hand and it grabbed for her, clinging like Mrs. Harvey's baby, and Noor yanked away. Pauline wasn't mewling anymore, just gurgling as pink bubbles rose out of her open mouth. Mr. Shattuck lay face down, twisted and silent. The ground was cold, the air cold, and Noor remembered she'd drawn into herself, separate from them and their brokenness, concentrating on holding her own fragments together.

"It was just a reflex," Noor's mother had assured her weeks later, when Noor described Pauline's sea anemone hand twitching. "She already had irreparable brain damage." Noor didn't tell her mother, or anyone, of how she'd wrenched away from Pauline's terrifying grip, of how she'd wanted her friend to quit making those noises, those wet whimperings. It was a long time before someone noticed them splayed on the side of the road, stopped in the dark, roared off for help since no one had cell phones yet. And then came the lights and ambulances, and in the hospital the nurses shaking their heads over Pauline's dad's poor judgment in walking that night with the girls in tow. Why hadn't he taken a road with a sidewalk, or better yet, borrowed a car? They must have thought Noor was sleeping when they said these things, but she was only playing dead to be with Pauline. Noor willed the memory back into the vault with its creaky, unlockable door.

"I've got to go," Noor said. "I'll let you know when I hear from my contact." She gathered her things and slid the book with Pauline's picture into her bag, so she could look at it in private.

Jaycee unlocked the door and peered out. "The going is good," she said. "Hey, you're Pakistani. Don't get caught with that stuff. They might think you're trying to raise money for Jihad. Like in Portland, you know? Car bomb little old Montpelier."

Nope, not as naïve as she pretended, Jaycee, or maybe just naïve enough to not realize how insulting that was. But probably true. Noor thrust back the little scale. "Here, you keep this in your pickle crock. Just in case."

Jaycee smiled and shut the door. Noor walked down the three steps to her car. It was a good thing, they later agreed, that she had handed back the scale, because no sooner had the door shut behind Jaycee than a cop car lurched clumsily onto the property, the brittle tops of winter weeds whisking against the car's belly. What was it with cop cars these days, Noor thought stupidly, recalling the scrape with the one near the airport, and then she wondered whether maybe she was only more attuned to their intrusions now. But she gathered her wits for long enough to whip around and walk right straight back into Jaycee's kitchen, popping open the cubby under the sink and stuffing her whole bag under the rusting pipes. A cat darted out from behind the bag and leaped between Noor's feet.

By the time the cop rapped on the front door, Jaycee had tossed the Tupperware into the trunk and Noor was peeing in the bathroom to cover up for having rushed so quickly from the yard. She gave a loud flush when she emerged into the kitchen, drying her still trembling hands. The female cop was dishwater blond with a frowsy bun and kept the crook of one finger curled protectively around a belt loop on Hil's trousers. Hil was pale as could be, dryer than toast, so depleted you could see the blood trying to make its way through him. He still clung to his piece of dirty tatting. Turned out he'd walked from Barnes Road, crossed Center Road, walked a few miles down Bliss Road, passing Noor's driveway, and headed off across a field into the valley below. He'd really made tracks since Noor had headed up to Hillwinds. The people on Bliss Road with the freshly built deck and the new garage had phoned 911, seeing Hill in the distance making slow circles and then sitting down amid the weeds with his antique farmer's dunce cap held high.

"He has pretty amazing posture, you know, and that can be deceiving. It makes it look like he knows where he's going. There's a creek in that direction," the cop advised. "They often head toward water, the Alzheimer patients, when they're wandering. It's a magnet to them, water is, some primitive instinct, go toward water the way animals do, so you don't die of thirst. You've got to keep a better eye on him, you know. This isn't the first time we've brought him back up here. If there were fines for neglecting a parent I'd fine you. Not that you don't have my sympathies."

I wish you *could* hand out fines for parental neglect, Noor thought.

"Jaycee, pay the kind taxi driver please," Hil requested, waving his soiled tatting like an aristocrat's silk handkerchief.

Like daughter like father, Noor thought. The world's their taxi driver.

The cop rolled her eyes. "You could trim his eyebrows once in a blue moon, too," she added, blushing, it seemed, when she noticed Jaycee's own bushy set. "They're just about scraping the cornea."

The cat twined around Noor and Jaycee's ankles as the cop drove away. Jaycee brewed more tea to try to calm their jangled nerves.

"I thought we were screwed," Noor said. "I thought we . . ."

"Hell with this," said Jaycee, fetching from the cellar a bottle of rum she said she'd hidden years ago from Mike and forgotten until now. The bottle was blanketed with dust, "Probably asbestos," Jaycee said, standing up in the kitchen and pouring a capful into each of their teas. Chamomile tea with rum—what the hell. "My bag will be ruined under that sink," Noor remarked, but she was shaking too hard to fetch it. It was a Yellowstone Collection Kangaroo Backpack from J.P. Ourse, the leather soft and buttery, the nicest she'd ever owned, an uncharacteristic splurge to add to the feed bills. In for a dime, in for a dollar. She mink-oiled it once a month, just as she cleaned and oiled the horses' tack. It turned out to be safe and sound. She slung both straps over one shoulder, un-backpacklike, the way she always carried it, watching the cat, its little heart locket swinging from the ring on its collar, slip back into the cubby. Other cats had gathered in the yard outside as if to sniff at the place where the cop car had parked on their favorite weeds. Noor sidestepped them on the way to her car. Before she turned her head to back down the driveway she caught a glimpse of Hil, who must have snuck back outside while she and Jaycee were having their drink. The old man was standing behind his house with his pants unzipped, peeing into the dead garden.

PART II
A Cool Drink of Water

CHAPTER FOUR

Hilary Emory, 1980

On a steamy August Friday, Hilary Emory stayed in his office after everyone at McLarren Publishing Children's Division had left early, headed for their beach house shares in the Hamptons or on Fire Island. He preferred the air conditioned hum of his office over the garbage stinking streets of Manhattan. Hannah had taken the baby to her parents' house at the Cape for two weeks. He had no invitations, no demands other than a sudden urge to plow through a stack of over-the-transom manuscripts that his assistant, Meredith, never seemed to get to. How many pages of unsolicited slush did one have to read before cramming it back into an S.A.S.E.? Meredith wasn't working out very well. Hil had already made it through the first, pathetic pages of a couple of Judy Blume knockoffs, a peculiar tale of a mortician's daughter that had unintended humorous moments—the heroine's father was always "freezing her out" and her mother was "stiff" and on occasion her best friend "died laughing" but mostly it was another one of the tedious line of "I lost my boyfriend but discovered my friends matter more" tale set in a mortuary.

The next envelope contained a wrinkled, coffee spotted, pale copy of something called "The Drinking Gourd" that Hil nearly tossed just on principle without even removing the rubber bands that held it together—"C'mon, people," he muttered, "have a little professional pride." Nonetheless, he read a few lines. Hil was still reading it in his apartment that night, on the table beside a glass of Dewars and a plate of cheddar and stoned wheat crackers. He felt like he was in a scene out of that Marilyn Monroe movie *The Seven Year Itch*, the husband alone in the city on a summer's eve except instead of Marilyn to seduce him it was a chapter book, un-illustrated, about a young slave boy from Georgia in the 1850s whose parents die of fever en route to Canada via the underground railroad and who continues north alone, hiding in haystacks with mice running over him, shivering with fever in a thunderstorm, making a spine chilling escape from a bounty hunter, stealing corn and eggs from unsuspecting farmers, fighting despair and measles, until he is taken in by a kindly farm family in upstate New York. It was brilliant—great young protagonist, historically solid, socially relevant, even timeless, probably, since when would a good book about a young escaped slave *not* be socially relevant? It would be a critical and maybe even a commercial success. A Newbery book, perhaps, used in classrooms across the country. It could raise Hil's stature in the slippery world of New York publishing, lead to a better, more lucrative position in another house with a smarter, cuter assistant who never misspelled Emory as Emery (like emery board) when she signed papers in Hil's stead.

There was no cover letter accompanying the manuscript, no phone number, merely a return address for a John Corgi at a Hotel Marquis in Elizabeth, New Jersey. Hilary poured himself a second Dewars to celebrate and immediately wrote to John Corgi praising his work and expressing eagerness to acquire his book. Without an agent the guy could probably be bought for five thousand dollars and think he'd hit the jackpot. As a senior editor Hil had the power to make an offer without needing to pitch the book to his colleagues, but even though he needed no marketing department input, he liked to use the *pluralis majestatis*, or Royal We, adding in his letter that Corgi's "socially relevant book has received the unanimous support of both our editorial and marketing staff here at McLarren's Children's Division." A younger acquaintance over at Scholastic, Jeff Parmenter, who dismissed such airs as missing the point, had regaled a cocktail crowd at the Miami Book Fair asserting that in ten years, publishing would be co-opted by large corporations, and that editors would no longer make their own decisions but would have to kowtow to all-powerful number crunchers in marketing, which no one else believed, of course, least of all Hil. A naysayer's delusion. What's more, in private, Parmenter proclaimed that one day, books would be supplanted by something in the airwaves; he couldn't say what; publishers would go bust; the big houses would be carried right out like in body bags, he said . . . all of which made Hil all the more glad that Corgi had sent his book to *him* and not the ambitious but deluded renegade Parmenter. "The Drinking Gourd" could be the career maker for which both men longed.

He decided he wouldn't even mention the book at McLarren until Corgi signed the contract.

On the following Thursday, Hil's second letter returned in the office mail marked "no known address." Hil got the number for the Hotel Marquis through information but the line was always busy or no one answered. Someone had to know where the guy was, a family member perhaps. But no Corgis showed up in the phone books of the Tri-state area. Apparently, Corgi was an uncommon name. Hil decided, on Saturday, with Hannah and Jacqueline Charlotte still splashing at Sandy Neck Beach, to take a drive to the hotel in Elizabeth and see what he could learn about John Corgi at his last known address. It was more inviting than continuing to shovel through the slush pile, doing Meredith's job, or reading any of the agented manuscripts sitting on his desk. So many people thought they could be children's book writers just because they'd read a few. Hil had wanted to do the same and had made some false starts—lackluster tales which he kept in folders in his filing cabinet under the label DOA. Hannah always encouraged his efforts though he'd never shown her the results, fearing her loss of respect. She'd been a French lit major, dance minor at Vassar.

He'd met Hannah at one of the many Bicentennial Celebrations downtown that summer of 1976 when the tall ships were making their appearance in the harbor and music groups and dance troupes performed in the streets. Hannah belonged to a woman's dance collective called Womb-Bat. He was dressed as Paul Revere in a ridiculous tri-corner hat, full-sleeved white shirt, woolen vest, and knee pants with stockings, hot as Revere's forge, and all the more ridiculous because the Bicentennial celebrated the creation of the Union and Paul Revere made his ride through Lexington a full year before anyone signed the Declaration of Independence, but McLarren was pushing children's history books in time for the big to-do and he was supposed to be shilling for a *Johnny Tremain* knockoff, only in the McLarren version it wasn't Paul Revere the kid helped but John Adams and he didn't get his hand burned in a silver works, he broke his leg falling under a carriage.

Hannah was dressed in a sexy interpretation of late eighteenth century meets the miniskirt with her breasts heaving above a tight corset and her long wavy blonde hair swinging free from its gauzy bonnet. He bought a soda and an Italian ice and offered both to her when her troupe took a breather, saying, "You look like you could use some cooling off."

"Thanks," she said, downing the soda and then reaching for the lime ice and sexily squeezing the little white fluted paper cup above her open mouth. "You must be hot in that outfit," she said, coming up for air and gesturing at his Revere suit. "I'm melting here myself." She flipped her curls fetchingly. Her combination of slender and voluptuous had struck him as perfect and the voraciousness of her thirst was a turn on. Then she had to start up the prancing and thrashing once again—as much as he could make out it was a feminist interpretation of Betsy Ross's sacrifice to male power. It was easy to find her through Womb-Bat's answering service the following Monday.

Now it had been two years since Jacqueline Charlotte was born and Hannah hadn't taken off the pregnancy weight. She still seemed to be eating for two, and she showed no interest in teaching dance at one of the many private schools in Manhattan. She belonged at home with their daughter, she said, and he supposed it was so, as whatever she earned teaching would be offset by the cost of a nanny, in opposition, he noted, to everything the now defunct Womb-Bat had stood for, or danced for, as the case might be. His friend Jeff Parmenter had the temerity to point out that the same might be said of Hil's salary being used to pay a sitter if Hannah was working, so Hil may as well stay home from work, too, but Parmenter liked to make a pain in the neck of himself so Hil made a habit of ignoring his dismaying proclamations, like the one about wasn't it possible someday that everybody would run out of stuff to want, so they ought to get out of this dead-end publishing shit and figure out how to invent something that people would just about die for if they couldn't have it. Hil didn't mention to Jeff Hannah's sudden affectation—a need to explore herself as "an artist"—though her first attempts at paintings, if Hil said so himself, were really quite good. She'd never painted before; it was only the gift of a set of watercolors that an uncle of Hil's, who didn't know babies, had prematurely sent them for the baby's first birthday, that got Hannah started. That, and her already considerable facility with calligraphy pens.

In any case, John Corgi was the real thing and if Hil didn't have what it took to write like that—*Henry looked up; the moon sprinkled goose light over the dazzled fields. Winking stars whirled in a pattern his Papa'd dragged into the raked red dirt of Master Arthur's yard. That same moon had shone through his cob plastered window when Mama was still a warm dark shadow, tucking the rag knot quilt over his twiggy legs*—Hil could recognize it when he saw it. Since Hannah had their elderly station wagon, Hil arranged a car rental and headed out of the city toward Elizabeth, New Jersey. It wasn't like heading for Connecticut or even north to the Catskills or Adirondacks; rather it seemed you were driving through the dirtiest, smelliest (the rental had AC, thankfully), most run-down and potentially gang-ridden parts of the city except that you'd gone through the tunnel and passed into another state.

Elizabeth, New Jersey was a lovely name for such a grubby industrial city. The haughtily named Hotel Marquis turned out to be an SRO, a single room occupancy flophouse, in a bad section of a town that appeared to be comprised of bad sections. Hil parked as near as possible to the blinking neon "OFFICE—Vacancies" sign and hoped that his rental car wouldn't be stolen or broken into. An emaciated hooker in hot pants with an incongruously pregnant belly gave him the once-over. A hooded youth peeled himself off the wall to approach but Hil quickly opened the hotel door. The "office" was a dark entry with stained indoor/outdoor carpeting. A man sat watching a miniature TV behind a bulletproof glass window with a shallow metal depression under the glass for handing out keys and taking in money. Another hooker, this one looking far too old for the job but adorned in platform shoes and silver mini, dug around inside a purse in front of a leaning soda machine. Hil had to rap on the glass to get the man's attention. The receptionist, if you could call him that, was in his sixties, thin and gray skinned, with brushed back, thinning black hair and the ground-down remains of a neglected set of teeth. His last job might have been as a whirligig operator at a sleazy carnival. "Yeah?" he said, glancing at Hil with little interest.

"I'm looking for someone named John Corgi and this is his most recent address."

"Was," the man said. "He blew his brains out ten days ago. Still owed me three weeks' rent. Did it in the shower."

"Corgi's dead?" Hil asked stupidly. Hil had just read his book. The boy slave was more alive than most of the people eyeing Hil's rented car from the corners of the lot. So how could Corgi be dead?

"You know anyone survived blowing his brains out? It wasn't pretty." The carny receptionist grinned.

Hil had missed Corgi by mere days. Now he'd have to find a family member who might or might not be willing to release the manuscript. There'd be no more brilliant books from Corgi, no series, no continuing relationship between the author and his esteemed shepherding editor. Hil sighed. He wouldn't be profiled in *Publisher's Weekly*. He wouldn't be interviewed at *The Times*. Chances were when he died he wouldn't even merit an obit there. "That's too bad," he said. It unnerved him how easily he went from hopeful to resigned, just as he'd felt when it was suddenly clear that Jacqueline Charlotte, age twenty-two months, was not one of those babies people paused to admire. Not even older ladies cooed at her. If they paused at the sight of him wheeling his newborn daughter along, it turned out it was the carriage that caught their eye, the black pram he'd rescued from an estate sale and spruced up with ribbon and polish, its giant spokes gleaming.

The carny/receptionist shrugged.

"Do you know if Mr. Corgi has any family I might contact?"

"Who wants to know?" The man gave Hil a meaningful stare.

The stare registered and Hil, after glancing over to see that the hooker was still busy—he didn't like showing his wallet in a place like this—removed a twenty from his wallet. Hil watched the man's bony hand—replete with tattooed fingers—grasp the twenty from under the glass.

"I never seen nobody come around when he was alive. That brother was always alone. But after he blew his brains out, a few days later some lady showed up, asked me to open up the room and took away some of his things. Could've been his mother only he was black and she was white. Too old for his wife. I ain't never seen her here before. She didn't shed a tear, anyway."

"Do you know how I can find her?"

"Nope. Police maybe."

"Do you know anything else about him?"

The stare again. Hil removed another twenty and slid it under.

"He didn't like it when it got noisy. Complained a few times. He was real quiet until he plugged himself. Just another crazy vet is what I figure. He wore a fatigue jacket."

"And about the woman who came here? Did she say anything about their connection, maybe?"

"I wasn't really listening. I mean, the dude was dead. I had no one to cover the desk here so I just let her throw some things together and out she went. Oh, yeah. Said she hadn't seen him in something like ten years. I threw the rest of the stuff in the trash. Wasn't much there, really. A few plates, cups, a mess of papers, paperback books—black history crap, nothing I'd want to read. Stuff like that."

"Uhh . . . a mess of papers?" Hil asked without hope, already resigned to the first book's sequel being buried in landfill.

Carny man shrugged.

"Could I see his room?"

"Been rented out already twice today." The receptionist glanced at a clock over his desk. "It's in use, if you know what I mean."

"Well, you've been very helpful, thank you." Hil hurried out of the Hotel Marquis, the hairs on his neck standing up as he turned his back to the street to unlock the car door, got into his rental, and quickly pushed down the door locks. He steered himself through the city streets, hoping to hell he wouldn't get a flat. So Mrs. Corgi existed. If it was Mrs. Corgi. She might have another name, a married name. Or she might not have a phone. But then again it might not be John Corgi's mother at all, but an old friend who read about the suicide in the paper, a social worker, a former teacher, a spiteful sister, even some debt collector with no legal connection at all, who knew? So, the next step would be to go to the police, he supposed. If they didn't know Corgi's next of kin then what? Social security or the IRS didn't seem appropriate for a guy living in an SRO. A private detective? He thought about making his way to the police station, waiting at another bulletproof window, being sent from department to department only to learn what he already suspected—no living kin, or a mom who'd be no help. Hil decided he'd call. That's probably what he should have done from the first. The trip out to Elizabeth was just a waste of time. He had a Newbery Award-winning novel and still no lead on acquiring it.

Hil drove Route 19 and NJ 139 traffic back to the Holland Tunnel past a blur of dead-looking factories, brick projects, and run-down houses. More cars were heading out of the city than into it on a hot summer Saturday. He kept mulling the situation. The woman who showed up at Corgi's room hadn't seen him in ten years; even if she were Corgi's mother (and how did you explain the white woman when Corgi was, as the carny receptionist called him, "a brother," a brother who wrote about escaped slaves?) chances were that she hadn't even known her son was writing a book at all. What a nuisance it would be to have to track her down and ask permission to publish it, which she might not even grant. And he was sure it would be a success—like John Kennedy O'Toole's posthumous *A Confederacy of Dunces*, made all the more popular because the author had offed himself before the book came out. But not if she said no. That's what he would tell her then. That publishing the book would give her son's death power and meaning, and make him live on.

In the fluorescent dim of the claustrophobia-inducing Holland Tunnel, a new idea began to form. He didn't need to contact the police. He didn't need to find this woman. John Corgi couldn't make his weekly rent; he probably didn't have enough money to photocopy. Maybe there was a carbon paper copy somewhere but he doubted that too. John Corgi probably lacked the savvy to know he should make a copy. He'd sent the treasure over the transom, after all. Not even an agent. Almost nothing surfaced from the slush pile. Okay, there was that picture book, *Jellyfish Jam*, that created a splash and ended up on the bestseller list, and now the editor had his own kid's book imprint and threw book parties at Universal Studios, but that was like winning the lottery.

Even if the woman was Corgi's mother how savvy would she be? What kind of mother lets her son waste away in a crappy flophouse living off veteran's benefits or disability or whatever it was he'd lived on? Why should such a negligent person get the proceeds from the book when she hadn't even had the wherewithal to cook supper for a depressed and desperate man? She didn't deserve even to know about her son's artistry, much less profit from it. But Hil deserved it. Not just as an editor, either. As a man. As a husband. As a father. As a person who'd done his part in writing go-nowhere books and kept his head up and got a respectable job, even if people tended to ask, "Don't you want to get out of children's books and publish *real* books someday?" Not that it was his dream to work on the children's end of things, but he'd been working as a low-level editor at Harcourt and when the opening for a senior position came up at McLarren he'd jumped at it. Hannah was pregnant at the time. Now he treasured the time he spent reading kids' books to his daughter even though she had that way of startling out of her slump whenever he turned the page.

As for "The Drinking Gourd," he could make some changes . . . the boy could become a girl to satisfy people like Hannah who wanted strong female characters. Hannah hated the way all the female characters in children's books tended to be hens sitting on eggs, or were akin to hens sitting on eggs—even Horton the elephant who hatched the silly bird's egg, was male. In fact, Hil had even read a book about a kangaroo taxi service in which the kangaroo, who carried customers in his pouch, was male. So, Corgi's boy could become a girl, the farm family could be in Vermont instead of upstate New York, the kid could have headed out from South Carolina instead of Georgia, a few switches here and there . . . and Presto, "The Drinking Gourd" would become Hil's book with maybe a catchier title. *The Cracked Vessel? The Spilled Drink?*

It would be a terrible shame for the book to go unpublished. So what if the book didn't have the cachet of being written by a dead war hero? It would still be a success. Here was a chance handed to Hil and he'd be a fool not to take it. Certainly Jeff Parmenter would jump at the chance. Why not Hil? He would be honoring John Corgi by allowing his story—altered of course, into Hil's story—to see the light of day. The drinking gourd in Corgi's title referred to the Big Dipper that slaves followed north. Hil wanted to keep the feel while dispensing with the exact words. How about *A Cool Drink of Water?* It could refer to a moment—already his imagination was firing up—when the child protagonist lands at the Vermont farmhouse and someone—another child perhaps—offers her a tin dipper from their spring. A symbol of acceptance, of sharing. Perfect. And the heroine's name—the little runaway slave girl replacing Corgi's Henry would be not Henrietta, but Elizabeth, Bitty. Elizabeth—his joking homage to the town in New Jersey that had turned Hilary Emory, secretly, into an esteemed children's author.

For one pinched moment he saw his mother's face, puckered with distaste, telling him, as she'd done when he was in sixth grade and had taken the UNICEF funds out of the little collection box he'd carried virtuously around the neighborhood on Halloween, that he was "a common thief," as if she thought it would be better for him to be an *uncommon* thief, a thief whose escapades she could be proud of, not just a sneak and a miscreant. He'd used the UNICEF money to buy himself a decent school shirt, for God's sake. He'd learned early that it was up to him to make his way in the world. His father, heir to an old family fortune, had wasted his inheritance on various harebrained projects that failed before they even got off the ground—like his plan to turn a silo into revolving condominiums with a constantly turning view of the newly developing countryside, and his impromptu run for governor on a third party ticket—further embittering his mother who'd probably only married his father out of a desire for the money (which hadn't been as much as she'd imagined in the first place, since the stock market crash had taken quite a bite out of the Emory fortune), and who'd never gotten over the death of Hil's older brother in Korea. She'd taken the term "crazed with grief" to new heights, having created a living memorial to his brother's "heroism" when Hil knew for a fact that his brother had been killed by "friendly fire" at Inchon.

So he'd bought a short sleeved button down shirt with UNICEF money, big deal. So he'd cheated on the occasional exam, plagiarized parts of his college honors thesis, barely embellished his resume—small potatoes, peccadilloes intended to help him along when no one else was going to give him a hand . . . and in his mother's eyes, unimaginative crimes, small connivances, when the big pickings beckoned just around the corner. Or maybe she really did want for him to be completely law abiding, but that didn't square with certain other things she'd mumbled when he'd stolen the UNICEF money, like too bad he hadn't visited more houses or had the sense to collect on high-end Prospect Street. "You could have bought *two* shirts with *that*," she said.

Yes, Hil had learned you had to take whatever opportunities came to you, not that too many appeared when you were an English major with a history minor working at a New York publishing house run by well-heeled hobby editors who could afford the poor but "respectable" salary and assumed that Hilary Emory, with his family name and apparently bespoke suits, which Hannah found at an Episcopal church thrift shop, not to mention his talent at squash, could do the same. His misdemeanors weren't causing bodily harm. You could hardly put his helping *The Drinking Gourd* see the light of day into the category of murderous robbery. No, it was more like skilled midwifery, bringing a stillbirth back to life when the parent was already dead and gone.

Hil was already hard at work transforming the coffee stained copy of *The Drinking Gourd* into his very own *Cool Drink of Water* by the time Hannah carried a sleeping Jacqueline Charlotte off the elevator Sunday night, both of them sunburned and cranky, spreading sand on the hardwood floors.

"Is there anything in the fridge to feed Jacqueline Charlotte?" Hannah wanted to know.

In response, Hil, enthralled by his newly discovered muse, merely grunted.

CHAPTER FIVE

Jeff Parmenter, 1989

Jeff was in his Broad Street office, checking the Dow and S&P 500 in the *Wall Street Journal* when the call came in from Emory. "Jeff, have you a moment? There's a detail I wish to confer about with you," Hilary Emory said in that fakey formal locution that always needled Jeff. Have you a moment? Wish to confer? Jeff translated mentally—*There's some crap I need to know about*—before answering.

"Yeah?" Jeff let his eyes keep running down the columns, always looking for another Gulf & Western, which had doubled in value the day after he'd bought it in 1985, the Reagan recovery really kicking into gear. But now, in '89, the Dow was in shit creek after an all-time high, all because of a bunch of stewardesses wreaking havoc with the airlines industry.

He waited for Hil to describe some inconsequential and easily reversible aggravation along the lines of his last calls—carpenter ants in the salvaged timber frame from the decrepit barn that would become the supposed Hillwinds Living History Books Inn and Enterprises gift shop, or a zoning issue or an itchy investor who wanted more evidence of the enduring success of the two-year venture—an aggravation that some artfully manipulated photos and pretty words would clear right up, which should be Hil's department given that he was the author, after all, not to mention on site. Jeff was only the red wheelbarrow on which everything else depended.

"Well, you see, one of our investors seems to have a problem. He thinks that our arrangement might actually be illegal. I know it's preposterous but he's quite adamant . . ."

"Not on this phone," Jeff said curtly. "I'm getting off now. I'll call you on our usual phone."

"When?" Hil sounded like some girl Jeff had taken home from a bar without assessing her appearance carefully enough. He grimaced, remembering the one with the bizarrely high hairline from a week ago. Shocking when he got up to pee at 4:00 a.m.

"Half an hour," Jeff said and set the receiver into its cradle. What the fuck? Was this just more of Hil's incompetence and paranoia or was there really some Hillwinds investor suddenly acquiring half a brain? God damn it to hell. Cold feet already? Didn't they get it? Even in a legitimate enterprise you can't hope for aggressive growth if you don't do risk, but if you sit on your cash, waiting for every Joe Schmo and his brother to come crawling for paper, you *can't* do risk. Jeff had appointments for the whole afternoon—accountant, broker, haircut and manicure—now he'd have to forego the gentle cuticle pushing and buffing of his nails by that cute Latina with the purple lipstick and the cleavage, what was her name? Wanda? Yolanda?

You could make calls out on the New York payphones but you couldn't get calls in on most of them, a measure to curtail drug traffic, but the payphones in Vermont were still innocently open. Jeff had the number of one at a gas station on Route 2 a ten-minute drive from Hil's house, through which they conducted their most important business. Hil seemed to think these precautions were ridiculous bothers; Hil didn't get it. And if Jeff could help it Hil *wouldn't* get it, because like all business models, Hillwinds was based on the appearance of solvency, and if Hil knew how leveraged their little business was, he *too* might get cold feet or some sort of stupid old-fashioned scruples.

Long distance would require Jeff using his calling card, which would mean records kept. To that end Jeff squirreled away coins. It was autumn, the nicest time in New York, the gingkos flapping their crooked fans in the brisk breeze that came off the East River. Gingko trees reminded Jeff of his daughter, Clea. She was the product of his only marriage, though he was embarrassed, sometimes, to still catch himself thinking of it as his *first*. When Jeff graduated from Washington University in 1972, he had a draft lottery number of just seventeen. His soon-to-be fatherhood, which didn't exactly thrill him for its own sake at the time, would earn him a deferment, and by the time the marriage ended, little Clea was two, the war was over and the army was volunteer again. Asian women had used to kneel beneath the gingkos lining the path to the Wash U. library, collecting the seeds to be cleaned and roasted. With their hair swept up in pink ball elastics, their hands in rubber gloves, and their noses handkerchiefed to protect them from the smell of the malodorous pulp, the squatting, reaching narrow-eyed ladies represented to Jeff the closest he'd ever come to being blown to smithereens in Southeast Asia. Saved. By Clea. He couldn't bring himself to make the effort to get in touch with his daughter now, though through various means he occasionally tracked down her whereabouts. It would hurt too much to see her, to speak with her. She'd be past her sweet sixteen. Jeff couldn't picture it. She'd be practically . . . what . . . a woman? She wouldn't recognize his face if he ever did show up at her mother's door, and besides, what if she ended up needing his help with college expenses?

The twin towers gleamed above the other skyscrapers. Jeff dropped into the South Ferry subway station and huddled with a handful of coins in front of a payphone. He knew it was ridiculous to call from a noisy subway station but it appealed to his boyhood obsession with Ilya Kuryakin of "The Man From Uncle." Hil answered on the first ring. He really was a sucker for their little rules, mainly because he actually cared with a capitol-C about something, even if that something was mainly himself. Jeff didn't care that much about anything anymore except maybe money, even though the stuff you ended up buying with it was never nearly as heart-stopping as the dollars themselves. He had lived with this paradox for years, though not unhappily. Still, he hoped for Clea's sake she was the opposite way. Even to care about which of your favorite shows was on TV that night used to have more rewards, Jeff remembered, than twisting his wrist to check the time on his new Rolex, which had a calculator, a stopwatch, and a scratchproof sapphire crystal. With a poke of his chin, he started the stopwatch. It amused him to time Hil's hemming and hawing, though Jeff had no intention of missing more than one appointment today.

"What's up," Jeff said.

"Well, this fellow has been taking some night school business courses and had the bad fortune of attending a lecture on the topic of investment fraud. He got to thinking and called me up with some very pointed questions. Seems he thinks we're operating something called a something scheme. Pyramid? Ponzi? Whatever that is."

Jeff was all attention now. "Does he want his funds back? What did he want? Did you remind him if he keeps the money in the whole ten years he's guaranteed money-good plus bonus income? Point two percent. Point two of the entire Hillwinds Living History Books Theme Park value at that time, or whatever it's called, Inn and Enterprises, Theme park, doesn't matter. Point two percent of the highest dollar value between then and now. Whichever is more. Plus tell him we'll throw in a handful of shares. Besides, if this joker takes out his money now, he forfeits all accruing income as per the original agreement," Jeff concluded. *We*, of course, was a loose term, since while Jeff provided input, Hil alone signed the so-called investment agreements with all their perks and stipulations, like on the ten-year date if you haven't taken income, you can withdraw the full principle even if the market had plummeted in the interim, and for twenty-five thousand you get your name or your face, your pick, in one of Hil's books, and for anything over forty you get your name on a bench. No one could deny it was a nice, rather lucrative arrangement, one that Jeff, especially, didn't want to see come to an end just yet. For although a portion of every dollar was invested with an eye toward generating investor income and maybe even actual project development since a portion of every dollar had gone into the purchase of the land abutting Hil's property and went toward the future buildings and operating expenses for Emory's little ego monument, yet another, perfectly acceptable portion would continue to go to Jeff in exchange for having the smarts to think up the arrangement and the cash to front Hil to get their little "dream" park rolling, and what Hil didn't know about wouldn't kill him. Besides, they were only doing their part. The whole economy depended on indebted entrepreneurs like them. Paper's worth zilch if no one's on credit; there needed to be debt to fuel the economy. There even needed to be lies, since bad times happen when risk-takers misunderstand the risk, and you can't have good times without the bad.

"He actually threatened me," Hil huffed. "He said he was thinking of going to the . . ."

Jeff jammed a finger in his spare ear when a train screeched and clanked into the nearly empty station—it was 10:15 a.m., time for all office slaves to be inside their high-rises by now."Hang on," Jeff said, cradling the dirty receiver into his shoulder and glancing at his watch—the call had gone on for less than two minutes. But two minutes could change the world, Jeff knew—he'd seen business deals flop in less than two seconds, and a million dollars made in the same amount of time—and for that reason it upset him to be away from his desk. You just had to roll with whatever inspiration came your way.In the momentary gap before the train chugged out again, he asked, "What? Couldn't hear you."

" . . . the authorities!" Hil said.

"Usually when they call up like this they just need reassurance. My broker gets these kinds of telephone calls all the time. You just have to talk them through it, show them the charts, the flow charts. You are keeping flow charts, aren't you, like we said?"

"Uhhhh," said Hil. "I asked him to wait until I discussed this with my partner. He said he'd wait one day. *Twenty-four hours* quote unquote," said Hil, as if twenty-four hours sounded more like a threat than just "one day." Jeff pictured Hil making that little quote gesture with two fingers of each hand, phone scrunched into his shoulder, his overturned bucket hat losing its balance on his head.

"Well then we'll go and meet with him," said Jeff. "Offer him a little scare tactics to calm him down."

"Scare tactics?" said Hil.

"Yeah, like he has to understand we're like an annuity, there's guaranteed income after ten years, and a death benefit secured at the highest value since the day you bought it even if it tanks the day you die! It's a win-win situation! But if he takes it out and puts it in the stock market, kablooie. Solvent today, Zombie tomorrow. Better yet, bribe him. Or threaten his wife and kid."

"Do what?" said Hil.

"That's a joke," said Jeff. "Look, I'm driving up this aft. You'll set up a meeting. Find out where he'll be, and we'll be there. And remember my name isn't Jeffrey Parmenter. It's Derrick Stamm."

"I'll try, Derrick Stamm," Hil said, like always.

"No, you've got to do more than try, you've got to make it happen." He stopped himself from saying, or we're both up shit creek. Hil wasn't entirely aware of the precariousness of the situation, and Jeff intended to maintain Hil's willful naïveté for as long as possible. Hil made it easy, with his outsized ego and a streak of loneliness that made him a sucker for thinking he was one of the boys. Plus, Jeff knew Hil's secret, the secret tipsily blabbered to him in a shared cab after a publishing Christmas party back when they were both still earning editorial peanuts, not long after Jeff had brought out Hil's first book, *A Cool Drink of Water*, to riotous pre-pub acclaim and burgeoning advance orders. Jeff would rather have a tall drink of water than a cool drink of water but when he made that joke Hil didn't get it and Hil's put-upon wife Hannah's residual streak of feminism was offended by it. The book was not yet in stores, not a day or two away from being shipped by the distributors out to eager shopkeepers, when Hil had made his confession. Hil hadn't actually written the book, he said. He'd told it all in a slobbery-collared rush, snow slapping the windshield, the cabbie listening in but like he'd heard it a gazillion times before, all the ways to fuck up and screw off and then beg for forgiveness.

"The kid shot himself in a shower stall," Hil had concluded his secret confession, just as the cab skidded sideways against a curb.

Jeff remembered being too stunned to open his mouth. But Hil wasn't asking forgiveness it seemed, only recognition. It was the kid's own fault, Hil said. If the kid who'd written the book about a young runaway slave hadn't offed himself before Hil, dipping into the slush pile while his assistant was on vacation, found it and wanted to buy it . . . Hil could hardly be faulted, "Can I?" he asked, and Jeff said, "Sure you can but so what?" After that they went back to print four times and then Hil had the great idea of swallowing his pride and asking Hannah for "help" with pictures. The new picture books came out and brought in some fine reviews, even a couple of movie options that didn't pan out, and all of that led to Hillwinds Living History Books Theme Parks Inn and Enterprises, or whatever the name was, since somebody had to reap the benefits and it might as well be him and Hil, and it *was* him and Hil, so everything was as it should be.

"A lot of folks don't appreciate the kind of shenanigans that go into good works," Jeff reminded Hil now as the next train groaned out of the station, the same banter he always used to lighten the moral load of Hil's perfidy as well as justify any upticks in Jeff's own consultation fees. "Listen, I'm the one who's got to get the car out of the parking garage, fight the city traffic, and drive five hours so you just have him ready to talk to me by four this afternoon, got it?"

"Let's keep this civil, Jeff."

"No doubt." The problem was that Emory wanted Jeff's know-how, his business smarts but he also wanted Jeff to stay the eager beaver English major from NYU working for shredded wheat at *Scholastic* who'd managed to make Hil feel like the proud author of a book he didn't actually write. And then Jeff had seen the writing on the wall of the publishing industry and decided to switch careers, learning to trade in the pits and then figuring out his own sweet little deals on the side. Hil wanted Jeff to keep talking characters and plot and *Cups Overflowing with Chowder* or whatever the next book would be called. There'd been too many books for Jeff to count, all with Hannah's charming pictures (Jeff used to wonder what other talents Hannah kept hidden up her voluminous sleeves, but now that Hannah was so voluminous herself he didn't bother) that didn't quite save them from suffering in comparison to the much better written original. Hil thought it impure to concern himself with percentages and points. But Hil wanted to keep that money flowing too, didn't he? Wouldn't he like to fix up that Cape he had his family camping out in, for starters? Let's keep it civil? Fuck. But it was funny too. A *Pyramid Scheme?* The things people come up with.

Jeff hung up, shaking his head. He'd have to get cash to take with him to Montpelier, enough to quiet this would-be vigilante who was calling up Hil. Hell, Jeff had other pots boiling, like the new Roderick Fellows Sanford Investment Securities LLC ("RFSIS"), which he was just about ready to get off the ground. Maybe it was time to just cut Emory loose, let him take the heat, let the project go to seed. Hil, fundraising with his moral compass in hand, really believed they were going to turn Hillwinds Living History Books into another Sturbridge Village without pulling any of that nice, freshly carded wool over the eyes of their investors. But it was a sweet little money tit and Jeff had been milking it quite happily. He hated to give up on a good gig like that without seeing what he could do with this Vermont hick crybaby with the big mouth. Let the guy accept a nice fat payoff and see what he had to say then. Jeff hurried back to his office to cancel the day's appointments.

Five hours later, Jeff turned off Center Road, onto Barnes, and on impulse took the right turn just before Hil's driveway, onto the freshly graveled drive that led to "Hillwinds," or *Ill Winds*, as Jeff had privately renamed it on the drive north. He'd see the progress for himself without Hil's boasting and yammering. The former hayfields were staked out with string and sticks to mark the locations of future blacksmith and spinning shops. The derelict, half-collapsed farm house that had loomed over the few outbuildings which would someday hold the working kitchen, kiln, and classroom, had been dismantled, its nineteenth century timbers on display in the spanking new mini-barn housing the first of the stage sets. To date, more had actually been developed at Hillwinds than

Jeff himself had counted on. Also, it was picturesque, if you liked nature and trees and that sort of thing. Too bad he hadn't found an all-season resort to solicit funding for instead, some place where he could play tennis or ski and order room service in the hot tub while watching over the suckers who came to check on the progress of their investments, and where every time you drove up the driveway you didn't need to avert your eyes from the sight of that giant boulder about to tip loose on the hillside and flatten you.

Jeff made a U-turn and headed back down the gravel drive to the road and into Hil's driveway. Apparently Hil was still holding off on fixing up the smaller of the two little colonial era cape houses. Jeff had heard a lot more about the house's potential than he cared to, like the plan to fix it up for the daughter to live in when she was grown, and if she married and had kids, God forbid, Jeff thought, but the house still looked as sorry as ever, squat and forsaken, the few remaining shutters, which were in the middle of being put up or taken down, propped against the foundation. He'd tried to explain to Emory that his interest was a supportive one. As chief financial backer, who, after all, provided the start-up funds, he'd leave the actual construction and running of the park to Emory and his minions, including his wife and that sad-sack preteen daughter who might have a passable ass some day if she didn't put on weight like her mom was doing.Hannah—what a waste of a bod. She had a fine mind though. It was she who had come up with the idea for the contest to name that precariously balanced boulder, a contest now underway in primary schools around the country. The kid that came up with the best name would win an all expenses trip for his whole class to Hillwinds, paid for by the modest, but still endlessly multiplying four dollars per kid entry fees, or $120 per class. The Emory family lived in the slightly bigger of the small cape houses, the one with an actual, new front stoop that showed up the tattered dormers. As usual Hil strode onto the stoop to greet him and just couldn't help enthusing over progress at Hillwinds before they got down to brass tacks, as if Jeff had made the trip just to see where the sheep pen was going to go. Hil directed him to the backyard and a rough little bench made out of timber ends where they sat looking over the dried-up autumn garden, and from where, at the top of the sloping fields, the Hillwinds grounds, with their crosshatch of strings and stakes, were just visible.

"So, your troublemaker investor, what's his name?"

"Eben Shattuck."

"Eben? What's he, a character in one of your books or something?"

"He works for the post office but he's taking classes as I mentioned. I think he plans to get his realtor's license. Son needs braces. His wife's a teller but her hours just got cut."

"So he's an asshole, blaming everyone else for his troubles. Big deal."

"I really can't say. He's always seemed a very nice man. His daughter comes to the house sometimes to . . . visit with Jaycee."

"Who?"

"Jacqueline Charlotte. Only she makes us call her Jaycee now."

About time, Jeff thought. Maybe the little sad sack had more of her stubborn mother in her than he'd figured.

"Well," Jeff said, "we need to visit with him and explain that he'll make a lot more money by staying with us than by going with a standard broker type. I've brought some cash if he insists on getting something now, but not his whole investment, just enough to calm his nerves before he asks for any more, enough for him to know we have it to spare." Jeff patted the breast pocket of his jacket, the envelope of hundred dollar bills that he had brought with him not only for this guy, Eben's, benefit, but for Hil's, in case Eben wasn't alone in needing reassurance. "Where and when do we meet him?"

"He's off at 4:00 and he works downtown so I told him we would meet him at the Capitol bar. If that is a satisfactory arrangement with you, of course."

"Okay, good." Jeff glanced at his Rolex. It was already nearing 3:00 and he was hungry. He hadn't even stopped for lunch he was so intent on getting up to Montpelier and taking care of business. But he knew better than to negotiate on an empty stomach. "I got to stop for a meatball sub on the way. But let's drop in on your wife a minute," he said, letting Hil lead the way to the front stoop again and into the house. "I always like to check in with Hannah."

Hil said, "I'm sure Hannah would be delighted to rustle you up some leftover squash loaf—we had it for lunch today ourselves . . .

"Nah, don't bother her," Jeff said, trying to hide his overactive gag response. Hannah came trundling out from Hil's study to greet Jeff as fast as her no longer gamine legs could carry her. As usual, Jeff found himself observing her behavior with care, wondering exactly what she knew about him and Hillwinds, in part because, to look at her you saw only the disappearance of her youthful charms, which had the curious effect of making her appear smarter than he once thought she was. Her arms were spotted with ink, and there was paint on her hands, the threads of dye bruising the tips of her fingers. Jeff noted a dab still marking one cheek, as if it was on purpose rather than by carelessness that she carried the vestiges of paint around with her all day. She did the slyest little jump when Jeff invited her to join him and Hil for lunch.

"Feeling flush today," he said, hoping he was right she wouldn't accept the invitation to lunch. She never did. She was smart enough to leave the men to their own devices. Besides, the little girl was at her schooling, her stubby head bent dutifully over the kitchen table, practicing multiplication. Had he watched over Clea's first attempts at math? Of course not, how could he? He hadn't seen her more than once or twice a year over Christmas and holidays, and what kid likes to do homework on Christmas? He remembered he taught her how to wrap presents, unless it was she who taught him that trick, the one with the scissor that made the ribbon curl.

"Up Straight!" Hannah ordered, taking another mouthful of corn fritter from a plate on the table. The girl stayed as she was.

❧

The meeting at the Capitol Hotel bar with Eben Shattuck didn't go well. It was late afternoon, which struck Jeff suddenly as being a bad time of day to meet a testy client, just like the joke about justice relying on how long the judge had been waiting for lunch.

Plus there was nothing more depressing than the forest of denuded trees hiding down the road from the clock tower and the Gulf gas station you could see out the window. Nothing worse than a tree but a naked tree, and nothing worse than a naked tree than a lot of them. And the guy, Shattuck, was one of those dads who shuttled their kids around town all day only now that his car hadn't started this morning he was doing it on foot. Practically the first thing he said was he needed to pick up "the girls" (as if Jeff knew who he was talking about) "from after school activity at the college auditorium at 4:45." As if one drink would be enough. But Eben Shattuck ordered Earl Grey tea, which came in a pot on a tray with a teaspoon. The skinny middle-aged man with the orange cowlick squeezing lemon juice into his Earl Grey tea struck Jeff as being an unlikely owner of balls. But Eben never backed down. He wanted his investment back and he wanted it now. The cowlick wagged. He'd invested with Hil for his retirement figuring that his government pension wouldn't cut it, but now he needed the money back because their furnace had died and their son needed special orthodonture, which the insurance company insisted was cosmetic, even though the poor kid could barely close his mouth. He'd taken too big a risk putting his wife's modest inheritance in Hillwinds Living Picture Books, he said, and then to add insult to injury, it was beginning to look like he'd been had.

"Living *History* Books, not *Picture* books," Hil corrected. Wasn't that just like Hil, Jeff thought. The world could be falling down around him and he'd still be correcting the spelling.

Jeff said, "You can fight the insurance company, Eben, you just have to get a doctor to say it's not cosmetic and then keep calling and bugging them until they give in and pay. That's how it always works. As for your furnace, I'm sure Hil knows where you can get a refurbished one, with all his remodeling know-how. Don't lose this chance to make real money, Eben. Your regular pension plan probably puts your dollars in equities, and with market fluctuations you could be out half of it before you're ready to retire. With us your money's more secure. Hil guarantees it. In any case, for the record, typically, most funds, redemption day is quarterly. We're in the middle of the quarter here, Eben. Most places there's a window, only 15 percent goes out per quarter. If everyone took out their assets at once, what do you think a dollar bill would be worth on the—"

"Guarantee? Really? Did you say guarantee? What you guaranteed was I could get my money out whenever I wanted. Whatever it's at. But it's been months now I been asking for it. My wife doesn't even know I put it with you, and she wouldn't like it if she found out. She—"

"And think ahead, Eben! Think of the kids' education. Although from what I hear from Hilary, your kids'll get by on academic scholarships alone," Jeff interrupted. "You and your wife won't need to spend a penny on colleges, which'll save on your retirement. Do your kids have red hair too?" But even tugging on the guy's paternal heartstrings didn't work. If anything, it only made Eben more bullheaded.

"It's fairly simple," Eben said. "I put in twenty-three thousand a year ago. Today, I ask for my money, I don't care what you call it, you can call it assets, you can call it funds, you can call it pie charts, you need to give me today's market value in *dollars*. Period. My kid needs orthodontics now, not in ten years. And the furnace needs repair. But it's none of your business why I want it. I don't need your permission. That's the rules. You owe me today's market value according to those statements you never sent out. Now. Tomorrow. If not, I bring the papers in to my professor. Not the one who taught the class about Pyramid schemes, yet, 'cause he's on leave. But this other professor's a county treasurer and she already said it sounds fishy what I told her and she has a cousin works at the State Attorney General's office."

Jeff sat up straight. Eben Shattuck's lousy twenty-three thousand wouldn't be impossible to come up with, but it would just be such a drag, not to mention a temporary absence of liquidity due to last week's fiscal emergency, which had required Jeff, or rather the so-called Derrick Stamm, who had signing privileges on the accounts, to borrow a handful of the Hillwinds assets to solve the burgeoning foreclosure of another of Jeff's start-ups of which Hil was unaware.

"You're making a real mistake," Jeff said to Eben. "You'll make money from this. That class you took had it wrong. A *pyramid scheme* makes money by paying investors to bring in more investors, a *Ponzi scheme* gives old investors new investors' money. We're obviously not a pyramid, and if we were a Ponzi, we'd have given you your money already, you can bet on it, take it right out of the next guy's donation. Eben, look at it this way. Your money is *venture capital!* You're a *venture capitalist! A visionary!* And this isn't some casino we're building here; this is cultural. Bringing history to life. A combination of literature and history, educational . . . for posterity. We're better than the Fed. The Fed can print money but they can't create value. We create value! Think of your grandchildren. Think of your name stamped on one of the cobbles."

"What cobbles?" Hil asked, but Eben was already on about the rate of interest seeming "too consistent," and repeating his whining about the statements not being provided. "Plus they're supposed to be quarterly, the statements, not annual. Listen," said Eben. "I don't want any trouble. I don't want to have to go the Attorney General on this. I got a lot to deal with. We got kids, a mortgage, my wife's got stuff going weird at work, we don't want to have to go to my professor's cousin who—"

"So you're studying to become a real estate agent? How about we help out with your licensing fee? Just consider it a little advance on the gains to follow." Jeff whipped out his wallet, opening it to the wad of bills, which no longer appeared as thick, to his eye, as it had before.

"And now you offer me a bribe! I'm sure the Attorney General will be interested to hear about that." Eben rose from his seat, the orange cowlick quivering, the little teapot clattering. He was not a large man, not an imposing figure at all, but he was steely and he meant what he was saying. "Who are you? *Derrick Stamm*!? What's your place in all this, *Mr. Stamm*? I looked you up. I couldn't find you anywhere."

"It's not a bribe. It's a no-fee cash advance. For incentive. You were one of our earliest . . . we just want to reward you for staying with Hillwinds. And I'm not in the phone books in these parts because I live in New York City," Jeff concluded, kicking himself for being dumber than Hil and giving away where he lived, even if under a different name. "I'm just an advisor," he said, "I'm not a *principal*," and this time he nearly believed it himself. "Your arrangement is with Mr. Emory, right, Hilary?

"Eben, I wouldn't have involved you in this if I thought there was anything . . . uhhh . . . mendacious going on," Hil said.

"What?"

"Fraudulent. Your Pauline is such a lovely, responsible girl, such a devoted friend to Jacq . . . to Jaycee." The barmaid (Jeff loved that term, but there were few places left that could carry it off like this place could) cleared the table of tumblers and cups before replacing the tea with a full pot and setting out fresh highballs for Hil and Jeff.

Later, after Eben put on his ugly yellow stocking cap, strode out of the Capital Bar and hiked the half mile uphill to the college to pick up the girls at their after school activity, Jeff said, "Fucking half-assed muckraker."

"Don't be harsh on him, Jeff. And if he really does go to the Attorney General they'll explain it takes a while, sometimes, for start-up companies to—"

"Are you out of your fucking skull? This guy could bring us down."

"I don't understand. We're running a legitimate, well-meaning—"

"Sure we're legit, Hil. Whoever said we weren't well-meaning? But don't you get it? We don't go to their clubs, so the big boys don't like us. Do you golf, Hil? No. Do I golf? No. Our little Hillwinds will just be a pile of boards in an empty field if Shattuck goes to the State . . ."

"You know what? You're right. We should golf," said Hil.

The rest was a blur. Both of them drinking, and then Jeff paid the bill. Bleary-eyed, he followed as Hil plodded off in search of the men's room, went off down a hallway, and opened a white bead-board door to a broom closet instead. For a long time afterwards, Jeff recalled the story of the rest of the night in two hazy, wobbly movements:

First, since they were driving the Buick, Hilary got in the driver's seat but Jeff kept his own fingertips at the wheel in a cautionary way, since Hil was drunk. Hil's drunkenness would be a huge, personal relief to him later, and so would Jeff's drunkenness, almost as big a relief as if Jeff hadn't nudged the steering wheel after Eben and his stocking cap came into view. Hil had been going on and on about how Eben was a reasonable guy and if only they might just catch up with him and try to talk some sense into him, it would surely do the trick.

"Whatever you think is best," Jeff had said, agreeing to this hopeless idea even though it was he who had put it into Hil's head in the first place. They'd ended up driving around the quad of the hilltop college campus past where a couple of maintenance guys struggled to carry an old beat-up piano from one building to another, and then headed into a landscape of forest, tall grass, farmhouses and patches of new building construction. Jeff was unsure. Were they headed back to Hillwinds? What a disappointment. But Hil drove past Center Road, and then after a mile they saw the yellow stocking cap trudging along in the near dark. Shattuck's holier-than-thou attitude really got Jeff's goat, when all Jeff wanted was to succeed in his chosen business, like everyone else.

Later, near dawn in New York, all keyed up from driving the unscathed Beamer home from Vermont, Jeff lay shivering between pressed, pinstripe sheets. How comforting pinstripes on a well-made bed usually were, as if you really could live on the straight and narrow . . . but not tonight, his eyes wide open atop the neatly tucked pillow. At last he sat bolt upright, opened the drawer, and popped two Valium, so after a minute it didn't seem that difficult to live with anymore, the girls showing up suddenly out of the darkness, the thump on Hil's fender, Hil's shriek like a subway coming into a station and life went on. The earth still turned. Neither good deeds nor bad deeds could stop it. Clea was still out there on earth someplace, and if he picked up the phone and dialed her number, it wouldn't be the end of either of them. But he would wait a little while, play it by ear. It was practically time for tomorrow's opening bell.

⁂

In a windowless washroom attached to Hil's study, Hannah dismantled the first of the two drawing pens, rinsed the feed and nib in the small dish of cleaning mixture, and then replaced the inky, strangely drinkable-looking bath with the one-to-four part ammonia to water solution she kept mixed in advance, no longer being as careful as she once had been to keep her yellowed, chapped fingertips clear of the ammonia. Really, she barely went out of her way even to wash her hands, anymore, cleaning them only indirectly, like when rubbing into the tufts of each day's watercolor brushes a lather of homemade soap. Since there wasn't a warm water tap, she used water mildly heated in the teakettle, and while in theory it rankled her to always be the person to clean the brushes, in practice she enjoyed the way the cleaning of the implements provided closure to the early morning hours of work, which were followed, daily, by the admittedly less satisfying hours that at her husband's insistence she needed to invest in Jaycee's schooling. It made Hannah feel guilty to think this way—that schooling Jaycee never matched in grace or power the images that Hannah might have created had she been granted the luxury of whole days to draw and paint. But cleaning the brushes reminded her of, years back, shampooing Jaycee's hair. They'd had a little vinyl brimmed cap with an open crown that sat atop the baby's head just over her ears, to keep the lather from sliding into her eyes as Hannah rubbed shampoo through the tufts of frizz. Jaycee was too grown-up to have her hair washed by her mother, now . . . but there was the schooling to make up for it, the girl's stolid embrace of facts and figures, her utter bafflement in the face of poetry, her ham-handed piccolo playing and her insistence on learning to write with her left hand as well as her right, or was it the other way around, Hannah wondered, unable to recall if Jaycee had been right- or left-handed before she'd succeeded at becoming more or less ambidextrous, her penmanship unkempt no matter which way you looked at it.

In her moistened palm, Hannah swirled and dabbed the brushes, rinsing each one clean and gently pressing out the excess. Finally she reshaped the sables and laid them on a scrap of old apron to dry, like putting the clean-smelling baby to bed at night. At last she returned to the pens, rubbing the soaked nibs free of the poisonous swirl of ink and ammonia before fitting the implements back together to be blotted on the outmost edge of a fresh sheet of testing paper. Before leaving the study, she paused to admire the new picture for *Lamb's Ear and Spiderwort*—a spiral of barn swallows with forked tails and pointy wings lifting themselves over the kitchen garden. It wasn't true she was a realist, even though realism was the thing for which her pictures were celebrated. The real birds at real dawn were never so precise as in Hannah's picture, their wings never so articulate, their flight so emphatic.

Then finally she paused at the sink again, ran hot water over a clean cloth, and wrung it out in her hand. That bump Hil'd got on his head just a few hours ago from driving the Buick into the barn would continue to need tending to, and she was glad, all said and done, to be the woman who was expected to hold a soothing washcloth to whatever injuries her husband caused himself. Boys will be boys, she thought fondly enough, if a little annoyed for how long he'd stayed out with his old friend Jeffrey Parmenter, wreaking their boyish havoc.

CHAPTER SIX

Hil, 2010

The ground begins to fall away from Hil's walking stick. The what you call it, the force Isaac Newton's apple fell. It helps speed up the peds. The downward thing. Don't forget, hold on to the purpose.They go easier on you if you turn yourself in.

Past the pink building people come to sleep. Betsy's B and B the sign says. A Victorian gingerbread painted a lurid pink. Benedictine and Brandy. That was a drink he'd once enjoyed. Why do they call these places B and Bs? Beds and Baths probably. The road is rushing away and now the sidewalk is on the other side. He'll just walk in the street, then. His peds are flying, the wind rushing by like a dog with its ears out the window. There's the old brick elementary school turned office building. Where do the children go to school now? Did Charlotte Jacqueline go there? No, of course not. They kept her home where she could get a proper education, where she wouldn't be corrupted and turned against them, taught the sarcasm of schoolchildren. There's another dirty little secret: a children's book writer who hates children. Better to let the daughter handle the children at Hillwinds; the daughter is better with the school groups than she is with the general maintenance. He didn't like the way that teacher leaned in so close to her at the Hill-winds blacksmith shop, trying to strike up a match.

The sidewalk reappears; where did it go? And the land stops falling away but flattens out again and the rushing, the wind, the speed disappear. Parking meters and parked cars. The café—La Brioche, rich pastries made by the culinary students. That means he's come to the intersection of Main Street and Capital Street but it makes a zigzag. Why couldn't they have straight angles? This must be a wrong angle. Which way? He should be at the bank instead of this other bookstore. Too many bookstores. What a thing for a famous author to say. One is used, the other new. But which is which? There are tray tables set out in front of this one with bargain books. Are his books bargain books, losing value? But no, he sees no familiar titles. No *Felicity Keeps the Fire Burning* or *Isabel's Days* or *Harvest Moon* piled there with the cheap paperbacks and dog-eared art books. He's safe.

There's City Hall. Yes, the police are in there. The station with its lovely brick arch and tower. Of course. Up the marble steps mined, perhaps, from the Barre quarry. Rock of Ages they called it or maybe Age of Rocks and in the semintary of the Italian carvers. Gravestones made to look like soccer balls and racecars. Ridiculous. Who wants to be remembered like that? Better to have a Hillwinds. Everyone should have a place. Except if they did he wouldn't be the only one. So better not. If he confesses then he'll be remembered for that and not for his place and his lovely books. He hesitates. No, the important thing is to remember his purpose. Confess.

But here's the station. Through the door. No officers but a big brass bell. Why a bell? Down the hall in darkness. The door opens to voices. Many seats and people at the bottom yelling. Lights glare on them. Is this an interrogation? A man jumps up from a darkened seat but he has no uniform. "We're in rehearsal," he says. He's wearing a sleeveless shirt, so unattractive with his skinny, hirsute arms. He says, "Sir, we're closed to the public today. That's a nice costume but we finished casting two weeks ago."

"Isn't this the station?" Hil asks.

"The fire station? That's next door. It has three big bays. You know, firetrucks?"

Hil shakes his head. It doesn't sound right. Fire. No, City Hall with the tower, the offices.

"Ohhh, did you mean the police station? Go back out, turn left at the bottom of the stairs, there's a road between the two buildings, head all the way back, and you'll see the cop shop and next to it is that gym, First in Fitness. It's two minutes away. Not even." The young man with the skinny arms has turned back to the voices on the platform below the many darkened seats. Hil remembers a play. Under the Milkwood, with Captain Cat and Rosie, but it's gone by the time he gets to the stairs.

Kids sitting on the stairs smooching. Grooming each other like monkeys. He's glad they never let Charlotte Jacqueline go to school. They probably let them act like this in class these days. Turn right or left? What did the man say? But it's gone already along with Hil's purpose.

"Excuse me please." He stops a young woman with a child in a stroller. "Uhhh, could you tell me where . . . uhhh . . . how to get to . . ." The place to tell.

"Where do you want to go?" the mother asks. She leans down to pick up the fuzzy toy her toddler has thrown onto the sidewalk. An unpleasant plastic thing bobs in the child's mouth. Why do they let their children suckle on those nipple knobs?

Damn. Hil raps his hat with his knuckles. "Where the men . . . uh, with uniforms. Guns."

"Soldiers?" she asks, perplexed.

"Not soldiers."

"Please?" She is cocking her head at an irritatingly sympathetic angle.

"What?"

She repeats the word more slowly. Po-lice. Police! Yes.

"Go back to the Lost Nation theater, you know, it's the old city hall, turn left and go all the way back. It's not far."

He nods his head.

She says, "Sir? Come with me, I'll show you."

"Uh, you were going . . . that way?"

"It doesn't matter. C'mon."

Women have always been the kinder sex. Despite what men say about catfights and jealousy. He never gave . . . what's her name, Charlotte Jacqueline's mother. He never gave her a reason to be jealous. Of his books perhaps, his work, his plans, his ideas for her drawings. But women? Never.

"Sir?" a lady with a toddler in a stroller walking beside him says. The stroller rattles annoyingly on the uneven sidewalk and the child's head bobbles. Children have such truly large heads.

"What's that?" Hil says. Why does she allow her child to suck on that gaudy plastic thing?

"Why do you need the police?" she says.

He starts to shape the word. Mother, he thinks, but that's not the word. Murder. That's it. But now he can't for the life of him think of why he would ever say such a thing. "Thank you kind lady," Hil says, bowing to her before he shambles away.

PART III

The Jump

CHAPTER SEVEN

Jaycee, 2010

The usual straggle of cats only barely made way as Jaycee stood in the yard upending parsnip peelings over the winter compost bin. Meanly she wiggled a parsnip tail in the cats' hungry faces, as if she might toss them a delectable rat to eat. Knowing her tricks, the two house cats, Warp and Weft, stayed back, their tarnished heart lockets, which Hannah had insisted they wear at all times ever since she'd come upon that lock of Pauline's hair and divided it between them, gently swinging from their collars.

"Mollycoddles," Jaycee said, beckoning the whole crew forward again for a lick from an empty tuna can. She wondered how many Good Samaritan points she deserved for throwing treats to stray cats when tonight's family supper would be a meager assemblage of glazed parsnips and pears, only minus the pears, to save money, from a recipe she'd modified after finding it a day or two ago in a *Good Housekeeping* magazine at the food stamp office, where she was filling out a food stamp application for her and her parents. At the food stamp office, she'd picked up the *Good Housekeeping* magazine to use as a lap desk, but then she needed to bring the application home because she didn't know her dad's social security number. Later that night, when she asked Hil what it was, he waved his arm in that flowery way he had of excusing himself, as a celebrated author, from needing to bother with such pedestrian concerns as social security numbers, or indeed, money itself.

What Jaycee really needed was to look into nursing homes, the kind you didn't have to pay for. Hil and his excursions, good-natured as they were, were getting harder to deal with, like a week ago when that kindly actor from Lost Nation Theater had found him lying with his walking stick in the lot behind the fire station and drove him to the emergency room, his pee-sodden clothing stuffed in an inadequately cinched-up bag. Jaycee had laid her satchel on a chair so as not to have to place it on the emergency room floor, but then she pulled the satchel up again and placed it on her lap, although it made her feel prim to sit that way.

But when the hospital social worker had started offering advice about how to finagle one's stubborn parents between the doors of a nursing home, Jaycee just shook her head, finding herself unready to consider so drastic a step. Even to seek power of attorney seemed drastic, whether because it confirmed her parents' infirmities or put Jaycee in charge of them, she couldn't say. But the event had marked the first time her dad ever wet himself, and Jaycee could surely guess what it harbingered. Nighttime visits to the Dollar Store, heaps of reeking diapers frozen in the trash, the cats indignant at the tang of them . . . not to mention . . . but no, she wouldn't let herself think about wiping him. She wondered when on earth he'd become so enfeebled, and where the line might be drawn between his currently insulated state of mind and the self-absorbed person he'd been before. Amazed by how poorly her parents had prepared for their dotage, she promised herself to be, decades from now, prepared for her own.

Showing no sign yet of renewed incontinence, Hil appeared to have forgotten his emergency room visit except for one thing. "Gonna catch that Mrs. Corgi," he'd kept saying at the hospital, and now she heard it again as she passed him in the yard on her way back around from the compost bin, her empty parsnip bowl in hand. "Gonna catch that Mrs. Corgi," Hil promised her, and waved his car keys in a jangle directly in her path.

Jaycee wrestled away the keys, planning to hide them in the soon-to-be-emptied jar of grape jelly, which she would use to glaze the parsnips instead of the pricey orange marmalade that was called for in the recipe. There was something incendiary about keeping a *Good Housekeeping* magazine in full view in a food stamp office, she thought, leveling a sideways kick at the last of the cats, a mangy fellow who was trying to follow her onto the porch.

"Go away," she told the cat. "I saw your cousins in Peru. You think you're a wild and crazy guy, but I'm sorry to inform you you're a kept man. Even the kitties in the church yards in Lima are more streetwise than you." Like the jungle cat she'd spotted along the Tambopata River, which bore an expression of faint disdain for all other living things—mice, weaver-birds, and Jaycee included—all cats made her think of Carlos. She thanked him in absentia for her identity as drug courier, even if it might only last a month or two, and even if it still found her swiping humble veggies into salted, boiling water. It was romantic being a courier, she thought, more romantic than her and Carlos's humid coupling. And even though they weren't still coupling, at least she was still a courier, or would be until she finally got paid.

Back in the kitchen, Jaycee opened the fridge and scooped up a clot of butter to melt for the grape jelly parsnip glaze. Her mom would lap it right up, she knew, for Hannah wouldn't be Hannah without her vice. A slender, low-calorie Hannah would be a fraudulent Hannah . . . and probably more trouble than this one was. The diabetes was only a diversionary tactic, like the killdeer (Hannah liked to pronounce the pretty brown and white bird, *Kill, Dear*) she'd taught Jaycee about in natural history class, and whose feigned broken wing was meant to distract you away from its nest.

Jaycee's mom had nests, too. Emotional ones. Little secretive assortments of hinged, tarnished keepsakes, elusive and unaccountable, like Pauline's hair inside Warp and Weft's lockets. Despite the invitation Jaycee had made to Noor about visiting Pauline's grave at the cemetery, the real reason she'd asked Noor to come was that she couldn't stand the thought of going by herself. The only times she'd ever gone there were with her mom, whenever she and Hannah got sick of pedaling the rattly old stationary bicycle for PE class. Hannah never cycled; she only barked out commands for miles-per-hour, and she never walked to the cemetery either, of course. She drove, and plucked a Kit Kat bar that had been left by a mourner—or a bag of Doritos or a can of Doctor Pepper—off one of the headstones, and sat and ate it in the car on a lane overhung with willow switches while listening to talk-radio and waiting for Jaycee to climb up the hill in her blue gym bloomers. It was a thirty minute walk from Hillwinds to Cutler Cemetery, just right for PE. After PE, Hannah would slide, groaning, over to the passenger seat to give the wheel to Jaycee for Driver's Education Class, since even when Jaycee wasn't of legal driving age yet, it was perfectly safe to practice on weekdays along the lanes amid the gravestones. The lesson always concluded with Jaycee practicing three-point turns near the pull-off to the utility shed while being quizzed by her mom about Vermont history, like was Vermont one of only a few remaining states in the Union not to have:

1. A governor,
2. An outbreak of polio,
3. A sales tax, or
4. None of the above?

"There's your babysitter's grave!" Hannah always interrupted her own quiz to point out, as mournful and excited as if the same grave hadn't been there last month and the month before. Then they'd step out to pay their proper respects, never pulling up the weeds, since that was something *mothers* did, Hannah said, except that Pauline's mother had moved away, leaving nothing but patches of thistle growing there.

"If you ever see it weeded, that means she finally came back to visit," Hannah would say, tearing open the wrapper of a beef jerky stick that had been carefully laid on a nearby headstone. You could see in Hannah's hunger the secret she was keeping, only not what it was. You could see in her lips a faint, moist swelling, and in her eyes a sort of swirling like a sink draining empty as she gnawed at the jerky. There were never any snacks on Pauline's headstone, except for, once, a single, wrapped horehound drop that had been left there by Jaycee when she was fifteen. Hannah, who'd watched her pull it from the depths of her gym bloomer pocket and balance it on the roughhewn top of the headstone, didn't take her to task for wasting food. Instead she said obscurely, "None of it's your fault."

"None of what's my fault?" Jaycee had asked, hoping that for once her mom might explain why she went along with Hil's schemes for Jaycee's weird upbringing, but instead Hannah said, "I checked for blood but there wasn't any. We're all of us flawed but we do what we can, and hopefully some of us do better than others. Don't forget I used to be a dancer. I wasn't much good. You could get a sizable National Endowment for the Arts Fellowship back then just for playing duck duck goose with audience members," she added wistfully, so Jaycee didn't have a chance to ask, "Blood? What blood?" and soon her mom trundled back to where the car stood open. Years later if Jaycee ever caught herself wondering, "Blood? What blood?" the only answer that came to mind would be menstrual blood and the twisted squares of bed sheet her mom had used to give her in place of "feminine products," a term that still made Jaycee wistful even though she'd been buying real pads on her own ever since the evening a shocked Pauline had told her of them. Pauline then died before she herself needed them, which struck Jaycee as the saddest thing, the thing Pauline might most have regretted.

⌁

Aside from working a little on the food stamp application earlier this week, there'd been a field trip to deal with. The visit must have been scheduled over the summer, and Jaycee had been surprised when the bus pulled in with its cargo of middle school kids enveloped in hormones. Her back to the door of the Maple Jug, sweaty from a morning's work scrubbing the shelves despite the woodstove's minimal heat—her mother's order not to waste wood—she was in a stretched-out tank top sponging the lids on some honey jars when they charged into the shop.

"Oh!" she started, dropping the sponge in the bucket, the water black with dust since the jars had been standing on the shelf already a year or two. You could buy better honey for less money at the Co-op, but with not-as-charming labels. She cursed herself for sneaking the old boom box into the shop and, worse, keeping it tuned to 104.7 FM, but the cute, bearded teacher didn't seem to mind the ousting of "Nearer My God to Thee," "Nelly Bly," "Maryland, My Maryland," or "When Johnny comes Marching Home" which was the kind of stuff that was supposed to be playing on the shop's old record player during open-for-business hours. 104.7 featured the alternative music Noor preferred, and the cute teacher even seemed to like it when one of the kids started hamming it up.

"Mine smell like huh, huh, huh, huh, honey, uh," the kid sang along, employing one of the honey jars in an unspeakably crotch-oriented choreography that reminded Jaycee of Carlos's thumbs corkscrewing into her groin. She made a show of drying her hands on an apron while putting it on, then gave a swipe of the apron on top of the desk where the day planner lay, in order to sneak a look at the schedule for this cute teacher's field trip. Unfortunately the field trip was all paid up, so no new cash would come in unless the kids had money for souvenirs. Still, the teacher's too-neatly trimmed beard didn't quite camouflage a reckless mouth, which Jaycee regarded as having the potential for compensation. On the other hand, it would be only a three hour visit before they started back to Middlebury. Damn. She took a longer time than usual doling out tickets in order to go over the featured event in her mind—an impromptu skit based on the chapter "Mystery Tea," from Hil's book, *Lost Loon*. It was one of the darker of Hil's books, although even the ones for primary schoolers included lurid depictions of hardships and grief. First they'd do the voice exercises and the relaxation exercise when you're supposed to turn your body into air, and then she'd ask the children to ad lib the skit aloud, assigning them roles as they went along. A show fit for a hen, as her former fiancé Mike used to say, referring to the chickens that once laid eggs at Hillwinds but were long since used up as Sunday dinner. The kids would throw together costumes out of stuff from the trunks, assemble the set from among sticks of furnishings huddled in the prop stall, and finally perform, leaving no time for Jaycee and the teacher to sneak into the blacksmith stall and fulfill her urge to untuck the bent wing of his plaid shirt collar. *Fair St. Agnes, play thy part,* went a rhyme Hannah once taught her for English Class:

> *And send to me mine own sweetheart.*
> *Not in his best or worst array,*
> *But in the clothes of every day.*

But: "I'm thrilled to introduce our new school trip feature," Jaycee announced, snapping open a camcorder thing she'd discovered one day in the lost-and-found box. She led the kids into the barn, where the prospect of today's skit being recorded on a camcorder turned out not to be the game changer she'd hoped it might be. A goody-goody sort of girl raised her hand to ask, "What's the point of being old-fashioned if we put it on a camcorder? They didn't have camcorders yet, in those days, did they?"

"Yeah they did," said another girl, whose cell phone had gone off six times since she'd been there.

"But then no one will be able to watch if we *don't* record."

"Who's gonna watch? Your goldfish?"

"I'd rather be dead than have somebody watch me play village idiot in a picture book."

"I'd rather be high. Let's drink some of the *Mystery Tea.*"

"You *are* the village idiot."

"Wait! It's a picture book?"

"Unless like it goes viral. Then we'll make like a million dollars."

"Viral?" asked Jaycee. *Were* these kids high? Would she even be able to tell? Again, just like when she was a kid herself, she felt left out of middle school.

"No, we won't make a million dollars. Besides, they didn't have *dollars* yet, did they?" the goody-goody girl asked. Even the teacher rolled his eyes.

"Sort of, but not dollar bills," Jaycee answered, glad to know at least one thing she could add to this volley of utterances. "Before dollars they used Continental Currency, but during the Revolutionary war too much of it was printed. In fact, so much currency was printed that the notes turned worthless. *Lost Loon* takes place when?" she quizzed, hoping to sidestep the troublesome question of what kind of money *was* used in the era of Hil's book. Greenbacks, maybe? Where was Hannah when you needed her? Asleep in her chair in the back of the store, a string of rock candy turning to drool in her open mouth.

"*Lost Loon* opens in 1793," said the other class know-it-all, a boy this time, less annoying than the girl because he had a port wine stain across one ear. Why hadn't his parents had it removed, Jaycee wondered, feeling for the kid because Hannah and Hil would have made the same choice. "But loons are not cousins to ducks, like it says," the boy continued. "Loons are Gaviiformes. They're more related to penguins than they are to ducks, or even to grebes. In fact—"

"Remember to raise your hands," the cute teacher had interrupted. Jaycee raised her hand flirtatiously, at once regretting the hiatus she'd slipped into that month as far as shaving her armpits. Eventually she picked a wallflower girl instead of a prettier girl named Samantha to play the lost loon, which wasn't really lost but was searching for a doctor because the Putrid Fever was coming. She picked an even shyer kid to play the terrible fever, and she herself played steam from a teakettle. It turned out to be one of those rare groups of school kids who seemed eager to travel backward in time, consenting even to leave their phones in a pile, minus the phone that they were using to record their skit for something called YouTube, since Jaycee had mistakenly left on the camcorder and worn down the battery. When the bus was loading up, she had felt bereft to see the cute teacher go. Everything had felt all mixed up. Her stretched-out tank top openings felt mixed with the openings of Carlos's shirt which felt mixed with Mike checking his fly as he walked out the door, and the cute teacher's bent collar aching to be smoothed felt tangled with Jaycee's apron strings. Her cumbersome boobs, the inconvenience and, let's admit it, her shame over the food stamps, her pity for the loon, her impatience with her dad, her adrenaline over the smuggled drugs, and Hannah clamoring awake in the shop corner wondering where she was, had all been part of the commotion.

"Bye," Jaycee waved. "Don't forget to download the performance on that Two Tube thing, and whoever wants to view it can view it, and whoever doesn't want to doesn't have to," she'd added, proud of this fresh trove of worldly knowledge.

"Upload!" they'd all jeered. "YouTube! And it's on there already!" they said, flashing their screens.

When the parsnips were done cooking, Jaycee reached over her kitchen counter, which smelled of the baking soda she scoured it with, and flipped back the curtain—plaid like the teacher's collar—to see if her mom had turned on their front stoop light to signal she was hungry. If Jaycee had succeeded in one thing this week, it was in postponing the permanent utilities shut-off, and sure enough the light was on, had likely been on for an hour or so. Yam Rock, illuminated in the dusk, looked like a lumpy phase of the moon had fallen onto the hill. The cats were playing soccer using some wretched creature—a mouse, it appeared—as the ball, and Hil was silhouetted nearby in the yard, shovel in hand, digging arduously away at the near frozen ground. A short while later, the tray of supper in her hands, she detoured across the brittle grass to where he'd been digging. The shovel was gone and not even his footprints showed anymore on the hard ground. At first glance the hole appeared to be empty, but then she noticed something under the clods of dirt, a lurid blue color she recognized—it was the folder containing the food stamp and disability applications.

"DA-AAD!" she whined, finding it hard to behave like the more adult of the pair when she was the only one listening. A parent's decline was supposed to make you sad, not piss you off. Balancing the dinner tray on her knees, she lifted out the folder, swiped it clean of dirt, and, trying not to despair of the mountains of paperwork that would come with looking after two elderly parents, she announced, "grape jelly glazed parsnips and leftover succotash garnished with stale toast triangles!" when she'd nudged open their door. Also on the tray stood the souvenir vase from Peru, which she'd stood between two old, very possibly leaded, plates on her parents' table.

Like the candlesticks and other of Carlos's wedding gifts she'd left behind at Frida's, the vase was wobbly and clumsily made. Tonight it held a twist of equally lopsided crepe paper flowers with pipe cleaner stems made by Jaycee in a fit of the same earnest daughterliness that she had practiced all her life.

"Jeopardy's in ten minutes," she said to her mother, who as if it were a restaurant was already there at the table awaiting her meal. Hil was in the kitchen supposedly washing his hands as Hannah had directed, though when Jaycee glanced in he was standing at the sink with the water running full force, reading the back of the dish soap bottle.

Jaycee shut the study door behind her and laid the file atop the clutter on the desk. Whatever wasn't squirreled away in drawers had been stuffed willy-nilly into cardboard boxes. Jaycee wouldn't have been surprised if there really was a squirrel in one of them. She wondered what Noor might say to this. Probably go ahead and cry as long as you buck up and get the job done. But what *was* the job, exactly? Jaycee took the seat at her father's desk and pressed the lamp button. In natural history class, along with the killdeers, Hannah had taught her about the importance of having a "search image," since an organism that knew exactly what it was looking for was more likely to find it, but Jaycee had no search image, and no clue at all about what she hoped to stumble upon. The best she could hope for was to locate a few questionable facts amid a bevy of unquantifiable figures that might help her file for something, anything, to keep the household from going under. That missing social security number, for instance? The more she'd searched among the boxes on her earlier visits to the study this week, the more it appeared Hil might never have paid taxes at all. Social security, Medicare, even Obamacare might be forever off-limits to the feckless Emorys.

The first desk drawer slid open too easily, since there was nothing in it but a newspaper clipping showing *Two Hens in a Hailstone*'s inclusion in the *New York Times Book Review Best Illustrated Children's Books* list. Hil thrived on this notoriety and at the writing conferences Jaycee used to attend with him he diminished Hannah's role by remarking on "my wife's surprising talent for bringing my vision" to life on the page. Jaycee's eyes skidded to a shelf where amid the cardboard boxes stood an empty box from Kraft with a slash of black marker over the not quite crossed-out word, CORGI. That was the name her dad had kept repeating to the hospital social worker and again this morning. Jaycee went to the carton, opened it, and started to read:

McLarren Publishing
Children's Division,
1932 Broadway, 15th floor, section 12
New York, NY 10019

August 2, 1980

John Corgi
Room 19
Hotel Marquis
417 Booth Street
Elizabeth, New Jersey 07200

Dear Mr. Corgi,

It is with tremendous pleasure that I report that we at McLarren Publishing would like to publish your book, The Drinking Gourd. Your historically solid, socially relevant book has received the unanimous support of both our editorial and marketing staff here at McLarren's Children's Division, who note that its tale of a young slave boy whose parents perish of fever while escaping to their freedom will touch the hearts of old and young readers alike, while proving equally gripping as educational. It's rare that we share such enthusiasm for a chapter book, and we are all eager to speak further with you; first, to ascertain that the book is still available (we certainly hope that the answer is in the affirmative!) and second, in order that we might discuss the very real possibility of a multiple book contract (dare we begin to imagine our un-paralleled delight on hearing that you have already written a sequel?!).

Please do let us know at your earliest convenience that you are as excited about McLarren as we are about The Drinking Gourd. Might

I add that the book's vivid realism—the scenes of the orphan stealing corn and eggs from unsuspecting farmers while fighting measles amid the onslaught of a terrible thunderstorm all in the context of a terrifying escape from the plantation south, for instance—puts us in mind of some of the great classics of children's cinema? Just fantasizing . . .

> *With admiration and respect, yours hopefully,*
> *Hilary Emory—Editor in Chief*

Jaycee snorted, amused. Her dad had been a senior Children's Editor at McLarren back in 1980, certainly never Editor in Chief, a source of some consternation to him even after he'd quit. And *dare we imagine our unparalleled delight* etc? What a fop he was then, and still was, she thought with a helpless allotment of fondness. Or was he really only a true gentleman? It was impossible to say, being his daughter.How strange, though, that it was a *Mrs.* Corgi, not the *Mr.* Corgi to whom the letter was addressed, whose name Hil had kept repeating all this week. And it was stranger still that Jaycee, who as a child had read so voraciously, remembered no book by any Corgi at all.

Maybe Corgi had used a pseudonym, she thought, recalling the authors of the books about African American children—Virginia Hamilton, Lillie Paterson, Pearle Bailey, Lucille Clifton, Walter Dean Myers—that she had enjoyed. Still, she did remember a book about a runaway slave, a girl, not a boy, and how the scenes with the dipper going into the pail had used to stir all Jaycee's senses, parching her with thirst, but then never slaking it. It was a thirst Jaycee felt now. She put aside the somehow touching acceptance letter to find another just like it but which had been mailed at a later date, and with Hil's faintly admonitory, *One can't help but wonder the reason behind our not having yet heard from you,* added in red fountain pen ink on top.

A thump and a yelp came from the dinner table. She rushed out to find Hil holding a chunk of the broken Peruvian vase, the twisted crepe paper flowers scattered on the floor among plastery shards on which the word, *souvenir,* was cut in two at the *v.*

"Oh," groaned Jaycee.

Like a baby Hil held the chunk to his lips and appeared to suckle the broken margin of it. A river of pee was in the process of pooling so broadly at his feet that Hannah's wheelchair was soon to be included in it. But Hannah didn't seem to notice. Instead her eyes were riveted on the word Corgi on the Kraft carton, which Jaycee had carried with her out of the study.

"Give it here, stupid girl!" Hannah cried.

But Jaycee took it home with her instead, nearly tripping on the cat's soccer ball, which turned out not to be a mouse but a shoulder strap change purse left behind by one of the field trip girls. It was made of magenta leather and contained a hundred dollar bill.

What girl brings a hundred dollars to school in a Coach purse? Jaycee wondered, sliding the pretty change purse, which was only a little worse for wear, in a pocket of her apron to be tucked later beneath the cash box in the Maple Jug until the girl came back to get it. Her dad would have kept the money for himself, she thought, and when she peeked at the next document in the Kraft carton, she was only mildly surprised to discover the meaning of it.

It read: *A Cool Drink of Water, by Hilary Emory*, and it was the book Jaycee remembered about the runaway slave girl slaking her thirst after her parents died of fever en route to their freedom. It was her dad's first book, the one that did so well by Hil that he was able to quit his job in publishing, take up life as a moderately successful author, and start the whole Hillwinds enterprise. But it had been written, Jaycee now understood, by a man named John Corgi. Her dad's whole life, not to mention *her* whole life, was predicated on an act of ego-driven greed that, now that she knew about it, should probably devastate her more than it was doing. She chewed on this fact while sitting at her table reading the familiar children's book, then heated her own supper and was just about to eat it when the telephone rang.

"Hillwinds Living History Books!" Jaycee answered, ruing her accustomed chirpiness even as she spoke, but then she wondered if her habit of being too nice to the customers was one of the few things she had ever actually liked about working there.

"This is Ed Best," said the man on the other end of the telephone. Jaycee said "Hi, Ed!" even though she didn't know an Ed Best.

"The teacher from yesterday's field trip," he added.

"Oh hi!" she said, surprised to hear the field trip had only been yesterday. A nuthatch made its way up a tree outside the window. She could feel the pulse and strobe of the nuthatch climbing as if it were climbing inside her throat, and very quickly in her mind she reconceived the night's supper, replacing it with Thai in white take-out boxes, and herself leaning delicately over with chopsticks to pluck a stray noodle from Ed Best's beard.

"I'm calling because one of my pupils appears to have left behind her change purse," Ed Best said. "It's pink. If you see it, will you call me, please? Her parents are making a scene about it."

"Bummer! Of course. I'll call you the minute I see it," Jaycee said, and took his telephone number by tracing it with her fingernail on the countertop. She pulled the coach bag from her apron pocket, removed the money, smoothed the hundred dollar bill into her own wallet, and hung the bag on a hook in the back of her closet. Then she sat back down to eat. The grape jelly wasn't so bad masquerading as marmalade, but parsnips were such homely things. All root veggies were homely, probably from being buried alive.

CHAPTER EIGHT

Noor, 2010

One thing about getting involved in a drug deal, Noor told herself, as she scraped the shovel along the cement floor of the pine scented shavings pit to fill a wheelbarrow for the stalls— the fear of getting caught and her anxiety about Dan finding out helped mitigate her distress over Mindy, about whom she still hadn't spoken with Dan. Or maybe it was the other way around— Dan's possible affair helped mitigate her anxiety over the drug deal. Although it had been nearly a week since she gave Gerry the "taste," she still hadn't heard back from him. She'd met with him in the dark, at a parking pullout under the highway overpass that crossed the Winooski River, to hand over the little samples, one for him, one for his dealer friend. They really did remind her of fortune cookies. She imagined what the little slip of paper might say—"big present come to you soon" or "don't look for trouble, trouble find you." She'd drawn up to the left of his dented navy blue Corolla, made a show of cleaning out the passenger side of her pickup (less recognizable, she hoped, than the Subaru), dropped stray wrappers and a Snapple bottle—horrors, should have recycled that—into a trash can. Overhead, semis and passenger cars rattled the bridge. Gerry brushed out his driver's side with an old glove, leaned across, winked at her, took the packets from her and tucked them into his wallet. Since then she'd been watching her phone for missed calls and unplayed messages, checking to see that the volume was on.She had even started worrying that their stash was a pile of counterfeit. Or maybe he'd just gotten himself a freebie. Despite her reassurances to Jaycee, as time passed she started having doubts about whether Gerry really did have an acquaintance who could sell the stuff. People change, after all. Dan was proof. She was proof. But if Gerry planned to stiff her he'd probably wait until he had the whole stash, not just a few tastes. And she didn't believe that Gerry would do that.

Distracted, Noor realized that she'd overfilled the wheelbarrow and was now leaving a pale scattering of shavings down the center aisle of the barn. She opened each cleaned stall and shoveled in new shavings, a bright bed soon to be trampled, pissed and pooped on. How much nicer it was to pick up after horses than it must be for Jaycee, cleaning up after her father. Noor found comfort in the daily tasks, the reassuring labor of maintaining the farm, though it was hard now to keep the hamster wheel of worry at bay. Only with her clients did her mind bend itself completely to the task at hand, forgetting even to think about money and bills.

This morning, on impulse, she'd asked Dan if he'd go see a marriage counselor with her. He'd looked up from spooning cold cereal into his mouth at the kitchen table.

"What for?" he asked.

Noor tried to assess the sincerity of his puzzlement. "Because I have this feeling we've grown apart." She knew how lame the words sounded, how cliché. But she wasn't ready to say *Because I think you're in love with llama bitch.* "We almost never eat supper together anymore . . . you used to stop by to eat with me before going back on calls. And the baby thing, trying to have one, it's messed everything up."

"We're just busy, Noor." Rapidly he started spooning up milky sludge. He had an irritating habit of picking up the pace of spoon against bowl as he got closer to finishing his cereal. When he was done he pushed back his chair and rose, reached for his cell phone, pager, and keys on the counter. Then he kissed her forehead as she stood there, her coffee cup in hand, a beggar hoping for one more coin, one more glimmer of encouragement. He said, "Listen, I really have to go now. We can talk about this later if you really want to."

"Tonight?" Noor asked, hating her own beseeching tone. But Dan was already in the mudroom putting on his overalls and boots. If *you really want to*, he'd said, so obviously he didn't want to, which wasn't surprising, given that he was a man and no man wanted to talk about a relationship. But a counselor might force the issue, might help her find out what was really going on, make it easier for her to ask and to face the consequences either way. Help them find a way back, maybe. Or a divorce lawyer. Of course he didn't want to go to a counselor. He was as cheerful as ever, while Noor lurked around looking for clues. Dan's call history in his phone had been deleted, Noor had discovered, sneaking it open in the middle of the night, which could mean nothing but might mean everything.

She couldn't imagine having sex with Dan when he might be sleeping with Mindy, but their conflicting schedules made avoidance so easy that Dan might not have noticed her keeping her distance. When it was time for her to ovulate she'd made excuses, pretending to have a stomach virus, making a show of slugging (water) out of an immodium bottle until the critical conception days had passed. Dan hadn't seemed bothered at all that they were missing another chance. Maybe he'd given up too, or maybe Mindy was keeping him satisfied. Or maybe he was just being a considerate husband. Exchanging the shavings shovel for a push broom, Noor told herself she needed evidence. And she needed to sell the coke, especially if the evidence turned out bad.

Sweeping up the spilled shavings, Noor kept turning over the morning's conversation. They were busy. But not that busy. They used to make time for each other, and for getting together with friends. Not making time for each other was Dan's fault, but Noor had to admit she'd been an even lousier social butterfly of late, not answering emails, declining invitations, letting her college gang and high school pals and riding partners and the few diehard women buds she used to meet for coffee slip away. She was just too busy, she excused herself, but Dan would say too busy and not interested enough and maybe even no fun to be with anymore.

"I spend all day helping people, wrangling volunteers and shoveling shit," Noor had said the last time he'd tried to get her to go out with his friends and their wives. "I'm tired at night. And who are you to talk? You've nixed all my attempts at new couples, like when Jan what's her name from the Co-op and her boyfriend wanted us to go out to Julio's that night. You said you didn't want to go out to dinner with two people wearing Earth shoes."

"Well maybe if they promised not to wear their matching cowry shell necklaces it would have been alright," Dan teased.

Noor had hid her own grin, since she hadn't really wanted to go to dinner with them, either. Though Dan worked way more hours than she did, he still, she had to admit, kept up with his biking and hiking buddies, whose wives and girlfriends just weren't Noor's type. They liked to organize get-togethers where the ones with kids talked schools and nursing bras and the girlfriends were either gung-ho-rock-climber-amazons or yoga and local food fanatics. She never wanted to drop in on those occasional potluck things they threw which always seemed to include three variants of pesto on gluten free pasta and for all she knew mother's milk veggie dip. Dan was right. She'd stopped being sociable, stopped being a friend. She had even stopped being a sister and daughter, practically, since there were only the weekly Skype session with her parents in Karachi, and her brother's rare emails. But she still had her clients, her horses, and her volunteers, while poor Jaycee had no one, only her crazy decrepit parents. Without the coke deal Jaycee wouldn't even have me, Noor thought, while hanging the broom back on its hook beside the barn door alongside the shovels and manure forks. Jaycee was a business partner, not a friend. Still, without the deal, Noor wouldn't have options if she and Dan broke up. And so the hamster wheel spun on—Dan/drugs/broke, Dan/drugs/money/broke—until her first client of the day arrived and freed her from its vortex.

Noor was expecting a new client that morning, her first paraplegic rider. Marta had told her over the phone that a car accident three years ago had left her with a C-7 break, use of her arms, nothing in her legs. Marta wasn't sure she wanted to ride but her doctor and PT and shrink all agreed it would be good for her, since, she'd said, deadpan, ice skating and tennis were out. She was twenty-six and weighed 110 pounds according to the intake paperwork they'd exchanged. She said she didn't mind the cool November weather.

At 8:45, Noor's newest volunteers, two physical therapy students from Champlain College, arrived. The college girls, in puffy parkas and matching French-braided brown hair, stood back and watched with Noor as Marta's specially outfitted handicap van pulled into the driveway. The maroon van door slid open and a motorized lift lowered her and her wheelchair to the ground. Marta wore a lot of eye makeup, big hair, and dangly jewelry perhaps to draw attention away from her spindly jeans-covered legs and hand-powered wheelchair. Fortunately she was as petite as her intake paperwork suggested, since Noor had no motorized lift to place her on a horse's back, like those owned by better-heeled therapeutic riding centers. She did, however, have a three foot high platform with a ramp she'd built herself, and her confusingly similar Champlain College interns, Jennifer and Jessica, to help.

"Hate to ruin the 'do," Marta said, fastening a helmet gingerly over her upswept blond hair. "Have to get it done again before I go out dancing tonight, ha!" She had a loud, braying laugh, plenty of bravado, and Noor liked her immediately. In the first twenty minutes, Marta learned to brush Daisy's flanks as far up as she could reach from her chair and, with help, picked manure and mud out of Daisy's hooves. "Smells like my ex-boyfriend's feet when he turned around and ran out the door," she remarked blithely. Still, light as Marta was, it was hard, even with Jessica's—or was it Jennifer's?—help, lifting Marta from her chair, holding her up, sliding her twiggy right leg over Daisy's back and easing her onto the cushioned vaulting pad with the large leather handles while the other J girl held Daisy's lead rope. Stirrups were beside the point. Marta kept a death grip on the oversized handles as Daisy dozed around the ring, her hooves leaving tracks in the half frozen sand.

"Try to relax your hands and let her carry you," Noor coached as she took the lead rope from Jessica/Jennifer and walked backwards. "Daisy won't go anywhere we don't want her to. Can you let go with one hand?"

"Are you crazy?" Marta asked, but she was grinning. Jennifer and Jessica each kept a palm on Marta's thighs to stabilize her but after a few loopy, tilting circles Marta straightened her torso—she had surprisingly good core strength. She'd been a gymnast at one time.

After twenty minutes Marta was willing to release the right side vaulting handle and let her gloved hand ride the air, as though she were sticking it out a car window, mimicking Daisy's slow roll. By the end of the session she was touching her hands to her head, leaning gently forward and back, twisting her upper body. Jessica and Jennifer applauded.

"You think they got some kind of saddle they can just lock me into?" she wanted to know when her session was over and she was back in her wheelchair. "So I can just learn to cruise around without the training wheels?"

"There are paraplegic riders who perform dressage in the Paralympics," Noor said. "And they don't have to be locked in. Stick with it and you'll be riding that horse by yourself."

"You think so?" Marta asked, the tough girl jokiness gone for a moment, the possibility lighting her features.

"I *know* so," Noor said. A brisk wind scattered dead leaves across the driveway. She shivered and said, "Brrr." She'd be working in her Carhartt quilted jumpsuit soon.

"Well, one good thing about being a 'plege," Marta said. "*My* toes don't get cold, ha!"

Noor watched as Marta maneuvered her chair down the drive, used her electric lift to raise her wheelchair into the minivan, rolled to the front, turned the ignition and backed out with a spray of gravel.

An unfamiliar ringtone. Noor slapped her left hip pocket for her cell—but it was the burner in her right. Gerry calling. Finally.

"Just a second," she said into the phone. "Thanks Jen, Jess," she called out to the Bobbsey twins lurking in the driveway, waiting for instructions. She pressed the phone into her down vest. "There's a pot of hot coffee in the house if you want some. Milk and cream in the fridge. Tea bags in the first drawer to the left of the stove." Her volunteers headed to the house. Noor turned to face the barn. "You still there? Sorry."

"I can call back later," Gerry said. His voice was husky with smoke. "Though I wouldn't turn my nose up at some of that coffee."

"You could hear me? Okay, they're gone. So? Where are you calling from?" she asked.

"Don't sweat it. Anyway, things went really, really well. You want to meet and make some plans?"

It was happening. She could feel her heart racing. "Did he say how much it . . ."

"Hey, not now, okay? Let's say we meet. *Share,* as they say in the program."

Of course, how stupid of her to ask for details. Thank god she hadn't called him by name. The thing was, they didn't actually have to meet this time. They didn't need a meeting to arrange their next meeting, the real deal, when they'd have to get together to exchange the money and coke face to face. They didn't have to be face to face to make plans. They both knew the only reason he wanted to meet was to see her. She ought to nix that, but she wouldn't. Seeing Gerry was entertaining and it kept him doing what she wanted him to. Nothing more except risky, maybe, if they were seen together and Gerry's past illicit ventures implicated her somehow. Or if someone told Dan they'd seen Noor with another man, if he even cared enough to get jealous. Funny to think anyone would imagine she'd be having a tryst with the unsavory looking Gerry Wilcox. But unlike Jaycee, he was *kind of* her friend. Gerry and she had history, slight as it was.

"How about at the first place?" Gerry continued, meaning the tower in Hubbard Park.

"Let me get back to you. I'll have to call my . . . uh, associate first. She has the . . . uh, information."

"No problem," Gerry said. "Call when you're ready."

"Okay. Oh, hey. A minute ago you said something about "in the program." Are you in AA or Narcotics Anonymous or something?"

"Not anymore," Gerry said.

Noor wondered if he'd stopped because the program didn't work or because it had and he hadn't liked the sober, pot free life. Or maybe it worked and he did like the sober, pot free life, in which case she was a bigger risk to him than he was to her. She hadn't noticed any booze on his breath or the stink of pot smoke on his clothes, just cigarettes. Anyway, the sale was going to happen; her guts twisted with excitement and anxiety. She was going to be a drug dealer. Noor Khan, felon. Well, not a felon unless she got caught.

Noor glanced at her watch. Only ten minutes before her next appointment. She had to call Jaycee about handing over the cocaine. She hurriedly got off with Gerry and dialed Jaycee, whose phone rang and rang. No answering machine of course. She was probably at the Maple Jug Mercantile selling comfrey poultices or something. Noor tried to ease her rapid breathing before Jennifer and Jessica came out with their matching coffee mugs, each with its matching dollop of cream, and wanted to know why she was looking faint. Now was the time to back out, before she got in any deeper. But she needed that money, and anyway she owed it to Jaycee to see it through. And Gerry. She owed it to Gerry too, she reminded herself, again seeing him smirking.

When she had a break Noor put the wagging Jiyah in the house even though the shaggy old dog would probably have preferred to stay out on the frigid driveway, believing she was standing guard. Then she drove the Forester up Bliss Road—such a promising name for the road on which she and Dan had staked their claim, set up house and home eight years ago. Had it felt like bliss? Noor wasn't sure she was someone capable of experiencing that emotion, but it had been good for a while. Against her will a memory came to her of the two of them stopping at the for sale sign on the empty farmhouse with its peeling yellow paint, peering in dusty windows, admiring the wraparound porch and the leaning but fixable barn, holding hands while sitting in the rickety porch chairs, Dan dreaming about their kids playing in the yard while Noor calculated the fencing requirements of the pasture and how many horses it could hold. Even then they'd had different priorities but it hadn't mattered; they'd been in it together for the long haul.

Noor sighed and forced away the memory of their younger, more hopeful selves. She stopped at the intersection of Center Road, where Hilary Emory made his walking error, swung right and then left onto Barnes. She turned at the Hillwinds sign, glimpsing in passing the two Emory houses, big and little, sitting side by side across their shared driveway like siblings on two sides of a church pew. Noor hadn't been in a church since she'd gone with Pauline; although her parents rarely made it to the mosque in Burlington they'd disapproved of her singing hymns in the Congregational Church with the Shattucks.

Noor drove up the quarter mile stretch of gravel road to the Hillwinds parking lot, empty once again, except for Jaycee's beige car, the usual troop of cats, and a new sign reading: ORDER YOUR ORGANIC THANKSGIVING FINGERLING POTATOES NOW! Thanksgiving. Ugh. Soon, on Vermont Public Radio, Susan Stamberg, brought back from retirement for the occasion, would be offering up Mama Stamberg's repulsive sounding cranberry sour cream relish. "It turns a Pepto-Bismol pink," Susan Stamberg would say gaily. Noor and Dan were invited to his boss's house for the holiday, as usual. She and Dan would sit side by side while the vets talked about the best way to suture a strangulated inguinal hernia, the partner's wife bragged about her job in the state legislature and everyone embarrassingly held hands and went around the table saying what they were thankful for, the hosts' teenage kids rolling their eyes, and Noor pretending she didn't know about Mindy Francis. And what would Noor say she was thankful for? Some really cool cheese she got from Peru.

Jaycee was in the Maple Jug sporting her floor-length dress and bonnet and dusting a row of empty glass bottles from her perch atop a stepladder. Noor banged through the door, tinkling the sleigh bells used year round in quaint Vermont shoppes to announce customers, setting a string of dried gourds rattling and startling Jaycee, who lurched off her ladder, nearly tripping over her skirt hem.

"Whoa, Nelly," Jaycee said. "You scared me. Hey, Noor."

Noor flashed on Dan calling Mindy a Nervous Nelly when she called the house that time. Maybe it was Jaycee who should have married Dan. "Hey," Noor said. "We're good to go. The guy liked the coke. I just need to pick it up and bring it to Gerry and he'll pay us."

A toilet flushed behind the closed door quaintly labeled "chamber pot room"—Mrs. Emory's touch, no doubt—there'd been a customer after all. A lean man in a track suit and running shoes—maybe one of Dan's friends with the La Leche wives—averted his gaze as he hurried past Jaycee and Noor, who stood frozen until the sleigh bells and gourd string announced his departure.

"Shit," Noor said, "I didn't see any cars in the lot. Couldn't you have shushed me? Do you think he heard?"

"He didn't hear. He's probably just embarrassed that we know he took a dump and didn't buy anything. Desperate runners stop in sometimes to use the toilet. Hey, I want to come with you to make the drop," Jaycee said, and pushed her granny glasses back up to the bridge of her nose.

"What's the matter?" Noor asked. "Why do you need to be there? You don't trust me all of a sudden?" It burned Noor that Jaycee was going to start doubting her now, after she'd taken all the risks arranging the sale. Not to mention her new lingo: *make the drop*? The girl must've watched her first cop show last night and wanted to try out her new street smarts.

"I trust you. Of course I trust you. I just want to meet him. I don't get to meet many people. Even here. Especially here."

"And you want to meet a *drug dealer*?"

"A drug dealer?" Jaycee grinned. "WE'RE drug dealers!"

"I thought you'd want to keep a low profile, for your own safety. But here, I'll give you his number and you can set up a meeting without me and I'll keep the low profile. Just don't call from your home phone."

"Noooo," Jaycee said. "I want us *both* to go. I thought we could maybe meet him in the cemetery, you know, where Pauline is buried, and we can visit her grave. Before he shows up. We can look at it together. Pay our respects."

Jaycee's boundless enthusiasm made Noor feel like a spoilsport but it pissed her off, too. Jaycee had no right to use Pauline's death for social glue. Noor looked away to the colored bottles on the shelves bending light into pretty spectrums across the floorboards. She couldn't help being a drag on things yet again by saying, "Oh, sure. We'll have a picnic on my dead friend's grave before we complete our drug deal. Shall we bring our Grey Poupon mustard?"

"You don't have to be mean about it. I didn't say anything about a picnic. And she was my friend too . . . sort of. *I* thought she was, anyway. I wanted her to be . . ."

"Fine." Noor tapped her foot in the middle of the spectrum. She half expected the colors to shatter into kaleidoscope shards but instead a rainbow stretched across her instep. "I'll set up a time with Gerry at the cemetery and call to let you know when to meet there. You'll bring the coke."

"Wait. How much money are we getting?"

"I still don't know."

"Shouldn't we have some say in the price?"

"Do we have any other options?"

Jaycee shrugged, then squinched her brows again. She really ought to deep-six that habit, Noor thought, borrowing from Jaycee's cop show vocabulary. The habit no doubt resulted from all the churning of butter the girl grew up doing: the crouching over ideas, the pounding of one thought into another until they all held together.

"Well, we won't let it go for *too* low," Jaycee insisted. "We'll tell them where they can stick it if it does."

Being the source of the cocaine was endowing Jaycee with new authority, Noor saw. Let her enjoy it while she could.

⟳

Gerry had decided that the Hubbard Park tower would be too busy on a Sunday, even on a cold late November Sunday, and Noor agreed. The strapping Montpelier denizens would be out in force, hiking or dog walking or biking like Dan with his spandex and racing stripes. Instead, Gerry suggested they meet in Sabin's Pasture, the hilly fields that rose behind the Vermont College campus. Gerry would park on the Route 2 border of the acreage and Noor could park alongside the quad on College Street and walk in behind the dorms. When she hit the brook that ran in the valley between dip and hillside she'd turn south toward Route 2, and they'd meet on the path that climbed the hill from the highway. Better not to park their cars side by side in daylight. Besides, she'd like the walk.

Noor noted that the fields below the dorms and rising up the hillside across the brook had popped up in weeds and thistle now that they were no longer hayed or brush hogged. In recent years the stands of pine at the tops of the fields and every other tree standing, no matter how worthless for lumber, had been ruthlessly logged in a dispute between the town and the landowners who had been refused a development permit. The town wanted to buy the land as a recreation site and wouldn't let the owners create a housing development, so the owners had trashed it out of spite. Stumps and shattered, upended trees littered the steep hillside. Now you could see that it hadn't been a very big plot of fields and forest to begin with—its former mystery lost to the saws and skidders. She hated to see productive grassland giving way to brush—soon it would be saplings and juniper and then pines. All that new weedy growth seemed like an insult to the farmers who had cleared these lands by brute effort. Still, the dried stalks made beautiful skeletons—starbursts of browned Queen Anne's lace, brittle gray milkweed boats with clinging fluff that had missed its chance to scatter seed, crisp goldenrod plumes rattling in the brisk wind. She'd snap off a bouquet and bring it home if she weren't afraid to import weeds to her own pasture. It felt good to be outside, striding along instead of walking backward leading Daisy or Moon Pie with a wobbly, ungainly rider, or slowing her steps so poor old Jiyah could keep pace. The overcast sky matched her mood but the cold restored her.

In less than a month people would be cross-country skiing or sledding back here or maybe they'd boycott the area after the way the owners had logged it.

Noor topped a small rise to see Route 2, fronted on its far side with shabby wooden and corrugated metal buildings; there was Gerry standing, smoking, beside his dark sedan. Noor waved and Gerry tossed his cigarette. She cut east so that he had to start climbing the path to meet her, away from the prying eyes of those traveling Route 2.

"This place is such a mess now," Noor said, gesturing toward the ravaged hillside. "It used to be so pretty back here."

"Hello to you too, thank you very much. Had some good parties up here, back in the day," Gerry said. "You ever go to any of those ones in the quarry?"

Noor squinched her eyebrows, then realized she was imitating Jaycee. She made her face smooth like a mask.

"S'pose not," Gerry said, laughing.

Wordlessly they kept walking up the main trail, now a skidder track with half frozen ruts. Noor listened to Gerry's breath go ragged. "My partner wants us to do the exchange in Cutler Cemetery. Do you know where it is?" she asked.

"You mean that old one across from the compost place before Main turns into County Road?"

"Yup."

"Alright. Shouldn't be any nosy neighbors there. When?" Gerry said.

"Would Tuesday at 2:00 work? Can you get the money by then?"

"Sure."

"Gerry, how come this guy is going to let you walk off with so much cash without a guarantee that he'll get his product?"

"He has a guarantee. He knows *I* know he'll hunt me down and disappear me if I don't show up with the stuff."

Noor stopped. "Jesus, Gerry." So this was the clean-hands-just-a-little-recreational-not-hurting-anyone business they'd gotten into. Sure, and the money to pay them would come from already fucked-up losers whose lives were a downward spiral no matter what Noor helped them put into their bodies. But she and Jaycee didn't think about the buyers. Or maybe Noor did think about them, secretly. Maybe she dreaded them, dreaded someday knowing just one of their names, their faces. It was hard to tell what she was thinking about and what she was pushing to the back of her mind, when just walking outside with Gerry felt so much better than standing at home in her kitchen pretending not to succumb to her suspicions of Dan.

Gerry laughed. "So you and your partner better be at that cemetery at 2:00 or it won't just be turkey getting cooked for Thanksgiving."

Noor nodded. Not much you could say to that. She fumbled a try. "What're you doing Thanksgiving, Gerry? I mean for real."

"I'll go get Taylor and take her to my mom's house. She likes to spend a night with Grammy now and then."

"Nice," Noor said. He'd be with family. She'd had a wild thought of cooking Thanksgiving dinner herself and inviting Gerry over. She could invite Jaycee and the Emorys and maybe the dealer guy from Burlington to top it off. Introduce Dan to her new social circle. And Dan could introduce Mindy and Mindy's pet, Whore-Hay. What a thrill *that* would be.

They walked another five minutes in silence, Gerry huffing now beside her like a hard-worked horse, until they'd reached the first plateau and the view of the mountains looming across the valley. Camel's Hump and its lesser cousins receded in dark undulations beneath gloomy clouds. Gerry leaned over and put his hands on his thighs and coughed. "This walking shit is bad for a guy's health," he said. He straightened up and put a hand on her jacket sleeve. "Why so glum, Noor Khan? Why do you always look like someone's run over your kitten? You've got cash coming your way, the coke is kick-ass, you're doing good work at your horse thing, you're helping your clients, you're hot, you have an apple pie picket fence husband, you've got the world by the tail. But don't mind me asking. You was always like that. Glum. A brooder. I remember in high school thinking them cheerleaders must'a not known something you knew. I like that, I admit it. It's sweet. It turns me on."

She didn't want to *turn him on*. Well, she thought she didn't, even though Gerry loosened her up, dislodged her negativity. She just felt better around him, and, okay, sexier. Across the valley a squall blew up, hiding the peaks, rushing toward them and then snow began to fall in large wet flakes. Dan would never say he liked her for her brooding, though he might have wished she was broody, like a hen. "I think Dan's having an affair," she said, the words coming out at last, as though she could say them more easily in this shroud of early snow.

"Yeah? Ken doll been running off with Skipper?"

"Gerry, it's not funny."

"No, it ain't. Come here, baby." Gerry pulled her into his leather jacket, into his powerful tobacco smell, acrid and comforting, and for the moment Noor let herself be pulled, let herself lean into his shoulder. Gerry put a hand on the back of her head, cradling her skull.

"Maybe you should have one of your own," he said.

"What?" Noor pulled back and looked up at him. She hadn't noticed in high school that his green flecked eyes were beautiful. A few first snowflakes were caught in his lashes, melting there.

"An affair," Gerry coached.

"Like that would help."

"You don't know. It might." Gerry pulled her back in, gently touched his lips to the top of her head, then raised her chin and kissed her, his lips just as they'd been that one time in high school, greedy but soft, yielding. Noor kissed him back and Gerry moaned. Then Noor pushed him away and started walking back down the hill. What was she doing? Gerry Wilcox?

"Hey, hey, easy," Gerry said.

"I can't do this," Noor cried. "I don't know what I'm doing, I don't even know what's going on."

"Easy, easy there," Gerry soothed. "You don't have to do anything."

"I *know* I don't," Noor snapped, striding downhill through desiccated nettles, burrs, Queen Anne's lace, spears of dead goldenrod, while the suddenly clinging snow turned everything into a strange black and white movie. This wasn't her life, wasn't her life, wasn't.

"Don't go getting your knickers in a twist," Gerry said and Noor shook her head at his dumb-ass phrasing. He grabbed her shoulder.

"Wait! I love you, little Noor Khan. Always have. I won't do shit to make you unhappy."

She could barely see Gerry's car outlined in the white-out but she could hear car tires hissing on Route 2, everything one big muffled gray blanket of a world.

"I know you won't," she said, and it was true.

❧

The day of the exchange was clear with a pale, late fall sun, the kind that offered little warmth but made the leafless trees appear more sharply defined, nearly brittle. Jaycee's car was broken down, so Noor had to pick her up in the farm truck because she needed to load up on feed and shavings on the way over. The feed store lady, who hung rhyming poems on the register each day extolling friendship, sunsets, cold weather, hot cocoa, and admonishing gossips and mean folks, wanted to chat about Poulin versus Blue Seal grains; it was all Noor could do to break away. Jaycee looked as excited as a kid en route to a birthday party—if kids at birthday parties wore earth-tone knitted ponchos over brown corduroy slacks that had once belonged to their fathers. Not too stylish today. Her hair was pulled into an incongruously perky ponytail and she'd flipped a colorful woven scarf over her shoulder—must be from Peru, as it was certainly outside Jaycee's normal dull palette. Noor wondered when she'd picked up tweezers. It should have pleased Noor to see Jaycee ever so slowly coming around to modern grooming habits (her hair less frizzy and her legs no doubt shaved under her dad's trousers) but somehow it made Noor uneasy, even unhappy. Could be she'd miss the old Jaycee when the new, done up one had fully taken her place, even though she'd been the one to encourage her. Still, tweezing and styling couldn't keep Jaycee from being her ineptly forceful, frumpy self. Noor hated to think herself so small-minded that she'd miss the upper hand she'd had by being the more stylish of the two. But no amount of style improvements could make Jaycee pretty, and that made Noor feel better. Guilty for being petty . . . but better for being prettier. What a schmuck she was. And it wasn't like her looks had kept Dan from calling Mindy a million times. Noor squeezed her eyes closed against another unwelcome tender image: Dan holding his sister's baby on his and Noor's last visit to his family in Ohio, bouncing on his toes, making goo goo faces and popping noises with his lips until the nine-month-old rewarded him with a one-toothed grin.

"Hey!" Jaycee said, freeing Noor from that bittersweet scene. Jaycee carried a large plastic pot of rust-colored chrysanthemums, pressed against the front of the furry beige poncho. A tote bag hung off her shoulder. "For the grave," she said, clambering in and settling her flowerpot on her lap. "My mom commented on you dropping by lately. She's happy I have a new friend."

Like Pauline, I'm getting paid to hang with you, Noor thought. She'd crossed the line from goody-goody to dope dealer with frightening ease. Until the coke in the cheese fell in her lap like manna from heaven she had never imagined she could be so criminal. Suppressed adolescent rebellion, anger at Dan, desperation, pick an excuse. "Where's the stuff?" she asked.

"In here, under the plant. I even brought a spade to plant it in the ground." She gestured to her oversized tote made of boiled wool. "The mums, I mean, not the, you know . . ."

"Pretty shrewd," Noor said, genuinely grateful that Jaycee had thought to bring along the camouflage of flowers, so if anyone drove by the cemetery they'd look like mourners. She backed out of the Emory drive and headed down Center Road with its November dulled fields—the early snow had disappeared the day after it fell—bare limbed maples, and occasional mini-mansions topping hillsides.

"So what's this guy Gerry like?" Jaycee asked. Poor girl had never had the chance to gossip about boys in middle school. As though Noor was only going to the cemetery in order to see him. "Just a guy I knew in high school who never did anything with his life."

"Oh. You mean like me," Jaycee said and Noor was instantly abashed. What a snob she'd become . . . had always been.

"Gerry said the coke tested out nearly 90 percent pure. The dealer didn't have to tell us that. Gerry said we'll get seventeen thousand dollars each. In cash. I don't know what his cut is or what his guy will make from it and I don't want to know. Let's just take our money and run."

"That's not so bad," Jaycee said. "The dealer doesn't know about this meeting, right? He's not going to come swooping down here to grab the goods without paying, then split the money with your friend?"

"You mean did Gerry set us up? He wouldn't do that."

"What makes you so sure?" Jaycee said.

When had Jaycee become so savvy to the ways of the world? "Because he's always liked me . . . too much."

"Lucky you," Jaycee said. "That's never been my problem."

Thinking of Dan and whatever he had going on behind *her* back, Noor looked straight ahead at the buckled pavement rising before them as they approached the top of the hill and then over the roller coaster swell down to the junction with County Road.

Halfway to the cemetery they passed Hil trudging along the shoulder of Center Road with his staff and village idiot hat.

"Oh God," Jaycee said. "There he goes. He walks out here all the time. I wonder why. Remember what that cop said the day we were weighing the coke about Alzheimer patients heading for water? Creeks and things. Except there's no creek here. I wonder what he thinks he's looking for. Maybe we should stop and take him home."

"We don't have time," Noor said. "And where are we going to put him, on top of the grain sacks and bales of shavings in the back of the truck?"

"Maybe he'll get tired and turn back," Jaycee said with a shrug. "One of the nurses told me they also visit places that were important to them once, where important things happened. Like if you're a cop and you're looking for a lost Alzheimer's patient, that's where you look first. Water, and then the church where they got married or the bank they robbed."

"Well nothing important ever happened at my house and he shows up there," Noor said, glancing at her watch. They were meeting Gerry at the cemetery at 2:00. She'd allowed fifteen minutes to visit Pauline's grave. Although Noor had consented to a graveside visit in deference to Jaycee, now that they were actually going to Cutler Cemetery, she longed to stand over Pauline's resting place by herself. Even if Pauline would be just a rectangle of grass.

It was a small old cemetery on what looked like a pasture hillside, with an earth flanked vault for the bodies of those who died in winter when the ground was too hard to dig up, marked by a simple sign hanging off granite gate posts that held no gate. It was only a few miles from Jaycee's house and not far at all from the crest of the hill where Pauline and her father had lost their lives in the hit and run. Noor realized she thought of it as *their* accident, not her own, as though her concussion and fractured femur and watching her friend die, had happened to *them*, not her. The place was empty, the stolid granite squares and the skinny, slatey older graves sporting leftover decorations from Veteran's day—stiff little flags, potted plants with withered stalks, plastic flowers incongruously garish in the leaf blown dullness. Noor ticked off the names: Noyes, Wheelock, Cutler, Dodge, Howland. Naturally, not a Khan or Musharraf among them. Not even a Goldberg.

"Here it is!" Jaycee announced, weaving expertly among the stones to point out two flat squares with plaques listing names and dates.

Noor took a sharp breath and tightened her shoulders in readiness. But of course, Pauline wasn't here, accusing Noor for still breathing, accusing her for hanging out with the girl Pauline had once babysat. Pauline was nowhere. Box of bones, that was all. And hair—no, don't think of that glossy, red-gold hair. Noor kneeled and brushed leaf litter from the cold stone.

"I'm sorry," Jaycee said, touching her shoulder. "I shouldn't have made you come here. Of course it would be harder for you than for me." She set the pot of mums where Pauline's head would be.

"It's okay," Noor lied.

Jaycee kneeled beside her. "Pauline made this, you know," Jaycee said, fingering her colorful wool scarf. "Well not all of it. One of the times she was over she saw my table loom and she wanted to try. She picked her colors and I strung the warp for her and showed her how to use the shuttle for the weft. I lost it like six years ago but now I found it again."

"She never mentioned learning to weave," Noor said. Maybe Pauline had been making the scarf for her, Noor. She remembered Pauline saying something to her about a birthday present she was making and that Noor would never guess what color it was.

"She didn't get to finish it before she died. I finished it for her." Jaycee lifted the scarf and ran fingers down its length. "See, her section is looser and the edges are uneven. That's just how it is when you first start to weave. It takes a while to get the tension right. My mother wanted me to pull her part out and do it right but I refused. I wanted to keep, you know, a piece of her."

So Pauline really had meant something to Jaycee and maybe Jaycee had meant something to Pauline, something Pauline wouldn't have admitted to Noor. She felt a pang of jealousy, and then of sympathy for this odd poky woman beside her. They'd both loved Pauline.

Jaycee wrapped the colorful scarf back around her neck. "My mom misses Pauline too, you know. She said, when I told her I was going to the cemetery with you—"

"You told your *mother*?" Noor snapped, interrupting her.

"Not about the *deal*, just that we were visiting Pauline's grave. She said, 'Thank goodness we still have a part of that poor girl right here in our house.' Hey, is that him?" Jaycee gestured with her chin toward a stretch of gravestones.

Noor rose and saw Gerry walking toward them, a cigarette in his mouth. His black leather jacket flapped open, his longish hair flopped over his forehead and he wore his trademark smirky smile as he put one hand on his pretend cummerbund and did a little Gene Kelly sidestep among the graves. Beside his dark blue Corolla, a black SUV was now parked. Noor felt a frisson of fear. Maybe Jaycee had been right, before. Maybe Gerry and his partner were going to steal the drug, leave the two women knocked out or worse in the cemetery. But Jaycee only whispered, "He's *cute*. You didn't say that." She smoothed her bulky poncho against her low breasts.

"Someone you knew?" Gerry asked, approaching Pauline's grave.

"Someone we both knew," Noor said. "A long time ago. Hey, Gerry, there's a car next to yours. Who . . ."

"Don't worry, he's just checking you out for next time. Nah. Making sure it all goes down the way it should. Hey, what do you think we're selling? Prom tickets?"

Noor glanced up at the parked SUV. The driver hadn't turned off the engine and puffs of condensed exhaust trailed from the muffler. Better than cops, she supposed. Jaycee nudged her.

"Gerry, this is Jaycee, my uh . . . partner."

Gerry extended a hand. "Glad to meet you Jaycee. Real glad." He smiled—turning on the dimpled charm. Of course he was glad, Noor thought: Jaycee was the source of their windfall. But then Jaycee blushed, and her sudden display of bashfulness posed a second, much more annoying reason for Gerry turning on the juice.

"Pleasedtomeetyou." Jaycee mumbled, actually dipping into a Jane Austen curtsy, shaking his hand.

"So, how do we do this?" Noor asked. "I mean, do you hand over the money first or do we hand off . . . I mean, I'm not up on the drug deal protocol."

Gerry laughed. "No protocol. No UN rules about who sits where or signs first. How 'bout I hand you the envelopes of cash, you count them," he glanced around the array of headstones to check for nonexistent lurking mourners before continuing, "and if you're satisfied you just give me the stuff." He pulled two thick envelopes out of an inner pocket in his scruffy leather jacket.

She thumbed through the stack of bills while Jaycee counted aloud beside her and Gerry rested his butt on a nearby upright gravestone. He plucked up a little flag and squinted at the stick. "Hey! Whadya know. Made in the US of A." He waited until they finished counting, then asked, "Are we cool?"

"This is really, really going to help with things," Jaycee said.

"How about you, Noor Khan? You good?" He searched her face.

"I'm good."

Jaycee yanked the mums and soil from the plastic pot, lifted a double wrapped white plastic bag and handed it off to Gerry, who tucked it inside his jacket. "I'll be right back," he said. Noor held her breath as she watched Gerry weave his way back through the headstones and hand the package through the lowered passenger window of the SUV. If this was a cop show someone would plug him in the chest and come for them but the SUV merely backed away, cruised out of the cemetery as Gerry turned toward them smiling.

"Done deal," Gerry said when he'd reached them again. He looked pretty proud of himself, as did Jaycee, Noor noted.

"Wait," Jaycee said. She dug in her boiled wool tote and withdrew a garden spade. She dropped to her knees and stabbed at the half frozen earth, lifting clods, then stuck in the mums, tamped the roots and potting soil so the rusty orange mums blazed in front of Pauline's stone. "They won't last long," she said wistfully, brushing off her knees. She rose, wiped her palms on the baggy hips of the corduroys, and shook Gerry's hand again, this time braving his eyes.

"No chance you could get your mitts on more of this?" Gerry asked.

"I told you it was a one-time . . ." Noor began.

"Yes," Jaycee interrupted.

"What? You've got more of this stuff?" Noor accused. Funny that Jaycee waited to mention it until she'd met Gerry.

"I didn't know, before. But then I started thinking. Well, remember I told you about the candlesticks and the other plaster wedding presents that guy Carlos gave me to bring to his sister in Lima along with the cheese that had the cocaine?"

"Cheese?" Gerry said.

"What about them?" asked Noor.

"Well, I remember a story I read about a sports trophy made of—"

"World Cup soccer trophy," Gerry said. "From Colombia. It weighed eleven kilos or something like that. Street value of close to a million dollars. I saw a photo of it."

Noor was surprised he knew this—did he read the news? Watch it on TV? Look up stuff on the internet? But then it *was* his line of work—well, no it wasn't, not before she'd come along. He'd been a humble peddler of weed.

"Right," Jaycee continued, "And I started thinking about the other gifts Carlos sent beside the vase my dad dropped. Those candlestick holders were huge. Big as wine bottles, practically. And a big heavy platter with a painting of a crying lady on it who looked just like Frida. It made *me* want to cry."

"Who's Frida?" asked Gerry.

"So I looked a little closer at that vase when I was trying to glue it together and guess what?"

"You got to be shitting me!" Gerry said.

"Nope," said Jaycee.

Noor said, "How could you tell?"

"Here, you can try it yourself," she said, and pulled a jagged fragment from her tote.

"Jeez," Gerry said.

"Oh, no! Look who's coming," Jaycee spluttered, putting the broken vase back in her bag.

Noor turned around, heart thumping, expecting cop cars or the mysterious dealer's thugs, but it was only Hil, waving his staff happily in their direction and starting toward them up the hill.

"At least he still recognizes me," Jaycee said. She rolled her eyes. "I've got to take him home."

"Well I told you I don't have room for him in the truck with all my feed and stuff. Unless you want him to sit on your lap," Noor said petulantly. Jaycee had been holding out on her about the rest of the coke, waiting to see if she freaked or went running to Dan for help.

"I can drive you and your dad home," Gerry said too quickly for Noor's taste. "Any friend of the lovely Noor Khan is a friend of mine."

"Oh, that would be great. Would you *really*?"

Settle down, Noor longed to say. Keep your bloomers on. He's mine! But then she corrected herself. Gerry wasn't hers, she didn't want him. She was married, for god's sake. At least she thought she still was.

"Daddy! Daddy! Over here!!" Jaycee shouted.

"I'll wait in my car," Gerry said. "Don't want to spook 'Daddy.'"

"Well this is the place for spooks," Jaycee said gaily, not even realizing how silly she sounded. Noor wanted to get away from Jaycee's father, away from Jaycee with her awkward flirtatiousness, take her cash and run, but she found herself headed toward Hilary alongside Jaycee, too civil to snub a crazy old man, even with drug money in her pocket. He stood by the granite gate posts with his head tilted like a dog listening to a whistle.

"So this concludes our business," Noor said to Jaycee. And, she added inwardly, our so-called friendship, and any need for either one of us to get together with Gerry again.

"No, no. You get half of the vase too."

"Why?" Noor asked.

"Because we're partners. Because I wanted us to come here together," Jaycee said. "Because of Pauline, you know, how we kind of shared her and I thought it was something we could share with each other. To make us better friends."

Jaycee looked at Noor with a naked, hopeful face, a face not unlike Marta's when Noor had told her about the competitive paraplegic riders. Noor was mollified by Jaycee's pitiful eagerness and the fact that she wasn't trying to edge Noor out of more cash, even though Noor wasn't sure she'd want to get involved further. "You better go get your father. But by the way, what was your mom talking about when she said that you still have a part of Pauline in your house? The pictures? The pictures your mom drew of her?"

"The cats' lockets," said Jaycee. "The hair in the lockets. My mom put it there. It's Pauline's."

"Oh please don't tell me that." Noor wheeled around, her eyes fixed in the direction of Pauline's resting place. "Take that back. Don't say that."

"Welcome to Emory World," Jaycee said.

CHAPTER NINE

Hil, 2010

Hortense has an eagle eye. Even when his wife is sleep-thinking beside him in bed, Hil can feel that eye peering, searching him out, and then when he gets up it follows him.

Hannah, not Hortense, she would scold. "But if you want me to be Hortense I'll be Hortense, for you."

Hil sings this like a jingle as he crosses to the bathroom sink and feels for the razor, not wanting to wake her by turning on a light. He'll need to jot down the jingle so he doesn't forget it. Carefully, he balances the razor back where he'd found it, and starts toward his study for paper and pen.

"Come back to bed," shouts Hannah from under the bedclothes. "But if you're shaving, use gel, not soap," she adds, even though she is drink-thinking. Yes? *Drink-thinking? Deeming?* Nope. Not it.

He starts back for the bathroom, splashes his face, and discovers his car keys in his bathrobe pocket. It pleases Hil to find those keys, ever since the daughter hid them in a what? A hatbox! Hah. He'll have to write that down. It's up to him to run the errands. He finds the car in the driveway and throws the car in reverse, making the same fancy, figure-eight maneuver that used to make the girls laugh. Mother and daughter. Whenever they were in the car, they used to plead for him to do a few figure eights, and even standing on the stoop they used to clap their hands to watch. The car follows the steep curves up and around. It's not necessary to jot down street names, since he knows the route by feel, by the spin and lag of the steering wheel. Druid-thinking? What's it called, for God's sake, when your eyes move in bed and you go places there?

One night the car drove him to Curtis Pond, but that's because the pond is in the Mad Hatter Valley. It vexed him to step off the duck thing into the muck. But what really peeves him off, to borrow a phrase from the younger folk, is when it drives him to Goat Haven B&B with its Maple Avenue and its sledding festivals and its Christmas Eve barn hoopla and its maple themed supper dances. Spence owns this place. Hil hates Spence. *Vermont Glory Days* my ass. Hil would rather call his next book Puke than Vermont Glory Days. Hillwinds never sugarcoats the past, even though people have a rollicking good time finding out how fucked it was to live back then. Hil digs for a match in his bathrobe pocket to burn Spence down, just as a light flicks on at the front of the house and the front door opens. He'll need to cover his tracks. He opens the car door, steps out, selects a turkey made of corn ears from the autumn display and flashes a thumbs-up sign.

"Thanks for the Big Bird!" he calls, cinching his bathrobe too late on purpose. Also in his pocket is the scrap of tatting from Hannah's dancer days, but now the tatting is filthy with bits of straw. There are always such clues, such leftover evidence. Hil wishes he had known this as a young man.

Spence gapes. The thumbs up isn't the only thing Hil flashed.

Except it isn't Spence, it's some younger, not-Spence guy, the same younger guy as last night with the mortified grin. "Sir! Can I help you with anything?" he asks. "Are you alright driving, sir? At this time of night? Can we fetch you a blanket? Is there someone we can phone? You really shouldn't be out here in . . . You're not properly dressed for in public, sir," the Not-Spence adds. Silly fellow. Wearing nothing but flannel himself.

"Uhhhh . . ." Hil picks up an apple-looking thing, a small one this time from the topmost reach of the spiral display and pitches a knuckler, striking the not-Spence guy in the face.

"Jeeez!" shouts the guy. "Get Outta Here, Man!"

"Don't mind if I do," Hil says. Oughtta jot that down.

He gets back in the car, shutting the door on a flap of his robe, and lets the vehicle carry him back the wrong way, its own way past the spot in the woods where a bad thing happened. In the distance as he drives, a siren starts up, like for a rare Vermont tornado. No one, not even a chicken, has ever lost his life to a Vermont tornado. And the siren as usual isn't for him. Instead the car deposits him safely at Hillwinds, where something made of mist and mirrors perches atop Yam Rock. Hil gives a wave with the scrap of soiled tatting, and the thing waves back.

PART IV

Hunger Mountain

Noor, 2010

The day before Thanksgiving, in the jammed aisles of the Hunger Mountain Food Co-op, Noor stood in front of the produce bins, lost in an eggplant's rich dark purple. Her own family, when she was growing up, had attempted an American holiday season but had always gotten it wrong—once substituting a large chicken for the turkey, another time a leg of lamb stuffed with rice, currying the sweet potatoes, serving paratha instead of Parker House rolls. Even though Noor preferred her mother's spicy cooking to the traditional bland Thanksgiving goodies, as a kid she'd resented her parents' fudged Americanisms, which seemed, even in retrospect, intentional on their part, as if what they wanted was to *try* to conform, but only as long as they didn't succeed.

Moving past the eggplant, Noor was tempted to make something so spicy that no one at Dan's boss's house could eat it but instead she settled for her promised Thanksgiving contribution— dark green, hard to peel, dense butter*cup* squash, not butternut, which could be watery. She put two heavy squash into her cart, collected milk, bread, and nearly caused an international incident at the bulk bins trying to get a turn at the roasted almonds and rolled oats. Finally she moved to the register, waiting in the long, slow-moving line. Out in the lot, the sharp wind pinked the cheeks of shoppers and the usually ultra-polite Montpelier drivers whizzed anxiously about, searching for spaces. Noor had to slalom her cart between them. And there, parked beside Noor's Subaru, was Jaycee, unloading a plastic wrapped, fresh Stonewood Farms All Natural turkey—a splurge with her new drug money, Noor supposed—into the trunk of the Emory Buick. Noor considered turning back to the store, pretending she'd forgotten something, so she wouldn't have to chat, but Jaycee looked up from the trunk, face flooded with joy. She was wearing her fuzzy poncho and the same colorful Pauline scarf but jeans this time instead of her father's cords. And a red beret set at a rakish angle. She looked like a wannabe bohemian high school art teacher, but kind of cute, too, in her peculiar frumpy Jaycee way.

"Hey! What a coinkydink! Noor. Crazy, huh?" Jaycee prattled. "We're both shopping on the *worst* day! Kamikaze shoppers everywhere."

Noor balanced both heavy grocery bags in one hand while she opened the passenger door of her Subaru and pushed them onto the seat. Naturally, one of the bags tipped and out rolled a squash onto the dog-haired floor. She turned to Jaycee and said dully, "Happy Almost Thanksgiving."

"You too!" Jaycee said with enough enthusiasm for the two of them. "Wearing my red," she said, touching the beret, "for walking between the house and Hillwinds, you know, hunting season." She dropped her voice to a stage-whisper. "I've been wanting to talk to you about how we'd get that stuff from Frida." Jaycee peered at Noor from beneath her granny glasses. "Hey, you don't look so good."

"I don't feel so good," Noor mumbled. She really didn't. She felt like shit. Like she had the flu except without the usual symptoms. Fatigued and achy, but in her soul instead of her joints. If she even had a soul anymore. According to her parents' religion—she didn't consider it her own anymore—the spiritual component of the soul was the size of a bee and shimmered like mercury when removed from the body. She could just imagine her soul buzzing away, but instead of winging it to paradise she imagined it breaking into separate beads like the contents of a broken thermometer, lost in the cracks between floorboards. She'd fractured it when she'd agreed to sell the coke, knowing it was wrong but letting anger at Dan and fear of losing her business direct her actions. Maybe it had weakened earlier, when she'd turned away from the dying Pauline. Or when she'd started making excuses to her parents for not visiting the mosque, a teenager questioning the logic of parents who believed both in science and Allah. But it wasn't the state of her soul, it was her fears about Dan that were making her ill. She knew *her* soul came second to the more prosaic dread of being dumped.

"Oh Noor, I hope you aren't getting the flu. I hear it's going around early. Do you need any help with anything?"

Jaycee's sincere concern weakened Noor's resolve. Having told only Gerry of her suspicions about Dan, she hungered for a confidante. She couldn't call her old friends after all this time to ask for a shoulder to cry on. And here was Jaycee, who would be thrilled to be that broad, fuzzy-ponchoed shoulder. Noor hoped she wasn't using Jaycee's desire to be a friend the way she knew she'd used Gerry's affection, but then it wasn't really using if the other person got what she wanted too. "My husband might be having an affair," she said.

"Ohhhh nooooo, I thought you had such a perfect life. That bastard!" Jaycee really seemed dismayed, no shades of schadenfreude at all, the schadenfreude Noor might feel if the roles were reversed. "Why would anyone cheat on you? They'd have to be crazy."

"I'm not even sure if it's true. I just found *a lot* of back and forth calls in Dan's phone to a certain woman. Way too many to be vet calls." Noor hugged her peacoat close to her chest. "She has a pet llama, by the way."

"Ahhh," said Jaycee, as if the Peruvian element explained Dan's recklessness. "Who is she?" she demanded. Noor shouldn't have said anything. Now Jaycee was all exercised about it, exer-cycling to the rescue. Still, it felt good to have someone on Noor's side against the mysterious, but certainly unpleasant, Mindy.

"In Calais. I don't even know what she looks like."

"She can't be as pretty as you. Do you know where in Calais?"

What difference did that make? Noor wondered. But she knew. She'd looked Mindy Francis up online, found her in public records, and tried to study a blurry image of her property on Google Earth. "Yeah," she admitted.

Jaycee slammed the trunk over her chilled turkey. "Let's go take a look. We can do a drive-by."

"A drive-by?" Noor tucked her ungloved hands into her armpits. "I swear you're watching too much crime TV these days." But the idea appealed to her. She wanted to see who this Mindy was. "She lives up some long driveway, the woman's got llamas, or llama, so a drive-by wouldn't work. We'd have to come up with a reason to knock on her door. I mean you. I'd stay in the car. I'm too recognizable as the exotic, alien wife."

"I know what," Jaycee said, getting into the spirit as though she were plotting some skit with a school group, "we'll dress up in Hillwinds clothing—you can be Bitty, the runaway slave girl; I'll be her Northrup sister, and we'll say we're looking for donations for needy children to visit Hillwinds."

"Oh sure, one of the many Pakistani slaves they had in this country circa 1860," Noor grumbled.

"We'll put a bonnet on you."

"Just get her to come to the door. I'll stay in the car. I want to get a look at her so I can see if I can picture it. Like maybe she dresses her llama in little costumes to match her own, or she uses hairspray or something. Dan's never been a big hairspray man."

"You're kidding, aren't you? This is going to be fun," Jaycee said, as though they were going to a costume party instead of trying to sneak a look at the woman who appeared to be replacing Noor in Dan's affections or, at least, in his cell phone. Jaycee seemed to think they were being goofy girls together, eleven-year-old pranksters . . . her chance to be *Noor and Jaycee* instead of the friendless Jacqueline Charlotte. Noor knew it was crazy to go over to Mindy's but she just had to see how this Mindy woman matched up with her seductive voice. And to say no now would disappoint Jaycee. . . .

An hour later they were headed for Calais from the Emory compound in Jaycee's unrecognizable, nondescript sedan, following Barnes Road until it hit County Road. Wearing her Hillwinds outfit, covered by necessity due to the cold with a puffy shit-brown, full-length parka that had been out of date so long it was back in style, Jaycee sat gripping the wheel, hands in her perfect ten and two position, though now you were supposed to keep your hands at nine and three, so you wouldn't punch yourself in the face if the air bag went off. Jaycee's car probably predated airbags. With her bonnet bunched into the hood of her parka, she totally looked the part, half Hillwinds and half real world, and Noor was impressed by Jaycee's gameness, her willingness to go out on limbs, not caring who thought what of her or what the consequences might be, after a lifetime, as she described it, of doing nothing but her parents' bidding.

Gerry had been very sweet to Jaycee when he had driven her and Hil home from the cemetery, Jaycee was saying. He had helped her with some firewood, and he had told her as they were stacking the wood about the bandit, Jesus Malverde, who was the patron saint of narco-trafficking and who had shrines built in his honor. Jaycee said cheerfully to Noor, "I really think Gerry's going to ask me out." Jaycee's habit of do-or-die optimism appealed to Noor as being something she herself ought to embrace. The girl should put an ad on the bulletin board at the Food Co-op amid the ads for *Dreamtime Healing, Holographic Kinetics,* whatever that was, and *Aromatherapy seminars.* But not so touchy-feely. She could coach mid-life women looking for a lifestyle change—ones who used to be dressage queens and now wanted to raise llamas or, say, deal drugs.

"What are you doing with your drug money?" Jaycee asked as she down-shifted for a hill. "You putting it in the bank or just hiding it in your house?"

"The barn," Noor said. The money, what was left of the seventeen thousand dollars, was wrapped in plastic like the coke itself and hidden at the bottom of a grain bin. She didn't want it to show up in a bank account and it was going almost too fast to bother. She had just paid off a credit card bill that morning, and next week had a date for a crown at the dentist's, where if you paid that day in full, they took off 10 percent. Or was it 5 percent? Yes. She was always disappointed, she remembered now, by how little that discount turned out to be. And disappointed that the crown cut into her new New Horizons operating budget. And her Dan divorce budget, if it came to that. "How about you?" she remembered to sound interested.

"Oh, here a little, there a little, here a pickle crock, there a bank account, Old MacDonald style." Jaycee laughed joyously, though she steered carefully along the sand-spattered asphalt. The early snow had not repeated itself but there'd been an ice storm a day earlier and the town had been out spreading salt-laced sand. Branches weighted with glassy jackets of frozen rain lined County Road all the way through Maple Corners, past the semi-frozen Curtis Pond where Noor had swum once with Pauline a million years ago. In Calais they followed Noor's smartphone GPS up a few slick dirt roads to Mindy's. Jaycee slowed to let a kink-tailed squirrel change its mind a few times before it skittered across the road and up a tree, as if its own GPS wasn't signaling properly.

As Google Earth had shown, Mindy Francis's driveway was long and curving, bounded by stone walls that had the look of recent landscaping rather than ancient pasture boundaries, and surprisingly, since it led off a dirt road, paved. It was probably heated too, as no ice remained on its asphalt. A yellow and black "Lab Crossing" sign announced its provenance as L.L. Bean. Generous plank-fenced, ice-crusted pastures spread out on both sides of the driveway. What a horse property it would make. And smack in the middle of what was once a hayfield—such a waste of good grass!— stood an oversized Lindel Cedar Home, with its ugly, jutting, windowed prow. An equally oversized silver Cadillac SUV, an Escalade, gleamed in front of the three bay garage. Did this woman live here by herself, alone with Whore-Hay the llama, who was probably lying on silk bedding inside the gorgeous cupolaed barn that flaunted a golden llama-shaped weather vane? Big money. Biiig Money. Noor imagined Mindy the divorced wife of an investment banker or a cardiac surgeon, or maybe she was still married to some much older rich man and just having a little fun on the side. Sexist! It could be Mindy's own money, earned on Wall Street, where for all Noor knew maybe Mindy worked as a commodities trader. It didn't matter. Large animal veterinarians and farriers were famous for getting involved with their female clients. Dan's very own sugar mama. But Dan hated these kinds of stylized farm manors as much as Noor did. They were so pretentious. She couldn't picture him feeling comfortable here.

"Holy crap," Jaycee declared.

They parked on the far side of the Escalade, where Noor hoped she'd be able to see without being seen. Jaycee got out, pulled on her bonnet and flounced her gingham dress under the parka. Then on second thought she removed the parka and slung it over her shoulders, cape style, to better show off her costume. She reached in back for a clipboard fluttering with paper.

"This is a stupid idea," Noor muttered. "I can't believe we're doing this. Look at you. She'll think you're some weirdo home-schooled religious nut."

"I *am* a weirdo homeschooled nut, just not religious," Jaycee said.

"What about the great god Hilary Emory?" Noor asked, regretting this cruelty the minute she said it, but Jaycee only answered, "Wish me luck," as usual, not in the least perturbed by Noor's attacks. Noor watched her plod up the steps, fumble with the heavy door knocker and wait in front of a huge golden wreath with spray-painted pine cones and Christmas balls, its red ribbon trailing all the way to the stoop. She bet there was a sprig of holly hanging in the front hallway for kissing under. Kissing Dan. Jaycee's long dress dragged over her cheap, imitation Ugg boots. Noor wouldn't be caught dead even in real Uggs—too Uggy.

Noor tapped her quickly chilling feet as Jaycee waited longer—why hadn't she realized that Mindy was probably away for the holiday or out shopping for the ostentatious feast (duckling or goose instead of turkey?) she'd lay out for her family—and then the door opened inward and a woman stuck her head out. She had spiky short blond hair—not how Noor had pictured a Mindy at all. A golden retriever dove for the open door but was dragged back by its collar. Jaycee's head tilted back and forth as she made up something to explain her presence. The woman—Noor couldn't see her all that well—gestured Jaycee inside. A moment later the two of them reappeared, shook hands, and Jaycee made a show of jotting down something on her clipboard. The woman closed the door. All Noor had seen were the bright blond spikes—bleached most likely—above a long red cowl neck sweater and slim legs in black leggings.

Jaycee was smiling when she came back to the car.

"Well?" Noor lowered her head until they'd turned around and headed back down the drive.

"She gave me a twenty dollar bill donation for some needy child to visit Hillwinds. Cash." Jaycee sounded pleased with her success.

"But what about Mindy? What was she like?"

"Oh, she's older than us. Maybe forty. Pretty. You know, well preserved. Good figure. Takes care of herself." Jaycee sped down the clear paved driveway and slowed to pull out onto the dirt road, resuming her usual thirty miles per hour.

"Great," Noor said. "Dan must like blondes after all. She sure has the money for botox or whatever."

"She was nice," Jaycee said. "She promised to come to Hillwinds someday. Maybe she'll buy that set of flour and sugar canisters."

"Oh, count me in on that field trip. Maybe I can teach her how to de-bristle pigs and scald them in an iron pot. Jesus, Jaycee, what kind of moral support *are* you? You're supposed to hate her. You're supposed to say she was a nasty bitch with a bad facelift. I don't even know why we came here. I still don't even know if they're having sex."

"Well she wasn't a bitch. Not to me. But she isn't gorgeous like you. And . . . oh . . ." Jaycee slowed the car and put a hand on Noor's arm. "She's pregnant. Just three months. She just found out this morning."

Noor's hand came to a stop in mid-air while reaching for the heater knob. "Did you ask who the father was, was he local, anything like that? Is she married?"

"That would have seemed too weird for me to ask."

"I suppose there's really no proof," Noor said.

As if on cue, the proof appeared, barreling towards them down the road in his mobile vet truck. They were a quarter mile from Mindy's and Dan had his left blinker on already as though he couldn't wait to make the first left into her driveway. Noor flattened herself below the windshield. You could bet he wasn't driving so fast out of eagerness to check in on Jorge.

"That's him," Noor said flatly, straightening up as the vet truck receded in the rear view mirror. "He's probably speeding right over to celebrate her pregnancy. *Their* pregnancy. Their baby."

"Shit," Jaycee said, "I didn't put it together. I'm such a dodo."

"We're both dodos," Noor said. Pregnant. Dan was going to be a father after all. Why wasn't she screaming, Noor wondered? But maybe she was. Maybe this weird high soundless whine in her bloodstream was a virtual scream. Maybe she just didn't want to show it yet, show the world how she felt. She'd thought he'd said, "I miss you," the last time they made love. What did he really say, or mean? Maybe he was only preparing to miss her, practicing what was to come. Or maybe he was really talking to Mindy while drifting off to sleep, not knowing he was saying it. They might have worked it out, might have worked their way back from an affair but not with Mindy pregnant. A child. So this was it. Her marriage was over. All over but the crying and, she realized, the division of assets. Vermont was a fifty-fifty state but, without a record, her new assets or what was left of them would go uncounted. She could use them to buy an expensive baby present for Dan and Mindy. Or gasoline to burn down Mindy's house. She could hear her soul-bees sizzling in the flames like mosquitoes in a bug zapper. But she'd never do anything violent; she was passive-aggressive, not aggressive-aggressive. Instead she'd think bad thoughts and take secretive actions, like the dope deal Dan would never learn about or sneaking up to Mindy's house with Jaycee.

"C'mon," Jaycee urged gently. "Let's go spend this twenty, go to Capitol Grounds and get cappuccinos. I'll treat."

She actually sounded like a normal friend and Noor nodded assent, unable to bring herself to speak yet. Noor had finally turned on the heater; the blast stung her eyes. She blinked, then told Jaycee, "You better change out of those Hillwinds duds first. Or maybe you could just stand on a corner and ring a bell like the Salvation Army and collect quarters while I sit inside crying into my coffee." She pictured Jaycee in a booth at Capitol Grounds, foam on her lip—Got Cappuccino?—her bonnet hanging cockeyed. For all Noor's disdain and grumbling, she didn't want Jaycee to change. And she didn't want to be alone now, either. She really did want company.

"You *could* comfort me you know," Noor offered.

"I'm doing the best I know how," Jaycee said. "I'll get better at it."

It wasn't until they'd finished two cappuccinos each that Noor realized that in addition to losing her husband and dealing drugs that week, they'd stolen a Hillwinds donation. Twenty bucks, twenty thousand, it was all part of the same spree, she thought, as Jaycee pulled the car into the drive-through teller line behind a bank. Maybe they were going to rob it.

"I put some of *my* money into my first ever checking account, but now I wish I'd stashed it all in a boot so I could count it whenever I feel like it," said Jaycee, who'd pulled up to the teller's window just to check on her deposit and make sure it had all gone into her account.

"*It'll* be fine," Noor said. "I'm going to be broker than ever, divorcing Dan. Do you have any idea what a lawyer costs, these days?" It wasn't really her, talking about the financial demands of a divorce instead of the alternating rage and sorrow that, mixed with the two foaming drinks, made her feel on the verge of puking her guts out. Just someone's voice coming out of her mouth. "One of my clients' divorce cost a fortune. I could get a Pro Se do-it-yourself divorce kit, 'cept a friend of mind once called it Pro Se screw-up-your-divorce-yourself kit."

That was Mara. They'd been pretty close, though, a long time ago now, before she'd met Dan. Together they'd housetrained their two new puppies, taking turns one winter sleeping over each other's apartments to let Jiyah and Arlo out to pee while the other girl slept. Jiyah'd been a rambunctious pup then, and now she was a stolid old matron with bad hips and Noor was a pre-divorcee.

Jaycee pressed the service button, opened the freshly returned canister, removed the slip of paper showing her account balance, grinned, waved the paper in the air, held it to her mouth and pretended to eat it as she drove away.

Noor's new non-Noor voice shaped the words: "So Jaycee, how're you planning to get those coke candlesticks and that big coke platter out of Peru?"

"Easy," said Jaycee. "I'm writing Frida a letter. Here! I can read it. You tell me what you think."

She pulled a piece of folded notebook paper out of her tote and started right in reading, like a kid at Show 'n' Tell, not even thinking to pull the car away from the teller window. Noor didn't have the heart to stop her.

"Dear Frida, or should I say, Director of the Speakers Series at Cultural Exchange International(?!),Que Passe, Amiga? Do you remember me? Just kidding, I hope. I enjoyed meeting you on the plane from Miami to Lima, hint, and I'm still grateful that you let me stay at your house, other hint.How is the bullfighting coming, these days? Did you finish sewing Hugo's matador costume? If you did, etc. Meanwhile I hope that your travels to Miami haven't etc. It must be rewarding to have a job in the arts. My new friend in Vermont has a cool job too."

Jaycee glanced meaningfully at Noor when she got to this part. *"She trains people to ride horses, even though they are in wheelchairs. The people I mean, not the horses. Ha ha. You would like her.*

Do you remember that man, Carlos, etc? Well, guess what? He intends to court me. Big surprise!I almost fell over. He already has tickets, maybe he's secretly rich anyway he will be here in two months. Would you believe I colored my hair? Auburn the only thing is, I am embarrassed to say that those pretty painted candlestick holders and that platter I gave you were really his gifts to me, but I—"

"The auburn hair looks nice," Noor interjected. As though hair mattered, as though anything mattered after seeing Dan heading to Mindy's. Still, it wasn't pity, she realized, that stopped her from telling Jaycee to stop reading the letter; it was fascination. How far would the girl go, she wondered.

". . . gave them to you since my bank card wasn't working and I couldn't buy you a proper Thank You gift for blah blah can you do me the gigantic favor of shipping them to Hillwinds blah blah give Hugo a hug from me and tell him I miss his maps blah blah some delicious

maple candies I hope they get to you in one piece. Well, not really since there are fifteen pieces in the box, but you know what I mean sincerely your friend—"

"Not Hillwinds," Noor said. "That's too risky. Have her ship it to . . . I don't know . . ."

"How 'bout I have her ship it to Gerry? *Not.* I know what I'll do. I'll ask her to ship it to her office in Miami. That way if Frida and her employers get caught with it they can make up something about a disgruntled artist who used the office address to get back at Frida for dropping the ball on his speaking tour. And if they don't get caught, I'll drive down and get it. I could use a good excuse to get off my butt and find a babysitter for my parents. What do you think of that? You could come with me. To Miami. Okay? I'll tell Frida it's a girls' night out kind of thing."

Noor stayed silent, unsure what she thought of anything, now, much less a downward slide cross-country to sell more drugs. Jaycee made a right turn onto State Street and up the big hill to where the day had clearly waned, even the shadows lost in the dark.

CHAPTER ELEVEN

Jaycee, 2010

June 17ᵗʰ, 1993
Mr. Hilary Emory
Hillwinds Living History Books Inn and Enterprises
Barnes Road
East Montpelier, Vermont 05601

Dear Mr. Emory,

Oh Dear. Please convey our respectful apologies to Mr. Derrick Stamm at Imperion, the Hillwinds Living History Books Fund fiduciary. He is, it turns out, absolutely correct. On looking over the Hillwinds Living History Books Fund paperwork, which is, as we have pointed out to you in our previous letters, rather difficult to follow, Houghton sees that I did indeed commit to the initial ten-year investment period, after which, for the record, it will be within my rights either to withdraw, as of approximately seven years from now on October 6, 2000, my full principal of $165,000 even if the investment value has gone down, or to reinvest the full principal for a second ten-year period with the assurance that the dividends will increase by 15 percent. Incidentally, I had thought that we were to receive our dividend checks on a quarterly basis, but since that has not been the case (our records *reveal that we have to date received just two dividend checks over the course of what has been, as of this writing, a twelve quarter period), we assume that Mr. Stamm has taken it upon himself to reinvest the payments(?).*

Mr. Stamm is also correct in assuming that, given that I was an early investor, we were never apprised of the comforting fact that my death benefit is to be fixed at the highest amount that the funds have achieved since my investment, even if the value plunges by the date of my demise. Goodness, I have never discussed these sorts of things before. But with the generous death benefit proviso in mind, Houghton and I have agreed to rescind our request for the withdrawal of my principle of $165,000 (a moot point, of course, we understand, given the ten-year proviso under which we first committed) and, in addition—please don't tell Houghton, this is my little secret—to make an additional small investment of $28,000, securing, I understand, Houghton's grandfather's portrait in the soon to be inaugurated Hillwinds Living History Proud Forbears Portrait Gallery, in honor of the continuance of our proud support of the Hillwinds mission. We are still grateful for the Hillwinds tour that you personally gave to me and my visiting sister, Rebecca, a year ago—the vegetable dye experience especially pleased us.

Yours sincerely (and, with a little of that candled egg on our faces, a plea that you at Hillwinds might find a way to make the paperwork not quite so confusing to those of us not schooled in such matters),

Houghton and Elizabeth Ann Greenwood

p.s. Yes, if we are reading your letter correctly, we accept your thoughtful offer of including the name of our grandson, Houghton Elliot Greenwood IV, in your next book, The Stove Piper. Little Houghton Elliot will be turning five this month, so there are still many wonderful years left during which he will be delighted to find a boy in your book named after himself. He has blonde curls, by the way, but I'm certain that he would be just as pleased if his namesake were an especially smart and athletically inclined (baseball is Houghton Elliot's favorite sport!) African American child.

Hilry Emry
Barnes Road
E. Monpelieer, VT

Dear Mr. Emry,

Your worse than I thought if you really accept me to stop asking my money back just so I can supposely get more later when I needed it a year ago already. If its the death benefit your all concerned about maby you better start concerning on your own.

Ill be calling my lawyer I don't hear from you this week. And I don't mean a letter aobut how proud I am helping teach teach kids to love literature here in our great history minded state of Vermont. that's five thousand dollars we put in and were waiting for it.

Mr. Mitch Waters
P.O. Box 922, Montpelier, Vermont 05601

May 6, 1998

To Hillwinds Living History Books Enterprises,

This is the seventh letter that I have needed to write to you so that we can properly care for our daughter, Nancy, who is dying of bone cancer. I did try driving up there to Hillwinds again in December but I got a flat tire and needed to rush back home to sit with her since my wife was at work.

Please find it in your hearts to be responsible to your investors at this difficult time. The immediate return of our fifteen thousand dollars won't solve our problems, given the doctor bills we are facing, but it would be better than not hearing back from you especially when you are a writer for children and it's our child, who used to love your books, who is dying.

Colby White
Route 2, Marshfield, VT 05658

c.olbywhite@aol.com

Jeff,

Hil writing. How does one write up a promissory note? The Channings' attorney says their trust requires one if their investment is to be rolloverable. Her letter is enclosed. Also enclosed you will find the blank credit card expense account checks as agreed, in order that you may remain in charge of running our Hillwinds into the ground. That was a joke, but, you're right, as the wife would say, the checkbook is better left out of her hands.

Hil.

CHOWSA—

THE CHANNING'S ATTOURNEY HAS HER HEAD UP HER HONEY POT. CAPPICE? AT PRESENT OUR PLAN IS TO RESPOND TO SAID PROBATE IF AND WHEN IT IS FILED.

SYONARA—*Derrick Stamm (i.e. if you recall my actual name is not to appear on the Hillwinds correspondence. What's more, let's agree that we destroy our letters after reading. Maybe someday you will find it in your heart to go on line and we can write these letters electronically. Hil, do you even know what I mean by that? Just asking.)*

Answer to a Marriage Proposal
for Ginny

I haven't had my fill of night
Ebon girded and sweet with sin
Earth and sky held close within your eyes
White heat lightning of what might have been.

I cannot weave this baubled thread of ecstasy
into a pattern, lusterless and dull
I cannot loose my grasp on—

November 30, 2006
Deborah Benjamin MD
1335 Ripley Road
Waterbury Vermont 05766

Dear Dr. Benjamin,

StefanPartners, LLP serves as the court-appointed claims agent for the liquidation of Roderick Fellows Sanford Investment Securities LLC ("RFSIS"). In early August, a laptop computer owned by Stefan-Partners was stolen from an employee's vehicle. You are receiving this letter because, as an investor in Hillwinds Living History Books Fund, you are entitled to receive immediate notification concerning any of the many investment vehicles in which Hillwinds, and indirectly, all of Hillwinds' individual investors, may have taken part. Although Hill-winds, under the eye of its fiduciary, Derrick Stamm of Imp-erion (it was, we are proud to say, Mr. Stamm who brought this matter to the attention of law enforcement authorities) withdrew all investments from RFSIS prior to the RFSIS bankruptcy in 2005, the stolen RFSIS laptop contains historical information which may include some inves-tors' personal information, including social security numbers and/or RFSIS account numbers (which are now defunct). However, Imp-erion provided no such personal information to RFIS at any time, so you can rest assured that your risk of having been victimized by personal identity theft is negligible.

Even so, StefanPartners takes this matter very seriously. We apolo-gize for any concern this incident might cause you. Based on conversa-tions with law enforcement, we do not believe that the information on the laptop was specifically targeted, as other vehicles were also broken into that day in the same area. The laptop is password-protected and there is no indication that the data has been accessed.

Nevertheless we have arranged services to help protect you. A toll-free help line, 1-888-862-7789, has been established to help you. The help line will be staffed 8:30 a.m.–5:00 p.m. Eastern Time, Monday through Friday. Also provided will be a six month membership in Qua-druple Advantage from ModernConsumerAdvice, Inc., an Imp-erion company, and the offer of a discounted membership for those wishing to purchase further protection from Imp-erion. Subscribers will also receive immediate on-demand access to their Imp-erion credit report. A description sheet for enrolling in Quadruple Advantage is attached.

Sincerely,
Stefan Partners LLP

January 2, 2000

To Our Fellow Visionaries:

This is Hilary Emory writing with tremendous pleasure granted by this unique opportunity to share with you news of the recent completion of The Hillwinds Living History Books role-playing studio, congruent with the marketing strategy that has for years been a hallmark of our parent corporation, Imp-erion. We hope that you and your families will join us in celebration at our Winter Solstice Feast and Fete, Friday, December 14th at 5:00 p.m.

Sincerely,

Hilary Emory, Author
Hillwinds Living History Books Fund

January 7, 2000

To Our Fellow Visionaries:

Indeed, as one or two of you have pointed out, our Winter Solstice Feast and Fete is to be held on Friday, **January 14th**, not December 14th, which is of course already past. My dear wife, Hannah, apologizes for her little mistake and for any and all inconvenience her absentmindedness might have caused.

She and I look forward to seeing you and your families all bundled up for winter activities.

Sincerely,
Hilary Emory

January 10, 2000

To Our Fellow Visionaries:

It is with true regret that I report that due to circumstances outside our control, we at Hillwinds Living History Books will need to
postpone this year's eagerly awaited Winter Feast and Fete. We will
update you shortly.

Sincerely,
Mrs. Hannah Emory

THE SOMEWHAT CONTRITE TALE
OF A MERE BUTTER KNIFE
By Emily Dickinson or should we tell them it''s Louisa May Alcott?

Susan stood in her Doorway—inebriate of Fog. She would not go with
him—she knew this as did he. She was vain before the Fog supposing
that it meant to plead with her . . . would She not reconsider her Principles? A Robin also joined in—a Mob of vain Pleadings—but his Waist-
coat had been swallowed up by gloom. Or should gloom be capitalized?
A Clatter came from the nearest chamber. It would be her fearsome
Niece. "Are you Dead?" Susan called. The Girl hesitated. "Just!" she
said, and at once the

Dear Sir,

Good Day. It is my honor and the pleasure of Roderick Fellows Sanford Investment Securities LLC ("RFSIS") , an Imp-erion Company,
to ask you will be able to help me .i have slave and brutally abuse for
longtime in col Muammar Gaddafi house and i have try to flee if i do

.col Muammar Gaddafi . will dehead me and my entire family. I took Seven Million And Five Hundred Thousand Euro from my boss secret safe to a bank escrow in far off. As is unwise for me to use my name so i decided to look for friend and fellow author. My partner at Roderick Fellows Sanford Investment Securities LLC ("RFSIS") , an Imp-erion Company, is God-willing to give you the 40 percent of the sum for your acceptancy. If you are please with this offer .please do contact me at yara.89991@yahoo.com for further instruction.

November 20, 2005

Dear Elizabeth Ann Greenwood -

Please accept Hillwinds Living History Books's deepest sympathy over the death of your dear husband, Houghton. Like you, we will miss him. In addition, we offer our apology for the confusion owing to our recent correspondence. As always, we will do everything possible to answer your questions.

For your grandson, Houghton Elliot Greenwood IV's investment portfolio single account F007, we have forwarded to you, under separate mailings, copies of the -4 suffix page with the long and short positions. For your own account, F0106, you were sent and should have received by now the October 2010 statement copies with both -3 and -4 suffix pages. Unfortunately the pre-2010 statements are unavailable until such time as our new digitization project at Laavark, Inc., an Imp-erion Company, is complete.

We hope that you find this clarification useful. Please don't hesitate to contact us, and please, as always, feel free to visit when your health allows and you find yourself back in the area.

Best Wishes,
Hillwinds Living History Books

Jaycee sat in disbelief among these and other papers in her father's study, like a child beneath a pile of fallen leaves toward which her own parent's car was blindly reversing out of a driveway. Her father with his misdeeds would run her over, then speed off not knowing what he'd done. But she wouldn't be flattened. She hoped. She would brush herself off and wave him away, and soon he would turn into one of those elderly people found driving in circles for days amid blizzards, subsisting on a sleeve of peanut butter crackers and a tube of cherry ChapStick.

His papers—their life, *her* life—were all such a mishmash.

You could pick it up and throw it and make it confetti.

Jaycee wondered if little Nancy White had survived or succumbed to her bone cancer. She could swear she'd seen a Nancy-like creature around town over the years—an anemic-looking girl with red eyes like in a horror movie, and a giant, unmoored kerchief flapping around her bald, sickly skull, her parents always right beside her in the aisles at Shaws and even once building a necklace at the bead store . . . but now that she thought of it, years had gone by since she had last caught sight of them. Surely other of her father's jilted investors crossed Jaycee's path every now and again. Just this week, an elderly couple walking a dog had stopped in their tracks for just a fraction of a second to stare at her with whispered disdain, and now she supposed they might have been one of them.

She found a file marked Property Deeds in large purple letters, but the file was empty. She found a notice of a fee for unpaid property taxes, but it was from a year ago already. She swiveled around in her dad's bumpy desk chair and found a driver's license renewal notice, due yesterday. She swiveled back in the other direction and found an overdrawn bank notice, and then a folder marked *miscellaneous* containing a years-old sketch of none other than Pauline, looking beautiful and wise, her red braids as neatly ribboned as if Jaycee herself had fastened them.

She shut the folder superstitiously, then opened it back up again, trying not to be overcome by worry. "You worry too much," Pauline had said, scrunching her face to demonstrate, but unlike on Jaycee, the expression brought depth to Pauline's face, her freshness in collusion with the weight of the world.

That night Jaycee dreamed that she was Pauline, and that she was babysitting a visiting group of senior citizens on a bargain charter bus tour to Hillwinds. "Why do you call it babysitting?" Jaycee asked in the dream, since in the dream she, Jaycee, was one of the old ladies on the tour. "Why don't you call it being our friend?" "Because I'm not your friend," said Pauline, not unkindly, while scissoring lengths of cheesecloth and twine for the day's activity, cheese making. Cheese making was always a hit with old folks, especially because it saved them from having to purchase a meal with the dregs of that month's social security check. The soft, spreadable cheese was Hannah's recipe. The problem was it took twenty dream hours between the time they whisked together the yogurt, sour cream, salt and chives and the time they would be able to eat it, during which the sacks of cheesecloth dripped a viscous, sour white secretion. The old dream ladies in pastel pant suits, and the few old dream men still alive, their trousers belted under their armpits, needed to carry the oozing, sopping sacks, which looked like lopped-off endocrine glands, home with them on the bus.

Where there's a will there's a whey, Jaycee thought when she woke from the dream. She thumped out of bed, stepped barefooted on something gritty and sharp, and bent to see what it was. It was a tooth, she thought, her fingertip flush on the gritty edge . . . except teeth weren't orange, at least not *this* orange. It was a piece of the broken Peru vase, she realized, like the piece that had made her sort of high the night before she met Gerry at the cemetery with Noor. She had hidden the rest of the shards in the pickle crock in the basement to keep them safe until Gerry arranged to sell them. She carried the fragment down the splintery cellar stairs to the pickle crock. Opening the lid she discovered a small chunk of the original coke that she'd hidden away for a rainy day. Now, without a second thought, as if it were stick of gum she'd discovered in the bottom of her tote one day, she opened the baggie, scooped up a crumble, rubbed it on her gums, then flattened a few more crumbles with a hammer and snorted them through a hollow reed from a cobwebbed Christmas wreath she'd made from cattails in one of the Hillwinds school workshops.

By the time she'd made it up the stairs all her worries were gone, and the best part was that she was aware of them going away, and when she wondered how much her mother knew about Hil's misdoings and his sad-sack investors and Derrick Stamm, the answer really didn't matter to her. It was just a curiosity, her mom's knowledge or not of the Hillwinds debacle, a passing thought, if you could even call it a thought, like a flutter of bruised rose petals. In no time Jaycee was dressed and driving, since her dad had not snuck off with the car and lost it somewhere the night before. She drifted left down the hill, and then, before she knew it, she was in the small village of Adamant, dreamily scouting the location for what would soon surely be her first date with Gerry, so when he called her, if he called her, he wouldn't need to be the only one thinking about where they should go.

Happily she recalled the visits she had made to Adamant with Hannah when they had gone there on field trips, which had made for some oddly pointless mother/daughter outings when all they did was sit in the screened porch of the general store, drinking root beers and watching the comely waterfall form a genteel stream through some bent-over grass. "It's not a town," Hannah had instructed in her homeschooling mode. "It's a village. The difference between a town and village is—you tell me." But the soft drinks were the real reason for the mother/daughter outings, since, because Hil disapproved of soft drinks, they needed to sneak away from Montpelier in order to drink them. The Adamant store wasn't open yet but the door to the screened porch was left unfastened, so Jaycee lay on the floor beneath where the same small lightbulbs and the same black flies made of beads and twisted wires as when she was a girl hung in tangles off the ceiling in honor of the local Black Fly Festival. The place would make for a quaint first date with Gerry . . . only she didn't want their date to be quaint. Her whole life was quaint, at least it once had been, and now maybe it wouldn't be, anymore. Adamant had used to be named Sodom, and the pond, a dull silvery marsh under a scrim of hoarfrost, still was. When he called, if he called, she and Gerry would pack a cooler with warm meatball subs and make muddy muskrat love on the cold banks of Sodom Pond, notwithstanding that all that had happened between him and her so far was that after Gerry drove her home from the meeting at the cemetery and helped her stack the woodpile, he had sucked on one of her horehound drops.

"Never ate one a' these before," he'd admitted, but then he'd made appreciative grunts while rolling the sticky brown lozenge over and under his tongue. Despite horehound drops being sometimes used as an appetite stimulant, he hadn't asked for another right away, had said, instead, "Maybe next time I'll try out that rock candy stuff."

Didn't that mean something?

If he called.

When he called.

"We really ought to get together sometime," Gerry had said.

Or did guys just talk like that when they wanted to let themselves off the hook?

That's what Noor had seemed to think, although she hadn't been so candid as to say it outright. Back in the car, cruising around the pond, Jaycee fumbled for her phone, preparing herself for the comforting sound of Noor's stud earrings tapping against the telephone, but instead she pulled over, closed her eyes and laid her head against the car seat. How tired she was, the drug asleep in her body like a separate, snoring animal. It seemed to take her forever to drive back home, where even the preparation of two Swanson's pot pies for her parents' lunch (none for herself; she wasn't hungry) required every atom of dredged up energy.

"I hope they pay up good muddy here," Hil remarked over his meal. The dementia was getting much, much worse, and now it mattered again to Jaycee, it did, and the worries came back, like how on earth would she support them, and would she ever be free of them, and what had happened to all the money Hil—they?—had stolen, and would she keep it when she found it or give it back to the people to whom it belonged?

She would give it to the sick girl, Nancy White, if Nancy White were still alive. The silly Greenwoods would have to take care of their own.

"I need to told you," Hil said, "Uhhhh . . . not blankie. We have thieves. Know that? Thieves stole my cock and brought it back grass roots. What happened to the other . . . uhhh . . . the other help at the home office tonight?"

"Just humor him," said Hannah. "Besides, for all we know, it's true."

I cannot take resilient pain, sword of love that wounds, not heals, Jaycee recalled as she rose to wipe the crumbs from the wooden table. It was a line from the poem, the poem she'd found in a cardboard box in the study, the poem her dad had once written to some unresponsive Ginny. Only what made Jaycee so sure Ginny hadn't responded? She wouldn't put it past her father to have run around on Hannah or even have another wife.

Instead of heading back into the study today, Jaycee climbed the steep part of the hill and sat on the bench looking over the sites where new homes were going up in the valley below, homes Gerry had told her he'd die before he lived in, though she wondered if that was sour grapes. What mattered was that she rather they lived in a cave, her and Gerry, than here at Hillwinds. She would rather they just dig a hole someplace, line it with ripstop sleeping bags, eat s'mores for their supper and kiss and make up—make up even if they'd never fought. She wondered if they would. Fight and make up. She supposed it was expected. She closed the fingers of one hand tight around this promise, then did the same with the other hand, then set all fingers free. How long, she wondered, were first dates expected to take before they finally happened?

CHAPTER TWELVE

Noor, 2010

The night before Thanksgiving Dan left a message saying he was performing emergency surgery at a dairy in Waitsfield and probably wouldn't be home until early morning. Noor considered calling all the dairies in Waitsfield to catch him in a lie, but it would be too humiliating, and too humiliating to call his office to check up on him. Noor rattled around the house all evening, inconsolable, furious, ready to fight but lacking a punching bag. Finally she threw the two buttercup squash she'd bought for Thanksgiving on the compost heap, which made too mushy a thump to be satisfying. Next she tried smashing them on the driveway under the halogen barn light, but they only dented, pale gashes in dark green skin, refusing to give way even when she hit them with the shovel and then jumped on top of them, which nearly sent her sprawling in the gravel. So she tossed them back into the compost. It was a sin to waste food but there was no way she could eat the squash meant for the holiday dinner she wouldn't attend. Maybe she would eat them in the form of fertilizer for next year's garden, when they'd broken down into slimy nutrients by which time she'd be a practiced single woman. Divorcee. The word sounded too pretty for what it meant, a lovely name for a child, maybe Mindy and Dan's child, little Divasee. Then they could have another one, named Alee-mona. She'd run into them on the streets of Montpelier, Dan carrying little Dee or Al in a chest pack, Mindy gripping Dan's arm possessively.

What a thought. Noor would have to move, start over somewhere else to escape the new couple. Except she already had the barn for the horses, the clients, whatever was left of her life here in Montpelier. And there was also the potential for more coke money, which would be, Noor thought, like a parachute designed to slow the downward spin on which Dan had pushed her. She would need to let Dan go. But he already was gone; she was sure that tonight he'd be sleeping in the ridiculously ostentatious house in Calais, arms around Mindy's baby belly, wondering—assuming he thought of Noor at all—how he'd break it to her, and whether or not she'd make a scene.

Noor wished she was the kind who could take a tire iron and snap all the spokes in the wheels of Dan's road bikes or take a chainsaw to his kayak. But she wasn't, and anyway she could imagine the laughter at his boss Ray's Thanksgiving table as Dan told his sad tale of the destruction of his toys by his crazed Pakistani wife, minus his affair, of course. Or maybe they already knew, the two other vets, the receptionists and techs, and pitied Noor or thought she had it coming. Or he wouldn't even go to the dinner himself, but spend the holiday eating pears and cheddar in bed with Mindy.

Noor couldn't lie down in their bed or even in the guestroom where Dan spent so many nights when he was on call, the pillows and sheets redolent of Dan's ivory soap scented skin, always fresh from the shower before he climbed in. It was only when they were making love that he got what they called his "goat" smell, an earthy odor, a musk of his own. Thinking about it made her crazy not with anger but with regret over not having indulged it more than she had, not having stuck her nose in it deeply enough. Some day she'd forget it, would be unable to replicate it in her mind. She went into the living room where she'd forgotten to keep the fire going, struggled with kindling and paper to bring the few coals back to life, then with small-diameter branches and finally full-sized cordwood. She pushed away the coffee table to make room for Jiyah on the rug and huddled under a quilt on the couch watching sappy Thanksgiving specials. Jiyah thumped her tail and looked mournfully at the thrashing Noor, who tripped over the dog each time she got up to pace the house.

After chores in the morning, with Dan still not home, another of his phony messages about "unforeseen surgery complications" left unanswered on the machine, Noor had to get out. She wanted to take Luna for a long ride in the woods but it was the last few days of deer hunting season, the most dangerous. And she didn't want to see anyone she knew. She put Jiyah in the car with a blanket in the passenger seat, drove to the interstate, and turned north. Jiyah curled up, her graying muzzle on Noor's thigh. At Waterbury Noor turned off the highway, following Route 100 through the unlikely named Moscow, where turkey cutouts graced windows of folks who had kids, and early Christmas lights sparkled in the gray daylight. At Stowe she drove through the gussied up village—half two-hundred-year-old farmhouses, half fancy restaurants, boutiques, and ski shops—and on up to the ski area. She pulled up at the Stowe resort. She hadn't been here since elementary school when the schools shut down each Thursday afternoon and the ski areas let the kids ski for free.

Up on the mountain they'd been making snow since it got cold and a few trails were open. Noor watched a chairlift hauling the early birds up the hill, and some bright pink and lime green figures crisscrossing the crystalline fake snow on snowboards and skis. A cross-country or perhaps telemark skier was racing *up* the slope under the chairlift. What was it that made people think it was fun to go up and down, up and down, or for that matter, around and around and around in a riding ring? The whole panorama of human activity seemed so aimless, an attempt to divert yourself from the nadir that awaited if you ever stopped moving. A modern Breughel masterpiece. If you had kids maybe you didn't feel that way, or meaningful work. She believed her work was worthwhile. She'd seen the kids' lives change. Seen kids who were nonverbal begin to talk, kids like Ricky become more responsive, less automaton. At least there was that. But she still felt as though she were struggling up some endless hill without ever reaching the top, never enjoying the long thrilling glide to the bottom.

Noor returned to the center of town and parked near the paved recreation trail which she assumed would be safe from hunters. She pulled on a red cap, didn't rebuke Jiyah for immediately moving to the driver's seat although she was supposed to stay on her own side, covered Jiyah with the blanket, muffled her own face with a scarf, gloved her hands, told the dog to "Stay" because, although the poor old mutt had no option but to do so, the command reassured Jiyah that Noor would come back, and set out walking quickly, across a small decorative bridge, and along the five-and-a-half mile trail. In the center of town the trail followed a brook past farm fields visible through the bare trees. A lot of people were out walking in family groups, working up an appetite before their Thanksgiving feast. She passed a young couple holding the hands of a pink snow-suited child, swinging her off the ground, wheeeeeee. Noor looked down as she passed. A vigorous older couple, the man lean and tall, the woman petite, wearing matching North Face fleeces, greeted her. She'd thought that was how she and Dan would grow old, though more likely he'd be out biking and she'd be riding a horse. Now, his future would be pushing the older Mindy in a wheelchair. She could hope.

Walking forced her to think, not just about Dan, but about what she'd gotten herself into with Jaycee and Gerry. She liked the money—who wouldn't like seventeen thousand dollars just for picnicking on the wrong wheel of cheese? The first deal was done and apparently they were safe from consequences. But she still had insomnia, not just from Dan. The heart palpitations, the trouble she had catching her breath some mornings. Gerry was right. What was it he'd said? Little Noor Khan with the homework done and the Ken doll husband is selling coke. She had screwed up big time, gone against her own principles, the habit of good citizenry instilled in her by her parents. It wasn't good. It wasn't *her*. She wasn't little anymore and she might have lost her Ken, but she didn't have to lose herself too. The new transaction would be underway with or without Noor's conscience or consent, but she would take no more money, she decided, and she wouldn't join Jaycee on the ride to Miami. No way she would. She wouldn't even answer the TracFone anymore, she hated the ringtone, a shrill buzz. Noor strode onward down the paved path between the bare trees, feeling resolute if ruined.

An hour and a half later, when Noor had completed the first circuit, she let Jiyah out to pee and then repeated the loop, so that she'd walked eleven miles in the cold before realizing she needed a coffee or a cup of soup to warm her up. Except for expensive prix fixe inn restaurants, there were few options on the holiday, the smaller diners and "Dutch Pancake" closed. She contemplated sitting at a table alone in the dining room of the Stowe Flake Resort or the elegant Lodge at Smuggler's Notch while a waitress counting the hours until she could get back to her family carried out plates overflowing with turkey and stuffing and squash. But Noor wasn't hungry or brave enough to face the pitying stares of the other patrons. Instead she settled for a tired cup of tepid chicken noodle out of a stainless vat in a gas station/convenience store and wondered how she would fill the rest of the day, the rest of her life. Would all holidays from now on be like today? She gassed up the car, bought a few greasy roller hot dogs for Jiyah and a bottle of water for the dog to lap out of the empty soup cup, and drove on.

At nearly 8:00, three hours late for evening feeding—she'd watched without watching a special showing of the endless, loud *Lord of the Rings* in Burlington—Noor was in the barn, dressed in one of the man-size thrift store down parkas she used for cold weather chores, scooping grain into plastic buckets—a small can of Vintage Senior for Daisy now that it was cold, whole oats for Luna, Trotter pellets for Moon Pie, each with their various supplements, selenium and vitamin E for Daisy, glucosamine for Moon Pie's arthritis, vitamins for Luna, to the accompaniment of nickering and impatient stall-banging in the aisle.

"You shouldn't let Moon Pie bang his door. It will exacerbate his navicular," Dan said, appearing by her side. He was wearing the blue knit sweater she'd bought him last Christmas and his charcoal wool overcoat she'd only seen him wear when he traveled for vet conventions. He looked annoyingly, heartbreakingly handsome. No "Sorry I didn't make it home last night." No "Sorry I got my mistress pregnant." Yeah, Noor needed to hang a stall mat on Moon Pie's door to pad it but she wasn't about to talk horse health with her cheating husband. She wouldn't ask him if he'd gone to Ray's house for dinner, or biked his annual Turkey Tour of the Valley with his buddies beforehand so they could feel virtuous about being gluttons.

Wordlessly, Noor reached over Daisy's stall wall to dump grain into the feeder before the mare, in her eagerness, could knock it out of Noor's hands. Under the row of bare, safety-caged light bulbs she continued down the aisle, dumping grain for Moon Pie and Luna as Dan followed.

"Where were you? You didn't leave a note. You had like ten calls on this thing." Dan thrust her TracFone in front of her nose.

Shit shit shit. She must have left it on the counter with her regular phone. This whole Mindy thing had made her careless. Or maybe on some subterranean level she wanted him to find it, wanted him to know she had her secrets too. "Did you answer it?" she asked. Jaycee or Gerry—had they left a message, hell, ten messages, which Dan had overheard?

"What's the deal with two cell phones, Noor?" Dan said. "What's that all about? Like you can afford it. And no. I didn't answer." Dan crossed his arms. Noor spun silent fake answers—I thought I'd try one of the cheap phones, cut my expenses, my regular phone wasn't working, I wanted to keep work phone separate for tax reasons—but instead she turned on him at last.

"Who are you to be asking questions? How's that llama in Calais, what's his name, *Whore*-Hay? And how's your rich bitch girlfriend with the spikey hair? I hear she's kind of a *whore*, too." Noor put the buckets on the floor next to a pile of bales she'd thrown down from the hayloft. She grabbed the knife hanging from a string on the wall over the stacked bales while Dan eyed her warily, but she only slit the twine on the top bale; the loosened hay fell into neat flakes. She picked up a tall armload and headed down the aisle, tossing a few flakes per stall.

"Come here and talk to me," Dan said.

"Why? We *need to talk*? Now? After I learn on my own she's *expecting*? You know what? I once read a letter in Ann Landers: *Dear Ann, I'm pregnant, my husband's having an affair, how do I know the baby is mine?* Leave me alone. I've got chores to do." She put the grain buckets back into the grain room, screwed a hose onto the lip of the water hydrant, and lifted the handle, waiting until she had the hose suspended over a stall wall to fill a hanging bucket before turning the attachment on the end of the hose to "on."

"Stop. She's *not* my girlfriend. I'm her vet. We're just friends. And, she's not just some rich bitch, Noor. She's from Brooklyn, her husband was a firefighter killed nine years ago and she got a big life insurance settlement. After September 11 she just wanted to get out of there. No one did a parade for *her* husband since *he* died on September 8. No one interviewed *her* on CNN."

Oh great, Noor thought, a woman with a sad story, wife of an unsung hero, a grieving widow who thought she had the right to steal another woman's husband because she'd suffered. "Don't tell me her history like it's admirable," Noor shouted. "She's sleeping with my husband, she's a bitch. She's having your baby. It was supposed to be *our* baby! At least that's what I thought."

"Noor, you've got it wrong."

"Oh, come off it, Dan. You call her all the time and she calls you all the time on your cell, and she calls here and you go racing out there like your life depends on it and you didn't come home last night. What am I supposed to think?" Now was the time for him to deny it, to say yes, okay, I had an affair but Mindy was already pregnant from somebody else, her carpenter or plumber or the guy who sold her the llama but *someone*. Not him. Not Dan.

"You've been checking my calls? You've been snooping on me?"

"Don't make *me* the criminal here." Even though I *am* dealing dope, she thought. It was good to be one up on him, have her own crime, her own folly. He had no idea how much snooping she'd done. Thank God he hadn't shown up at Mindy's while Noor was there, hunched in the front seat of Jaycee's car. Noor's nose was running from the cold. She swiped her face with the back of her glove and moved to the next stall with the hose. Daisy had already finished her small allotment of grain and stood nosing in her hay flakes. Noor watched the water swirl to the top of the five gallon, flat-backed bucket. She flipped the hose nozzle to off and moved to the next stall. "Just tell me the truth, Dan," she ordered. She continued filling the last two buckets, then hauled the hose back to the hydrant, unscrewed it, let it drain, and hung it in the small heated tack room so it wouldn't freeze overnight.

When she closed the tack room door she was surprised to see that Dan had slumped down on the low stack of bales. It would be tough to get the hay off that fine wool coat, she thought inanely.

"Do you really even care, Noor? It's not like you're interested in me anymore."

"You're not getting out of it by making this *my* fault," Noor said, wanting him to stand up, to not look so pitiful slumped there, his feet in loafers not meant for this kind of cold. And she *had* cared. She still cared.

Dan looked up, all blue-eyed remorse. "I'm sorry Noor. It just happened."

"Just happened? You let it happen. You wanted it to happen. You didn't even want to try to make this work, go through counseling or something."

"It's too late for that."

"What do you mean? You're in love with this person, this Mindy?"

"She's pregnant and it's my kid."

She thought she'd already gotten the kick in the gut in the car when she saw him on Mindy's road but having Dan admit it made it real: he was having a child with someone else. She felt like one of those farmers who fell into a grain silo and suffocated in a shifting tower of corn, flailing, all the while knowing it was hopeless since there was no one to hear your cries.

"I guess you better go live over there in that big house with her, then," Noor said, walking past Dan, heading out and shutting the barn door behind her. "By the way," she shouted, "any chance you would have told me before the kid was born if I hadn't been such a snoop?"

Dan followed her into the house, into their bedroom where Noor had thrown herself down on the bed, not even bothering to take off her boots or jacket.

"Noor, you haven't wanted to make love in I don't know how long. The only time is when you're—and what's with that Trac-Fone? Okay, I did listen. I heard a call from some guy named Gerry who wants to get together. Soon."

"Gerry's nobody, Dan. Believe me, it's a work thing."

"Yeah? You've got your secrets too. What have you been up to? Why do you have to always be so fucking sphinx-like? Is it a Pakistani thing?"

Noor turned over, rage rising, and spit out, "Yeah, it's 'cause I'm a Paki, Dan. I'm a terrorist! You should know that by now. And sphinxes are Egyptian, you racist."

Her father had warned her and she'd laughed. But it always came down to that in the end, didn't it? So Dan had said the unforgivable. After he'd done the unforgivable, made another woman pregnant.

"I want you gone," Noor said. She sounded like she was on a soap opera, one that had moved from daytime to evening viewing, but that was the thing about these sordid dramas, not even primetime could make them fresh. She sat up and said with icy reason, "Dan, you're portable. You have an office and a mobile vet truck. My business is here. You can go. So go."

"You can't support this place alone."

"You have no idea what I'm capable of. And haven't you heard of alimony? That shouldn't be a burden considering your sugar mama."

"It doesn't have to be like this. I mean, we could stay friends."

"Friends?! Oh great, what a novel idea. You are so ridiculous. How long did you think you could keep this a secret? Until you came home with the kid in a Baby Bjorn? What am I, the auntie? Kid, meet your Auntie Noor. She should have been your mom but *it's too late it just happened besides she's a Paki.*"

Dan opened his arms wide and smiled a sheepish, besotted smile. "Noor, she makes me really happy."

"Shut up. Get OUT!"

But it was Noor who got out, cruising the frozen streets of Montpelier while her engine warmed, and her heater attempted to defrost the scrim of ice crystals on the windshield that she'd barely scraped. She hunched to peer through the half-moon of clear glass just above the dashboard vent.

Where could she go? To Jaycee's? Was Jaycee her only friend anymore? What had happened, why had Noor let go of Ellen and Ruthie and Mara? She couldn't call them after all this time when she was so needy—it would be an affront to them, especially to Mara, who'd been having her own string of troubles—positive mammogram, lapsed health insurance—last time they'd all met, after which Noor, unforgivably, had forgotten to check up on her. Even though she cringed at the thought of facing Jaycee's cockeyed attempts at girl talk right now, Noor was just about to call her, knowing how thrilled Jaycee would be to get her first-in-a-lifetime sobbing-girlfriend phone call, when instead, she checked the first of Jaycee's string of sixteen messages. "Hey. It's me, Noor. I mean Jaycee! Jeez. I can't believe I just said I was you. Sorry! Don't mean to—" Noor deleted the silly, staticky message midway.

Without admitting to herself where she was going, she drove to Barre Street to park as naturally outside Gerry Wilcox's apartment house as if she'd parked there a million times before, except there was a bus stop in front of Gerry's decidedly ugly two-story, asphalt shingled, mustard-trimmed apartment building. So Noor turned the corner and parked behind in an alley of garages and storage sheds that backed up to the railroad tracks, and beyond the tracks the incongruous, swooping rooflines of the Food Co-op whose holier-than-thou attitude always rankled her even though she liked shopping there. A not new, but not too beat-up, red pickup with a seven-foot Fisher plow had been backed into one parking space. She wondered if Gerry had gotten a start on that plowing business he'd mentioned. She hadn't really taken him seriously at the time. She hadn't ever really taken him seriously, period. Next door was the slick new Central Vermont Community Land Trust apartment complex. Public housing. Why hadn't Gerry moved there instead? His reported income surely would qualify him. If he even reported his income. From this vantage Noor saw laundry lines crisscrossing the cluttered, sagging second-story porches of Gerry's building. One unit sported dead house plants and another early flickering Christmas lights with missing bulbs—not Gerry's apartment, she was sure. The building might have made an effort at elegance at one time—there were decorative wooden corbels holding up the roof beams—but its location near the granite factory—where the sign read ANITE without the GR in the beam of its security lights—and the separate front doors indicated that it was old factory housing.

Noor walked resolutely around to the front. Ice, melted and refrozen into footprints, hadn't been cleared from the sidewalks. A bent metal pipe served as railing for the cement steps. On the tilted porch, lit by an overhead bulb, stood white plastic chairs; a flimsy aluminum ashtray, spotted with ash but with the butts dumped out, sat on an empty plant stand. Behind a screen door that should have been changed to a storm door by now, the house was unlocked. She entered a narrow hallway. There was no list of names, no buzzers, just closed doors with numbers behind which she could hear thumping bass, a shrill TV laugh track, a woman shouting. This was crazy. He might not even be home. Or he might have someone with him, some Charlene or Kelsey from down the hall. Noor knocked softly, then louder, on the door with the thumping bass. The music turned lower and the door opened halfway. A kid who couldn't have been more than twenty, with multiple piercings in his eyebrows and lips, and one of those ugly hole-in-the-middle ear plugs spreading his left lobe, cocked his head.

"Yo," he said.

"I'm looking for Gerry Wilcox," Noor nearly whispered.

The kid shrugged. He didn't know a Gerry Wilcox.

"Thanks," Noor said but when the door was already closed and the music thumping again, she knocked a second time. "Sorry. The man with the black leather jacket. Longish hair, sort of?"

The kid still had no clue.

"Smokes unfiltered Camels."

"2B," the kid said.

Noor climbed a narrow staircase with several missing balusters and a bare two-by-four serving as a railing. Upstairs was quieter, just a hum of TV voices coming from 2A, and no smell, like downstairs, of overcooked Thanksgiving turkey. Noor knocked on Gerry's door, which was painted dingy white, the stick-on numbering misaligned, the 2 higher than the B. She waited a beat, thought of retreating while she still had time, and then the door opened and Gerry stood there in a faded black Metallica T-shirt, a frozen pizza box in one hand and a puzzled look on his face. Sting's mournful "The Hounds of Winter" played softly in the background. Noor watched while his surprise turned to astonished delight, his mouth creasing into that Gerry grin, his green eyes radiating a web of premature crows' feet.

"Can I come in?" Noor asked.

Gerry gestured her in with the pizza box. "I forgot my manners for a sec. Didn't expect to see *you* here. What's up? We got a problem with our transaction or something? Little Noor Khan having a change of heart, wanting to undo the deed already?"

"It's not that." Noor looked around the living room, which was pretty much what she expected—a sagging plaid couch in front of a plasma TV, a small square table with peeling veneer pushed into one corner holding an outdated boom box CD player and a spill of CDs, uncurtained windows with pull-down vinyl shades, a car hubcap leaning against one dingy white wall—except for the electronic keyboard standing in front of a folding chair. It was a new chair, she noted, the price tag from the TJ Maxx in Burlington still affixed. Probably brought his daughter along as well and bought her a new overnight bag and a bubble bath set.

"You play keyboard?" Noor asked.

"Naah, I just fool around. Here, give me your coat."

"I'm in my barn clothes," Noor said, settling on the couch without removing her parka. "I probably smell. I didn't even change."

"Who wants you to change?" Gerry pretended to sniff the air discerningly. "Mmm, sexy. Pine shavings, with a piquant essence of hay and earthy undertones of horse shit."

Noor snorted. "Is that your plow rig outside?"

"It is. Thanks to you and your friend and our friend in Burlington. I've got a few driveway jobs set up already. Hey, want a beer?" Gerry asked. "I ain't got nothing fancy, just Bud. None of those boutique Bicycle Built for Two Dancing Frogs brews here."

"Fine," Noor said and waited while Gerry rooted in a fridge.

"Hey, that friend of yours, the one I drove home from the cemetery? She's got it pretty hard with that dad of hers and his old-timers disease."

"Yeah," Noor called back, "And what's with asking her out? Are you going to?" she added but Gerry didn't hear her. Just as well. She wasn't up for thinking about Jaycee's problems when she had a massive crisis of her own. What were her parents going to say when they heard? No one divorced in their family, even though all it took, for a man, anyway, was to turn around and say three times, "I divorce thee, I divorce thee, I divorce thee."

Gerry came out and sat down on the couch beside Noor, making the sunken springs creak. They clicked their cans and Noor took a gulp of the sour foam. "So what's with you?" Gerry asked. "You look like someone shot your dog."

"It's always animal death with you, Gerry. 'Run over my kitten, shot my dog.' Dan's gotten someone else pregnant. He's going to move in with her."

"The stupid, stupid bastard," Gerry said, shaking his head. "Jesus. I can't believe he was willing to risk losing you like that."

"I don't think he considered it much of a risk. I think he wanted it to happen. He said I acted like I'm keeping secrets from him too, and he's right. He even said something about me being secretive because I'm Pakistani."

"Now I gotta kill him," Gerry said. "Run him over *and* shoot him."

Noor looked up, startled, thinking back to the guy in the black SUV at the cemetery. "You're joking, right?"

"Yeah. Sort of. C'mere you. Take that big thing off before you overheat in here." He reached out and tugged on one of the padded sleeves, stripping the oversized coat off her easily. He tossed it on the small cable spool that served as a coffee table. Noor studied her knees, covered in flannel lined jeans, and the toes of her insulated barn boots.

"Still dressed too warm," Gerry said, shaking his head. "I'm heating up just looking at you."

Noor glanced at him, expecting a smirk but Gerry was smiling, guilelessly it seemed, eagerly. It was funny, Noor thought, that Gerry believed she had come over here for *this,* as if she had dressed on purpose in layers the better for him to peel them away from her. Under the parka she wore a gray fleece, a cotton turtleneck, and under that a silk long john top. Gerry unzipped the fleece and tugged that off by the sleeves too. Noor sat still like a child being readied for bed, which she supposed she was. Why not? She didn't owe anything to Dan now. But she was numb, the day's surreal turn spinning in her mind. She pretended obliviousness to Gerry's intentions and the fact of him being so close to her. It wasn't until he went to lift the turtleneck and discovered the long john top, joking about her weird religious undergarments, that Noor closed Dan out, leaving the day behind, and allowed herself to feel Gerry's hands on her ribcage. They slid up and then around her back to unhook her bra, the warmth of his rough palms spreading through her. It was like high school, she thought. They might have been still in high school, after the prom, to which he'd invited her even though he knew she wouldn't accept.

He stopped. "You're okay with this, right? I don't want to take advantage of your being all upset or nothing. We don't have to do this. But if we don't, I'll just jump out that window over there. I knew I left it open for some reason."

Noor reached out and grasped the back of Gerry's head in both hands and pulled him toward her, hungry now for his cushy lips, his faintly beery breath, his heat, her heat. Their beer cans tipped in their hands; the microwave was dinging in the kitchen.

"Wait, wait," Gerry said, and yanked his T-shirt over his head, then leaned in so that his chest—boyishly smooth in contrast to the wear on his face—was hard against her breasts, his hands around her hips, peeling her jeans, unlacing her boots and throwing them to the side, sliding off her panties, groaning when she wrapped her legs around his back and squeezed with riding-strong thighs.

"Not so fast, not so fast," Gerry murmured. "I waited a long time for this. Let me see you." He slid to the side and ran a hand from her crown down her face, her neck and collarbones, between her breasts, over her belly and into her pubic hair, smiling when Noor shivered, then tormented her by pulling his hand away, sliding it down first one thigh and calf, then the other. "Perfect," he said. "You're perfect." Then he swung back over her and buried his face in her neck, able to do so because he was so much shorter than Dan, so much more suited to burrowing into her. He pushed inside, gentler than she would have expected, sweeter, maybe too sweet. He was making love but she was just making oblivion. She put her hands on his ass to urge him on. He had a tiny butt, mushroom white. Maybe she could come to love that butt, love the unknown Gerry who played the rickety electric keyboard, who had dreams she'd never even considered, who plunked down his coke middleman money for a truck with a plow rig so he could earn a living aside from selling weed, love him the way she loved the slow rhythm that was tricking her out of this godawful day, tricking her into nothing but now.

∽

Noor woke, stiff and cramped beside Gerry on the couch, the room lights blazing. It was dark outside the windows. Her watch read 3:27 a.m. She found her way to Gerry's bathroom with its mildewed shower curtain, its hairy razor and cap-less toothpaste tube on the sink edge. A snapshot of an otherwise naked woman in thong panties, serving her breasts up like fruit on a platter, smiled coyly for Gerry from the wall across from the toilet. Was this the mother of his daughter or some other, long-lost girlfriend? Did he use it for masturbation? Probably not. He would regard it with tender nostalgia. Maybe he would want a picture of Noor next. She hadn't even thought about a condom it had been so long since she needed one. Jesus. Who knew where he'd been and whom he'd been with. Stupid. She made herself sit on the toilet seat instead of hovering over it like in a public bathroom—hadn't she just had sex with the man? Then tiptoed back to the living room where Gerry had spread himself out, face down, on the couch, the no longer so endearing mushroom butt glowing as if phosphorescent. As silently as she could, she slid her clothes back on, zipped and laced, smelled spilled beer on her parka, hoped she wouldn't be stopped by a cop, and let herself out of his apartment and down the rickety staircase, out the wooden and screen doors, onto the street and around the corner to where her car sat frosty under streetlights.

Thankfully her battery, iffy of late, hadn't drained. It would be terrible to have to go wake Gerry to give her a jump while explaining why she'd sneaked out without a goodbye. All she knew was she had to get out of there, be alone right now, she couldn't risk Gerry waking happy to see her, wanting to take her out to some 24/7 breakfast place where he would make googly eyes at her and she would study the smeary laminated menu for too long.

Noor scraped the windshield while the engine rumbled and the heater blew cold air. Then she drove home, whatever that meant. Dan wasn't there, and for a nanosecond she forgot she had kicked him out. Jiyah, however, was overjoyed to see her. Had the dog ever before spent a night alone? "Sorry, sweetie," Noor said, letting Jiyah out for a long awaited leak. She checked the closets and drawers to see what Dan had taken—a few pairs of jeans and tee shirts, his gray North Face fleece, clean coveralls, his work boots, his parka, and, oddly enough, a sight that knocked the air right out of her, his suit and dress shoes, the outfit he'd probably wear when he married Mindy someday. He'd taken his electric razor and toothbrush from the bathroom—a bathroom with clean tile walls and no photos of affectionately unclothed girls. Except for her toothbrush sitting alone in the holder and the neatly folded towels on the rack, the bathroom was as empty as the rest of the house would be from now on. There was no point in pretending she'd get back to sleep. She made coffee and waited for it to get light enough to start her barn chores.

At 8:30 she was huddled in an armchair under a blanket pretending to watch Bridget Jones whine about her food and alcohol unit intake when she heard knocking on her door. Shit, now who? She didn't want to see Gerry or Dan. But it was Jaycee, turning the knob to let herself in, full of busy cheer. Noor didn't get up but she clicked off the remote.

"Are you okay? Did you get my messages? You need to hear what I found in the papers in my dad's study. The stolen book wasn't the half of it. It was only the tip of the iceberg. There was a scam sort of thing—some investment thing at Hillwinds. All these people screwed over. But wait a second. You look really weirded out," Jaycee said, pulling off her hairy poncho and under it an enormous hunter orange down vest, before plopping herself on the couch. How wound up she was, Noor thought with annoyance. Would somebody please unspin her?

"Yeah, I was feeling kind of crazy last night. Dan moved out. Mindy *is* having his baby."

"What!? Oh no, I'm so sorry Noor. You'll drive down to Miami with me, at least, to get away and talk. Frida's nice. She'll—It'll be good for you to—" Jaycee made a move to come over and hug her but Noor kicked the blanket off her legs and slipped out of reach. She headed to the kitchen where the coffee maker had long overheated the pot. "You want a cup of burnt coffee?" she called with forced bravado, feeling as if she'd rather drown herself in it than drink it.

"Sure, two teaspoons of sugar please. Do you have raw milk? No, forget it, any milk's okay. That really sucks. You must have had a bad night," Jaycee said.

"Yeah, kind of a weird night. I couldn't reach you"—had she tried? She couldn't remember now—"so I went over to Gerry Wilcox's to be consoled."

Jaycee didn't respond. Noor tipped the coffee pot over a white mug emblazoned with the wordy green logo Northeast Bovine/Equine Veterinary Conference 2008, threw in two spoonfuls of sugar, and poured another one for herself in an ordinary blue mug, black no sugar. She returned to the living room.

"I was so screwed up." She thrust a cup at Jaycee, who looked up at her with stricken eyes. Gone at once was her manic enthusiasm; it was as though she'd been slapped.

"You slept with him." Jaycee's voice went dull. "I thought you weren't interested in Gerry anymore."

"I wasn't. I never was. I'm not. I mean, not serious interest, I just needed, you know, solace." She'd needed someone to *want* her. "I'm sorry, Jaycee, I wasn't thinking clearly."

"You mean you weren't thinking about me. I told you I thought he was going to call me." Jaycee had popped up and now started struggling back into her hideous orange down vest and fuzzy poncho. "It's not just me," Jaycee said. "Don't you think you might have hurt *him*? Gerry, I mean? Using him to get back at Dan? You already know he always had a thing for you. What do you want? Him to jump off a cliff for you?"

Noor glugged a harsh mouthful of coffee. "Oh, come on, Jaycee, Gerry'll get over it, don't you think? I bet he'll still call you."

Jaycee headed for the door, then stopped and turned back, her face pinkly distorted, her eyes teary. "I told you we had a nice ride home that day, Gerry and me. We were going to be like, I don't know, friends, first. We were taking it slow." Jaycee stomped through the mud room, knocking into something—a broom maybe—sending it crashing to the floor, and fled.

Noor groaned. She really hadn't thought about Jaycee when she slept with Gerry. She'd been so wrapped up in her marriage imploding that she hadn't stopped to think of anyone's feelings. Couldn't she blame it on the fact that she'd had so little sleep in the past forty-eight hours? She ran out to the stoop in her sock feet. "Jaycee, wait. Please. I'm sorry. I didn't know . . . I'll come with you to Miami. I will. I will." But Jaycee backed the beige Buick down the driveway to the road, where she narrowly missed being hit by a passing plow truck—not Gerry's, thank god—before gunning away.

It had snowed overnight, Noor noted in some distant part of her brain. She stood on the stoop, inviting the cold to punish her. Jaycee was right. Noor had whirled through all their lives like a damaging tornado. At least Dan was happy now, free of her. What was the matter with her? Noor stared out at her barn, the overcast winter sky, the naked tree line, waiting for an epiphany, something to shock her beyond self-knowledge into being a better person, into a reversal of her years-long habit of caring only for horses, dogs, and clients, but it was just too damn cold for that, so she went back inside.

PART V

Things Live On Each Other

CHAPTER THIRTEEN

Hil, 2011

The more Hannah works at the Maple Jiggle the more household errands fall on Hil's shoulders. Today on the road he spots the child again, the one he's been looking for, wearing the usual hooded sweatshirt. He puts his foot on the brake, slowing down the Buick so as not to frighten her again as he frightened her last time. So as not to overtake her, he makes a few decoy loops like onto Arsenal Road where the snow is poorly plowed so drifts block the slideways, which makes it hard to turn the big, square Buick around without crashing into mailboxes. He needs to keep better watch. That's the errand for the day. And yesterday too. And for tomorrow if she is still walking alone/along through slush, in her trashy what are they? The things you put on your peds. Tenny shoes. Where has he seen that girl before? Someone really ought to learn to keep her safe where she belongs. But now here she is again, wearing her pretty braid looped out of sight under the peaked cotton hood where it won't be recognized, like hiding a kitten in a pocket so it won't be drowned in a bucket. He oughtta jot that down. She looks familiar from behind, like Jiminy Cricket. Hil should know her by name. Or she should know him. It's when he gets up close there'll be a thing, he expects. What kind of thing?

He feels it coming on, squeezing his mindboggle. He hates when this happens. You never know. But then the words bird away and you can see them on the wire, little black scratchy wings that don't mean nothing. Hil laughs. He doesn't talk like that! He has impeccable whatever. But soon they won't mean shit.

The girl is too busy tip-peddling the slushy even to glance up at the car. Her mother is a fat hippopotamus, sending her into this not-spring weather. It's only polite that Hil follow a ways, like the dads on Hallows Eve the way they trail their scary goblins. But the girl doesn't startle, never betraying her thing, that thing that rattles girls' nerves when the car's too big, and soon she waits for Hil's Buick to cut her off between the painted white crossing, her face pinched by the hood, of which the faded mint color makes it clear she's trailer trash. He passes by slowly instead of waving her on, and finds it hard to find a parking space at the old college gym since it's Farmer's Wife Market in there this morning.

After he parks, he climbs the ramp to the gym, feeling sorry for the engine heads who designed it for being so without basic know-way that they built it going up instead of going down. The three doors are slathered in glossy so thick you could peel it up in one carpet and roll the undernourished chirp right up in it and hide her someplace where she won't be forgotten. Diligently he follows, searching for a sight of the little pinched hood amid the food malls displaying their aromatics. When Hil pauses to study a warming tray, the stall keeper offers, "Would you like to try a sample?" bringing to Hil's attention a plate of smaller morsels pierced by skinny wooden sharpies.

"I'd be . . ." he pauses, but he can't call it up. "I'd be defiled." Delicately he picks up a sharpie, like someone lifting a dime from the floor. She's not a slumpie, this stall keeper, like most of the rest in the Farmer's Wife Market, which is filled to the brim with their hand-knitted neck things. Soon he hurries past the stall of metal trinkets women wear, and past the table of heavy clay things for breaking, and then he spots her in her sweatshop tasting a square. Breakfast. Straight to the gullet. And at the baker stall, lunch. Her fat mother really oughtta be snipered. But when the girl stops for a third supper sample, the hood slides from her face and comes to a drapey rest on her shoulders, revealing her to be the same middle-aged hussy she turned out to be last week, the one with the fear of being pushed off a bluff. What an awful thing to need to be worried about, being pushed off a bluff in your pearl gray twin set in your own car. Hil shrugs, used to it all by now, the way the birds flap close and then veer away, the way he used to smoke white things but not anymore. He plucks another bite of food off the thing in front of him, pops it in his mouth, and thoughtfully chews.

"Sir," says a slumpie. "That's not the sample tray, sir. You need to pay for those cookies! Are you barefoot, sir? Are you by yourself?"

"With someone," he answers, catching sight of the strumpet going out the back door of the jiminy, her faded mint color sneaking past where the heavy blue draperies swing closed on skit days. The acoustics are lousy in this place. Hil wouldn't throw a skit in here if he was a basketball. He oughtta jot that down. He follows the wildebeest down a close cement tunnel, hating the way she keeps trying to trick him, looking sweet at first but then they turn out to be bad tricks like at the bluff in Rhinebeck. It's a good thing he threw her overboard, except he never did check she went deep enough down.

Hil curdles and sweats. There's a stewer in the hallway with rings on a rod. I'd be delighted. That's the term. He's been here before, having his nice hot stewer. There's no drying things however, just squares of coarse paper. He finds the wildebeest pedaling an exercise thing in a whitewashed cell at the end of the tunnel filled with old clunky exerclods.

"Can I help you, Sir?" she asks. "Sir, are you looking for someone? What have you—" and suddenly she's pushing past him to get out the door.

Outside, all the buildings are raining now and he swerves to the center near Arsenal Road so as not to hit the poor thing racing along, a skinny, freezing child sent into the cold wearing nothing but jeans and a negligent teacher, trying hard to stay safe with one shoe untied. Her mother should be flat. He pulls close to offer the girl a ride. For how gallant he is. But maybe a tad of a simpleton, too. The little cricket, Jiminy, was cleverer in some versions than he was in others. In some versions, he didn't even have a name, but in others he was strangled in the first chapter.

"May I kill you?" Hil asks, reaching for the girl's pretty straw-melon braid. Except he's forgotten to put on the brake. The car slides away sideways, still chugging. Stuck. Away the little girl races, not even glancing at Hil lying there. Above him the inks fly back to their wires. How cold he'll be. Somebody stop. Somebody stop me and help, he says.

CHAPTER FOURTEEN

Jeff Parmenter, 2011

The words, *Things lived on each other—that was it*, courtesy of Theodore Dreiser, courtesy of Jeff's long-ago Washington University English Prof, Elsbeth Picone, flared onscreen as it did every morning before ceding itself to the bright, brisk lines of Jeff's home page. Ms. Picone had been the first and only *"Ms."* of all Jeff's teachers, predating even *Ms. Magazine*. Among Jeff's classmates a rumor once circulated that the reason Ms. Picone lost her tenure fight was that she insisted on being called Ms., but the real truth was she was ugly as a banshee and if banshees smoked, she smoked like one, too. Her ugliness was downright combative, and even in the days when smoking ruled in college classrooms, brown teeth and jaundice didn't. In honor of her skinny, sooty, droopy, charred appearance—a resemblance to a roasted Jerusalem artichoke that she herself once lamented aloud during class time—the Dreiser quote, which was her mantra, had stayed near Jeff all these years, like a soul, he sometimes thought, and, now that she was dead— her name's appearance in Wash U's *In Memoriam* posting surprising Jeff only in that it had taken her so long to die—the quote became his screensaver.

Jeff's home page was Yahoo Finance Research in Motion Limited (RIMM), but since today, a Monday, was Martin Luther King Day, it showed the same value (16.17%) it had all weekend, just like Apple (419.81), Sysco (29.47), Motorola, Oracle, Adobe, Click Software, Juniper Networks, Microsoft, Riverbed, Johnson and Johnson, United Health, Exxon, Dutch Oil, Ford, GM, GE, Mindax. (God, he hated that name, like Tampax, why'd he ever buy it?) and Google (Why *hadn't* he bought it? Why *didn't* he, still?). His typing finger hovered in a replay of Saturday's dismay at not having bought the search engine at 474 six months ago, or 262 three years before that. How he hated long weekends (since the markets stayed closed, there was nothing to *check*) but he had to admit to feeling a certain release of tension as well, since all values stayed the same, his wins and his losses momentarily suspended, RIMM's losses foremost among them. He had bought RIMM at 88.58 on January 18, 2008, a day immediately followed by several small successive boosts which afforded him added confidence in snapping up other stocks at *their* supposed lows, some of which really *did* go up in value, so in fact, by purchasing RIMM in the first place, he hadn't lost as much as it seemed he had. For instance, without the illusion of having picked a winning buy date on RIMM, he might never have had the stomach for buying, say, Qualcomm, now worth 56.64 up from 38.27. Not to mention Oracle. He loved that name. Why hadn't *he* come up with it? The real tragedy of RIMM was that he'd bought it with a windfall, money that shouldn't by rights have been his but his ex-wife's, from a clause amid Jeff's retirement papers her lawyer was too much of a screwup to find. But for now it appeared the windfall was wasted. Too, Jeff had a theory that the usual market fluctuations—plunging after skyrocketing, climbing after sliding—didn't apply after three day weekends, so things never got really interesting again until Wednesdays.

For the same reason he would never consider a job in finance for one of the biggies on the West Coast, not even in the valley, not that he'd been offered. You'd have your whole day ahead of you but the markets would have shut down hours ago.

He checked Apple for the second time today even though it was a holiday, and this time he really did suffer a quasi-heart attack, he could feel it in his jaw, at the sight of the value having plummeted since just a few minutes earlier, since by mistake he'd typed APP instead of APPL. Tomorrow he'd buy American Apparel, since how could it not be at a low if it was less than one percent? That said, if his jaw was still throbbing tomorrow he wouldn't buy, since he never bought or sold when he was having a heart attack.

Never buy while you're dead again, he sometimes thought. And then, *Things lived on each other—that was it.*

He jumped up for the bathroom, since it was almost time to leave. He shaved, combed, brushed, buffed, and applied some of the new expensive Clé de Peau Beauté Men's Concealer in Ocher, which would be expensive at seventy dollars for a quarter of an ounce if it didn't cause him to require less eye crème (forty-five dollars at Sephora.com) than was required by the cheaper Manajji. Then he drank a glass of Pom Wonderful, put on his anorak, and paused to look himself over in the full-length mirror. Since the lady he was seeing had a habit of huddling under the covers on days off, she wouldn't notice him at the mirror or drinking her Pom. Her name was Clea, same as Jeff's daughter. For some time last night, half awake and half nightmarish, he'd pondered the nagging possibility that maybe she *was* his daughter, her being all of twenty-two and with blue eyes like his and his ex's, until he'd realized that the real Clea must be in her forties now. He felt a pang of resentment of the passage of time, for both their sakes. At least he didn't look like a guy with a middle-aged daughter, not including those icky yellow markings showing up recently on the flesh around his eyes. He took another slug of the juice, grateful for this sudden influx of beta-whatevers into his life, washing down its bracing siltiness with more of itself. As if it would save him. And Clea, too. After all it was a womanly concept, that hourglass shape with the forces of gravity rushing through it—time running out.

Jeff shut the door softly behind him so as not to interrupt his overnight guest's type A pretense of taking the day off and rode the empty elevator to the parking ramp, glad to have something that needed to be done on this otherwise pointless Monday. On the highway he had hours to practice his lines, banging his hand on the dashboard for emphasis but not with enough force to injure himself.

"Why would you think it was *okay* just to throw—to throw out—to break—to dick around with tradition after all these years—to hang onto the expense account checks after sending them to me for all these—Have I disappointed you in some way, Hil?"

But that was too pathetic and altogether not hair-raising enough, Jeff thought, knowing Hil responded better to threats and falsehoods than to reasoned pleas.

"What the FUCK, Hil, what the FUCK?! For what, Hil? So you . . . so your wife can buy more Vermont Lentil Stew mix tied with blue ribbon to put in her gift shop nobody shops at? Is THAT what you're buying with my expense account funds?! Mine? Your idea man? Your . . . your numero uno?"

Hil would pretend not to know what Jeff was talking about. Or else he really wouldn't know. Jeff couldn't decide which was worse. The bottom line was Jeff had to get hold of those credit card checks, which Hil hadn't been sending him lately, which between Hil and Jeff were known as the expense account checks, which provided Jeff, or rather, Derrick Stamm, access to Hillwind's ever-shrinking credit limit, which came in handy when Jeff was buying lunch or drinks for would-be investors at one or another of his more promising ventures. Rumor had it Derrick liked the feel of the blank checks in his wallet, the slight heft they provided, liked even the scant weight of the pen in his hand when he was filling in the blank line with the number he needed. Jeff wondered if other people harbored rumors of themselves like Jeff did, uncorroborated inklings of the things they might be feeling.

"They're not that big a deal, those checks, but they're a big deal to me," Jeff said to the car, practicing anew, the sky vast against the windshield, the steering wheel coming up a little harder than expected this time against the palm of his hand . . . and then Hil would remember where he'd put the checks, this time, and he would walk flat-footed into the house to retrieve them, and maybe even bring Jeff some bonus, like last time, when he delivered to Jeff a rolled up copy of Elizabeth Greenwood's dead husband's social security check, though God knows why the woman had sent it to Hil in the first place.

The smallest details were often more important than the ones you staked your life on, Jeff realized with discomfiture. Something was off kilter. He righted his pinkie ring, reminding himself he had the upper hand here. Or rather, Derrick Stamm did. Jeff would miss that made-up fellow. He would miss his lofty signature and the feeling Jeff got when he penned it that he, Jeff, really was committing a forgery, as if there really were a man named Derrick Stamm with a Dracula cursive and a Mont Blanc Meisterstruck le Grand Rollerball Engraved Pen, a man with whom Jeff would soon be required to sever all bonds . . . like if he and Derrick ever played Squash they wouldn't anymore, or if they ever had a drink or even liked the same girl or the same novel, they couldn't anymore.

Jeff eased the car over the flat wooden beam bridge spanning the untamed froth of some poor excuse for a scenic waterway, taking a second to roll down the windows in order to show off the tinted window screens to the denizens of the state capital, even though the cold made his teeth chatter. He bypassed his usual stop at the Subway shop where he always chose the six-inch meatball parmesan, since he hated the sight of the so-called *Sandwich Artists* pawing at veggies in their hospital gloves, instead turning onto State Street to park down the block near the railroad trestle, where a gas station sold individual cigarettes out of a mug on the counter. If you were quitting you could buy just one cigarette at a time instead of a whole pack. Jeff wondered why R. J. Reynolds hadn't come up with this themselves by now; they could sell a pair of cigarettes for five bucks easy to quitters like him, since even though they'd bucked the habit before they hit their twenties, they still liked having one once in a while. He paid five pennies for a book of matches, then stood in the parking lot far from his car so if the lit match broke, it wouldn't damage the paint job. Soon he put the cigarette out on the pavement amid scores of other butts and, with the help of Montpelier's pedestrian-friendly traffic laws, which Jeff couldn't stand because of how earnestly drivers obeyed them, he crossed the street to the Chinese place that looked like a lopped-off corner of the adjacent Laundromat. He ordered at the Formica counter then carried the tray to a table that might once have been used for folding freshly washed undies. The food was surprisingly tasty here. The soup was just the right mix and the Kung Pao crackled. A fire engine drove past outside and a large lady seemingly unfazed by being the wearer of a thick mustache lumbered up to the counter for take-away, the upturned cuffs of her overalls spilling a trail of birdseed behind her all the way to the feed store across the road.

After lunch he used the restroom, where he was rescued from prodding at the yellowish marks on the flesh around his eyes by there being no mirror. Had he really read something about those marks being warning signs of heart attack, or had he only made it up? Or had some girl or other told him? Probably made it up herself, he thought, in the car again and gazing at the spots in his rear view mirror, even as he drove. Since it was still lunch hour and he didn't want to run the risk of interrupting the Emorys drooling over their barley stew, he took the steep hill to the college for a look-see. Somehow one of his names had ended up on a list of potential college donors, and a letter had reached him asking for help in a capitol drive raising funds for new campus residence halls. He'd sent the letter back Addressee Unknown and now bit down gingerly on all his near misses, wincing in advance of the pain in his jaw.

Ridiculously high snow banks edged the gravel expanse of parking lot behind the boxy college dormitories that looked like orphanages, orphanages that even if they *were* orphanages would be in need of refurbishing. A freshened-up library might not be such a bad idea either, Jeff noted, although he had to admit the building had charm. It was red brick with white pillars. While from the outside it looked like it could hold maybe ten books, inside it felt capacious. The air smelled dry but fecund, papery with the thoughts of the immortal dead. Jeff breathed in deeply to see if he if could smell them—their hair, their spirits, their nails, their loves. He had used to be able. This was the smell that had started him off in publishing when he was in his twenties, and it didn't surprise him, sucker that he was, to find that the smell still held some of the same deceptively romantic sway over him, like sniffing glue, he reasoned, since there was glue in the bindings. With some misgiving, he approached the HELP desk, where a young man wearing fingerless gloves shivered over his own beard as if studying the Talmud. Jeff waited with uncommon patience to be noticed by him.

"Can you help me?" Jeff finally asked, and the young man led Jeff through a warren of shelving until, after searching around among microform files, he preceded Jeff down a hallway to a windowless room containing one wooden chair and a surprisingly cool-looking microfiche reader, which was the only technology Jeff ever dared use to look up his daughter, since if he let himself get in the habit of spying on her via computer he'd be doing it hourly. Though microfiche remained a meaningful technology, the librarian said, it was best kept under cover of rear rooms. He took the chair himself, removed the long knitted scarf that had been trailing all along from his rear jean pocket, wrapped it around his neck, inserted the microform, and activated the scan.

"Is there an app for that?" Jeff asked.

You could never get away with hijacking the Help Desk at Yale, he knew. Or Harvard. You'd be found wanting and would be turned away, sent home more ignorant than you were before. A distant cousin of Jeff's once rose to fifteen minutes of fame by helping to capture an infamous book thief who smuggled rare books and priceless old manuscripts past security posts in an array of public and university libraries, but as far as Jeff was concerned, this do-gooder cousin was on the absolute wrong side of the law.

"You work here at the college?" the librarian asked.

"Donor," Jeff lied. "I pay your boss's salary. Hell, I calculate his worth."

"Her," the guy corrected, but his face lit up on learning Jeff's position. Maybe Jeff would put a word in for a hot water dispenser for tea, his expression seemed to say.

"Is this the person you're looking for?" he asked, tilting his beard away from the scan to give Jeff a better view. Jeff couldn't say for sure . . . but then all at once he knew. It was the first up-to-date photograph he had seen of her in years. The last had been a *Long*

Islander engagement photo, and before that an acne-ridden group portrait commemorating the Suffolk County Middle School Entrepreneurs Club. Twin funnels of white eyelet spilled from the sleeves of her tailored suit jacket, and more eyelet cascaded at the modest neckline. Her haircut was feathers. Like her dad she had her teeth professionally whitened. There was lots of chunky jewelry not in bad taste, but Jeff's eyes smarted at the sight of the missing wedding band. She was either divorced or widowed, then. He hoped not widowed. He hoped not divorced. He also hoped she wasn't the kind of person who took her ring off for public appearances in hotel conference centers. A banner proclaiming the Rotary 2010 Milwaukee Wisconsin Keynote Address adorned the wall behind the podium where she stood. She was a public speaker, then. His heart splintered with pride. According to the article under the photo, the title of his daughter's speech was An Assessment of the Rotary's *Four-Way Test*, and the test went like this:

Of the things we think, say or do . . .

1. Is it the TRUTH?
2. Is it FAIR to all concerned?
3. Will it build GOODWILL and BETTER FRIENDSHIPS?
4. Will it be BENEFICIAL to all concerned?

From a place setting marked by a crumpled napkin where her luncheon plate had been, two men vied for a view of the spot behind the podium where her skirt might show. She would have, Jeff imagined, a Madam's heart. She would have a passable singing voice. She would be three years running Businesswoman of the Year. She'd be fun at roasts, but she would suffer secret heartbreaks, multiple unpaid parking violations, a home pedicure spa, a supply of Stella D'Oro Breakfast Treats, and a shelf of bound journals filled with nightly attempts at poetry writing. He wondered if she knew what a sad little pointless ironical verse the two of them, errant father and earnest daughter, might make together.

Are we the truth? the verse went.

Are we fair to all concerned?

In your dreams. Things live on each other—that was it.

⁓

By 2:00, after a bit more searching, he'd left the library with his daughter's home address and phone number in his anorak pocket. Soon, with just enough time to face down the Emorys and get back to New York before the streets were too eerie and lonely to drive on, he reached the Hillwinds turnoff. A shocking number of cars were parked in the lot in front of the shop, but as he made his way toward them Hil's big Buick barreled past, a grungy circle of fabric snagged on one headlight. Hil was all hunched over, rummaging. Then down rolled the window and Hil tossed out a barn cat that landed on the hood of Jeff's car before leaping away. Jeff flashed a resigned palm—Stop, it said—but Hil's gaze was fixed on a whirl-wind of sun motes blizzarding his windshield as he careened to-ward town. It must be more fun to *be* Hil than it was to be *near* him, Jeff supposed. The man might have been a stock car racer on Mars for all the attention he paid to Earth.

Later, lying on the floor of the Maple Jug, it was important for Jeff to accept that there might not *be* a later . . . at least not for him.

It was Hannah who saved him, Hannah who kept in her cleav-age a boob-warmed medicine pouch containing a miniature bottle of aspirin, just one tablet of which, in the nick of time, secured Jeff some ability to go on looking at the ceiling. He *could not fig-ure out,* just as Drieser's Frank Cowperhood was forever unable to figure out, *how this thing he had come into—this life he had been tossed into,* as Dreiser put it—*was organized.* At first it was only the usual jaw ache that clamped down on Jeff, but before he knew it there was God's whole knee pressing the oxygen out from under his ribcage and then he fell to the floor with Jaycee kneeling over him struggling to remember CPR. People often got it wrong. The CPR for drowning victims on TV was often fatally flawed, as was the procedure for choking victims in restaurants in movies. Jeff's ex-wife, who was a medic, knew these things. A well-trained EMT would first flip the victim onto his belly to let the water gush out, and would only then roll him onto his back to open the airway and begin compressions. And in a restaurant, you never back-slapped a choker, lest the force of the slap send the trapped chunk of rib-eye only further down the windpipe.

Lying on the floor of the Maple Jug, Jeff worried he might shit himself or worse, confess everything, not just the scam, but the muddier, stinkier stuff that surrounded it: His own tipsiness and Hil's drunkenness that night on the road. Eben Shattuck's yellow cap, the sudden appearance of the two little girls, the road swollen with trees, the way Jeff hated trees even more when he was tipsy than when he was sober. How Hil got that nasty bump on his forehead from not buckling his seatbelt, and how the car, the old Buick, the same car Hil was driving today, became a dented, bloodied mess. And how together, back at Hillwinds, they had sprayed it with a garden hose then driven it on purpose straight into the barn, wrecking the timbers and banging it up the more, and had the ruined barn as alibi should one be required. But one never was.

"You know who I am?" he asked Jaycee, the floor hard against his back, his anorak pinned by the weight of his arms. He meant . . . he didn't know what he meant, Jeff Parmenter or Derrick Stamm? Better if she thought of him as Derrick, no, better if she thought of him as Jeff.

"Oh for god's sake she's known you since the day she was born," snapped Hannah from her chair, the wheels nearly at his face.

He had found Jaycee and Hannah in the shop shelving small paintings of maple leaf syrup bottles and maple leaf cookie cutters and maple leaf potholders and even paintings of maple leaf cupcakes, a funny thing to try to make a go of when you were hardly treading water businesswise, notwithstanding the more than twenty customers who were in the crowded shop, pulling paintings off the shelves the split second things went up. There were also some small painted slaves setting out amid the painted merchandise with their painted belongings slung over their shoulders and even their painted dreams and despairs in tow. Amid facsimiles of Vermont-made Chamomile Rag Rug Shampoo bottles, some inch-high children blew soap bubbles with whip-wielding overseers trapped inside them.

"Welcome to Hillwinds Art Minutes!" Jaycee had kept chirping.

"Art *Minute,* not minutes," Hannah had kept correcting.

"Welcome to Hillwinds Art Minutes," Jaycee had repeated.

Then, all it once, it seemed, packages in hand, the happy shoppers left the shop. Jaycee shut the door behind them and stood at the till, counting the lucrative Art Minutes take as the parking lot emptied.

"If you sell stuff for months, everyone takes forever to saunter in and then not buy anything, but if you sell it in a minute, they all rush to pay, except a minute's not enough so you have to make it seven or eight or so," she'd explained to Jeff lightly, her tone so out of keeping with his practiced lines that he thought he'd better chat awhile instead of launching right into the reason for his being there. He thought maybe he would offer to put up a few storm windows to soften her and Hannah up before he asked for the checks Hil'd neglected to send him, not to mention a piece of today's till, since he was fiduciary, after all, not to mention Saul Greenwood's or whatever his name was social security checks, in case they were still showing up somehow. He would set it right, he'd tell them, send the checks back to social security or better yet deliver them in person if there even was an actual office anymore.

"But the real reason they rush to buy my paintings is because they're good," said Hannah, still capable, at sixty, of flashing her eyes, the paint from the slaves as fresh on her fingers as if she'd last washed her hands in charcoal and oils.

After that, mother and daughter had simply kept going about their business, though what business there was was a mystery to Jeff since there was nothing left to sell. The shelves were not only bare but entirely gone, the brackets empty on the walls and even the cash register had appeared to him then as being a painted, unreal object despite the very real cash Jaycee was shuffling. The girl would make a fine card player, he noted with worry, since card players, even those dressed in hook and eye buttons and bonnets, made for wily antagonists. It was possible, he thought, she was planning to sell the property before he'd managed to persuade the ailing Hil to put him on the deed. He flipped open his phone and rechecked Friday's closings so as not to look beholden to the change in her hair style, which, unlike the severe part she'd worn as a child, seemed to fortify her, and make her whole.

AAPL (419.81), SYY (29.47), MSI, ORCL and so on. Though it was all as Jeff remembered, and it had once seemed like enough, it didn't anymore. A chill went down his spine.

"If I wanted to I could call up Elizabeth Ann Greenwood right now and she could drive up and ID this joker and tell us how he scammed Dad and made Dad betray the trust all those poor people put in him," Jaycee then said.

"Oh please," said Hannah. "Anyone who puts their trust in your father, God strike me dead, gets what they have coming," and then she'd smoothed her faded skirt and the man's shirt she wore, a pilled blue flannel. Soon she wheeled her chair nearer, and she and Jaycee leveled their wire-rimmed spectacles at Jeff's suddenly perspiring face, the sweat climbing into his hair and boring moist stinging tunnels into his ears. If he had once been in thrall to Professor Picone and her horn-rimmed glasses, he could only imagine what this amalgam of mother and daughter forged by bright round spectacles might teach him. And then his legs had folded under him and he fell to the floor, the open phone skittering.

"Oh god Mom, stop," Jaycee had said, for Hannah had begun reciting lines from *Charlie and the Chocolate Factory*.

"Violet, you're turning violet," Hannah said, reaching into her cleavage for the little drawstring pouch of aspirin. Jeff had closed his eyes on the sight of the white tablet. There had come a thumping in his ears and then a pinging of pipes with heat trapped in them and he could see his wife pushing the carriage with their daughter papoosed in a yellow blanket along the path to the library amid the gingko trees at Washington University. He could see his first car, a yellow Fiat, and then his second car, an Eagle Talon, and finally the first of the countless Beamers. He saw himself in middle school burning the cookies on the day they switched Shop Class with Home Economics so the boys could do girl things and vice versa, and he heard again the Home Ec teacher with the Boston accent saying, "We have farty kids in this class so make farty cookies," since she mispronounced "forty," and he heard Dreiser's Frank Cowperwood scolding himself for not being well enough organized. It wasn't true your life raced past you when you lay dying. Instead it stood right next to you for hours. You'd be dead before you finished watching the movie. An ambulance was already en route to Hillwinds, the siren throbbing in the floorboards.

"Your dad was driving," Jeff said now to Jaycee, whose face hovered above him moonlike and contemplatory, including no anger that he could see.

"He still has his license," she conceded.

"No, I don't mean that," Jeff said. "I mean in 1989. On—"

Hannah clapped her hands over Jaycee's ears.

"Eben Shattuck knew too much," Jeff said, his face sweating out the words. "Your dad was driving but I . . . we didn't know it was the girls on the road with him, we thought it was trees."

"Eben Shattack was Pauline's dad," Jaycee said with horror, and then her back went straighter where she knelt, as if all of her parts worked separately.

"Later on you drove the Buick into the barn," Hannah accused. She kept her hands on Jaycee's ears but Jaycee had heard it all: Jeff could see it in her face—the rage, and then a click of utter sadness, and then the way she stepped away in her mind from the story, not in order to dispel it but simply to have nothing more to do with him than was going to be required, just like Clea.

The ambulance was nearly there. The cops. They were racing up the hill. Yam Rock trembled on its rocky balance beam and then the EMTs were at the door. Two women and one cop and a defibrillator. A cat leapt in beside them, buoyant with its many lives. Jeff knew a lawyer who died of a heart attack because the defibrillator had happened to be broken at the courthouse that day. He readied himself for just such an outcome, but instead the EMTs laid down the defibrillator and asked him how he was feeling.

"Won't anyone please call my daughter?" he said, gesturing at his phone with her phone number on it, her home stunningly nearby in Hanover, New Hampshire. She could jump in her car and be in Burlington in time to greet him at the hospital. Surely they would take him to the hospital in Burlington, not the one in Barre. He hoped Clea knew that. It sickened him to think that he and Clea might cross paths on the highway with the moose-crossing signs between them, the giant animals stepping from the trees.

Jaycee called Clea's number as the EMTs crowded to record Jeff's vitals and attach a monitor. He could hear the phone ringing in Jaycee's hand and then his daughter picked up, her voice nothing at all like Jeff remembered only just like her mom's. Jaycee explained the circumstances in an unsteady voice and held the phone to Jeff's ear. "Clea," Jeff managed.

"I'm sorry, Dad, I'm not here," said Clea. "I was, but now I'm not. I'm sorry. I must have just gone out somewhere," she said. Then she hung up, and when Jaycee redialed, nobody answered

"Can you tell us your name?" asked an EMT.

"My name is Derrick Stamm, Jason Longfellow, Stephen Klom, Mitch Boss, Guy Rosen, and Serge Dominico," said Jeff. "Oh, and Jeff Parmenter."

PART VI

Bliss Road

CHAPTER FIFTEEN

Noor, 2011

Noor pulled out of the driveway of Canterbury Stables. Starting mid-December, she'd decided, with her cocaine cash, to board Daisy there for a couple of expensive winter months in order to continue lessons with her hardiest clients who didn't mind twenty or thirty degree weather as long as it was in a windless indoor arena with soft footing. She was glad she didn't have to lead a horse around her ring in fourteen inches of snow. She waited for a silver Toyota Tacoma and a green highway department truck to pass. The afternoon sun, already low on the horizon, lit the tops of the hills and shadowed the valley, this morning's shimmering blanket becoming a dull gray spread. To her left, rising out of a drift of new snow, a signpost bore the elaborate but unnerving Canterbury Stables sign in which a riderless but saddled horse jumped over a three rail fence, each rail announcing Canterbury's services: boarding/lessons/training. Not a good advertisement, in Noor's view. Where was the missing rider, in a ditch somewhere? The sign also sported a set of unlit Christmas lights. She picked up her to-go cup of now cold coffee. The sipping well held a skim of ice.

Noor waited for an approaching red pickup with a plow to turn left into the drifted driveway across the road. When it came even with her she saw that the magnetic sign on the truck's passenger door read *Wilcox Mowing and Plowing Services* with a Montpelier phone number. Gerry. For a moment Noor considered speeding away on the plowed and salted asphalt. It had been two months since the Thanksgiving night Dan had moved out, the night she'd snuck out of Gerry's, and lost Jaycee's odd, and unexpectedly missed, friendship. That loss had been temporary, it turned out, since Jaycee had called Noor to "request" an apology, and Noor had found herself to be relieved to comply. She was less relieved that she'd promised to go to Miami with Jaycee in February but hoped the trip would fall through before it came to pass. Still, she'd never apologized to Gerry for running out, never even seen him until now. Sighing, Noor backed the Forester into the plowed space behind the sign, and turned off the ignition. Across the street Gerry's red plow truck scraped, clanked, and smashed snow into a gravelly pile at the end of a driveway. She crossed the road and waited beside the mailbox as Gerry backed his pickup to the road and made another rattling pass. Snow curled off the end of his seven-foot plow in a compressed white wave. She supposed she shouldn't be surprised if he was ignoring her, punishing her. He had to look behind him, didn't he, before backing up to the street? Noor hunched her shoulders inside her insulated Carhartt overalls and stepped from foot to foot, hands shoved deep into her pockets. She'd left her gloves in the car. She still wore her wedding ring, the diamond no less brilliant for being discredited.

Gerry put the rumbling truck into park. White clouds of condensation puffed from the tail pipe. Apparently he hadn't been indoctrinated into the Montpelier eco code: never let a vehicle idle. He stuck his head out the window and tipped a finger to his black knit cap. Noor approached like a kid in a doctor's office about to get a shot, except that her parents had always administered shots at home; she'd never actually been in a doctor's office until after the hit and run.

"So how's Noor Khan keeping these days?" Gerry asked. "Last time I saw her—wait, I didn't see her, she disappeared."

Noor avoided his eyes, studied the driver's door handle. It had key scratches all around the lock just like her father's sedan in Karachi. Gerry probably had bought his truck from an old man who fumbled. "You're pissed at me," Noor said.

"Not pissed. Disappointed there, for a bit. But *Say La Vee*, right?"

Noor swiped her nose with the back of her hand. It was freaking cold out here. "I see your business is doing well." His gloved hand rested on the shift stick and under the black steering wheel his thighs were parted—just relaxed, she supposed, but she looked back up so quickly from the crotch of his jeans that he probably noticed her embarrassment at being caught with her eyes on the prize.

"Long as it keeps snowing. You want to hop in here and warm your toes while we talk?"

"I better not. Got to get going . . ." not that she had anywhere she needed to be. "Listen, Gerry I'm sorry about Thanksgiving night. It was just too much all at once, you know?"

"*I'm* not sorry it happened. I enjoyed the snot out of it myself."

How was it that Gerry could enjoy something that had ended with her sneaking out to avoid him? In Noor's book, if you were going to lose something it was better not to have it, or think you had it, at all. Better not to want it, either. Noor looked behind her at the sound of an approaching car, then back to Gerry. "I just wanted to, you know, apologize for being a jerk."

"You weren't a jerk." Gerry smiled that killer smile. "An asshole, maybe, but not a jerk."

"An asshole." Noor nodded. "Alright."

"Naah, just kidding. You ain't a jerk or an asshole, Little Noor Khan, you're just scared. Scared to care."

"That's what Jaycee said. You and she cook that one up together?" Now that he and Jaycee were psychology experts, they could hang up a therapy shingle and teach everyone how to be as well-adjusted as they were.

"Me 'n Jaycee been cooking up some stuff together, but not that. She invited me over for supper one night, not long after you took a powder, and it was pretty nice being around someone who was willing to admit she wanted me there. Nice change of pace you could say. I wasn't crazy about the parsnip loaf she made so a few days later I brought over some steaks and baking spuds, enough for her old folks, too, and we put on the *feed bag* and then *took a roll in the hay* over at her place—ya like my horsey metaphors? Remember Mrs. Russian in eleventh grade with the Met-a-phors and the Sim-iles? 'Remember sim-ile cuz it's sim-i-lar.' Anyhoo, been seeing Jaycee steady since then. Jaycee's a great girl, you know. She cracks me up with those homeschool stories. She's pretty keen on you, you know. Good thing you two worked it out."

Noor was peeved by the idea that it was her supposed "fear of caring" that had led Jaycee and Gerry to get together. And it wasn't news that Gerry and Jaycee were getting it on—of course Jaycee had told her. Gerry just needed to rub it in. Still, what a shit she was, reject a guy then feel jealous when he found someone who actually wanted him. But, she thought, good for Jaycee. Good for the two of them.

"You don't like taking risks." Gerry just wouldn't stop talking about it.

"How can you say that? I risked trusting you with the coke, didn't I? I risked getting arrested, losing everything."

"Noor, I've always been scared of horses. My grandfather logged with them and I seen what they can do, seen 'em take out a bunch of good sized young trees just swinging a twitch log around too fast. You don't weigh more'n 110 pounds, probably, and you got no fear of half ton pea-brains. But when it comes to taking a chance on stepping away from who you think you're supposed to be, or the person you think you're supposed to be with, you can't do it. I get it. Don't like it, but I get it. Anyway I'm into other things now, someone who's not scared of anything, so far as I can tell."

He was right of course. She could quote his words back to him, she too didn't like it but she got it, finally. She was scared. Had always been scared and it led her to do mean, uncaring things. Even now their two streams of condensed breath commingling in the cold air felt entirely too intimate. She wanted to be away from there, back in her Suburu, at home with flatulent Jiyah and a warm woodstove. She'd apologized. Fine. "Tell Jaycee I have the name of a lady who does intake at one of the nursing homes that she and I were talking about. Good luck with the plowing," Noor said, stepping back from the truck window.

"I *love* plowing." Gerry winked, put the truck into gear and lowered the plow to the driveway. "It's like playing with my new toy truck in a big white sandbox." He lurched forward into a long gritty scrape. Noor turned back to her car behind the Canterbury Stables sign. The Christmas lights now twinkled gaily although it was only three in the afternoon.

⤝⤞

When she pulled into her driveway, Noor saw Dan's mobile vet truck parked in its old space. "Oh no," she groaned. "Not two in one day." He was probably over here gathering more of his things. She considered backing out and continuing down Bliss Road until enough time had passed that Dan would have left the property with whatever electronic equipment and college sport trophies he deemed vital to life at Mindy's. Then she saw Dan, jacketless, bent backed, using a shovel to broaden the path she'd stomped in the snow between the house and the barn. Sighing, she got out of the car.

"Dan, what are you doing?" Noor called.

He didn't hear her, his ears covered by his red plaid earflap hat and his breath probably huffing as he threw snow mechanically over his shoulder. The path he was shoveling had neat upright walls and sharp edges but his face was uncharacteristically covered with stubble.

"Dan? DAN!"

Dan put down the shovel and turned toward her. His cheeks were pink with the cold but, strong as he was, not with exertion, his blue-gray eyes pale beneath the red hat. Noor shifted a bag of groceries in her arms—groceries for one. She had asked the man in produce to cut her half a cabbage, and even that looked too big. "What are you doing here?" she repeated as Dan approached her.

"I need to talk to you," he said.

"Let's let the lawyers talk," Noor said.

"No, not about that. Can I come inside?"

"What for?"

"'Cause it's cold out here?" He smiled sheepishly.

Noor turned and led the way to the mudroom. She was an idiot to talk to him.

Jiyah, left inside to stay warm, was all over Dan. Noor tried to ignore the joy her old dog experienced as Dan rubbed behind Jiyah's ears and scratched her chest, tried not to feel vicarious enjoyment in Jiyah's pleasure over Dan's homecoming. Dan dutifully removed his boots in the mudroom as though he intended to stay, or, as though he'd never left.

Noor set the groceries on the kitchen counter and squatted before the woodstove in the living room. She opened the damper and wedged in a few more logs. The fire had burned down to coals while she was teaching. It would take a while for it to catch.

"Wood holding up?" Dan asked.

"It's only January, Dan. You know how much wood we stacked. What do you want?"

"Mindy terminated," he said.

For a moment Noor thought he meant Mindy had kicked him out. She realized what he meant a second before he added "The pregnancy."

Noor unzipped her insulated coverall, kicked her way out of it, and sat down in an armchair. It was chilly in the room. "Why?" she asked. "Your baby-mama change her mind?"

"Noor, please, I know you're mad. The amnio showed the baby had Down's Syndrome. Mindy already has two kids in college and didn't want to take on that responsibility. Which is understandable . . ." he faded off. "She's in Saint Croix now. Maybe for the winter. She asked me to go with her for a few months but I couldn't. You know, work. But I didn't want to." Dan was still standing in the doorway, hands at his sides, looking pitiful.

What was Noor supposed to say? Sorry your little dream life went sour? Why was he telling her all this? Was she supposed to comfort the man who'd cheated on her and left? "I can't really picture you with a developmentally disabled kid, Dan. You never had much patience for my clients."

"I would have taken *any* baby," Dan said. Then his voice dropped. "Noor. I'm really sorry. I fucked up big time."

"Yeah," Noor said. "You did. I see you're not wearing your wedding ring," she said, flashing her own. She didn't want him to think she wore it because she was pining for him, but she also didn't want him to know she wore it to stave off other men's advances. She wasn't going to ask him to sit down, offer him tea, make him any less uncomfortable than he appeared.

Dan took the seat she didn't offer him and glanced at his bare ring finger, then at her. "I miss you Noor."

She turned away from his pale earnest eyes. "You want me to feel sorry for you because you lost your baby? Okay, I do. That's a terrible thing. But you walked out on eight years of marriage. Listen, I've got to put those groceries away." Noor strode into the kitchen and started tossing groceries onto the counter. A quart container of pricey Greek yoghurt slid off the counter and exploded on the floor, splashing her fleece-lined jeans and her wool socks with white goo.

Dan appeared at the kitchen threshold. "Let me help you," he said.

"I don't . . . Please Dan, just go. I can't handle this right now."

Dan stared at the mess on the floor. "Can I come back some other time?" he asked.

"I don't know . . . Dan, I've got to clean up. Just go, okay?"

She stacked six soup cans on a high shelf, and when she turned around Dan was gone. Noor slid to the floor, just missing the cracked container. After two months she'd gotten—if not used to the idea of Dan being gone, or of Dan having a baby with Mindy, at least used to living alone, and now he was back, asking her forgiveness, perhaps asking to come home. It wasn't fair. And it wasn't fair about him losing another child . . . Did she want him back? Her ego said no way. He'd humiliated her, betrayed her. He'd acted like a total sneak but then, so had she, and he was still Dan. Her head hurt. She felt like she was getting a migraine though she'd never had one before.

"Jiyah, come here," Noor called, then rested her face in the old dog's fur while Jiyah lapped up the spilled yoghurt.

CHAPTER SIXTEEN

Jaycee, 2011

"Frank stepped forward and laid his hand on the exposed engine. *"Joe, it's still warm,"* he said. *"The accident occurred a short while ago. Now keep Smuff here and keep out of trouble ourselves."*

"I'd rather keep Muff here than Smuff here," said Gerry, putting his hand on Jaycee's own engine, which was still purring, although she'd already pulled back up her fishnet pantyhose. Gerry kept the whole dog-eared Hardy Boys series on a low shelf in his bedroom, saved from when he was a kid, and he had been reading aloud to her from his favorite, *The Tower Treasure*. "Sonia Sotomayor is a Supreme Court Justice because she read Nancy Drew when she was a girl. I'm a snowplower 'cause I read Hardy Boys. Ahh, the power of literature," he said, pulling at the waistband of the pantyhose until Jaycee said, "Tonight. Not now. You can't always get what you need."

"Want," he said.

"Want," she repeated. He was teaching her songs.

"Want what? Go on."

"You can't always eat what you get but you can eat what you need if you try. Just kidding," she said, biting his shoulder. Jaycee had worn her blue jean mini-skirt from last night's pre-Valentine's Day celebration, the whole time they were in bed, and Gerry's obvious enthusiasm for the scant, fringed hem didn't hide the other kind of enthusiasm he clearly had for Jaycee. He liked her. He even seemed . . . Jaycee hunted for a word . . . if not yet totally smitten, serious. Jaycee was smitten *and* serious, and to protect herself from being wrong about his affection for her, she regarded it as if it were one of several admirable surprises about him, like his expert reading aloud ability, which, she had to admit, wasn't the sort of skill you'd expect of him. He read smoothly and with clarity amid bursts of perfectly modulated drama . . . much the way he made love.

"Oh wait a minute, my TracFone is ringing."

"Go for it honey," Gerry said, reaching for his pack of cigarettes. "Now that I know it turns you on so much, I'll call you every day."

She squatted over her boiled wool tote bag and fumbled for the phone. It was Frida saying she was travelling for a few days, visiting family outside Lima before flying to Miami.

"Oh good," Jaycee said. "We'll be on our way soon to meet you there in Miami then, me and Noor. See you soon then! Bye!"

"Mira!" said Frida. "I decided not to mail your candlesticks and platters because the mail in Peru is not reliable. I put them in my suitcase. They're heavy but that's good for my exercise. See you in Miami."

Then she hung up, leaving Jaycee with nothing to do but tell Gerry about it.

"So your naive friend," said Gerry. "This trusting lady you like so much, who has a son and a husband and a good job, is on her merry way to the drug sniffing capital of the world with two pounds of your coke in her suitcase. Call her back. Tell her to get her bag back and get outta Dodge. If nothing else she might think twice next time someone asks her to smuggle crafts, poor chump. She shoulda known better than to carry who knows what hand-made recreationals through customs."

"It's more like three pounds, not two," Jaycee said, "And I made it through Newark with the coke in a cheese without a problem."

"You're white with a US passport. She's not. Besides, that was Newark."

"Yeah but she goes through Miami all the time," Jaycee said. "They probably know her by name there." Still, he was right. Frida didn't have a clue what she was maybe walking into, but when Jaycee called her back, the connectivity was gone, as it was likely to remain, given that her relatives lived up in the mountains. Blinking back sudden tears, not about Frida so much, she had to admit, but in response to Gerry's drubbing, she dug in her tote again for the nugget of coke she'd hidden before coming over here. She scraped it with a fingernail, then held it out—a gift—to Gerry.

"Hey, how much of that stuff you been doing? No wonder I get tingly every time I kiss you," said Gerry, regarding Jaycee with a wary dismay, the Hardy Boys novel falling closed on the page. "What is it with women these days?" he wondered. "Every time I think I know someone I find out I don't. Can you do me a favor? Be careful, okay? I mean, once in a while for a little fun is fine, but I know lots of people who got into trouble with the stuff."

"I don't do it much. I'm the girl who never even drank coffee, just chamomile tea, until she was practically thirty already. And maybe you shouldn't think you know someone you just met. I hardly know my own father and mother," Jaycee said. She had finally put her dad into a nursing home, and Hil's partner, Jeff Parmenter, was on his way to indictment for fraud. Hannah, whose claims to have been in the dark about everything had the unfortunate consequence of making her appear stupid to other people, spent a lot of time talking smartly about plans either to sell Hillwinds, declare bankruptcy, pay the delinquent taxes, or maintain a lawyer, whichever Jaycee could manage. But the way Jaycee saw it, her life was her own now, period. At last she was out from under the thumbs that had been keeping her down, and it occurred to her now that no matter how smitten she was with Gerry, she wasn't about to let him control her. She told him that. It made her sad to declare her independence from him but there was more future for the two of them together if they were sometimes apart, and she told him that too.

"What song's that?" he said.

Jaycee grinned. She carried a couple of plates to the kitchen, wolfed down a slice of pizza in compensation for the coke she'd have to wait to enjoy, then rinsed the plates. Here was another surprise about Gerry; there were no dirty dishes in the sink. Then she put on her coat, stuffing her blouse in the pocket but leaving her bra on the floor for him not to forget her. When she was at the door he said, "Wait a minute, Jaycee. I didn't say that like I wanted about the coke. What I should say is I hope you don't need to keep doing that shit. I'm not bossing you around. I should, but I ain't. But be careful, okay? Keep your wits about you. Especially on this thing to Miami. You and Noor. If you can't warn off your friend before she shows up at customs at least look out for yourself."

"Okay," said Jaycee. "Thank you for saying that, Gerry. Happy Valentine's Day."

"You too. Happy heart day," Gerry said.

Jaycee stood a minute in the open door, her head smarting already with cold from the landing and from the notion that Frida was a chump. *Her* chump. Her and Noor's. Some kid outside had been yelling all morning at his plastic sled for it failing to slide down the mountain of plowed snow that marked the far edge of the parking lot—"You suck!" the kid shouted—and now he might have been shouting at her and Noor.

"I was thinking, Ger," Jaycee said, to take her mind off Frida. "Would you look after my mom when I'm on my trip? Would you be able to stop over there a couple of times and make sure she's eating properly, like not just cookies?" Another kid joined the one playing outside; there were whoops of derision and then success.

"No cookies. Done. Say please and I'll do anything," said Gerry.

"Hey that should be a line from a song," said Jaycee.

CHAPTER SEVENTEEN

Hannah, 2011

True, there was the problem of *A Cool Drink of Water*—the fact Hil didn't write it.

Plus, there was the thing about her drawings and paintings— they were better than Hil's prose warranted.

But these issues, Hannah wondered, with some difficulty wheeling her chair down the hall to their bedroom, where she had a death errand, that is, a task that had to do with preparing for death so when it came she wouldn't wail or flap or panic but would "die with abandon" like when she was a Womb-Bat and the troupe had been required to die while dancing—did these issues of Hilary's, she wondered, make him a fool? Or did they make *her* the fool?

Hil had been a decent father to Jaycee, not *there* enough, but too pushy by far so it was good he wasn't there enough, and as for being a husband, except for pairing his not-so-compelling stories with Hannah's remarkable paintings, he'd never taken from her anything she had no wish to give, nor given to her anything she had no wish to take. Hannah's frontispiece for *Tossed Sallet and Pinched Goosefoot* might have garnered a Caldecott Honor Prize had Hil's dialogue been not so prim and old-fashioned, but as he liked to point out, he had never faulted *her* for not winning that prize. Plus he wasn't a disaster in bed except for his eyes in the tilt of the floor mirror, watching himself instead of her, like when he ate what Hannah cooked there was always *Hil eating* but never *Hannah's food*, never "It's good, Hannah, thanks," but just Hil chewing over his thoughts, and later, his non-thoughts. The pointed farmer's hat he favored made him look like a fool, but it also made him lovable, at least to Hannah, the way, as a girl, she chose the most hopeless boys to have crushes on, like the boy who polished his apple by rubbing it so vigorously against his pant leg that his hair stood up when he took a bite of it, and the boy who fell into fits of hysterical laughter at the sight of his own boogers.

Still, why was it always the writer who rushed off to get famous when the illustrator stayed home at the kitchen table to school the child? Hil's fame laid claim to *her* pictures. It claimed her rabbits, her minks, her barns, her loons, her deer, her persimmons, her woodstoves, her chimneys, her wisps, her wasps, her clouds, her plows, her looms, her hearths, her children, their braids, their brightness, her rain, her storms, her goats, her pies, her soups, her moons, rooftops, horses and wagons. Now that Jaycee had put him in the nursing home in Waterbury, saying it was too hard for her and Hannah to keep him safe anymore, and the world safe from him, Hannah supposed she could just paint whatever she wanted if only she knew what she wanted to paint, but this wasn't what was really bothering her either, she realized, as she wheeled herself over the bedroom threshold to complete her errand. As if it knew what she was after, the armoire stood waiting, like a coffin only upright.

She hadn't thought about the lock, so long had it been since she had put on jewelry, but she found the key at once in the aspirin pouch she kept hidden in her cleavage, although for cramps and other ailments they used lineaments, vapors, unguents, powders, mustards, poultices, tinctures, and teas. The key was smaller than a cricket, and when she dropped it, instead of falling to the floor it jumped backwards into her sleeve. Inside the armoire lay the mothy scrap of newsprint she was looking for, and all the worn velvet chambers containing wearable trinkets (you couldn't call them jewelry) for which Hannah had sentiments, since Hil had bought them for her and Jaycee had used to help with the fasteners. Jaycee wigging out on her filial duties by sticking Hil in a nursing home in Waterbury wasn't what was bothering Hannah, either, but that she couldn't get the Buick out of her mind, nor the dents in Pauline, after all these years of not thinking of them in order to keep Jaycee from knowing. And now Jaycee knew, but from the look on her face when Jeff opened his mouth, she wasn't exactly shocked by the news, only freshly, more vigorously sorrowful, her sadness turning to anger.

Kansas City, Missouri (Kansas City/AP), Penny Wise and Not So Foolish, Hannah read, having pulled the mothy clipping from inside the armoire and not needing her glasses to see it:

> *In Kansas City on Thursday a six-year-old boy became a wealthy man after the penny he found in a souvenir coin-in-a-bottle sold at auction for $250,000. The lucky little boy broke the tiny bottle with a hammer because, he says, he wanted a penny for his new piggy bank. His mother recognized that the penny was unusual because of the date and the chain of linked rings decorating one side and the image of Lady Liberty on the other, but, she said, "I never imagined it would pay for Mikey's entire college education!"*
>
> *The penny was minted in Philadelphia in 1793, the first year the US minted its own coins. Similar coins from other years are not nearly so uncommon. The mystery remains how such an extremely rare and valuable coin ended up in a souvenir penny bottle bearing the stenciled words "A penny for your thoughts."*

Hannah folded the little story back up, regretting it instantly because the seams were so worn they were practically disintegrating, and reached behind an old charm bracelet for the box with the slot where a ring would have gone, except instead of a ring was a penny. Hannah pulled the coin free, looking first at the worn-off circle of links, and then flipping it over to regard Lady Liberty, her high forehead a blur but the aquiline nose and combed-back tresses still lovely to look at. The date was 1793, same as the setting for Hil's *Lost Loon.* Because the loon in that story was supposed to be lost,

Hannah had included no loon in her pictures for that book, only an absence from pond and sky showing several whirling echoes of faintly brushed, birdlike, lunatic motion. Hil's editor baulked, and Hil, brandishing the letter, had stood over Hannah until she relented and drew in the bird. It was the worst thing he'd done to her, even worse than never quite telling her outright about the money he stole from their investors. Hannah had learned of the fraud on her own by sorting the mail and then played dumb so long she only felt stupid. The penny had belonged to the girl, Nancy White, who died later on from bone cancer. It was taped to the corner of her parents' first investment check, the single cent the dying girl's one proud contribution to what was to be hopefully her own college savings. Hannah had removed it from the corner of the check and replaced it with a usual penny showing Abraham Lincoln.

"Would you like to go to Waterbury later on?" Gerry startled her by asking from the bedroom doorway, causing her to drop the penny into her sleeve. Not wanting to put it back in its box while Gerry was watching, she tipped the coin into the cinched open aspirin pouch that she wore around her neck, and followed him out to the table for one of his expertly grilled cheese sandwiches. He stood brandishing the plastic spatula he insisted on bringing over to cook with instead of using their rusty old cooking tools. He never buttoned or rolled up his shirt cuffs, she'd noticed, as if he liked to risk them catching on fire. By Waterbury, he meant should they visit the nursing home, and after lunch they drove out there, even though Hil might embarrass her again by ordering the most buxom of the nursing aides to get down on her knees and spit-polish his shoes.

Hil was the only resident who appeared to be awake in the TV room, but even after Hannah said "Hello, dear" he refused to turn his head away from Raymond Burr demanding justice in an old episode of "Ironside." Only when Gerry wheeled her right in front of him did Hil look at Hannah coldly and announce, "She's blocking my view. Off with her head."

"Who are you, the Red Queen?" Hannah asked.

But Hil only lapsed into one his trances. His eyes turned to fog and his mouth hung open. Words sloughed out, but they made no sense. The only sense he had left was to stay upright in his chair.

"How 'bout we cut our losses and stop at Dunkin' Donuts to pick up some of those munchkins things you been wanting," Gerry asked Hannah.

Hannah said yes, knowing Gerry would buy. He always did.

"Oh shoot do you have a penny?" Gerry asked at the drive-through where they were buying the munchkins, and when she opened the aspirin pouch, there one was.

"Here," she said, beaming.

CHAPTER EIGHTEEN

Hilary Emory, 1982

En route to a reading in Rhinebeck, New York in early December—still snowless here though at home they already had half a foot—Hil bought himself a tuna sandwich and corn chowder at a diner on the Taconic Parkway. He had just turned forty, and though he'd never much used to enjoy driving, he had found, over the last few weeks of new book-related travel, that the solitary time behind the wheel of the beige Buick, an unobtrusive car bought to replace the dying station wagon in hopes that it wouldn't attract thieves when they still lived in New York City—was one of the unexpected perks of success. He enjoyed the bucolic Parkway, with its forested margins and distant fields, which he had chosen because it was neither the shortest nor longest route, and he drove smoothly but carefully, peering for deer crossing the peculiarly pale pavement. He'd seen a few does with their oversized ears but none, thankfully, had come past the edge of the woods. There were so many more deer in Dutchess County than in central Vermont, where Hil now lived with Jacqueline Charlotte and Hannah, because more of Vermont was still open to pasture and hayfield while Dutchess County had reforested. Of course Vermont wasn't anywhere near as open as it had been in the eighteen-fifties, the setting of his troublesome sequel-in-progress about the Northrups of East Montpelier, Vermont, the family that had taken in the runaway slave, Bitty, in *A Cool Drink of Water*. Despite being darker complected, Bitty was just one of the Northrup girls now, sharing in the haying and sugaring, gardening and milking, baking, washing, carding and spinning. Period drawings and later photographs showed the land skinned clean of forest, except on the rockiest ridges, and the bare pastures were crisscrossed with stone walls like in rural Ireland or fondly remembered Yorkshire, where Hil and Hannah had spent their honeymoon.

Off the highway and wending through towns lit with Christmas-y electric candles in the windows, ribbonned wreaths and strands of colored lights, Hil noticed the squat second story windows on the old houses of Dutchess County, so different from the symmetrical window arrangements on New England colonials. The Northrup family lived in a flat-fronted colonial with an ell and an attached barn. Hil had always liked those severe, flat-fronted colonials, perhaps, he'd told Jeff Parmenter, because he'd had a severe, flat-fronted mother.

In Rhinebeck, a village catering to the whims and needs of New York City second-homers where Hil hoped to cash in on the brisk Christmas trade for children's books, he parked in the rear of a lot behind the row of brick-and-frame storefronts, as far from the bookstore's back exit as possible to avoid being caught up in unnecessary post-reading chats with customers or store staff. Experience had taught him a clean getaway was best and he still had another hour-and-a-half drive down to Nyack for tomorrow's reading or, as he preferred to think of it, tomorrow's *appearance*.

He spent half an hour window shopping to avoid pre-reading conversation with the bookstore employees. Once he stepped inside the bookstore he'd assume the mantle of the kindly children's author, but not a minute before. The Christmas displays of pricey fur-lined boots and expensive kitchen gadgets laid out on sparkly fake snow annoyed him. There was nothing here he'd want to buy for Hannah or Jacqueline Charlotte, not even a hand-cranked ice cream maker; nothing reminiscent of the richly laborious lives of the Northrup family. Okay, he didn't expect Jacqueline Charlotte and Hannah to make soap from lye and potash—though why not, now that he considered it? They could sell it with the books, attached to the covers with calico ribbons. It pleased him to think that Jacqueline Charlotte wouldn't ever have to choose to remove herself from the world in which he and Hannah had been raised. They could keep her pure; pure enough that when she was interviewed as the daughter of the author of the Hil's Books—say, when he was dead—she would refer to him as Papa and tell stories of how he had treated her episode of infant whooping cough with two spoonfuls every three hours of boiled Hysop, horse-heal (an herb, she would titter, when the interviewer mistook horse-heal for horse heel), and brown sugar. Shuddering, Hil turned away from a store devoted to bath luxuries and expensive lingerie. He now liked his women in cleanly starched muslin, the scorch marks of irons vaguely sepia-toned, like on the Shroud of Turin.

The poster on the storefront glass of Chaucer Books announcing his reading from *A Cool Drink of Water* showed a fair likeness, Hil thought. Distinguished mid-life children's author—kindly and approachable.

The poster duly advertised the fact that *A Cool Drink of Water* was a *New York Times* best-selling children's book. He hoped for a Newbery medal but at least the book had done well enough for Scholastic to send him on this tour, thanks to Jeff Parmenter who raced it through production to be ready in time for Christmas. Parmenter was getting testy about the sequel, which was overdue. The trouble was, Hil hadn't realized how hard a sequel would be to write without someone else's draft to adapt, or *inspire* it, as Hil preferred to think of it. Unfortunately, Bitty's just being one of the Northrup family wasn't very dramatic. He was struggling to invent complications, though so far all he'd come up with was a punishing flood and a bout of, yes, whooping cough. Thank god Hannah listened to his good ideas, since really she was just putting on paper the very pictures that had already taken shape in Hil's mind, the pictures Hil would make if his hand weren't shaky. She channeled them, Hannah. She had a talent for that, for getting his pictures out of his head in all the right lines and colors.

Inside the bookstore, wooden racks bedecked with tinsel displayed hardback best-sellers—*Gorky Park*, *Rabbit is Rich*, *Hotel New Hampshire*, Steven King's drooling *Cujo* and Toni Morrison's *Tar Baby*, as well as paperback literature from Austen to Zola, racks of note cards, coffee table photography books of the Catskills and Adirondacks. In the midst of it all stood a podium and folding chairs, a table piled high with copies of *A Cool Drink of Water*. He couldn't help but be proud of the gleaming cover with the painting of water spilling past the lip of the tin dipper, and all the dark and light faces reflected in the spilling water and filling the dipper above. The actual drinking gourd of the original title would not have worked; children wouldn't connect with gourds. The tin dipper was much better. A stroke not of genius, he thought modestly, but of insight and restraint. He had brought a tin dipper with him, in fact, as he did to all of his appearances, to be filled with water and drunk from by the children, passed mouth to mouth, like communion. He pulled it out of his jacket pocket and placed it on top of the stack of books, then continued his perusing.

The children's section was crowded with plush toys, cheery posters, and gleaming picture and chapter books. Hil waited to be recognized by his hosts while peering coolly at the competition through the gummy itch of his contact lenses. The previous year's Newbery medal had gone to a New England girl's journal from 1830, which might hurt Hil's chances this year. They probably wouldn't pick two New England nineteenth century heroines (damn, he should have left Bitty a boy after all) two years in a row, even though last year's winner lacked the drama or social relevance of *A Cool Drink of Water*. This could be a problem for the sequel as well. What a shame he hadn't been able to get *Cool Drink* out in 1981, when an escaped slave surely would have trumped a motherless girl from New Hampshire.

Well, he wouldn't be writing about slaves anymore. He'd had to become knowledgeable about the underground railroad so as to answer any questions raised by audience members, interviewers and table mates at awards banquets. The kids were the worst—"Mr. Emory, what did Bitty use for toilet paper?" one of them wanted to know. What a load of giggling commenced when he answered corn cobs. Although wouldn't the husks have made more sense? Come to think of it he wouldn't be averse to requiring that his family use husks themselves, though not the visiting tourists once his idea of the theme park got underway, for which there'd be a bathroom, he had to concede, and a septic system.

"Mr. Emory!"

"Yes," he said, turning to see an eager bespectacled woman in a denim wrap skirt and nubbly ochre sweater beaming at him. He assembled his professionally benevolent smile and said, "You must be Connie?"

"Oh, no, Connie had a family emergency. I'm Nita, second in command. I'm so excited to meet you. I wish my daughters could come tonight, they just love your book, but they're with their father alternate weeks . . ." She blushed, flustered to admit to her divorce. "Would you like a tea or coffee? May I take your coat? We have another fifteen minutes. I was getting worried. I mean, I knew you'd show up but still—look, the seats are already filling up."

"No tea, thanks but could I trouble you for a cup of water to fill this little tin dipper?"

"Oh, no trouble. I'll be sure to make it cool."

"Excuse me?"

"You know, a cool drink of water . . ." Nita flushed at her lame joke.

"Ah, yes, ha ha." His laugh sounded fake even to him. "But if we could fill this tin dipper . . ."

"Well certainly. I'll put a cup of water right next to the stack. I won't bother you; you probably need a moment to compose yourself after your long drive. Do you have a new book in the works, by the way? We do like to know," she said, at which he told her of the sequel to *A Cool Drink of Water*, a book this time with pictures "owing to my wife's skills with pen and ink and watercolors," he boasted to the blushing Nita, in order to cover up the fact that he'd stalled in the writing of the sequel.

"Oh yes, I've read that she had never had an art class! Maybe you can talk about that a little," Nita said.

Hil bowed his head in mute concurrence.

When the reading was finished—he'd chosen the dramatic scene in which Bitty was hidden in a flour sack in the root cellar to escape the bounty hunter—and he'd answered a few of the usual questions, Hil signed books for the twenty or so librarians, teachers, mothers and kids who stood in line across the table, their coats draped over their arms, their scarves wrapped around their necks, the younger kids with their mittens clipped to their sleeves. He signed with a fountain pen—a quill would have been better—note to Hannah, find him a goose quill pen. Each buyer got a moment of eye contact, a thank you, and the question—would you like me to inscribe it to anyone in particular?

A few shy types just wanted his signature, but a well-groomed, sixtyish matron in a pearl gray twin set—long sleeve sweater with matching sleeveless shell underneath—a style Hil remembered fondly from the girlfriends of his youth—leaned forward over the table. Hil caught a surprising whiff of alcohol on her breath.

The woman hesitated. She seemed to be studying him and so Hil, growing impatient, studied her in return. Her hair was dyed a too-youthful russet, but the pearls around her throat looked genuine. Her pleasantly even features were marred by twin marionette lines bracketing her mouth. Probably quite pretty in her day.

"You can make it out to John. John Corgi," she said.

Hil stiffened, unnoticeably he hoped, then forced himself to smile while not quite meeting her eyes. "How is that spelled?"

"You know. Like the dog?"

"Certainly." Hil inadvertently pressed too hard on his fountain pen nib, splooging a stain of black ink onto the pristine title page of *A Cool Drink of Water*. John Corgi. It was a name he barely thought of, a name he had hoped so fervently never to hear again that he had nearly forgotten it. It had to be a coincidence. What would this well-dressed if out-of-date matron with a string of pearls know of a depressed Vietnam vet who'd shot his brains out in the shower stall of a flophouse in New Jersey? Hil pushed the signed book back to her, forcing himself to meet her eyes. They were as gray as her sweater set and unnervingly fixed on him. She was drunk, he thought, but whether to find this comforting or foreboding, or maybe even enviable, he couldn't decide.

"You'll want to hold that page open for a few minutes to let the ink dry," he advised. "Next?" he said, pointedly smiling at the line behind her and stopping himself from fussing with his contact lenses. The woman lingered half a moment longer before giving way to a black girl of about ten years old who'd asked him, in the Q & A after his reading, why he'd written about a slave girl when he was white. He'd gone on with the usual bit about the power of imagination and how all historical fiction involved writing outside your own experience. He watched the gray twin set lady heading for the door.

"Make it out to Meleesha, that's M-E-L-E-E-sha," the child instructed.

Hil looked over Meleesha's head to see Mrs. Twin Set slipping out the door. Forget about her, Hil instructed himself. Just a coincidence, an aberration.

"Here you go, Meleesha," he said heartily. "I hope you enjoy the book." Ridiculous names these people saddled their kids with. He caught the cold engine sounds of a few cars leaving the parking lot, one of them, he hoped, carrying away Mrs. Twin Set.

After the small talk—"That went well, don't you think?"—Nita and the other employees began folding chairs and Hil headed for the rear door, feeling, as always, a little queasy about not staying behind to help the little coven of well-meaning, dull women who always hosted his appearances. A brisk wind had picked up. Hil drew on his leather gloves and wrapped his itchy beige scarf—knitted by Hannah with homespun yarn, her first attempt at a Vermont handicraft—around his neck. He winced at the thought of his cold car and slipped out. Lights were off or low in the other stores that shared the lot—9:05 being past bedtime for Rhinebeck on a winter Wednesday night, apparently.

Just as Hil started across the nearly empty lot someone appeared at his side. He spun his head to see the twin set woman falling into step beside him. Oh shit, he intoned silently, shit shit shit shit shit. She must have flattened herself against the brick building so he would neither see nor hear her coming. What was she wearing, moccasins? Pearl gray to match her outfit? She was wearing no coat. She must be frozen, he thought, or just cold blooded.

"You didn't think you could get away with it that easily, did you?" she said.

"I'm sorry, I don't know what you're talking about," Hil replied.

"I think you do." Her voice was polite, modulated, educated even.

"You're mistaken, Madam. Oh dear, I seem to have left my fountain pen on the table," Hil attempted, but when he veered as if to make his way back inside she took hold of his elbow with a Doberman Pincer grip. Soon they had crossed the lot, lit by one streetlamp in the far corner and one light on the bookstore's rear exit. Next to Hil's Buick, a pale elderly Cadillac, replete with double shark fins, listed to one side. Why would anyone park beside the only other car in the lot? But of course, she'd recognized his Vermont plates.

"I want you to acknowledge you stole my son's book," the woman said. "Publicly. I want my John to get his due."

Well that would be hard, considering John Corgi's brains went into the sewer system several years ago. And how could Corgi be her son? Corgi was black, impoverished, desperate. How could this suburbanite be his mother?

"I really don't know what you're talking about. And if you'll excuse me now, I really do need to be on my way." Hil drew out the car key, turned his back on his inquisitor, and bent to unlock the Buick. It was then she pushed something hard into his back. This matron couldn't have pulled a gun on him, could she? It was too ridiculous, too unreal, too network television. (Hil and Hannah allowed themselves only public television and Jacqueline Charlotte wasn't and wouldn't be allowed any TV at all.) Hil froze, nevertheless. It felt like a gun. Would she use it with the same amount of self-possession she'd probably shown when she'd put on her pearls that morning?

"I'm sorry," she said, "sorry it has to come to this, but you've given me no other option. You're going to get in my car and we're going to go for a little ride."

Run for it, Hil told himself, but Hil found himself fighting with the sprung passenger door of the old Caddy, then sliding onto the torn front seat while Mrs. Corgi, keeping the pistol trained on him, slid in behind the wheel. Hil looked longingly at the back of the bookstore, hoping for Nita to come to his rescue. His captor switched the gun to her left hand but still pointed it his way, while turning the key expertly with her right. The car coughed, ground, coughed—giving Hil a moment's hope while she tapped the accelerator—then turned over and roared its V-8 might. She fiddled with the steering column shifter, put the car into reverse, and, without looking over her shoulder switched the gun to her right hand and backed out of the space. "Thank god for automatic transmissions," she said as if making cocktail party chatter, though she was about to drive him off to god knew what fate.

"My husband so wanted a manual but I refused to learn how to use a clutch. It would be quite impossible to do all this and shift gears as well," she said as they rolled out of the lot, past the quiet Rhinebeck shops, onto Route 308 east.

"Where are you taking me?" Hil asked, watching his breath turn to an icy scrim on the passenger window. He automatically reached for the seatbelt and found none. Not that an abductee should put on a seatbelt, probably.

"Oh, it will be a surprise. Do you like surprises Mr. Emory?"

"Not really."

"Well, I'm afraid you gave me quite a surprise too."

She turned left onto Route 9 North. He must keep watch, he told himself, he must keep track of where she was taking him so he could find his way back if he got the chance. Another left and signs for Northern Dutchess County Hospital appeared. They were headed west now, their combined breaths fogging the windshield, enclosing them in creepy intimacy.

"Do you have a heater in this decrepit rig?" Hil asked, shivering.

"Now, now Mr. Emory. No need to be insulting. Haven't you done enough to hurt me already?"

"Done what? I've done nothing. Surely you're making a mistake." He ran scenarios through his mind—knock the gun out of her hand. She wasn't a large woman. He could overpower her. But he remained hunched in his seat watching the bare trees slide by. How quickly the town gave way to countryside—fields, fences, barns, silos. How easily he reconciled himself to what might happen. Because it would happen. And frankly, he deserved it.

"I'm quite sure I'm not mistaken, Mr. Emory. I know you stole my son's book because I have a copy of John's original manuscript right here."

"How do you know that he didn't steal *my* book, then?" Hil asked. He couldn't keep from swinging his head around to see the manila envelope on the back seat. But what could she prove? He'd been careful to change enough that only the broad outlines of the original story remained. Though, and he hated to admit it, the language, too, was John Corgi's, but that had been out of respect, Hil thought. Hil's short-lived reputation would be ruined. He'd get an obit in the *Times*, after all, and be written up as the editor that stole the story from the Vietnam vet suicide. Hil wouldn't even get a job as a copy editor after this. What could he do in Vermont, teach high school? Toss hay bales? Join the salesgirl who taped her couplets—*Don't neglect to fill the bath, for birds not wet are birds of wrath*—to the cash register at the feed store? And what would he tell Hannah, who had backhandedly complimented him by saying, when she'd read Hil's version of Corgi's manuscript in bed one evening, Hil's name typed modestly on the title page, "I wouldn't have guessed in a million years I had married a man with this kind of talent, Hilary. I wouldn't even have bet a nickel on it." Then she'd reached for him under the sheets, something she'd rarely done since Jaycee was born.

"It's all I have left of him," Mrs. Corgi was saying. "That and this gun. The police released it to me after they ruled John's death a suicide. A morbid memento perhaps, but handy. Don't think I won't use it if I need to Mr. Emory. You know why? Because I have nothing left to lose. I've lost my son, my husband, and soon I'll lose my house. *I'm* not getting any royalties, you know. Do you know what grief feels like, Mr. Emory? Do you know how a mother feels when her only child enlists for Vietnam? Do you know the worry, the terror? Every time the phone rings, every time there's a knock on the door. And then to have him come back a different man than when he left, a ruined man? He shot himself in the head with this gun Mr. Emory, but I suppose you already know that. You stole his book when he sent it to you to publish it and then you refused it and then he killed himself. With this gun," she repeated, tilting the muzzle in the direction of Hil's hat. "You probably told him his writing wasn't up to your lofty standards. You told him how sorry you were that he'd probably have to wash dishes instead for the rest of his life. You broke my son's heart, Mr. Emory. You broke my son's spirit."

No—I never refused it! Hilary nearly said, but he caught himself in time to say, "I'm very sorry to hear about your son's suicide, but I had nothing to do with it." Another road sign slid past. Montgomery Street. "Your grief has confused you," Hil added, hoping to make points here with sympathy. He almost did feel sorry for her. Her son was dead. And Hil hadn't refused the book at all. He'd loved it from the start. He would have bought it if John Corgi had only waited a few days before bringing his gun into that shower.

"Don't you dare tell me I'm confused," she hissed. The car swerved, knocking Hil uncomfortably against the door. "Don't you tell me what I feel or what I am. I had enough of that in my marriage. And when he was a teenager John started in, he said I couldn't understand him because I was white and he was a black man. Can you imagine what that feels like, Mr. Emory, to have your own child reject you, the child you carried in your womb—reject you because of the color of your skin? He was such a sweet, sweet boy until he grew that Afro, Mr. Emory. It wasn't easy for him. We lived in a suburb and he was the only dark-skinned child; other kids were mean sometimes. His stepfather wasn't beyond a nasty joke or two at John's expense. But *I* always, always loved him. And the thing is—I know he was getting ready to reconcile."

"What are you talking about?"

"Because Henry . . ."

"Who is Henry?" Hil interrupted. They'd traveled several miles and now they were climbing on some small road, passing a long entrance to a compound of some sort—Hil recognized it as the road to the turn-of-the-century Beaux Artes Astor mansion, Ferncliff. What the hell was she doing headed up there? He twisted his gloved hands anxiously.

"Henry? Don't you remember Henry, Mr. Emory? That was John's character, the little slave boy, before you changed him to Bitty. Anyway, Henry gets taken in by the family in upstate New York. He's rescued by *white* people. Don't you see? That's surely a sign that John had overcome his feelings about not being able to connect to me because he was black. If Henry had been rescued by black people then I'd know John was still upset with me for being white. Don't you see? But since his rescuers were white it meant he was ready to reconcile."

She was insane. That wasn't how it was at all. Insane with rage and grief. Insane and probably drunk. Her booze breath had intensified in the confines of the old Cadillac. Did he have the guts to flip the door handle and roll out the door? But she was going too fast, even on this dark Ferncliff drive. What would happen if he rolled out of a car at forty miles an hour? And couldn't she stop and shoot him while he was lying on the road?

"My husband wasn't John's father. John's father was a lovely young man . . . well, that's better left in the past, Mr. Emory. Just a chance occurrence, one of those things one does in youth . . . Let's just say that my husband was never much of a stepfather to John."

"Please drive me back to my car Mrs. Corgi. Please let me go. I'm very sorry for your suffering but I've played no part in any of it." Hil wondered fearfully if that was the best tack, the most likely path to her releasing him unharmed. Maybe he should admit his part with a little tweaking? Tell her that he had in fact received and read John's book, put it aside, forgotten about it and months later written his own book without realizing that John had been his muse? No, she'd probably just be angrier that he had "forgotten" her lost son's work. Better to maintain a claim of innocence, as he'd claimed innocence when accused of plagiarizing the paper about Frederick Jackson Turner's "Frontier Hypothesis" in college. Although really he hadn't plagiarized that paper, just paid a smarter friend to do his research and write a basic draft. Lawsuits were expensive—it wasn't likely that this woman who was losing her house and drove a twenty-year-old wreck would have the money to fight him. Better to maintain his innocence and try for sympathy. "I have a wife and a child of my own, Mrs. Corgi. They'd be devastated if anything happened to me, just as you're devastated by the loss of your son."

"Oh, no," she said. "You stole it then you plagiarized it then you killed him and we're going to finish this off. We're going to get things straight. I read his book. I was looking for something of him in it. It's all I have left of John. But then I heard the radio, I always listen to NPR, that program with the librarians recommending Christmas gift books, and I heard them talking and I just knew it was John's book. You made a few little changes but it was *John's* book. And John never made a penny from it. John never got on the radio. Can you imagine how different his life might have turned out if he'd been the one celebrated, if he was the one going to bookstores and reading his book to teachers and librarians? He might have met a nice girl, settled down, bought himself a house, given me grandchildren. I'm sure the money you've earned from the book bought you quite a nice little hideaway in Vermont for your wife and daughter, didn't it? I read about that. Yes, it must be nice to have money."

"Is it money you want?" Hil asked with an uprush of hope—he could buy her off. It would be hard explaining to Hannah where the money went, but he'd manage. He'd tell her Jeff Parmenter was in a jam and needed cash. "I can help you out. If you drive me to a cash machine I can . . ."

"Oh, I could use money . . . My car needs a new transmission, and I'm behind in my mortgage payment, they're taking my house, you know, they've taken everything—*you've* taken everything from me, except for my pride and my determination. I'm a very determined woman, Mr. Emory—but you can't buy me off with John's blood money. No."

The car was slowing. Now, he told himself, now jump out. But he sat there, too panicked to move. Clouds had parted and a half moon punctured the sky. The gummier of the contact lenses appeared to have fallen out. He could see okay, but just with one eye. She pulled to a stop. Through the dim light Hil realized they'd parked near the edge of a drop-off. His fear ramped higher. Through leafless trees he saw train tracks far below and beyond them the cold glitter of a giant silvery knife. The Hudson River. She turned off the ignition.

"Where are we?" Hil asked, trying to control his quavering voice.

"We're not far from Rhinecliff. Do you know Rhinecliff, Mr. Emory? It's not so far from Rhinebeck."

He did. He'd once been a guest at the weekend place of an author he was editing; Hannah and Jacqueline Charlotte had come along. How would they survive without him? "Be reasonable," Hil pleaded. "I had nothing to do with your son's death and I didn't steal—perhaps his book and my book share some similarities—I wouldn't know—but many books are written about similar subjects. There are dozens of runaway slave narratives. No offense to your son but it's not an original topic, Mrs. Corgi. Now you want to blame someone, me, for your misfortune."

"I wasn't sure exactly what I was going to do when I drove out here earlier. I've been scouting the right place all afternoon. Don't you think this is a nice spot? It's at least eighty feet down to the tracks and the river. Don't you think you'll feel better once you admit your wrongdoing? Would you like a drink first? I'd like another drink." She pulled a bottle from under her seat—Chivas, he couldn't help noticing—fumbled with the cap while still holding the pistol in the other hand, and took a long swig. She extended the bottle to Hil.

"No thank you." He had to keep a clear head. But then he reached for the bottle. I can't be faulted, he thought. *Sure you can but so what*, he heard Jeff say, as he had said in the cab the night Hil confessed to stealing the book.

"Well, then. I guess we've completed our business, Mr. Emory. I apologize to your wife and child. I'm sure none of this was their fault."

She wouldn't, she wouldn't. She was faking, feinting. It was a ploy.

In panic Hil grabbed for the key, the shifter, anything to stop her from gunning the car over the edge. She pushed the pistol into his chest—now it's done, Hil told himself, quite calmly, already resigned to the force of the blast and the relief of knowing there was nothing he could do anymore to stop things—but when Mrs. Corgi pulled the trigger, it merely clicked. Nothing. A misfire. He was almost disappointed to have to relinquish this admirably Zen acceptance of his own death.

"No bullets," she said sadly. "I have his gun but not the bullets. I insist you make a public apology, Mr. Emory, and give credit where credit is due."

The newfound peace vanished. "Why you contemptible bitch." Hil yanked the keys out of the ignition and made sure the car was still in park. "You just wanted to scare the shit out of me."

"Give me my keys," she said indignantly. "They're mine. And you don't need to curse." She reached for the dangling keychain.

Instead, Hil backhanded the empty revolver out of her hand, catching her under the chin and slamming her head against the car window. "You crazy bitch," he said to the woman, who now lay against the driver's door, her head outlined by the spider-webbed window. Threads of blood began to trace the cracks.

Hil breathed hard, shook himself, trying to make sense of what had just happened. Empty gun, car in park, he had the keys. Despite the leather gloves he was wearing, his knuckles hurt on his right hand. More blood seeped around Mrs. Corgi's poorly dyed hair. Her chest rose slowly. He just had to think. It was silent here, no cars passing on this dead end spur off Ferncliff Road through the empty woods.

He had to make a plan.

She'd said she was going to drive herself off. She was useless, miserable, she'd said herself she had nothing left to lose. He had a family to protect, a reputation. It would be quick, clean, he'd walk back to Rhinebeck, it couldn't be more than four or five miles despite all her zigging and zagging. He'd get his car and be out of there. She'd be judged a suicide, like her son. What other option was there for a parent of a suicide? Would anyone make the connection to her coming to the reading, recognize the inevitable obit photo in the paper? Still, they couldn't tie him to her death.

Think. He'd never taken off his gloves in the freezing car. No fingerprints. His scarf was safe around his neck. What other evidence might there be? He reached into the back seat and grabbed the manila envelope that supposedly held Corgi's manuscript, along with the inscribed copy of *A Cool Drink of Water*. What else? Any other papers? He flicked on the overhead light, then, terrified, flicked it off again. He had to get out of there. He screaked the stiff passenger door open and scrambled out. Her head injury would be ascribed to the Cadillac's fall and the absence of seatbelts. If he was lucky the car would burst into flames.

But what if he was too much of a ninety-eight-pound weakling to push the car over? He opened the passenger door again, reached in, averting his eyes from the woman who was moaning now, the flow of blood slowing, the wound seeming to clot, and slid the shifter rod to neutral. He put the key back in the ignition. He pushed on the door frame. The car sat still. He put it back in park, kicked away any rocks or sticks that blocked the front tires, shoved the shifter back into neutral and threw his weight against the trunk. This time the front tires edged past the lip of the embankment. Then it was gone, as though the embankment had crumbled away beneath the tires but it hadn't; the car was falling, thumping and crashing all the way down, down, cracking saplings, shrieking metal. After what seemed like a long time he heard a great thump, and then a dense, wintry silence.

Hugging the book and envelope to his chest Hil took to the road. Once he'd left the Ferncliff drive behind and hit a main road, he ducked behind trees the few times headlights approached. He listened for sirens but heard none. He kept walking east toward Rhinebeck. He had to do it, she'd threatened to take him with her. (But what if that threat had been as empty as her gun? What if?) No, she was a suicidal maniac. Like son, like mother. It was self-defense. He had a right to protect himself. And really, she *was* suicidal. By the time he'd gone a few miles he'd nearly convinced himself that it was all her doing, he'd merely assisted her in reaching her goal, just as he'd assisted John Corgi.On the hoar frosted pavement dry leaves tumbled in the moonlight. He heard nothing but his own footsteps, wind soughing in the bare trees. Once the muffled tattoo of horses running in a field. A dog barking.

In less than an hour and a half, Hil was back in the parking lot behind the bookstore in Rhinebeck. Had anyone noticed his car sitting there all alone for no apparent reason with all the stores closed down? Perhaps there was a tavern still open and he hadn't wanted to move the car down the block. Whatever, it was nobody's business and there was nothing to be done about it now. He locked the manuscript envelope and the inscribed copy of his book in the trunk of the Buick, started the car without turning on the lights, then reconsidered—attract no notice—and turned them on. He had a reading tomorrow in Nyack, a confirmed hotel room waiting for him only an hour and a half south. How good it would feel to stretch out on a hotel bed and shut his eyes.

Hil drove carefully out of the lot and onto Route 308. The car heater worked just fine as the engine warmed and he headed toward the Kingston bridge, following his own two cones of light. Had he really done it? He'd done it. Now everything would be different, and everything would be the same.

Still, halfway to Nyack, Hil couldn't shake the feeling that he'd forgotten something, left something unfinished, something *dangling*. The tin dipper, he realized. What had he done with the tin dipper? Had he left it in the bookstore? Or in Mrs. Corgi's car? He could call the bookstore tomorrow but if it wasn't there perhaps it would be better not to draw attention to it. Hil gripped the wheel of the beige Buick more tightly. He had the feeling he might never let it go.

PART VII

Not You and Me

CHAPTER NINETEEN

Noor, Jaycee 2011

Noor had a secret. It lay curled inside her, infinitesimally small and fragile, too easily lost. She curled around it; she hadn't thought she wanted it but here it was, for now anyway. When she closed her eyes she didn't see the lines of traffic, the malls and industrial complexes, the winter killed fields of this portion of Interstate 95, but a day when she lay in an overgrown pasture of timothy and clover. Beside her Dan had fashioned a crown of white clover blossoms. "Here," he'd said, and Noor turned toward him so he could place it on her head. "Princess Noor," he proclaimed. "There's already one of those, isn't there?"

"Queen Noor. Of Jordan. But her crown isn't as nice as mine."

Dan had run his hand down the buttons of Noor's shirt, slid his fingers under the cloth onto her still flat belly. "Our baby will display hybrid vigor," he joked, referring to the breeding principle of mingling two long separated genetic lines to generate offspring superior to either parent. He kissed her belly and Noor had closed her eyes, sighed. Dan rolled onto her and she opened her mouth to him, enclosed him in her arms. All around her the smell of sweet clover, the buzzing of bees, and Dan's long body pressing into her, between them their future taking shape in her belly. Noor opened her eyes when Jaycee suddenly swerved.

"Sorry," Jaycee said. "That jerk in the U-Haul veered too close."

Careful, Noor thought. Baby on board. She closed her eyes again but she couldn't recapture the day in the clover and she decided she didn't want to think about Dan fondly; it hurt too much and confused her. He was the guy who said Mindy made him happy; he was the guy who begged to come home. She'd wanted to rub her pregnancy in Dan's face out of spite but now that he was grieving his own offspring she couldn't. Spite was a base emotion; Noor wanted to be better than that. Anyway, it wasn't Dan's baby this time, but Gerry's—enough reason for ambivalence without the fact that Jaycee would be destroyed when she learned about it. *If* she learned about it, Noor told herself. Was there any reason to tell Jaycee while the baby's—the fetus's—fate remained so uncertain? She'd never made it past the first trimester before. Two miscarriages didn't mean she'd lose the third pregnancy—for all she knew her eggs had dissed Dan's sperm and would like Gerry's just fine. Could she picture herself a single mother, her parents in Karachi horrified that not only was she divorcing her husband—if she was, in fact, divorcing—but having another man's baby, a shame they wouldn't be able to endure if they lived any closer to her and this new grandchild. But it was easier to picture raising the baby alone than envision terminating, to use Mindy's word, a pregnancy after two miscarriages.

Noor squeezed her eyes shut and damned her wishy-washy self. She used to want to remake frumpy Jaycee in her own image but now she realized she could use some of Jaycee's singularity of purpose, her large and unequivocal desires, her habit of being so consistently, unapologetically herself. Everything about this trip was fraught with ambivalence. What was Noor thinking, heading to a drug assignation in Miami when she hadn't even planned to share in the profits? But she *wanted* the money, as shameful as that sounded. If she were to become a single mother, not to mention going through with a divorce, she'd need it. Noor imagined herself explaining to the police: *No officer, I had no idea, I just thought I was on vacation with my friend. She wanted to take me to this Cuban restaurant.* Yeah, that would fly.

Noor rolled her jacket into a pillow and leaned into the passenger window, hoping for sleep to overtake her. Jaycee was happy enough to take two turns at the wheel to every one of Noor's. Noor was suffering from first trimester, progesterone-induced sleepiness, while Jaycee seemed positively electric, tapping her feet, jiggling her legs as she drove. Too much coffee, Noor decided. The girl needed to cut down. Too much coffee and the excitement of a big payout.

In Virginia, in the late afternoon, Jaycee insisted on buying a sack of boiled peanuts at a gas station, despite the briny low tide smell of the boil pots, which would have made Noor gag even if she weren't pregnant. Jaycee choked down a few and threw the rest into the trash before settling into the passenger seat. Noor snickered. "Not your usual Jiffy, huh?" It was her turn to drive and she pulled carefully onto the ramp and into the torrent of highway traffic.

"What's Jiffy?" Jaycee asked, revealing another of those lacunae in her upbringing. The Emorys probably smashed their own peanuts with a stone. "Hey," Jaycee said, shrugging, "you got to try everything, right?" Apparently everything included the countless sexual positions with Gerry about which Jaycee had been rhapsodizing since the George Washington Bridge. She'd prefaced it with, "It doesn't bother you if I talk about Gerry, does it? I mean, since you didn't want to do the nasty with him again and all."

Noor had shaken her head no. It *did* bother her but she knew she had no right to be bothered and Jaycee had every right to enjoy Gerry's gymnastics, but she wished Jaycee could be less persistent, less graphic, and just plain less Jaycee: Poor girl thought she was being hip by saying "do the nasty," but she sounded like one of the Golden Girls Noor had watched on *Nick at Night* when she was twelve. So far Jaycee had informed Noor that they enjoyed incorporating whip cream and Nutella (Jaycee knew Nutella, if not Jiffy) into their sexual games and also dressing up in costumes from the Hillwinds prop trunk. Gerry looked so cute, Jaycee reported, in an 1850's farmer's blousy shirt and woolen vest and button trousers, but she wouldn't let him wear the domed felt gnome hat because it was Hil's signature headgear and she didn't want to feel like she was playing pony with her dad. Noor would have thought that those kinds of games were reserved for later in a relationship when sex cooled, not that she and Dan had ever tried them, but if Jaycee and Gerry enjoyed starting off their courtship with props as well as varied locations—they'd already done it in the Hillwinds blacksmith shop, the bathtub, and even behind a flimsy panel screen room divider in Wood Art Gallery at the college—then that was their business, not Noor's. Noor wondered why Gerry had been lacking in such theatrics when he and Noor had settled for the couch in his apartment; he hadn't even eaten a frozen pizza off her. Maybe he didn't need extras with Noor like he did with Jaycee, she thought meanly. All he'd done extra was get her pregnant.

Noor glanced into the rearview mirror as she passed a slow blue Corolla. "Are you going to call Frida to make sure everything's okay?" she asked when she could see the Corolla behind her in the mirror.

"I tried in the gas station. I just got her voicemail. She says "please leave a message" in Spanish and English. Isn't that cute? It's too noisy to call on the highway."

"I sure hope she has the stuff with her. I'd hate to drive down here for nothing."

Jaycee looked hurt by the idea that their girlfriend trip could ever be for nothing, but to cover up she patted the dashboard and said "At least we're getting out of the cold and snow."

"And sitting in a car two days each way looking at the ass end of tractor trailers."

"It's a *road trip*," Jaycee declared. "I've never been on a road trip. It's an adventure." She tapped the steering wheel to some inner beat, then said, "Did you know that the state bird of Virginia is the cardinal?" Two stops ago she'd picked up a kids' book of state birds, flowers, and mottoes through which she now flipped. "You'd think it would be something you don't see at home but I see cardinals all the time. It's also the state bird of North Carolina. And of West Virginia. And Illinois, and Kentucky and Ohio. What an overused bird. Delaware has the blue hen chicken."

"Fascinating," Noor grumbled. "Why didn't you take Gerry with you? Why me?"

"Gerry can't leave his new plowing business in February," Jaycee replied with the possessive, wifely pride she'd developed since she and Gerry had become an item. "Besides, he's looking in on my mom, making sure she eats right. I certainly wouldn't have asked you to do that. You would've said yes, and then I would've never heard the end of it."

Noor shrugged off the correctness of this remark. It must be awful to be tied to a place that had wrecked people's lives like Hillwinds had, even if you'd have to sell it in order to keep your dad in his nursing home. But Jaycee didn't seem to want to talk about the investment shenanigans or her parents at all anymore, except to point out that she herself was all but broke again. Even the little cape house was almost surely a goner, she said, upending a bag of gas station Virginia mints in her lap. But then, as if the plucking of spilled mints from between her thighs inspired her, all she wanted to talk about was Gerry and his Marshmallow Fluff-capades.

Billboards advertising "SOUTH OF THE BORDER" and "COME VISIT PEDRO'S FIREWORKS" passed like mile markers: PEDRO'S WEATHER REPORT: CHILI TODAY—HOT TAMALE! On the next sign the stereotyped bandito advertised hot dogs: YOU NEVER SAUSAGE A PLACE! EVERYONE'S A WIENER AT PEDRO'S! Noor pulled off at the first exit that offered facilities and rolled into a gas station. They each hustled to the restroom with its unpleasantly rust-stained toilet and dripping faucet, then Noor stood at the pump while Jaycee went in to pay, coming out with a supersize coffee for herself and Noor's large decaf. Noor began pumping regular into her salt-stained Forester.

"I don't see what good decaf will do you" Jaycee said, sticking her cup into the drink holder.

"Did you try Frida again?" Noor nagged as they headed back onto the highway.

"No luck yet but maybe her phone's not charged. Or she left it in her apartment in Miami. Hey, there's another one," Jaycee announced, referring to an eye-catching double billboard: REPENT

AND YOU SHALL ENTER THE KINGDOM matched with ADULT BOOK STORE! TRIPLE XXX! NEXT EXIT!

"The paradox of the South in a nutshell," Noor said. Her dark complexion had gotten some darker looks the last few stops. The birds had changed too. They'd seen crows and hawks, sure, and even the ubiquitous cardinal, but now Jaycee identified a black-billed snowy egret standing one-legged in a patch of swamp between the south and northbound lanes of traffic, a fluorescent yellow foot curled below its black leg, the cloak-like plumage gently swaying.

Later, Jaycee nodded off, a barely-nibbled Hostess Ding Dong crumbling in her lap—it was kind of cute how Jaycee delighted in all that had been denied her growing up chez Emory. Kind of cute and kind of fattening, except, now that she thought about it, Jaycee had actually trimmed down. Noor flicked the radio on low and slowly turned the dial.

"*. . . can't expect Obama to care about Christian concerns when . . .*"

"*1-800-ROCK105 if you have the answer to . . .*"

"*. . . two cups karo syrup and a pound of . . .*"

"*feliz cumpleanos a Carmelita Diaz en Greenville*"

"*Baby, Baby, can't get you out of my . . .*"

"Oh for God's sake," Noor said and flipped the radio off. She tucked in an Emmy Lou Harris CD, crooning softly to "Wrecking Ball." Dan had found Emmy Lou's quavering voice annoying. But the sadness of the songs and the rhythm of highway miles relaxed Noor. Driving was a form of limbo, in which all responsibilities disappeared and she could forget for a moment her unresolved problems. At every stop the air temperature was warmer, the breezes caressing. And, on the downside, her breasts more tender.

Funny, how "tender" was another word for "painful." It was all a matter of degree, she supposed, a spectrum of hurt from ouch to agony. Childbirth was supposed to be nearly unbearable, but most women bore it, even the weak and the wimpy, and then there was the love that resulted, another kind of tenderness. She hoped she'd bond with her child, not turn away. Turning away had been her modus operandi for a long time. But from a child? That would be unforgivable. If she and Dan had had a child, she might have turned away from both of them. Or maybe she would have grown more tender.

The first palm tree appeared at the last rest stop in North Carolina where Jaycee took the wheel. In South Carolina they finally approached SOUTH OF THE BORDER and PEDRO'S FIREWORKS. "Want to pull off for a few minutes?" Jaycee asked. "It looks fun."

"Don't even think of it," Noor warned. Sighing loudly, Jaycee steered the car past the neon signage, the 165-foot Pedro tower, a dormant Ferris wheel and multiple mustachioed Pedro statues with serapes and sombreros. "Besides being stupid," Noor said, "it's grotesque. How do you think they'd portray *my* family, with a statue of a suicide bomber strapped with explosives? They could have signs: COME VISIT AHMED'S. YOU'LL HAVE A BLAST!"

Feeling a little ashamed of her hyperbole, Noor agreed to play another in a series of games of "alphabet." They giggled stupidly at a truck with the business name "A. Duie Pyle" stenciled on its sides and a bumper sticker admonishing: *Don't Drive Faster Than Your Guardian Angel Can Fly.* They groaned, not laughed, at a billboard showing an enormous luminous fetus gripping its umbilical cord under banner letters: CHOOSE LIFE!

At the next gas station, Noor sat down to pee in the restroom, and was faced with the sight of her panties spotted with rusty blood. She began to hyperventilate. It was happening already, a miscarriage. But she hadn't even cramped. Was she going to lose this one here in some nameless gas station on Interstate 95, a tiny room with broken hardware where the lock should be? Noor gripped the toilet paper holder on one side and the edge of the dirty sink on the other for support, neglecting to hold the door firmly shut with her foot. Slow down, she told herself. Breathe. Spotting didn't mean a miscarriage; lots of women spotted during pregnancy. She'd had awful cramps the last two times. No cramps were good cramps. But spotting? She'd have to buy panty liners. Or pads if it got worse. She'd be relieved if she lost it, she told herself. But it wasn't relief Noor felt, just panic, along with the nearly infinitesimal seepage. She chanted silently, certain now: *I don't want to lose this baby. I don't. Please don't let me lose this baby.* It was a visceral prayer; so much for all the cogitations, the indecision. The sight of blood had whisked her maternal ambivalence away. Someone pushed the door open; Noor kicked it back shut. She wiped, washed her hands, zipped up her pants and walked gingerly to the car.

They had driven from dark to dawn, through daylight, twilight and long into dark again before collapsing at a cheap motel paid for in cash and backed up with the fake license/ID Jaycee had purchased from Gerry's downstairs neighbor who made them for underage drinkers as a sideline to his job at Tire Warehouse. Vermont still didn't require picture licenses. In the room, Noor turned on the heater fan to dull the sound of highway traffic and burn off some of the smell of mildew. Jaycee tried Frida's cell again even though Noor had been brought up to never call anyone past 8:00. She imagined Frida gently sleeping, jumping at the vibrations of her phone, fearing for her little boy in Lima.

"Don't worry, Peruvians stay up late, even when they're in this country," Jaycee said, but neither Noor nor Frida answered. "Maybe she turned in early tonight. She does have to work Miami hours," Jaycee amended.

Despite being tired, Noor lay a long time on the lumpy mattress, detecting no new seepage, but afraid she'd wake up to a gush of blood between her legs, a trip to an ER perhaps, like last time, and the cat out of the bag *vis-a-vis* Jaycee. But she hadn't had cramps yet. There was that.

Noor woke to more spotting, but no gush and then they were back on the road.

Highway signs flashed overhead like some slow green strobe light as the miles unraveled, the sun traveled its low winter arc above acres of thirsty looking pines, and a vast assortment of what looked to Noor like getaway cars, drug dealer cars, and human trafficking vans passed or were passed. Jaycee had her head in her guidebook and was finally, blessedly, quiet. In the tailgate-facing seats in a maroon Dodge Durango with *Keystone State* Plates that was passing too close on Noor's left, three little kids opened mouths full of chewed-up food for her appreciation. Noor laughed, showing her own mouthful of gooey pastry stolen from Jaycee's stash. One of the kids pushed a handful of crackers into his mouth, refueling.

Twenty minutes further they were in a traffic jam, cars backed up ahead, taillights winking as they creeped and stopped, creeped and stopped. Jaycee looked up from her book. "What's happening?"

"Must be an accident." They inched along, eventually passing a blazing road flare, then firemen in fluorescent yellow bunker gear gesturing them into a single lane past ambulances with flashing lights, fire trucks and then a quick glimpse, down a small embankment, of an upside down maroon SUV with its tail hatch smashed in, doors splayed open.

"Oh my God, it's the car with the kids," Noor cried, catching sight of the Pennsylvania plates. "Those kids were making faces at me. Oh my God." Noor's hands started shaking on the wheel and her breath turned jagged in her chest, her foot like vapor on the pedal.

"Drive, Noor," Jaycee ordered. "They're waving you on. You have to go. Those kids might be fine, you don't know. It doesn't look that awful," she said doubtfully.

Someone honked. A cop motioned angrily for her to get going. Both women faced forward as Noor white-knuckled the wheel and forced her feet to return to where they belonged. Newly vulnerable, her belly pitched beneath her seatbelt.

When they were back up to speed, Jaycee said, "Accidents must get to you worse than they get to most people, I guess. That makes sense. If I were you I guess they'd get to me too."

Noor still couldn't speak. Where were those kids with their happy mouths full of cracker gunk? Trussed up on backboards, headed to the hospital? On their way to the morgue?

"You want me to drive?" Jaycee asked. She was bouncing in her seat again with too much energy.

"I'm okay," Noor said, "but you better cut down on the coffee."

Half an hour later, Jaycee, conferring with her guidebook, said, "Hey, we could stop for an hour at Little Talbot Island State park. It's hardly out of the way at all. Don't you want to see a beach that isn't covered in condos and hotels?"

Since she'd already nixed Pedro's and a side trip to Disney World and a search for a motel with a pool despite Jaycee's wheedling, Noor figured she couldn't say no to everything. "One hour," she warned.

Jaycee navigated them onto 1-A, and after a half hour of pretentious ocean-front real estate and gussied up golfing and sea resorts, the buildings thinned out and then they were traveling along magnificent salt marshes decorated with stilt-legged egrets and herons. Small live oaks bore Spanish moss, and palmettos fanned their green blades.

They paid the day rate at the Little Talbot Island State Park ranger station. Noor had to pull Jaycee away from the exhibit of taxidermied seabirds and a yellow-eyed bobcat in the ranger's office so they could park in the broad expanse of a near empty lot. Noor made a stop at the bathhouse/bathrooms, with their showers and flush toilets—how strange to think water could be kept running in uninsulated buildings in winter. She dropped her pants in a stall—was that fresh spotting or just what had already occurred? She changed the panty-liner to keep track. They walked the boardwalk through dunes fenced off to protect nesting seabirds, to a platform with a long set of wooden stairs that brought them down to the beach. She couldn't help but imagine her child—unborn, perhaps never to be—digging in the sugary sand with a pail and shovel. Then she remembered the kids in the smashed SUV who might have been on their way to this same beach. Don't think of them, she told herself, and she set off north up the beach, away from a steam-spewing power plant in the southern distance, Jaycee hurrying beside her. A line of brown pelicans glided above the green curl of waves, nearly touching the surface with their bellies. A seal popped up as they trudged the cold sand. It might be Florida, but it was Northern Florida in February, and brisk. The sky puffed big white high clouds and the breeze whipped their hair.

Along the dune edge of the beach they came to skeletal oak trees, some standing, some lying with tangled root balls reaching as high as their branches, burnished pewter by long past storms. They sat down in the lee of a tipped trunk, protected from the wind and warmed by the sun, facing the sea. Unbidden, Dan's face appeared in Noor's mind. He'd been so gentle when treating the horses, tender even, giving them their spring vaccinations. Her new vet Erickson, who came out to inject Moonpie with steroids for heaves, had thrown a twitch chain over the fearful and balky pony's sensitive upper lip, twisted it tightly, and demanded that Noor hold the wooden baton to which the chain was attached. What did Erickson's wife think of him? Did he frighten her too, manhandling her most sensitive parts, for what he no doubt called *her own good?* Noor wouldn't let the man on her property again and was angry at herself for not stopping the procedure the minute he brought out the twitch. She wondered if there'd come a time when she and Dan would be comfortable enough that he could be her vet again, if not her husband. Only what would he think if he knew why she was in Florida? He wouldn't want to be her vet, or her husband.

Noor pushed thoughts of Dan away. It would be nice to just lie here and forget everything for an hour, but instead she pictured Frida, dressed for success, smooth nyloned legs scissoring toward the risk she had no idea she was taking. But how much risk could it be? Jaycee had walked through customs with a whole stinking coke-filled cheese. And no doubt Frida had weathered customs before, her laptop examined in dingy back rooms, the names and addresses of her cultural exchanges causing consternation all around.

"Too bad they don't let you cramp right here," she heard Jaycee cogitate, taking a second to figure out she'd said camp, not cramp. "The campground is across the highway in the woods.

It would be nice to stay here with Gerry. The brochure says that, aside from the beach, 'maritime forests, desert-like dunes and undisturbed salt marshes on the western side of the island allow for hours of oral sex.'"

"What?" yelped Noor. "It does not."

"Yup, 'The diverse habitats in the park host a wealth of positions for fornication, including river otter style, marsh rabbit style, bobcat style (on a tree branch, I guess), and the skinny legged, airborne couplings of a variety of native and migratory birds.'"

Noor laughed. Jaycee was a good mood changer. She sat up to watch little white and gray birds race up and down the waterline on their spindly legs. What were they, plovers? What would Jaycee's imaginary guidebook say about plover-style sex? Run away as fast as your backward knees can carry you. Noor dug her sneaker heels into the yielding sand. Her butt and legs would be covered with grit, and then so would her car but she didn't care. The car was already trashed with wrappers and food bags. She slid all the way down and let her hair get sandy. The ocean sighed and the small waves hissed amid the scribbled tracks of the plovers. Noor shut her eyes, then sat up and shook the sand from her unwashed hair. "Jaycee," she said. "I'm pregnant." She hadn't meant to say it, but all at once there it was between them.

"That's great!" Jaycee crowed, sitting up beside Noor.

"It isn't Dan's," Noor interrupted, although she couldn't fathom Jaycee's enthusiasm even if it were Dan's.

Jaycee cocked her head in confusion, then her eyes welled.

"I'm so sorry," Noor said, reaching out to put a hand on Jaycee's knee. Jaycee was wearing those old purple velour sweatpants for traveling clothes and the sand stood out against the fabric's worn nap. "I didn't think I would ever need birth control. I won't tell Gerry. I promise. I wouldn't ask anything from him, and I won't do anything to get between you and him. That's a promise, Jaycee. I swear."

"You don't know!" Jaycee sobbed into her lap, her back bent in such a way that she looked, for once, fragile, breakable beneath a thin windbreaker that might have been her father's. "You don't know. If you have the baby Gerry would want to be involved. He'd be your baby's father, and what would I be, the peculiar spinster aunt?"

It was what Noor had asked Dan about his and Mindy's baby. Non-baby. "Jaycee, I promise. I'm not going to take Gerry from you. We'll tell him the baby is Dan's, like you thought."

"But you know he'll know. And he'll come running."

"No, he wouldn't. He's with you. He wants to be with you. Look on the bright side," she said in a strangled voice. "I've already had two miscarriages. I'll probably have another. By the time we get back to Montpelier this whole conversation will be moot." Why had she even brought it up, then, she chided herself. But she'd had to.

"He'd go back to you because he'd love his kid if you had it, and he'd go back to you out of shared grief if you lost it." Jaycee's face was already streaked with tears. "It won't be the same anymore. It will all be ruined."

"Jaycee. I'm spotting. I've been spotting since yesterday. I'll probably lose it."

"No! You can't. That's Gerry's baby! A little Gerry running around with a toy snowplow would be so cute! You can't lose it. CHOOSE LIFE!" Jaycee shouted, like the billboards they'd passed with the monstrous, glowing fetus. As though Noor could reach out and clutch her baby's umbilicus.

Noor started to laugh, it was just so ridiculous, and then she was crying too. She was in trouble no matter what. If she kept the baby she'd be interfering with Jaycee's romance and making things even weirder with Dan; if she lost the baby they'd all be heartbroken. Yes, all four of them, heartbroken.

Jaycee jumped up and walked toward the sea. She stood at the water's edge kicking at rocks and driftwood while Noor watched, then returned and plopped back down.

"I have a secret too," Jaycee said. "I wasn't going to say anything because I knew it would upset you, but since we're letting it all hang out, I will. You know I told you that slime bag Jeff/Derek had that heart attack? Well, before he had it he told me something really, really bad, even worse than all the other stuff. Way worse."

"Well what was it?" asked Noor, when they had watched a line of plovers escape an incoming wave. And then another incoming wave, before Jaycee spoke up again.

"That my father was drunk. And was driving the car."

"Big deal." Noor shrugged. What on earth was Jaycee going on about now? Of course her dad was driving the old car around. That's why he'd ended up in the nursing home. Probably would have driven straight into the building on his own if they hadn't put him there first.

"That doesn't bother you?"

"Why should it bother me that your dad finally drove around recklessly enough to get him in the nursing home where he belongs? He didn't hurt anyone, did he?"

"Not now! Then! The hit-and-run. The—*that night*! You know, *Pauline*. Wow, that is so bizarre. I had the same misunderstanding as you just did, when Jeff told me."

What? What was she going on about?

"When Jeff was having the heart attack, before the medics came when he thought he was going to die and it was just us, just me and him and my mom, he said it was Dad, drunk, who killed Pauline and her father and, you know, hit you too. But then Jeff said he'd been drunk too. He said he "nudged" the steering wheel. He said Eben Shattuck knew stuff he wasn't supposed to know. About Hillwinds, you know, Eben Shattuck was one of the investors there, and my mom already knew. I could tell she knew everything all along. Of all the bad things he's done—they've done, I mean—Pauline is the one thing I'll never forgive. Even if it wasn't just Dad's fault, he never took responsibility. I thought he was as bad as he was going to get, and I thought I could handle it. But this?"

Noor was speechless. At twelve years old she'd been diagnosed with post-traumatic stress disorder and survivor's guilt by a therapist who wore baggy linen dresses and made her rake a tabletop Japanese sand garden. Another therapist Noor saw briefly in her twenties theorized that Noor's survival of the hit-and-run was why she didn't invest deeply in relationships; she wasn't about to open herself to further losses. That therapist, an avuncular man named Oscar, had wanted her to smack a pillow with a foam baton to "get out her anger" and "free the love." She'd told Oscar she'd given up her adolescent rage at the unknown hit-and-run driver long ago and there was enough free love in the world already, then refused to make another appointment even after he called her up three times like a jilted boyfriend. But now there *was* no unknown hit-and-run driver. There were those two old sorry bastards who weren't even worth the effort of her taking a swing at them.

"Just don't tell me your *dad* didn't know he'd hit us," Noor said in a strange cool voice that didn't feel like her own. Underneath it something was building, something ugly. She felt like she'd throw up and then she did throw up, right there into the sand. They stared at the pool of vomit until Jaycee kicked sand on top of it.

"Alright I won't," Jaycee said. She reached over and took Noor's hand, held onto it when Noor tried to pull away, held it firm the way you'd steady a frightened horse, the waves suddenly quiet, the shorebirds motionless and perplexed, as if waiting to be sent scurrying away again.

Halfway down the Florida coast that evening they pulled off the highway to fill the tank. Next to the gas station a motel advertised, in tilting letters on a plastic marquee, LIVE BAND! SEVENTIES NITE! COME ROCK WITH RICKIE AND THE RAKERS! FIRST DRINK FREE!

"Let's go dancing," Jaycee said.

Noor snorted. "You're kidding, right? Very funny."

"No, just for a little while. C'mon. Let's go rock with Rickie and the Rakers."

"Rakers? What does that even mean? A bunch of guys who do lawns?" Gerry did lawns when he wasn't plowing, Noor reminded herself. Hush.

"Let's find out," Jaycee said. "C'mon, first drink's free."

"Like I can drink while pregnant," Noor said. "And I don't think I should risk jumping around when I've been spotting. Besides, you really think it's appropriate to kick up your heels when Frida's carrying—"

"Then sit and watch me. I've never gone dancing. I only danced by myself in my room with a little transistor radio that Enrique left behind. And Mike, my fiancé, wouldn't dance. Which was probably a good thing. Just ten minutes, okay?"

The path to the *American Owned* Peach Tree Motel's Quasar Lounge was lit with tiki torches—a mix of images that would boggle the mind if Noor had any mind left to boggle. Inside the lounge was dark, as expected, though the Quasar Lounge quasars (disco balls with spikey Science Fair projections) flashed dizzyingly. Rickie and the Rakers were three gray-haired white guys in big lapelled shirts and white polyester *Saturday Night Fever* suits—a bassist with huge sideburns and mustache to match, a guitar player/vocalist, and a drummer with a big console whose dials he kept twisting.

The dance floor consisted of a small square of linoleum directly beneath the largest quasar, in the midst of dark booths and café tables. A few middle-aged couples tricked up in seventies clothes— the women sported big hair and floral banlon dresses tight across the butt; the men had pointy collars on wide lapelled, slick shirts— boogied to the Rakers' rendition of "Witchy Woman."

Noor and Jaycee bellied up to the bar where they ordered a Cuba Libra for Jaycee and a cranberry juice for Noor from a bartender who barely glanced at them. No wonder. A bummed-out chick with beach head and a homeschooled hausfrau wearing an EAT MORE KALE tee-shirt and bagged out velour sweatpants. "No one's going to dance with us here," Noor said. "Look at us."

"I thought you weren't dancing. Anyway, look at *them*. We're thirty years younger than anyone else in the room. That should count for something. C'mon," Jaycee said. She led Noor to a booth.

They hadn't been parked there for more than a minute before a wiry guy with slicked back hair and a shiny blue suit, a TV-perfect used car salesman, came to their booth. He looked from Jaycee to Noor, then back to Jaycee and asked her to dance. Jaycee leaped up eagerly. Surprised to be second choice, Noor guessed she was too dark for him. She slid to the back of the booth and nursed her cranberry juice, grudgingly admiring Jaycee's galumphing, joyful attempts to keep to the beat of "Staying Alive." How was it that Jaycee could feel awful about Noor being pregnant with Gerry's baby and then get up and stomp around like a maniac? And these couples, married thirty years or more, divorced, remarried maybe, or just middle-aged dating, out there on the dance floor whooping it up as though nothing mattered—their underwater mortgages, their dull jobs, their high cholesterol and unemployed stay-at-home adult children who didn't clean their rooms. She imagined Jaycee chiding her: *How do you know everything in their lives is crap? Why do you have to be so negative? Maybe they're happy.* Maybe they were. They looked happy for now, and they would say now was what mattered. But that's how people let themselves off the hook, wasn't it? People like Hilary Emory and Jaycee and Noor.

"Hello."

Noor looked up to see a thick-bodied black man in his late fifties or early sixties, with gray hair cropped close, smiling down at her. Deep creases ran from his nostrils to the corners of his mouth in his round face. He wore a white, short-sleeved shirt tucked into neatly pressed jeans, above which rose a sizeable paunch. What would a black guy be doing listening to awful seventies tunes by an even more awful band, she wondered.

"Why's a pretty lady like you sitting here all by your lonesome?"

"I'm actually here with my friend," Noor gestured with her drink at Jaycee, who was doing a frenetic butt wiggle into the crotch of her scrawny partner. Not exactly seventies moves. Noor blushed. Of course Jaycee had to be grinding at the moment Noor pointed her out.

"How 'bout we show them up?" he asked.

Noor said, "Sorry, but I'm pregnant and my doctor said I have to avoid strenuous exercise. I think that includes stamping, screeching, bouncing, and waving your arms." And grinding, she didn't add.

"Congratulations on your good news, honey. Maybe these musical geniuses," he winked, "can be convinced to take it down a notch for just one song."

"Maybe," Noor said. She didn't want to dance, fast or slow, but she didn't want him to think she was rejecting him because his skin was darker than hers. She gave a suck on the straw of her near empty glass, producing a rude rattling noise.

"Sounds like you need another, darling."

"I'm good," Noor said quickly, then added, "it's just cranberry juice," as though it mattered that this stranger might disapprove of a pregnant woman drinking. Where the hell was Jaycee when she needed her?

"How about I come back when they play a slow song?"

"Okay," Noor agreed, hoping she'd be on the road by then.

He touched his temple as though tipping a hat and walked away.

A few minutes later Jaycee flopped down in the seat across from Noor. "Wow. I'm soaked." Her limp hair was wet and tousled. She pulled her sweaty kale-colored tee-shirt away from her saggy breasts. "At least I must've worked off my drink by now. You know, for driving." Jaycee tilted the melted ice from her Cuba Libre into her mouth.

"Had enough?" Noor asked. "Let's get out of here before—" The Rakers had started warbling the Bee Gee's "How Deep is Your Love." "Shit," she whispered. Her slow-dance partner was weaving between tables, headed their way.

"Ready?" he asked, offering a hand to the cowering Noor.

Noor looked at Jaycee for help, but Jaycee only waved at her. "Go *on*. I want to dance more anyway." Jaycee was up, eagle-eyeing the crowd for her next victim.

Noor's partner propelled her to the dance floor with a light hold on her elbow, then, sliding a hand on her back, guided her around to face him in the midst of other hugging, swaying couples. Noor set one hand on his shoulder and he pulled her uncomfortably close to his large stranger's body. He took her other hand in his. "My name's Freddy," he said as they moved in a slow, rocking step that Noor thought might actually soothe her baby. "What's yours?"

"Noor."

"That's a pretty name, Noor."

"What are you doing here, Freddy," Noor asked, "in the middle of all these white disco buffs?"

"I was just on my way home, been on a business trip. I wanted a drink, sign said first one free, sounded good to me." Freddy shrugged. "Can't say disco's my favorite music, but it don't matter to me how people get their kicks. What about you? I'd guess you're not a Bee Gee's fan yourself. Let's see . . . I bet you like something more downbeat, hmmm, I'd say sad lady ballad stuff."

Noor laughed. "Could be."

"Emmy Lou Harris," Freddy guessed. "Tracy Chapman. In a pinch, what's that new girl's name? Adele."

Noor laughed again.

"And you're here because?" Freddy asked.

"My friend just had to go dancing."

"Good for her," Freddy said, "but looks like she's been doing some of that wacky dust to get in the mood."

Noor glanced skeptically over at Jaycee who was now dancing alone, way faster than the beat. No way. That was just Jaycee being Jaycee, thrilled to knock another item off her endless bucket list of things she'd never done. Freddy readjusted his hand on Noor's back, and Noor stiffened, thinking, oh no, here comes the part where the old guy tries to feel my butt, but Freddy simply continued to hold her lightly. Relieved, Noor allowed her face to rest against his white shirt. His solid belly pressed against the buttons, the way hers would in a few months . . . Freddy smelled of cologne, cigarettes, whiskey, laundry soap. Beneath the Rakers' croon, she could hear the steady ba-dump, ba-dump of Freddy's heartbeat. His hands—one holding hers, the other resting below her shoulder blades—were exceptionally warm. Noor felt a strange flush moving through her arms, her legs, her breasts, her belly, her face on his chest. Not arousal, but *awareness*—of this living, breathing person who happened to be cradling her in his arms. She let herself relax into Freddy's impermanent, but very real, touch. His courtly embrace felt like swaying in a warm bath accompanied by the thump of bass from a distant boom box. It was, she realized, exactly what her baby might be feeling and hearing, sloshing in her womb.

"That's right, honey," he said, "that's good."

When the song ended and the Raker's started up Clapton's "Lay Down Sally," Freddy propelled her gently, hand on the small of her back, to Jaycee who was bouncing on the seat again.

"Thank you kindly, Noor," Freddy said, tipping his imaginary hat again.

"My pleasure." Noor could feel the silly grin on her face.

She tracked Freddy's return to the bar. From the back she could see a bald circle in the midst of his grizzled hair, and that his heavy walk rolled as much sideways as forward, but still she could have stayed longer in his arms, sharing his warmth, his pulse.

Jaycee crunched the last of the melted ice from Noor's glass and thunked it down on the Formica table beside her own empty. "Your old guy has a nice booty," she said.

"Jeez, Jaycee, booty usually refers to women's butts." Noor followed Jaycee as they headed to the door past a trio of polyester-clad, big-haired matrons emerging from the ladies room.

"My bad," said Jaycee.

"Jaycee, don't say that either . . ."

"Why not?" said Jaycee. "I thought it was what people say now."

"Yeah, but not *us*. Not you and me."

Jaycee went quiet at the sound of that "you and me" like a child who had been given a lollipop.

⁓

Late that night they were lost in Miami, cursing MapQuest, trying to find a motel, any motel, that didn't look like it was servicing hookers or drug cartels. They found their way, finally, to West Miami, skipped the questionable West Haven Motel and Trailer Park, guessed that the Starlite West Motel with its reassuringly high hacienda style wall would be too pricey, and continued further west until they settled for the Tamiami Trail Motor Inn. Even this ugly lump of a motel sided with Texture-111 fake wood panels was rich with exuberant greenery—the office nestled in a welter of palms and palmettos and lushly flowering plants. They paid an ancient crone wielding dangerous looking knitting needles behind a glass shield and stumbled up to a balconied second floor, opening the door with an untrustworthy key instead of a pass card in the loose-sounding lock. Jaycee headed for the shower. Neglecting to take off the spread, Noor fell across the closest bed and buried her face in the stale, smoky fabric. She needed to sleep so badly it felt like being dead.

They didn't wake until 9:40 when a chambermaid's vacuum knocked into their door. The half-open blinds were gray with dust but the sun streaming through was painfully bright. The room was more dismal than Noor had realized last night. Two sailboats that looked as though they'd been painted by someone's drunken neighbor keeled nauseatingly over the beds. Noor wondered how it was she had a hangover when she hadn't been drinking. She'd never even undressed or crawled under the covers. She needed a shower.

Noor went to pee in the cramped pink-tiled bathroom, relieved to see that there was only one new, faint blood spot on her panty liner. She looked in the bathroom mirror: greasy black hair, puffy eyes, a white tee-shirt with sweat stains. Nice. A shower and a change of clothes. Now.

"You're coming with me, right?" Jaycee called through the closed door.

Noor pushed open the door. "You're Frida's friend. I'm not. And two people would be more readily recognized if something went wrong. Not to mention look at me."

Jaycee was hopping on one foot, pulling on a pair of too-tight capris. "Are you kidding? There are tons of brown people around here. *I'm* the one who stands out."

Noor supposed Jaycee was right. "Pleeeeease," Jaycee implored, "I need your moral support. I thought we were in this together. You don't have time to shower, by the way."

No shower, damn. Well, if she was going to share in the profits Noor supposed she should share in the risk. She wondered if Frida would bring the big candlesticks wrapped, or bagged, or just out there for the world to see, along with the tray and the miniature picture frame that was probably barely worth selling. It was kind of mean for Jaycee to have Frida take away the gift she'd given to Hugo, but better than if he started crushing and snorting it one day with all his little boy pals. What kid wanted a picture frame anyway? Noor threw down the towel she'd picked up and left the bathroom. She stared at Jaycee, who looked more haggard than Noor's reflection in the bathroom mirror, more haggard than you'd expect even after the long drive. "Jaycee, have you been doing coke on this trip?"

"No! Well, just a little. And we don't have time for this now," Jaycee snapped. "We're already late for Frida. Take your stuff. We might not get back in time for motel check-out." She was busy stuffing gear into her wool tote bag.

Noor shook her head. Great, just what they needed. Jaycee chipping into the profits, not to mention messing herself up when she finally had a chance to get free of her parents. Well, Noor would insist they talk about it, once they were on the highway, safe. They really were late.

They dropped the key at the cramped office, garnering no notice from a texting teenage receptionist who had replaced Senora DuFarge, and headed for the parking lot, where Noor's car was the only dirty vehicle in a row of shiny late-model numbers, surprising at such a dump of a motel. Any loser can make car payments, she supposed, chastising herself again for being such a heartless snob.

Jaycee drove. Twice, they circled the park with the statue of Jose Marti, then hit lights at nearly every block in a gauntlet of nail emporiums, Auto zones, cafecitas, banks and eateries. Despite the strip mall effect, the spaces between buildings were as verdant with tropical foliage as was their dodgy motel. Frida's office, located in the heart of Little Havana, was tucked between a hair salon and a tiny coffee shop called Manuela's, where they were to meet. The sign at the office read, simply, Cultural Exchange International, blue on white.

"I thought it was going to be a more impressive place," Jaycee conceded as they parked. "I kinda pictured a real office building, not a strip plaza storefront. I mean, they fly her over from Lima once a month."

Noor shrugged. "Come on, she must be waiting for us."

Manuela's looked no wider than a horse trailer, just enough room for a counter with seats, and a row of little half tables that appeared to be hung from the wall, like Murphy beds. A hand lettered sign offered plantanos, tostones, beans and rice, a spicy goat stew, and roast pork sandwiches along with café cubano, café con leche, and flan. A couple of men at the side tables eyed the two women curiously, then returned to their coffees and conversation. Noor and Jaycee sat down in the back of the narrow room at the one actual round table with space enough for three. It took them a while to figure out that they had to go up to the counter to order. Noor watched while Jaycee tried out her too-loud-and-not-very-convincing Spanish on the sixty-ish woman, perhaps Manuela herself, with tightly coiffed dyed black curls and a flowery pink apron, who worked the counteter. Jaycee returned with two tiny steaming cups of caramel colored *café cubanos*.

"Probably not the place to find decaf," Noor said.

"I asked for descafe but she said no es or something."

"Sorry baby," Noor said to her belly. "Just this once, I promise." The coffee was syrupy sweet but delicious.

They sat for twenty-five minutes while Jaycee slugged a second, then a third coffee, Noor playing with the little red plastic stirrer in her empty cup. Jaycee had seemed irritable and glum earlier, but now, after a trip to the bathroom, she was wired. Probably gotten back into her stash. Jaycee nattered on about how Peruvians had no clue about Mexican food—they couldn't cook it to save their lives, the so-called Mexican restaurants didn't know the difference between Catsup and salsa—but maybe Frida liked Cuban, or maybe Manuela's was just convenient, being next door to the office and all. Her eyes darted to the wall clock. "I guess it's not just that she's on Peruvian time," Jaycee said more loudly than was necessary. "Maybe she came in before we got here and had to go back. Oh, my god, hang on a second, did I tell her 10:00 or 11:00?"

"Nice going," Noor said. "Well, we can't hog this table for an hour," though she wanted to say, let's just chuck it, let's head home, something's not right, but Jaycee had already jumped out of her chair, all but clapping her hands with decisiveness, forgetting, it seemed, how hungry she had claimed to be in the motel.

"I'll just run over to her office. You wait here in case she shows up," said Jaycee.

"I don't even know what she looks like!" Noor protested but Jaycee, bumping past the men at their tables, excused herself loudly and headed for the door. Noor went up to the counter. She bought a grande plate of rice and beans along with a flan, for the milk it contained. An older man sipping a café con leche grinned at her. "I like girls with big appetites," he said.

"I'm pregnant," Noor said, surprising herself with the pleasure of saying it to another stranger. Soon Dan would be the only one who didn't know. "Eating for two." She carried her heaping plate of rice and beans and the flan back to the table. Frida might not show up, but at least Noor and her baby wouldn't go hungry. Baby Eric/Erica. Or Jasper/Jasmine. She'd get her child a Shetland pony and teach it to ride as soon as it could walk. Then Dan could help it learn to ride a bicycle, Gerry could show it how to drive a plow truck, and Jaycee could teach it . . . what? To be unfazed, unstoppable. Noor smiled and turned to her meal. The rice and beans were delicious and the caramel topped flan looked so tempting she ate it first.

⟨∽⟩

Inside the third floor office of Cultural Exchange International, which looked as shiny-paneled and rinky-dink as one would expect from the exterior, only decorated with large colorful posters of petticoat-flashing dance troupes and a portrait of Mario Vargas Llosa with his Nobel Prize, Jaycee was informed by a chubby, gloating co-worker with sparkly eyeglass frames that Frida was not available for their appointment to discuss a musicians in the schools project—Jaycee had hurriedly come up with an alibi—*because*, and the woman positively gloated as she leaned conspiratorially closer to whisper, "Frida was arrested yesterday at Customs carrying in some heroin. They deported her! Back to Peru. She's lucky it's not Guantanamo," the co-worker added. "I never trusted that girl. She was always too nice. Too perfect. You know what I mean," she added, as if Jaycee, who was decidedly not too perfect, would understand exactly what the woman meant.

Jaycee resisted an impulse to scream. Instead she tut-tutted numbly and backed out of the office, then nearly killed herself going weak in the knees as she thundered downstairs, forgetting she'd put on the dressier of her two pair of shoes to greet the well-dressed Frida. Frida's coworker had said heroin, could you believe it, Jaycee muttered to herself, that's how rumors get started. Heroin? thought Jaycee. It was only coke! She would need to extract Noor from the café and get out of Dodge, as Gerry would say. Jaycee dialed Noor but no answer. Damn her, she always turned off her phone. And of course Frida would have told the authorities about Jaycee tricking her into carrying the goods into the country. And even if she didn't know Jaycee's full name it could be found in the manifest of the LAN flight they'd shared. She and Noor were screwed if they didn't get out of here now. Come to think of it, they were probably screwed even if they did.

Through the glass front door leading back to the street from Frida's office building, Jaycee saw a pretty Latina in a silvery gray business suit, carrying two large, cumbersome shopping bags, step out of a dark sedan. Although she looked grim, not the effervescent woman who'd once taken her in, Jaycee recognized Frida. So she hadn't been arrested! Just as Jaycee was about to open the door and shout Frida's name, she saw a man with close-cut hair seated in the car Frida had exited, watching. In a flash Jaycee got the picture. Frida was a decoy. It was Jaycee they were gunning for. She stood there, frozen for a moment. Through the glass, the parking lot pavement wavered with heat, and Noor's Forester, with its damning Vermont plates, despite the salt and dust scrim, glowed a neon green in that lot full of plates decorated with Florida oranges. And though she couldn't see her, she could picture Noor waiting inside the coffee shop, a sitting duck.

Jaycee spun around. At the end of the hallway an exit sign marked a rear door. She cracked it, saw no one, let herself out into an alley separating Frida's building from the rear of another. She hurried down the alley and out to a busy street. Look normal, she told herself, just like she'd told herself hopelessly all her life, only today there was much more riding on it. Half a block down Jaycee saw a woman holding a baby waiting on a bench under a bus stop overhang. A bus with *S.W. Eighth Street-Tamiami Trail* on its banner drew into the stop. Jaycee kept her pace slow, even while climbing the bus steps behind mother and sleeping child, paying the two dollar fare, and taking a seat near the rear of the bus, which soon pulled back into traffic and headed west.

The shedding palms, the half-filled parking lots, a restaurant advertising Executive Lunch Only $5.99 slid past as she scrabbled in her purse for the remnants of her stash, panicked for a moment when she thought it was gone, sighing when she found it. Noor wasn't going to help her even if Noor got off. And Noor *might* get off. She could say she didn't know anything about it, she was only along for the ride. She could tell them she was getting a divorce, pregnant, needed to get away, knew nothing of Jaycee's reason for the trip. And Frida, maybe they'd believe her that she too knew nothing. After all, she didn't. She was telling the truth. Meanwhile she'd rat Jaycee out. And why shouldn't she? All power to her. To both of them. But Jaycee would have to flee.

Call Gerry, she thought. Maybe he'd run away with her, or maybe he'd pretend he didn't know her but at least send money. She found herself smiling at the thought of being on the lam, a fugitive, with or without her man. Meeting the eye of the woman with the child she smiled more broadly in her direction, but the woman only laid her head against the bus window and closed her eyes. Jaycee tried out the words: I've lost everything. But she didn't feel bereft. She felt excited. Everything? What was everything? Hillwinds? Her parents? She only regretted losing Noor and, she hoped not, Gerry. She removed her fake driving license/ID from her wallet and studied the name Gerry had given her as a joke: Veronica Snow. Snow for coke! She got it now. He was so funny. She would miss him if he didn't come. But she'd escaped Jacqueline Charlotte and Jaycee Emory and the cats with their lockets and if she changed buses often and dodged well enough she'd escape this too. She could take up residence in a hidden cabin in a swamp like that woman Marjorie Kinnan Rawlings who wrote that book about the boy and the deer. Or she could buy a fake passport and slip over borders and sign her new, assumed name with her right or left hand. Across the aisle the sleeping baby stirred and started to cry, waking its tired mother, who jumped up, startled, yanked the signal cord and hustled off at the next stop, dragging the diaper bag and the folded umbrella stroller with her but leaving behind a ragged stuffed animal shaped like a mollusk. Veronica Snow grabbed the moth-eaten creature and hugged it close. There were teeth inside the mouth. The teeth turned out to be a zipper but Jaycee didn't pull it open. "Holy schist," she whispered, and settled in for the ride.

Noor, 2013

Just like last year, all the birthday guests had left except for Gerry. He was carrying two-year-old Afia around on his shoulders, chanting "FEE-Fi-Fo-Fum, I smell the blood of a little one!" Afia shrieked at the mention of her nickname, Fee, and kicked Gerry's sternum with joy. It was hours past her naptime, and even though she was beyond wound up, with the birthday excitement, the gifts and cake, Noor didn't have the heart to chide Gerry when father and daughter were having so much fun. Instead she bustled about the tiny caretaker apartment over the Gelmans' barn, shelving gifts and smoothing wrapping paper for reuse. Dan had brought a savings bond and a book of farm animals that mooed and squawked at the press of a button.

"I hope it doesn't have any llamas in it," Noor had joked.

Dan's girlfriend Kathleen, a Washington County superior court judge, wanted to know, "Why doesn't she like llamas, Danny? I find them incredibly appealing," and Noor and Dan, eyes meeting, kept from laughing.

Kathleen had brought a lovely mirror for Afia's room. Gerry'd brought a package of plastic hotdogs and hamburgers that Afia had smooshed onto everyone's cake-filled plates. Taylor, Gerry's nine-year-old daughter, driven all the way here by her mother, had given her adoring half-sister a Barbie tricked out with a homemade punk haircut and a navel piercing. Fee's only tears of the day came when Gerry's ex came back early to hustle Taylor home to Burlington.

Alice, Noor's former cell-mate, out on parole, had sent a pretty painted tea set, and a letter regaling Noor with anecdotes about her recovery. Two good things had come out of the whole cocaine mess: Alice, and the fact that despite the stress of incarceration, the absence of barn chores in jail had probably helped her maintain her pregnancy. No, there were three good things: without the cocaine she wouldn't have slept with Gerry, and without Gerry she wouldn't have Afia, who was everything. Thank god Dan had come through with selling the house and providing Noor money for such a great lawyer, since without copping to a lower plea and being spared a trial, she'd probably be in prison all through Afia's girlhood, especially being Pakistani-American. She hoped Frida was so blessed, but Noor was forbidden contact with Frida and Frida's family. Her own family too was off limits to Noor, scared to come back to the States to visit and Noor wasn't allowed to leave. They hadn't even met Afia yet.

Noor retrieved a plastic sweet pickle from the floor and picked up the jack-knifed Barbie, who was doing a credible downward dog. She set Barbie on a high shelf with the other things she hoped Afia wouldn't remember for at least a few days. There was the make your own beads kit, or should they call it make your own choking hazard, dropped off by a teenage girl from the Phoenix House addiction center whom the court had recently authorized Noor to give lessons to on the Gelmans' pony, and next to that a trio of odd presents sent yearly by Jaycee. The first was a ragged but clean clam-shaped stuffed animal that had shown up shortly after the baby's birth. Panicked, Noor had slashed the seams, afraid the cruddy little toy held contraband. It had come via Gerry, with no return address, and a note saying "Sorry about everything but at least you got a baby! Love your mystery friend." Why she hadn't just burned the clam Noor didn't know, except that its smell of fresh dryer sheets made her feel like she ought to look after it. Jaycee's next birthday present was a reversible doll that you could turn upside down and another doll appeared beneath its skirts: under one skirt, a fuzzy brown bull, and under the other, a bullfighter swinging a red cape. Did that mean Jaycee was in Mexico or Spain? Or Peru again, or anywhere else there was bullfighting? And this year she'd sent a gold charm bracelet with a single charm, a gold heart holding a costly ruby or a chunk of red glass. The jewel was either precious or fake, like the gold itself, like Noor's friendship with Jaycee. Noor guessed it was an attempt to send money, something Noor might pawn in order to pay bills. Probably Gerry knew where Jaycee was, but she never asked and he was too discreet to offer. His discretion was one of the things she liked most about him. Even with Dan he was gallant, never rubbing it in that the baby was his or that he knew what an asshole Dan had been. He hadn't even guffawed at Noor's llama joke, and when Dan and Kathleen left he'd stepped out for a minute to have a smoke and see them on their way.

Noor glanced at the clock. Nearly 5:00, time to feed the Gelmans' horses. "Gerry," she called, "I'm just going to run downstairs, can you . . ." but there was no answer. She peeked in the door of Afia's room. The two of them lay cuddled up on the bed, Dan's birthday book open on Gerry's chest, Afia's lids fluttering over her green eyes, Afia greedily sucking her thumb as if it really did give nourishment. Gerry put a finger to his own lips and Noor left to do the evening chores, chores for which she received the right to live rent-free in the Gelman's caretaker apartment and even fulfill her community service requirements there on their property, using their horses. She had secretly despised the Gelmans at first—Gentlemen farmers!—but in just a short time she was grateful for their open minds, their way of, though not overlooking her history, tolerating it. It was likely they wouldn't have welcomed her at all had she not had a record—Bleeding hearts!—but if she had to rely on do-gooders in order to do any good in the world herself, so be it.

When she got back upstairs, Gerry was just putting his sneakers back on and the door to Fee's little room—really only a storeroom—was closed.

"We throw great parties," Gerry said, reaching out to massage Noor's shoulders. Noor relaxed into his touch, then remembered herself and pulled away. Better to keep things simple and clear: Afia, the barn, the Gelmans' horses, the no longer so bothersome probation, her dwindling UA's (she only needed to pee in front of an agent every six months now, though she still felt like someone was watching her every time she squatted over a toilet. How ironic that she had to take pee tests even though she'd never *used* drugs), her tiny cluster of friends, mostly other single moms she'd met at the landscaping job Gerry had found her and at Afia's day care.

"Thanks for helping, Gerry," Noor said. "You want some coffee or something?"

"Nah, got to go. But I got Fee for the Fourth of July parade, right?"

"Sure," Noor said. "She'll love it."

"You want to come with us?" Gerry asked. "I hear they're going to have a great 'JUST SAY NO TO CRACK!' float with a bunch of low-pants plumbers showing their backsides. How can you miss that?"

"I'll think about it," Noor promised. She listened as Gerry thumped down the wooden staircase into the barn aisle, eager to get outside and light up another cigarette, and then she pulled the door closed and sat on the couch in the quiet dark. Afia's real birthday would be on Tuesday, and tomorrow Noor would take her to the mall in Berlin, avoiding the fancy toy store in downtown Montpelier, to buy her a rocking horse. Noor thought of the horse as Afia's first, but maybe her daughter wouldn't like horses. Maybe she'd like dolls, or trucks, or soap bubbles, and that would be fine. On the other hand, Noor mused, looking out the window at the Gelman's summer pastures, horses *were* the best. One of the Gelman's horses stamped a hoof in a stall below, as if it had something to say in the matter.

READER GUIDE TO
A WELL-MADE BED

Note to book groups: If you would like Abby and Laurie to meet with your book group via skype, you can message them on the facebook page of A Well-Made Bed.

1. What would you call the most crucial scene or event in the novel? Which is the most disturbing?

2. If you had to drive to Miami or somewhere else far away with one of the characters in this book, who would it be? Dan, Gerry, Hil, Jeff, Noor, Hannah, Jaycee, Carlos, Frida or somebody else? Why?

3. In the absence of their crime, Noor and Jaycee likely would never have become friends at all. As it is, they grow closer the more entangled they become in their crime and its consequences. Have you ever found yourself growing fond of a person as a result of the two of you breaking a rule, or a law, together?

4. Often, when people are caught doing things that are wrong, they apologize by saying that they made "a mistake," or by saying that "mistakes were made." What do you think of this kind of apology?

5. Did Hil and Jeff make a "mistake" in committing their crimes? Did Noor and Jaycee? What is the difference between making a mistake and choosing to do something that you know is wrong? Or does it only become a mistake once you're caught?

6. Do you think that Gerry is a good influence or a bad influence on Noor and Jaycee?

7. Who gets a worse rap in this novel, men or women?

8. What do you think Hannah knows about Hil and his crimes? When do you think she learned about them? Do you consider Hannah to be complicit in Hil's crimes?

9. Describe the kind of person you think Jaycee would be if she had not been raised at Hillwinds by parents determined to prevent her from being like other modern-day children.

10. What do you think will become of Frida and her family?

11. Do you think Jaycee will suffer consequences for her actions? What do you think will become of her? What do you hope she does next?

12. Laurie and Abby have very different writing styles. Were you able to distinguish between the two?

13. If the people in your book club like to cook, plan a potluck composed of foods that you think Jaycee might have helped Hannah cook when she was a girl. Or if all you want is a yummy spread for crackers or bread, here's a recipe for a batch of the soft breakfast cheese that Jaycee prepares with the elders visiting Hillwinds:

   3 cups plain nonfat Greek yogurt
   1 and ½ cups light sour cream
   ½ small onion, finely diced, white or red
   ¾ cups fresh chives, finely chopped, or ½ cup dried chives
   1 teaspoon fresh minced garlic
   1 tablespoon salt—*this amount is necessary to extract the liquid from the mixture*

Mix everything up together very well in a bowl. Lay a large rectangle of cheese cloth onto a cutting board and fold the cloth over to double it. Spoon the yogurt mixture on top, cinch the edges of the cheese cloth into a ball, fasten it with cooking twine, and hang it over a sink or over a large, deep pot for 12 hours at room temperature until the liquid has drained off. Remove the cheese from the cloth and keep it refrigerated in a covered container until you serve it.

BIOGRAPHICAL NOTE

Abby Frucht has received two National Endowment for the Arts fellowships. She has published five novels and two collections of stories, and been awarded a Quality Paperback Book Club Prize, the Iowa Short Fiction prize, and a Best of the Web citation. *A Well-Made Bed* is her first collaborative work. She was raised in New York, lives on a lake in Wisconsin, has raised two sons, teaches at Vermont College of Fine Arts, and counts her friendships among women as one of the driving inspirations of her life.

∽

Laurie Alberts, the author of three previous novels, a story collection, two memoirs, and a book on the craft of writing, has long been driven by her obsessions. Commercial fishing in Alaska, life in Russia under tyranny, the lonely downfall of a former love each impelled her books. *A Well-Made Bed* came from a different source. The pleasure of brain-storming, arguing, shaping and revising a novel with another writer whose sensibilities, process, and style are drastically different from her own taught her that fiction can arise from the joy of collaboration.

Books by G.A. McKevett

Savannah Reid Mysteries

JUST DESSERTS
BITTER SWEETS
KILLER CALORIES
COOKED GOOSE
SUGAR AND SPITE
SOUR GRAPES
PEACHES AND SCREAMS
DEATH BY CHOCOLATE
CEREAL KILLER
MURDER À LA MODE
CORPSE SUZETTE
FAT FREE AND FATAL
POISONED TARTS
A BODY TO DIE FOR
WICKED CRAVING
A DECADENT WAY TO DIE
BURIED IN BUTTERCREAM
KILLER HONEYMOON
KILLER PHYSIQUE
KILLER GOURMET
KILLER REUNION
EVERY BODY ON DECK
HIDE AND SNEAK
BITTER BREW
AND THE KILLER IS…
A FEW DROPS OF BITTERS

Granny Reid Mysteries

MURDER IN HER STOCKING
MURDER IN THE CORN MAZE
MURDER AT MABEL'S MOTEL

Published by Kensington Publishing Corp.

G.A. McKevett

And the Killer Is . . .

A SAVANNAH REID MYSTERY

KENSINGTON
PUBLISHING CORP.

www.kensingtonbooks.com

KENSINGTON BOOKS are published by

Kensington Publishing Corp.
119 West 40th Street
New York, NY 10018

All Kensington titles, imprints, and distributed lines are available at special quantity discounts for bulk purchases for sales promotion, premiums, fund-raising, educational, or institutional use. Special book excerpts or customized printings can also be created to fit specific needs. For details, write or phone the office of the Kensington Special Sales Manager: Attn. Special Sales Department. Kensington Publishing Corp., 119 West 40th Street, New York, NY 10018. Phone: 1-800-221-2647.

The K logo is a trademark of Kensington Publishing Corp.

ISBN-13: 978-1-4967-2014-6
ISBN-10: 1-4967-2014-8
First Kensington Hardcover Edition: May 2020
First Kensington Mass Market Edition: July 2021

ISBN-13: 978-1-4967-2015-3 (e-book)
ISBN-10: 1-4967-2015-6 (e-book)

10 9 8 7 6 5 4 3 2 1

Printed in the United States of America

For Tracie,
the sister my heart adopted

Acknowledgments

Thank you, Leslie Connell, my dear friend and faithful copy editor, who read my stories before *anyone* else and set my mind at ease, telling me that they were good and getting better all the time. You will never know how much that meant to me.

I wish to thank all the fans who write to me, sharing their thoughts and offering endless encouragement. Your stories touch my heart, and I enjoy your letters more than you know. I can be reached at:

sonja@sonjamassie.com
and
facebook.com/gwendolynnarden.mckevett

Chapter 1

"Hey! What the bloody hell do you think you're doin' there, woman?"

Savannah Reid turned to her enraged husband, sitting next to her in the driver's seat of his old Buick, and thought she had seen happier expressions on felons' faces who had just received a sentence of fifty years to life.

"Bloody hell?" she asked calmly. "Since when do you say 'bloody hell'?"

Detective Sergeant Dirk Coulter thought it over a moment, looked a tad sheepish, and admitted, "Okay. I dropped by Ryan and John's restaurant and had a pint with John earlier. That British accent thing of his is almost as bad as your southern drawl. Rubs off on you. I'm around him ten minutes, and I start talking about dodgy weather and how knackered I was after givin' some nutter a bollockin'."

"Do you drop by ReJuvene regularly?"

"Naw. Maybe five or six times a week."

"These pints you're downing—they're free, no doubt, considering Ryan's and John's generous natures."

"Of course they're free. You wouldn't expect me to drop into a swanky establishment like theirs and plunk down my hard-earned cash for a beer, wouldja?"

"No, darlin'. Never crossed my mind that you would do such a thing as pay for a drink you could get for free."

"Good." He looked relieved for a moment, then seemed to remember his former complaint. "But don't think you're distracting me. I still got a beef with you, gal."

She glanced around, trying to determine what faux pas she might have committed. After all, she was doing him the enormous favor of keeping him company on an afternoon stakeout that was as exciting as eating a mashed potato and white bread sandwich, followed by vanilla pudding.

The locale wasn't anything to quicken the pulse either. They were parked on a nearly deserted residential street in one of the few unattractive and unsavory neighborhoods of sunny little San Carmelita—otherwise known as "the picturesque seaside village where native Southern Californians themselves go to relax and play."

Instead of sunlit beaches, boutiques, gift shops, and upscale restaurants, this part of town had ramshackle buildings, barred windows, signs warning of fierce dogs who could run faster than any trespasser, graffiti-smeared cement block walls, and burned-out streetlights. From what Savannah could tell, this section of San Carmelita possessed no virtues whatsoever, except those held by the souls who lived there—strength, courage, pride, and determination born of desperation.

Over the years, Savannah had seen more than one glorious flower bloom on this side of town, thriving in poverty's mud and squalor. But there were still a lot of places she'd prefer to be and things she'd rather be doing.

Considering the price she was paying to keep her bored cop hubby company, she couldn't imagine how she had managed to offend him.

She wasn't painting her fingernails—an activity he despised, claiming he was deathly allergic to the odor.

She had brought a tin of fresh-from-the-oven chocolate chip and macadamia nut cookies and had been considerate enough not to eat more than her rightful half of them.

She had allowed him to choose the music on the radio and, as a result, she had spent the last hour listening to Johnny Cash.

In truth, she liked Johnny quite a lot, but there was no point in letting Dirk know that. At the end of this tour, she wanted him to feel sufficiently indebted to her to take her out for a nice dinner. Otherwise, he would assume he could buy her off with day-old donuts and stale coffee . . . which he would also manage to finagle for free.

"Sorry, sweetcheeks," she said, her down-in-Dixie drawl a bit slower and softer than usual. "I don't know what sort of sins I've committed to get you all in a dither."

He nodded toward the dash, where she had set her empty soda can.

"Yeah?" she said, genuinely confused. "It's not going to spill, if that's what you're frettin' about. It's empty."

"You better make sure," he told her in a tone that was uncharacteristically bossy for him.

Over the years, she had trained him well.

He knew better.

She figured it must be mighty important to him, for him to risk riling her. So, she snatched the can off the dash, then began to roll down the window.

"What do you think you're doing?" he snapped.

"I'm gonna see if I can squeeze a drop or two of Coke out of this here can that you've got your willy all tied up in a Windsor knot about."

"You go pouring it out like that, some could splash on the outside of the door and ruin the paint job."

For a few seconds, she stared at him, calculating how much energy she would have to expend to cram a soda can into a highly annoying husband's right ear.

She figured, in the end, she could get the job done, but Dirk wasn't one to quietly submit to having items inserted into his orifices without offering resistance, and she was tired, so she abandoned the plan.

Instead, she rolled the window back up, opened the door, leaned out, bent down, and shook the three remaining drops of soda onto the curb.

Then, with much pomp and circumstance, she shut the door and handed him the can. "There you go. Feel free to shove this . . . wherever you're putting your garbage, now that you no longer hurl it over your right shoulder and onto the floorboard, the way you did for years and—"

"Until your brother restored this car to cherry condition!" he snapped, grabbing the can from her hand. "After all the work Waycross did on my baby, do you think I'm gonna let her get all dirty again? No way. You could do brain surgery back there on my rear floorboard now."

"Unsettling thought, but possibly necessary if this conversation continues," she muttered.

"You could lick ice cream off these seats."

"Knowing you, if you dropped your cone, you probably would," she whispered.

"What?"

"Nothing. I'm glad you're so proud of how clean your car is now, after years of slovenliness."

"Thank you. I guess." He crushed the can flat with his hands, reached behind her, and lovingly placed it into the fancy-dandy auto litter receptacle attached to her headrest, hanging behind the passenger's seat.

The bin was lined with a deodorized plastic bag, and Savannah was pretty sure she could detect the scent of bleach.

Her baby brother, Waycross, had restored Dirk's old Buick after it had been all but totaled in a severe accident. Before, the car had been pretty much a trash heap on wheels.

But since Waycross had surprised Dirk with the perfect "resurrection model" of his formerly deceased vehicle, Dirk was treating the car even better than Savannah babied her red 1965 Mustang. That was saying quite a lot, since she sometimes used dental floss to clean its wire-spoked wheel covers.

While she was glad to see Dirk finally give a dang for a change, embrace a passion, and abandon his former lifestyle—a study in untidy apathy—she found his new obsessive cleanliness annoying, to say the least.

"Be careful what you wish for," she murmured. "Lord

help you if you happen to get it." Under her breath she added, "Maybe I could get Waycross to remodel the area around my toilet."

"What?"

"Nothing."

Twenty minutes and several cookies later, both Savannah's and Dirk's banter had turned to silence born of acute boredom. Not even Johnny's rousing rendition of "Folsom Prison Blues," recorded in the infamous jailhouse itself, was enough to keep Dirk from nodding off.

"I could be home right now, you know," she told him, confident that he was sound asleep and wouldn't hear a word. "I could be watching TV or reading my new romance novel."

Surveilling a drug house was seldom a joyous occasion, and the one they were observing was even less exciting than most. They weren't even sure the occupants inside were selling drugs. Dirk had received a tip that they were a high volume, well-fortified operation. But the informant had a reputation for being less than honest, especially when offering information to avoid arrest.

Dirk's objective was simple: determine whether the tip was legitimate before going to the trouble and expense of sending an undercover cop into the house to score.

So far, other than a pizza delivery, no one had come in or out of the place, and it looked like any other run-down bungalow in the neighborhood. Quiet and reasonably law abiding.

To the point of boring.

"Yeah. I could be relaxing in my comfy chair, petting my kitties and shoving raspberry truffles in my face," she continued, berating the sleeping man. "Instead, I'm sitting here, my butt numb, listening to you snore like a warthog with a head cold and . . ."

Her complaint faded away as an old van with battered fenders and rust-encrusted paint pulled in front of the house in question. After jumping the curb, driving onto the grass for a moment, then down, the vehicle managed to park.

A woman exited the driver's door, nearly falling on her face in the process. Even from where Savannah sat and without any sort of sobriety test, she could tell the gal was strongly under the influence of something.

Savannah grabbed her binoculars off the dash and took a closer look at her. She paid special attention to the woman's haggard, anxious expression, her drug-ravaged body and shaky, fidgety movements.

She was painfully thin and dressed to reveal as much skin as possible in a teeny bikini top and short shorts that suggested the goods she was displaying were for sale—or at least for short-term rental.

"As Granny would say," Savannah whispered, "you can see all the way to Christmas and—glory be!—New Year's Eve, too."

When the woman walked around the rear of the van, on her way to the sidewalk, she paused to bang her fist on the back window several times. She yelled, "You stay put! Set one foot outside this van and I swear to gawd, I'll whup your tail good when I get back."

A rusty old bell clanged deep inside Savannah's personal memories. For a moment she was a twelve-year-old child, sitting in the open bed of an ancient pickup truck filled with her younger siblings, watching their mother stumble across a dark alley and enter a tavern's rear entrance. She felt the chill of the night air, the ache of hunger in her belly, and the crushing weight of responsibility, knowing that she alone would be responsible for keeping them all safe for the next four or five hours.

Warm, fed, or entertained . . . those were impossible luxuries.

Safety would be the only gift she might be able to afford.

But even that could prove difficult, considering the drunken patrons coming and going through the bar's back door. Not to mention the older children's propensity to ignore her orders, climb out of the truck, and play in the unlit parking area strewn with broken glass, discarded hypodermic needles, and used condoms.

Adjusting the binoculars' focus, Savannah saw a small face appear at the van's rear window for a second, then duck back down.

Deep inside her, among the dark memories, a presence stirred—a being that had been born long ago in that lonely, dangerous alley. A child with a woman's fierce maternal instincts, who carried a sword that she named Justice and a shield that was wide enough to protect not only herself, but any and all innocents she could gather behind it.

"Don't worry, darlin'," she whispered to the little one with the frightened face she had seen in the window. "Tonight . . . your life changes for the better. I promise."

Chapter 2

Savannah nudged the sleeping Dirk. "Wake up, sugar," she told him. "Your nap's over. Time to get to work. You don't want to miss the show."

Dirk stirred, glanced around with sleepy eyes, then managed to focus on the retreating woman's backside as she walked away from them, stumbling up the sidewalk toward the house they were surveilling.

"Eh," he said with a dismissive shrug. "I've seen way better butts than that—like this morning, when you bent over to take the biscuits outta the oven."

Ordinarily, Savannah would have been flattered and happy to receive the compliment. Of Dirk's numerous, endearing qualities, one of her favorites was his attitude that "more is more" when it came to feminine curvature.

But under the present circumstances, considering the child in the van and the fact that the woman entering the drug house could barely walk, let alone drive safely, Savannah had other things to think about than her husband's unabashed enthusiasm for his wife's ample backside.

"Is that her van?" Dirk asked, nodding toward the decrepit vehicle.

"Yes," Savannah replied.

"Was she drivin' it?"

"Rather badly, but yes."

"Good. When she comes out, we'll let her drive a couple of blocks—far enough away that the dealers in the house won't see. We don't wanna tip them off just yet that we're watching them. We'll get her on a DUI along with the junk, assuming she scores some."

"That would be nice, if only it was that simple," Savannah said with a tired sigh.

"Whaddaya mean? Maybe I can get 'er to talk. If I withhold her goods for a few hours, she'll flip."

Savannah watched as the woman tripped over her own feet, entering the house. "She looks like a flipper all right. Five minutes with you in the sweat box, she'll fold like a shy oyster."

"Exactly. Instead of messing with setting up an undercover buyer, we'll use her statement, and maybe a couple of others to get a warrant and come back next week with a full team to roust the house good and proper. No problem."

"She's got a child there in the van. From what I could see, a little one."

Savannah watched as the reality of the situation dawned on her husband, along with its implications.

"Damn," he said.

"Yeah. We can't let her drive away with a youngster in

the van and her drunk as Cooter Brown. Not even a few blocks."

"But if we remove the kid she'll notice he or she is gone, throw a fit, and alert the house that we're out here. They'll figure out that they're being watched."

"Exactly."

She could tell from his grimace that Dirk's brain was spinning as fast as hers, trying to form a plan.

Reaching a conclusion at the exact same moment, they said in unison, "Call Jake."

Dirk reached for his phone, punched in a number, and waited for his fellow detective, Jake McMurtry, to answer.

Since she was only a few feet away and Dirk always had the volume up on his phone, Savannah could hear Jake's drowsy tone when he said, "Yeah, Coulter. What's happenin'?"

Her husband wasn't the only one who nodded off on stakeouts. It was an occupational hazard. One that could cost a cop their job . . . or worse.

"You still sittin' on that house in the projects?" Dirk asked him.

"Yeah. Nothing's going on here. I think I'll pack it in."

"I'm at the house on Lester with Savannah. Turns out we may have to bust them now. Get over here as quick as you can."

"Call for backup."

"I will. Move!"

As soon as Dirk had placed the second call for reinforcements, Savannah said, "We have to get that young'un out of that van now. I'll bring the kid back here to the car and babysit till y'all are done doing what you gotta do."

"Yeah. Okay."

Both bailed out of the Buick and hurried up the sidewalk to the van, trying to stay behind the vehicles as much as possible in case someone in the house was looking out the window at that moment.

"Where did you see 'em?" Dirk asked. "Front or back?"

"Looking out the rear window. I'll try the back door, and you open the driver's side. I didn't see the mother lock it."

"Watch yourself," he said. "There might be someone else, another adult, in the back with the kid."

"I already thought of that. But thank you."

"Maybe I should take the rear."

As she had many times, Savannah reminded herself that Dirk hadn't done the protective male thing years ago, when they had been partners on the force. Back in "the day" he had treated her as an equal.

He still did. For the most part. But she had been shot and nearly died in his arms.

Near tragedies like that changed everything.

It had certainly changed him . . . her . . . them.

Eventually, skin, muscle, and bone healed. But the scars left by fear on the human psyche—those were forever.

"I got it, darlin'," she told him, her southern drawl soft but confident. "If there's a problem, you'll come scrambling between those bucket seats, into the back, and save me."

"Well, okay. But don't open the door till I give the word."

"All right. But not your usual one. It needs to be G rated for the kiddo."

He chuckled, a bit nervously. "Yeah. Gotcha."

They ducked as they scurried to the back of the van, keeping wary eyes on both the vehicle and the house.

Once Savannah was crouched at the rear door with her head beneath the window, her fingers around the handle, Dirk rushed to the driver's side.

A few seconds later, she heard his authoritative but, thankfully, suitable for all ages command, "Go!"

She twisted the handle, yanked hard, and the door came open with some difficulty and a loud, creaking sound, like an ancient, partially buried, dirt-encrusted casket opening in an old horror movie.

Peering inside the dark, cluttered interior, she saw nothing at first. But her eyes quickly adjusted, and she could see a small, frightened child with heartbreaking, large, frightened eyes staring at her.

"It's okay, sugar," she said, holding up both of her hands in a surrender pose. "Everything's all right."

The little head whipped around to watch Dirk as he climbed into the driver's seat and turned to face them.

"She's right. You're okay. We're just here to help you," Dirk said, using his "soft, sweet" voice. It was the one he usually reserved for his three favorite creatures on earth—Cleo, the gentler of their two cats at home, Vanna Rose, their red-haired, toddler niece, and of course, Savannah . . . when they weren't quarreling.

As Savannah climbed into the rear of the van, she could see the child better and realized it was a boy, about six years old.

Even in the dim light she could tell that he was underfed and barely clothed in only a pair of dirty shorts and flip-flops. He was in dire need of a good bath, a shampoo, and a haircut.

"My name is Savannah," she told him, holding out her hand to him. "What's yours?"

The boy hesitated and glanced down at her outstretched hand. Then without accepting the handshake, he looked her square in the eyes and said in a strong, confrontational tone and a southern accent even stronger than her own, "I'm Mr. Brody Greyson. But I'm not supposed to talk to strangers, especially ones that's just broke into my momma's van."

Something about the boy's squared, bony shoulders touched Savannah's heart, not to mention his Southern twang. His thin arms were crossed over his chest and his chin lifted defiantly. But she could see he was trembling.

She glanced out the side window of the van toward the house. The path was clear. No sign of Mom. At least, not yet.

"That's good advice your momma gave you about not talking to strangers, but in this case—"

"It weren't my momma that said it. My teacher tells us that."

"Then good for your teacher," she told him, "but in this case, it's okay, because that fella there is my husband, Detective Sergeant Coulter, and he's a policeman."

Dirk pulled his badge from his pocket and held it up for the child's inspection.

But instead of being impressed and comforted, Brody Greyson whirled on Dirk with a vengeance and shouted, "A cop? You're a stinkin' cop? Then you'd better get your smelly butt outta here right now, before my mom comes back! If she catches you in her van, she'll whup you up one side and down the other! She's mean as mean can be, and she *hates* cops! She says you're nothin' but a rotten, stinkin', lousy bunch of—"

"Now, now, Mr. Brody Greyson," Savannah said. "If

you make a habit of speaking to police officers in that disrespectful manner, your life's bound to get complicated real fast. You could find yourself in a whirlwind of trouble, even at your age!"

"I don't give a hoot! You clear outta here, before I knock you into next week myself! My momma left me in charge of her van, and if she finds out I let you in here, she'll thrash me with her belt. I'd a heap rather *you* get a whuppin' from *me* than *I* get one from *her*!"

"How about if nobody gets any whuppin' at all?" Savannah said, placing her hand gently on the boy's shoulder. "There's no call for anybody to get hurt. We're just going to talk and sort out some problems, all nice and peaceful. Would you like that? Would that be okay with you?"

She glanced over at Dirk and saw the sadness she was feeling in his eyes.

Something told her that a woman who had raised her son to be this aggressive and opposed to peace officers wasn't likely to be taken into custody gracefully.

"If you try to talk to my momma 'bout anything, it ain't gonna be nice *or* peaceful, I guarantee you," the child stated with deep conviction, echoing Savannah's thoughts. "She ain't known for 'peaceful,' and she's not all that nice either, even to people she likes, and she hates cops more than anything in the world. 'Cept maybe preachers."

"But if Detective Coulter treats her with respect—"

"Won't make a bit of difference. She says she'd be happy to skin every cop in the world alive and roast 'em all for dinner."

Savannah winced, then faked a laugh. "There's a lot of police officers in the world. If she tried to roast them all, she'd find herself busier than a one-eyed cat watching nine mouse holes."

"She's got a lot of energy, my momma," Brody said, nodding solemnly. "She'd get 'er done."

Savannah looked at Dirk and noticed he was watching the front door of the drug house intently. She wasn't surprised. The woman had been inside for several minutes now. Certainly long enough to do a quick drug deal. Most likely, she'd be coming out at any moment.

Behind Dirk, through the windshield, Savannah saw two police cruisers coming down the street toward them, their lights off. They pulled to the curb and parked, half a block away.

"Backup's ten-twenty-three," she told him.

"What've we got?"

"Two units."

His cell phone dinged. He glanced at the text message. "Jake too," he told her.

He didn't have to tell her that the time for conversation with young, but old for his age, Mr. Brody Greyson was coming to an end.

"Listen, son," Dirk told him, "I'm going to have to ask you to go with this lady and do everything she tells you to do. We've got some important business to tend to here at this house, and it would be best for everybody if you go with her until it's all over with."

"I ain't goin' nowhere!" the boy said, shoving Savannah's hand off his shoulder and scrambling to the other side of the van, away from her and Dirk. "I know what you're fixin' to do. You're gonna bust my momma and her friends and lock 'em up."

Savannah's brain tried to process what she was hearing. How could a child possess such street smarts at this "tender" age? She decided to be honest with him. There was no point in trying to sweeten this bitter cup of coffee.

"How this goes down," she began, "pretty much depends on your mother, what she's done, and what she decides to do in the future. If she cooperates with—"

"She doesn't cooperate with nobody," he said. "Ever. 'Bout nothin'."

For a moment, Savannah could see the sadness, the vulnerability in the boy's eyes. Briefly, she saw the fragile child behind the hard exterior.

"I'm sorry to hear that," she told him.

"It's gonna be bad," he whispered.

"Then come with me. I'll take you to a safe, quiet place. At least, then it won't have to be bad for *you*. Something tells me you've had enough of the bad stuff already. Right?"

She saw the nod, faint as it was. Quickly, she moved toward the boy, took his hand, and coaxed him toward the rear of the van.

She jumped out herself, then lifted him down and closed the door.

"I could've done that myself," he said. "I get out all the time without any help. Been doin' that since I was a baby."

She looked back at Dirk, who had also exited the vehicle and closed the driver's door. He gave her a slight, sad smile and a thumbs-up. Then he glanced over at the house. The door had opened, and Brody's mother was coming out.

"Come along, young sir," Savannah said, grasping Brody's hand tightly and rushing him down the sidewalk toward the Buick.

"I think I should stay here and help my mom," he said,

his voice quivering as he resisted and tried to pull his hand free.

"You can't, darlin'," Savannah told him, her own tone shaky as her throat tightened. "Adults have to take care of themselves, make their own decisions, sink or swim."

"She's bound to sink. I know her. She always sinks . . . 'specially when it comes to cops."

He tried to stop, to pull his wrist from her tight hand, but she held him fast and rushed him along.

"If she does, then it's on her, sugar," she told him. "Not you."

They had arrived at the Buick. When she reached for the rear door handle, he tried even harder to wriggle away. "This ain't no cop car!" he yelled. "Are you sure he's a cop? Are y'all just tryin' to kidnap me?"

She glanced behind her and saw that Dirk was standing on the sidewalk next to the van, talking to the boy's mother. All seemed to be going okay.

Two houses away and out of sight of the surveilled house, Jake and four uniforms watched from behind a neighbor's thick shrubs, waiting to see if they might be needed.

Everyone would try to remain low-key for as long as possible, rather than alert the house there was a problem outside.

Okay, so far, so good, Savannah thought. There was no need to grab the kid up and toss him into the car, further exacerbating his fears, if she could just talk him into going peacefully.

Sinking to one knee, to be at his eye level, she said, "No, Brody. We're not going to kidnap you or hurt you in any way. Detective Coulter is a real cop, a good cop. I swear. I used to be a police officer, too. All we want is for you to be safe. If we're lucky, maybe we can get your momma some help, too. Then you could be both safe *and* happy. Now, wouldn't that be a fine thing?"

Outside the dark van, Brody's small face was clearly visible, and Savannah could see with heartbreaking clarity the child was a mess.

His hair was long and badly matted, and his gaunt cheeks were smudged with far more grime than a child would normally accumulate during a single afternoon of roughhouse play.

Savannah didn't want to think about how long it would take to get a pair of shorts that filthy.

Even through the dirt, she could see copious bruises in various stages of healing on his legs and arms, not to mention a dismaying array of untended cuts, scrapes, and scratches.

But it was his eyes that held her and her heart captive.

Throughout her career with the San Carmelita Police Department, she had seen a lot of sad, neglected, abused children, but she never got over the pain of it. She was sure she never would.

Years ago, she had been a sad, neglected, abused child. Back in the tiny rural town of McGill, Georgia, another policeman—brave and strong, with a heart that hurt when he saw sad children—had rescued her and her siblings from a situation much like this child's.

She knew exactly how Brody Greyson felt. She could see the same pain in his big eyes . . . eyes filled with innocence, hope, and grim, worldly knowledge far beyond what any child should have to carry.

"Hop inside the car, Brody," she said softly. "Take a chance. Brave guys like you get rewards for their courage."

"What kinda rewards?" he wanted to know.

"They get better lives."

For a couple of seconds, he smiled at her, and Savannah was struck by the otherworldly beauty of the boy's face. Beneath the pain, the dirt, the poverty, the anger, and the fear, he had a cherubic quality that belied the harsh statements he had spoken and the quarrelsome attitude he had displayed earlier.

In that moment, Savannah believed—based on Granny Reid's religious instruction—that she was seeing what Brody Greyson's Creator had lovingly designed . . . before the child had been reshaped by his troubled environment.

"Come with me, sugar," she said. "You'll be so glad you did."

"Okay," he said softly. "Let's go."

"Atta boy." Savannah pulled the door open and motioned for him to get inside.

"Just hop in there and get buckled up, so we can—"

At that moment, they heard a scream, like that of a screech owl with its tailfeathers caught in a fox's mouth. The sound was so loud it literally caused Savannah's ears to ache. But it had a far more devastating effect on Brody.

"Momma!" he screamed as he broke away from Savannah and raced toward the van. His mother and Dirk had somehow gone from what appeared to have been a civil conversation to an all-out, no-holds-barred wrestling match on the sidewalk next to the vehicle.

Savannah ran after Brody, but he was a spry little fellow and managed to arrive at the scene of the vigorous action before she, Jake, or the uniforms could intercept him.

Dirk had gotten the upper hand and was kneeling

astride the wayward mom, who was displaying an impressive amount of strength for so tiny a woman as she flailed and kicked, screamed and cursed with an impressive vocabulary—even if it was mostly four-letter words.

On the sidewalk was a ragged backpack, its flap open and contents strewn across the concrete—sandwich bags filled with pills of every color, packets of white powder and crystals.

Even with Savannah's prior experience, which included a stint in Narcotics, she was impressed by the magnitude of the haul. It was obviously far too much for a personal stash. Momma Greyson had to be dealing, as well as using, and during her brief visit inside the house she had scored, big time!

For all the good it was going to do her.

At that moment, it appeared Dirk might be able to accomplish the task of flipping her over and onto her stomach, maybe even cuffing her. But the situation took a dark turn when the enraged boy jumped onto his back, wrapped his skinny left arm tight around Dirk's neck, and began to pummel his face with his right fist.

Though shocked and horrified, Savannah couldn't help being impressed with the kid's ferocious fighting skills. Apparently, Mr. Brody Greyson wasn't a lad to be trifled with, and it appeared "trifling" included attempting to arrest his mother.

"Let go of my momma!" he yelled at Dirk. "Get off her, you lousy, pig-nose, skunk butt!"

"Tear his face clean off, Brody!" Momma screeched. "Tear it off and shove it so far up his—"

"That's enough!" Savannah shouted as she grabbed the boy by his shoulders and, with considerable effort, peeled him off Dirk's back. She lifted him off his feet and pulled him close, his back against her chest in a tight bear hug. With his arms pinned to his sides, all he could do was struggle—and, unfortunately, administer some well-aimed kicks to her legs.

"Stop, Brody," she whispered in his ear. "Just stop. Take a deep breath and calm yourself, darlin'. Make the good choice. Swim. Don't sink."

After what seemed like forever to her and her shins, he ceased to struggle. She lowered him, so he could stand on his own feet, then turned him to face her, so that he wouldn't see what was happening behind him with his mother.

Jake and the uniformed cops had joined Dirk in the effort to place the woman under arrest. Even with enforcements, the scrimmage had become a battle that law enforcement appeared, at least for the moment, to be losing.

Savannah suspected that Dirk was holding back in his efforts, treating his suspect far more gently than he would have a male perp whose child wasn't nearby.

She had seen him take a gentler approach before when there were youngsters present. His generosity was often to his detriment.

"Gentle" wasn't going to cut it with this gal.

She had elbowed one of the uniforms in the face. Hard. He was kneeling beside her, holding his hand over his right eye, rocking back and forth and moaning something about how he was "never gonna see again."

In her spare time, Ms. Greyson had managed to kick Jake squarely in the solar plexus. He was lying on his side in the road next to the curb, gasping like a salmon who had managed to swim the entire journey upstream to the spawning ground, only to be grabbed by a famished grizzly bear, intent on having him for lunch.

But worst of all, their would-be captive had a handful of Dirk's hair and was pulling it as hard as she could—a particularly egregious thing to do to a fellow who literally counted his front top hairs every morning to see if he'd lost any and how many.

Savannah debated whether to join them, to see if she could add anything worthwhile to the mix. But she didn't want to turn Brody loose, for fear of what he might do. The last thing she needed was to have to chase a frisky, frightened, angry child through a shady neighborhood with miscreants galore.

When Savannah saw one of the uniforms reaching down to his utility belt to retrieve his Taser, she knew it was time to get Brody out of the area. At any moment, his mother, who had graduated from slapping and kicking to clawing and biting, was likely to be flopping around in a manner that no child should witness.

Savannah glanced over at the house and saw that several faces were peeking from between drawn curtains at the windows, but no one appeared overly eager to rush outside and rescue their most recent customer.

Savannah had a feeling, based on experience, that the plumbing inside that building was being taxed at that moment by the number of drugs being flushed through its pipes.

Considering the quantity of pills and paraphernalia that had spilled out of Brody's mom's backpack, and since she hadn't been carrying the bag when she'd entered, Savannah knew that Dirk would have ample cause to, at the very least, knock on the door and have a serious conversation with the inhabitants before the evening was over.

He was going to have a busy night.

Not to mention the time and effort he would expend booking the reluctant Ms. Greyson.

It would be hours before Dirk would be coming home and seconds before Brody's mom was going to be zapped. Savannah decided it was the perfect time to leave.

"Come along, darlin'," she told Brody, grabbing him by the hand and dragging him back to the car. "We've got better things to do and nicer places to be than hanging around this mess."

"But, my momma . . ."

"I wouldn't fret about her none." Savannah glanced back just in time to see the woman on the ground kick the Taser gun so hard that it flew out of the cop's hand and hit Jake in the head, adding to his already considerable agony—and fury. "I think that little momma of yours can take care of herself just fine."

Once again, Savannah shoved him into Dirk's immaculate backseat and instructed him to buckle his seat belt.

She could tell by the awkwardness of his movements as he did so that he wasn't accustomed to even this, the simplest of safety practices.

She added that fact to the growing list in her head of serious reasons Ms. Greyson could be considered, at the very least, an inadequate parent.

Savannah and Brody were in the Buick and a block away when they heard a series of yelping shrieks that reminded Savannah of how her cat, Diamante, had reacted years ago when getting her tail caught beneath the back-porch rocking chair.

She looked in the rearview mirror at her passenger to see how alarmed the boy might be at knowing his mother was having a serious and personal encounter with a Taser.

To her surprise, he looked quite resigned to the fact. His voice was even calm when he said, "Guess she done made her decision, like you said, to sink or swim. When it comes to my momma, you can pretty much figure on her sinkin' ever' time. That's just how she rolls." He took a deep breath and sighed. "I wish I could say different, but . . ."

"I hear ya, sugar." She locked eyes with him in the mirror and gave him a weak smile. "Try not to feel too bad about it. She's not all that different from a lot of folks I've known in my day."

To her surprise, he smiled back—a mischievous little grin. "I'm feelin' okay. But if that's true, you must've had a pretty crummy life."

"You have no idea, puddin' head. Like we say in Georgia, it's been a tough row to hoe, and it's not showing any signs of letting up."

Chapter 3

"Wow! You live *here*? You must be rich!" Brody Greyson exclaimed when Savannah pulled her husband's Buick into the driveway of their small Spanish-style house with its white stucco walls and red-tiled roof.

She glanced around at the somewhat middle-to-lower-income neighborhood and wondered how bad Brody's home must be for him to be so impressed with hers.

"Rich?" she said, shaking her head. "Not so's you'd notice it, kiddo. My husband being a cop and me a private detective who's out of work most days, we do well to make ends meet somewhere in the middle."

Her denial did little to dampen the boy's enthusiasm as he pressed his face to the window, taking in every detail of the yard.

"But y'all got grass and flowers and stuff, and your house is white and clean as a hound's tooth."

Savannah chuckled, enjoying a bit of nostalgia at hearing the child's accent and terminology. Despite his scrape with Dirk and some of his too-adult language, the kid was positively oozing with charm, and his southern drawl was a bit of pecan and coconut frosting on the German chocolate cupcake.

Slowly, carefully she parked the Buick—heaven forbid she should get a scratch on that virgin paint!—next to Granny Reid's old Mercury panel truck. Until that moment, she had forgotten that her grandmother had asked permission to drop by this evening and use her kitchen to bake a coconut cake for the church picnic raffle.

Granny had never complained about living in the old mobile home that had once been Dirk's. Before moving in, she had tossed out his "furniture," which consisted of a school bus seat "sofa," TV tray "end tables," and "storage" units made of stacked plastic milk crates. Then she had set about decorating in earnest, adding enough floral fabrics, ruffles, and lace doilies to make her "castle" her own.

When Gran woke at dawn every morning, the first thing she did, even before having coffee, was say a prayer of thanksgiving that she now lived among the palm trees in a seaside town in California. It had been a lifelong dream of hers, to live by an ocean with a palm tree in sight, and she never got over the wonder of it all. . . .

Until it came time to bake something.

"That blamed trailer oven's got a lot of gall even claimin' to be one," she had told Savannah. "You can't put a mite-sized pan of brownies in that dinky thing, let alone one of my triple-layer coconut cakes. Mind if I come swing by and bake it in yours?" she had asked.

Since her grandmother was one of Savannah's favorite people on earth, she had quickly given her permission.

"Speaking of hounds' teeth," Savannah said as she turned off the car's ignition, "you're about to meet an honest-to-goodness hound dog by the name of Colonel Beauregard the third. But we just call him 'the Colonel.'"

"What kinda hound is he? There's all kinds, you know," Brody shot back with great authority. "Redbones and blue-ticks and basset hounds and beagles, too."

"Hey, you know a lot about hounds."

"I know a lot about dogs. I like dogs. Cats too. It's just people I don't like."

She chuckled as she got out of the car, opened his door, and helped him unbuckle his seat belt. "I can't argue with you there, kiddo," she told him. "I'm a bit partial to folks who wear fur coats and walk on four feet, like my two cats, Diamante and Cleopatra, and my granny's dog, the Colonel. He's an honest-to-goodness blood-hound."

"Really? Like they have in the movies that go chasin' people through swamps and stuff?"

"Sure as shootin'!"

"With long, floppy ears and one of them wrinkly faces?"

"Yes, and he can howl loud and long enough to curdle milk and send shivers up and down your spine."

Together, they walked up the sidewalk to the house. Savannah was surprised and pleased when he slipped his hand into hers. He seemed quite a different child from the one who had been pummeling her husband such a short time ago.

As they stepped onto the front porch, she noticed that

he was particularly interested in the giant bougainvillea vines that grew from two large clay pots on either side of the door.

"How did you get them flowers to do that?" he asked, pointing to where they intertwined in a glorious crimson arch above the doorway.

"I planted them, and they grew. That twisting themselves together business—they just sort of did that on their own," she told him. "That's why I named them Bogey and Ilsa."

He gave her a look of total confusion.

Chuckling, she said, "Maybe someday, you'll watch a fine old movie named *Casablanca* and then you'll understand."

After thinking that over for a moment, he scowled, shook his head, and said, "Naw, I don't think so. If it's about plants getting tangled up together, it's probably a mushy movie. I ain't big on them."

"No, I don't suppose you are." She unlocked the door and ushered him inside. "At your age, I reckon it's ugly monsters out to destroy the world and superheroes trying to stop them."

"Well, yeah. Duh."

Once inside the foyer, she called out, "Gran! I'm home, and I brought company."

"Hey, darlin'! In the kitchen. I'll be out in a minute," was the cheerful reply from the rear of the house.

Still standing in the foyer, next to the coat closet door, Savannah hesitated a moment, then said to Brody, "You go on into the living room, while I put away my purse," she said. "Look around and see if you can find a black cat or two."

"You've got lotsa pets! You're lucky!"

"I certainly am," Savannah said as she watched the child scurry into the living room, in search of furry faces.

Once he was out of sight, she opened the closet door, shoved some coats aside, and punched in the number combination on the small wall safe's pad. With one more glance over her shoulder to make sure he wasn't watching, she opened the door, removed her Beretta pistol from her purse, and put it inside the safe.

In the olden days, when it had just been her living in the house and with only a few adult visitors, Savannah had simply placed her weapon on the closet's top shelf, far back in the corner. But her quiet little house had become far busier in the past few years, and children had been added to the mix. With two firearms in the family, she and Dirk had decided to install a safe and use it faithfully.

With a child like Brody visiting, she was glad they had done so.

Both she and Dirk had witnessed the tragic aftereffects of careless, unsafe gun storage practices.

With so much at stake, there was no point in taking chances.

Her weapon locked away and her purse on the top shelf, she closed the closet door and walked into the living room.

Not for the first time, she was surprised when she saw what Brody was doing. He had found one of her two black mini-panthers lying on the windowsill cat perch. The cat was soaking up the last bit of afternoon sun as the boy leaned over her, scratching behind her right ear, whispering sweet nothings to her.

Savannah was shocked to realize it was Diamante, the less friendly, far more aloof of the two sister kitties.

Strangers simply did *not* pet Diamante. It was unthinkable. She just didn't allow such things.

Cleopatra was affectionate to a fault, usually making a nuisance of herself by begging for pets, belly rubs, and ear scratches.

Diamante, on the other hand, deigned to allow Savannah, and *only* Savannah, to pet her. When absolutely necessary. For short periods of time. *If* she was in the mood.

This new turn of events was even more miraculous because Diamante had an ear infection and, as a result, was even grumpier than usual.

"Oh, watch out!" Savannah warned him, rushing to the window perch, ready to rescue her juvenile guest, if necessary. "Her ear's been bothering her lately, so she's not—"

"I know, I know," he said calmly, still stroking the cat. "But the right one's the sore one. That's why I'm just touching the other one."

Once again, Savannah was surprised. "How did you know that?"

"When I walked in, she was scratching the right one. Then she shook her head hard, like they do when they've got a bum ear."

He bent down and peered into the ear in question. "I don't see no mites. That ain't the problem."

"No. It isn't mites. The vet decided she had an allergic reaction to some new food I bought them at—"

"A food they never ate before?"

"Yes. I had a coupon and—"

"Yeah. Food allergy. That's what I woulda said, too.

No mites and both ears are nice and clean. A change of food . . . that could do it."

Savannah could barely suppress a snicker at his somber little face and oh-so-grave tone. A prestigious cardio surgeon couldn't have been more serious or confident when diagnosing a complex artery disease.

"Did your vet give you some stuff to smear inside there?" he asked.

"Um, yes, as a matter of fact. An antibiotic cream. But she—"

"Hates it. Yeah, I know, and you probably have to put it in there a couple times a day."

"Yes. Twice."

"Next time she needs it, you just tell me, and I'll do it for ya, okay? I'm real good at it."

"No way! She'd claw your eyes out." Savannah reached down and pulled up one sleeve to reveal fresh scratch marks on her arm. "This is what I wound up with, and that was just because she saw the tube in my hand."

"Then I won't let her see the tube. I got a system. Really."

"Who's your new friend, Savannah girl?"

Savannah turned to see her grandmother standing behind her. She was wearing an old-fashioned apron over her bright tropical-print caftan. Her cloud of soft silver hair was tied back from her face with an equally colorful scarf, twisted into a headband.

A smudge of flour on her nose and a dusting across her cheeks suggested she had been cooking—along with the amazing aroma of fresh-baked goods scenting the air.

Her bright blue eyes sparkled with good-natured humor as she smiled at the boy and held out her hand. "I'm Stella Reid, but everybody I know calls me Granny, so you might as well, too," she told him.

The child accepted her hand and gave it a hearty shake. "I'm Mister Brody Greyson. Glad to make your acquaintance, Miz Reid," he replied with all the mannered graciousness of a well-bred southern gentleman.

"And yours, young man," Granny replied. Turning to Savannah, she said, "He's a real whiz with cats, it 'pears. Could've saved you a vet bill, if only you'd known."

Again, Savannah watched as Granny's sharp eyes swept over the boy, from head to toe. This time, Savannah could tell she was noting his soiled, worn, inadequate clothes. It took more than a pair of shorts and flip-flops to keep a child warm on a cool beach day. Then there were the unattended scrapes and cuts, not to mention the lack of basic sanitation.

Savannah watched her grandmother's smile fade into something more akin to sadness, tinged with anger. Gran harbored strong feelings for innocent children who were neglected—and toward those who should have been caring for them.

"How do you know so much about animals and their ailments?" Savannah asked Brody, as he continued his ear rubbing on the purring and highly contented Diamante.

"One of my friends is a vet. She helps me with my animals," he replied matter-of-factly.

"I thought you said you didn't have any pets."

"I don't have pets. But I take care of the cats and dogs out in the alley behind a motel we stay at when we've got the money. If they're hurt, I take 'em to Dr. Carolyn, and she fixes 'em up for me. I pay her back by helpin' her there at her clinic. I clean up after the animals and sometimes I help her hold them still while she works on 'em."

"No wonder you know so much about ear infections and the like."

"Yeah. I told her I'm gonna be a vet, too, when I grow up, so she's givin' me a head start."

"She sounds like a fine person," Granny said, "as are you, for helpin' out them poor alley cats and stray dogs."

Brody shrugged his bony shoulders. "It ain't as good as havin' pets of your own, but we can't."

"Why's that?" Granny asked.

"'Cause sometimes, when my momma can't pay the motel, we get kicked outta our room on our ears. Then we gotta sleep in our car on the beach. Can't have your own honest-to-goodness pets with that happenin' all the time."

"No, I reckon not," Granny said. "Animals need stability. Children too," she added softly.

Instantly, Brody bristled. "My momma ain't bad. She does the best she can!"

"I've no doubt that she does, son," Granny replied. Looking down at his skinned knees, she added, "But once in a while, life gets extra hard and folks need a helpin' hand."

A hard, cold look came over his otherwise sweet face. It occurred to Savannah that it was an expression seldom seen on one so young and usually observed on street-hardened criminals.

The thought also crossed her mind that, unless someone intervened soon, this boy, whose heart was tender toward animals and who wanted to be a veterinarian when he grew up, would probably never fulfill his dream. Unless his present path was drastically altered, he would probably be wearing that bitter expression behind bars.

The very thought broke her heart.

"As much as both you and that cat are enjoying that

petting," Savannah told him, "I promised you an intro-duction to a real-live bloodhound."

Instantly, he brightened, and she was grateful for the change.

He abandoned Diamante and rushed around the room, looking up the staircase, behind the living room furniture, and then into the kitchen. "I forgot about the hound dog! Where is he?"

"He's out in the backyard," Granny said. "With Dia-mante feelin' poorly, her ear hurtin' and all, I didn't have the heart to lock the kitty cats upstairs all by their lone-some so's he could run around loose downstairs here."

"They don't play good together?" Brody asked.

"No," Savannah assured him. "Years ago, when the Colonel was just a pup back in Georgia, our neighbor's mean old cat darned near beat the tar out of him, and he never got over it."

"Hates cats?"

"Despises them."

"Can't be around 'em?"

"Not for a second."

Brody shook his head solemnly. "Then we wouldn't want them to run into each other. If he killed one of them . . ."

Savannah chuckled. "Oh, they've fought a few battles over the years, and the cats' lives were never in any dan-ger. The Colonel's, maybe. It's his safety we're worried about."

"His snout and eyes?"

"Exactly." She reached over, placed a hand on the boy's shoulder, and guided him toward the kitchen and the back door. "You skedaddle on out there and introduce yourself to him."

"He won't bite me, what with me bein' a stranger in his yard?"

"Naw," Granny replied. "He ain't gonna chow down on you. You're a young'un, and the Colonel loves little'uns. He thinks they're all puppies for him to play with. He'll be tickled to have yer company. You'll see."

"I'll go out and introduce you, if you like," Savannah offered.

He considered it, then straightened his shoulders and, looking both doubtful and eager, said, "That's okay. I got this. I can handle a hound dog any day and twice on Christmas."

With that, he hurried toward the back of the house and out the rear door, slamming it closed behind him.

Savannah and Granny rushed to the kitchen window to watch the meeting.

It went as Granny had predicted. The Colonel met Brody halfway across the yard, jumped up, put his massive feet on the child's shoulders, and gave him an enthusiastic, wet slurp across his cheek.

Laughing, Brody wiped off the canine slobber with the back of his hand, and the women heard him say, "You cut that out, Colonel What's-Your-Name, or I'll lick you right back."

"That dog's 'bout as tall as that child is," Granny said, laughing. "But lookie there. The boy stands right up to him and tells him what's what."

"Oh, Mr. Brody got grit in his craw to spare. I had to pull him off Dirk earlier. That boy was, as we say, 'stompin' a mudhole' in my husband and 'walkin' it dry'!"

The normally calm and cool octogenarian gasped and turned to her granddaughter with a genuinely shocked expression on her face. "You had to rescue your big, burly policeman husband from a scrawny, underfed young'un like that?" she said.

"I'm dead serious. I swear. He was on Dirk's back, riding him like he was a rodeo cowboy and Dirk was a Brahma bull, and the boy was socking him in the face the whole time he was on him. I had to peel him off him like he was an overly sticky bandage on a hairy leg."

Granny looked out the window again at the child, who was now rolling around on the grass with the bloodhound. He was laughing, the Colonel was howling, and all appeared right with the world—or, at least, in Savannah's backyard.

"Hard to imagine such a thing," Gran said. "What brought *that* on?"

"Dirk arresting his momma, who'd just walked out of a drug house with more pills in a backpack than your average pharmacy's got on their shelves."

Granny nodded somberly. "That'll do 'er. Dirk don't look kindly on such goings-on."

"None of us do. Especially now," Savannah added, her voice heavy with sadness.

She stole a quick sideways glance at her grandmother and saw the same sorrow reflected on the older woman's face. Savannah wished she hadn't said it. The last thing either of them needed was to be reminded of her brother's struggle with drug addiction. At the moment, Waycross was doing well, attending meetings and staying clean. But they all lived in fear that he might relapse.

They knew, all too well, that addiction was a monster who could never be buried in a grave and forgotten. It had a terrible habit of resurrecting itself when its victims least expected it. One could never consider the battle won and relax. The disease was incurable. Though, thankfully, in some cases, manageable.

With the help and support of his loved ones, Waycross seemed to be managing.

That was enough. For today.

One day at a time.

"Is that why you brung the child home with ya?" Granny asked, nodding toward Brody, who was running around the yard, trying to hide from the dog with no success whatsoever. The Colonel was, after all, a bloodhound. "Was it because his momma's in jail?"

"I brought him home because when I took him to CPS, the intake gal there told me she didn't have a foster home for him to go to. She was fixing to stick him in juvie hall, so I asked her if Dirk and I could just take him for the night. Maybe something would open up for him tomorrow. It took some convincing, but I finally talked her into it."

"Good for you . . . and for him."

They watched and laughed as the hound grabbed a mouthful of the back of the boy's baggy shorts and took him to the ground, where he playfully mauled him like a stuffed toy, Brody squealing with delight the whole time.

"I'm going to have to get him some clothes right away," Savannah said. "He can't run around all over Kingdom Come in those filthy shorts."

"Looks like he has been. For a long time, too."

"I know, and we're putting a stop to that. Like you always told us, 'No matter how poor a body is, there's no excuse for dirtiness.'"

"That's for sure," Granny replied. "He desperately needs an introduction to Mr. Soap and Miss Bath Water before he's much older."

"I hate to interrupt his good time though," Savannah said, watching the boy try to teach the dog to retrieve the stick he had thrown. The Colonel was great at chasing any thrown object and picking it up with his massive mouth, but he was loath to return his prize to the pitcher. Instead, he pranced around the yard, stick in mouth, head high, showing off his treasure.

"Yeah, if the child had a tussle with the law earlier today, he's probably in need of some rest and relaxation."

"Not to mention a good meal. I've got some leftover fried chicken and potato salad in the fridge. I'll ply him with that."

Granny glanced away, looking a bit guilty. "I must admit, you ain't got quite as much as you had when you left the house earlier today."

Savannah laughed. "That's okay. I knew I was taking a risk when I left you alone with it. Us Reid women can't resist leftover chicken."

"I'll make it up to you though. I baked two of them coconut cakes. Had you in mind for the second one."

Savannah thought it over a few moments, weighing the pros and cons. "Let's see now . . . A drumstick in exchange for one of Granny Reid's prizewinning coconut cakes. I'd say I came out ahead in that deal."

"A drumstick *and* a thigh. I was plumb starved to death."

"Still a bargain." Savannah headed for the refrigerator. "Let me get that food on the table, and then I'll call him in to wash up and—"

Her cell phone rang, just as she entered the kitchen, and she didn't recognize the chime as any of her "regulars."

For a moment, the thought occurred to her that the intake official might have found a foster home for Brody, and she had to admit that she was a bit disappointed to think that was the case.

To her surprise, she was actually looking forward to having the boy around for the evening, feeding him a good meal, getting him cleaned up, finding some decent clothes for him, "treating" him to some of the simple pleasures of life that, sadly, might be luxuries for him.

That would be a more fun and worthwhile way to spend an evening than reading a few more chapters of her romance novel. Surely, Lady Wellington and her new coachman hottie could wait yet another day to consummate their torrid love affair in the hayloft.

She pulled the phone out of her pants pocket and instantly felt better when she saw the name. In fact, she felt a bit of a thrill that, she had to admit, was a tad more exciting than a married woman should get when answering a call from a man who hadn't given her the diamond ring on her finger.

But she quickly consoled herself with the thought that literally millions of women would have been thrilled to death to receive a call from this particular man.

Ethan Malloy—Academy Award–winning movie star, heartthrob, leading man in the fantasies of lust-besotted fans worldwide—had once been Savannah's client and was now her treasured friend.

Just before clicking the on button to receive the call, Savannah turned to Granny and mouthed the single word, "Ethan."

The gleam that lit Granny's eyes in an instant was testimony to the appeal the actor held for all ages. No one, young or old, could resist the charms of Ethan Malloy.

"Hello, Ethan. So nice to hear from you," Savannah

said, suddenly conscious of the fact that she had just put on her sexiest phone voice . . . and sounded pretty darned silly in the process. She wondered if he heard that sort of thing a lot and considered her and her "type" ridiculous.

No, Ethan was much too kind for that.

Long ago, Savannah had decided that his gifts, which included standing at least six inches taller than the average male, a voice a full octave deeper than most, and pale blue eyes that reached into the soul of every person they studied, hadn't ruined him. This Texas boy, son of a moderately successful rancher, seemed to have no clue about his effect on women. His modesty, along with his calm, soothing, deep voice, might have been his greatest charm.

But he didn't sound calm or soothing when he said, "I'm sorry, Savannah. This isn't a social call. Something bad—" She heard his voice break and he struggled to speak. "Very bad, has happened. I need help."

Again? she thought. *No, please, not again!*

The last time he had spoken words like that was upon the occasion of their first meeting. Ethan's wife and young son had gone missing, and he feared they were victims of foul play.

"Not Beth and Freddy," she said, almost afraid to even think it, let alone say it. For days she had searched for the two, afraid that, when and if she found them, she might be too late.

Fortunately, that hadn't been the case. She had located and rescued them, but not before blood had been shed. It was a case that would haunt her forever.

"No," he said. "Freddy's okay, and Beth. Well, you know we aren't together anymore."

"Yes. I know. I'm so sorry."

How could she not know? Everyone in the world

knew, thanks to the tabloid magazines that had splashed the gory destruction of their personal lives across the covers of newspapers and gossip rags from one side of the globe to the other.

It wasn't surprising to her. The marriage had been in trouble even before the tragic kidnapping. Few couples would have survived their ordeal and managed to stay together.

"What's wrong, Ethan," she said, "and how can I help?"

"I thought maybe you'd heard already. What with your husband being a detective. We called the police, of course. I was the one who found her."

"Found who, Ethan?" she asked, her heart pounding. "What's happened?"

"It's Lucinda Faraday."

Savannah searched her memory banks and recalled a woman with platinum blond hair, bobbed short and wavy. Big, doe-like eyes and thin, arched eyebrows. A silver-screen star from the late forties and early fifties. In particular, Savannah recalled a famous picture of her, lolling on a satin chaise lounge in a provocative pose, dressed in a peekaboo chiffon negligee with marabou feather trim, smoking with an opera-length cigarette holder.

There had been a scandal of some sort attached to her name, but at the moment, Savannah couldn't recall it.

"Yes," she said. "I remember her. The old movie star?"

"Yes. She was an accomplished actress. She was also a wonderful person. My friend."

"She *was*?"

"Yes. She's . . . she's dead."

"How?"

"Murdered, I think. It was me who, who . . . I found her. About a half an hour ago."

Savannah could tell he was crying. Her heart ached to think of this kind, gentle man in the midst of yet another tragedy of some sort.

Some people just never seemed to get a break. Not even those who appeared to be good, law-abiding folks.

"Where's the body?" she asked.

"In her home."

"Her home. Oh, yes. I remember. It's that old mansion out in Twin Oaks, right? With a funny name I can't pronounce."

"Yes. Qamar Damun. It's a beautiful old place. Used to be anyway. She's lived here for years."

"*Here?* You're there now?"

"Yes. Like I said, I found her. We called the police already, but I'd appreciate it so much if you'd come out here. You know a lot more about . . . this kind of thing than I do. I'd feel a lot better if you were here."

Savannah looked out the window at Brody, who was still wrestling his new canine friend. How could she leave this child, so in need of simple, basic care? And yet, this friend of hers was hurting and frightened. . . .

"Ethan, I'd like to help you," she said, "but . . . can you please hold on for just a moment?"

"Yes, of course," he replied.

"Go," Granny said quietly. "If that young man needs help, you go help him."

"But—"

"No 'buts' 'bout it. If there's anything I'm still perfectly capable of doin', it's takin' care of a young'un. Go do whatcha gotta do."

"Are you sure?"

Granny propped her hands on her hips, squared her shoulders, and lifted her chin. "Do I look sure?"

Savannah couldn't help grinning, despite the circumstances. "Okay. Thank you, Granny."

"It sounds like you're busy, Savannah," she heard Ethan saying. "I'm sorry. If it isn't a convenient time, I can—"

"That's the thing about murder, Ethan," Savannah said, her tone nearly as sad as his. "There's never a convenient time for evil like that."

She drew a deep breath and shifted mental gears from a stand-in mom for a night to a private detective and former policewoman. "I have to explain the situation to a young fella, and then I'll head right out there. I'll arrive inside half an hour."

"Thank you, Savannah!" He sounded so relieved. "You have no idea how much I appreciate this."

She knew exactly how much. She could hear the heart-deep gratitude in his voice, see the confidence in her grandmother's kindly smile, and she knew she'd made the right decision.

"I know you do, Ethan. Now listen to me carefully. Do you have any reason to believe that the killer might still be there on the property?"

"No. I don't think so. She looks like—" She heard him make a gagging sound. "—like she's been . . . gone . . . a while."

"Okay. You said 'we' called the police. Who's there with you?"

"Mary Mahoney. She's Lucinda's housekeeper. More like a companion, really."

"That's it? Just the two of you?"

"Yes. Just us."

"Then don't touch anything. Neither one of you. In fact, you two just go outside. Is your car there?"

"Yes."

"Good. Then sit in your car and wait for either me or the cops, whoever arrives first. Okay?"

"Okay."

"I'll get there as quick as I can."

"I know you will. Thank you."

"You're welcome, sugar. Try not to worry. Everything's going to be okay."

There was a long, awkward silence on the other end. Finally, she heard him say, "Except that my friend is dead."

Savannah felt like a jerk. Platitudes, so ineptly uttered, were worse than worthless under such dire circumstances. When would she learn not to let them just fly out of her mouth like bats out of a cave at sundown?

"Yes, I'm sorry, darlin'," she said, as softly as she could. "You're right. Nothing can ever make that okay. Or even close to all right."

Chapter 4

As Savannah drove Dirk's precious Buick through the quiet little beach town, then into the canyon leading eastward and away from the ocean, she could feel the tension in her body. It was a nasty and unwelcome presence that tightened her muscles, strained her nerves, and caused her heart to beat faster than it needed to.

In her twenties, Savannah hadn't noticed such things. Or if she had, she had chalked such symptoms up to "excitement."

In her thirties, she had noticed, but not minded so much. Again, a heightened pulse was a small price to pay for a life fueled by adrenaline. Challenge, conflict, and even the occasional life-threatening drama seemed acceptable, if that's what was required to follow one's passion.

But now, well into her forties, Savannah found that she

didn't recuperate as quickly as she had before from these tussles with her fellow human beings. The sore muscles, frayed nerves, and resulting exhaustion tended to linger for days afterward, causing her to wonder if, perhaps, she might have accomplished the same ends with more peaceful methods.

Peace.

With each passing year, she realized the value of that rare commodity and found new ways to pursue it, embrace it, and enjoy its rewards.

As she crossed the city limits and entered the canyon, Savannah rolled down the driver's window and slowly, deeply, breathed in the fragrance of the countryside. The beloved, familiar scents of the desert—the dry smell of the dust, the pungency of wild sage, and the rich perfume of eucalyptus—filled her lungs and calmed her soul.

The trauma of the arrest and her concern about leaving a troubled child in the care of her elderly grandmother began to fade away with each exhalation.

Savannah reminded herself that Brody Greyson's mother wasn't a problem that she could fix. The woman herself was the only person with the power to do that, and something told Savannah that even she might not be able to save herself at this point.

Although Granny Reid had taught her grandchildren to never give up on anyone, that no one was beyond redemption, Savannah had seen far too many people who had traveled their dark, rocky roads so far and so long that only a miracle would bring them into the light.

Miracles happened, of course. Every day. But, having seen the worst of humanity, Savannah didn't hold her breath waiting for them.

She just whispered a prayer for the person in need of divine intervention and kept moving.

Peace.

It had a lot to do with figuring out what you could fix and what you couldn't.

As she wound deeper into the canyon, leaving most of civilization behind, she allowed the serenity of the place, unspoiled by humanity, to seep into her soul. She also released the fear and guilt of leaving Brody with Granny. Her grandmother had laughed at her when she'd asked if she thought she could handle the boy.

"If there's one thing I'm durn good at—other than bakin' goodies, that is—it's handlin' young'uns," she'd told her.

"But Brody's not your average kid," Savannah had started to explain, "and—"

"*No* child is average. Plus, remember, I managed to raise your sister, Marietta, and both of us lived to tell the tale."

"True," Savannah had admitted. Surely, anyone who had managed to rear a child like Marietta Reid and keep her out of jail and the graveyard could handle the likes of Brody Greyson. Especially with some help from an overly energetic bloodhound.

Savannah took another relaxing, deep breath and released her concern about Brody and Granny. That was just needless worrying, and surely, she could find something more pressing to worry about.

Like a murdered movie star.

As she approached the outskirts of the tiny town of Twin Oaks, Dirk's car phone rang. As she answered it, she silently thanked her brother, Waycross, for at least the hundredth time for this additional, loving gift. Last Christmas he had installed hands-free phones in both of their vintage vehicles, making their lives easier and considerably safer.

Her little brother was one of Savannah's dearest blessings. Every time she thought of him, which was many times a day, she was grateful for his love and that he, himself, had found his way back to a life of sobriety. She would be forever thankful that her little brother was one of those rare miracles.

She glanced at the caller ID and smiled. "Hey, you," she said. "Did you get her booked in and locked down?"

"Finally," Dirk said, sounding tired and grouchy. Even a bit more than his usual degrees of haggard and disgruntled. "I've arrested rabid grizzly bears that were more cooperative."

"Did you have to go to the ER and get patched up? Gashes stitched, bones set, brain scan done?"

"Ha, ha. Aren't you funny. No, but I've got a serious shiner from that ankle-biter kid of hers. Did you get him settled in with CPS?"

"Um. Not exactly."

"What happened?"

"Let's just say, we have company tonight. Maybe for a few nights, until they find a foster home to take him in."

"Ah. That's why your grandma said she was busy and couldn't talk when I called the house."

Savannah gulped. "Uh-oh. Did she sound okay?"

"She sounded fine, laughing her head off. But I could hear the Colonel howling like a hyena in the background."

See there, Savannah told herself. *You were fretting over nothing. No wonder you're sprouting new gray hairs every day.*

"She did have time to tell me that you're on your way to Twin Oaks," he said. "A homicide?"

"Yes. Ethan called me and asked if I'd come up here. The victim's a friend of his. I just got into town, passed that big fruit stand that sells apple cider. Where are you?"

"Right behind you."

She glanced at the rearview mirror and saw a police cruiser rapidly approaching, its blue lights flashing.

She laughed and said, "Let me guess. You caught the case."

"Yep. So much for our quiet, romantic evening together at home. Huh, darlin'?"

Savannah momentarily considered what a "romantic evening" with Dirk entailed. Plenty of salty snacks and cold beverages to wash them down, served by the lady of the house. Then some form of baked goods, also conjured into being by the on-premises chef, and all the while, a boxing match on cable TV.

"Romantic," indeed, she thought.

But she decided to be kind. Pointing out the obvious wasn't always the best way to assure domestic tranquility.

"I figured they'd give it to you," she told him. "That's why I drove the Buick out here instead of the pony. Reckoned you'd show up and prefer to have your own car to drive home."

"How considerate of you. Wouldn't be that you actually enjoy driving her, now that she's all cherried out."

"Oh, right. I'd choose a boring Buick Skylark over my smokin' hot Mustang. Get real. This was an act of true love. Pure self-sacrifice. Nothing else."

The heavy silence on the other end of the phone told her she'd gone too far. The day might come when Dirk could take a bit of teasing over his beloved, returned-from-the-grave ride.

Apparently, it had not yet arrived.

She decided to return to the former topic. "Yeah, no romantic, stay-at-home evening for us," she said. "Considering all the rumpus and commotion you heard that's going on back there, a simple murder scene might be more peaceful."

More silence on the other end.

She hated it when he threw her olive branches into the wood chipper, as he was inclined to do.

But she soon realized he had more on his mind than just pouting, as he quickly pulled alongside her, then shot past her, leaving her figuratively "in his dust."

She heard him chuckling as he said, "See ya later. When you finally get there. What's your ETA? An hour? Two?"

"Yeah, yeah. You've got lights, a siren, and a police cruiser. While I'm pedaling this crummy, *boring* old Buick."

"Hey, you'd better watch what's comin' outta your mouth there! That's *my girl* you're talking smack about!"

"I thought *I* was your girl!" she shot back.

But he didn't hear her.

Detective Sergeant Dirk Coulter had already ended the call. He and his cruiser with its powerful engine and flashing blue lights were far down the road, then around a sharp curve and well out of sight.

He'll beat me to the crime scene with a minute and a half to spare. Woo hoo, she thought, grinning and shaking her head. *The dude's easily impressed. With himself.*

Chapter 5

Even with his lights and siren, Dirk hadn't beaten her to the mansion by much, Savannah realized when she reached the end of the long driveway and saw him climbing out of the cruiser.

Of course, he would still count it as a win. Like horseshoes and dynamite, "close" was enough.

But all thoughts of their little competition left her mind the instant she turned her attention to the home itself. Certainly, she had heard of Qamar Damun, the art deco mansion whose Arabic name meant "Blood Moon." It had been built in the 1920s and, over the course of the past century, had been inhabited by some of Hollywood's brightest luminaries.

The Moroccan-style castle set high upon a secluded mountaintop enjoyed quite a history. It had a colorful reputation and not only for its brilliant stained glass windows, complex brick and stone work, and massive arched entryway.

Usually, when the estate was discussed, it was with hushed tones, and the stories were of decadent, violent parties, attended by movie stars, mobsters, highly influential politicians, and wealthy adventure seekers.

The mansion's darkest crimes had occurred during its first thirteen years, in the era of Prohibition. But over the past hundred years, it was widely believed that every one of the basic Ten Commandments had been broken, some more than once, within its marble walls with embossed bronze friezes.

The phone call Savannah had received earlier caused her to consider the idea that Qamar Damun might have returned to its evil ways. Or at least, someone within its walls had.

Savannah parked behind Dirk's cruiser and saw that he was walking toward her, a jaunty swagger to his steps, a grin on his face.

For a guy who had gotten his butt whipped only a short time ago by a kid who was knee-high to a duck, he was acting far too frisky in her opinion.

But he didn't have time to do much bragging, because before he could reach her, Ethan Malloy had climbed out of a GMC Sierra Denali parked nearby and was hurrying over to greet them.

Normally, on any given occasion, when Savannah first laid eyes on the world-renowned movie star, she was taken aback by his good looks and innate charisma.

But the stricken look on his handsome face and the sadness in his famously blue eyes caused Savannah to remember the first time she had met Ethan Malloy.

Once again, Ethan's fame, fortune, and the adoration

of millions had not protected him or those he loved from life's harshest realities.

She hurried to meet him halfway and folded him into a hearty embrace, which he returned. For a moment, she could feel him melting into the strength and compassion she was offering. Not for the first time, it occurred to her that for all the fan adoration, Ethan Malloy was a terribly lonely man.

"I'm so sorry," she told him. "You were the one who actually found her?"

He nodded. "Yes. Mary called me and told me she was missing. I came right over, and we looked for a long time. You'll see why, once you're inside the house, and I was the one who first saw her."

He shuddered, and for a moment his face turned so pale that she thought he might faint.

She couldn't blame him. There were scenes in her memory that still haunted her, causing her to feel the same way when she made the mistake of recalling them.

Dirk approached them and shook Ethan's hand. "I just heard you say, 'We' were looking for her. Who's 'we'?" Dirk asked, wearing his most officious detective expression.

"Mary Mahoney and myself."

"Who's that?"

"Lucinda's housekeeper, though she's more like a companion—as you'll also see when you go inside."

"Where's she now, this Mary gal?" Dirk wanted to know.

Ethan passed a shaking hand over his face. "In her quarters. She's a mess. I told her what you said, Savannah, about staying out of the house, but she was crying so hard that she could barely walk. She just wanted to lie down on her own bed, and I didn't have the heart to force her to—"

"No, of course not. I understand. As long as she isn't anywhere near the body."

"Not even close. Lucinda's in the ballroom," Ethan told her. "The servants' quarters are on the opposite side of the house, in the rear."

"When exactly did Mary call you?" Savannah asked.

"A couple of hours ago. She said she hadn't been able to find her all day. I came right over. We've been looking the whole time. It wasn't easy. You'll understand why when you go inside."

"When did Mary last see her?" Dirk asked.

"I think last night, when they both went to bed. She said when she took her breakfast to her, she couldn't find her."

Savannah noticed he was shivering, even though he was wearing long sleeves and the night was fairly warm.

"We were afraid something like this might happen," he said, "what with her being so old and in poor health, and the house being so . . ."

Dirk craned his head, looking up at the massive, four-story high brick and marble facade with its ornate geometric bands of patterns. "This *is* a big place," he said. "I can see how somebody'd get lost in a joint like that. You'd have to carry a sandwich in your pocket if you decided to go from one side of it to the other. By the time you got there, it'd be time to eat again."

Savannah could see that Ethan was spending far more time and effort trying to figure out what Dirk had just said than the comment deserved—especially under the circumstances.

"Why don't you show us where the . . . she . . . is, if

you're up to it," she said, slipping her arm through his. "Or, if you don't want to have to see her again, you can just point us in the right direction, and we'll find her."

"No, you won't. Not without help." He looked up at the massive arched entrance and the sick expression came over his face once again. "You'll never find her on your own. I'm surprised that I was able to."

As they approached the doorway, Savannah quickly became aware of what they were going to find on the other side of the eight-feet-tall carved and inlaid doors, even before Ethan opened the one on the right and waved them inside.

There was no mistaking that smell. To her knowledge, there was only one thing that stank like this combination of terrible odors: garbage, decaying food, dust, mothballs, rotting wood, mildewed cloth, moldy plaster, as well as copious other unidentifiable, toxic substances.

A hoard.

Thankfully, this particular blend lacked the added horrors of urine and feces. But it was especially strong, dense, and overpowering, as though the door and windows hadn't been opened and no amount of fresh air or sunlight had entered in many years.

Once they passed through the door, the enormity of the mess inside was all too apparent.

They were unable to take three steps inside without having to walk upon a layer, at least six inches deep, of accumulated garbage.

Although the giant foyer was as large as that of a glorious old theater, they had to make their way along a narrow path, barely wide enough to accommodate them, walking single-file, between towering piles of assorted boxes, furniture, clothing, rotting household items, and miscellaneous trash.

Savannah's claustrophobia rose with each halting step she took, as she tried to follow Ethan and not fall behind.

A dozen comments sprang to her mind, but she kept them to herself, recalling that this was the home of someone who had been Ethan's dear friend.

As Granny would say, "If you can't say something nice . . ."

Ethan was grieving. He didn't need anyone to state the obvious, horrible as it might be.

"Ho-leeeshee-it!" Dirk exclaimed, following close behind her. "What sorta nut job lives in a trash heap like this?"

Okay. So much for discretion and sensitivity, she thought, shooting him a warning look over her shoulder.

Ethan stopped, turned around, and gave Dirk a look that was neither threatening nor angry, but his voice was decidedly firm when he said, "In this case, it was a beautiful, loving lady, who battled depression for many years and lost the war. Lucinda suffered many devastating losses in her life. Eventually, they took their toll."

"Not every ship can weather every storm," Savannah added.

"Sorry," Dirk mumbled with more humility than Savannah would have expected. "She's your friend. I shouldn't've said anything."

Ethan gave him a half smile. "I understand. For the record, I didn't know until today that she was living like this. I'd never been inside this house. No surprise that I was never invited. I was as shocked and horrified as you must be. Probably more."

He turned and continued to lead them along the narrow path through the clutter and grime of Lucinda Faraday's life.

It reminded Savannah of the tunnels that ants created to navigate through their hills. In places, the piles of junk were well over their heads, seven or eight feet high. She couldn't help but wonder how on earth anyone could even reach up that far to stack it.

"This isn't just gross. It's downright dangerous," Dirk said, obviously still unable to grasp the importance of delicacy and diplomacy. "This mess could've caved in on her and mashed or suffocated her. Are you sure that's not what happened? Maybe it wasn't a homicide after all, but more like an avalanche of—"

"Murder," Ethan snapped back angrily. "She was murdered! Okay?"

"Yeah. Yeah. Okay. Sorry."

Dirk gave Savannah a sheepish look. It told her that Mr. Sensitivity finally realized he needed to shut up. At least until they saw their victim.

Ethan led them from the foyer into an enormous room that Savannah decided must be the ballroom. Like the entry, clutter obscured most of the floor. Although there appeared to be more pathways through the mess, and the piles on either side were mostly only waist high.

Here and there, Savannah could actually see a patch of worn, filthy parquet.

The only evidence that it had once been a glorious room was the coffered ceiling with intricate panels decorated with plaster vines, leaves, and roses. The graceful design spiraled toward the center of the ceiling, to a magnificent crystal chandelier, almost completely covered with dust and cobwebs.

"She's over here," Ethan said as he headed toward a far corner. "I searched this room, and all rooms on the first two floors, three times before I finally found her."

"Any particular reason you only looked on the lower floors?" Savannah asked.

"Mary told me that Lucinda hadn't been on the third and fourth floors for years." He paused, looked uncomfortable, then added, "Apparently, the two uppermost floors are even worse than these."

Savannah couldn't imagine such a thing, but she kept it to herself. Ethan seemed to be not only grieving but embarrassed on behalf of his deceased friend.

Suddenly, he stopped and stepped as far to the side as the narrow walkway would allow. "I don't want to see her again if I don't have to," he told them. "Setting eyes on something like that once in a lifetime is more than enough. I don't know how you people can stand to do that sort of thing for a living."

"I'm sure it helps if the bodies aren't someone you knew and loved," Savannah said as she and Dirk maneuvered around him, then headed deeper into the corner, where he had pointed.

Dirk pushed ahead, working his way through the piles of clothing. Some garments were filthy and crusty with mold and mildew, while others still had tags and were in their original designer packaging.

After coming to the end of the trail, facing a wall, he said, "I don't see a body back here." He turned to Ethan. "Are you sure you—"

"Under that pink satin comforter thing," Ethan replied.

A warning bell went off in Savannah's head. "Is that how you found her, Ethan?" she asked as she spotted the gaudy flamingo pink throw. "Was she covered up like that, or did you . . ."

"I covered her," he said. "I had to. I couldn't just leave her like, well, you'll see."

She saw another violent shudder go through him, and for a moment, she was again concerned that he might pass out. She decided he was in too fragile a state for her to lecture him about how unwise it was to tamper with a crime scene in any way at all. Even to modestly cover the body of a woman you held in high esteem.

Why make him feel any worse than he already did?

"Don't *ever* mess with a crime scene, man," Dirk barked. "Especially a murder. At a time like this, catching who did it is a lot more important than guarding a woman's modesty. It ain't like she's gonna mind at a time like this, huh?"

Savannah cringed. In all the years she had spent with Dirk, she had yet to impress upon him the value of civility. He considered "tact" a waste of time at best, and at worst, evidence of a weak, sneaky character who didn't possess the courage to speak their mind.

No, Dirk Coulter was a manly man who had never entertained an unspoken thought. No filter whatsoever. No pesky childhood training like Granny's "If you can't say something nice, say nothing at all" to cramp his style or burden him with the nuisance of forethought or the onus of empathy.

But you always knew where you stood with Dirk.

Whether you wanted to know or not.

Savannah moved closer to the covered body as Dirk took a couple of pictures of it and the surrounding areas with his cell phone.

She noticed that one foot was sticking out from beneath the duvet. From the skin texture and the condition of some of the toenails, it was obviously the foot of an older woman. But the nails were meticulously painted in a crimson polish, and the high-heeled slipper was a black satin mule, accented across the top with marabou feathers.

A long-forgotten image stirred in Savannah's memory. The red toenails. The glamorous black footwear. But before the full picture could form in her mind, she was distracted by Dirk pulling some surgical gloves from his inside jacket pocket and handing a pair of them to her.

"Don't touch anything if you don't have to," he grumbled. "The scene's been interfered with enough already."

She glanced over her shoulder at Ethan and saw him wince. The verbal dart had found its mark, to be sure.

"I think enough's been said about that already," she whispered to her husband. "If it hadn't been for Ethan, you'd probably be searching through this hoard by yourself, looking for the missing woman. What a grand, fun time that'd be, huh?"

"Yeah, well, whatever," was the lackluster reply.

"I'm going to step away now, if that's all right with you guys," Ethan said. "Like I said, I really don't want to have to see her again."

"No problem," Savannah said. "You can wait for us outside if you prefer."

"Or better yet," Dirk added, "you could go get that gal, Mary, and tell her I'll meet her out front in a few minutes. I'm gonna have to ask her some questions, whether she feels like talkin' or not."

"Okay. I'll do what I can."

Ethan disappeared in an instant, and Savannah couldn't blame him—on so many levels.

She turned back to Dirk, a couple of choice statements on the tip of her tongue. But she quickly swallowed them, because he had uncovered the body.

It was a sight that she would never forget. A vision that she was quite certain would reappear in nightmares for a long time. Maybe for the rest of her life.

Chapter 6

"It's the pose," Savannah said, studying the body sprawled atop the garbage on the floor. "Her famous calendar girl shot."

"I ain't got a clue what you're talking about. How famous could it be?" Dirk said as he tossed the hot-pink satin duvet that had covered Lucinda Faraday onto a pile of clothes next to her body.

Savannah took her phone from her jeans pocket and began an Internet search. A moment later, she shoved it beneath Dirk's nose. "That one," she said. "It was taken back in the forties."

"Oh, yeah. I remember seeing that," Dirk replied, squinting at the small screen. "I think I heard a lot of the Second World War GIs had it on their lockers or whatever. Pretty racy stuff for back then."

Savannah took the phone back and read the caption

beneath it. "Says here they found out later that she was underage when she posed for it. Barely sixteen."

"She sure didn't look sixteen."

"No, but she certainly looks like she does here, pose-wise anyway." Savannah pointed at the body, which had been placed in the same suggestive position as the old photo.

Savannah could better understand why Ethan had felt the need to cover his friend. The overtly sexual position-ing had been considered inappropriate by many censors in its day. But the same pose on a ninety-year-old gave the impression that the killer had arranged the corpse that way to dishonor the woman, to insult her memory.

Savannah hated to think what the papers would do with this information if it leaked . . . and it was bound to. Such salacious details almost always came to light sooner or later, especially if they involved a celebrity.

"She's even holding the long cigarette holder," Savan-nah said, comparing the picture with the smoking tool in the body's hand.

"The killer obviously wanted to make a point of some sort."

"They wanted to embarrass her."

"Embarrass her? She's dead. How can you embarrass a corpse?"

"Spoken like a true guy. We women have the ability to be mortified about our appearance and a lot of other things long after death. Believe me."

He shrugged. "Okay. If you say so."

She put her phone away and turned her attention to the body. The negligee's chiffon had some holes in it and the lace edge was ragged. The feathers on the slippers were sparse and limp. The carved ivory opera-length cigarette holder was stained from years of smoke.

"Her clothes," she said. "They're old, like antiques. If I didn't know better, I'd say they're the exact same ones she wore in the picture."

"She saved them all these years?"

"Probably. You've been wearing that same Harley-Davidson T-shirt since I met you."

"I'll have you know I replaced that first one ten years ago." He pointed to the logo on his chest. "*This* is a *second* edition!"

"Oh, okay. I stand corrected."

She tried to move closer to the body, but the limited space and a large wire bird cage stuffed with Christmas decorations prevented her from getting a good look at the head and face area. All she had was a vague impression of a blond wig, sitting askew, maybe even backward, atop the victim's own gray hair and some garish red lipstick and turquoise eyeshadow, smeared around the mouth and lids.

"Any obvious cause of death?" she asked him. "Blood maybe?"

"No blood, but it's not hard to figure out the cause of death."

Carefully, he stepped into a plastic milk crate containing a dozen or more assorted ashtrays to make room for her to move forward.

Shining the flashlight from his phone onto the head and neck area, he said, "I'll take a wild guess and say it was strangulation."

She gasped when she saw what he was illuminating for her benefit. A stocking was wrapped around the victim's neck, then knotted. It had been tied so tightly that, in places, the cloth was actually embedded in the flesh and invisible.

"Wow. I'd say whoever did that relished the task, if you know what I mean," she said.

"It was personal, that's for sure," Dirk replied. "Nasty. Also, the killer was strong."

"Or at least, quite revved up at the time."

Savannah turned on her own phone's light and looked closer. "That's an old stocking, too," she said. "Silk, not nylon."

He bent beside her and looked closer. "How can you tell?"

"It's seamed, a matte look, not shiny like nylon. I'd say . . . silk crepe, extra fine forty-five gauge with a dull luster. Color, Toffee Apple."

"Seriously?"

"Absolutely."

"Wow, you know your stockings. I'm impressed."

"Don't be. That's all written on the bottom of the foot."

She stood up, turned off her light. "Like I keep telling you, boy, you gotta download that magnifier/light app. In your line of work, it'd come in handy."

"Yeah, yeah. Whatever." He began to punch in a number on his phone. "Might as well call Dr. Liu. Get 'er over here."

"She's not going to be happy that you moved the duvet. How many times has she told you not to—"

"—move the body or anything over it, under it, or around it?"

"Yes. That. She gives you the same speech every time you get to a scene before she does."

"Goes to show, you can't make that gal happy. If she gets her liver in a quiver over a little thing like that, it's on her."

"O-o-kay." Savannah clucked her tongue and shook her head. "But I've gotta question the wisdom of getting on the bad side of an ill-tempered woman who makes her living by cutting up bodies with a scalpel."

"Good point."

When Savannah and Dirk finally made their way through the maze of mess and out the mansion's front door, they found Ethan sitting on the bottom porch step.

A woman sat close beside him. He had one arm around her shoulders and was holding her hand in his. She had short salt and pepper hair, and was a slender woman, possibly in her late sixties. She wore a crisp white blouse and black slacks with sharp creases. It occurred to Savannah that the garments had been carefully ironed and had the look of a manager's uniform.

Ethan said something to her in a low, comforting tone, and she responded by laying her head on his shoulder.

But when Ethan heard them close the door and step onto the porch, he immediately released her, stood, and turned to them.

His eyes searched Savannah's, then Dirk's. "Did you get what you needed?" he asked. "Did you see what I saw? Why I knew it wasn't an accident?"

"Yeah," Dirk replied. "I've called the county medical examiner. She and the CSU are on their way."

Ethan looked relieved. "Oh, good," he said. "I guess they'll take Lucinda, I mean her body, to . . . wherever. . . ."

"To the morgue for the postmortem," Savannah offered. "Then, after that, they'll send her to a mortuary to be prepared for burial or for cremation, as she preferred."

The woman, who was still sitting on the porch, her back to them, stirred a bit. Ethan seemed to remember she was there.

"Oh," he said, turning to her, "I'm sorry. Mary. These are friends of mine, Savannah Reid and her husband, Detective Sergeant Dirk Coulter. Savannah and Dirk, this is Ms. Mary Mahoney. She's, um, *was* Lucinda's housekeeper and companion."

"Companion," Mary said. "As I'm sure you can tell, there was no housekeeper for years. Not since I gave up trying."

Mary struggled to stand until Ethan reached down, placed his hands on her waist, and lifted her onto her feet.

Savannah watched her closely and noted that she grimaced, as though she was in terrible pain, even from such a mundane action. Her hunched shoulders, the way she moved, all indicated that her muscles and tendons might be tight, her bones and cartilage brittle, resisting even the smallest shift in position.

Savannah knew better than to offer her a handshake. Having met too many people suffering from severe arthritis, she knew the friendly gesture could cost the woman dearly in pain.

"How do you do, Miss Mahoney?" Savannah said instead. "I'm so sorry for your loss. A terrible thing to happen, and right here in your home."

"Oh, I don't live there!" she said as though she had just been accused of a terrible crime. "I have my own apartment in the back of the house. It has a separate entrance and everything." Her already florid face flushed even darker. "I would never. I could never live like—"

"I understand," Savannah said, feeling sorry for the woman, who was obviously embarrassed by her mistress's lifestyle. "I'm sure your apartment is nice and tidy."

"Not like the rest of this dump heap," Dirk chimed in.

A heavy, awkward silence descended on the porch. As Savannah waited, what seemed like years, for it to end, she thought how many times her husband had created such an unnatural vacuum.

Too many to count.

It was just part of the wonder that was Dirk.

He wasn't a cruel man. Quite the contrary, in fact. But he had never felt the need to weigh words before spitting them into a room, or across the front porch of an art deco mansion with the hoard from hell and a murdered woman inside. Who would have thought such circumstances required delicacy?

Certainly not my *husband*, she thought. *Nope. Not ol' Blurt-It-Now-and-Think-About-It-Later-If-At-All-Dirk.*

"How long has the place been like that?" he continued. Obviously, still not thinking.

"For years," Mary whispered.

"Well, yeah." Dirk nodded solemnly. "I mean, you sure couldn't accomplish something like that in one day!"

"I used to try to keep it clean. But the last twenty years or so, she got worse and worse. Finally, she wouldn't let me throw anything away. Nothing. Not even real garbage."

Suddenly, Mary was overcome with a coughing fit that turned her face from red to a deep purple. Savannah was alarmed. It wasn't a normal, mundane chest cold or the hacking brought on by allergies. It sounded like the deep, strangling lung spasms that would come out of someone who wasn't long for the world.

"Are you okay, Mary?" Ethan asked her, seemingly as alarmed as Savannah.

Mary nodded, unable to speak.

"We can drive you to the hospital, if you need to go," Savannah offered. "You should probably have that looked at."

Finally, Mary recovered and said weakly, "I'm okay. I've been to the doctor about it. Not much they could do, what with me living here, you know, in that."

"What'd you keep workin' here for?" Dirk asked. "If breathin' that mess was causin' me to hack up a lung, I'd be movin' on."

Tears flooded Mary's eyes. She crossed her arms over her chest and grabbed her upper arms tightly, as though giving herself a badly needed long, hard hug.

"I don't have any place to go," she admitted, "and after all the years I'd spent taking care of Miss Lucinda, I couldn't leave her. She wouldn't have made it this long without me. She doesn't have a lot of friends or family."

"Yeah, I was gonna ask you about that," Dirk said. "We'll need to inform the next of kin. Who is it?"

Both Mary's and Ethan's faces darkened at the question. Savannah knew it wasn't going to be a cheerful reply.

"She had a great-grandson," Ethan said. "But the way she spoke about him, I didn't get the idea they were close."

"He's still around, and they weren't at all close," Mary added. "Far from it. In fact, they hated each other."

"Any particular reason?" Savannah asked.

"Yes." A look of intense anger crossed Mary's face. "Because he's a horrible excuse for a human being. That's why. She disowned him years ago, and I don't blame her one bit. He gave her no choice."

"All right," Dirk replied, watching her intently. "I'll keep that in mind when I inform him of his loss. Anyone else that she was close to?"

Ethan thought for a moment, then shrugged. "Not that I know of. She and I did a movie together about three years ago. That's how we met. It was her last role, a cameo appearance. She was amazing. Took me under her wing and taught me everything she knew. But I didn't get the idea she had a lot of friends or family."

"She had nobody," Mary said. "She either chased them away, or they ran off on their own steam for their own reasons. Lucinda was alone and lonely. Had been for years."

"That's sad," Savannah observed, thinking of the picture of the vulnerable fifteen-year-old, exploited for her exceptional beauty, her innocence robbed, her life forced down an unsavory, dangerous path before it had even begun.

Savannah recalled seeing headlines that proclaimed Lucinda Faraday the most beautiful woman in the world. "Every man wants her! Every woman wants to be her!"— or so said the publicists, as they scrambled to sell her to adoring throngs.

Seeing Lucinda Faraday back then, at the height of her beauty, who would have thought she would end up like that? Savannah wondered. *Murdered and thrown onto the refuse heap that had come to define her life?*

Savannah could see a convoy of white vehicles turning from the highway and heading toward the mansion. The vans' sides bore the county's official seal and the letters *CSU*.

Dr. Liu and her crime scene unit had arrived.

Savannah didn't envy the medical examiner and her crew the job that lay before them. Trying to gather evidence at the scene of any homicide was difficult, no matter what the circumstances.

But, considering what lay inside the walls of Qamar Damun—the strange, formerly beautiful house with its dark past and exotic name—their task was unenviable at best. Savannah was afraid that their search for the truth of Lucinda Faraday's violent death might prove all but impossible.

Chapter 7

"Okay," Dirk said, "we inform this dude that his great-grandma's dead, and then we go home and to bed. That sound okay to you?"

Sitting next to him in the Buick's passenger seat, Savannah nodded. She could feel the fatigue and the stress of the day weighing heavily on her. Ten years ago, she wouldn't even have noticed. It would've taken a week's worth of rotten days to slow her down.

Now, well into her forties, a ten-minute encounter with a quarrelsome, druggy mother, while trying to keep her son from witnessing that quarrel, had left Savannah drained and in need of her comfy chair, a steamy romance novel, and some serious kitty purring and petting.

Add a homicide—like the maraschino cherry on the melted sundae—and Savannah felt twice her age.

"Good idea," she said. "I was hoping to get back in

time to tuck Brody in and tell him good night." She glanced at her watch and realized it was 9:10. "No doubt Gran's already put him down. She's always been dead serious about getting kids to bed on time. Says it stunts their growth if they don't get enough sleep."

Dirk laughed, but there was no mirth in it. By the lights of the dashboard, Savannah could see his grim expression when he said, "Didn't seem to affect my growth none. I did well to get four hours' sleep on a good night there in the orphanage."

As usual, when Dirk mentioned his childhood, Savannah felt a pang of sadness. In all the years she had known him and the countless personal things they had shared, she could count on her fingers the times he had said anything at all about his upbringing.

Dirk Coulter was a man with a well-established reputation for complaining constantly about everything—that his free coffee was stale, that he had to wait longer than five seconds in a grocery line, that it was raining or not raining as he desired. So, the fact that he had so little to say about being raised in a no-frills, poorly regulated orphanage told Savannah a lot.

She was almost afraid to ask. But, as usual with her, nosiness won over courtesy. "Why weren't you able to sleep?" she wanted to know.

"I could've. But you close your eyes, you take your chances."

"Of what?"

"At least, gettin' your junk stole."

"And at worst?"

"Gettin' jumped."

"At night? When you were in bed?"

"That was the best time to settle whatever happened earlier in the day. No adults around to put a stop to it. If they could be bothered. If they weren't too busy, gabbing with each other or sneakin' off for a smoke."

"Important stuff like that."

"Yeah. Right."

They rode on a few more blocks in silence. Then he continued, "At night, the lights are off. The other kid's got his eyes closed, not on guard. If he's all the way asleep, you could get three or four licks in before he'd even know you were on 'im."

"Wow," she said quietly, shaking her head. "You sound like an expert there."

He grunted and shrugged. "I gave as good as I got. Usually better."

She didn't hear any pride or satisfaction in his words. Just a flat, matter-of-fact delivery of the facts as he saw them.

Reaching over, she placed her hand on his thigh and patted it. "I'm sorry you went through that, sugar," she said. "No kid should've had to grow up that way. It wasn't fair."

He turned and gave her a sweet smile. "Yeah, well, you and me both know that 'fair's' got nothin' to do with nothin'."

"True."

"Grown-ups, they've got a lot to say to kids about how important it is to be fair. But then, you notice that they aren't fair even half the time, and life itself is even less fair. Good things happen to rotten people. Rotten things happen to good people. That's just the way it is. Nothin's fair about nothin'."

"I like to think that, in the end, everything works out. The good people get rewarded, and folks who hurt others get their comeuppance, sooner or later."

"That's because you got them rose-colored glasses on, Van. From what I've seen, there ain't a lot of justice in this world. What little there is comes later, a lot later, rather than sooner."

"But it does come."

"If you say so."

"Granny would say so, too."

"She would. That's true. You and your grandma are two special women. Both of you went through hell and back when you were growing up. There's no denying that. But I figure the suffering you and her went through, it's what made you who you are—the two best people I've ever known in my life."

He reached down, lifted her hand from his leg, and tenderly kissed it.

Savannah could feel her throat tightening and some tears wetting her eyelids. Leave it to him to get all mushy when she was extra tired. It was a dangerous combination—romance and exhaustion. If she didn't watch out, she'd be reduced to a blubbering ninny in the next five seconds.

That wouldn't do because they were approaching the house where Lucinda Faraday's great-grandson lived with his fiancée. Making a notification was tough enough without arriving in tears because your hubby had said something sweet a minute before.

As Dirk pulled the Buick up to the curb in front of the tiny Spanish-style house with its beige stucco walls and clay tile roof, Savannah was a bit surprised to see that Lucinda Faraday's heir lived in a place that was even smaller than hers, not to mention that it was in worse shape.

Savannah had repainted hers and had some missing tiles replaced within the past few years. Even with only the fading light of the setting sun to illuminate the house, one look at the old structure told Savannah that no one had done any improvements since it had been built, decades before.

The yard was equally neglected, as was a rusty old SUV sitting in the driveway.

"That thing's seen better days," Dirk said.

"A few decades ago," Savannah added. "Like the house."

"From the looks of this place, it was back when the old lady and her great-grandson had their falling out. When she cut off the money."

"If she ever gave him any in the first place," Savannah added. "Just because folks are rich, that doesn't mean they pass it down."

"Not till they're dead and got no use for it anymore."

"Something to consider, since he's the sole heir, huh?"

"Yeah. We'll have to keep an eagle eye on him when he gets the bad news. See if he takes it hard, gets weepy and all that."

"Or refrains from dancing a jig."

"Exactly."

They got out of the car and headed for the house. It was dark inside, except for the glow of a television coming from the living room window.

"Looks like somebody's home," he said. "I hope so. I don't wanna have to go running around town lookin' for the guy in bars and pool halls."

Savannah grinned and thought, not for the first time,

that Dirk had never noticed that San Carmelita's last official pool hall had closed over twenty years ago. Now the town's miscreant juveniles tended to while away their idle hours in the food court at the local mall. Much to the distress of shoppers and the mall security team.

As they were about to step onto the porch, Savannah glanced around to the side of the house and saw something that stood out in sharp contrast to the rest of the property. A shiny new black Porsche, whose price tag would have exceeded the value of the house and land combined.

"Hey, hey, hey," she said. "Nice ride."

Dirk sniffed. "If you like those fancy foreign jobs. I'm partial to American-made myself."

"Made in America back when the buffalo and the dinosaurs roamed."

"Yeah. Like your Mustang."

"Shush about my Mustang. I noticed you were happy to leave the cruiser with one of the uniforms back at the Faraday place, so's you could drive your Buick home."

"Yeah, well. Can't have *you* drivin' it everywhere."

"Might spill a drop of Coke on the dash."

"I know! I break out in a cold sweat just thinkin' about it."

He knocked on the door—a bit more softly than his usual cop-pounding barrage. The nearby windows didn't rattle, and he didn't shout, "Police! Open up!"

Savannah was proud. Who said a husband couldn't be taught a bit of civility by a highly determined wife?

He had to knock twice more before someone finally opened it a crack and looked out.

"Yes?" answered a meek voice. A woman's voice.

"Yeah, hi," he replied, pulling his badge from his jacket

pocket and holding it up to her eye level. "I'm Detective Sergeant Dirk Coulter with the San Carmelita Police Department." He nodded toward Savannah. "This is Savannah Reid. Can we come in for a minute?"

"Why? What do you want?" she asked, her voice almost squeaky with timidity.

"To talk to Geoffrey Faraday," Dirk told her. "Is he here?"

"Um." She glanced back over her shoulder. "Yes. But he's busy."

"Then tell him to get un-busy and come to the door."

Savannah noticed that Dirk had dropped his nice-guy tone and was about to go flat out Aggravated Cop. From experience, Savannah knew that wouldn't bode well for Miss Squeaky Voice behind the door.

Savannah stepped forward and in her most "down home" Dixie tone said, "Please, ma'am. This is important. Detective Coulter has a matter of serious family business to discuss with Mr. Faraday. Something he needs to hear."

When the woman hesitated a moment too long to suit Dirk, he called out, "Faraday! Come to the door! Now!"

Sooner than Savannah expected, Dirk's new tactic worked. Almost instantly, the door opened halfway, fully revealing the timid lady of the house, who was standing there in a pair of pink pajamas with cartoon teddy bears on them. She appeared to be in her late twenties and in desperate need of a shampoo. Her dark hair hung in limp, greasy strands nearly to her waist. Other than a smudge of mascara beneath both eyes, she wore no makeup. Just a frightened, nervous look.

Next to her stood a guy, maybe ten years older than she was. He was as overly dressed and meticulously groomed as the lady of the house was slovenly. His thick strawberry-blond hair was so heavily gelled that Savannah was sure not a strand of it would budge, even in an EF5 tornado. He was wearing a charcoal suit that, even to her relatively untrained eye, appeared to be of the highest quality with a contemporary, physique-flattering cut. A crisp white shirt and designer tie completed his ensemble. She was sure she could have paid off her mortgage several times over for the price of his platinum, diamond-accented watch.

He flashed them a smile as gaudy as his jewelry and said in an oily smooth voice, "Good evening, Detective Coulter, Ms. Reid. I'm Geoffrey Faraday." He waved a casual hand toward the woman standing beside him. "This is my fiancée, Brooklynn Marsh. How can we help you?"

Instinctively, Savannah knew he had been standing right behind the door the entire time. That and her instincts caused her to distrust and dislike him instantly. Most law-abiding people, if visited by a representative of law enforcement, were curious, concerned, and open. Not guarded, nervous, and scared, as Brooklynn appeared to be, or fake-friendly and suspicious like Geoffrey.

People with nothing to hide didn't hide behind doors.

"We need to come inside and speak to you, Mr. Faraday," Dirk was saying, even as he put his hand on the door and pushed it farther open. "It won't take long."

"Good, because I'm going out for the evening," Faraday said, adjusting his gold cuff links in such a way as to give them both a good, long look at them.

"Maybe you are, and maybe you aren't," Dirk told him, not bothering to hide his annoyance. "That depends on how our little talk goes."

Savannah shot Dirk a warning look. After all, this man

was about to hear that a member of his family had been murdered. Since they had no evidence to the contrary, they had to assume he knew nothing about it and would probably be devastated.

"Could we all sit down, sir?" Savannah asked.

Faraday glanced behind him at the cluttered living room, then gave his fiancée an angry look. "I guess you could," he said, "if there was somewhere to sit in this place."

Instantly, Brooklynn sprang into action, scurrying around the room, grabbing dirty clothes, magazines, and a pizza box off the sofa and tossing it all behind a recliner. "There," she said. "All clear. Sit down."

Faraday picked up a bra from a nearby chair, gingerly, with thumb and forefinger, and tossed it behind the recliner with the rest. Then he took a seat on the edge of the chair and waved Savannah and Dirk to do the same on the sofa.

They did. Though Savannah made a mental note to toss her slacks into the washing machine the moment she arrived home. The place stank of urine, which she hoped was from unseen pets and on the carpet, not the furniture.

"What's this all about?" Faraday asked as Brooklynn sat down, cross-legged, on the floor at his feet.

Dirk cleared his throat and then plunged in. When forced to do something he hated, he didn't waste time. "I'm sorry, Mr. Faraday, but you must prepare yourself. I'm afraid I have some bad news for you."

Faraday didn't seem particularly alarmed, or even all that curious, Savannah noted as she watched his face, taking in every nuance of expression, as he said, "Oh? What news?"

"It's about your great-grandmother. Mrs. Lucinda Faraday."

"Okay. Let's hear it."

Hardly the normal response, Savannah thought. Most folks were frozen in terror by this point in such a conversation.

"I'm afraid she's passed away," Dirk said with more compassion than she thought him capable of mustering under such strange circumstances.

Brooklynn gasped and clamped her hand over her mouth.

Faraday, on the other hand, sat quite stoically until Dirk clarified his former statement. "She's gone, sir. I'm sorry, but she was found dead in her home a few hours ago."

"I guess it had to happen sooner or later. Great Granny was old. Old as dirt, as they say," Faraday stated quite matter-of-factly. "It's not like we weren't expecting it."

"Yeah, okay." Dirk leaned forward, his elbows on his knees, unabashedly staring at the not-particularly-bereaved great-grandson. "But were you expecting her to expire due to foul play?" he asked.

Again, his fiancée on the floor at his feet made a small, choking sound, while Faraday registered hardly any reaction at all.

"Foul play?" she said with a half sob. "Do you mean, like someone . . . hurt her?"

"Yes, very much so. Someone killed her, ma'am," Dirk said. "I'm sorry. I'm sure that makes the news much harder to hear."

She nodded, then covered her face with her hands. "It's horrible!" she said, beginning to cry in earnest. "She was a difficult person, but for someone to actually . . . Oh, it's just awful! Who would do such a terrible thing?"

"That's what we need to find out," Dirk said, studying

Geoffrey Faraday like an owl eyeing a rat he was contemplating having for dinner. "We will. But first, we need to know if your great-grandmother had any enemies that you're aware of, sir."

"Enemies?" Faraday gave an unpleasant little snort. "Yes, she had enemies."

"Who?" Dirk asked, reaching into his jacket and taking out a small notebook and pen.

"Who *wasn't* her enemy?" Faraday replied with a shrug. "I don't think I ever heard her say a kind word to anybody. She was ill-tempered, conceited, opinionated, and ruthless when it came to getting her way. Which she always did."

Brooklynn looked up at him, her mouth open in shock. "Geoff! Don't say that about your great-grandmother! Miss Lucinda could be nice . . . when she wanted to be."

"When it served her purpose, you mean," he replied. "She managed to anger, insult, and alienate everybody from her housekeeper, to the guy who delivered her newspaper, to her local congresswoman." He paused to take a deep breath, then added, "Let's just say, she's not going to be missed. Quite the contrary, in fact."

Savannah turned to Dirk. She could see his mental wheels spinning, taking in all of this, trying to make sense of it.

Geoffrey Faraday didn't appear at first glance to be a stupid man. Yet, with every word he was uttering, he was making himself look, more and more, like their number one suspect.

"Okay," Dirk said. "Nobody's going to grieve her passing? Everyone she knew could have wanted her dead?"

"Absolutely. Most people will probably be relieved."

"That's a horrible thing to say, Geoff," Brooklynn said with a sniff, twisting a strand of her long dark hair around her finger. "I'm not happy she's gone. Now it's too late for us to ever make peace with her. I'm sad it had to end like this."

There was a long, awkward silence in the room as Geoffrey glared down at his fiancée.

Finally, Dirk said, "Okay. Was there anyone in particular you can think of who might have had a worse-than-average grudge against her? Anyone she had a confrontation with recently? Anybody who might've threatened to do her harm?"

"Nope. Afraid not." Faraday gave Dirk a little smile that set off alarm bells in Savannah's head. It was a mocking grin, almost as though he was daring Dirk to challenge him.

Not smart, Savannah thought. *Not when my man's tired and hungry.*

Dirk was almost always one or the other. Often both.

Suddenly, Dirk snapped his notebook closed and shoved it, far more forcefully than necessary, into his jacket pocket. He stood and said, "Okay, Mr. Faraday. If you don't want to help me figure out who killed your great-grandmother, I'll take it from here myself. The first person on my suspect list is going to be the one who has the most to gain from her passing."

Faraday looked up at Dirk blankly, his mocking grin gone. He didn't reply.

Savannah stood and followed Dirk to the door. But before they left, Dirk turned back to Geoffrey and said, "Oh, yeah. I understand you're Lucinda Faraday's sole heir. That makes you number one on my list. Congratulations!"

As they left the house and Geoffrey Faraday with an unhappy look on his formerly prissy face, Savannah couldn't help thinking how glad she was that she'd married a policeman, instead of a certain banker's son she'd fancied herself in love with, years ago.

She had nothing against bankers or their sons, of course. No doubt many of them were exciting, fun guys. But she was pretty sure her own life was more interesting, hanging out with her favorite cop.

Chapter 8

Nearly an hour later, when Savannah and Dirk arrived back at their house and pulled into the driveway, she saw the living room lights were on.

"Granny's still awake," she said, feeling a tug of guilt to have kept her grandmother up past her bedtime.

"Of course she is," Dirk said as he parked the car and shut it off. "When did you ever come home, after being out late, and find your grandma snoozing?"

"It happened. But I could probably count the times on one hand. She used to say, 'A mama hen cain't close her eyes to sleep till all her chickees are safe and sound in the nest.'"

As they got out of the car and walked to the front door, Dirk draped his arm over her shoulders and pulled her against his side. "I just hope that little ankle-biter didn't give her a hard time tonight. If he did, him and me's gonna tangle."

Savannah laughed, slipped her arm around his waist, and gave him a squeeze. "I hope not, too. It purely traumatized me, watching my beloved husband get the stuffin' beat out of him by a squirt that doesn't weigh as much as his thigh."

Dirk sniffed. "I had my hands full with his wild hyena of a mother. I've taken down bikers on PCP who gave me less hassle than that woman. I'll be happy if the only time I ever have to see her again is from the witness stand at her trial."

"You think she's going away?" Savannah asked, as the harsh truth of the boy's situation hit her.

"Oh, she's goin' away for sure. No doubt about it. That gal's rap sheet's longer than my"—he gave her a quick, suggestive grin—"my right arm."

She snickered. "Well, as long as it's your right arm and not your third leg."

"That's for sure. If that was the case, she'd be goin' away for life."

He unlocked the front door, opened it, and stood aside to allow her to walk through before him.

That was one thing she deeply appreciated about her West Coast boy. He might not be a son of the old South, but he had good ol' boy manners when it came to how to treat a lady.

Best of all—after the many years they had been together, first as partners on the force, then best friends, then husband and wife . . . after all the intimate knowledge they had of each other, gleaned from circumstances that were anywhere from deeply romantic interludes to dealing with the effects of bad chili cheese dogs—he still considered her a lady.

His lady.

The fact that he treated her as such, even when performing the simple act of going through a doorway, was one of his more endearing qualities.

She was also pleased that, without her even asking, he immediately took the precaution of putting his own weapon into the closet safe, rather than placing it on the top shelf.

When it came to kids, Dirk took no chances. Not even with ones who had given him a shiner earlier in the evening.

As they walked into the living room, Savannah glanced to the left, expecting to see her grandmother sitting in the most comfortable chair in the house, Savannah's infamous "comfy chair."

Like most of the Reid women who sat in it, the chair was soft, pretty, feminine, and overstuffed. The large, cushy footstool, also covered in the same rose floral chintz, was usually inhabited by one or both of her sister cats, Diamante and Cleopatra. Like bookends covered with silky black fur, they provided comfort and love in the form of purring foot warmers.

But, to Savannah's surprise, the chair was empty.

For half a second, she thought something might be wrong. Perhaps she shouldn't have left her elderly grandmother in the company of a juvenile delinquent, whom she had known for only a couple of hours.

But one glance toward the sofa put her mind at ease.

Granny sat in the middle, an open, well-read copy of *Peter Pan* in her lap. To her right was Cleo, curled in a ball against her thigh.

To her left sat Brody, his head on her shoulder, his eyes closed.

He looked like a different kid from the one Savannah had left in her grandmother's care earlier. This kid was clean. Shockingly clean. His dirty blond hair was now three shades lighter, definitely blond without a speck of the dirt. Sun-bleached, no doubt from spending a lot of time outdoors, his long hair was now fluffy and curly instead of straight and greasy.

Brody Greyson was the poster kid for Southern California Surfer Boy.

He was wearing Savannah's Mickey Mouse T-shirt, one of her many souvenirs from Disneyland. It was far too large for him, hanging down to his knees.

Savannah could see only a bit of his shorts beneath the shirt. But like the boy's hair and the rest of his body, the shorts had undergone a transformation in Granny's expert hands and were far cleaner than Savannah would have guessed they could ever be.

On the boy's lap was Diamante, curled into a contented, purring, snoozing circle of ebony fur, like her sister. Although the boy appeared to be asleep, too, his fingers were lightly stroking the cat's neck.

Granny was still reading the book, her voice soft and low. She glanced up at Savannah and smiled, the personification of peace.

"Hi," Savannah whispered. "I see you have everything under control, as expected."

Granny quietly closed the book and set it aside. "Nothin' needed controllin' 'round here tonight," she said. "The child was good as gold. Not a cross word or a disrespectful action outta 'im. He wanted to bring the Colonel indoors with him once it got dark. But I explained how

that could result in a hound dog with no nose on his face."
She nodded toward the cats. "He dropped the subject, we
put the hound in the utility room on his bed, and we sailed
through the rest of the evenin' with nary a problem."

"Then you did better than me," Dirk said, taking off
his tennis shoes and kicking them under the coffee table.

Granny looked up at him and squinted, trying to see
him clearly in the dim lamplight. "Mercy sakes alive,
boy. Is that a black eye you're sportin' there?"

Dirk nodded. "About as black as it's ever been, I hate to
admit," he told her. "Don't let that angelic look there fool
ya. That little runt can be a tear-cat when he wants to be."

"I ain't asleep, you know," Brody said, his southern
accent thick and drowsy. He opened his eyes halfway. "I
can hear everythin' you're saying. I ain't no runt, and I
ain't a tear-cat neither, 'less you're puttin' a whoopin' on
my momma."

"Yeah, and I'm an officer of the law," Dirk shot back,
"not a lousy, pig-nose skunk butt neither. Your momma
was resistin' arrest and encouraging her boy to rip my
face off, which I might remind you, you were tryin' your
best to do."

Granny cleared her throat and looked down at the
child next to her, a frown on her face and a distinct twinkle in her eye. "Brody Greyson, tell me the truth, 'cause I
don't abide no lyin'. Did you call Detective Coulter a pig-
nose skunk butt?"

"I did."

Brody didn't appear embarrassed. Not even a little. Savannah didn't know whether to be amused or concerned.

She decided she was both.

Granny continued, "Okay, thank you for your truthfulness. Did you lay your hands upon him in a violent manner, intendin' to do him bodily harm?"

Brody thought it over for a minute, then said, "I jumped on his back and started whalin' on him for all I was worth, intendin' to rip his face off and shove it where the sun don't shine—just like my momma was tellin' me to do."

He looked up at Granny with eyes that were filled with more innocence than might have been expected from someone who had just delivered such a damning confession. "Is that what you mean by 'bodily harm'?" he asked.

"Yessiree bob. That there's exactly what I meant." In one practiced move, Granny reached for the child, grabbed him by the shoulders, and spun him around until they were eye to eye.

The awakened and unhappy Diamante jumped off his lap and joined her sister on Granny's right side.

Granny looked deeply into the boy's eyes and said in a gentle but firm voice, "Young man, you and me gotta get somethin' straight right now. Detective Coulter there is a policeman, and in this household, we hold police officers in high regard."

The boy bristled. "Well, me and my momma don't like 'em. They're mean, nasty, monkey—"

"Stop! We don't allow no name-callin' in this house!" Granny took a deep breath, then having gathered a modicum of calmness, she continued. "You may have met some mean police in your young life. I'll grant you that. There's no-goods in any group of people. You line up a bunch of plumbers, teachers, even preachers, you'll find a dud or two among 'em. Cops ain't no different that way. But the vast majority risk their lives ever' day to keep us all safe, and we won't have nobody bad-mouthin' 'em in this house, let alone raisin' their hand to 'em. You hear me?"

With his nose only a few inches from hers, Brody continued to glare at Granny for what seemed to Savannah an eternity. But the older woman's steady, gentle gaze finally wore him down. He nodded and looked away.

Granny smoothed his hair back away from his eyes and placed a quick kiss on his forehead. "Detective Coulter is part of my family, Brody," she said. "A precious part. He's like a son to me. If you and me's gonna be friends, you'll have to treat him with respect. Understand?"

Savannah glanced over at Dirk and thought she saw a tear in his eye. She couldn't be sure because the black one was bloodshot and swollen. But she could tell that Gran's words had found their way to his heart.

As she had countless times already in her life, Savannah felt infinitely grateful to have a grandmother like hers.

So what if her childhood, her parents, hadn't been all they should have? She wouldn't trade her own upbringing for anyone's. Not if it meant losing Gran.

Savannah walked over to the sofa and held out her hand to Brody. "I think it's about bedtime, young man," she said. "I know it is for us old folks."

"That's for sure," Dirk grumbled. "But I've gotta eat something first. I'm about to starve. Is there any of that coconut cake left?" he asked Granny.

"It's in the icebox," she told him. "We saved you both big slices. Why don't you two eat 'em whilst I put our youngest to bed upstairs in the guest room?"

Surprised, Savannah looked at her grandmother. "No, no," Savannah told her. "The guest room is for you, like always, when it's late and you stay over. I'll make up a bed for Mr. Brody here on the couch."

"But . . . but he's the guest of honor tonight," Granny argued.

"Yes, he is," Savannah agreed. "As a gentleman, he would be honored to give you, his elder and a lady, the best bed while he holds down the couch and keeps it from floating away."

Savannah gave Brody a wink and a grin. "He's tough, aren't you, darlin'?"

Instantly, the boy gave her a broad smile. "I sure am. Tough as they come. I'm used to sleepin' on the floor in the back of my momma's van. Sleepin' on a couch ain't no big deal to the likes o' me."

Granny stood and whispered in Savannah's ear, "Are you sure? I don't mind bein' down here on the—"

"Sh-h-h. We won't hear of it," Savannah told her. "I had a feeling you'd be staying the night when I left earlier. I put fresh sheets on the futon, so the guest room's all ready for you."

The two women embraced and kissed each other good night. Granny hugged Dirk tightly, gave Brody a peck on his cheek, then disappeared up the stairs.

Savannah began to take the back cushions off the sofa and set them aside to make more room for the boy to sleep.

Dirk walked into the kitchen, and Savannah assumed he was headed to the refrigerator and the coconut cake. But a moment later he returned with his arms full of bedclothes from the utility room closet.

He waited until Savannah had removed the last cushion, then he spread the sheet and tucked it in.

"Lay down there, kid, and be quick about it," he told Brody with gruff playfulness.

The child grinned and scrambled to do as he was told.

As Savannah spread the second sheet and a blanket over his legs, she couldn't help thinking what an improvement that was over his and Dirk's earlier exchange.

"There's just one thing I'd really like to have," Brody said as he sat on his newly made "bed," his arms crossed over his chest.

"Whaddaya want now?" Dirk asked. "Oh, I know. A pillow fight!" He smacked the boy soundly with the pillow, knocking him onto his back. "Oops! Fight's over," Dirk told him. "I won."

Brody roared with laughter, grabbing the pillow away from Dirk and shoving it under his head.

Then the child turned to Savannah, his eyes filled with a longing that went straight to her heart.

"What is it?" she asked. "You want a glass of milk to help you sleep or—"

Brody shook his head. "No. Your grandma gave me so much to eat, I don't think I'll ever be hungry again. What I'd really like is . . . Do you think I could sleep with the kitties?"

Savannah and Dirk looked at each other for a moment, then Dirk said, "Actually, they're *our* bed partners. I sleep with Cleo, and Savannah cuddles up with Diamante."

The boy looked crushed, but he busied himself fluffing his pillow. "That's okay. I understand," he said. "They're used to sleeping with you guys. They'd probably be scared if we changed things up."

Savannah reached down and scooped up the still-pouting Diamante from the floor, where she had been placed when they had started making the bed. "Oh, I don't think Di would be scared to sleep with you. She likes you a lot, after you paying so much attention to her hurt ear and giving her all those good pets earlier. We've got two cats, and we aren't stingy folks. I reckon we can share with you."

Brody Greyson's bright, grateful smile was the only reward Savannah needed for her sacrifice of a purring, furry bed warmer.

She handed Diamante over to the child and watched him cuddle the contented feline close to his chest. Then Savannah bent over and gave him a kiss on the forehead.

"See there," she told him. "I promised you earlier that you'd be rewarded for being brave and making the right choice. I told you your life was going to get better. Remember?"

He nodded solemnly. "I remember. I'm always gonna remember that. Forever and ever."

Dirk reached down and rubbed the kid's head with his knuckles, rustling his hair. Dirk nodded toward Savannah and said, "This gal here, I've known her a long time. When she makes you a promise, you can take it to the bank and cash it."

"Okay." Brody grinned, tucking Diamante's head under his chin, while being careful of her ear. "You two are married, right?" he said to Dirk.

Dirk laughed. "Figured that out all by yourself, didja? Maybe we'll make a detective outta you someday."

Brody snorted. "That'll be the day. My momma'd pitch a fit if I was to ever become a cop. She'd rather me be a bank robber."

Dirk opened his mouth to say something, shot a sideways look at Savannah, and mumbled, "No comment."

As he ambled off to the kitchen, no doubt in search of

coconut cake, Savannah hurried over to the end table near Brody's head and switched off the lamp.

"Good night, sugar," she told him. "If you need anything at all, don't be afraid to come up and get me. Upstairs, down the hall, last door on the right. Next to the bathroom in case you need that, too."

"I'm fine," he said. "I don't get scared, and I'm used to holdin' it."

Savannah felt her heartstrings twang. "You're in *my* house now. Everybody here gets scared once in a while. It's nothing to be ashamed of, and when you're under my roof, you go when you need to. It's not healthy to . . . 'hold it.' Okay?"

"'Kay." He glanced toward the kitchen. They could hear knives, forks, and plates rattling. "That cake your grandma baked is the best I've ever ate. You better get in there quick, before he eats it all."

Savannah laughed. "How did you know?"

"He's the kinda guy you gotta watch your food around. Believe me, I can tell."

Savannah recalled something Dirk had told her once about literally having to fight for food back in the orphanage.

She looked down at her little guest with his gaunt cheeks and too-thin body. "You two boys have more in common than you probably think," she told him sadly.

"Me and him? Naw. We're nothing alike at all."

She gave him a final tuck in. Then, as she walked away, she whispered, "More than you might think, little man. In fact, more than you could ever imagine."

Chapter 9

"Your new boyfriend was lookin' pretty sharp this mornin'," Dirk told Savannah the next day as she drove him to the county morgue. "How much did all those new clothes set ya back?"

"More than you'd think," she replied. "Outfitting a young'un from head to toe with a week's worth of clothes—even a little kid—it's not cheap."

"Lemme know how much it was, and I'll pay it," he said, much to her shock. Since when did Ol' Stingy Pants fork over money without being asked nicely? Asked nicely while being prodded with a red-hot pitchfork or being hung upside down by his toenails.

"Seriously?" she asked, sure she had heard wrong.

"Yeah," he replied, moderately grumpy. "Most of the time I make more money than you. I don't mind pickin' it up this go around."

She thought her heart would burst with tenderness. He really could be a sweetie when he wanted to be.

"You don't have to," she said. "Ethan gave me a big retainer. But I appreciate the thought. A lot. Thank you."

"Sheez. Dodged that bullet," she heard him whisper.

"Yeah. You get credit for offering, but don't have to actually shell out any real cash."

"I know! Best of both worlds."

They rode on in silence awhile, leaving the picturesque residential area where they lived, passing the hospital and the junior college area.

"How hard was it to enroll him in school?" Dirk asked. "Did they give you a hard time about it?"

"Yes. They did. I had them call CPS, and by the time the gal there was done with them, they seemed pleased to have him."

"Was he okay when you left him? Was he happy to be there?"

"He's a kid whose mother's been letting him play hooky and hang out on the beaches for most of the school term. What do you think?"

"Did he say he misses the ol' gal?"

"No. He didn't mention her one single time."

"Good."

"I take it as a positive sign. Beats him crying his eyes out over her. Is she asking about him?"

"Not that I heard."

"Good."

Savannah turned off Sunset Avenue and headed toward the less touristy, more industrial part of town. There were hardly any palm trees in that area and no ocean views to speak of. Instead of quaint Spanish-style architecture, the buildings were enormous square boxes made of cement and steel with flat roofs, few windows, and loading docks.

Savannah hated that area. She considered it soulless. But mostly she resented the fact that countless acres of orange and lemon groves had been destroyed in order to build these monstrosities.

Not once since the orchards had been ravaged had she driven into this area and not recalled the dismembered trees bulldozed into giant piles and burning, the black smoke staining the turquoise sky.

"You know how much I hate coming down here," she said, beginning her well-worn complaint.

The one Dirk had heard far too many times.

"Yes, I know. I know," he said. "You're still pissy about them cutting down the trees."

"Not pissy. You are minimizing my feelings there, boy. I'm bereaved. Bereft and bereaved."

"And bemoaning the fact ad nauseam," he mumbled, turning away to look out his window.

"What?"

"Sorry to hear that you're in pain, darlin'. Again." He sighed. "Next time, I'll drive, and you can wear a blindfold. Then you won't have to belabor the point that you're beset with bereavement."

She turned and shot him a withering look. "Keep that up and you might *be* smacked upside the head."

He grinned at her and winked. Obviously terrified by the threat. "What're we gonna have for dinner tonight?"

"Whatever the kid wants, I reckon," she said.

"How come *he* gets to choose?"

"'Cause *you'll* eat anything."

"True."

*　*　*

When Savannah pulled the Mustang into the morgue's parking lot, she steeled herself for the ordeal ahead.

It wasn't the prospect of seeing a dead body. She had certainly seen more than her share of those. So many, in fact, that if she didn't know them personally, it didn't bother her that much anymore.

Except for the smell.

That she couldn't handle. No amount of pungent mentholated ointment spread generously inside a surgical mask could cover the stench of decomposition. It was an odor that went through the nostrils, straight to the stomach, and caused many people who smelled it to need to purge. Instantly.

Savannah was sure that the sink near Dr. Liu's autopsy table had been used for that purpose more often than for washing hands and disinfecting instruments.

It was the main reason that, fascinated as Savannah was by the miraculous design of the human body and as intrigued as she might be by the amount of forensic evidence it might provide during an autopsy, she wouldn't have done Dr. Liu's job for a million dollars.

Per autopsy.

Even worse, there was the gruesome task of dealing with Officer Kenny Bates, who manned the front desk.

Since she had Dirk with her, she doubted that Kenny would turn the full force of his "charm" in her direction. Not long ago, Dirk had assured Kenny that, if he didn't leave Savannah alone and refrain from making lewd suggestions in her company, Dirk would rearrange his digestive system so thoroughly that he would have to sit on his plate to eat his lunch.

Considering that Dirk was a head taller, ten years

younger, leaner and far meaner than Bates, good old Kenny had taken the threat to heart and behaved himself thereafter. As long as Dirk was present.

But as luck would have it, just as they were approaching the building together, Dirk received a call on his cell phone from the police chief.

"I wanna take this call first, before I go inside," he told her. "Are you gonna wait for me?"

Savannah smirked and shifted the plastic container filled with macadamia chocolate chip cookies under her arm. "Naw. I think I'll go ahead. I'll get Dr. Jen softened up for you. One bite of my cookies and she'll be putty in your hands."

"Yeah, right. In *your* hands, maybe. But *mine*? Never. Watch out for Bates."

"*He'd* better watch out for *me*."

She left Dirk to deal with the chief, glad that was no longer part of her job description, and walked through the front door of the county morgue.

As expected, Officer Kenneth Bates was wasting the taxpayers' money, making himself utterly useless at the front desk, watching some sort of television program on his computer screen while shoveling an enormous ice-cream sundae into his face.

His was a face that had been acquainted with far too much ice cream in its day, not to mention pizza, chips, dips, and doughnuts. Since he was not in the habit of changing and laundering his uniforms regularly, anyone with even minor detecting skills or a morbid curiosity could determine what he had eaten in the past week, simply by looking at his shirt front.

That, along with his askew, threadbare toupee, rendered Officer Bates totally resistible to most human beings. Especially females with a modicum of discernment and taste.

The bright smile that crossed his face the instant he saw her walk through the door might have been heart-warming, had it not been for the chocolate sauce running down his chin.

The thought of being held in such high esteem by one of her fellow humans might have proven at least a bit flat-tering in most circumstances. Over the years, Savannah had enjoyed more than her share of male attention. Al-though the fashion industry might have considered her to be overweight, men seemed to be attracted to, even fasci-nated by, her generously proportioned curves.

Then there was Kenny.

Kenny wasn't just attracted or fascinated by her.

Kenny was head over heels in lust with her. Deeply, hopelessly obsessed.

Even with a husband the size of Dirk threatening him, and in spite of the fact that Savannah had once beaten him soundly with his own rolled-up porn magazine, Kenny's ardor had not cooled one bit.

He wanted her, and he wasn't going to stop until he got her—or died in the process.

Savannah was hoping for the latter, as the former was unthinkable.

"Savannah!" He nearly dropped the tub of ice cream he was holding as he rushed to the reception counter. "I haven't seen you for so long!"

"Uh, yes," she said, reaching for the clipboard with its sign-in sheet and pen. "My luck was bound to run out, sooner or later."

"I was worried about you," he said, moving quickly into her personal space by leaning much too far over the counter. "I asked everybody about you, if something bad had happened to you, like a car wreck or something."

"Nothing quite as trauma-inducing as walking in here just now and laying eyes on you, Bates," she said in a silky smooth, semi-sexy tone meant to confuse him.

Confusing Kenny Bates was so easy it was hardly even worth the effort. But then, a gal had to take her entertainment where she could find it.

"I told a bunch of people, if they saw you, to give you my love," he said. "To tell you I was worried sick about you. Did they? Did anybody tell you I said that?"

"No. They didn't mention it." She picked up the pen, glanced at her watch, and jotted down her arrival time in the appropriate space. "They wouldn't dare."

He appeared puzzled, so she clarified. "A few years back, a patrolman told me that you'd asked after me. He made the mistake of repeating, in sordid, grotesque detail, what you said you'd like to do to me on a date."

"Oh yeah?" Ken brightened considerably. "What'd you tell him?"

"Nothing."

"Nothin' at all?"

He looked so disappointed. It was all she could do not to guffaw.

Donning her most solemn "Would-I-lie-to-you?" face, she told him, "Let's just say that by the time I finished with your little messenger, he was blind, deaf, lame, and unrecognizable to his loved ones."

"Oh. I guess that's not good."

"I reckon not. People talk, Bates. That sort of thing happens . . . word gets around. That might be why no one's willing to play Cupid for you anymore."

She glanced down at the sign-in sheet, paused to contemplate the possibilities, then scribbled the signature, "Et Durt AnDi."

For a moment, she thought she was finished with Kenny Bates. But no, Ken's deviant desires knew no bounds. He never seemed to know when he was ahead.

"That stuff the patrolman told you I wanted to do to you," he said, a hopeful gleam in his eye. "Didn't any of it sound fun? Like maybe you lickin' peanut butter offa my—Ow-w!"

She had shoved the clipboard at him just hard enough to knock the tub of half-melted hot fudge sundae all over the front of his already filthy uniform.

"You did that on purpose!" he shouted, looking down at the ruination of his snack, which was running down his legs into an unappetizing puddle on the floor.

Behind her, Savannah heard the front door open and close. She assumed and hoped that Dirk had entered just in time to witness the calamity.

He had.

"Nope," her husband assured her tormentor. "She didn't do it on purpose. If she had, your teeth would be down there on the floor next to the maraschino cherry."

Dirk walked up to Savannah, slipped his arm through hers, and gave her an admiring look. "Anything else you'd like me to do to him?" he asked her. "Just say the word."

Savannah thought it over, then shrugged and said, "No. I think I got it covered. But I appreciate the thought. You've always been my favorite backup."

They left Kenny Bates, standing in the melting mess of his destroyed dessert, bemoaning his loss . . . bereaved and bereft.

Chapter 10

Savannah and Dirk opened one of the two swinging doors at the end of the hall a crack and peeked inside the autopsy suite. As expected, they saw Dr. Liu exactly where they thought she would be, standing over the stainless-steel table that bore the remains of a star of the Golden Age of Hollywood.

But Lucinda Faraday didn't look like a glamorous star. She barely even looked human.

It always hurt Savannah's heart to see someone's body on an autopsy table. It certainly wasn't the way anyone would want to be seen on their final day on earth, robbed of their dignity, their identity, their clothing, unique grooming and jewelry—all that had defined them in life.

But at least Dr. Liu had the sensitivity and decency to keep the private areas of her "patients" covered whenever possible. As a result, Lucinda Faraday had a snowy white cloth draped across her, concealing her body from neck to knees.

Savannah knew that, by now, Dr. Liu would have completed her examination. Therefore, the cloth also hid the large Y-shaped incision that had been made from shoulder to shoulder, and all the way down the chest and abdomen.

Normally, a person as old as Ms. Faraday, or anyone who had been sick and died from natural causes, would not have received a complete autopsy. But seemingly healthy people who might have left the world at the hands of another, or their own, were required to be examined as thoroughly as modern science allowed.

If there was a story of murder to be told, the Great State of California wanted to know every detail of their passing.

Morbid though the autopsy process might appear, Savannah had seen profound truths brought to light from one simple fact, uncovered during such an examination.

Savannah believed that most victims, if they had been alive and able to speak on their own behalf, would want the details of their murder known and their killer brought to account.

Even precious things like dignity and privacy seemed insignificant when compared to the need for justice.

"Let me go in first," Savannah whispered to Dirk, as they stood by the doors. "I'll butter her up for you with the cookies."

"Of course," Dirk grumbled. "How would I do my job without my wife and her famous cookies?"

Savannah elbowed him in the ribs and grinned. "Not nearly as well. That's how. You can repay me later."

"Repay you? I thought you were on Ethan Malloy's payroll now. You're not helping me. You're working for a client. I don't owe you squat."

"Hm. That's a shame." She gave him a naughty grin. "The payment I had in mind involved whipped cream."

He perked up considerably. "On apple pie?"

"Nope. On something you like even more than apple pie."

"Damn."

"Yeah. You missed out, big boy."

The grin he gave her suggested that he was less than bitterly disappointed. He knew her too well. Well enough to know that Hard to Get wasn't a game that she played with skill. Unfortunately, she was as fond of whipped cream as he was.

Looking through the crack between the doors, Savannah could see that the medical examiner was removing her gloves and the protective clothing she wore while performing the more gruesome duties that her job required.

The exotic beauty looked more like a model than a coroner. Tall and thin with a lovely face and figure, Dr. Liu didn't bother to hide her attractiveness. No, she celebrated it, wearing short skirts and stilettos that showed off her legs to perfection. Her long, glossy black hair was tied in a ponytail, out of her way, with a colorful silk scarf.

Savannah had seen how men, even her own man, watched Dr. Liu move across a room. While Dirk wasn't ill-mannered enough to ogle females in public, Savannah couldn't blame him for looking when it came to Dr. Liu. Even other women stared at Dr. Liu.

Like that moment, as they both watched her peel off her lab coat, revealing a cold shoulder blouse and snug, short pencil skirt.

Next, she pulled the scarf from her hair, letting it flow over her shoulders. Savannah heard Dirk catch his breath when she turned away from them and bent over to remove the paper protectors that covered her high-high heels.

"Okay, enough of this," Savannah whispered to Dirk. "Wish me luck," she added, pushing the door open.

"You don't need luck. You got cookies," he replied.

"True."

When Savannah walked inside, Dr. Liu turned, saw her, and smiled warmly. "Good morning, girlfriend. Nice to see you. Especially since you come bearing gifts," she added when she saw the container.

"We figured it might be about time for your midmorning break. Thought you might need an infusion of chocolate to keep you bright eyed and bushy tailed."

The doctor's eyes sparkled for half a second at the mention of chocolate, then she scowled. "We?"

Savannah nodded, and Dirk stepped inside the suite.

"I couldn't let her come see my favorite M.E. without me tagging along," he said in his worst, least convincing kiss-up voice that Savannah never heard him use.

Or at least, not since the last time he had visited the cantankerous doctor whose findings were almost always critical to his cases.

Dirk had no problem dismissing most people who irritated him with a curt zinger. Unfortunately for him, Dr. Jennifer Liu seemed impervious to his zings, considering him little more than a nuisance to be dealt with as quickly and infrequently as possible.

Worse still, she didn't mind if he knew it.

As the doctor tossed her used, bloody gloves into a biohazard waste receptacle with a bit more vigor than the task required, she said, "No, of course you'd come along. Getting a bit of one-on-one time with a good friend and not having to share my cookies with a brazen glutton, that was clearly too much for me to hope for. Huh, Coulter?"

Dirk sighed and shook his head. "Sometimes I think you don't like me, Dr. Jen, and I just don't understand it. I'm always nice to you, but every time we meet up, you go outta your way to hurt my feelings." Savannah watched as Dirk painted a "deeply wounded" expression across his face. Of course, she knew it was fake. She had actually seen Dirk hurt a few times, but he was a tough guy, and it took a lot more than a sarcastic M.E. to get beneath his thick hide.

Unfortunately, Dr. Liu knew that, too.

"You most certainly are *not* always nice to me, Detective," she snapped back. "You pretend to be pleasant when you're trying to get something out of me. When you want me to put your examinations in front of other cases, when you want me to rush lab results, when you want me to tell you, 'Who done it?' in thirty seconds when I arrive at a scene."

"Yeah, well, that'd be nice once in a while," he said, dropping the Nice Guy facade. "But I ain't gonna hold my breath till it happens."

"Go ahead." Dr. Liu tossed her white lab coat into the bin with the dirty gloves. "Hold your breath right now. For ten minutes. I'll rule your cause of death 'Asphyxiation' and the manner of death 'Suicide by Temper Tantrum.' It'll only take me five seconds. Case closed."

Calmly, slowly, Savannah opened the container of cookies and offered one to the M.E. "How about we stop squabbling and get down to the serious business at hand—eating some of these?"

"Sounds good to me," Dirk said, peering into the box.

Dr. Liu grabbed the box and hugged it to her chest. "Me too."

"Finally!" Savannah exclaimed. "The two of you agree on something. It's a miracle!"

Later, Savannah, Dirk, and Dr. Liu were settled in the M.E.'s office, munching cookies and discussing the preliminary findings from Lucinda Faraday's autopsy.

Dr. Liu sat at her desk, Savannah and Dirk on nearby no-frills folding metal chairs.

The county had been in the midst of a budget crisis when they had originally "decorated" the M.E.'s office. That had been decades ago. Medical examiners had come and gone. The first female M.E. had been appointed. Time had marched along, but the now-rusty, rickety metal chairs remained.

Savannah couldn't help noticing, as always, that once the conversation turned professional between her husband and the medical examiner, the bickering stopped.

"No big surprise that it was strangulation," Dirk said. "I figured that out as soon as I saw the stocking around her neck."

"Whoever put it there didn't intend for her to survive the ordeal," Savannah added.

"No kidding. The ligature was so tight it literally cut into the skin, several millimeters, here in the front of the neck." Dr. Liu tapped her glossy crimson nail on an eight-by-ten photo on her desk.

Savannah winced when she looked closely at the picture, the dark brown line, broken by a red incision where Dr. Liu was pointing.

"That much violence," Dirk said, "has to be personal."

"Or a pervert's frenzy," Savannah suggested. "Was she sexually violated?"

The doctor shook her head. "No."

"Are you sure?" Dirk asked.

"Absolutely certain. Not one mark or bit of evidence to indicate she was in any way."

"That's a relief," Savannah said, thinking how glad she would be to report that to Ethan. He would be grateful that his friend had been spared additional misery and indignity. "Considering the suggestive posing of the body, it seemed likely."

"It did," Liu agreed. "I fully expected to find she'd been raped. I was surprised to find the body unharmed. In that way, at least."

"How about other kinds of injuries?" Dirk asked.

"Other than the obvious strangling, I found nothing at all."

Savannah frowned, puzzled. "Not even defensive wounds?"

"Not a single one. There was a Band-Aid on her ankle. Beneath it was a mostly healed scrape of some sort. Definitely not perimortem. I'd say it was at least a week old. Probably older, considering how long it can take for someone her age to heal."

"She didn't fight even a little?" Dirk said. "That's unusual."

"It certainly is," Savannah agreed. "When someone's being strangled to death, they fight for their life. Violently."

"I know. Every strangulation victim I've examined had the bruises, scratches, you name it, to show they fought."

"They also inflict wounds of their own," Savannah added.

"Very true." The doctor reached for the last cookie in the container. "Many have their attacker's skin under their nails."

Dirk watched her bite into it with a look of deep sadness, then said, "One of the first things I do is check out a suspect's face, neck, chest, and shoulders for scratches. It's a dead giveaway."

"Why on earth didn't she fight?" Savannah said, more to herself than the others.

Dirk nodded. "It would have taken some time. What, Doc, fifteen seconds or so?"

"Depends on a lot of factors. It's hard to say for certain, but it wouldn't have been instant, for sure."

Savannah leaned back in her chair and folded her arms over her chest. Just thinking about Lucinda Faraday, or anyone, dying that way made her feel heartsick. "Even if, for some strange reason, Lucinda was willing to die, her natural instincts would have probably kicked in at some point, and she would have resisted."

"I agree," Dirk said. "Even if it was some sort of assisted suicide, I can't imagine she or her accomplice would have chosen a nasty method like that. There's always pills."

Unpleasant memories flooded Savannah's mind, pictures that would haunt her forever of people who thought they were taking an "easy" way out by swallowing pills. They hadn't understood the body's determination to survive and what it did to save itself, even if its owner wanted to leave.

"I've seen a lot of dead folks in my day," she said sadly. "I have to admit, other than those who die of natural causes, I have yet to see a passing that appeared easy."

Both the doctor and Dirk nodded solemnly.

"But now that you mention pills," Liu said, "I'll remind you that we won't be getting the toxicology report for a couple of days. I half suspect there may have been some drugs in her system."

"You saw signs of addiction?" Dirk asked.

"No. Her liver showed that she drank quite a bit, but it was still healthy for her age."

Dirk looked puzzled. "Then why are you thinking drugs?"

"You think someone else might have given her drugs?" Savannah guessed. "Maybe sleeping pills?"

"It could account for the fact that she didn't fight her attacker," Liu replied. "If someone slipped her some sort of sedative, she might have been unconscious through the entire thing."

Savannah felt a shiver go through her. "That would indicate a clear case of premeditation on the killer's part. No spur of the moment, in the heat of an argument, provoked fit of rage, or whatever."

"True." Dirk picked up the photo from Dr. Liu's desk and studied it as he said, "That'd have to be a pretty cowardly murderer—to be so afraid of an old lady that he'd drug her first before killing her."

"A coward," Savannah said, "or maybe some sicko's idea of compassion?"

Dr. Liu picked up yet another photo off her desk and

looked at it. Savannah could see it was a picture of Lucinda Faraday, lying on her bed of garbage, provocatively posed.

"We already know the killer is cruel," the doctor said. "If they drugged her before murdering her, I don't know what their motive was. That's for the two of you to figure out. But I can tell you one thing. . . . It most certainly wasn't an act of mercy."

Chapter 11

When Savannah and Dirk left the morgue, Savannah wanted to return to the Faraday mansion with him. But she couldn't.

"Why not?" he asked her. "If you wanna check out the crime scene with me, I'm happy to have you come along."

"I promised Ethan I'd meet him on the pier at noon and catch him up on what we've got," she said, trying to hide her disappointment.

"What we *ain't* got is more like it," Dirk said as he turned toward their neighborhood instead of the freeway that would take them to Qamar Damun.

"I know, but he's paying me well, so I owe him the nothing he's paying for."

"What?"

"Exactly. Then when I'm finished with him, I'm going

to ask Tammy to meet me at the house. I can get her started on the background checks for Geoffrey, Brooklynn, and Mary."

"Good. She does a lot better job than that new gal we got at the station house. That dingbat couldn't find a Boeing 747 if it was parked in her driveway."

Savannah laughed. "I never thought I'd hear you compliment Tammy while calling someone else a dingbat. Have you gotten soft in your old age?"

"Naw. I ain't soft. She's gotten better. She probably *could* find a 747 in her driveway, if all four of its engines were running. But don't tell her I said that. Wouldn't want her to get a swelled head or nothin'."

"I'll resist the urge to share," she replied.

"You gonna pick up the rug rat from school at three o'clock? It's only a few blocks from our house. I'm sure he could find his way. The kid seems, uh, quite streetwise, to say the least."

"I know, and Gran offered to get him. But I wanted to, it being his first day and all. He was nervous this morning, when I left him. He didn't say so, but I could tell. He acted like he'd never been to school before."

"Maybe he hasn't."

"He said he went to kindergarten and first grade there in Georgia. Said his mom just hadn't gotten him enrolled here yet."

"She probably figured she'd get around to it. Once she got her drug situation sorted out. First things first, you know."

Savannah thought it over for a moment, then groaned. "He had no clothes but those shorts and flip-flops. He said they were living out of their car. He's obviously undernourished."

"But she had a bagful of drugs, plus several cartons of cigarettes and all kinds of booze in her van." He shook his head. "A lady with her priorities in order. Obviously."

"We don't even know for sure if he was in school in Georgia. When I was registering him, they were having a hard time locating his records." She felt a knot forming in her throat. "Poor kid. All the more reason why I want to be there to pick him up when school lets out. I'll take him for an ice-cream cone or whatever. See if he'll open up to me."

Dirk gave her a little smile as he pulled into their driveway. "You're a good woman, Savannah Reid," he said. "Did I ever tell you that?"

She leaned over and kissed his cheek. "You might've mentioned it once or twice."

"If I get off work early enough, I'll take him over to my barber and get him shorn."

"I think he looks kinda cute with his hair long. Like a little surfer dude."

"Then I'll tell my guy not to take off much, just spruce him up. We want him looking sharp over at that new school."

She gave him another kiss. Longer this time and on the lips.

"Thank you," she said. "I appreciate your help."

"Hey, as long as the squirt's under our roof, he's my problem, too. Plus, your granny seems keen to help."

"I know. Isn't she great with him?"

"She's awesome. But more than anything else, I'm just sayin'—it ain't all up to you, darlin'. Takes a village and all that."

Savannah sat there, looking at her husband. His scruffy beard that he shaved once a week, whether it needed it or not. The faded second generation Harley-Davidson T-shirt. The bomber jacket that looked like it had actually had a few bombs land on it in its long lifetime.

She was on her way to see Ethan Malloy, a man adored by millions of lust-besotted women, whose face had graced the world's best-known magazines, who had been named, more than once, the sexiest man living.

But she wouldn't have traded Ethan or any other guy for the one sitting next to her, the man who frequently told her she was the best person he had ever met.

Bulging biceps, broad shoulders, a perfect smile, a deep voice, and piercing blue eyes were all nice.

But as any woman with a degree of wisdom or insight was well aware, the sexiest feature any man could possess was loyalty.

As Savannah and Ethan walked the length of San Carmelita's beloved wooden pier, it occurred to her, not for the first time, what a pain in the butt celebrity must be.

Yes, Ethan's was one of the best-known faces in the world. His size alone set him apart from most of the people around them. It was impossible for such a large man to hide in a crowd when he was a head taller than most.

Even wearing sunglasses and a baseball cap, he was recognizable. At least half of the people they passed gasped when they saw him, then pointed him out to their friends and family.

Cell phones were lifted, and pictures taken—photos and videos that would, undoubtedly, appear within minutes on the Internet.

Those were the nice people.

The not-so-nice ones ran up to him, grabbed his arm,

shook his hand, hugged, and even kissed him. Savannah quickly lost count of how many autographs and selfies he had granted before they had walked the fifteen-hundred-feet length of the pier.

"I don't know how you stand it," she told him. "I'd go plumb crazy if I had that many strangers snatching at me all the time."

In a tone of voice that sounded like exhausted resignation, he said, "It's part of the job. Goes with the territory and all that. If getting their picture taken with me or owning a piece of paper that I scribbled on means that much to them, who am I to say no?"

"A lot of celebrities do—say no, that is."

He shrugged. "That's their right. But it's not me. I can spend ten seconds and give somebody a memory that'll last them for a lifetime. That's an honor and blessing I'll always be grateful for."

At that moment, a couple of teenaged girls spotted him and came running over to greet him. One grabbed his arm in a death grip, while the other jumped up and down several times in front of him, trying to kiss him.

Savannah was about to reach out and smack her when Ethan bent down and turned his head, allowing her a quick peck on the cheek.

"Oh, Ethan! I just *love* you!" the smoocher said, when she finally managed to catch her breath. "I'm not just saying that. I mean, love! *Really, really love!* I watch your movies every single night before I go to sleep."

"Um, that's nice. Thank you," he replied, moving into position for the selfie the other one was trying to take.

Once the girl who had confessed her "really, really love" got her giggling fit under control, she stood, gazing up at him with adoration and something that looked to

Savannah like pretend sadness. She was a bad actress. "I was so sorry to hear that you and Beth broke up," she told him. "I can't believe she'd be so stupid. To leave a man like *you*. Why on earth did she do such a stupid—?"

"Okay! Enough with the rude questions!" Savannah said, giving the girl a hearty push that would have landed her on her rear, had she not collided with her friend. "You got your hug, kiss, and picture. Scram."

The girl's face flushed red with anger. "Oh yeah? Who are you? His new girlfriend? I read everything they write about Ethan, and I don't remember anything about *you*!"

"I'm his bodyguard, and if you don't want your butt Tased, you'll get outta range. Pronto!"

Savannah made a big show of reaching into her purse, and in seconds, the teens were halfway down the pier, heading for the beach.

Savannah heard Ethan chuckle. She turned to see him watching her, a smirk on his face.

"You're my *bodyguard*?" he asked.

"Yeah. I throw that in with the private investigating."

"Good deal! Two for the price of one!" He glanced down at her purse. "Do you really carry a Taser in your pocketbook?"

"No. The most lethal thing I've got in there is a bottle of spray perfume." She pulled her jacket back a bit, revealing her holster strap. "I do, however, carry a Beretta here."

"Then, if I'm attacked by marauding, overly curious teenagers, you can obviously deal with the problem."

"You betcha. Relax, Mr. Malloy. You're in good hands."

"I never doubted it."

They continued walking toward the end of the pier, which was thankfully less crowded. The sun was hot, but it was a windy day. A stiff breeze was blowing cool ocean spray up onto the pier and wetting their faces as they stood, looking out at the horizon.

Savannah breathed in the smell of the sea and, as was her habit, thought how grateful she was to be living in a place of such beauty and restoration.

"Do you ever miss Texas?" she asked him.

"No," was his instant reply. "Do you miss Georgia?"

"No." She paused and reconsidered for a moment. "Well, some of the people. The peaches. The pecan pies. That's about it."

They shared a companionable chuckle, then the view for a while. Then it was time for business.

"I'm so glad to hear that Lucinda wasn't, you know, hurt. That way," Ethan said.

She found it endearing that this man of the world still possessed his Texas good ol' boy sensitivities and was uncomfortable discussing indelicate subjects with a lady.

"Yes, me too," she assured him. "It's hard to imagine anything that would make a murder 'better' somehow, but I guess that does. A bit."

He nodded. "After seeing her body, you know, like that, I figured she'd been violated, too. I was so hoping she hadn't suffered that fate. Again."

"Again?" Savannah gave him a quick sideways look.

"Yes. Again."

She gulped. "When?"

"Long ago. Back when she first arrived in Hollywood. She was just a kid."

"I'm sorry to hear that."

"More than once."

"Oh, no. Really?"

"I'm afraid so."

"If you don't mind me asking, how do you know this?"

He gave her a half smile, glanced in both directions, and said, "I don't mind you asking me questions, but I have this rabid bodyguard who—"

"Has spray perfume in her purse and a Beretta on her side? Yeah, yeah. She ain't that tough. I could take her."

Ethan smiled, but it quickly disappeared. He sighed, removed his baseball cap, and ran his fingers through his hair. "I told you that Lucinda and I did a movie together some time back. That was the first time I'd ever met her, though I'd admired her work for years. One night, they were taking a really long time setting up a particularly difficult shot, and she invited me back to her trailer. She said that, if I wouldn't be offended, she could give me a couple of pointers about how to play to the camera."

"How nice of her."

"You have no idea. We became friends that night, and I can't tell you how much she helped me, as an actor and a person."

"You must have become close, for her to share something with you as personal as a sexual assault."

"Like I said, she wasn't victimized only once. She was passed around like a piece of candy, from one high-powered jerk to another, while she was still just a kid. Studio heads, politicians, mobsters, you name it."

"She had no guardians to watch over her?"

"She had a mother who sold her to the highest bidder."

Savannah winced, thinking how many times she had seen that scenario play out on ordinary, mean streets. "Unfortunately," she said, "Hollywood doesn't have a corner on that market. Some folks who should be protecting their young sell their innocence all day long."

"True." He drew a deep breath. "I just wanted to say that I'm relieved her death didn't include that particular horror. It's bad enough that someone murdered her."

"It certainly is."

"Do you have any suspects?"

Savannah shook her head. "We've interviewed her great-grandson, Geoffrey, and his fiancée. He's Lucinda's sole heir, and I wouldn't give you two cents for him. But neither of those things mean he's a killer."

"Yeah, I heard about Geoffrey. Lucinda couldn't stand him, great-grandson or not," Ethan said. "We had a few long talks about him over some fine Irish whiskey." He smiled wistfully. "Lucinda did enjoy her Irish whiskey."

"Any particular reason that she didn't like him?"

"She said he was lazy, worthless. Then there was the illegal stuff."

"What kind of illegal stuff?"

"I don't know exactly, but she mentioned that he spent some time in prison. More than once, I believe. She bailed him out and paid for his lawyers a time or two. Then she gave up on him and disowned him."

"Disowned? How about disinherited?"

"Probably that, too. I don't know for sure. Lucinda was a generous person, but she was smart enough to watch who she gave to and who she didn't."

"Wasn't one to throw her pearls before swine, huh?"

"Not at all, and I'm pretty sure she considered her great-grandson an oinker."

Savannah thought she might be seeing a glimmer of light in a dark crawl space.

"I'll sic Tammy on him right away," she said. "Between her and Dirk, they'll find out why he served time and maybe some other times when he should have but didn't get convicted. Tamitha's great at uncovering skull-duggery of the, shall we say, well-hidden variety."

"I have total faith in you and your team, Savannah." He looked down at her with a depth of affection that touched her heart. "I'll never forget what you and your people did for me."

She reached over and patted his hand, which was resting on the top rail. "I was so sorry to hear about you and Beth divorcing. Unlike that silly kid, I really mean it."

"Thank you." He turned to stare out at the ocean again. "We'll never get back together again. I'm sure of it. But we aren't bitter enemies. We've decided to stay friends, for Freddy's sake."

"I'm not surprised. You're both good people with kind hearts. You'll do the right thing."

"We try. I guess we succeed. Sometimes."

"I don't know if it helps to know this, but most marriages wouldn't survive what happened to your family."

He took off his sunglasses, passed his hand over his eyes, and turned to face her. "To be honest, Savannah, the marriage wasn't going to last anyway. It hadn't been working for a long time before . . . that . . . happened."

"I understand."

More tears took the place of the ones he'd wiped away, as he said, "Everybody and their cousin's dog thinks they want to be a celebrity, Savannah, a big star. They think fame and fortune is what it takes to be happy."

"Yes, that's the rumor going around, I hear."

"It's a lie. Along with the prestige and the expensive toys, fame and fortune bring a lot of misery. Rich, successful folks have every problem that everybody else has."

Savannah thought about the tough times she'd endured because of a lack of funds. She saw his point but couldn't fully agree.

Experience had taught her: money might not buy happiness, but poverty could sure cause a heap of suffering.

"But rich folks don't have money problems," she gently argued.

"You might be surprised," he told her. "They have bigger incomes, but most of the ones I know also have bigger bills and wonder sometimes how they're going to pay them. Besides, life's worst problems, the ones we all have, can't be fixed with money."

She ran down a quick list in her mind of what she considered life's worst problems to be. Sickness, betrayal, shattered marriages, aging parents, wayward children, natural disasters, guilt, regret, and fear of the unknown.

"I reckon that's true," she said. "Money helps some situations, but it can't make anybody immune."

"It sure doesn't. Or Lucinda Faraday would have lived a bit longer and died peacefully in her bed, surrounded by people who loved her, instead of . . ."

"I know." Savannah nodded and patted his hand again.

There was no need to state the obvious.

Chapter 12

Savannah intended to phone Tammy the moment she got home and ask her to drop by for what Tammy liked to call a "sleuth briefing." Never in her life had Savannah known anyone who used the word "sleuth" as frequently as her best friend and assistant, Tammy Hart-Reid. Nor had Savannah had the pleasure of anyone's company who was actually more obsessed with private investigating than she was.

Therefore, Savannah wasn't exactly shocked when she pulled up to her house and saw Tammy's hot pink Volkswagen bug parked in the driveway. No doubt, Tammy already knew more about the case than she did. Granny's panel truck, parked next to the bug, told Savannah that there had probably been a "sleuth briefing" already.

In the Reid family's hometown of McGill, Georgia, there was a saying regarding Granny: "If you want to pass a bit of juicy gossip around town, quick-like, there are three sure ways—telephone, telegram, or tell-a-Stella."

Granny was the soul of discretion, *if* you actually asked her to keep something to herself. Ancient Babylonian torture techniques couldn't have wrenched your secret from her. But if you failed to mention that it was a private matter and not for general consumption, you could expect to be questioned about it by everyone in town, from the mailman to the grocery store clerk, the very next day. They probably already knew more details about your personal business than you yourself.

As Savannah walked into her house, it occurred to her, not for the first time, that maybe giving a key to everyone she knew and inviting them to "Just drop by and make yourself at home anytime you've a mind to" wasn't the best life strategy.

On the other hand, Savannah was seldom lonely. At any given time, there were usually at least five human beings and three furry critters inside her walls.

Plus, they were always hungry, and Savannah was never happier than when she was creating good food and shoving it into the mouths of her grateful loved ones.

"Yoo-hoo," she called out as she tossed her purse onto the piecrust table and stowed her Beretta in the safe. "Who's here?"

"Me!" yelled a cheerful voice that could only be Tammy. Savannah would've never allowed anyone else to be that obnoxiously vivacious on her turf. At least, not in the morning.

"Me too," called Granny from the kitchen. "Y'all wash your hands and come sit down to the table. I've got dinner ready—or 'lunch' as you Yankees like to call it."

Savannah grinned. In Granny's estimation, unless you were born and raised south of the Mason-Dixon line, you were a "Yankee." To her, Alaskans and Hawaiians were Yankees, and therefore needed to be cut a lot of slack when it came to their questionable manners. Not having been "raised up proper," they couldn't help it. Bless their hearts.

Savannah walked into the living room and saw Tammy seated at the rolltop desk in the corner. The office computer was on, and she was flipping from one Web page to another with dizzying speed.

On her lap was one of Savannah's favorite creatures on earth, a tiny, copper-curled fairy-child named Vanna Rose. Savannah's namesake, niece, and very heart.

The baby had already heard her aunt and was struggling to get down from her mother's lap, giggling and waving her chubby arms wildly.

"Okay, okay," Tammy said, laughing as she slid her down to the floor. "Go on. Show Auntie what you've learned since you saw her last Thursday."

Savannah watched, spellbound, as the child stood, wobbling on her miniature feet. She had a look of intense concentration on her face, as she held her arms out to each side as though she was getting ready to take flight.

"No way!" Savannah said. "Don't tell me she's learned how to—"

"Okay. I won't tell you. You can see for yourself in a few seconds. You might want to stand a bit closer though and get ready to catch her."

Savannah did as Tammy suggested and watched, her heart filling to overflowing, as the baby lifted one chubby little foot and, as carefully and dramatically as a tightrope walker balancing a hundred feet above the circus arena, daintily placed it in front of the other. She wobbled for what seemed like forever, then seemed to realize she had "landed" it and let out a squeal of triumph.

Her own joyous cries were joined by Savannah's and those of Granny Reid, who had come to watch at the kitchen door.

Savannah hurried to her and scooped her into her arms. Planting kisses on the child's dimpled cheeks, she exclaimed, "Lord've mercy! Did you see that? She's on her feet! Look out, world! There's no stopping her now!"

Savannah danced around the room with her niece and, for a moment, grim topics like murdered movie stars left her mind, releasing her, allowing her to enjoy a bit of light to balance the darkness.

Finally, Granny called a halt to the celebrating. "Okay, the beans are gettin' cold and the corn bread's gonna set up, hard as a brickbat. Skedaddle in here and stuff your faces."

As Tammy stood and turned off the computer, Savannah noticed that she had a twinkle in her eye that could only mean one thing.

"Gran filled you in on the case, and you've already found something, right?" Savannah asked her.

"I sure did. Wait till you hear it!"

"I 'sleuth briefed' her on all the important details," Gran said as she started to lift a large bowl of white beans, cooked in a savory broth with onions, carrots, celery, and tomatoes.

"I'm sure you did," Savannah replied, relieving her grandmother of the heavy bowl and placing it in the center of the table.

Granny set a small cast iron skillet containing the corn bread on a trivet beside the beans, next to the butter dish.

"Don't wait for me," she said. "I'll just get the sweet tea from the icebox."

Granny turned to Tammy, who was buckling her daughter into her high chair. "Don't worry," she told her, "I've got some lemons cut up in mineral water for you and the punkin', and I didn't stick no ham in the beans neither."

Savannah couldn't help smiling at the concession her grandmother had made for their health-conscious vegetarian guest. Like Granny, Savannah held the opinion that any pot of beans without a few ham hocks thrown in for "seasonin'" was hardly worth cooking, let alone eating.

For the first few years of Granny's and Tammy's friendship, Gran had lived in dread that Tammy might fall over in a dead faint at any minute, considering how little "fat she had on her bones." It had taken a long time for Tammy to convince Gran that drinking unadulterated water instead of Georgia style sweet tea was a good idea.

But after watching their svelte, athletic friend run for miles every day—even after bringing a baby into the world—and perform every task known to modern womanhood with boundless energy, even Gran had to admit that "clean eating," as Tammy called it, might not prove fatal after all.

Once Vanna was settled in her chair, Tammy crumbled a bit of corn bread around the tray for her.

Granny laughed when she saw the child begin to cram the tiny pieces into her mouth as quickly as possible. "Boy, look at that! Don't ever get between a Reid woman and her corn bread. You might lose a finger or two!"

When they were all settled around the table and had begun their midday meal, Savannah decided she couldn't wait any longer. She turned to Tammy and said, "Well, what did you find out? Spill it."

Tammy grinned, obviously proud of herself, which gave Savannah hope. Without a doubt, Tammy was the most skilled and enthusiastic techno-researcher Savannah had ever seen, and every day, Savannah was grateful to have her as a member of her Moonlight Magnolia Detective Agency.

Especially since the height of Savannah's computer skills was her ability to cut and paste a block of text or copy an image.

If Tammy was wearing her self-satisfied smirk, Savannah knew she had something juicy.

"Okay." Tammy pulled her electronic tablet from the baby's diaper bag on the floor next to the high chair. "As soon as I heard who the victim was, a wealthy woman with a ton of assets, I checked out her heirs, you know, to find out who had the most to gain by her passing."

"She only has one," Savannah said.

"I know. Sometimes you get lucky."

"Dirk's running a background check on him right now."

"Then Dirk-o's probably getting pretty excited. Geoffrey Faraday's a bad boy. A serious record. Prison time and everything."

"Mercy!" Granny said, slathering butter on her corn bread square. "Whatever for?"

Tammy's pretty face grew serious. "He served five years for human trafficking."

"Wow!" Savannah recalled the annoying but impeccably dressed young man they had interviewed earlier. Somehow, it defied logic that a man wearing such a pretty suit would have committed such an ugly crime. She also took into account that her "logic" might be a bit fashion-biased. "I didn't see that coming. I was thinking bad checks or tax evasion maybe."

Granny shook her head solemnly. "That human trafficking, it's an awful business, to be sure. Evil like that is bound to darken a body's soul. Though some might say it's hard to imagine somebody having a soul and doing such a thing to another human being."

"That's for sure." Savannah turned back to Tammy. "Got any particulars on that?"

"I do. Apparently, he was in cahoots with some really bad guys who were bringing women in from Thailand to, supposedly, work in nail salons. But as it turned out, those parlors were fronts for prostitution. They were offering massages in cubicles in the back of the salons, areas they claimed were for waxing, etc."

Tammy shot a quick look at her daughter, who apparently couldn't care less about bad guys and their misdeeds, as long as she had plenty of corn bread crumbled in front of her.

"Let's just say," Tammy continued, "folks were getting more than their feet rubbed and their brows waxed in those private cubicles."

"I hate human traffickers," Savannah said, feeling a wave of fury, hot and turbulent, rising in her soul. "Back in their victims' native countries, they promise them palm trees and golden beaches and money flowing through their hands. Except, of course, they don't get to keep the money, let alone send it back home to their homeless, starving families."

"That's the main reason most of them leave home in the first place," Tammy interjected.

"True," Savannah agreed. "The minute they arrive, these jerks take their passports and shove them into a filthy apartment, ten to a room. The only time they get out of those horrible places is when they're herded into a windowless van and hauled somewhere to work a sixteen-hour day."

"I was reading about that," Tammy said, blinking away some tears. "The traffickers take their passports and any money they might have. Then they guard them every minute to make sure they don't run away."

"Wouldn't do 'em any good even if they did get away," Granny said. "Most of 'em probably don't speak English. They wouldn't even be able to tell somebody what they're going through or that they need help."

"They don't run to the police for assistance either," Savannah said. "In many of their countries the police are corrupt and cruel. They have no reason to think it's any different here. It would never occur to them to risk their lives breaking free of their captors, then run to the authorities for help. For all they know, the cops would take them right back to their tormentors, who would beat them . . . or worse."

"Do you think that sort of wickedness goes on much?" Granny asked Savannah.

"More than you might think. It's a terrible thing that's hiding in plain sight all around us and getting worse all the time. Like I said, some of the nail salons, massage parlors, and even the restaurants we eat in. You'd be surprised how many of the people who serve your food or bus your table or wash your dishes or harvest the food you're eating are slaves in every sense of the word."

"What I don't understand," Tammy said, "is why there isn't more being done about it."

"Don't look at me," Savannah told her. "I don't understand it either. It's an outrage for a so-called civilized society to just overlook such a thing, we who claim to be so concerned about human rights and dignity. It defies explanation."

The women continued to eat their lunch in silence, but the celebratory mood that Granny's meal had provided was gone.

Savannah felt bad, mostly for Granny. But considering the topic they had just discussed, the people who were suffering in silence and fear, she decided that maybe having a bit of a damper thrown on their family gathering might be a small price to pay in exchange for a bit of heightened awareness.

Finally, she turned to Tammy and said, "Exactly what was Geoffrey Faraday convicted of? What part did he play in this mess?"

"He owned the crappy house where the women were being held captive. Once in a while he'd pop over there to, well—"

"Get his mustache waxed?" Granny said.

"Something like that," Tammy said. "He was convicted and given five years. He served a little over three before they let him out."

"Three years for a crime like that?" Savannah shook her head. "That's what I mean. He probably would've gotten a longer sentence for writing bad checks."

Savannah thought of Brooklynn Marsh and how she'd seemed more upset that Lucinda had died than Geoffrey. "I think I need to have a private talk with that guy's fiancée. From the little she said when Dirk and I informed them, I got the idea she might have a more sensitive conscience than ol' Geoff."

"Wouldn't take much," Granny said. "I reckon even the majority of scallywags behind prison bars right now would draw the line at slavery. They got mothers and sisters and wives. How'd they feel if they was treated like that?"

"If only society itself would draw the line," Savannah said. She sighed and pushed her half-eaten bowl of beans away.

It was one of those rare occasions when she lost her appetite in the presence of Granny's fine cooking.

Chapter 13

Eager to tell Dirk what Tammy had found out about Geoffrey, Savannah tracked him down at the Faraday estate.

She arrived to find one of the crime scene unit's vans parked in the driveway, the mansion's front door wide open, and CSU techs trudging in and out, carrying brown paper bags filled, no doubt, with evidence. Or at least what they hoped would prove to be meaningful.

They looked disgruntled, and Savannah could easily guess why. On a day like that, with such a difficult scene to process, she figured they were reconsidering their decisions to pursue forensic investigation as a career.

There were certainly plenty of days when she doubted her own choice and wished she had followed her childhood dream, married Little Joe Cartwright, and become a cowgirl.

But then, of course, if she had married Little Joe and lived on the Ponderosa, she would've missed being Detective Sergeant Dirk Coulter's wife.

As she walked through the front door of the mansion, she could hear her husband's deep, booming voice in the distance as he instructed his team, a true alpha male, using his manly-man authority to impart his extensive knowledge of all things concerning law enforcement.

"Come on, people! What the hell's going on here? Get the lead outta your boxers! This ain't no Sunday picnic for any of us, ya know!"

Yes, she thought, *that's my man, all right. Tactful and kind, strong but gentle, a truly inspiring leader.*

"I ain't got all day to hang around here and babysit you guys," he continued. "For now, just bag up all this crap and haul it back to the lab. Eileen can help you test it there."

For a moment Savannah imagined the look on Eileen Bradley's face when her crew returned to the laboratory with two hundred bags of garbage that Dirk wanted dusted for fingerprints. Eileen hated Dirk only slightly more than Dr. Jennifer Liu did. For the same reason. Like every other detective working on a case, Dirk wanted results from the morgue and the lab ten minutes before the crime had been committed. Unlike other detectives, he wasn't the least bit shy about making his expectations known, loudly and in no uncertain terms.

Fortunately for Dirk, both women could be bribed with homemade baked goods containing chocolate, and he had a wife who didn't mind providing the goodies and delivering them with a smile.

Lucky him.

On a good day, Savannah didn't mind either. It kept

her in the action, which she'd missed since parting ways
with the SCPD.

Once again, Savannah found her way through the
hoard tunnel, fighting her claustrophobia as she did so. At
one point she met one of the male techs in a tight spot. He
was a large fellow, both tall and wide, and his arms were
filled with evidence bags.

Savannah broke what appeared to be a hopeless im-
passe by climbing onto a pile of clothing. When her hand
brushed something furry in the heap, she instantly decided that it was some luxury item of clothing made of
fur.

It was either that or scream bloody murder, like a hysterical woman who had lost her wits, in front of and within
earshot of the entire CSU team. She never would've lived
it down.

Having a vivid and easily manipulated imagination
could be a blessing, she decided, once the man had
moved past, and she had scrambled down from the clothing pile. As she hurried away she could swear that she
saw the garments she had just touched move a bit.

It's just that fur stole settling back into place, she told
herself, as a shiver ran down her back.

Or, at least, she hoped it was a shiver.

*Yeah, yeah. That fur stole's just getting comfortable
again,* said the anti-Pollyanna realist in her head—the gal
who could be a sarcastic bitch when she wanted to be. *Be
sure to use a ton of bleach and a steel wool scrubber on
that hand, first chance you get.*

As she worked her way across the enormous room toward the far wall and the area where the body had been
found, Savannah heard the occasional curse and a few

yelps of terror and discomfort from the CSU team members who were trying to maneuver through the maze.

"Guess they found some fur stoles, too," she muttered. "God knows how many of them are scattered among this junk."

Finally, she saw the opening in the mess and the area where Lucinda's body had been. Dirk was there with a couple of the techs.

Instead of surgical gloves, they were wearing substantial leather work gloves to protect their hands.

They even had dust masks over their mouths and noses.

That was a first for her tough guy hubby. Although he would deign to wear the mandatory surgical gloves when handling things at a crime scene, she had never seen him put on a mask before.

She could certainly understand him wearing it. After her close encounter with whatever that fuzzy thing had been in the clothing pile, she'd vowed that, if she came in here again, it would be wearing a full head-to-toe hazmat suit.

Dirk was picking up handfuls of the debris that had been a makeshift "bed" for Lucinda's body and shoving the garbage into large, grocery-store-sized paper bags. He looked absolutely miserable, as did the others doing the same job around him.

"How much of this are we going to take, Sarge?" asked the young female squatting next to him. She looked around, her eyes wide with wonder and alarm. "There's just gotta be an end to it . . . at some point."

"Keep goin' till we get everything that woulda been under the body. Once you guys have processed that back at the lab, if you find something useful, good. If not, you'll be back here, bagging up more."

The tech groaned like a teenager who'd been asked to wax the family car and clean out the garage on her first day of summer vacation.

"Yeah," Dirk told her, "think about that when you're mowin' through this crap back at the lab. Don't miss nothin'!"

Out of the corner of his eye, Dirk saw movement behind him. He turned and barked, "Yeah? What?"

She knew the exact moment he recognized her, because his eyes softened in an instant.

That was a common occurrence. No matter how bad his day might be going, Dirk's mood always seemed to improve when his wife appeared.

Savannah loved that.

"Oh. Hi, Van," he said. "I thought you were one of these knuckleheads."

He waved a hand in the direction of the two closest techs and, once again, she marveled at how her husband managed to consistently endear himself to those around him.

The miracle was that no one had bumped him off some night in a dark alley. She was pretty sure that, if she had ever worked under him, she might have done so. Fortunately for her, Dirk was a far better husband than boss.

He stood up, groaning as he did so, and placed his gloved hand on his lower back. She could only imagine how long he had been in that position, squatting on that dirty floor, scavenging through the garbage.

But she had come prepared. She knew what it took to coax her husband out of a cranky mood and onto the sunny side of the street.

Unfortunately, it would violate several laws to do that sort of thing at a crime scene, so she had brought food instead—his second greatest passion in life.

She leaned close to him and whispered in his ear, "There's a double chili cheeseburger and a large fry waiting for you in my car out front, if you can manage to tear yourself away from this fascinating place."

He ripped off the mask, revealing the dazzling smile of a true glutton. "Coffee?"

"The giant thermos full."

"I adore you, woman," he said, seeming not to mind one bit if his underlings heard.

They did. Savannah heard them snicker and saw them exchange some seriously dramatic eyerolls.

They should be so lucky, she thought, as she and Dirk found their way out of the mess and into the sunlight. How many people could buy unadulterated adoration— for the price of a burger and fries?

Later, when the food and half of the coffee were only a fond and distant memory, Savannah said something to Dirk that caused his mood to plummet once again.

"What if she wasn't killed there in the spot where we found the body?"

He stared at her for a long time without answering. Finally, he said, "You know, if I want to get depressed again, I could just walk back into that garbage dump of a house. I don't need you to do it for me by saying something like that."

"Sorry. But it's true. You guys could be combing through that area, bagging up all that junk, and you don't even know for sure that's where the deed was done."

He groaned and rubbed his eyes. She had no doubt they were burning from the lack of sleep and the dust he had been sorting through. "I guess she coulda been killed somewhere else in the house and then dragged or carried to where we found her, like a secondary dump site in a regular murder."

"We should probably consider it."

"But why? What makes you think the killer did that?"

Savannah took a deep breath and tried to think of the simplest way to make her point. He was tired. She had discovered that tired men—and women for that matter—had problems understanding what was being said to them. Especially when what they were hearing might mean even more work for them.

"Because," she said, "the place where she was lying, it didn't look like a bed of any kind. Even people who live in the worst of hoards usually have a mattress or a chair or a pile of bedclothes, or at least one blanket, where they tend to sleep. Something resembling a bed. There was nothing like that under her or anywhere in that area. It was just junk and garbage and the body."

"Okay. What makes you so sure she was murdered in the bedroom—or wherever she sleeps?"

"Dr. Liu said she believes Lucinda was given a sedative."

"Yeah, I remember. No defensive wounds and all that."

"Exactly. When would you be most likely to give someone a sedative?" she asked.

He nodded thoughtfully. "When they're going to sleep."

"Right. When they're retiring for the night or getting ready to take a nap."

"But either way, they'd probably be in their bed—or whatever passes for a bed."

"I should think so."

"But what would be the point in killing somebody in one place of a house and then dumping their body in another room?" he asked.

"I don't know for sure, but I'd think for the same reason as any killer uses a secondary location to dump the body."

"To keep us from investigating the actual murder scene."

"Yes. Because they're afraid we'll find something there that points to them."

Dirk slugged back the rest of the coffee in one gulp, then screwed the top back on the thermos. "Okay," he said. "Time to go back inside. First order of business, we find Lucinda's bedroom."

"Even if it's the dining room or the bathroom."

"What?"

"You know what I mean. Mary should be able to tell us."

They got out of the Mustang and, as they were walking up to the mansion's front door, they encountered a CSU tech coming out, her arms laden with evidence bags.

She gave Dirk a dirty look over the top of her mask as they passed.

He nudged Savannah in the ribs and said, "If I go missing, don't stop searching until you find me. I'll be somewhere in the heap."

"Why? You afraid it's going to collapse on top of you?"

"Yeah, about thirty seconds after I tell this team that we've been baggin' up all that stinkin' garbage—I mean, valuable evidence—from the wrong place."

Chapter 14

When Savannah and Dirk entered the mansion, they realized that, other than the foyer and the tunnel that led into the ballroom, they had no idea how the mansion was laid out.

"Mary said her apartment is in the back of the house," Savannah reminded him. "If we just work our way toward the rear . . ."

"Yeah, easier said than done. We need a map of all the tunnels, where they lead, and how to get out of them in an emergency."

"A GPS would be nice."

"Or Mary's cell phone number, so we could just call her and ask her to come get us."

They gave each other a look that was mixed with humor and disgust.

"We're pathetic," Savannah said. "Two seasoned detectives who can't find their way from one end of a house to another."

He nodded and took her hand. "You're right. This is ridiculous. Come on."

They looked around and found what appeared to be a path leading in the opposite direction from the ballroom.

As he headed that way, he squeezed her hand and said, "If we get stuck and starve to death, at least we'll die together, and my last meal was a pretty good one."

She chuckled. Leave it to Dirk to worry about food at a time like this, or at any time for that matter.

"Or," she said, "if we get attacked and eaten by a fur stole."

"What?"

"Never mind."

The new tunnel, narrow as it was, did appear to be leading somewhere that they hadn't been before. They passed through a graceful archway trimmed with decorative tiles in shades of tangerine, bright yellow, and cobalt blue.

On either side of the arch were sconces made of delicate metal filigree and stained glass of the same brilliant colors.

"What a shame," she said, "that this house is so badly neglected. It must've been glorious in its day."

"Yeah, weren't we all?" he grumbled.

"Seriously. Tammy told me that she did a little research on the mansion itself, after she dug up that dirt on Geoffrey. Super famous movie stars, rich folks, and even hard-core gangsters partied here back in the twenties, thirties, and forties. *Serious* partying, too. All sorts of illegal stuff."

"Was our victim part of that scene?"

"In the forties, she was. She bought it in the fifties, when her career started to slow down, and she didn't need to spend as much time in Hollywood."

Savannah paused for a moment and looked around at the items stacked on either side of them in this new area.

"Apparently, at one time, Lucinda was big on decorating for the holidays," she said, pointing out the boxes of Christmas ornaments and tinsel stacked on top of other boxes and containers with labels that read, "Easter" and "Halloween."

A lot of it appeared to be cheap junk, but Savannah saw a miniature train and snow-covered village with animated additions like a carousel and townsfolk skating on a frozen lake. She imagined what it must have been like when this magnificent house was fully decked out for the holidays. Decorated by someone who, obviously, enjoyed celebrating life and its special occasions.

"How," she asked, "does someone get from setting up beautiful little villages at Christmas time to . . . this?" She waved her arm wide, indicating the hoard.

Dirk looked around, thought it over for a moment, and said, "A little bit at a time, I guess. It probably sneaks up on you, and you don't notice until it's too late. Nobody in their right mind would just wake up one day in a clean, neat house and decide they wanted to live like this instead. It has to be some kind of illness that causes it."

"I agree. It must be miserable, living with the disorder like that. Most people can hide their problems for a long time. Things like alcohol and drug addiction, gambling, infidelities, obsessive-compulsive disorders—those can be hidden for years. But the only way to hide all this is to never invite anyone to your home. To lock yourself in your own prison of mess and disorder in total isolation."

Dirk nodded. "True, and if those closest to you find out, they probably just tell you that you're being stupid or lazy or whatever, living like that."

Savannah remembered Geoffrey Faraday's impeccable grooming. Apparently, appearances were very important to him. "Can you even imagine the conversations that must've passed between prissy Geoffrey and his great-grandmother? They were probably brutal. He didn't strike me as a nice guy who would pull his punches in an argument."

"Or any other kind of fight, for that matter." Dirk gave a nasty little chuckle. "You know, before I became a married man and a bit more civilized, I would've looked for a reason to clean that guy's clock. Especially once I found out about the human-trafficking crap. He's probably good at bullying weaker, disenfranchised people. I'd like to teach him what it's like to tangle with somebody stronger than him for a change."

"Before this is all over, you might get your chance. Though I'm not recommending that, of course."

"No, of course not." He gave her an evil little grin. "Don't worry. I'll make sure I'm not in uniform at the time."

"Except for a couple of copper funerals, you haven't worn a uniform in ten years," she said, pointing out the obvious.

"See? Nothing to worry about."

Once they had passed through the arch, Savannah looked around and decided that, perhaps, they had entered a living room of some sort. Like the ballroom, it was large with a ceiling that was breathtaking, adorned with intricate plasterwork. But instead of a chandelier, this room had been lit with a series of Moroccan style lanterns, like the ones that lined the walls of the house and lit the exterior gardens.

The giant marble fireplace sat at the opposite end of the room. For a moment Savannah tried to imagine all of the junk gone, the place decorated for Christmas, and one hundred or more guests milling about in the vintage attire of yesteryear. Women in silk beaded gowns and men in black tuxedos with tails, crisp white shirts, and top hats.

What a sight they must have been to behold.

But at that moment a rustling sound over in the area of the fireplace caught her attention and gave her a shiver. She could still feel that fur brushing her hand. She suspected she would feel it, at least in her vivid memory, for years to come.

"What's that?" Dirk asked. "Did you hear it?"

She lowered her voice to a whisper and said, "I heard it. I think it's over by the fireplace."

"I hope it's Mary," he said.

"I hope it's human."

"Huh?"

"Whatever. We still have to find out."

There was a turn in the path ahead, and since the pile on either side was head high, they couldn't see who or what was there.

They headed that direction, walking softly, trying not to make any sound as they went.

She wasn't exactly sure why they were trying to sneak up on whatever it was. If it was human, it was probably Mary, and they were looking for her anyway. If it was vermin, the last thing she wanted was a friendly meet-and-greet with a rat. Especially one that was large enough to be mistaken for a fur stole.

By the time they finally reached the crook in the path, the noise around the corner was much louder. It sounded like someone or something was rummaging around in a careless, maybe frantic, manner, looking for something and not finding it.

They turned the corner and saw Mary Mahoney, on her hands and knees, tearing through a stack of junk that looked mostly like papers and old photographs.

She hadn't seen Savannah and Dirk yet, and the look on her face was one that Savannah could only classify as desperation.

"Damn," they heard her whisper as she looked over a paper, then tossed it onto the floor with a bunch of other discarded sheets.

Silently, with more than a little curiosity, they watched the frantic search. Mary seemed genuinely upset as well as frustrated as she picked up each page, looked it over, and dropped it onto the already sizable pile.

Savannah also took the opportunity to study the space itself where Mary was conducting her search. It appeared they had come upon Lucinda's "bedroom," after all.

Although it had been a living room—or a "parlor" in its earlier days—that particular nook had obviously been used for sleeping. There was the pile of bedclothes that Savannah had noticed missing in the ballroom.

Next to the makeshift bed were several boxes that contained neatly folded clothing. These particular garments appeared clean and in better condition than the ones in the hoard itself. They looked as though they had actually been worn and laundered recently, and the styles were more contemporary and fashionable than those discarded in the piles.

Savannah also noticed a dozen or so books near the
bedding that were neatly stacked rather than thrown into
heaps like the others she had seen.

As an avid reader who possessed a beloved To Be
Read stash of her own, Savannah recognized the careful
arrangement.

Assuming the assortment was Lucinda's, Savannah
felt a bit closer to the victim than she had before. Book
lovers considered themselves part of a massive, worldwide club, kindred spirits who understood the necessity
of escaping regularly into other worlds through the pages
of a book. The mark of a true book lover was a substantial, well-organized stash.

At that moment, Mary Mahoney noticed them . . . and
that they were watching her. She jumped and squealed in
a tone that sounded both frightened and angry.

"Oh!" she said, dropping the papers from her hand.
"What on earth? I didn't know you were . . . What are
you doing?"

"We were looking for you," Dirk told her.

"We were also looking for Lucinda's bedroom," Savannah said. "Looks like we found both at the same time.
This is where she slept, right?"

Savannah scrutinized Mary's face, her eyes, and could
tell that the woman was considering what her answer
should be. More importantly, Savannah could tell that
Mary was deciding whether to tell them the truth or a lie.

All day long, as a police officer, Savannah had seen
suspects weigh the pros of lying versus the cons of telling
the truth. In the end, when they made their decisions, they
had usually lied.

But the look of resignation that crossed Mary's face

told Savannah she had decided to take her chances and tell the truth.

"Yes," she said. "This is where Lucinda wound up sleeping in the end. After she couldn't get into her bedroom anymore."

Savannah winced. "How sad."

"Oh, please. There are a thousand sad things about how Miss Lucinda lived. Eventually, she had to start using my bathroom. Her own toilets, tubs, and showers were, well . . ." She shrugged. "Let's just say they were unavailable to her."

Dirk grimaced. "As the housekeeper, you couldn't keep even one of hers clean enough to—"

"Stop! Don't you dare judge me!" Mary shot up off the floor with far more energy and nimbleness than Savannah had seen her exhibit before on the front porch with Ethan. Apparently, rage could override the disability of arthritis. At least for a moment, in Mary Mahoney's body.

Dirk held up his hands in surrender. "Sorry, Ms. Mahoney. I didn't mean to get on your bad side. It just seems like—"

"You know absolutely nothing about my life, Miss Lucinda, or this house, Detective," Mary told him. "I'm not interested in hearing how you think things seem."

"Okay. Heard and noted," he said.

But that wasn't enough for Mary Mahoney. Her otherwise pale complexion turned red, then purple as she continued to rant. "Unless you're the one who's put up with a miserable, cranky, nasty woman, who also happens to be one of the world's worst slobs, you have no idea what I went through with Miss Lucinda. I tried! God knows, I tried! And this"—she waved her hand, indicating the garbage-packed room—"this is the result. This is the reward for all my efforts."

Savannah stepped forward, and in a voice that was as calm as the other woman's was irate, she said, "That must have been almost unbearable for you. I'm sure you're a very clean, organized person yourself. To be responsible for keeping a beautiful mansion tidy and presentable to anyone at any time, that would have been an enormous responsibility."

"It was, but I didn't mind. I loved this house! Loved it like it was my own. I worked day and night for years trying to keep on top of what she was doing to it. But she'd go out to garage sales and flea markets like most people go to the grocery store. I'd walk into the house to find the room I'd just cleaned filled up with dirty, half-rotten junk she'd found by the road or in a dumpster somewhere."

"That must have been terribly upsetting."

"Of course it was. She wouldn't listen to reason when I tried to tell her the junk she was collecting was nothing but garbage. She wouldn't let me throw any of it away either. I tried, and she would have a fit! I was afraid she'd suffer a heart attack someday during one of those horrible tantrums of hers. Then I'd get blamed because I tried to throw out a moldy old pizza box that she said she was going to turn into a work of art."

Savannah gave Dirk a sideways glance to see if he was seeing what she was—an enraged, bitter woman who obviously harbored some very strong resentment toward her employer, the victim.

He returned Savannah's look with a quirk of his eyebrow. Yes, they were of the same opinion.

"I can't even imagine what you went through with her," Savannah said in her best big sister voice meant to console even the most distraught child. Or adult, if necessary. "Doing your best, working so hard, and yet, having people think it was your fault, since you were officially the housekeeper."

Mary burst into tears. From her extreme reaction, Savannah figured it might have been the first time anyone had said such a thing to her, and she was desperate to hear it, to receive some sort of understanding, even if it was from someone who hardly knew her.

"It was awful," Mary said through her sobs. "Nobody will ever know how bad."

"Plus, you had to live in this mess," Savannah said. "You, a professional housekeeper, who values cleanliness above all else, and—"

"Yes! You're right! That was miserable, too! Although I made her keep her junk out of my rooms, in the servants' quarters in the back. Anytime she brought anything in there, I'd toss it out one minute later. I didn't even care if she threw one of her temper tantrums. That was *my* home! *Mine!* The only time I'd even let her come in was when she needed to use the bathroom—to bathe or shower or, you know, do her business."

"I believe that was very generous of you, under the circumstances," Savannah told her.

"You do? Really?" Mary seemed afraid to believe her good fortune in finding this boundless source of sympathy.

"Absolutely!"

"I'm so glad you understand."

Savannah knew the empathy she was offering the woman was self-serving, and she felt a bit like a hypocrite for slathering it on so thickly. But she wasn't lying to her. She did understand the housekeeper's frustration and anger with all she had endured at her employer's hands.

But Savannah had also interviewed enough people in her day to know that a little compassion could pay handsome dividends in the long run. People felt comfortable with those who showed an interest in their tribulations, and they were more likely to share information with them than with someone like Dirk, who relied on intimidation.

Sometimes she felt Dirk's method, while less popular, was more honest. But when trying to expose a cold-blooded killer, she decided the end justified her means.

So, she continued to soft-soap Mary Mahoney, but figured it was time to add a few interrogation-type questions to all that consolation.

"I can't blame you a bit," she said, "for feeling the way you do about Ms. Faraday, may she rest in peace. But I'll bet you, if she was half as difficult as you say, and I'm sure she was, there were other people who weren't particularly fond of her."

"Oh, of course. Like I told you before, when you first came over and Mr. Malloy was here, she chased everyone away by being mean and insulting them. Plus, as you can imagine, people don't enjoy spending time in a place like this. The smell alone can make you sick."

"It sure can," Dirk replied. "Speaking of that, would you mind if we continued our talk in your nice, clean apartment instead of in here?"

Savannah watched Mary closely as the housekeeper's eyes scanned the area around them. Whatever she had been looking for earlier, she still wanted to find.

What could be that important? Savannah wondered.

Whatever it was, it had to be paper, or she wouldn't have been scanning and discarding one after the other.

"I believe you were looking for something before," Savannah said softly, knowing she was pushing her luck.

"If you like, we could stay in here long enough to help you look for it one more time. We can help you, too."

"No, that's okay," was the abrupt reply.

"We don't mind," Dirk chimed in. "I think I caught a case of the Creeping Crud-itis from being in here already."

"No!" Mary turned and started down a path that they hadn't noticed; it appeared to lead even deeper into the house. "Let's go," she said. "I'll make us some tea. Miss Lucinda always liked her afternoon tea."

When Mary looked back over her shoulder, probably to make sure they were following her, Savannah was sure she'd seen some tears in her eyes.

Savannah decided to take a chance and see if Mary Mahoney had any mixed feelings at all about her mistress's passing.

"Did you have tea with her, Mary?" she asked. "Was that something that the two of you shared together every day?"

Just for a second, Savannah saw the agony of loss cross the housekeeper's face. She nodded ever so slightly. "Yes. Every day. We did enjoy that."

Then, as though catching herself being sentimental when she didn't want to be, Mary sniffed and lifted her chin a couple of notches. "We had to have it in my apartment kitchen though," she said as they headed down the new path. "She hadn't been able to set foot in hers for years."

Chapter 15

Savannah and Dirk expected Mary to lead them on through the mansion toward the rear of the residence to her quarters. But instead, she took them back out the front way, and the three of them walked around the house, and through neglected gardens that flower-loving Savannah could tell had once been beautiful.

"The back of the house is worse than the front half," Mary explained, shamefaced.

"Do you mean to tell me the hoard is more dense in the rest of the place than what we've seen already?" Savannah asked, unable to believe it.

Mary nodded. "She started upstairs, worked her way down, filled up the back of the first floor, and then finished with the front part, where you were."

"Where on earth do you even get that much stuff?"

Dirk asked. "I can't believe that one little woman was able to fill up that huge house like that!"

Mary gave a dry chuckle and shook her head. "You didn't know Lucinda. She was a real fireball in her day, had more energy than anybody I ever knew. She lived ninety years—nearly a century. When you're determined, you can get a lot done in that much time."

"I guess so," Savannah agreed. "My own granny's been alive almost that long, and she's moved mountains in her day."

She decided not to point out the obvious—that Granny had raised children and grandchildren and made an enormous, positive difference in many people's lives.

As they continued to walk around the huge mansion, it occurred to Savannah that the ninety-year-old Lucinda had made this trip every time she wanted to use a bathroom.

"It must be terrible, having a hoarding disorder," she said. "It impacts a person's life so negatively in so many ways. Surely, Lucinda would have stopped if she could have."

"I don't know about that," Mary said. "I can understand how you'd think that. But I spent a large part of my life trying to help her get out of this trap she was in. I can't even tell you how tightly she clung to her lifestyle. She refused to do anything at all to change, even tiny steps."

"Eh, people are weird," Dirk said. "Who knows why anybody does anything?"

*   *   *

Ten minutes later, Savannah and Dirk were sitting in Mary's cozy kitchen, sipping tea from delicate antique china cups.

"Lucinda gave them to me for my sixtieth birthday," Mary had told them as she'd set the cups on the table and filled them with a fragrant jasmine tea. "She gave me the silver set last Christmas. We'd been using it for years, and she told me she wanted me to have it. I think she might have sensed that she wasn't going to be around much longer."

"Any particular reason?" Dirk asked, unimpressed with teacups or silver teapots.

Mary shrugged. "Not really. Just that she was getting up there and realized she wouldn't live forever."

Savannah studied the silver service set, admiring it. All three pieces—the teapot, the sugar bowl, and the cream jug—were heavy gauge silver, embellished with elegant rococo designs. Their interiors were gilt. "It's the most beautiful silver set I've ever seen," Savannah told her, resisting the urge to mention it must have been worth a fortune.

"It meant a lot to Lucinda," Mary said, running her fingertips along the top of the sugar bowl. "It was given to her when she was very young by a Russian ambassador. They were . . . friends. Very good friends," she added with a grin. "In her prime, Lucinda was quite friendly. With a lot of powerful, rich men."

"I'm sure she had a lot of stories to tell," Savannah said.

Mary nodded excitedly. "I told her that! I encouraged her to start a book years ago, all about her adventures, but she never got around to finishing it. I told her she should. Boy, she had some juicy stories. There were scandals back in the 'good ol' days' that would make today's gossip magazines look like church bulletins."

"I've heard Hollywood was pretty wild back then," Savannah said.

"Whatever you've heard, it was way worse. Lucinda told me things that would curl your ears."

"Do you have any idea where that book is now, the one she started?"

"I saw it a few days ago, there under her pillow where she was sleeping. But when I looked today, it wasn't there."

"Okay, enough about old stories. No recent juicy stuff?" Dirk said, getting back to business. "We need to find out what she'd been doing lately, what might have gotten her killed, not what happened sixty or seventy years ago."

"Nothing salacious lately, I'm afraid," Mary replied. "I guess she was a bit past all of that at her age. Even a woman like Lucinda Faraday has to slow down sooner or later."

Savannah decided to take Dirk's lead and move the conversation back to the investigation. Surely, they had established a significant amount of rapport with her and could take a chance.

Jumping right in, Savannah leaned across the table in the housekeeper's direction and said, "Mary, if you don't mind me asking . . . What were you looking for so frantically there in Lucinda's sleeping area? Whatever it was, you seemed quite eager to find it. Some sort of paper?"

Mary looked as though Savannah had just delivered a karate chop to her solar plexus. For the longest time, she said nothing. Then she opened her mouth and—

There was a banging on the kitchen door so loud that

all three of them jumped. Mary even knocked over the sugar bowl, spilling it all over the lace tablecloth she had spread in their honor.

"What the hell?" Dirk said, getting to his feet, as still another barrage of loud pounding began. He turned to Mary, who was pale from the double shock of Savannah's unsettling question and the angry attack on her back door. "Were you expecting somebody?"

"No! No one at all!" she replied.

He strode over to the door and jerked it open.

Savannah was on her feet at that point, too, and was standing beside her husband when they saw who was calling.

"Geoffrey!" they both exclaimed, surprised to see him and equally put off by his manner.

"What the hell are you two doing here?" the erstwhile great-grandson of Lucinda Faraday demanded.

"Investigating a murder. Why?" Dirk shot back. "Did you commit one?"

"I'm done talking to you. If you want to ask me something, speak to my lawyer."

Geoffrey tried to push past them, but if Savannah and Dirk were good at doing anything together, it was filling up a doorway. Nobody got around or through them uninvited.

"I'm here to talk to Mary, not you," Geoffrey complained. He stood on his tiptoes, trying to see over their shoulders. "Mary? Are you in there? Get out here. We have to talk!"

Mary tried to step up to the door, but Savannah placed her hand on her arm and gently pushed her back.

"You don't need to talk to him," Savannah told her. "At least, not while he's acting like a horse's rear end."

"She does too have to talk to me!" Geoffrey bellowed, his spray-on tan looking strange on top of his red, flushed cheeks. "Mary, I'm giving you notice to vacate this property immediately! It's mine now, and you aren't welcome here, so get out! I'm giving you twenty-four hours before I send the sheriff out to evict you!"

"Wait a damned minute," Dirk said, holding one large hand in front of Geoffrey's face in his best Cop Directing Traffic style. "She doesn't have to go anywhere. She lives here and has for years. You can't throw someone out of their home with nothing but a twenty-four-hour notice."

"Not only that," Savannah joined in, "but who says this property is yours now?"

"Of course it's mine!" was the quick and angry response. "I'm Great-Grandma Lucinda's sole heir. Whose would it be? Everything that was hers is mine now. That's the law."

"Actually," Dirk replied, "a judge will probably be the one deciding who inherits your great-grandmother's estate. She may have left a will. She might've had other people she preferred to leave it to. But either way, you can't come around here harassing this lady who took care of your great-grandmother while you ignored her."

"Ignored her? She's the one who abandoned me!" Geoffrey said, his face getting darker by the moment.

Mary managed to work her way around Savannah until she could see Geoffrey. The rage on her face matched his as she shouted back, "Miss Lucinda abandoned you? How dare you accuse her of that. She bailed you out of jail more times than you can count and paid your attorney fees, time and time again."

"She didn't that last time!" Geoffrey yelled. "She

wouldn't raise a finger to help me when I needed it most!"

"It wasn't until you committed a crime so hideous that it made her sick to even hear about it that she cut you out of her life," Mary countered. "That wasn't abandonment. That was her coming to her senses and realizing what a monster you are!"

Geoffrey stuck his finger in Mary's face and shook it. Savannah got ready to grab the offending digit, give it a twist, and listen to it crack. But he lowered his hand and his voice when he said in an ominous, low tone, "*You* are the one who turned my great-grandmother against me, you bitch. You told her bad things about me and started the trouble between us. Don't think I've forgotten that. I haven't, and you're going to pay for it. Big time. Somehow. Someday, you're going to be very sorry for what you did to me. I promise you that!"

Dirk reached out and grabbed a fistful of Geoffrey's nicely pressed, expensive shirt. He jerked the smaller guy off his feet and pulled him against him, until they were almost literally nose to nose.

"What kind of idiot are you," Dirk shouted in his face, "to threaten a woman right in front of me like that? I'm the cop who's investigating you for murder, and you threaten someone in my presence? Are you completely stupid?"

Geoffrey went from enraged to terrified in an instant. He shook his head and muttered something that sounded like an apology under his breath.

Dirk pushed him, maintaining his grip on his shirt and backing him away from the house. "You leave this property right now, Faraday," he told him. "If this lady tells me that she even saw you looking in her direction from the other side of a street, we're going to have a long, serious talk, you and me. Do you understand?"

Geoffrey nodded feebly, and the instant that Dirk released his hold on him, he scrambled away, nearly tripping over his own feet as he stumbled to the black Porsche they had seen before behind his house.

As he drove away, Savannah heard Dirk mumble, "If there was any justice in this world, that man wouldn't be driving that car. He doesn't deserve it."

"Or the air he breathes," Savannah added, equally disgruntled.

They turned back to the kitchen and saw Mary collapsing onto one of the dining chairs, her face white, her breathing labored. A moment later, she began to cough again, those deep, wracking spasms that they had witnessed when they first met her, talking to Ethan on the front porch.

The attack went on for quite a while, alarming them both. Savannah stood behind her chair, her hands on the woman's shoulders, feeling helpless, unable to assist or even comfort her.

"Are you okay?" she asked, knowing how inane it sounded. Obviously, she was far from okay.

Savannah looked over at Dirk and realized from the alarmed expression on his face he was just as concerned as she was.

"Mary," he said, dropping to one knee beside her chair, "can we help you? You want us to call nine-one-one? Get you an ambulance?"

Mary continued to cough but shook her head emphatically.

"Okay, we won't then," Savannah assured her. "Just try to breathe, darlin'. In and out." Again, she felt stupid for even suggesting the obvious and momentarily worthless advice.

Finally, the spasms subsided. But they had taken their toll on Mary. She leaned forward, folded her arms on the table, and laid her head on them.

Savannah rubbed her back as Dirk tried to reassure her by saying, "Don't worry about that piece of crap, Ms. Mahoney. Really. I know his type. He's all mouth. He's not going to come around here bothering you anymore."

"But if he does," Savannah added for good measure, "don't you even open the door to him. You don't have to. You just call us, and Dirk'll deal with him. Believe me, Detective Coulter can get a lot rougher than that with him if he needs to."

Finally, Mary recovered herself well enough to speak, though in a shaky, weak voice. "I'm not scared of him," she said. "Not physically anyway. But I'm afraid he'll do exactly what he said, kick me out of my home."

"Try not to worry about that now, Mary," Savannah told her. "You can cross that bridge when and if you need to."

"I know I shouldn't get upset. It brings on those coughing fits. But I've lived here for so many years now. I can't imagine having to leave. Especially at a moment's notice, like he was saying."

"You won't have to," Savannah said, wishing she could believe her own words. She shot Dirk a questioning look, which he returned with a shrug of his shoulders.

Not reassuring.

Maybe she was advising the woman to be too complacent. Perhaps the threat was real.

"I think you should talk to a lawyer, Mary," Savannah said. "Just to set your mind at ease. An attorney who specializes in this sort of thing can tell you what to expect and how to protect yourself. Even one appointment could make a difference, give you some peace of mind."

Mary shook her head. "I don't think it would help. Like he said, he's her next of kin, her sole heir."

Dirk cleared his throat and said, "To your knowledge, did Ms. Faraday have a will?"

"Yes. She did."

"And . . . ?" Savannah asked.

"She left everything to him."

"Oh." Savannah glanced at Dirk, who was shaking his head and looking as disgusted as she felt.

Mary lifted her head and turned in her chair to face them. "But that was before he got arrested and convicted for holding those poor women who were being trafficked in the basement of that old house of his in Barstow."

Savannah perked up a bit. "Oh yeah?"

Mary looked up at her with frightened, sad eyes. "Yes. After that, she sat me down, here at this table, and told me that she didn't consider him family anymore."

"Understandable," Dirk muttered.

"She said I was the only person she trusted, the only one who had ever been kind to her, taken care of her. She told me I was her family. She said she had written a new will and left everything to me."

Suddenly, a light dawned in Savannah's head. "That's what you were looking for," she said.

Mary nodded. "That's what I was looking for. I've been looking for it since Ethan found her yesterday."

"A new will!" Dirk said, far too cheerfully. "Well, there ya go! You don't have anything to worry about."

Savannah rolled her eyes at him and gave Mary a comforting pat on the back.

Nothing to worry about?

Mary's future depended on a single document. A piece of paper hidden in a sixteen-thousand-square-foot mansion. Filled with countless cubic feet of garbage.

All Mary Mahoney had to do was find it.

No, she had no reason for concern, nothing to worry about. Not a blamed thing.

Chapter 16

As Savannah sat, parked in her Mustang, watching Brody run across the schoolyard toward her with a big grin on his face, she felt a rush of happiness. Other than little Vanna Rose squealing at the sight of her, having a child so thrilled to see her wasn't a joy Savannah had experienced much in her life.

Sometimes, Diamante and Cleopatra were especially excited when she came home, and they expressed their pleasure by making furry figure eights between her ankles as she walked from the front door, through the living room, to the kitchen. But she knew they were far happier that the Bestower of the Kitty Kibbles had arrived than that Beloved Mommy had made it home safe and sound.

They were gluttons. Pure and simple. She harbored no illusions about the fact that their love for her was based primarily on food. Petting, scratches behind the ears, and mumbled sweet nothings about how they were the world's smartest, sweetest, and most beautiful cats qualified as a distant second on their list of priorities.

Until that moment, sitting in the Mustang and watching Mr. Brody Greyson race across the grassy field toward her, Savannah had never fully experienced what Granny must have felt all those years ago when she had collected Savannah and her siblings from their school.

With her windows rolled down, Savannah could hear him yelling, "Hi! Hey, hey, Savannah!" from halfway across the field. She saw the light of happiness in his eyes and something even more important—peace. After less than twenty-four hours in her care, Brody looked like a different kid.

She couldn't recall ever feeling more deeply satisfied than she felt at that moment, as though she had accomplished something truly great.

"'Hey' yourself, kiddo," she called out to him as he approached. "Get in this car right now and tell me all about your day!"

He jerked the door open, tossed his backpack onto the floorboard, and plopped himself on the passenger's seat.

The sneaky little smirk he gave her told her that he was deliberately trying to pull one over on her.

"You'll have to get up pretty early in the morning to put the shuck on me, boy," she told him.

His eyes widened with fake innocence. "Huh? Whaddaya mean?"

"Backseat," she told him.

"Huh?"

"Munchkins ride in the backseat. It's the law and a good one at that."

His face screwed into a scowl. "No way. My momma lets me ride in the front seat."

She turned toward him and laser-trained her intense blue eyes on his. "Don't even start with that 'But my momma lets me' junk. I'm not your momma, and it won't work. When you're with me, we do things my way. No arguments. Got it?"

He sighed and, acting as though his britches had a brick or two in each pocket, climbed out, pulled the seat forward, and slid into the rear.

He sat there, giving her the evil eye, as she glared back at him in the mirror.

"Don't look at me like that, boy," she told him. "You know darned well we wear our seat belts in this car. Buckle up."

"I don't know how."

"We both know that's a big ol' fib," she said. "You've done it several times since I met you. I saw you."

"I done forgot how."

"You'll remember. You're a fart smeller."

He giggled. "You said it wrong. You meant 'smart feller.'"

"Whatever. That's you. Get that seat belt on before you're a minute older. We've got a couple of cones waiting for us at the drugstore's ice-cream counter . . . if you were good at school, that is."

Two seconds later, she heard the metal snap of the seat belt.

"See there," she said, starting up the Mustang. "You're farter than you thought."

He giggled. "I was good at school, too. A perfect kid!"

"Glad to hear it. I was looking forward to a double scoop cone, fudge and butter pecan."

"I want chocolate chip mint and licorice," he said.

"Yuck. You lost me with the licorice there, puddin' head."

"Hey, it's what I like, and I was good! All day! It wasn't easy, neither. My teacher was cranky. I think she must've had her underdrawers on backwards or somethin'."

"Oo-kay. Whatever you say. Let's make tracks."

Half an hour later, they pulled into Savannah's driveway, both holding towering cones and wearing ice-cream mustaches. Hers chocolate. His licorice.

She saw two familiar vehicles—Gran's panel van and Ethan's GMC Sierra. She had company. Again. Granny hadn't yet left, and Ethan had dropped by.

Her house was full of love.

Long ago, she had decided that, if one wanted privacy and a personal life, it was best not to open a business in your house. Or have relatives who thoroughly believed the old saying, "My home is your home."

"Yay, Granny's here!" Brody shouted, nearly dropping his ice cream.

Savannah was more than pleased to see him so excited about seeing her grandmother again. Who said kids didn't appreciate the older generations?

But then he added, "If she's here, then the Colonel's prob'ly here, too! He's my favorite dog ever! He's a darned good wrestler!"

"What exactly constitutes a good dog wrestler?" Savannah asked as they got out of the car.

"He grabs hold of you with his big ol' mouth and throws you all around, but he doesn't hurt ya."

"I see."

"But he does slobber all over ya. If slobber was poison, you'd be dead as a three-day-old road-kill possum after a tussle with the Colonel."

"I can imagine." She shuddered. "Lord knows, I don't want to when I'm still eating my ice cream, but unfortunately, I can."

He continued to prattle on. About what, she wasn't sure, as she was wondering why Ethan had dropped by.

Probably not to wrestle with the Colonel.

If he was here for an update on the progress she had made so far, she didn't have a lot for him. Considering how generously he was paying her—at his insistence— she wished she could give him a great deal more.

Like the killer . . . tied up with a bright red bow.

Especially if it was rotten old Geoffrey, who was her favored suspect, as well as one of her least favorite people.

As soon as they stepped onto the front porch, a familiar and loud noise erupted from the backyard. A hound's plaintive, excited baying.

"The Colonel!" Brody shouted. "He heard us!"

"Smelled us is more like it," she replied, laughing. "He *is* a bloodhound, after all."

"He wants me to go back there and play with him."

"He does, and that's an excellent idea. But you go upstairs and change out of those new school clothes first. I don't want them ripped up the first day you wear them, by a champion wrestling hound dog."

"Okay!"

They entered the house, and the boy bounded up the staircase, looking as excited as the dog in the backyard sounded at the prospect of their next bout.

Savannah peeked into the living room and saw Granny

sitting in her comfy chair, and Ethan on the sofa. Both were holding a coffee cup and balancing plates on their laps with generous slices of coconut cake.

Ethan saw her and jumped up to greet her, nearly dropping his refreshments in the process.

"Take it easy there," she told him. "That's some of the best cake on the planet. If it hits the floor, you'll cry, for sure."

"I would," he said, setting the plate and mug on the coffee table. "I've enjoyed a few bites already, and I'd agree with you. It *is* the best!"

He hurried over to hug her. She stood on tiptoe to kiss his cheek and thought of the teenage girls at the pier. She wondered how many women in the world would have been thrilled to see Ethan Malloy in the flesh twice in such a short period of time.

She certainly was.

Glancing over at Granny, she could see her grandmother was getting up, vacating the chair for Savannah.

While Savannah was touched and honored by the gesture, she wouldn't have it. Gran had raised her too well.

"Sit still," she told her grandmother, waving her down. "I'm going to snag a piece of that cake and some coffee and join you."

Granny eased herself back into the chair and said, "What's wrong with that hound dog out there? I haven't heard him bay like that since the cat next door at the trailer park got into his food dish and ate part of his supper."

"He wants Brody to come out and tussle with him again," Savannah told her. "The kid's as keen on it as the hound. I think you can safely say they've bonded."

"I had a redtick hound myself when I was about his

age," Ethan said. "One of the best friends I ever had. He went everywhere with me. Slept with me. Even ate with me any time my mother wasn't looking."

"Boys and their dogs," Granny said, reaching down to pick Cleo up from the floor and set her on her lap. "They're best friends. Like a grandma and cats."

Savannah went into the kitchen and was in the middle of cutting herself some cake when Brody bounded through the kitchen, racing toward the back door. He was wearing his old shorts, which were now, at least, clean.

"Hey!" she called after him. "You want a piece of cake before you head out there? You might need some energy with all that tossing and tumbling you're about to do."

Brody hesitated, and she could see he was sorely tempted. But another bay from the Colonel sent him over the edge. "Naw. I'll have some when I come back inside," he said before he raced to the back door and disappeared.

Savannah headed back into the living room, her treats in hand. Sitting on the sofa, she turned to Ethan and said, "I was happy, as always, to see your car in the driveway when I came home. But I hope you didn't drop by for a 'murderer reveal' like on TV. We're good, but we take more than an hour to catch the culprits, I'm afraid."

He gave her a reassuring smile. "I'm sure you do. I have no expectations of a quick resolution here."

"Of course, we can always hope," she said. "But unless the killer's standing over the body with blood on his clothes and the murder weapon in his hand, it usually takes longer than sixty minutes."

Watching him take a sip of his coffee, then squeeze the mug tightly between his hands, Savannah could feel the stress radiating from him in waves.

"Truthfully," he said, "I'd be satisfied if I thought

you'd be able to solve this case in two months. Even two years. Ever. I'm afraid you won't be able to, and Lucinda will never receive the justice she deserves."

"I understand. I won't lie to you, Ethan. That's always a possibility. Some murders are never solved."

Granny spoke up, adding, "Sometimes ever'body knows who done it, why, and with what. But for one reason or another, the police just can't nail the killer and put 'im away for good."

"That's true," Savannah said. "Knowing 'who done it' and proving it in a court of law are two very different things."

The look of sadness and anger on Ethan's face went straight to Savannah's heart as he sighed and said, "That's undoubtedly true. Bringing a killer to justice, I'm sure, is a lot harder in real life than it is on television or in the movies."

"It is," Savannah assured him. "Much harder. That's why detectives—private ones and cops alike—lose a lot of sleep during some cases. Believe me, we don't want to see a killer walk either. The thought that they're still out there and could do it again makes us crazy."

Ethan set his mug down, reached into his jeans pocket, and pulled out his wallet. "That's why I came over here this afternoon," he said. "After we talked there on the pier, I had a feeling this was going to be one of those cases that's really hard to solve."

"Okay," Savannah said. "You're probably right about that. But put your billfold away, boy. Your initial retainer was overly generous. We haven't come close to running through that and probably won't. I reckon I'll owe you money in the end."

"No. I won't be accepting any refunds from your

agency, whether or not you catch the killer. Whatever happens, I know you and your team will be doing your best, and that's enough for me."

He reached into his wallet and pulled out a check. He placed it on the sofa cushion between them. "That," he said, "is a little extra effort on my part to catch this guy."

Savannah looked down, saw the amount, gulped, and said, "That's a mighty effort there, darlin'. What are you fixin' to do with that much moo-lah?"

"It's a reward," he explained, "for information leading to the arrest and blah, blah, blah. If anybody tells you anything that takes this investigation forward, they get that. If a second, separate party comes forward with something else, I'll give them the same."

"Goodness!" Savannah nearly choked on her cake. "That's . . . wow! You really do want this guy caught."

"You have no idea. The more I think about it—the fact that Lucinda managed to live such a full, long, adventurous life, that she made it out of all sorts of dangerous situations and thrived, only to have her amazing life end in that pathetic, cruel way—I can hardly stand it."

"I hear ya, son," Granny said. "Not because I'm an old gal myself, but there is something particularly sad about an elderly person's life being taken that way. Like they lived all that time, maybe a good, peaceful life, and then, that's what their legacy is. What they'll be remembered for. It ain't right. Not a'tall."

"Exactly!" Ethan's face flushed dark with rage. "Lucinda should have been able to die naturally and peacefully with someone she loved holding her hand, not a murderer strangling her. She should have been allowed to keep her legacy, her reputation as a glamorous woman, a gifted actress, someone who inspired and helped a lot of people. But her killer robbed her of that, along with whatever years she had left. He stole her from us and the times we might have spent with her. I want him to pay for it."

Ethan paused, and Savannah could tell he was trying to get control of his anger.

She also knew he never would. Not about this.

"Murder is far more complex than the killing of a human being, as horrible as that is," she said softly. "There are always multiple victims. One person dies, but so many other lives are damaged, too. Some beyond repair."

"Catching the killer, convicting them, it's a good thing," he said. "I was so grateful to you and your team for bringing the murderer who ruined our family to justice. But it didn't bring back our dead, and we're still suffering the aftereffects of what happened. We always will."

Savannah studied the young man sitting next to her and thought of all he and his wife had endured. She grieved the loss of his marriage, his life as he had known it before they had been victimized.

"I'm going to do all I can for you," she told him, "and for Lucinda." She reached over and picked up the check. "This may help. There may be someone out there who knows something. The thought of a substantial deposit in their bank account might inspire them to share it."

Granny chuckled. "More than once, I've seen a person become inspired to do the righteous thing for a pile of filthy lucre."

Ethan looked confused. "Lucre?"

"That's Bible talk for money, son," Gran told him. "I'm just sayin', the Lord moves in mysterious ways."

Chapter 17

Once Ethan had left and Granny had settled down for a nap in the upstairs bedroom, Savannah decided to take a glass of lemonade out to Brody, who was still playing with the Colonel.

The boy had found a ball and was playing fetch with the hound. Although he was getting a bit frustrated. The Colonel was good at catching a thrown object, but he had never been inclined to bring it back to the human who had tossed it for him. He seemed to be of the opinion that, if he'd gone to the trouble of catching his prize, he should be able to keep it.

As a result, Brody was spending more time chasing the hound and prying the soggy ball out of his dripping jowls than throwing it.

The moment she stepped outside with his lemonade in one hand and a glass of tea for herself, she found the child standing, hands on his hips, glaring at the dog and giving him a piece of his mind.

"You ain't so good at this," he told the Colonel, who was prancing around the yard, his tail held high, the ball in his mouth, and a self-satisfied look on his long face. "You're supposed to bring it back to me so's I can throw it again, you knucklehead!"

Savannah laughed, took the glasses over to the wisteria-draped arbor near the back of the property. "The Colonel doesn't always play by the rules," she told Brody.

"No kidding. He seems to think it's a lot of fun for me, watching him run around with the ball in his jaws. He ain't got the hang of this a'tall."

"I hate to tell you this," Savannah said as she set the drinks down on an accent table between the chairs, "but he's been doing that since he was a pup and his father before him and his granddaddy, too."

"You knew the Colonel's granddaddy?" Brody asked, amazed.

"I sure did. This is Colonel Beauregard the Third. His grandfather was our first Colonel. Granny got him when I was a kid."

"My age?"

"A mite older than you."

"Did you play ball with him, too?"

"I tried. He was as obstinate as his son, and his grandson after them. Seems that particular brand of contrariness runs in the Beauregard hound dog family."

Brody laughed. "I don't care. He's still fun. Watch this."

He scampered over to the dog and got down on his hands and knees. Immediately, the hound dropped the ball, ran to him, and with his nose, bowled the boy over onto his side.

Brody grabbed the dog around his saggy neck and dragged him down on top of him.

That was when the battle began in earnest. Pseudo-fierce growling on the Colonel's part, a lot of squealing from Brody, as they rolled back and forth across the grass, neither willing to let go of the other.

Savannah laughed, enjoying the moment of innocence and levity, having had little of either for the past twenty-four hours.

What is it about kids and dogs? she thought, watching them. *They bring out the best in one another.* Recalling all she had seen and heard at the Faraday mansion last evening and today, she added, *Too bad adult humans can't do the same.*

At that moment, she saw something that caused her to collapse in a fit of laughter. Colonel Beauregard III grabbed a mouthful of the seat of Brody's shorts, gave a mighty tug, and pulled them halfway down the boy's buttocks.

"Hey!" Brody yelled, trying to pull them up. "Knock it off, dog! Those are my britches! Let 'em go!"

But his struggles only added to the fun for the hound. He tugged at the cloth with typical canine enthusiasm, as though they were playing tug-of-war with a rope toy.

Savannah got up from her chair and sauntered over to give the boy a hand in retrieving his clothing and his dignity. "What's the matter, Mr. Greyson?" she teased. "Looks like he's getting the better of you. Or at least of your drawers."

She reached down to pry the dog's jaws apart, but before she could, she saw something that made her gasp and freeze, her hand on the animal's massive head.

"Stop! Colonel, drop it! Leave it!!" she commanded.

Normally the hound would have been reluctant to quit a game he was enjoying so much, but he seemed to sense the urgency in her voice. In an instant, he did as he was commanded, backed away from the boy, and sat down on his haunches, whining softly.

"What's the matter?" Brody said, sitting up and readjusting his clothing. "Why'd you make him quit? We was havin' fun!"

Savannah felt her knees go weak, so she sat down, abruptly, on the grass beside the boy.

Her mind raced, taking in what she had seen and frantically trying to think of the best way to discuss it with the child.

In the end, she decided to just be honest and forthright. But gentle.

"Brody, darlin'," she said, reaching over and smoothing his tousled hair. "Just now, when you and the Colonel were wrestling. I saw something."

He looked totally confused and only moderately concerned. "What are you talkin' 'bout? Did you bring me somethin' out here to drink?"

"Yes. I brought you lemonade, and you can have it in a minute. But I have to ask you about something I saw, there on your backside."

Instantly, the boy's smile disappeared, and his color deepened as he blushed. "Ain't nothin'," he said.

"I think it is, and I'm sorry, but we're going to have to talk about it." She stood and offered him her hand. "Would you prefer to go over there?" she asked, nodding toward the arbor, the chairs, and table with the drinks on it.

"No!" He refused her hand, sat up, and crossed his arms over his chest. "I don't want to go there. I want to go home. Call my momma and tell her to come get me right now!"

Savannah's heart sank. This was going to be even worse than she'd feared. "I can't, sweetie," she told him. "I can't call her where she is. Your mother couldn't come and get you right now, even if I did call her."

He started to cry. "But you tell her it's important. She said I should always call her and not say nothin' because—" He choked on the rest of the words, put his hands over his face, and sobbed.

Savannah felt a rage welling up inside her, stronger, darker, and uglier than she could recall in her entire life.

But she pushed it down, deep inside, so the child wouldn't hear it when she said, "Your mother told you that if anyone ever saw those marks, those sores on your bottom, you should call her?"

He nodded.

"And not tell anybody how they got there, right?"

"Yes," he whispered.

"Did she tell you that something awful would happen if you told anyone what happened to you?"

He looked up at her and seemed to be somewhat surprised that she knew.

"Yes," Savannah said. "I know about marks like those. The long ones are from a belt. From somebody giving you a whuppin' . . . a really hard one."

When he didn't reply, she continued, "Brody, I used to have bruises like that on me, too. On my bottom and on the backs of my legs. My momma made me wear long skirts, and long socks that came all the way up to my knees, even in the hot summertime, so the neighbors and the kids and teachers at school couldn't see them."

This time the boy was more than surprised. He was shocked. "You *did*?" he asked incredulously. "*You* did?"

"Yes. I sure did, and I remember to this day how bad those whuppin's hurt."

He nodded but offered nothing else.

"I saw something else on your bottom, too," she said softly. "You had something else done to you, too, besides the whuppin'. Something I didn't have done to me."

Staring down at the grass, he gave another little nod as teardrops rolled down his cheeks.

She took a deep breath and fought back her own as she said, "Those round, red sores, and the ones with black scabs on them . . . those are cigarette burns, aren't they?"

"I can't say anything," he protested. "My momma said, if I did . . ."

"I know. But you didn't tell me anything. You don't have to, darlin'. I was a police officer, and I know what causes marks like that. I also know who does it to kids. You didn't do anything wrong. You didn't tattle on anybody. I figured it out on my own. Okay?"

"Yeah. Okay. But she said if anybody saw them or if I tell anybody, something bad will happen. The cops will put me and her both in jail."

"That's not what's going to happen, honey. Nobody's going to put you in jail. I promise. Nothing bad is going to happen to you. Nothing like that is ever going to happen to you again."

She reached out her arms to him, and to her relief, he

threw himself into her embrace, burying his face against her chest.

Even the bloodhound joined in by walking over to them and nuzzling the weeping child with his big nose and whining his sympathy.

"See there," she said, kissing the top of the boy's head. "The Colonel is letting you know that he's going to protect you, and I'm going to, and Detective Coulter, and even Granny, too. We're all plumb fierce about protecting kids and keeping them from being hurt. You don't have to worry anymore."

She felt him sag against her with relief, and that was what caused her to lose the fight with her own tears.

She held Brody Greyson, rocked him, and cried along with him. She wept for him and for the wounded child she had been so many years ago. She cried for all the children who bore the marks of adults' pain, frustration, and rage on their precious bodies.

Later, inside the house, Savannah left Brody snuggled up to Granny's side on the sofa as she read to him from one of Savannah's favorites, *The Blue Fairy Book*. She went upstairs to her bedroom, washed her face, and phoned Dirk.

She dreaded the call terribly. She knew he would be as upset as she was over this awful development. The last thing she wanted to do was tell him over the phone.

He sounded cranky when he answered with, "Yeah. Hi."

"Where are you?" she asked, anticipating his answer.

"This stinkin' place, sortin' through the stinkin' junk. That's what my life is now. Stinkin' garbage. Why?"

"I, um, I—" She swallowed, fighting back the tears that were threatening to resurface.

"What is it, babe? What's wrong?" he asked, all signs of grouchiness gone in his concern for her.

Don't tell him on the phone, her instincts warned her. *Life's best and worst words should be said face to face.*

"I know you're working, honey," she said. "I know you're busy. But could you . . . could you please come home?"

There was a long pause. "Now?" he asked.

"If you can, I'd appreciate it."

"Okay." Another lengthy silence. "Can you tell me what it is?"

Tell him, another voice in her head said. *You can't expect the poor guy to worry himself sick all the way home.*

In this case, the truth is worse than whatever he would worry about, argued another voice.

"Don't worry, darlin'," she told him. "It's not a life and death emergency. I just . . ." The tears started to fall. A knot rose in her throat, and it was hard for her to speak around it. Or even breathe. "I just need you."

"I'm on my way."

He hung up, and she clutched the phone to her chest, feeling his essence, his love and concern.

She knew her husband. She knew he was, as he said, on his way.

Bless his heart, she thought, *being Dirk, he's probably already halfway here.*

Chapter 18

When Savannah descended the staircase, she could hear Granny reading. Having practically memorized the book in her youth, Savannah could tell that Gran was near the end of the story.

She walked on into the kitchen, pulled a bag of dry dog food from the pantry, and took it back into the living room with her, arriving just in time to see Brody give Gran a hug around the neck and thank her for the story.

Not for the first time, Savannah marveled at the capacity children had for love. Even those who had dared to trust, only to have that trust violated, found the courage to reach out, again and again. Unlike most adults, who became bitter and withdrawn.

She walked over to Brody and placed the bag of dog food on his lap. "Would you do me a big favor?" she asked him.

He looked down at the sack, grinned, and said teasingly, "You want me to eat a bag of dog food?"

"Yes, absolutely," she replied. "If it's a bit dry for you to gag down, there's ketchup, mustard, and maple syrup in the fridge. Put enough of that stuff on it and it'll slide down nice and easy-like."

"Oh, yum." He giggled. "Or I could go feed the Colonel for you."

"Yeah, there's that."

Granny gave her a questioning look. Usually Gran fed the Colonel, as she was more aware of his dining schedule. The bloodhound had always been inclined to overeat if left to his own devices.

Not unlike the rest of the Reid clan.

But Granny said nothing as Brody jumped up from the couch, tucked the bag under his arm, and headed toward the back door.

"Also, while you're at it," Savannah called after him, "would you give him some fresh water? You can fill the big stainless steel bowl there at the water faucet."

"Okay," he replied. "I don't mind earnin' my keep around here. Next thing, you'll be askin' me to chop firewood and plow the back field."

In spite of his pretended complaint, Savannah noticed that he had a certain swagger to his walk that she hadn't noticed before. She thought of what Granny had always told her grandkids: "Honest work don't hurt you. Tacklin' somethin' hard and doin' a good job of it—shows you how strong and smart you are."

What better work was there for a child than caring for an animal they loved?

"What's goin' on, Granddaughter?" Granny asked,

reaching for her hand and pulling her down beside her on the sofa.

"I had to get him out of the house for a minute, so I could tell you."

"That's what I figured. Let's hear it."

Savannah paused, steeled herself, then let it out. "Dirk's on his way home right now. I called him and asked him to come."

"Okay. Why?"

"Because we have to take Brody to the hospital."

"Lord've mercy!" Granny's eyes, usually calm and gentle, searched Savannah's with obvious alarm and concern. "What on earth for? He seems fine to me."

"I know. He seemed okay to me, too. But when he was playing in the backyard earlier, the Colonel pulled his britches down, and I saw that he's been whipped. I don't mean a get-your-attention, run-of-the-mill spanking either. They're big, ugly bruises. He was beaten. Looks like a belt."

Granny closed her eyes and shuddered. "Oh, no. Poor child. I can't bear it!"

"I know. Me either, and there's more."

When Granny opened her eyes, Savannah could see tears in them. "What else?" she asked.

Gran's tears prompted Savannah's own. She wiped them away, glanced toward the back door, and said, "That bitch has burned him with cigarettes."

"No!"

Deep in the recesses of her mind, Savannah realized that she had just used a word that, out of respect and a healthy portion of fear, she had never spoken in her grandmother's presence. But Gran didn't seem offended, at least, not by the word.

She was too busy being outraged by the offense against a child who had already found his way into the centers of their hearts.

"Heaven forgive me," Gran said, shaking her head, "but hearing that makes me want to beat the tar outta that woman myself."

"I know. Don't worry. I'm sure Dirk will deal with it."

For a moment, Granny looked alarmed. Savannah quickly added, "Legally, of course."

"Of course." Gran mulled it over for a while, then said, "It'd be more satisfyin' to yank her bald, but I reckon that's against the law here in the fine state of California, where you can't even drink your soda pop with a plastic straw."

"They'd frown on yanking somebody bald, I'm pretty sure. You want to get away with that, you'd have to move back to Georgia."

Savannah glanced toward the door again. "I have to ask you something before Brody comes back in."

"What's that, darlin'?"

"Last night, when you bathed him, you didn't see those marks?"

Gran shook her head. "No. 'Course not, or I woulda told you for sure. When I offered to come into the bathroom with him, shampoo his hair and scrub his back for him, he let me know in no uncertain terms that he didn't want no female scrubbin' no part of him."

"Can't blame him for that, considering it was his own mother who hurt him."

"That's for sure. But I thought he was just bein' modest, and I aimed to respect that. He was old enough to be in a tub alone. I sat down the hall in the guest room with the door open and kept my ears out on stems, just in case he got in trouble."

"You did fine, Gran. I was just wondering if you'd noticed anything then. I didn't think you had, but I wanted to make certain."

"I understand, Savannah girl. You're doin' right by him, for sure. But why do you think he needs to go to the emergency room?"

"I don't think I could get an appointment this late in the day with a pediatrician I've never used before. Some of those cigarette burns looked red, like they might be infected. Can't take a chance with things like that."

"True. Infection can spread fast, especially in a little fella like that, who's not been taken care of properly. He don't look as healthy as he should to me. Like he ain't thrived or somethin'."

"I think so, too. All of this has to be documented to bring legal proceedings against his mother, to make sure the boy doesn't wind up back in her care again."

"Heaven forbid."

At that moment, Savannah heard the front door open, then slam closed. She knew, within seconds, her husband would charge into the room.

Some knights arrived not on a white horse but driving an old, restored Buick. Sometimes, their armor was a faded Harley-Davidson T-shirt and a battered bomber jacket.

She was right.

In only a few heartbeats, he was in the room, and she was in his arms. He hugged her tight against his chest. Then he pulled back a bit, looked down into her eyes, and said, "Okay. I'm here. What the hell's goin' on?"

*   *   *

Convincing Brody that a trip to the hospital was both necessary and in his best interests proved more difficult than Savannah had anticipated.

When she first told him, he flatly refused. But, to her surprise and great relief, Dirk took over and, in his own gentle but firm manner, convinced the boy it was going to happen whether he wanted it to or not, but wouldn't be nearly as bad as he feared.

Dirk also assured him that they would both be with him every step of the way, to make sure he was well treated.

In the end, Dirk sealed the deal with a promise to take him to a Dodgers' game and buy him a cap and Dodger dog.

Savannah had often thought that bribing a kid was a lazy form of discipline. But after one thirty-minute battle with a child as determined as Brody Greyson, Savannah thought perhaps she should be less judgmental of parents who purchased their children's cooperation with cash and prizes.

Her new motto, concerning the raising of children, consisted of: "Whatever it takes."

Considering the fact that it was Dirk who had won him over in the end, she wasn't surprised when, upon arriving at the hospital, he had chosen Dirk to be his guardian and protector against probing doctors, nurses who insisted that he put on a paper gown, and anything even resembling a needle.

As Savannah waved good-bye to them and watched them disappear down the hallway, hand in hand, she decided she was happy to leave them both in the care of professionals.

The doctors were the ones with the fancy degrees and the paychecks to match. Let them find a way to haggle with the kid, now that Dirk had already played the Visit to Dodger Stadium bargaining chip.

She wished them luck, said a quick prayer, and headed for the one place in the hospital where she actually enjoyed spending time. The Serenity Garden.

When her brother, Waycross, had been in an accident, she had waited in that lovely, peaceful place for news of his condition.

The lush tropical paradise in the middle of the hospital complex had soothed her soul during that difficult time. Settled on a comfortable chair next to the koi pond, she watched the fountain send its glittering drops into the air and the lotus blossoms float on the swirling, crystalline water, along with tiny brass bells that chimed melodiously when they met.

Savannah found the place just as charming as it had been before. Possibly even more so, since the twilight version of the garden twinkled with tiny flickering fairy lights, adding to the magic of the place.

Sitting on the comfortable, cushioned chaise, Savannah realized how exhausted she was. Long ago, she had learned that there was no labor on earth as draining as dealing with human drama. She would have gladly picked cotton in the hot Georgia sun for a week rather than deal with something as upsetting as seeing the aftereffects of child abuse in her own home.

Her rage and sorrow wreaked havoc in her own body, leaving it aching from the stress.

Like Granny, the less evolved part of her brain desperately wanted to lay hands on Brody's mother and exact a generous measure of revenge on his behalf. Let her find out how it felt to be at the mercy of someone bigger than you, stronger than you, and definitely more outraged.

"She probably had it done to her, too," Savannah whispered to the enormous black and gold koi nearest her. "She can't help it. She just doesn't know any better."

Yeah, go on, make excuses for her, replied another less conciliatory voice in her head. *Of course she knows better. She knows full well what she's doing to her kid is wrong. Otherwise she wouldn't threaten him to keep his mouth shut about it. She's worried about getting busted by the cops for abusing him. But she's not worried about the pain she's causing him—and, by the way, if it was done to her, then she, of all people, should know how bad it hurts.*

Savannah's brain kept replaying the vision of those cigarette burns in her head. One particular detail screamed out to her that those wounds had been inflicted with cruel deliberation.

They weren't random.

They were carefully placed in precise, straight lines, equally spaced.

When Savannah thought of how much effort had been taken to do that, to methodically torture a precious, innocent, no doubt squirming child, her vengeful thoughts turned much darker than simple hair yanking.

She hated it, hated having such blackness in her own soul.

"Savannah, are you okay?" said a deep, kind male voice from the shadowed pathway nearby.

"Yes, love," said another, decidedly British, fellow in the darkness. "We called your house to speak to you, and your grandmother answered. She told us you were here and why. We came to see if we could help."

Savannah looked up and felt her heart rising from its black, angry abyss.

"Ryan!" she shouted, jumping up from the chair. "Oh, John!"

She rushed to greet two people she simply adored. Before she knew it, she was in the midst of a tight, loving three-way hug. "Thank goodness you're here," she said, melting against them. "You have no idea how relieved I am to see you guys!"

Chapter 19

Two and a half hours later, everyone, including Ryan and John, was back at Savannah's house, sitting at her kitchen table, happily making the rest of Granny's pot of beans disappear.

Although Ryan Stone and John Gibson were restaurateurs, who had traveled the world and enjoyed its best cuisine, they were chowing down on the southern countryfolk staple as though it were the finest French cassoulet.

"Have some more corn bread," Granny said, passing the basket to John.

The elegant, silver-haired, lushly mustachioed gentleman dug into the bounty with uncharacteristic enthusiasm. "I do believe I'll have another," he said in the posh, melodic tone that could only be achieved by British aristocracy.

Turning to his partner—in the restaurant business and in life—John said, "This corn bread is divine, so light that it will float out of your hand if you aren't cautious. Have another piece?"

"I most certainly will," Ryan replied. "This is the best corn bread I've ever had. The bits of onion and peppers really give it a nice kick, Granny. You've outdone yourself!"

As tall, dark, and utterly gorgeous Ryan helped himself to another piece, Granny blushed from all the praise the two were heaping on her. But then, Ryan and John caused a lot of females to blush . . . mostly because of the risqué thoughts they entertained about them. Fantasies that were mostly centered around the theme of reordering their sexual preferences.

At the other end of the table, Savannah grinned, watching her grandmother act the coquette as she exchanged flirtatious banter with them.

All seemed to be enjoying it, so there was no harm done.

Except, perhaps, to Dirk. Though he would never have admitted it, he resented the amount of attention the handsome twosome received from females.

"What a waste," he'd expounded on more than one occasion to Savannah during their private moments. "Gals throwing themselves at 'em, right and left, and them not even inclined to put on a catcher's mitt and nab one."

Savannah turned her attention to the little guy sitting next to her. Even Brody, after the tough day he'd had, was mowing through a bowl of beans as quickly as he could.

Ryan and John had attempted to engage him in conversation several times, but the boy seemed far more interested in filling his belly than making new friends.

Amazing, she thought, *what serving dinner a couple of hours late does for the appetite.* She had always considered "starvation" to be the best spice in her pantry.

When Granny offered the corn bread basket to Brody, she told him, "I'll be headin' on home tonight, so's you can sleep in the guest room in a proper bed, instead of all crunched up on the couch."

Instantly, Brody's face crinkled into a frown. "You ain't going home just so's I can have the bed, are you?"

Granny looked surprised. "Well, I—"

"Don't be goin' home on my account," he assured her. "I mean, if you need to, go on ahead. But if I had my druthers, I'd sleep on the couch and have you here."

Granny gave him a playful grin. "Don't go butterin' me up, boy. It's the Colonel you're frettin' 'bout. I know you and him's gotten to be fine friends."

She gave Savannah a helpless shrug and questioning look.

Savannah nodded.

Gran tousled the boy's hair. "I reckon, I could leave him here a couple days, and you two could—"

"No! It ain't just the hound dog," Brody protested. "He's a bunch o' fun, but I like you, too. Why don't you stay? Make yourself at home?"

Ryan and John burst out laughing, and so did Savannah. The boy's precociousness along with his ever-buoyant spirit were irresistible.

"Granny, if I may weigh in here," she said, "I think that, unless you've got a good reason for going home, like you miss your fine neighbors there at the trailer park . . ."

"The ones cooking meth or the hookers?" Dirk mumbled.

Savannah ignored him and continued, ". . . you should

stay here with us as long as you, Brody, and the Colonel want to. With this case going on, we'll be out and about a lot anyway. It'd be nice if someone was here to keep an eye on the place."

Both Brody's and Granny's faces lit up.

"That sounds like a brilliant plan," John chimed in. "See what can be accomplished when great minds come together?"

Savannah was quite sure that, if the Colonel had been in the room, instead of snoring in his oversized doggy bed in her utility room, he would have been smiling, too.

An hour later, Brody was tucked into the upstairs bed, with the promise that Dirk would carry him downstairs and put him on the sofa once their company had all gone home and Granny was ready to retire.

"We don't want to keep you awake with all our chitter-chatting," was the explanation given to the boy.

It sounded so much better than, "We're going to have a meeting of the Moonlight Magnolia Detective Agency at the kitchen table, and we don't want to discuss the unsavory details of a murder a few yards from a kid on the couch who, instead of sleeping, would be lying awake in horror."

Savannah put a plate of cookies on the table, along with the obligatory coffee, and tea for John. Tammy and Waycross had been summoned, to complete the team. Savannah had mineral water for her, and a six-pack of root beer for him.

Baby Vanna Rose was snoozing, draped across Waycross's lap. Both the baby's and her daddy's fiery red hair glowed in the warm light of the stained-glass lamp. Unlike the overly streetwise Brody, the toddler wouldn't understand the morbid topics being discussed, even if she should wake.

"Let's start with you, Tamitha," Savannah said. "Did you dig up anything else on our principal players?"

Tammy grabbed her electronic tablet and referred to her notes. "Brooklynn Marsh is an interesting lady."

"Really?" Dirk said. "I didn't notice."

When Tammy gave him a long, confused look, Savannah said, "She's a pretty sad case."

"Plain. Mousy. Lackluster," Dirk interjected.

Savannah searched for kinder words but couldn't find any. "She struck me as a worn-out, dragged down, faded version of whoever she might have been if she hadn't hooked up with a jerk like Faraday."

"As unpleasant as that evaluation might sound," Tammy said, "I'll have to admit you may be right. She was a successful professional, the managing editor for a major magazine. Very fit and attractive, too, I'd say, judging from her earlier social media photos. She made a lot of money, owned a nice home. But then she met Geoffrey and her life took a major turn for the worse."

"In what way, love?" John asked as he added another bag of Earl Grey to his cup.

"Did he run them into debt?" Ryan asked.

Tammy nodded. "He certainly did. She spent all her money on his legal problems. Especially after his great-grandmother cut him off and refused to foot the bills for his shenanigans anymore. Brooklynn took out a second mortgage on her beautiful beachfront house to pay his attorney's fees."

"But he was convicted anyway," Savannah added.

"That's right. She even spent a couple of months in jail herself for 'obstruction of justice' when they figured out she'd lied and given him a false alibi. That led to her losing her job and therefore her home. Where they're living now is a cheap rental." Tammy laid her tablet down and took a sip of her water. "The poor woman's life has gone to the devil in a wicker basket since she hooked up with that guy."

"I don't doubt what you found there," Dirk said. "It may all be true, but he's driving a sports car now that cost more than a house."

"Let's just say"—Savannah turned to the always sharply dressed Ryan and John—"the two of you would covet his wardrobe. His suit, Ryan, is almost as nice as your bespoke Giorgio Armani."

Ryan gasped with pseudo-horror. "No! Tell me it isn't so!"

"But not as fine as my Brioni," John said.

"Oh, no. Of course not," Tammy assured him. "The suit has never been created that's as lovely as *your* Brioni."

John gave Ryan a nudge in the ribs and a good-natured laugh.

"If you guys don't mind," Dirk said, rolling his eyes, "we're supposed to be discussing murder, not fashion."

"We're determining the financial status of our major suspect," Savannah told him. "That's important."

"Yeah, yeah. Okay." Dirk threw up his hands. "The guy who couldn't pay for his own attorneys, whose fiancée is broke because she did, is now rolling in dough. That might be something we should check out."

"I'm on it," Tammy said.

"He's probably into something crooked," Waycross spoke up. "Sounds like he couldn't hold a job if it had a handle on it."

"Sounds like the only thing he's good at is livin' off womenfolk," Granny said.

Waycross nodded. "Yes, he does seem pretty good at that. But if he's got a lotta money and no job and his woman's flat broke, he's prob'ly come by it through skullduggery."

"Like he did before with the trafficking," Savannah said.

Ryan held up his hand. "We know a guy in the bureau who specializes in human trafficking. We can ask him to check around, see if maybe this guy's returned to his wicked ways."

"Thank you," Savannah said gratefully. As wonderful as it was to have successful restaurateurs for friends and part of her team, it was even nicer that they were former FBI agents.

"How 'bout that Mary Mahoney lady, the house-keeper?" Waycross asked. "She's got more access to the dead woman than anybody else. Also, not ever'body likes their boss. There mighta been some bad blood between them two."

"Oh, there was a bit," Savannah told him. "I think there was affection, too. She claims Lucinda made a second will, leaving the estate to her. But that doesn't always rule out murder."

"Could even be a motive," Gran said, "if she decided that the Good Lord was takin' too long to call Miss Lucinda home. She mighta got impatient to collect that inheritance and rushed things along."

"True," Savannah said. "A lot of killers have love-hate

relationships with their victims. Those two emotions aren't mutually exclusive." She turned to her little brother. "You check her out, darlin'. See if anything pops up. Okay?"

Waycross blushed and said, "Sure. Glad to help."

It touched Savannah's heart that her brother was so grateful to have a place on the Moonlight Magnolia team. He was a valuable addition to their group. But since childhood, Waycross had never thought of himself as even worthwhile, let alone a precious commodity. His recent troubles with a prescription drug addiction had caused what little self-esteem he had to plummet.

But the entire family, even Dirk, had rallied around him. Especially his loving wife, Tammy. Little by little, he seemed to be coming around.

"Look, guys, we need to wrap this up," Dirk said, "or I'm gonna have to run out on you. I've gotta get back to work."

"You do?" Savannah asked, dismayed. Then it occurred to her that her earlier call had interrupted his workday. Instantly, she felt guilty. "I'm sorry, sugar. I'll go with you, help you shovel the garbage."

He gave her a sweet, understanding—if exhausted— smile. "You don't have to be sorry. Especially 'shovel garbage' sorry. You did the right thing calling me. I needed to come home for that business with the kiddo. I had to talk to him, question the doctors, take pictures, and all that."

"Are you gonna arrest that no-good momma of his for child abuse?" Granny asked, keeping her voice low.

"She's already under arrest," Dirk said, "behind bars even. Surprise, surprise, she couldn't make bail. But I'll be adding to her charges, big time. What she did to that kid—" His voice broke. He closed his eyes and shook his head. "I've seen way too much of that crap in my career, but this is one of the worst. He's such a sweet kid, too. It makes me crazy."

Granny reached across the table and placed her hand on Dirk's. "I know, son," she said. "It's a heartbreaker, for sure."

Tammy looked down at her baby, sleeping on her husband's lap. She said tearfully, "I'm quite sure I would kill somebody if I had to in order to keep them from doing something like that to my child. I can't imagine how a mother could . . ."

Waycross wrapped his arm around his wife's shoulders, leaned over, and kissed the top of her golden hair. "At least we don't have to worry about Brody's momma doin' nothin' like that to him ever again." He turned to Dirk. "Do we?"

"No. She'll be serving time for the drug charges, and now this? Any halfway sensible judge will make sure she's behind bars for most, if not all, of his childhood. She won't get her hands on him again. At least, not until after he's a grown man."

"And a lot bigger and stronger than she is!" Tammy added.

Dirk winced, reached up, and touched his badly bruised eye that Brody had pummeled. "Having wrestled with her and gotten punched by him, I'll tell you now, that family knows how to fight! I hope I don't have to tangle with either one of them again."

Dirk rose from the table, stretched, and popped a couple of cookies into his pocket. "Like I said before, I've gotta get back to the mansion, spend a few more hours rummaging around before I put this day outta its misery."

Savannah looked over at her grandmother and wondered if she dared impose on her again.

As always, Granny read her mind. "Go on along and help your husband. I can tell you're dyin' to. I'm stayin' the night anyway, since Mr. Brody invited me so sweet-like. Don't take more'n one of us to take care o' a sleepin' child."

Ryan gave John a questioning glance and John spoke up, as well. "We can come, too. Make a party of it. Four of us have twice as good a chance of finding something as two."

"Really?" Dirk looked like he couldn't believe his good luck. "Wow! Thanks!"

Tammy looked wistfully down at the baby sleeping on Waycross's lap. "Well, you guys have fun," she said, a plaintive tone in her voice. "You know we'd pitch in, too, but we're parents now, so—"

"So, nothin'," Granny said, reaching for the tiny red-head, who didn't stir at all as she transferred her from her grandson's lap to her own. "Get outta here and go catch a bad guy. The young'uns are gonna be asleep, safe and sound, the whole time. Remember, when it comes to takin' care o' kiddos, I'm a champion!"

Tammy didn't bother to hide her glee as she wriggled about, doing her "happy dance."

Dirk was astonished. "I never saw anybody so happy to wallow in trash as you are, Miss Fluff Head."

"Oh, shut up, Dirk-o," Tammy shot back. "You aren't the only one who takes their life's work seriously."

"Okay, okay." He held up both hands. "Since Gran's being so generous and willing to sit on the rug rats, I'll bring the kid downstairs and put him on the couch, then we can take off."

"I'll get the bedclothes for him," Savannah said. "Tammy, would you check under the kitchen sink and grab as many of those rubber cleaning gloves as you can find? Ryan, would you collect some trash bags? Lots of them. John, please run upstairs and get those bottles of hand sanitizer out of the bathroom cabinet. Waycross, in the utility room cupboard, in the earthquake emergency stash, there's a whole box of those little flashlights. Would you fetch 'em?"

They all stood, staring at her in amazement.

Finally, John said, "Is it truly that revolting, the Faraday mansion, the hoard inside it?"

"Oh," she said, "you have *no* idea. I'd suggest you all stop at home on your way there and change into work clothes. Clothes you won't mind burning later."

They stared at each other for the longest time, eyes wide, mouths open. Savannah thought she might have overdone it, lost Dirk the assistance he so needed.

Then Tammy said, "Wow! This sounds awesome!"

"Smashing!" John said. "I can't wait!"

A second later, they took off in all directions to collect the supplies.

Four minutes later, the four self-appointed crime scene assistants raced out the door.

Savannah watched as Dirk, black eye and all, gently laid the sleeping boy on the white sheet, made sure the pillow was fluffed under his head, and covered him with the blanket.

Reaching down, Dirk scooped up Cleo, his favorite feline sleeping partner, and tucked her securely under the child's arm.

"Good night, Brody," he whispered. "Tomorrow will be a better day."

Then he bent down and kissed the boy on the head.

As she watched, it occurred to Savannah that, in all the years she had known him and in all the situations she had watched him deal with people, she had never loved and respected her husband more than she did at that very moment.

Chapter 20

"There's an old sayin' we use down south." Waycross paused to wipe the sweat off his forehead with his shirtsleeve and catch his breath. "It goes, 'I'm up to my eyeballs' in whatever."

His fellow searchers welcomed the interruption, small though it might have been, to take a breather of their own. They laughed.

Not uproariously, by a long shot. Just dry chuckles.

Waycross and Tammy, Ryan and John, Savannah and Dirk, and even Mary Mahoney, had been searching the hoard for two hours.

The magic had worn off for all of them after the first twenty minutes. Since then, they had all been operating on pure work ethic and determination to find something, anything, to reward them for their efforts thus far.

Savannah looked across a pile of ancient magazines at her little brother, all grown up. His mop of red curls was the same as the little boy who used to tag along behind her, looking for opportunities to either amuse or annoy her.

The mischievous sparkle in his eyes had become more subdued with the years. Other than his beloved Tammy and their magical red-haired fairy fay, life had been more difficult than kind to Waycross, and it had taken its toll.

Savannah missed the jolly little guy who had frequently hidden frogs in his sisters' underwear drawers and who drew long, curly mustaches on every photo he could get his hands on—celebrities on yet-to-be-read neighbors' newspapers, wanted posters in the post office, Adam and Eve in Granny's family Bible.

But Waycross Reid was a good man. A devoted husband, father, grandson, brother, and brother-in-law. He was far more important than he realized.

He deserved a generous helping of self-confidence.

Savannah considered it part of her life work to help him attain it.

She laughed at his comment and said, "You never thought you'd literally be up to your eyeballs in garbage, huh?"

"None of us did," Tammy said, as she shined her small flashlight around the area at her feet. "I still haven't seen the floor yet!"

"I caught a glimpse of it about an hour ago," John piped up from his and Ryan's area, closest to where Lucinda's bed had been. "It's a beautiful hardwood parquet. Quite lovely, if I do say so."

"Along with the rest of the house." Ryan shifted an

armful of clothing to one side, then had to grab a stack of books that threatened to collapse on him. "Obviously, this place is in need of some TLC, but—"

"No," Dirk said as he shoved a pile of papers into a brown evidence bag. "It's not in need of TLC. Our garage floor's got some grease on it and should be scrubbed. That's 'in need of some TLC.' This place doesn't need tender lovin' care. It needs somebody to set a match to it. Once we get our evidence outta here, that is."

John gave him a scandalized look. "Torch it? This magnificent, historical work of art? I hope you're in jest, lad."

"I agree," Ryan said. "If you can look past the mess, this home is an art deco masterpiece! Not to mention the treasures that are scattered among the junk at our feet."

They all looked down. Other than John, everyone wore a doubtful frown.

"I hate to contradict you, Ryan, but I don't know about that," Tammy said, "unless there's a market for used toothpaste tubes, empty cold cream bottles, and naked paper towel rolls."

Ryan held up a book as Exhibit 1 of his argument. "This, for instance, is a 1902 copy of *The Hound of the Baskervilles*, by Sir Arthur Conan Doyle. It's easily worth between five and ten thousand dollars."

Dirk gasped and so did the rest.

"Seriously?" Waycross asked. "I'm up to my eyeballs in junk worth thousands of dollars?"

"You're practically swimming in dough, mate," John told him. "Makes you see things a bit differently, no?"

"Yes!" Waycross returned to his task with renewed vigor.

"Good," Dirk said. "Maybe you'll find that will Mary was talking about, or a threatening letter, or a scandalous diary."

"To heck with that," Waycross said, digging in up to his elbows. "I'm fixin' to find another book like that 'un!"

Half an hour later, the search team heard someone coming through the tunnel in their direction and glass clinking, along with what Savannah thought sounded like the tinkling of ice.

Refreshments? she thought. *Somebody's brought us energy-restoring, soul-refreshing goodies? What a delightful idea.*

"Do I hear food?" Dirk said, turning to face their new arrival.

"Just beverages," said Mary Mahoney as she appeared around the curve in the path. She had a tray in her hands, loaded down with what Savannah hoped with all her heart was lemonade.

It was. Fresh squeezed and well sugared. Savannah's all-time favorite.

Other southerners could extoll the virtues of sweet tea, and of course, she loved it, as well. But there was nothing like real lemonade to quench the thirst and recharge a dehydrated, calorie-deficient body.

"You've been working a long time," Mary said as she found a reasonably clean spot atop an old overturned laundry basket to place the tray. "I thought you might need something to wet your whistles, as Lucinda used to say."

"Lucinda drank a lot of lemonade, did she?" Dirk asked, a sarcastic tone in his voice.

Savannah suggested his skepticism might have something to do with the enormous amount of empty Irish and Scottish whiskey bottles they had uncovered in the hoard.

"Not really," Mary said. "My lady preferred beverages with a little more kick, to be honest. But back in the old days, when we entertained frequently, she would ask me to make lemonade for our guests."

"I can't imagine how beautiful this place must've been back then," John said as he hurried over to help her pour and serve the lemonade. "It's such an elegant estate, and those were such glamorous times."

Mary's eyes sparkled as she handed Ryan his glass. Like most females, she looked him over thoroughly from head to toe, taking in his dark hair, pale green eyes, and his body, which many hours on the tennis court had honed to perfection.

"Oh," Mary said, "you wouldn't believe the people she entertained here. Everybody who was anybody came to Qamar Damun in its heyday. Everybody wanted an invitation to this place. Some arrived even without an invitation. If we invited fifty people to a party, a hundred would show up. They weren't all well behaved either, if you know what I mean."

"We've heard tales," Savannah said, accepting the tall, frosty glass that John was handing her. "I understand some not-so-nice things happened here, too?"

Mary nodded solemnly. "It's true. I won't deny it. Let's just say, the police became very well acquainted with Miss Lucinda and her guests."

Dirk took a long drink from his glass and wiped his mouth with his sleeve. "Something tells me she might have crossed quite a few cops' palms with silver on a regular basis back then."

"Silver, gold, Rolex watches," Mary replied with a grin. "Not to mention, regular invitations to the best parties. But those were usually reserved for high-level law enforcement officials. State prosecutors, county judges, important people like that."

Tammy gently refused when offered the glass full of sugar and said, "Tell us, Mary, of all these people who came and went in this house over the years, did Ms. Faraday have any disagreements with any of them, arguments, hurt feelings, stuff like that?"

"Of course she did," Mary admitted. "Ms. Faraday was a spirited, opinionated, feisty woman who said exactly what she thought at all times. That's not always the best way to make and keep friends."

"Did she have any friends, serious friends?" Savannah asked.

Suddenly, Mary looked sad, as if remembering something unpleasant. After refilling Dirk's glass, she cleared some clothing off an old chair and sat down on it, groaning slightly as she did. Apparently, her arthritis was acting up.

"Miss Lucinda did have a friend, a best friend, for a long time. Delores Dinapoli."

"I guess she's dead now," Dirk said with his usual tactful, delicate manner.

"No, Miss Delores is still around. She's over twenty years younger than Ms. Faraday. They got along well for a long time. I'd even say they loved each other like a mother and daughter. Better than some mothers and daughters."

Considering how sad Mary looked to be discussing this topic, Savannah thought it might be important.

She probed a bit deeper. "May I ask what happened between them? Did their friendship end at some point?"

"It did. With a bang, so to speak."

Now she had everyone's attention.

"What happened?" Tammy asked.

"The same sort of thing that happens in too many friendships. Betrayal. Of the worst kind."

"Who betrayed whom?" Ryan asked.

"I'm ashamed to say it, but my lady was the one who destroyed that relationship, as she ruined others. She was a flawed person in many ways, but the best I ever knew."

"You're a loyal person, I can tell," Savannah said softly, taking a step closer to Mary. "I know it must be uncomfortable to say unflattering things about your former employer and friend. But right now, we need to know all we can about her and her relationships."

"I understand."

"Good, because unfortunately, when a murder occurs, luxuries like privacy go out the window. Sometimes, having one seemingly small secret revealed can solve a case."

Mary looked up at Savannah and nodded thoughtfully. "I'm sure it does happen that way sometimes."

"Then, if you can bring yourself to do it, would you tell us what happened between Delores and Ms. Faraday?"

Savannah could tell that Mary was struggling with her conscience, but in the end, practicality appeared to win the battle.

"Miss Delores was married to Dino Dinapoli, a very wealthy man, a good-looking man. He was an extremely sexy man, if you want me to be honest."

"We do," Dirk assured her. "That's exactly what we want. Go on."

"That was how Ms. Faraday liked her men—good-looking, sexy, and wealthy."

"Lemme guess," Waycross said. "Ms. Faraday took a serious likin' to Miss Delores's husband."

"She did," Mary admitted, "and she made sure he felt the same."

Savannah did a bit of quick math in her head. "Was Dino closer to Lucinda's age than Delores's?"

Mary shook her head. "No. He and Miss Delores were about the same age, which, yes, means that he was around twenty years younger than Ms. Faraday."

"Wow," Tammy said. "That Ms. Faraday must've really had a way with men, to be able to seduce somebody twenty years her junior."

"Oh," Mary said, "she had a way with men, all right. She had *her* way with them. I never saw her go after a man she wanted and not get him. She just had a way of pulling them in, like a fish on a line. She'd bait them with that whole glamorous silver-screen star facade, slather them with all that buttery flattery, and the next thing you knew, they were her next tasty dish. Of course, once she had eaten what she wanted, she threw the leftovers into the garbage, wiped her mouth, and pretended nothing had happened."

"Unless a wife found out," Dirk said. "Then the meal might end badly."

"It did. Frequently. Ms. Faraday wasn't nearly as discreet as she thought she was. Pretty much everyone around her knew exactly what was going on at any given time. I'm sorry to say she ruined quite a few marriages."

"Are any of those wounded parties still alive, other than Delores, that is?" Savannah wanted to know.

"No. Just Miss Delores."

Mary paused to take a sip of her own lemonade, and Savannah noticed that her hands were trembling. She used both to hold the glass, and even then, she nearly spilled it.

"A few years back," Mary continued, "I remember Miss Lucinda telling me, 'All of my enemies are dead now.' I thought how strange it would be to say that. Even to think that."

It would be strange, Savannah thought. To have lived so long that almost everyone you knew, all of your contemporaries, at least, had passed on.

She imagined it must be a lonely feeling. Though, apparently, a relief, if most of the people you knew had been enemies rather than friends.

"I don't doubt she said that," Dirk added. "But I wouldn't have to be a detective to tell you, I saw her body, and Lucinda Faraday was wrong. She still had at least one enemy left, for sure."

Chapter 21

The next morning, when Savannah returned from dropping Brody off at school, she pulled together a small breakfast of cinnamon rolls, miscellaneous fruit, freshly squeezed orange juice, and percolator-brewed coffee.

Just as the cinnamon rolls were coming out of the oven, the members of the Moonlight Magnolia Detective Agency—plus Ethan Malloy and his three-year-old son, Freddy—began to arrive.

Since the weather was crisp and cool, and because she thought Freddy and Vanna Rose might enjoy playing on the grass in the backyard, Savannah ushered everyone out the back door and over to the picnic table beneath the wisteria arbor.

Granny and Tammy helped her put the goodies on the table, while Waycross and Ethan introduced the children to each other and the joys of rolling about on Savannah's lush lawn.

"You're still using only natural fertilizers on your grass, right?" Tammy asked, checking out the nearly perfect and weed-free green expanse.

Savannah couldn't help herself. Tammy brought out the worst in her. She gave her a wicked smile and said, "I've used only organic fertilizers since that long conversation we had last spring. Except for the dandelions, of course," she added. "A good squirt of arsenic is the only thing that gets rid of those stubborn, nasty things."

Tammy gasped and nearly dropped the cinnamon rolls. "Arsenic? You're kidding, right? But you shouldn't be, because nobody should joke about arsenic. Do you know what that stuff does to the human body?"

"As a matter of fact, she does," Granny said, rescuing the rolls and conveying them safely to the table. "My granddaughter knows more about poisons and ugly stuff that kills people than 'most anybody I've ever known. 'Cept me, of course. Being part of a private detective agency, I have to keep up on that sorta thing."

"Of course," Tammy said, simmering down almost immediately.

That was something else that Granny knew more about than Savannah did, and Savannah was the first to admit it. Granny could calm a mad hornet who'd just been stepped on and turn him into a honeybee in three seconds flat.

It was a gift that Savannah wished she had inherited, knew she had not, and had surrendered any hope of developing herself.

She looked over at her brother and Ethan and saw, to her delight, that the two men were rolling around on the grass with the kids. Even the Colonel had joined in the fun. She noticed that the hound was being far gentler with little Vanna than he had been with Brody. Like most good dogs, he sensed that she was smaller and more delicate, a puppy to be coddled and not wrestled.

He was nudging her with his soft nose, his long velvety ears brushing her pink cheeks, causing her to squeal with delight.

Ethan reached out and grabbed his three-year-old son, who was trying to climb on top of the dog's back. "Watch it there, Freddy boy," Ethan said. "That's a hound dog, not one of your granddaddy's packhorses. You might hurt him."

Freddy threw a tantrum, kicking his legs and screaming as though he were in agony, rather than being cradled in his father's arms.

"I know, I know," Ethan told him. "I'm a cruel father, not letting you ride every dog you get your hands on."

Ethan looked up and saw that Savannah was watching. He said, "I took him to my dad's ranch for Christmas and made the mistake of going riding with him. He loved it."

"There aren't a lot of horses to ride here 'bouts," she said.

"Tell me about it. That's why I have to watch out for any dogs that cross his path."

Granny walked over to Ethan and Waycross, holding a plate that she had filled with strawberries, orange slices, banana slices, and grapes cut in half. She sat down on the grass beside the children and told their fathers, "You fellas get over there to the table and have some breakfast before you start discussin' business. I'll watch out for these young'uns. I'll even keep that cowboy there off the hound dog."

"You don't mind, Granny?" Waycross asked his grandmother. "Seems like you've been doin' nothin' but babysittin' lately. We don't wanna wear you out."

Granny laughed and offered a bit of strawberry to Vanna. "Don't be silly. At my age, I'm plumb thrilled to death to be of some use to somebody."

She looked down at the children with a light of joy and purpose in her eyes. "Just a few years back, I was askin' the Good Lord why He was keepin' me here, walkin' above grass instead of layin' under it. I wasn't sure what I was supposed to do with my life. Then, one day your little Vanna Rose showed up, and now some others, too, and all of a sudden, I know exactly what I'm here for."

She pointed over to the table, where Savannah, Dirk, Ryan, John, and Tammy were sitting down and helping themselves to the refreshments. "Y'all got an important job to do, a holy mission, looking for justice. If I can help you in any way to get 'er done, I'm grateful for the chance."

Ethan stared at her for a long moment, then said, "I think I'm in love with you, Ms. Reid."

She blushed and tittered like an eighth-grade girl who'd been asked to her first prom. "Why, Mr. Malloy. You say things like that, you'll turn my head."

"How's about I adopt you? Is that a possibility?"

She gave him a flirtatious grin that surprised everyone who saw it. "Oh, I reckon somethin' could be arranged, sir. We'll work on it."

Savannah chuckled and shook her head as she listened to the exchange. *You can take the belle outta the South*, she thought, *but you can never take the South outta the belle.*

"Good thing," she whispered, "'cause what a loss that would be."

Before long, the last cinnamon roll had been sent to Pastry Heaven, the coffee and tea were mostly gone, and thanks to the children and Tammy, the fruit had disappeared.

With the important tasks finished, it was time to get down to business.

"Okay," Dirk said, leaning back in his chair, his hands behind his head. "We all know what we didn't find last night."

"The will," Tammy replied. "I must say I felt bad for Mary. It's so important to her. I really wish we had been able to locate it for her."

"We haven't abandoned the task yet," John added. "I, for one, would be glad to go back there today and look again."

Ryan nudged him. "Yeah, we know what you want to go back and look for. The possibility of finding more first editions, not to mention that amazing coin collection and the Ming vase you uncovered last night."

"That was brilliant!" John exclaimed. "I'll remember that moment for the rest of my life. If it's authentic, and we can find the will that leaves the mansion and its contents to Mary, she could be a wealthy woman just from that one vase alone."

"I so wish we'd found that document," Tammy said. "Mary seems like a good person. She took care of Lucinda, and we all have a feeling that wasn't an easy job, for all those years. It's only fair that she would be the heir, not that worthless great-grandson who never even visited Lucinda."

"Unless he wanted her to bail him out or pay his attorneys," Dirk added. "What a dirtbag. You guys are hoping to find the will. I'm hoping I can lock that guy away again. Maybe this time, he'll stay behind bars, where he belongs."

"Hear, hear," John exclaimed. Lifting his teacup, he said, "A toast to better days for Mary and far worse ones for our friend, Geoffrey Faraday."

Everyone toasted with whatever beverage they had in hand. But a moment later the enthusiasm, the levity died down, and reality set in.

"Okay," Dirk said, "it's not like we came up empty handed last night. Waycross kept us from getting totally skunked with his find of the evening."

Savannah lifted her coffee cup again and said, "To Waycross and the discovery of the night. The diary!"

"To Waycross!" everyone exclaimed. "To the diary!"

Everybody at the table went wild with applause and cheers, except for Dirk, who simply smiled and nodded. He was somewhat phobic when it came to overt expressions of approval. Unless, of course, he was watching a boxing match and his favorite fighter knocked his opponent to the mat.

In that case, all hell broke loose, and the otherwise reserved Dirk could be heard baying more lustily than the Colonel in the act of treeing a giant raccoon.

Savannah looked across the table at her ginger-haired brother, who was blushing almost as red as his curls. She wasn't sure if he was wallowing in the joy of his team's recognition or if he was embarrassed half to death. She decided it was probably a bit of both.

"Actually, Sis," he said, "it was *you* who found it, not me."

Savannah shook her head. "You pointed to the box that was under my feet and told me you had a hunch it was in there. I opened it, and there it was. But believe me, I wouldn't have if you hadn't suggested it."

Ducking his head, he said, "Aw, shucks. Quit it."

John reached over and gave the young man a shove that nearly knocked him off his chair. "Learn to take a compliment when it's given to you, lad," the older man told him. "Not that many sincere ones come a man's way in a lifetime. Embrace them whenever possible."

"Okay. Thanks." Waycross lifted his head, straightened his back, and said, "It was my pleasure to help out. I'm just glad we've got it. I remembered Miss Mary sayin' that whiskey was one of Miss Lucinda's favorite things in the whole wide world. With the diary bein' so personal and all, I just figured the two might go together."

"You figured right, little brother," Savannah said. She felt the urge to glance around her backyard, just to make sure no one was eavesdropping. But, as always, her property was private, thanks to the high fence she had installed and the thick shrubs she'd planted. Privacy, and the resulting ability to walk outside on one's own property in your underdrawers at any time, day or night, was important to Savannah.

But the topic she was about to broach wasn't one they wanted to share with the public at large—or anyone outside the Moonlight Magnolia team. Except in this case their client, Ethan Malloy.

She lowered her voice and said to Tammy and Waycross, "Did you guys get a chance to read it last night? Did you find anything good?"

Tammy also gave a conspiratorial glance around herself before whispering, "We read it and found good stuff!"

Waycross turned to Dirk and quickly added, "We did exactly what you said though. We wore those stupid, hot, sweaty as all git-out surgical gloves the whole time."

"I didn't even let him eat potato chips over it while we were reading," Tammy added proudly. "Didn't want to get any crumbs between the pages."

Dirk groaned under his breath and mumbled, "Good. I can just imagine what cranky Eileen there at the lab would say when she found those. She'd be all over me, griping about 'chain of custody' and all that junk."

Savannah raised one eyebrow. "All that junk? It's kind of important, keeping evidence from getting contaminated."

"Yeah, yeah. But how many times have you seen Eileen chowing down on some of those cookies you take there to bribe her and get on her good side, while she's checking out the interior of a suspect's vehicle, or looking at some bloody gunk under the microscope?"

Savannah nodded. "True." She turned back to Tammy and Waycross. "We've established that you didn't get potato chip crumbs inside the diary or your fingerprints on the cover. That's important. But what did you actually find inside?"

Tammy and Waycross looked at each other, and Savannah could have sworn they both blushed. She also thought how charming it was that there were two people left in the world who actually blushed anymore, and that they happened to be married to each other. What a sweet couple. She glanced over at the baby on the lawn, who was lying beside the big sleeping hound, her head on his neck.

Savannah thought of Brody and wished she could somehow infuse a bit of that sweetness and innocence into his life, poor kid.

"Tell us what you found," Savannah told her brother and his wife, "and don't hold back any of the salacious details out of modesty or courtesy or anything like that."

"Yeah," Dirk said. "None of that courtesy or modesty stuff allowed around here." When Savannah gave him a funny look, he added quickly, "Not in the middle of a murder investigation anyway. Spill whatcha got."

Tammy and Waycross stared at each other, as if waiting for the other one to begin. Finally, Tammy sighed, crossed her arms over her chest, and said, "We read all night and got through most of it. I can tell you now, Lucinda Faraday was a very unhappy lady."

She glanced over at Ethan, saw a sadness on his face, and added, "I'm sorry, Ethan. I know she was your friend, and you had a lot of affection for her. I'm not saying she was a bad person. From a lot of the things she said in the diary, I can tell that she cared about other people and tried to help them as much as she could. There were certain things that really hurt her in her life. Some she never really got over."

"Like what?" he asked.

Tammy gulped and looked down at the table. "The one thing that seemed to bother her the most was an abortion she had years ago, when she was only sixteen. She wrote about it, there in her diary, off and on for the rest of her life. She never got over the hurt of it, her pain of losing that child."

"What made it way worse," Waycross added, "was the abortion wuddin' her choice."

"What?" Savannah was horrified. "They did it against her will?"

"Absolutely," Tammy assured her. "Her manager insisted, said an unwanted pregnancy would end her career. He wasn't going to let one night of her being stupid ruin all he'd done for her."

"What he'd done for himself is more like it," Ryan said.

"He set it up and forced her to go and even helped to hold her down when they did it."

Ethan put his hands over his eyes, as though trying to unsee what he had just heard.

Savannah reached over and placed her hand on his shoulder. "I'm sorry, sugar," she said. "This must be hard for you. It's hard for the rest of us, and we didn't even know her."

He rubbed his eyes with his fingers, then turned to her and said, "It's just that I remembered something she said one time when she'd had a bit too much to drink."

"About this?"

"Maybe. I asked her if she had children. She said two, a boy and a girl. When I asked her their names, she said the boy's name was Martin, but she wouldn't tell me the girl's name. She just said, 'She died.' I felt so bad for her. I could tell she was in a lot of pain when she said it. I just figured it was an older child. Not something like this."

"Forgive my ignorance," John said, "but could she have even known the gender of the fetus?"

"It would depend on how far along she was," Savannah told him.

"She was only a little over two months pregnant,"

Tammy said. "Savannah's right. She couldn't have known at that point. Certainly, not back then. In those days, nobody knew the child's gender until it was actually born."

"Then how did she . . . ?" Dirk asked.

Tammy shrugged. "From what I could tell, reading what she wrote, she just had a sense it was a girl. A very strong sense. Years later, she even described the child in the diary as having long, curly blond hair, pale skin, and light blue eyes. She wrote that her little girl loved strawberry jam, white kittens, and ballet. She said her daughter was funny and sweet and could dance and sing beautifully."

"How sad," Savannah said. "It sounds like Lucinda's lost pregnancy was a lost child to her in every sense of the word. She believed she knew her daughter intimately, as she would have known her had she been born."

"She was so young," Ryan said. "It would have been very difficult for her to raise her child on her own."

"She knew that," Tammy told him. "She says so in her diary. She was fully prepared to carry and deliver the baby, then give it up to a good family to raise. But she said her agent wouldn't let her do that either. He said the baby's father wouldn't allow it. Apparently, he was a celebrity of some sort, too, and had a reputation to protect. She mentions the father was there the night the procedure was done but was no comfort at all to her. Quite the contrary, in fact."

Savannah imagined Lucinda grieving for the child she had never known, then she thought of Geoffrey. "But she had a child at some point," she said, "and a grandchild. Or she wouldn't have a great-grandson."

"She did," Tammy said. "I checked some family tree records and found them. She had a son named Martin.

Must have been the one she told you about, Ethan. Martin died in his forties of alcoholism. Martin's only child was Jeffrey. He was killed in an automobile accident, driving drunk. Also in his forties. Geoffrey was a teenager at the time."

"Those must be some of the losses that Mary referred to, that Lucinda had suffered," Savannah observed. "Losing a son and a grandson, both in their primes, and to alcohol."

"Apparently, it runs in the family," Ethan said. "Though we never discussed it plainly, I have no doubt that Lucinda was an alcoholic. I believe a lot of her depression was rooted in that. Or vice versa. It's always hard to know which comes first with that disease."

They all sat in silence for a moment, letting the information sink in. Finally, Savannah said, "As tragic as all these things were, I'm not sure how losing her sons to alcoholism or an unwanted pregnancy and horrible termination about seventy-five years ago would have anything to do with her being murdered today. Her sons are gone. The participants in the abortion—her manager, the baby's father, whoever performed the procedure—are probably long dead by now."

"True," Dirk said. "Let's move along. What else was in the diary?"

Waycross looked down at his notes. "The other thing that seemed to upset Miss Lucinda somethin' awful was what happened between her an' her good friend, Miss Delores. She never did get over that neither. Was writin' about it up to the very last."

"What did she write?" Savannah asked.

"Mostly that she felt she'd done a terrible injustice to her friend." Waycross shrugged. "I wuddin' argue with the lady 'bout it. You could tell by what she wrote 'bout ol' Dino, he wuddin' worth warm spit."

"Then they weren't in love?"

"Not a bit. She just thought he had a wicked eye, and she was gettin' old and didn't get looked at that much anymore, so she crooked her finger, and he was on 'er like a duck on a June bug."

Dirk mulled that over for a moment. "A duck enjoying a bit of hanky-panky with a June bug, whatever the hell that is."

Savannah turned again to Ethan. "I hate to ask this, but was that sort of thing routine behavior for Lucinda?"

"What? Sleeping with men much younger than she was?"

"Something like that."

He thought it over for a minute. "I guess so. She didn't worry much about age. It wasn't an issue for her either direction, older or younger. I never saw anybody turn her down because she was older than they were. Men were pretty happy to be invited into Lucinda's boudoir." He winced and added, "Back when she had a proper bedroom, that is."

When a silence settled over the table, Ethan looked around, lifted his chin, and said, "Since nobody's going to ask, but apparently everyone wants to know—the answer is no. I guess she drew the line at a guy young enough to be her great-grandson. Either that or she just didn't take a shine to me."

Savannah looked him over and grinned. "The former, darlin'. I assure you."

"Yes!" Tammy said, far too enthusiastically.

"Absolutely. Without a doubt," Ryan and John agreed in unison.

Dirk rolled his eyes, "Oh, good grief. You people are shameless."

Savannah turned to Tammy and Waycross. "Was there anything else we need to know about in the diary? Like, did she mention if Delores Dinapoli threatened her?"

Tammy nodded. "If you call it a threat to tell somebody, if they don't stop what they're doing, you're going to rip off their arm and beat them to death with it."

Savannah thought it over for a moment. "Naw, parents down south use that threat on their kids all the time. It's just an affectionate, colorful . . . promise, of sorts."

"I read some of that stuff she wrote during that time, too," Waycross said. "I figure Miss Lucinda was a mite scared of her friend. I don't think Delores meant it the same way Granny did when she used to threaten us."

"Okay. I think I should go pay a visit to Delores Dinapoli," Savannah said. "I'll shake her tree and see if any ripe fruit falls."

"Sounds good," Dirk said. "Thanks."

Ryan raised a hand. "We just want you to know that we followed up this morning with our friend in the bureau. The trafficking guy. He said he was well aware of Geoffrey Faraday and the circles he used to travel in. He swears everybody but Geoffrey's still behind bars. Neither he nor anybody he spoke with on our behalf has gotten so much as a whiff of Geoffrey since he's been out."

"Darn," Savannah said.

"Yeah," Dirk added. "I was really hopin' to go after him."

"You can," Tammy told him. "In fact, you should."

"Oh yeah? Why?"

"Because I checked him out this morning, too, after I

uncrossed my eyes from reading that diary most of the night. I was able to go even deeper than before."

"You hacked into his bank accounts," Savannah said. She knew Tammy. Fortunately, she fought on the side of the angels. If she ever turned to the dark side, heaven help humanity.

Tammy giggled. "Let's just say I know more about him than I'll bet his fiancée does—or she'd probably leave him."

"Did you find anything good?" Savannah asked.

"Something intriguing and inexplicable."

"Let's hear it."

Tammy looked down at her electric tablet. "All of a sudden he's turning up with all sorts of expensive stuff. That suit, the watch, the cuff links, and of course, the Porsche. Not bad for a guy who, a month ago, didn't have two nickels to rub together. Meanwhile, his fiancée, who spent all her money on him, is now flat broke. I find that curious."

"Me too," Dirk said. "I'm going to put Jake on him, have him tail him for a few days, see who he's meeting where and when. Maybe we can at least find out what sort of nastiness he's up to this time."

"With any luck, it'll be something really bad," Savannah said. "It'd be so much fun to watch you arrest him."

"Ah-h-h . . . the stuff fantasies are made of."

Chapter 22

As Savannah drove to Delores Dinapoli's home in Malibu, she decided that being a private detective had to be the best job in the world. At that moment, the primary reason she thought so was the Southern California coastline.

Miles of beach that varied between smooth, golden, and sandy to rocky and strewn with tide pools, home to all sorts of exotic sea life. Then there were the palm trees that lined those beaches. The oleander bushes that lent a feminine softness to the borders of the otherwise soulless freeways. The crimson bougainvillea that draped itself over a multitude of manmade structures, lending those concrete and steel buildings their gentle beauty. Then there were Savannah's favorites, the wildflowers that grew in profusion on the hillsides, due to the extra heavy spring rains.

She especially loved the poppies. She couldn't think of another place in nature that particularly vivid shade of orange existed.

Yes, if being a PI meant she "had" to drive along the Pacific Coast Highway, smell the salt sea, admire the flowers and palms, all while passing the homes of the world's most beloved movie stars . . . oh, well, she'd find a way to suffer through somehow.

With clear skies and the sun shining brightly, the ocean sparkled as though it had been sprinkled with a million tiny crystals. The "diamonds" seemed to dance on the water as the tide brought them to the shore, where they appeared to melt into the sand.

If I were back in Georgia, she thought, *I'd be waiting tables at the Burger Igloo or doing the books at Butch's garage. There's nothing wrong with waitressing or working in a garage if that's what you want to do. But for me, this is better. Way, way better.*

She thought of how she'd told Brody that he would be rewarded for his courage with a better life.

Oh, how she hoped she could help him receive that reward. She wasn't sure she had ever met anyone, man, woman, or child, who was braver than that little boy.

He was just a kid and yet, she admired and respected him more than most adults she knew.

She was looking forward to going back home to him, once her business was completed.

Delores Dinapoli's home wasn't hard to find, like some of the estates tucked away in the hills to the east of the highway. Nor was it difficult to access, like the mansions with high, impenetrable fences and 24/7 manned security gates.

Her house was a simple gray Cape Cod affair situated

right on the edge of PCH. It looked like it would feel more comfortable on a beach in Maine than in an area where the majority of the homes were stucco with red tile roofs, like in San Carmelita and, farther up the coast, Santa Barbara.

As she pulled onto the gravel driveway, Savannah looked eagerly for any indication that someone was home. She hadn't called first. Years ago, she'd discovered that it was easier to tell a person, "No, I don't want to talk to you," on the phone than in person.

With that in mind, she had come to visit Delores Dinapoli unannounced, hoping she would be home and willing to be coerced into a conversation that she probably wouldn't want.

The first sign that she might be in luck was the late model SUV parked in front of the house. Its back door was open, and a woman was unloading tennis rackets and an oversized ball bag.

She recognized the woman as Delores Dinapoli from several pictures that Tammy had found on social media and sent to her.

She was tall, lean, and deeply tanned. Her blond hair was cropped short and she moved with a powerful, no-nonsense strength that might have made her appear less than feminine. But her grace more than made up for it.

She spotted Savannah right away, tossed the equipment back into the SUV, and waited for Savannah to park the Mustang.

Then she walked over to the car, peered at her with strange golden eyes, and said, "Hello. May I help you?"

"I certainly hope so, Mrs. Dinapoli. In fact, I'd say you might just be my last hope."

That was enough. She was invited inside.

* * *

Although Delores wasn't the warmest woman Savannah had ever met, she was friendly enough to invite her to sit down when she told her she was a private investigator.

Savannah suspected her hospitality was born of curiosity, if nothing else. Few people had a PI call on them, and they found it intriguing. Thankfully. Otherwise Savannah's job would have been much harder.

Delores offered her a seat on the sofa and a cold drink. Even though Savannah was about to float away from all the coffee and tea she'd already had that day, she accepted a soda. Experience had also taught her that some people were too polite to throw someone out of their house who was holding a beverage they had just given them.

Accepting a drink usually bought her the amount of time that it took her to consume it.

Savannah could sip a standard twelve-ounce can of soda for a minimum of fifty-seven minutes. She could also find out most of what she wanted to know in that time.

But once she had the security of the frosty drink in her hand, she stopped beating around the oleander bush and admitted to Delores Dinapoli the true reason for her visit.

She had a feeling the proverbial manure would hit the fan blades and become airborne.

She was right.

One mention of Lucinda's name and, as her southern, non-cussin' lady granny would say oh-so-delicately, "The pooh done flew."

"You've got a lot of nerve coming to my home to discuss something like that with me!" Delores shouted at her as she jumped to her feet and charged toward her, stopping only a few feet away from the sofa. "You get your rotten, stinkin' ass outta my house! Now!"

Apparently, Savannah thought, *Delores Dinapoli ain't a southern lady.*

But she *was* clearly enraged, and Savannah was surprised to realize how unsettling it was to be the subject of that rage.

Savannah even took a second to remind herself that her Beretta was in its holster, should she need it.

If she had been honest, she would have admitted that, even though she was twenty years younger and quite a few pounds heavier than the other woman, and trained in karate and standard police defense and offense tactics, she was a wee bit scared of Delores Dinapoli.

Go figure.

"It's truly not my intention to offend you, ma'am," she said, holding the soda in front of her and hoping the outraged woman was persnickety enough about her housekeeping to not attack her and risk having soda splash all over her furniture, rugs, floor, and silk accent pillows. "I just thought you might prefer to speak to me before you have to talk to the police. Maybe I can get you up to speed, before they come knocking on your door."

"I have no idea why you or they would knock on my door about anything having to do with Lucinda Faraday. She's been out of my life for years now. Good riddance too. The last thing in the world I want to do is talk to you, the cops, or anybody about *her.*"

"Do you know that she's dead?"

Delores stood still, completely void of expression, displaying one of the best poker faces Savannah had ever seen. Either she hadn't heard and wanted to hide her surprise, or she did know and wanted to conceal her feelings on the topic.

Finally, she whispered, "Yes."

"How did you find out . . . if you don't mind me asking, of course."

"I saw it on the news. Like almost everyone else, I suppose. Lucinda didn't have contact with many people. She'd lost almost everyone who ever meant anything to her."

"Including you, and I don't blame you," Savannah said softly.

She could tell Delores was taken aback by the gentle reply, but she quickly recovered herself and charged ahead. "If you can say that, then you must know the circumstances under which our friendship ended. Therefore, I'll tell you again. You have a lot of audacity coming here to talk to me about something as personal and painful as that."

"Actually, you said 'nerve' the first time, not 'audacity,' but you're absolutely right. I have a lot of both. As, I suspect, do you. I think a woman has to have more than her share to get by in this world, don't you?"

Again, Delores seemed shaken. Savannah could tell. Under different circumstances, Savannah believed Delores might have actually liked her. Kindred spirits, and all that.

As Savannah was waiting for Delores to decide whether to slug her or have a conversation with her, the cell phone in Savannah's jacket pocket began to play the frantic, annoying little tune she had chosen for Dirk.

"Don't worry. I won't answer it," she told Delores, who was still standing less than a yard away from her, glowering down at her. "This is too important for us to be interrupted."

The cell phone finally quit, but the two women still stared at each other, waiting.

Only a few seconds later, the phone began again. Two calls in a row, one right after the other. That was her and Dirk's code for: This is serious! Pick up!

"I'm sorry, Delores," she said, reaching inside her pocket. "Apparently, it's important. I'll only be a minute."

Before the other woman could reply, Savannah answered with, "Yes, Detective Sergeant Coulter. How can I help you?"

"Are you still intending to drop in on that Dinapoli gal?" he asked.

"No, sir, I'm in Malibu with a Mrs. Delores Dinapoli. How can I help you?"

"Oh, gotcha," he replied. "Well, watch yourself with her. She could be dangerous."

"Just a pleasant conversation about the case you and I are both working on. She's most cooperative."

"Yeah, I'll bet she is. I wanted you to know that Ryan and John just called me from the mansion. They found two boxes of letters in the heap. One's full of love letters from that gal's husband to Lucinda. Over-the-top gushy stuff. The second's stuffed with some of the nastiest threatening letters you'll ever read, and they're from that gal there."

"Yes, I told her you'll be wanting to question her. She'll be happy to speak with you, sir, I'm sure."

"Watch her close, Van. Anybody who'd even write the sick crap that's in those letters is nuts."

"I'm sorry, but I won't be able to do that, Detective.

Anything Ms. Dinapoli tells me is confidential. If you want to know anything about her and Ms. Faraday, you'll have to question her yourself."

"Yeah, yeah, yeah. Get outta there as quick as you can and call me the minute you're on the road."

"I'm sorry, Detective Coulter, but that's my position. Good-bye."

As soon as she replaced the phone in her pocket, Delores walked over to a chair and sat down. "Okay, what do you want to know?" she asked.

"Please tell me when you last communicated in any way with Ms. Faraday."

"It will be fifteen years ago on the tenth of June. That's when I told the woman I loved like a mother that she had broken my heart and shattered my life. That was the day when I lost the two most important people in my life— my husband and my best friend. I'm not likely to ever forget that day."

"No, I'm sure you won't. There is no pain quite like betrayal, and that has to be one of the worst kinds."

Delores studied her for a long time, then asked, "Has it happened to you?"

"Yes."

"A husband?"

"A fiancé."

"Did he do it with your best friend?"

"Three of them."

"Ouch."

"Yeah. He was stupid. Couldn't figure out how to close a zipper."

They both laughed. A little.

Delores picked up a pack of cigarettes from a nearby

table. She removed one and offered it to Savannah. When Savannah shook her head, Delores lit up, her fingers fumbling with the lighter.

Once she'd drawn several long drags, she asked, "Did you leave him?"

"Moved to the other side of the country. If I'd gone any farther, I'd have fallen into the ocean."

"I hear you."

"I gather you divorced yours."

"Naw." She released the smoke slowly from her nose.

"Oh?" Savannah couldn't hide her surprise. Delores didn't seem like a woman who would continue to cohabitate with an adulterous husband.

"He fell down a staircase. Broke his neck." She grinned. "Oh, darn."

Their eyes met, and a shiver ran through Savannah, colder than she could recall feeling in a long time.

"Oh. Wow," was all she could manage.

Delores's weird smile was as chilling as her strange gold eyes. "You asked when I last communicated with Lucinda, and I told you. Now, ask me when I last communicated with that worthless jackass of a great-grandson of hers."

Savannah felt her pulse rate jump. "Oo-kay. When did you last communicate with dear, darlin' Geoffrey?"

Again, the cold, creepy smirk. More smoke pouring out of her nostrils. "Yesterday."

Chapter 23

The instant Savannah pulled onto the Pacific Coast Highway, she used her hands-free car phone to call Dirk.

He answered with a breathless, "Are you outta there?"

"Yeah, safe and sound. But that woman is one creepy freak-o and a half. She's got me thinking she might've even murdered her own husband."

"We can check into that later. Did she kill Lucinda?"

"I'm honestly not sure. But she told me something you've just got to hear."

"Okay, lay it on me."

Savannah was so excited that she had to concentrate and remind herself that she was driving. The Pacific Coast Highway was beautiful, but it was dangerous, too. The sharp curves were fairly unforgiving, especially to someone who didn't travel it every day and hadn't memorized every twist and turn.

She drew a deep breath, held it, and slowly released it. Then she said, "Geoffrey Faraday is blackmailing Delores Dinapoli."

"Get outta here!"

"I'm not messing with you. That's what she told me. Showed me the e-mails and everything."

"What's he got on her?"

"What he's got is his great-grandmother's tell-all manuscript, the book that Mary told us about. The one she said Lucinda was working on for years. Her autobiography, including all the craziness back in the good old days."

"Let me guess," Dirk said. "There's a chapter in there on the Lucinda-Dino affair?"

She laughed. "Did I ever tell you that I married you because you're smart?"

She could hear the smile in his voice when he said, "You never mentioned it before. But I'm glad you finally came to that conclusion."

"Oh, that's not why I married you, darlin'. I just wondered if I ever told you that."

"Smart-ass. I want to hear more about this blackmail scheme of Geoffrey's. How did he contact her? How much did he ask for?"

"Like I said, with an e-mail. She showed it to me. He even scanned the pages of the chapter that talked about them. She let me read them. They weren't very complimentary to either Delores or Dino."

"In what ways?"

"Lucinda called Delores a frigid witch who neglected her husband, physically and emotionally, and she wrote something about Dino's dicky-doo being 'dinky' and 'stinky.'"

"O-o-o-o, brutal!"

"He wants half a million for the manuscript."

"Does she have any intention of paying him for it?"

"No way. I got the idea she's been called a frigid witch and worse a few times already and doesn't mind that much. I also have a feeling she pushed ol' Dino down a staircase and broke his neck, so I doubt that she cares if someone says she neglected him or if they denigrate his wiener."

She could almost hear the wheels in his head spinning, as hers had been for the last half hour.

"Okay," he said. "Here's the plan. I'm going over to Geoffrey's house—or should I say his mousy little fiancée's rental—and ask him what the hell he thinks he's doing."

"He'll deny it."

"Of course he will. But I can get a read on him, and I can shake him up, letting him know that I'm onto him."

"Sounds doable. Want company?"

"I want *you*. Always. Even if you don't think I'm smart."

"Oh, you misunderstood me. I think you're *brilliant*. But that's not why I married you."

She heard him chuckle and the deep sound went right through her. "Tell me why," he said, "my good looks, my charm, my impeccable table manners."

"Certainly not the latter."

"Then what?"

"Many reasons. Lawn maintenance. Cleo likes you. Granny adores you. You set the garbage cans out on the curb every Thursday."

"Gee, I can feel my head swelling by the minute."

"But mostly, I married you for your not-at-all-dinky, never-the-least-bit-stinky dicky-doo."

"Yay! I knew it!"

She ended the call and continued to maneuver the treacherous curves of the Pacific Coast Highway, still enjoying the beautiful view, still proud of herself for taking a chance and moving to California.

But mostly she was glad she had married Dirk—a guy who was so easy that one silly little joke could set his world right.

"Easy" was good. Almost as good as "peace."

Savannah and Dirk rendezvoused at a corner, a block away from Geoffrey and Brooklynn's house, then drove the rest of the way in the Buick.

When they got out and walked up the sidewalk, both were too excited to even speak.

At the door, he gave his customary Papa Bear knock.

Savannah could feel her heart pounding as they waited. As usual, under stressful circumstances, she found herself thinking the silliest things. Like: *Will Geoffrey be wearing a different amazing suit, or does he wear the other one all the time? Even to bed? Will Brooklynn have washed her hair yet? For cryin' out loud, stop it! What are you, the Queen of Stupid Questions?*

The moment the door opened, one of those questions was answered instantly.

No, poor Brooklynn hadn't washed her hair or changed out of her pink teddy bear pajamas.

Savannah couldn't help feeling sorry for her. Depression was a hideous disease, as evidenced by the woman standing in the doorway.

"Hello again," Dirk said with more congeniality than Savannah had expected. "Is Geoffrey at home?"

"No."

"Where is he?"

"At work."

Dirk gave Savannah a quick sideways look. "Where's *work*?" he asked.

"He has a job now. An important job, and he makes a lot of money."

Seeing that Dirk wasn't getting anywhere fast, Savannah decided to give it a try. "Have you ever been to this place where he works, Brooklynn?" she asked with as much patience as she could muster.

"We drove by it once. I didn't go in, but I saw it."

"Was there a sign on the building?"

"Yes."

"What did it say?"

"City Hall."

Again, Savannah and Dirk exchanged looks. Sure. Geoffrey Faraday, ex-con, was now working at San Carmelita's City Hall, performing some important job that paid megabucks. Enough to buy diamond-encrusted watches and top-of-the-line Porsches.

And if frogs had wings, Savannah thought, *they wouldn't bump their little butts when they hop.*

"May we come inside, Brooklynn?" Savannah asked. "We'd just like to talk to you for a minute. No big deal."

Brooklynn looked back over her shoulder at the living room behind her. "The place is kinda messy. The girl who comes in to clean forgot to come this week."

"Don't you just hate it when that happens?" Dirk said as he opened the screen door.

His body language said he was coming through, so she stepped back and allowed them to enter.

Once inside, Savannah could tell that Dirk was anxious to get down to serious business before Geoffrey appeared. Finding him gone was a stroke of luck that just might pay off handsomely.

Brooklynn started to clear the debris off the sofa, when Dirk said, "Oh, don't bother with that, ma'am. We're not gonna stay long if Geoffrey's not here. It's just that we need a certain item, and we think Geoffrey might have it. I was going to ask if I could borrow it from him."

"Oh, right. Hm-m-m." She glanced around and said, "If you tell me what it is, and I know where it is, maybe I could get it for you."

"Sure." Dirk brightened considerably. "It's a stack of papers. A manuscript. Does that ring a bell?"

She thought it over but looked confused. "Not really."

"It might be in a box," Savannah offered. "Or some kind of manila folder, or . . ."

"No. I haven't noticed anything like that lying around."

Dirk pasted on his sweetest, most benign smile. "Would you mind if I just looked around a bit? I wouldn't ask, but like I said, it's really important, and I'm super busy today. It'd be great if we don't have to wait until Geoffrey comes home."

Again, she glanced around at the clutter and looked embarrassed. "I don't mind if you look around," she said. "As long as you don't yell at me about the mess. Geoffrey always yells at me about the mess, but he never picks up anything himself. Just drops stuff wherever he wants and leaves it."

"Men!" Savannah said with a laugh that sounded fake even to her. "They'll leave their sunglasses in the toaster oven and their socks in the freezer if you don't watch them every second."

She shot a Get-on-With-It look at Dirk.

The legal renter, whose name was on the lease, had just given him permission to search the place.

This is no time to let moss grow on your backside, she thought, giving him a knowing nod toward the bedroom.

"If you can just find that manuscript," she told him, "we can get out of here and leave this poor woman alone. I'm sure she has other things to do than chat with us."

Brooklynn shrugged. "Not really. My show's coming on in half an hour, but until then, you're welcome to hang out and do whatever you need to do."

"Oh, then maybe I'll help Detective Coulter search, if that's okay with you," Savannah said.

"Sure. Whatever. Do what you gotta do."

Savannah turned to Dirk. "What the heck, Sarge. Let's do what we gotta do."

They both headed into the bedroom. No time to waste. The master of the house might come home at any moment, and for all they knew, the lady of the house might come to her senses.

Heaven forbid.

When Savannah and Dirk emerged from the bedroom Savannah was carrying a small silver laptop, and Dirk had a bright red leather satchel under his arm.

Brooklynn was lying on the laundry on the sofa, her feet up on its arm, watching a soap opera. She smiled when she saw them. "Oh, you found something! Is it what you were looking for? The manuscript?"

"Yes. It's here in this." Dirk held up the satchel.

"Oh, right! *That* thing! I didn't know what was in that, but Geoffrey brought it home the other day. I think it's new. He's been buying so much stuff lately. He likes nice things."

Instantly alert, Dirk said, "He brought this home the other day? Which other day, exactly?"

"Um . . ." She squinted her eyes, thinking. "It was the same day you came by here to tell us about poor Great-Grandma Lucinda's passing. He was gone for a while. When he got back home he had that with him. He took it into the bedroom. I didn't know there was a manuscript in it, or I would have told you about it. Where did you find it?"

"Between the headboard and the wall," Savannah told her.

"Really? What a weird place to put it. That Geoffrey!"

"Yes. That Geoffrey." Savannah tried to laugh with her, but it was all just too strange.

"We're leaving now," Dirk said, heading for the door, his prize under his arm.

"Tell him we said hi. That we're so proud he landed that important job at City Hall," Savannah added. "Maybe you can put some of that money he's making toward the wedding or a nice honeymoon."

Brooklynn smiled broadly and pranced across the room toward them, her hand held out. "That's done taken care of," she said. "The deed is done!"

It took Savannah a while to notice that there was a tiny, modest band next to the equally nondescript engagement ring. Not that there was anything wrong with inexpensive wedding sets, but a guy who wore a diamond-studded platinum watch and gold designer cuff links should have done better, in her humble opinion.

However, the bride seemed thrilled, so who was she to judge?

For some reason, Savannah recalled how many abused women had told her that the real mistreatment had begun right after they'd said, "I do." Sometimes, the first blows were struck on the actual honeymoon.

She looked down at the PC she was holding and was pretty sure it was Geoffrey's. It was a high-ticket model. Brooklynn wouldn't have owned anything so expensive.

She thought about how Geoffrey was going to react when he came home and realized they had come and taken his property without a warrant. If he found out Brooklynn had given Dirk permission to search . . .

Savannah handed the laptop to Dirk, reached into her purse, and pulled out one of her cards. When she handed it to the woman, she said, "Brooklynn, I hope you never need this. But if you ever find yourself in any trouble. Any kind of trouble. With anybody. Like maybe even Geoffrey. Promise me you'll call me. I can help you. Detective Coulter can help you, too, and we will. Okay?"

Brooklynn looked puzzled as she stared down at the card. Finally, she said, "Yeah. Okay. I don't think I'll need it."

"Just hide it away someplace where nobody but you will see it. Remember it's there, and don't be afraid to use it, any time, day or night. Got that?"

"Yeah, okay. Thanks."

"No, thank *you*. You have no idea how much help

you've been," Dirk said. He looked like he was about to break into song and dance at any moment.

Savannah decided to get him out of the house before he did.

Considering the hell the woman was going to catch for what she had done, it just didn't seem appropriate.

Chapter 24

"Lord have mercy! As a fan of romance novels, I've read a lot of steamy stuff in my day, but this here plumb takes the cake!" Savannah looked up from the pile of papers on her lap and over at her grandmother, who was sitting on the sofa, the other half of the manuscript on hers. Both wore surgical gloves.

From the expression on Granny's face, Savannah could only imagine what Gran's half of Lucinda Faraday's tell-all book contained.

Granny glanced up from her reading, held up a traffic-cop hand, and said, "Sh-h-h. Don't interrupt me. I just got to the good part. I mean, the bad part." She reconsidered for a moment. "No, the good part. Oh, mercy, I'm all twitterpated."

"I know! Here I thought y'all used to behave yourselves back in the old days. This stuff is worse than we ever—"

"Hush!"

Savannah giggled. "Okay. Sorry."

If the manuscript had been a published, bound hard-cover, she couldn't have convinced her grandmother to read a sentence of "such filth." But along with being a modest woman who guarded the sanctity of her eyes, mind, and soul, Granny Reid was a true detective, a card-carrying member of the Moonlight Magnolia Detective Agency.

When Dirk had left an hour before, his instructions were, "Get that thing read as quick as you can. I gotta know what's in it and who else Geoffrey Numb-Nuts might be blackmailing."

Savannah had made a huge pitcher of sweet tea, piled some cookies on a platter—Reid women needed fuel for their tasks—and she and Gran had settled down, each with a cat cuddled next to them, and applied themselves with a fervor.

Tammy sat at the rolltop desk in the corner, her daughter asleep in her lap, the computer on and ready to go. Every few minutes, Granny or Savannah would bark out a person, place, or thing for her to research. So far, she had studied the life histories of at least thirteen of Lucinda's lovers, with whom she had shared from one night up to a year.

All were well dead and unlikely to care, let alone kill her.

"Okay, Tams, how about this fella?" Savannah said a few minutes later, having found a story that was darker and more disturbing than the others. "A guy by the name of Jacob Stillman. I gather he was in his early forties in 1948."

Tammy turned eagerly to the desk computer. "Then his birth date would have been, let's say, 1900 to 1910. Got a location? Anywhere he might have lived?"

"Los Angeles."

"I'm on it."

Granny looked up from her pages. "That rings a bell."

"It does," Savannah said. "It sounds familiar to me, too. But I can't quite place it."

"What'd he do?"

"He and Lucinda spent some, um, quality time together when she was fifteen and he was forty-two."

"Jerk. Oughta had his tallywhacker tied in a knot."

Tammy added, "Around his neck."

They all had an instant mental vision of Lucinda's body and made a face. "Sorry," Tammy said. "My anti-child-molester zeal got the best of me there. Since I've become a mother, my live-and-let-live attitudes have flown out the window. I'm starting to sound more like you Georgia gals."

Savannah smiled and nodded, but she was barely listening, as her eyes skimmed the pages. "She was in love with him," she added. "Very much in love."

"Of course she was," Gran said with a sniff. "She was fifteen. You don't fall a smidgeon bit in love at that age. It's head over hiney or nothin'."

"What else?" Tammy asked, typing away at the keyboard and staring at the various Web pages popping up on the screen in rapid succession.

"He was the father of the baby that was aborted."

"Apparently, he didn't mind having sex with a minor,"

Tammy said, "but he wasn't ready to marry and raise a child with a teenager. Nice guy."

"He wasn't a nice guy, and not just for what he did to Lucinda," Savannah said, studying the papers in her hand. "He worked for Lucinda's manager, who was a gangster himself. Definite ties with organized crime."

"Back in those days," Granny added, "gangsters were the roughest ruffians around. They were shootin' the puddin' outta each other on a daily basis. They had the police and politicians and judges in their hip pockets. Them that weren't cops and governors and judges theirselves, that is."

"Lucinda writes that Stillman didn't want her to have the baby and give it up for adoption because he intended to be a judge when he grew up someday. Figured he could help out his mob buddies if he was in position to rule on cases against them."

"Of course he could," Tammy said. "That'd make him an extremely popular, and no doubt wealthy, fellow in that time and place."

"Nothin' like havin' a squad o' rich mobsters on your side back then," Gran agreed. "He'd have been set for life. Did he ever get to be a judge, heaven forbid?"

Tammy nodded. "He did. In 1949. Served for the next twenty-two years."

"That was twenty-two years of corruption and judicial misconduct, I'm sure," Savannah said.

"Oh, that's not all," Tammy said, sounding most excited. "That was the turning point for his particular branch of the Stillman family. They did quite well for themselves after that."

"In what way?" Savannah asked.

"Every way! He married into a wealthy family and had

two sons. One also served as a judge, the other built an extremely successful shipping company."

"Wait a minute! I got it!" Granny exclaimed, startling the sleeping Cleo curled beside her. "That nice-looking young man who wants to run for governor, Mr. Clifton J. Stillman. Wasn't his daddy a super-rich guy who made his money in shipping?"

Tammy gasped. "That's right! Clifton's on fire! They say he's the rising star of his party here in California. Some are saying he could be president someday! I've watched him debate a couple times, and he's brilliant. I think I heard him say his grandfather was a judge. That his family is all about public service and justice."

"Not to mention a bazillion bucks from shippin' and who knows what other skullduggery," Granny added.

Savannah listened with one ear, but she had reached a part of the manuscript that was so horrifying, she could hardly breathe. She read it as quickly as she could to the end.

Laying the pages down on her lap, she reached for her tea, her hand shaking. As she was taking a long drink, to wet her dry mouth, she heard Granny say, "Savannah girl? You okay, sugar?"

"Not really," she replied, "and when you hear this, you won't be either. I've gotta call Dirk."

Savannah, Dirk, and Granny sat at the kitchen table, while Tammy sat on the sofa, close enough to join in the conversation, as she nursed her daughter.

"Are you absolutely sure about all of this?" Dirk asked. "'Cause if I move on it with a guy like Stillman . . ."

"If Lucinda's manuscript is true, and it sure has the ring of authenticity to me, then it's true," Savannah told him. "That's the best guarantee I can give you."

"Run it past me one more time before I leave. If I'm gonna go rattle the cage of a guy who might be president someday, I gotta be well informed."

"Okay." Savannah drew a deep breath and began. "Lucinda got pregnant by this older guy, Jacob Stillman, who was in cahoots with the mob and wasn't the least bit interested in raising a baby with a kid."

"I got that much. Go on."

"Her manager and Stillman were mob buddies. The manager arranged to take Lucinda and Stillman out on a high-level mobster's yacht. They also invited a girlfriend of Lucinda's, named Belinda, along. Belinda was sixteen and she was also pregnant. The father of her baby was the mobster who owned the yacht."

"We didn't hear about Belinda in the diary," Tammy spoke up from the living room.

"No," Savannah said. "The tell-all is a lot more forthcoming than even her personal diary. Anyway, they told the girls that it was going to be a party, and they didn't bother to mention that they had also invited an abortionist. Not a real doctor, of course."

Dirk shook his head with disgust. "Of course not. A coat hanger, back alley kinda guy."

"Tragically, yes." Savannah took a long drink of her tea and realized that her thirst was from her nerves, not dehydration. No amount of liquid was going to wash away the terrible taste left behind by what she had read. "If you want all the gory details," she told Dirk, "you can read the manuscript. It's quite graphic. Very sad. But the upshot is: Both girls received abortions that neither of them wanted. Lucinda survived hers, obviously. Belinda did not. She was, I guess you would say, 'buried at sea.' Lucinda witnessed everything that happened to her friend, as well as suffered her own loss."

"Damn," Dirk said.

"Yes," Granny agreed. "That poor little Belinda, and no wonder Miss Lucinda was haunted by that night for the rest o' her days. Somethin' like that'd scar the mightiest of souls, to be sure."

Dirk sat back in his chair and crossed his arms over his chest. Savannah recognized the gesture all too well. He was guarding his heart.

Unfortunately, in a cop's world, if you had a heart at all, protecting it from the tragedies you witnessed every day was impossible.

"Okay," he said, "what else?"

"I don't know how true it is," Savannah continued, "but Lucinda wrote that some months later, Jacob Stillman had the nerve to actually blackmail the mobster who owned the yacht. He threatened to go to the cops about the murder if the mobster didn't use his influence to help Stillman get the judicial appointment he was after. I guess the mobster decided it would be handy to have a guy like that in his pocket. They formed a sort of sick, symbiotic, parasitic relationship, each feeding off the other. The mobster even invested in Stillman's son's shipping company, guaranteeing its success."

Dirk nodded thoughtfully. "So, we have this guy now, Clifton Jacob Stillman, the grandson, with his family's wealth and judicial experience—not to mention who knows how many unsavory connections—getting ready to run for governor of California. Nice."

"He might be," Tammy piped up from the living room.

"I like him. He seems to be a real man of the people with a lot of compassion."

"That's a rare commodity in the world of politics," Savannah said. "But maybe he doesn't know his family's history. Maybe he doesn't realize that their wealth and influence began that night on a yacht where a couple of girls had their babies stolen from them, and one lost her life."

Dirk stood, picked up his phone from the table, and shoved it into his pocket. Turning to Savannah, he said, "I'm off to Los Angeles to find out how much he knows and doesn't know. You want to come with me?"

She glanced at the clock. It was twelve-thirty. The drive to Los Angeles could easily take an hour, maybe more. Plus, who knew how much rigmarole they would have to go through to see a man as important and busy as Clifton J. Stillman?

"I don't think we could make it there and back before Brody gets out of school," she said. "I'd better stick around here."

She saw the disappointment in her husband's face. The same disappointment she felt at having to turn him down. There was nothing she wanted more than to be there and watch this interview. She owed it to Ethan if nothing else.

"Oh, for heaven's sake," Granny said. "Have y'all forgotten already that you have a built-in babysitter here, one that's more than willin' and eager to take that little guy off your hands?"

"But you'll have to pick him up from school and everything," Savannah replied.

Granny put the back of her hand to her forehead and feigned a dramatic faint. "Oh dear, oh dear, whatever shall I do? I've never picked up a child from school before, and it's a whole, what, two blocks away? I might get lost or plum wore out before I get there and back."

Savannah laughed. "Okay, okay. That's enough. I'll leave him in your extraordinarily competent hands, Gran."

"I'll probably just walk over with the Colonel and get him. Somethin' tells me Brody'll score points there at his new school by showin' off his four-footed friend."

"I think that's the best idea ever. Thank you, Granny."

"My pleasure, darlin'." Gran turned to Dirk. "Go to Los Angeles and talk to that Stillman man. I'll bet you dollars to doughnuts that weasel, Geoffrey, already has."

"We can hope," Dirk said. "Never hurts to hope."

As they headed for the door, Dirk stopped and looked back at the brown paper evidence bag on the kitchen table that held the manuscript. "You're absolutely sure," he asked Savannah, "that you and Granny are the only ones who touched that thing."

"Yes, and before you ask, we were wearing gloves the entire time."

"Good." He rushed over to the table and scooped up the bag. "After we get back from LA, I'll drop this over to the lab and make Eileen dust every single page for finger-prints."

Savannah gave him a *tsk-tsk*. "And you wonder why that gal's not a fan of yours?"

Chapter 25

Traffic was light on the way to Los Angeles, and Savannah and Dirk had no trouble at all finding Clifton J. Stillman's campaign headquarters. His operation was not being run from a shabby first-floor converted bodega in a tough part of town, like some politicians who claimed to be "for the people."

No, Clifton Stillman didn't bother to hide his wealth. His headquarters covered the entire fifty-third floor of one of the tallest buildings in downtown Los Angeles. Glass and steel, and an atrium four stories high with full-sized palm trees and a waterfall announced his wealth to anyone visiting the heart of his operation.

"I hear they have a penthouse suite in this place that would knock your socks off," Savannah told Dirk as they walked to the elevator bay and watched as herds of rich

Californians, dressed in their ultra-expensive pseudo-casual attire poured out of the various doors.

Savannah felt a little underdressed in her simple white cotton shirt and her linen slacks and jacket. She decided she should have at least worn heels instead of her trusty loafers.

As they stepped into an elevator, she looked Dirk over, taking in his standard uniform: faded jeans, Harley-Davidson T-shirt, bomber jacket, and scuffed running shoes.

He must really be embarrassed, she thought. But only briefly before remembering—he was Dirk.

He did fill out those jeans quite nicely, though she doubted that would impress Clifton Stillman as much as it did her.

She had always enjoyed walking behind Dirk, and since he walked twice as fast as she did, she frequently got the opportunity to savor the view.

It took a while for the elevator, fast and modern as it was, to get to the fifty-third floor. It wasn't a particularly pleasant trip, as neither she nor Dirk enjoyed elevators. Usually, they were alone when riding one, and they passed the time and reduced the tension by making out.

She supposed they could have followed their routine. Californians weren't known for being overly judgmental about those things. But with a dozen other people inside the tiny enclosure, riders constantly getting in and out and jostling for positions, she decided it would hardly be worth it.

She looked over at Dirk and saw he was grinning down at her. The twinkle in his eyes told her he was thinking the same thing.

He bent his head down to hers and whispered, "Thanks for the thought anyway."

She chuckled. "You too." Then she added for good measure, "Don't worry. This'll go okay."

"I know," he said with typical Dirk nonchalance.

Not for the first time, Savannah wished she could feel as confident about anything, even once in her life, as her husband did about almost everything.

How nice it would be not to have inherited the Reid Worry-All-The-Time and the Second-Guess-Yourself-Every-Dang-Chance-You-Get genes.

She would never know. She suspected those two anomalies made up 90 percent of her DNA.

Finally, they arrived at the appropriate floor and exited the elevator to find themselves in an expensive, elegant office foyer.

The design and furnishings were ultra-contemporary. A lot of industrial style cement, black leather sofas and chairs, a gas fireplace, and one of the biggest widescreen televisions she had ever seen. It was showing, predictably, Clifton J. Stillman giving a speech and looking quite gubernatorial, even presidential, doing so.

To their far right, behind a black and chrome desk, sat a beautiful young woman, impeccably dressed in a designer suit that even Geoffrey Faraday would probably approve.

They walked over to the desk, and Dirk took his badge from his jacket pocket.

Holding it out for her inspection, he said, "Good afternoon. I'm Detective Sergeant Dirk Coulter. I need to speak with Mr. Stillman."

Savannah couldn't help noticing that he had neglected to mention the fact that he was with the San Carmelita

Police Department. She didn't blame him. Nothing could be gained by drawing attention to the fact that you were from another jurisdiction.

The young woman smiled, showing a full set of perfect teeth. "Is Mr. Stillman expecting you? Do you have an appointment?" she asked.

"No, I don't," he admitted, "but—"

"Oh, what a shame," she said with a sympathetic shake of her perfectly coiffed head. "Mr. Stillman is extremely busy today and won't be able to see anyone without an appointment."

"I understand," Dirk said in a tone that suggested he was anything but understanding. "Ma'am, this is concerning a very serious matter, and I assure you that Mr. Stillman would want to know that I'm here."

The young woman looked both irritated and curious when she said, "May I ask what this is regarding?"

Dirk gave her a chilly smile and said, "Just tell him that it's about Lucinda."

"Lucinda?"

Savannah watched her closely to see if she appeared to recognize the name. If she did, she gave no sign of it.

"Yes," Dirk assured her. "Tell him it's critically important, and it's about Lucinda."

The receptionist picked up the phone, punched in a few numbers, and after a brief pause said, "I'm so sorry to bother you, Mr. Stillman, but there is a gentleman at the front desk, a Detective Coulter. He doesn't have an appointment, but he says he has a matter of critical importance to discuss with you. He says it has to do with Lucinda."

She listened briefly, and Savannah watched as the semi-smirk slid off her face, to be replaced by incredulity.

"Yes, sir," she said. "I'll send him back right away." Again, she listened for a few seconds, then replied, "Of course, Mr. Stillman. I'd be happy to escort the detective and his companion directly to your office."

She ended the call and walked around from behind the desk. Savannah could tell that it irked her a bit, but she pasted a smile on her face, gave a gracious wave of her hand, and said, "Follow me, please."

As Savannah and Dirk fell into step behind her, he turned to Savannah, gave her a wink, and whispered, "He knows."

She nodded vigorously, resisting the urge to giggle. "I know . . . that he knows. Cool."

The receptionist led them into the center of the action, and unlike the quiet reception area, this part of the campaign headquarters was abuzz with activity.

The enormous room was filled with busy, bustling people and the cacophony of phones ringing constantly with myriad ringtones. On the wall to the right were several televisions, most of which were tuned to news stations. One was showing the same speech as in the reception area.

Another wall was decorated with a large American flag, as well as a California flag and a gigantic calendar. All sorts of Post-its and notecards were stuck to its various squares. Some areas had lines drawn through them. *Perhaps when Mr. Stillman is out of town?* Savannah wondered.

On the third wall was the largest map she had ever seen. It was the state of California, showing all of the voting precincts. They were color coded in a way that made no sense to Savannah, but she assumed they were crucial to the campaign.

No one even looked their way as they followed the receptionist to the far end of the room. Savannah couldn't remember ever seeing so many people so busy.

She reminded herself to never work on a political campaign. It appeared to be the exact opposite of peace.

Finally, after what seemed like a major hike, they arrived at a glass-enclosed office in the very back of the room.

In an instant, Savannah recognized the man inside, sitting behind the desk. It was the handsome, dynamic, up-and-coming Clifton J. Stillman himself, in all his glory.

Although he didn't look particularly glorious when he glanced up and saw them walking toward him. In fact, he looked quite worried.

She took that as a good sign.

Anything but have this long trip turn out to be a fool's errand with her playing the major nitwit.

The fact that Stillman appeared bothered, rather than simply curious, told her that he knew exactly who Lucinda was.

At least, she could hope.

The receptionist started to knock on the door, but Stillman waved them inside.

The three of them entered. She announced Dirk, who then introduced Savannah, and Stillman gave the receptionist a dismissive nod.

At first, Savannah thought he wasn't even going to invite them to sit. Then, he seemed to decide a cooperative approach might be best.

"Would you like a cup of coffee, Ms. Reid, Detective?"

"I'll pass," Dirk said, plopping himself on a chair without waiting to be asked.

Savannah sat a bit more gracefully and said, "No, thank you."

Dirk pulled his badge from his pocket and quickly showed it to him. Again, he wanted to show his authority but not necessarily his jurisdiction.

But this time, he was dealing with a candidate with his sights on the White House, not a receptionist.

Clifton J. Stillman was a sharp cookie.

"You're with the San Carmelita Police Department?" he said, his intense gray eyes taking in every detail of their attire, sizing them up in an instant.

It made Savannah uncomfortable and reminded her that she and Dirk did the same to people every workday.

"Yes," Dirk replied. "How did you know that, sir?"

Savannah was sure Dirk hadn't given Stillman time to read any of the fine print on his shield. It was a good question. She could see the man struggle for a moment to come up with an answer. Her only question was: would he be honest?

Something about the way he sighed and dropped his shoulders, as though in defeat, suggested to Savannah that he had chosen to be truthful.

"A couple of days ago," he began, "I saw on the news that Lucinda Faraday had been found dead in her mansion, Qamar Damun, in Twin Oaks, which I believe is still part of San Carmelita. I assumed you're with the SCPD."

"You're right. I am," Dirk admitted. "I appreciate you taking time to talk to us."

Stillman turned his intense gaze on Savannah. "May I ask what your involvement in this case might be?"

She decided to be completely honest with him, too. It would only make things simpler for everyone.

"I'm a private detective, also from San Carmelita . . . and Detective Coulter's wife."

"You're helping your husband solve his case?"

"I'm trying, sir. I formerly served with the SCPD. We were partners, in fact. However, I'm investigating this murder on behalf of a client."

"Who?"

"I'm not at liberty to say, Mr. Stillman. Someone who was very fond of Ms. Faraday and wants to see her murderer brought to justice."

"Okay."

His brow furrowed with concentration, and she could tell he was evaluating everything they'd said, as well as their demeanor.

She could also tell he had a lot at stake. For all of his cool alpha male demeanor, she sensed he was highly stressed.

"Mr. Stillman," Dirk said, leaning forward in his chair, "could you tell me what personal knowledge you might have of Lucinda Faraday?"

Stillman sat back in his chair. Way back. He laced his fingers together over his belt buckle and said, "Before I heard about her murder, I knew very little. That she was a pretty lady, an old-time movie star, who did some sort of racy calendar shot back when she was still underage. Maybe in the forties?"

Savannah nodded. "Yes. When she was fifteen."

"That's disgusting," Stillman said.

"You don't know the half of it," Dirk added. "Or maybe you do."

Stillman just gave him a deadpan stare that said nothing.

Dirk returned the stare with his own, and as Savannah watched, she was glad she had never been on the receiving end of that.

Dirk was very good at glowering. He watched a lot of Clint Eastwood movies and practiced in front of the mirror.

He denied it, of course—all that rehearsing. But finally, his efforts paid off; Stillman caved first. "If you have questions for me, Detective," he said, "please ask them. I have a very tight schedule."

"Okay. We'll get right to it then," Dirk told him. "Do you know a guy named Geoffrey Faraday?"

Savannah saw and heard Stillman's sharp intake of breath. The question seemed to both surprise and maybe even frighten him.

It took too long for him to answer with, "I don't know him personally."

"Have you communicated with him in any way lately?"

Again, she watched Stillman wrestle with the decision: lie or tell the truth?

He held his hands up, almost as though he were surrendering, and said, "I have."

"Thank you. I appreciate you telling me the truth. We'll get along a lot better that way. Would you please tell me about that communication? I need details."

Stillman looked past them, through the glass at the people working in his giant war room. Several of them were staring at the office, as though trying to discern what was happening.

The floor-to-ceiling glass hid little.

Transparency may not always be the best policy, Savannah thought.

Stillman stood and walked around his desk. For a moment, she thought he was walking out on them. The expression on Dirk's face told her that he thought so, too.

But when Stillman got to the door, he turned his back to the glass.

At least his employees and volunteers couldn't see the distress on his face when he said, "Detective, I'm being blackmailed."

"By Geoffrey Faraday?" Dirk asked.

"Yes."

"With a tell-all manuscript?" Savannah asked.

"Yes. Apparently, Lucinda Faraday wrote one of those kiss-and-tell books before she died, and it included some stories about my grandfather that were . . . unflattering, at best."

"I know," Savannah said. "I've read them."

"Then perhaps you can understand why I'm upset. With me running for office, this is the last sort of publicity I need."

"I'm sure it is," Dirk said dryly.

"But the worst part, the most painful aspect of the whole sordid thing is that I loved and respected my grandfather. He was an old fellow and died when I was a kid, but I remember him as a loving, funny grandpa. He was a good man, who left the world a better place than he found it. He instilled that same conviction in my dad and in me. I'm devastated to hear about this other side of him."

Savannah couldn't help pitying the man. The pain in

his eyes convinced her that he was telling the truth. Whatever he might be lying about or faking, the hurt was all too real.

"When did Geoffrey Faraday contact you?" Dirk asked him.

"The same day that they found her body. Late that evening, actually." He sagged against the glass behind him, as though too exhausted to stand. "To be honest, if you hadn't come here, I think I would have contacted you anyway. I almost did this morning. It occurred to me that he might have actually been her killer. I know he's her great-grandson and all, but he wouldn't be the first sonuvabitch to murder someone in their own family."

"How did he communicate with you?" Savannah asked.

"An e-mail."

"Can we see it?" Dirk asked.

"Yes." Stillman took his phone from his pocket, found what he was looking for, and turned it around so they could see the screen. "That's the e-mail," he said, "and those are the pictures he attached. They're the pages of the manuscript that pertain to my granddad."

Savannah looked them over and told Dirk, "These are the same as the others. The threats are almost word for word. Just different pages, of course."

"Others?" Stillman asked, intensely curious. "What others?"

"Let's just say you aren't Geoffrey's only target," Dirk told him. "That tell-all book is bad news for more than just you and your family."

"The guy needs to be stopped," Stillman said.

Dirk handed his phone back to him. "I absolutely agree." He pulled a card from his pocket and handed it to

Stillman. "My e-mail is on there. Would you please forward those to me?"

"Sure. Anything else?"

Dirk stood, and Savannah did likewise.

"Yes. If you hear anything from him or anyone, or if you remember anything we haven't discussed here already, call me right away."

"Okay, I will. Thank you."

As they headed for the door, Stillman offered his hand. When they shook it, he said, "Detective, Ms. Reid, I'm torn. Do I pay him? I can't stand the idea of having this campaign destroyed before it's even begun. Too many people have worked too hard. So many will be hurt. My whole family devastated."

Savannah watched Dirk struggle with the answer for a long time and appear to come up with nothing.

She decided to step in and rescue him, even if she couldn't rescue Clifton J. Stillman. "No one can tell you what you should or shouldn't do, Mr. Stillman. You're the one whose future is on the line. If you decide to pay, be sure to let us know exactly what's going on and when. Maybe we can nab him in the process."

"Yeah," Dirk said. "Meanwhile, we'll keep workin' day and night to put the guy away. Then you won't have to worry about it at all."

Stillman looked sick—to his stomach and in his soul. "I hope you do, Detective, put him away, that is. But something like this—it's out there now or will be very soon. There's really no stopping it."

Chapter 26

As Dirk drove them home from Los Angeles, Savannah decided it was less stressful to call the office than concentrate on his city driving and flinch, gasp, and grab the arm rest every fifteen seconds.

Peaceful, it was not.

"Tell me something good," she told Tammy, when she got her on the phone.

"I thought *you'd* be the one with good news," Tammy replied. "You both seemed so hopeful when you left. Downright cheerful, and we both know a Cheerful Dirk sighting is a rare occurrence, indeed."

"We do have good news, actually. Stillman was pretty open with us, told us that Geoffrey's blackmailing him, the same way he did Delores Dinapoli. Showed us the e-mail and everything."

"Great, and by the way, I found a dozen or so versions,

like practice runs, of those blackmail letters and the pictures he took of the pages on the laptop that Dirk left here. I hope that'll be enough for Dirk to arrest him for blackmail while he's building the murder case."

"Good work, Tams. I'll tell him what you found. But he'll probably want to tie up a few loose ends, just to make the case as tight as he can. He'll drop me off at the house in a few minutes and then he's going to take Lucinda's manuscript to the lab for fingerprinting. Geoffrey's prints should be all over it, and that'll be another nail in his coffin."

"Good deal! This case is turning out to be fun!" Tammy sounded so positive, so bouncy, that Savannah could hardly stand it.

As always, Savannah had to balance her joy for her friend that she was so darned healthy with wanting to tie her down and take a transfusion of all that energy for herself.

"How's Mr. Brody?" Savannah asked. "Did Gran have any problem picking him up?"

"No. She took the Colonel with her when she picked him up, like she said. He was thrilled to death."

"I'll bet. What are they doing now?"

"I just took a peek out the utility room window. The three of them and Vanna, too, are in the backyard. Brody and the Colonel are running around on the grass while Granny squirts them with the water hose. Vanna's crawling, watching the circus and laughing. They're all in heaven."

"I'm sure they are. I'm sorry you have to work."

"I *love* to work. Tell Dirk-o that I checked out City Hall, and there's no way anybody there hired a dirtbag like Geoffrey Faraday. That can't be where he's making the money to buy all that expensive stuff, like he told his girlfriend. Like we ever thought it was, duh."

"He's not making it from his blackmailing career either," Savannah said. "Stillman hasn't paid him anything yet, and Delores told him to take a hike. I guess he'll have to find another line of work."

"Or keep doing whatever he's doing that's paying for those clothes and that car."

"Stay on that, would you, sugar? See what you can dredge up."

"Sure! I love it when you keep me busy."

"Thanks for everything, puddin' cat. We just passed the pier. See ya soon."

"Toodles."

As Dirk pulled up to the house to drop Savannah off, she felt a twinge of regret to be sending him off on his own.

"This isn't the way we usually do it," she said with the door half open and one foot on the ground.

He looked a little sad, too, as he leaned over to give her a second good-bye kiss. "I know. But as long as the kiddo's staying with us, we'll both have to put some time aside for him. You go play with him now, and I'll take him off your hands when I get home."

"Okay. Sounds like a plan."

"One more thing," he said, grabbing her arm. "Did you call the CPS gal today to see if they've found a foster home for him yet?"

"Um, no."

Savannah searched his face to see if he was angry. He looked more relieved.

"Good," he said. "Why don't we just leave her alone. Wait for her to call us. They get really busy there and—"

"Wouldn't want to bother them, make a nuisance of ourselves. They'll call us when they're ready. Until then . . ."

"Yeah, till then. Go have fun. You deserve it."

Savannah could hear Brody's squeals of delight and the Colonel's unearthly baying coming from the backyard, along with Granny's and Vanna's laughter. "Okay," she told Dirk, "I will. Thank you."

"Thank *you*, babe."

As she walked up the sidewalk to the front door, she turned to watch him drive away. She waved. He beeped the horn a couple of times. She smiled.

Marriage was turning out to be nicer than she'd thought it would be.

Once inside the house, Savannah headed straight for the desk in the corner of the living room, where Tammy was slaving away at the computer.

Savannah placed her hands on her friend's shoulders and gave her a quick rub. "Can I ask you for a favor, darlin'?" she asked, knowing the answer. Even without a massage, Tammy was always eager and ready to please.

Savannah was convinced that if the Chinese had a Tammy to help them build their Great Wall, it would have sprung up overnight.

"Could you get Mary Mahoney's phone number for me? I've misplaced it, and I'd like to make a quick call to her."

"Sure! No problem."

Savannah was sure it wouldn't be. Tammy Hart-Reid could tap into bank accounts and most government service records in less than ten minutes. A phone number, no challenge at all. Savannah would have bet she'd have the number before she got back from the utility room.

She passed the washer, dryer, and noticed the cats' filled water and food bowls. *Brody's doing*, she thought. At the window, she stopped and looked outside.

The scene was every bit as charming as Tammy had described. Only now, Granny was holding Vanna Rose in front of her and Vanna was doing the squirting with the hose gun. She had a pretty good aim for a toddler, and both boy and dog were completely drenched and utterly joyful.

"One phone call and I'll be joining you," Savannah whispered.

Then she heard Tammy shout from the other room, "I've got it, your phone number, that is!"

"Of course you do," she replied. "What would I do without you? What would I do without any of you?"

Savannah settled into her rose-print chintz chair to make the call to Mary. She knew she wouldn't be enjoying it long, but lately, she'd had to snatch "comfy chair" moments as often as she could. They were few and far between.

Mary answered after one ring. "Savannah! How's it going?"

"We're cautiously hopeful, ma'am. So far, so good. I called because I have a few quick questions for you."

"Okay. Let's hear them."

"First, I want to double check on something you told me earlier. Where did you say you last saw that tell-all manuscript that Lucinda was writing?"

"It was under her pillow, there where she was sleeping."

"Is that where she usually kept it?"

"For as long as I can remember, even when it was only a few pages, she'd tuck it under her pillow. I think she wanted to make sure no one saw it until she was ready to show it to the world."

"Okay. Can you remember exactly what day it disappeared?"

"No, I'm sorry. I know it wasn't long ago. Days ago, not weeks."

"Did you see it at any time after she died?"

"No. Definitely not."

"Okay, thank you. My next question is very important. To your knowledge, when was the last time Geoffrey was in the house? For any reason. Even for a moment."

"It's been a long, long time. Before he went away to prison. He and that fiancée of his—"

"His *wife* now, actually. They tied the knot."

"Foolish girl."

"I know."

"They came by here to try to talk Lucinda into paying for his bail and his attorney. She wouldn't. They stormed out in a huff. Well, the girl wasn't the sort to storm or huff anywhere. But he was furious."

"Was the house"—Savannah struggled to find the words—"in the condition it's in now?"

"Upstairs, but not downstairs. Lucinda entertained them in the parlor, and it was clean and neat at the time."

"Did they see the rest of the house, any of the messy part?"

"No. I'm sure they didn't. I was with them the whole time. They were only here about ten minutes."

"Okay, and now, one last question: Is there any chance Geoffrey has a key to the mansion or knows a way in?"

"A key? No. A way in? Sure. The place is falling apart. Right now, you could find at least a dozen places where you could walk or crawl in, if you wanted to. That's part of why I refuse to live inside the big house itself. That and the filth. At least, my apartment door has a sturdy lock on it and windows that lock. I wouldn't feel safe in there."

Savannah thought of Lucinda, strangled in that house only a few days ago, and stated the obvious. "You're absolutely right to be concerned. As it turns out, Qamar Damun isn't safe at all."

When Savannah had finished her call with Mary, she debated whether or not to phone Ethan, as well. She knew he was eager for any tidbit of information she could give him.

However, there were a little boy and a baby girl in the backyard who she knew would be delighted to have her join them, even for a few minutes. Not to mention a grandmother whose face always lit up at the sight of her.

A strange feeling was creeping over Savannah, trickling through her veins. Born of a dilemma she'd never faced before.

She felt torn. Guilty.

She hated it.

She took pride in the fact that she followed her grandmother's teaching: "Whatever your hand finds to do, do it with your might." She had lived by that and found satisfaction in doing so.

But now she didn't know what to do. How could she

give all of her might to being both a private investigator and a guardian for a child who needed her? There was only one of her, and when she had to juggle those two responsibilities, both would surely suffer.

She glanced over and saw that Tammy was watching her from the desk in the corner. "It's tough deciding between working or doing the 'mommy thing,' huh?" her friend said, with eyes that were kind and wise for her age.

Savannah nodded. "It sure is. How do you working mothers do this, handle both roles?"

"We don't. Nobody can," Tammy replied. "We do one at a time, back and forth. We try to find a balance."

"Every day?"

"Every hour. Sometimes every minute. It's really hard."

"How do you ever feel good about yourself? How do you take pride in having done a great job?"

"Do a *good* job. *Great* is overrated. Good is fine. You can take pride in the fact that you did your best. Be proud that you tried."

"Does it ever balance out?"

"Sometimes you can have all the balls in the air, going around and around and not dropping. But most of the time, like I said, you just try. That's enough."

Savannah thought again of her career, her number one reason for living most of the years of her life. She thought of Dirk, of how little he asked of her and how grateful he was for whatever she gave him. She thought of little Brody out there, having fun. But not as much as he'd be having if she would join him.

"I gave enough to my career for one day," she said. "I'm going outside to play."

"Good for you," Tammy said. "I'm proud of you."

"Balance, you say. Just try."

"You got it!"

Savannah disappeared upstairs and returned two minutes later, wearing her swimsuit top, a pair of shorts, and flip-flops. Her hair was pulled back and fastened with a barrette.

As she sailed through the living room, past the desk, Tammy yelled, "Whoopee! Look at 'er go! Teach those kids how to properly use a garden hose sprayer!"

"Let's just say, you won't need to give Vanna a bath tonight, not when Auntie Savannah's done with her!"

Savannah bounded out the back door, and, if she had entertained doubts before about how she should spend the next hour—work or play?—those concerns evaporated the instant she saw the love lights in those three precious people's eyes. Even the Colonel bayed joyously, ran to her, jumped up and put his big, muddy feet on her shoulders. The next second, she received the wettest kiss ever given to her by a male.

"Ew-w-w!" she yelled. "Dog slobber! Quick, gimme that hose! Quick!"

Considering the attitude of the crowd gathered in her backyard, she realized that was a poor choice of words as a jet of ice-cold water filled her left ear, then hit her full in the face.

"No! No! Oh! Dadgum!" she spewed and sputtered, trying to shield herself from what felt like a fireman's hose blasting away her eyebrows, nose, and ears. "That's *not* what I meant! Turn it off! Oh-h-h, when I get my hands on that hose, you are so-o-o gonna regret—There! Yeah! How do you like *that*!? Yeah, you'd better run. Run, you turkey butts! Run! Run! Run! A-ha-ha-ha!"

Chapter 27

Tammy had just set the table, and Savannah and Granny were dishing up the fried chicken, gravy, and potatoes, when Dirk walked through the back door.

"What happened out there?" he asked, pausing in the utility room to remove his muddy sneakers. "That backyard looks like somebody tried to fill the swimming pool and then realized we don't have one."

Savannah paused halfway to the table with the platter of chicken to give him a kiss. He looked at her stringy, damp hair and flushed cheeks. Then he glanced around the room and saw that everyone else, except Tammy, had the same wet, flushed appearance. Granny, Brody, and Vanna all looked like someone had dunked them in the ocean, then left them on the beach to dry in the noon sun.

"We had fun," Savannah said simply.

"Obviously," he said. Then he noticed the chicken and thoughts of anything else fled. "Oh, wow, does that ever look and smell good. I thought I was starving before, but now . . ."

He headed straight for the table, pulled out his chair, and plopped down on it. Picking up his knife and fork in his fists and pounding on the table, prison dining hall style, he said, "I want some grub! I want some grub!"

Brody scrambled onto his seat, grabbed his own flatware, and joined in the chant.

Savannah just gave her husband a sad look and shook her head.

"What?" he said. "I'm setting a bad example for the kid? You don't approve, and I don't get dessert?"

Brody giggled, but Savannah still wore the same grim expression.

"You're not sending me to bed without my supper, woman. I'm not kidding. It's been so long since I've eaten that I'm fartin' cobwebs."

"Dirk!" Granny shouted. But when she clamped her hand over her own mouth everyone could hear her giggling.

Brody nearly fell off his chair, helpless with laughter.

Savannah was still unmoved. She walked over to the kitchen counter, picked up a paper lunch sack, and handed it to him. "I knew you'd be starving," she said, "so I made this up for you."

"What is it?"

"Same as this," she said, waving her hand to indicate the table and its bounty.

"But why would you make me a sack lunch? I hadn't even come home and misbehaved yet."

Savannah turned to Tammy and said, "Go on. Tell him."

Tammy ran over to him and parked herself on a chair beside him. She produced her tablet and began to scroll down its screen. "Savannah told me to try to find out how Geoffrey's making all that money. He doesn't have a job and is failing miserably at blackmail."

"Okay. And I'm still hungry."

She shoved the tablet under his nose. "See this charcoal suit? Does that look like the one he was wearing?"

Dirk looked. "Yeah. I guess so."

She searched, then showed him the screen again. "Is that the diamond-encrusted platinum watch he had on?"

"Looks like it," he replied, moderately interested.

She displayed Exhibit C. "His gold cuff links, also with diamonds?"

Dirk sat up straight in his chair. "Yeah, I believe it is."

"And the coup de grace." She showed him a picture of the Porsche.

"Where did you get these pictures?" he demanded. "Come on! Stop playin' with me here. What's up?"

Tammy laughed. "You're about to apologize to me that you ever called me a bimbo, an airhead, a dumb blonde, a—"

"Hey, hold on! I never called you a dumb blonde. Savannah'd smack the crap outta me if I did. Now what have you got?"

"A luxury menswear shop was burglarized a week ago. A trio of three guys broke in and stole numerous high-end suits, including that charcoal one, jewelry, including that watch and those cuff links, the owner's laptop, which is sitting in there on the office desk. Yes, I'm sure. I checked the serial number against the one that was stolen. Then, the frosting on the cake . . . they took his Porsche. I have the VIN number if you'd like to make a comparison."

"Wow! Thank you! I will never call you a fluff head again."

She gave him a "yeah, right" look. "I've heard that before."

He sniffed. "Then you should probably take it with a grain of salt."

Savannah leaned over the table and patted Tammy's hand. "Go on, kiddo. Tell him the very best part."

"This cake has *two* frostings?" Dirk asked.

"The other two guys were caught."

"Did they rat him out?"

"Not yet. But they all three shared a cell together in prison."

Dirk leaped out of his chair and, without a word, raced out the back door.

A few seconds later, he ran back inside, his stocking feet soggy with mud. He grabbed his shoes off the floor, snatched the lunch bag out of Savannah's hand, and took off. Again.

Other than a ten-minute period, when Savannah snuck away to her bedroom to call Ethan and give him a quick catch-up, she had the privilege of enjoying what she found out later was commonly called a Family Movie Night.

She was astonished that it could be so much fun for the three of them—Granny, Brody, and herself—to lounge around in the living room, devour bowls full of home-made savory popcorn, washed down with root beer floats, and watch an old Disney classic together.

They allowed Brody to choose, since he was the most recently added guest, and he picked *Aladdin*, because as he put it, "That blue genie dude just cracks me up!" Though he did put one of Savannah's best accent pillows over his face and make mooing sounds during the romantic scenes, smearing popcorn oil on the pillow's silk cover in the process.

When the evening was finished, and both Granny and Brody were in bed, Savannah retreated to her upstairs sanctuary, the bathroom, and pampered herself with a luxury she hadn't enjoyed for days. Her ritual bubble bath.

Dressed in her fluffy white bathrobe, she took her latest romance novel, her phone, and clean undies and went into the room that she had decided long ago was the most peaceful place in the world.

Her world, anyway.

Running steaming hot water into the tub, she added a generous squirt of bubble bath scented with star jasmine.

Having pulled down the blinds, she lit several pink votive candles and set them, here and there, around the room. Then she flipped off the light.

Standing in the middle of the room, she took a moment to look around, as she had hundreds of times, and enjoy what she had done. Because she, alone, had created this lovely space.

It was as feminine and soft and dreamy as her life was hard and harsh and all too real at times. She felt like a woman within these walls, even after a day when she had wrestled a bad guy to the ground, blending her sweat and sometimes her blood with his.

The wallpaper with its tiny red and pink rosebuds, the mahogany wainscoting beneath it, the black and white ceramic tiles on the floor, the Victorian pedestal sink, and her favorite, the claw-foot tub, all drew her into a magic world that soothed all of her senses.

Even her taste buds were to be pampered. On a tiny china saucer sat two dark chocolate, raspberry-cream-centered truffles.

"Ah-h-h," she said. "You did good today, Savannah. Well, you tried. You did the best you could, and Tammy says we all get credit for that. So, enjoy."

She dropped the robe and lacy knickers on the floor and slipped slowly into the sparkling pile of bubbles. The water was hot, almost too hot, but that was exactly how she liked it.

She lay back in the suds and wondered why she didn't just insist on living here, 24/7. Never, never, ever to step out of that tub again.

She closed her eyes, drew a deep breath . . . and the phone rang.

"Damn it!"

She cursed herself for not turning off the phone, although she knew she never had and never would. She had too many people who loved her and might call her, desperately needing her help. She'd been a cop. She knew what could happen to perfectly innocent people out there. She could never allow herself to be truly "off duty."

She leaned as far as she could, trying to reach the phone, which she had left on top of the wicker hamper.

It was too far. She'd have to get out.

If that loved one in desperate need on the other end wasn't already dead, she was going to kill them.

Finally, she retrieved the cell phone and instantly melted when she saw the caller ID.

Alma Reid.

Savannah didn't want to admit that she played favorites with her siblings, but she did. Absolutely. Hands down. Waycross was her favorite between her two brothers, and sweet, gentle, smart, and funny little Alma was the only sister she liked.

She loved them all, of course. There was some rule book somewhere that said you had to. That you were a rotten person if you didn't.

But she actually *liked* Alma, too. She enjoyed her. She missed her.

"Hello, darlin'," she said into the phone as she settled back into the bubbles that were about half gone. "I'm so glad it's you. I've been missing you lately somethin' fierce. Even more than usual, that is."

"I've been missin' you a bunch, too," said the soft, gentle, southern voice, so like her own . . . when she was in a good mood and not irked at anyone.

"When are you going to come out for a nice California vacation? I'm working on a case now, and I've got some extra money. I'll pay your way."

"Actually, I was thinking of doing that. But you wouldn't need to pay my way. I've got some saved back."

"That's wonderful! Tell me when you're coming, and I'll bake a cake!"

"One of your German chocolate ones with the pecan and coconut frosting?"

"Any kind your little heart desires."

"Okay. How does next week sound?"

"Oh, don't toy with me, girl! Don't get my hopes up and—"

"I mean it. I'm so tired of living here in McGill. I miss you and Granny so much it hurts. You're my people. Well, you're the ones I like."

They shared a hearty laugh at their siblings' expense.

"You know I feel the same way," Savannah told her.

"Why don't you pack several suitcases and a few boxes, too, and spend a long, long time?"

"Do you mean, like, move there?"

"It's been done."

"You and Granny and Waycross are braver than I am."

"Hey, it's only change, and change won't kill you."

There was such a long silence on the other end that Savannah thought they might have been disconnected.

"You there, kiddo?" she asked.

"Yes. That's the problem. I'm here, and I'd much rather be there. With y'all, and the sunshine, and the beaches, and Disneyland."

Savannah felt as if her heart was overflowing. "Oh, honey," she said. "Do it! I'll help you any way I can."

"I know you would. I think about it all the time. But it's hard to leave everything you know. I've spent my whole life here."

"All the more reason to try something else for a change. If for any reason you find you don't like it, McGill ain't going anywhere. You can always go back. You've got nothing to lose and maybe a whole new life to gain."

"I'm going to!" she said. Savannah could tell by the joy and excitement in her voice that her sister had made her decision.

"Oh, darlin', that is wonderful! Wonderful! You have no idea how glad I am that you're doing this! Thank you!"

Suddenly, the bubbles in Savannah's tub sparkled more brightly and their jasmine scent was sweeter. She was pretty sure that if she bit into one of those truffles it would taste better than anything she had ever put in her mouth.

Happiness just did that to you.

Chapter 28

Savannah was never more contented with her lot in life than when she was in her kitchen, cooking good food for her loved ones. The only thing she enjoyed more was when she was in the backyard barbecuing for them.

So, that was exactly what she did the following evening.

All of her California family was present: Granny, Tammy, Waycross, and Vanna Rose. Ryan and John were there, as well as Ethan and little Freddy.

Savannah and Dirk had billed the occasion as an opportunity for everyone to get to know Brody better.

While that was true, the grown-ups were in a particularly festive mood for a reason they weren't sharing with the children.

Geoffrey Faraday was in jail! Not for murder, as they were still building that case. But Dirk had him dead to rights for blackmail, burglary, and grand theft auto. Considering his previous record, there was no doubt that Geoffrey Faraday would be incarcerated for a very long time. Unless, of course, they could nail him for first-degree murder, and then he would be going away forever.

Ryan and John had brought a set of horseshoes and were showing Brody how to play the game. Unfortunately, more than once, the Colonel had mistaken their intentions when throwing the horseshoes and had scampered after them, trying to pluck the heavy metal objects from the air.

"Don't do that, you fool hound dog," Brody yelled at him. "If you catch one of those things, you're going to knock your teeth out. You'll be the only bloodhound in town sportin' dentures."

Savannah had solved the problem by luring the dog over to the barbecue grill with tiny bits of the tri-tip she was cooking. After one bite, he had no interest in sinking his teeth into a horseshoe.

Dirk was tending the barbecue. Outdoor grilling was his only foray into the world of cooking, but he was getting better at it all the time. Although lately, he had decided it kept the meat moist if he poured some of the beer he was drinking over it from time to time.

Savannah decided to call it "basting" and hope her guests wouldn't object to eating food that had been splashed with one of Dirk's half-consumed beers.

When she saw Tammy staring at him as he performed the ritual, Savannah whispered, "The heat burns off any germs that might be on the meat. Don't you think?"

"Sure," said the ever cooperative and nonjudgmental Tammy. "You bet. But I'm a vegetarian. I wasn't going to eat it anyway, and I'm certainly not going to with Dirk-o spit on it."

Ethan was talking to Waycross, while Vanna and Freddy played on the grass nearby. Freddy found a dandelion that had escaped Savannah's scrutiny. He picked it and attempted to stick it in Vanna's bright red curls. Unfortunately, his little friend would have no part of it. She reached up, pulled the flower out, and promptly stuck it in her mouth.

Savannah saw Tammy give her a dirty look.

Shrugging, Savannah said, "What? I only put arsenic on the ones in the front yard, so what's your problem?"

"Very funny," Tammy said, reaching around Dirk to put one of her vegetarian burgers on the grill beside the tri-tip.

"Hey," he complained, "get that wanna-be burger off my grill. Only manly man stuff gets cooked here."

Tammy crinkled her nose at him. "Your manly man tri-tip *and* my veggie burger. That's what's going to be on your grill, and don't spill any of that spit-polluted beer on my burger."

"I don't spit in my beer! Who the hell do you think I am? I'll have you know I have perfect control over my saliva. It goes where I tell it to and when."

"He does," Savannah assured her. "I know. I've seen him spit on bugs in my garden before. He's surprisingly good at it."

Tammy rolled her eyes and walked away to join Waycross, Ethan, and the babies.

Dirk motioned for Savannah to come closer. He whispered in her ear, "Is it really a bad thing for me to pour my beer on the tri-tip? Or is that just her being persnickety?"

"She might have a point," Savannah said. "Why don't you open a new beer and just use it exclusively for the meat."

He thought about it for a minute, then said, "If there's anything left in that meat-only bottle, can I drink it when I'm done?"

"Of course, darlin'. When I bake a cake, I get to lick the beaters and the bowl. We cooks need a few perks for slaving over hot stoves."

As she walked away, she saw him head for the cooler and another beer, grinning all the way.

He was so easy.

But just as he was lifting the bottle out of the crushed ice, she heard his phone ring, and she knew who it was by the Alfred Hitchcock theme song ringtone.

She hurried over to him to see what Dr. Liu would have to say. This was the phone call they had been waiting for. The final nails in Geoffrey Faraday's coffin. He was a murderer, and they wanted to make sure he didn't just pay the price for burglary, blackmail, and car theft. That particular conviction was the only thing that would have satisfied Lucinda Faraday—murder in the first degree.

"Yes, Doctor," Savannah heard him say. "Whatcha got for me?"

He put the phone on speaker, so Savannah could hear the conversation, too.

"I have lab reports on Faraday. They show there was a drug in her system. Quite a lot of it."

Savannah said, "I'm here, too. What kind?"

"Hi, Savannah. It's a prescription strength sleeping pill, called dimazepin. It's one of the strongest ones, a controlled substance."

"How much had she taken?" Dirk asked.

"Ten times the amount it would have taken to kill her."

"Wow, then there's no way that was an accident," Savannah said.

"Absolutely not."

Savannah wondered about the strangling, which seemed like overkill if you had already given a woman ten lethal doses of medication.

"Why didn't he just let her die from the pills?" Dirk asked. "Why the strangling? Why the posing?"

"He was cruel," Savannah said. "He didn't want her to die peacefully or easily."

"I agree with Savannah," Liu said. "The pills were just so he could kill her more easily."

Savannah glanced around the yard and realized almost all of the adults were watching them, Ethan in particular. They had known that calls from Dr. Liu and the lab were imminent. She could tell they were waiting to hear, and at this point, she didn't know if this was good news or bad.

"I have another piece of information for you," the doctor continued.

"What's that?" Dirk asked.

"I heard from Eileen at the lab. She asked me to call you."

"Why didn't she call herself?"

"She isn't speaking to you. She's furious with you for sending over so many items for them to process. She says it'll take six months, and frankly, I don't know if she'll do ten percent of it."

Dirk mumbled something that sounded moderately obscene under his breath.

Savannah stepped in. "Did she at least take time to search the manuscript for fingerprints?"

"Yes. Apparently, that's what she's maddest about. Said it was a waste of time."

Savannah didn't want to hear that! "How?" she asked. "A nuisance I can understand, but a waste? Really?"

"She didn't find one print on it that belonged to your suspect, Geoffrey Faraday," Liu told him. "It was covered with prints. The victim's."

"Obviously," Dirk said. "She wrote it, so she would have handled every page."

"And one other person, which we thought is a bit strange."

"Who?" Savannah asked.

She waited for what felt like an eternity for Liu to say the words. Finally, she did. "The prints that were all over it, other than the victim's, belong to Brooklynn Marsh. Geoffrey's new wife."

The backyard barbecue had turned into an emergency meeting of the Moonlight Magnolia Detective Agency.

Savannah and Dirk quickly filled everyone in on the latest developments, especially the one about them having a brand-new number one suspect.

"Who woulda thought Miss Mousy had it in her?" Dirk said, shaking his head as they gathered around the picnic table beneath the arbor.

"I agree," Savannah said. "She didn't look like she'd be able to say 'Boo' to a goose."

"I always wondered about that southern phrase," Tammy observed. "Do you people down there go around scaring geese a lot?"

"You mean more than here or in Maine or North Dakota?" Savannah asked.

"Do you mind?" Dirk barked.

"Sorry." Savannah cleared her throat. "Hearing this new thing about the fingerprints on the manuscript, it makes sense. If I was engaged to a horse's rear end like Geoffrey, I'd be looking to get rid of him, too."

"Yes, and the woman invested years of her life with him," said John. "She'd be looking for some sort of pay-off."

Ryan added, "She bankrupted herself for him. Lost a career. She'd want major financial compensation of some sort, if she could manage it. Probably emotional payback, too."

Savannah glanced over at Brody and saw that he was trying to teach the two toddlers how to throw the horse-shoes. They seemed oblivious to the adult conversation taking place on the other side of the yard.

She was glad for that, at least.

Turning her attention back to the group, she said, "If it was a woman who killed Lucinda, it would make even more sense that she would drug her first. No struggle, less work that way."

"Is Brooklynn large and strong enough to carry Lucinda from the bed area to the place where I found her?" Ethan asked.

"Hm. I'm not sure about that." Savannah tried to recall the woman's basic build. It had been hard to tell under the baggy pajamas. "We'll have to think about that one."

"I'm still not sure why she got moved from her bed to there anyway," Dirk replied. "Doesn't make sense."

"Maybe I was wrong and the whole thing went down right there where the body was found." Savannah turned to Ethan. "You said that Lucinda liked her Irish whiskey."

He nodded. "A lot."

"Did she have a nightcap?"

"Every night without fail. Told me she'd never get to sleep without it."

"Tell me about that. If it was a nightly pleasure for her, she probably had some sort of ritual."

He nodded. "Yes. She did. She had a special cut-crystal glass. Short, wide, with red flashing around the top and a gold edge. Beautiful. She told me a lover gave it to her. She didn't say which one. I had the feeling it might have been her son's father. Anyway, it meant a lot to her. She always drank her nightly whiskey from that."

Savannah turned to Dirk. "Did the team find a glass like that at either the bed location or where her body was found?"

"No."

"Are you sure?"

"Yeah. A fancy glass like that would've stood out in all the ugly garbage. I'll check with the CSU team, but they were all showing me anything they thought was different or special. There was nothing like that found in either place."

Waycross had been sitting quietly, adding nothing to the conversation, stroking Colonel's glossy copper ears and keeping an eye on the children. But he turned to them and added, "If I wanted to put somebody to sleep, big time, and I knew they downed a glass of whiskey ever' night before they called it a day, I'd spike that whiskey. Then after I'd done the stranglin' thing, I'd been sure to get rid of that bottle and glass, 'cause they'd have a bit o' that poison in or on 'em. That's prob'ly why we didn't find 'em there. If that Brooklynn gal was the killer, she'd a took 'em with her."

Savannah mulled that over and thought it made perfect sense. She said to Ethan, "If that glass is half as pretty as you say it is, I don't think she'd throw it away, either."

"If she pulled this off," Tammy said, "on some level, I think she'd be feeling proud of herself. She'd want to keep it as a little souvenir, don't you think?"

One by one, the team members thought about it, then nodded.

"I'd keep it," John said.

"Me too," Waycross added.

"Even I probably would," Dirk admitted, "though it'd be stupid. You'd just kinda have to, to remind yourself of what you'd got away with."

A cold determination started to build in Savannah. She thought of the old woman whose life had been difficult already, taken from her by a young one whose only motive would have been greed, pure and simple.

She stood and turned to Dirk. "I don't like the fact that, if she did it, she's feeling proud of herself. I want to upset her apple cart, right and proper. Would you mind if I go have a little talk with Miss Brooklynn?"

"Not as long as you're wearin' a wire, and we're in the van right outside."

"Overly protective, are we?"

"We are that," Ryan said. "Especially where you're concerned."

"We're fond of you, love," John added. "In case you hadn't noticed."

"I've noticed," she said, feeling a blush coming on. "I appreciate it, too. Apparently, our Miss Mousy ain't as timid as we thought."

Chapter 29

When Dirk dropped Savannah off, a block from Brook-lynn's modest Spanish home, he said, "One more time."

She sighed, knowing the microphone John had hooked inside her collar was working fine. But Dirk was a worry-wart. At least where she was concerned.

That was endearing and occasionally annoying.

"Testing, testing. One, two, three, four, five, gonna skin that man alive . . . if he doesn't let me get out of this here vehicle and go do my job."

In her earpiece, she heard Ryan say, "Loud and clear, Dixie Darlin'. Go get her."

"They've got it," she told Dirk.

"Yeah, me too," he said, adjusting his own earpiece.

She leaned over, gave him a kiss for luck, and left him to listen and worry.

She knew, between the two of them, she had the easy part.

Crossing her fingers and saying a little prayer that their gal would be home, she hurried up the sidewalk and onto the little house's porch.

One more time, she ran the details of her plan through her mind. What she would say and when.

Yeah, like it matters, she thought. *No matter how prepared you think you are, the plan always flies out the window in the first ninety seconds.*

Savannah knocked on the door, and it took quite a while for it to open. When it did, she could hardly believe what she was seeing.

Standing there was Brooklynn Marsh-Faraday, but she was a totally different woman. Savannah was shocked by the transformation that a stylish outfit, makeup, and hairdo could make.

Brooklynn was wearing a figure-hugging dress, tights, and booties that showed she did, indeed, have a body and was quite physically fit. Her makeup was impeccable, accenting her slightly slanted eyes, and giving them a beautiful, exotic quality. Her hair was not only washed, but styled, full and glistening as it flowed over her shoulders to her waist.

Brooklynn was a knockout! Go figure!

"Wow," Savannah said. She almost added, "You clean up good," but changed it to, "You look very nice. Going somewhere?"

"Just hanging out," was the casual reply.

Savannah thought she smelled alcohol on her breath, but she couldn't be sure. If it was booze, the gal had started a bit early in the day.

Celebrating, perhaps?

"May I come in?" Savannah asked.

"Oh, yeah, sure."

Brooklynn opened the door and stepped back so she could enter.

The house had gone through a transformation, too, though not as drastic as the lady herself. Some of the clutter had been put away and the smell of urine was less. Apparently, some kitty had a newly cleaned litter box.

"What's up?" Brooklynn asked, motioning for Savannah to sit and doing the same herself.

"I've been thinking about you. Wondering if you're doing okay."

"Really?"

Savannah noticed that the look on her face wasn't one of appreciation, but suspicion.

Brooklynn gave her a not-so-pleasant smile and added, "How nice of you."

Savannah couldn't recall hearing the word "nice" spoken with such sarcastic coldness.

Yes, this was definitely not a mousy miss sitting in front of her. This gal was hard, cold, and for some reason, no longer trying to hide it.

Savannah took a deep breath and got a nearly dizzying, strong smell of alcohol.

Whiskey.

No doubt about it. A lot of it.

"I've been thinking it must be hard for you," Savannah continued, "what with Geoffrey being arrested. Again. You all alone here. Again. With you just a newlywed. I'm sure you were hoping for more."

"Much more," was the simple, blunt answer.

"Are you going to be okay?" Savannah asked. "Do you have anyone to support you during this—"

"I don't need support. I'm fine. But thank you for caring."

Again, with the sarcastic tone.

This Brooklynn was the exact opposite of the one who was sitting on the floor, weeping about never being able to repair their relationship with Great-Grandma.

Was the change in her personality due to drinking? Savannah wondered. Some people turned into someone else as soon as they downed alcohol.

But Savannah didn't think the strong stench was coming from Brooklynn. She only had a bit on her breath. This smell was so powerful, Savannah would have been reluctant to strike a match.

"I suppose you're wondering about the estate," Savannah said, venturing into dangerous territory.

"What's to wonder about?" Brooklynn said. "She died, he's going to jail, we're married, I don't have to worry about paying the bills anymore. Or his ridiculously high attorney bills."

"I see."

For just a second, the harsh exterior seemed to slip, and Savannah thought she saw a bit of fear flit across her face.

"You do?" she asked in a voice more like Timid Brooklynn.

"I think so. You put so much into this relationship. Years, money, time, effort. I can't imagine Geoffrey was easy to live with. If you wind up benefiting from his great-grandmother's passing, and he doesn't . . . oh, well."

A broad smile lit up Brooklynn's face. Apparently, it felt great to be so "understood."

"That's exactly what I was thinking," she said. "I'm sorry she died, but still, some good should come from it."

A slight breeze came through a nearby window and Savannah got another strong smell of whiskey.

Wow, that girl must've bathed in it this morning, she thought.

Then the breeze shifted slightly, and she realized the smell was coming from behind the sofa.

She flashed back on their first visit, when there had been a flurry of activity tossing things into the corner behind the furniture.

Slowly, Savannah stood, knelt on the couch, and looked behind it. "I'm sorry, darlin'," she said, "but I think you might've spilled something back here. Smells like vanilla flavoring or—"

That was when she saw it. An empty bottle of whiskey, a large, fresh puddle of the stuff on the floor, clothes, and other items that had been thrown there. But more importantly, there was a beautiful small crystal glass with ruby flashing along the top, finished off with a stripe of gold.

Savannah reached into her pocket, pulled out a surgical glove, and slipped it on. "Oh, lookie! What have we here?" she said, reaching down and retrieving the glass.

She held it up for Brooklynn to see. For the sake of the men waiting outside and listening, she said, "A lovely glass with a red top and gold trim. How nice! Where did you find something like this, Brooklynn?"

For a long time, the women stared at each other. Brooklynn wavered between a "mouse in a trap" look and her cold, nasty persona. In the end, the icy gal won.

"I think you know where I found it," she replied. "I think we both know what it means."

"We do." Savannah took a small brown paper bag

from inside her purse and slipped the glass inside it. "It means Geoffrey's done a lot of bad stuff. But it was you who drugged and strangled his granny and left her in that awful pose. You wrote those blackmail e-mails. All the while, you were framing Geoffrey for it, bringing that manuscript over here and giving us permission to search. Very smart, lady."

Brooklynn gave a slight nod. "That's an interesting theory you have there. Do go on."

"I can understand what you've got against Geoffrey. But how about Lucinda? You acted as if you liked her the other day."

"She was horrible to me. Treated me like dirt the first I met her. She looked me up and down, and she decided right then I wasn't good enough to be in her family. Knowing what a pig Geoffrey is, you can imagine how offended I was."

"Of course. He didn't deserve you."

"So true! Then after I found out what a mess she was living in over there, I knew she was crazy to pass judgment on me."

"That must have been when you went back to scope out the place and plan the murder."

"What?"

"The last time you were there as Lucinda's guest, you only went into the parlor, and it was still clean. If you saw the mess firsthand, it must've been when you went there uninvited. When you broke in, looked around, memorized those stupid tunnels, and planned how you were going to do it."

Brooklynn said nothing, but gave her a funny little smile, as though she was enjoying herself.

Savannah could tell she was aching to talk about it.

Killing another human being is the biggest event in most murderers' lives. They always want to share it. With somebody. Anybody. Especially someone who understands.

"I understand, you know," Savannah assured her. "I probably would have done the same thing."

"No, you wouldn't. You're a *nice* person."

Again, "nice" was spoken as though it was the most horrible word in the English language.

"I'm nice to people who deserve it. Not to people who don't. Geoffrey didn't deserve good things. His great-grandmother had a ton of nice things, but see what she did with them? You worked hard your whole life, and thanks to him getting in trouble and her not helping him, you lost it all. You deserved reimbursement, one way or another."

"Yes! That's exactly what I thought!"

"She wasn't going to live that much longer anyway."

"Exactly!"

"What good was her money doing her . . . her living there in a landfill."

"I know!"

"By knocking her out with the drugs first, she wouldn't even feel it."

"Well, that was the plan." Brooklynn slumped back in her chair, less jubilant than before. "It didn't work out the way I'd hoped."

"I hate it when that happens. You think you've got it all worked out and then . . ."

"One little thing."

"What went wrong? Looks to me like you covered your bases just fine."

"She passed out before she could show me where

the . . . where something was that I wanted. That was actually the reason for drugging her. I thought if she was woozy enough, I could tell her to give it to me or else, and she would. Plus, she wouldn't fight me so much. She took me to the area she said it was in, but then she passed out and wouldn't wake up."

"Oh, man! That must have been frustrating!"

"It was! But nobody's gonna find it . . . that thing . . . anyway in all that mess, so it all worked out okay."

"The will, you mean. The new one that leaves everything to Mary Mahoney."

Brooklynn looked dumbstruck. "You know about that, too?"

"Let's just say there are two very smart women in this room right now. One of whom is going to be very, very rich."

They shared a laugh, then Savannah said, "How did you get Geoffrey to marry you so fast? I mean, you needed to be married so you'd have the money once he went off to prison."

"That was the easy part. He heard those guys he'd done that burglary with had been arrested. He figured they'd be giving him up any minute. I told him if we were married, they couldn't make me testify against him. Now that was a stroke of luck. I think it was the Man Upstairs looking out for me, don't you?"

"Oh, I'm sure He's watching . . . and listening, too."

A small voice in her earpiece said, "Every word. We got it all."

"There's just one thing I can't figure out," Savannah continued.

"What's that?"

"If you gave Lucinda a fatal dose, and she'd already

passed out, she was dying anyway. Why the strangulation? Why the posing?"

"That nasty old bitch made me feel really bad when she put me down like she did. Even after I left her that day, I kept seeing the disgust in her eyes. I saw it constantly, from the time I woke up in the morning until I went to sleep. I saw her eyes, and I thought how I was going to get even with her. When I'd start feeling bad, I'd imagine what I was going to do to her someday and feel so much better."

"So, when the time came . . . ?"

"I couldn't just let her go to sleep. Nice people die that way. No, it had to be *my* way, exactly the way *I* imagined with the world seeing her for what she was—a dead, old, ugly slut."

"Okay. That's it."

Those were the code words for Dirk to come in and take over.

In seconds he'd come charging through the door, and that was a good thing. Because Savannah desperately needed to go outside and get some fresh air. She thought there was an excellent chance that she was going to be sick.

Chapter 30

Since their previous backyard celebration had been interrupted, the Moonlight Magnolia gang, friends and family, decided to throw another party a week later. Life was good. They had so many wonderful things to celebrate.

It was a group affair with everyone contributing in their own way. Dirk was manning the barbecue by popular demand. Several bottles of meat-dedicated, room temperature beer had been placed tactfully within his reach by the grill. Loathing a warm brew as he did, there was no chance he would be stealing sips from it.

Tammy brought trays of fresh fruit and vases of wildflowers, picked in the hills that morning. After Freddy stuck several of the blossoms in Vanna's curls, she decided to decorate the Colonel by putting daisies in his collar. Brody quickly intervened on behalf of his buddy, telling her, "I know you mean well, Miss Vanna, but no self-respectin' hound dog wears flowers. Not a *boy* hound, anyway."

The moment she turned away, Brody removed them and set them aside. He promised to help her decorate Cleo's and Diamante's collars later.

Waycross supplied the music. He rigged up a set of powerful car speakers to a battery, and, as self-appointed DJ, was playing tunes chosen for everyone present: Johnny Cash, classical, rock, and the staple—good ol' California beach songs from back in the day.

Ethan provided a tent, for those who might prefer to be out of the sun. Inside he had set up a high-tech audiovisual presentation that was a memorial to Lucinda, showing the highlights of her life. The positive ones. The sunshine and none of the darkness.

Mary Mahoney sat in the tent, watching, weeping, and laughing with the others who ventured inside to view. She had helped Ethan assemble the photos and videos into a loving remembrance of a colorful life, flawed as it was, lived with gusto and courage.

Savannah had prepared a dozen side dishes the night before. Everything from her signature potato salad to a few southern favorites, salads that contained nary a vegetable, but plenty of fruit-flavored gelatin, whipped topping, and marshmallows. She set them out on the table, knowing that Tammy would soon be pointing out the folly of calling something a "salad" that contained nothing but man-made chemicals.

Granny had insisted on doing the baking. Savannah suspected it was so she could enjoy the company of her favorite kitchen assistant, Alma. The younger Reid sister had arrived the day before, and Savannah felt her home was now complete, just having the dark-haired, blue-eyed, gentle beauty under her roof.

So much to celebrate!

As John passed around the trays of exquisite gourmet hors d'oeuvres from ReJuvene, Ryan offered some to the group standing around the grill. When he got to Savannah, he said, "I'm so happy to know your sister. She's absolutely delightful. Sort of a mini Savannah."

"No, she's her own person," Savannah said, though pleased with the compliment. "Younger."

"Well . . ." Ryan shrugged.

"She's a lot nicer, too," Savannah added.

"That's for sure," Dirk said, earning him a swat with a dish towel.

John walked up to them and said, "Is it me, or does there seem to be something going on between your little sister and our Ethan?"

He nodded toward the makeshift dance area where Waycross was playing a sweet love ballad. The only couple on the "floor" was Alma in her brightly flowered sundress, her hair in a graceful updo, slowly swaying to the music in the arms of Hollywood's leading man.

They were chatting away, giggling, lost in their own world.

Savannah could hardly believe her eyes when she saw Ethan rest his cheek on the top of Alma's head and close his eyes, a look of pure bliss on his face. To watch them, she could imagine they had been dancing together for years.

Could it be? Her little sister and Ethan Malloy?

"Holy cow!" she said. "Can you imagine? What if they . . . ?"

"Don't look now, but I think they already have," John said. "What a fine thing. She's just what he needs."

"She is?" Savannah thought of her sister, the darkness of their childhood, the poverty, her total lack of what the world would consider "sophistication."

"It would be wonderful, but they're so different," Savannah told him. "She's just a simple country girl, and he's a man of the world. She's a one-eighty-degree turn from Hollywood."

"That's exactly why he'd want her. Why he needs someone like her. She's real."

They watched as little Freddy walked up to the dancers, reached up, and tugged on the leg of his father's slacks.

Startled out of their reveries, Ethan and Alma looked down, saw the child, and laughed.

"Hey, are you cutting in on me, young man?" they heard Ethan say to his son as he picked him up in his arms. "You want to dance with my girl?"

As though understanding exactly what his father meant, Freddy held his arms out wide to Alma.

She laughed and eagerly took him, placed their arms and hands in the appropriate dancing positions, and waltzed him across the lawn.

As everyone cheered, Ethan threw his hands up in surrender and walked over to join them by the grill. "Did you see that?! I change that kid's dirty diapers, and he goes and steals my girl!"

Something about the way he'd said "my girl" caused Savannah's heart to soar. John was right. She had introduced Ethan to her sister three hours ago, and he was already calling her his girl.

She glanced over to the dessert table to see if Granny was watching and saw that she was taking it all in and grinning broadly. When the two women's eyes met, Gran laughed, put her hands together as though in supplicating prayer, then raised them, palms up, to the heavens, as if giving praise.

Savannah laughed. For years, Gran had been praying for a good man for her little Alma. If there was one thing Savannah knew, it was that sooner or later, the good Lord always answered Granny's prayers. Savannah suspected it was because she wouldn't quit until she plumb wore Him down.

Ethan reached over and took hold of Savannah's elbow. "Excuse me," he said. "I don't want to take you away from your hostess duties, but could I have a word with you?"

"Sure."

She led him over to a bench behind the vegetable garden, farther away from Waycross's speakers and all the gabbing going on around the food area.

As they sat down on the bench, she saw him cast a couple of looks at Alma and Freddy, who were still enjoying their waltz. They had been joined by Brody and Vanna and, considering that the toddler had just learned to walk, Brody was doing a pretty good job of showing her how to sway back and forth, standing on one chubby baby foot, then the other.

"I hope somebody's getting that on video," she said. "It's about the sweetest thing I've seen in a long time."

"It certainly is," he said. But Ethan wasn't watching Brody and Vanna. He was enjoying the sight of his son and the pretty girl who was twirling him around and around, making him squeal with joy.

Ethan seemed to make an effort to pull himself back to the business at hand. He shook his head, reached into his pocket, and pulled out a check. He took Savannah's hand, opened it, and placed it in her palm.

"This is for you," he said. "Don't even start to make a fuss because—"

She glanced down at the sum and gasped. "No way! You already paid me! I got the bank transfer three days ago!"

"This is a bonus, and that is the fuss I just warned you not to make."

"But it's too much, really," she said, trying to shove it into his tightly closed fist. "I can't possibly take it."

"Well, I'm not taking it back, so you're stuck with it." He gave her a warm, brotherly look and said, "Savannah, please let me do this for you. For your family. You do so much for others. It would make me so happy if you'd take this money and spend it on something special. Maybe something you've wanted for a long time but couldn't . . . you know."

"Afford?"

"Yeah. That. Isn't there something you'd really like to have for yourself, or someone else you love?"

Savannah looked across the yard at the people who mattered most to her in her life. Such good people. So deserving. So content with so little.

"There is one," she whispered.

"Good." He smiled his big famous breathtaking smile. "I'm so glad. Thank you!"

"No, thank you!" She leaned over and kissed his cheek.

She saw him cast yet another lovesick look over at Alma and Freddy, who had ended their dance and were clapping along with everyone who was watching them. "Wait a minute," she said. "This isn't a bribe . . . so that I'll put in a good word for you with my sister, is it?"

His eyes followed Alma as she led Freddy over to Tammy's fruit table and gave him a chocolate-dipped strawberry. "No," he said softly and quite seriously. "That's a situation I hope I can handle all by myself."

"I think you can, too, big boy."

"Yeah?" He looked so hopeful, like a little kid on Christmas Eve.

"Oh yeah. I know her. I know you. Go for it!"

The next thing she knew, she was sitting alone on the bench, and he was headed for the fruit table.

"Hm," she said to herself. "Reckon he's got a powerful hankering for a chocolate strawberry!"

Savannah lingered on the bench long enough to make a telephone call, collect some information, and solidify her plans. Then she strolled over to the magnolia tree, where Granny was sitting in a chaise, enjoying the shade and a glass of lemonade. The Colonel lay beside her chair, snoring as she stroked his back.

She raised her legs, vacating a seat for Savannah on the foot end of the chaise.

Savannah sat down and pointed to the hound. "He's worn to a frazzle from all this socializing with energetic kiddos."

"It's good for 'im. It's good for all of us. Kids keep ya young."

"Looking at you, I believe that. We were your fountain of youth."

"You and Alma and Waycross were. The rest . . ."

They laughed.

Savannah reached over, took her grandmother's hand,

and folded it into hers. "I've got some good news to tell you," she said.

"Oh, I done heard about how Mary found that will, right where you told her, where that lady's body was."

"Yes, that's good news, but—"

"I know she might sell the mansion to Ryan and John, too. They asked her, and she said she'd think about it. That she prob'ly would, 'cause it wouldn't be the same for her if Miss Lucinda ain't there. Plus, she don't think it's good for her health, bein' there."

"I hadn't heard! How wonderful! Can you imagine what Ryan and John could do with that place, with all their good taste and sophistication! It would be glorious!"

"Once they got all the junk out."

"Well, yes. There's that. But neither of those things are my good news."

"Oh, I know. Waycross and Tammy done invited Alma to stay at their house till she finds a place of her own. Your house's about full to the brim."

"I don't mind one bit and neither does Dirk. But that's not my news."

"I'm plumb outta ideas. What is it?"

Savannah looked down at the hand in hers and remembered when it had far fewer lines. When its veins had not been purple but had been smooth. When there were no age spots or misshapen knuckles.

She thought of all that hand had accomplished in its eighty-plus years. All the diapers it had changed, noses it had wiped, wounds it had tended, backs it had patted, troubled heads it had soothed, meals it had cooked, and broken things it had mended. Including hearts.

She wouldn't have changed one thing about that hand, lines, veins, or spots. Or the woman who owned it.

"I was just given a gift," Savannah began. "A very special gift that I didn't particularly deserve and certainly wasn't expecting."

"That's wonderful, child! I'm happy for you!"

"The person who gave it to me told me to use it to do something good for my family. Something I've wanted to do for a long time."

"Really! Bless their hearts! Although I'm sure you deserved it. You're my Savannah girl, and you deserve more than this whole world could give you."

"So do you, Granny. That's why I'm so happy to give you my good news."

"What's that, child?"

"I just made a phone call to that beautiful mobile home park down on the beach."

"The one that's right on the water?"

"Yes. The one that I know you've had your eye on ever since you moved here."

"Oh, sugar." She chuckled and squeezed Savannah's hand. "That's just a daydream for me. One o' them fantasies you play around with in your head that you know ain't never really gonna happen. It's just nice to think about. Livin' right there by the water, where all you gotta do is walk out your door and there's the Pacific Ocean! Feelin' them fresh breezes all day and all night. It's just a dream."

"But we Reid girls believe that dreams can come true."

"Sure, we do. Just look at us, livin' here in California and—"

"In a rusty trailer that's parked among a bunch of ya-hoos making meth and turning tricks and who knows what else."

"I'm contented. Nobody's gonna bother me. I got the

good Lord watchin' out for me, and if He ever dozes off on the job I got the Colonel and a twelve-gauge shotgun full o' rock salt."

"That's all well and good. I'm glad you're contented with what you have. But I want you to have more than living in Dirk's old rusty trailer. I want you to live in a nice mobile home in that wonderful park. I want you to walk barefoot on the beach every day, just like you've dreamed, for the rest of your life and watch every sunset and soak up as much of that sunlight and enjoy as many of those breezes as you can."

Tears filled Gran's eyes as she clung to Savannah's hand. "Granddaughter," she said. "I know you mean well, and I love you for it. But I won't go into debt at my age, and I refuse to let you either. There's no way we could—"

"We can. We will. Pay cash, that is."

Granny gasped. "That was the gift you got? Enough money to buy a mobile home and a space in a place like that?"

"Yes, and we'll furnish it any way you like. I called the park, and they have three units for sale. Would you like to go with me tomorrow and pick one out?"

Granny didn't answer. She couldn't. She was blubbering far too hard to speak as she grabbed her granddaughter and folded her into a breath-robbing hug.

Savannah happened to glance across the lawn, and who did she see watching their exchange but Ethan. Of course, he couldn't know what his gift had bought, but he knew who had received it, and he obviously approved.

He smiled, nodded, and threw her a kiss.

She reached up in the air, "caught" it, and held it to her heart. Where it would remain. Forever.

Chapter 31

As Savannah stood at the picnic table, scooping left-overs into plastic containers and sealing others in zip bags, she remembered one of the reasons why she loved her younger sister so much.

Alma helped with after-dinner cleanup.

"If you'll toss me one of those bigger bags, I'll stick the leftover corn on the cobs in it," Alma said from the other end of the table.

Savannah slid the box of bags down to her and said, "This brings back memories, doesn't it? All those dishes I washed. All those pans you dried?"

"It sure does." Alma smiled across the table at Savannah with eyes the same cobalt blue as her own. "I can't say I enjoyed it all that much at the time. Mostly because I was frettin' about the fact that the others weren't lending a hand. But now that I look back on those evenings, I wouldn't give them up for anything."

"Me either. But only because of you. You actually managed to make kitchen cleanup fun."

"You too. When we were little, we blew bubbles at each other. Then when we got older, we talked about boys. Told each other our secrets. That was always fun."

Savannah glanced around to make sure no one was listening. "Speaking of boys, I couldn't help noticing that you and Ethan seem to be getting along well."

Instantly, Alma's eyes twinkled even brighter. "Oh, we are, Savannah. I knew he was handsome, of course, and a great actor, but I had no idea he was so nice."

"I'd say he's even nicer than he is handsome, and that's saying something. It looked like you were enjoying each other's company."

"We were! The dancing was just . . . Oh, wow, Savannah. His little boy is a sweetie, too. We took to each other right away."

"I could see that. I'm excited for you, Alma. You've barely arrived in California, and you're already fitting right in."

"Thank you for telling me to come. I don't think I would've had the courage otherwise."

"*You?* Lacking in courage?" Savannah shook her head. "Oh, Alma. Do you remember that time when I had gone out with Granny, and you younger kids were home all alone, and Cordele set the house on fire?"

"I'm not likely to forget that. Ever." She shuddered. "It was the scariest thing I ever went through."

"I'm sure it was. But you got all the rest of the young'uns outside and put them under the old tree in the front yard, like Granny told you to do if there was an emergency like that."

"The worst part was when I couldn't find Jesup. Momma hadn't put her to bed before she left for the tavern. I finally found her laying on some dirty laundry in the bathtub."

"Yeah, Shirley wasn't much of a tuckin' in kinda mom."

"I didn't think I was going to get us out of there alive. I kept thinking Jesup's gonna die, and she's only six years old! It's gonna be all over for her before she even gets started!"

Savannah pictured the sweet little girl with the bright blue eyes and dark hair, who had dragged her sister to safety that night with no concern for her own. "Yes, Jesup was only six, just starting out. But do you know how old *you* were at the time, darlin'?"

She could tell by the way Alma stopped and considered it that she'd never given it any thought. "I'm two years older than Jes, so I must have been eight."

"You were just starting out yourself."

"When you put it like that, I reckon I was."

"But you got her out. The firemen were so impressed that you were able to carry her like you did through all that smoke and heat."

Savannah stepped closer to her sister, wrapped her arms around her, and drew her close to her heart. "If you had enough courage to risk your life and save another at the age of eight, sugar, you could move mountains now. There's nothing you can't do!"

"Thank you, Savannah. I love you. Always have."

"Same here, sweetpea. Same here. Now, let's go grab

some more of those amazing cream cheese swirl brownies you made before that new fella of yours makes every one of them disappear!"

After a few more brownies, after a few more dances, and after saying good night to Mary, Ryan, and John, Waycross the DJ announced that he was about to play the last song of the evening.

Ethan just about overturned the picnic table, jumping up and running over to ask Alma for the pleasure.

On the other side of the table, sitting next to Savannah, Dirk snickered. "Man, that guy's a goner."

"He is, isn't he?"

They watched as Ethan and Alma practically ran to the dance area and melted into each other's arms.

"They'd better watch out or Granny'll be after them," Dirk said.

"I know. I don't think you could slide a potato chip between them right now." She watched a bit longer, then said, "I know women do, but do men ever fall in love that quickly? Love at first sight, and all that?"

"I did. But it might need to be a Reid woman."

"Aw, the perfect answer."

"Wanna go see if anybody can wedge a chip between us?"

"Sure! We'll show the kids how it's done."

Fortunately, the last song of the night was a waltz, so they were able to show off their Fred and Ginger routine.

One of the nicest surprises Savannah had discovered about her husband was that he had a passion for ballroom dancing. Even less predictable, he was actually good at it.

He pulled her into his arms and they began to glide, turn, and slide across the grass, using the full expanse of the lawn.

"Hey, we haven't forgotten how," she said.

"Never. But I think we should do this more often, just to make sure we don't."

After a few more turns, he bent his head down to hers and said, "I was going to tell you this later, but now's as good a time as any."

"What's that?"

"The phone call we've been waiting for, the one about our foster parent status for that mini ruffian we've been feeding and watering . . ."

"Yes?" she asked, her heart in her throat.

"It came through about an hour ago. I was inside the house, taking a leak upstairs, and I thought I heard the phone ringing, but I wasn't sure so—"

"Are you gonna tell me what they said, or am I gonna have to slap you nekkid and hide your clothes?"

"Yes."

"What? Yes? You're gonna tell me?"

"Yes."

"You are living dangerously, boy."

"They said *yes*. That CPS gal rushed the paperwork through, and the state of California has declared that me and you are able and fit foster parents. Officially. Done deal."

"Oh, Dirk!" She stopped dancing in midstride, and if he hadn't caught her, she would have fallen. Then she burst into tears.

He laughed, but when she continued to cry, he got concerned. "Um, you're happy about this, right?"

"Yes!"

"Just asking, 'cause you Reid women cry when you're mad, sad, or happy."

"We've been told that before."

"Sometimes, it's really hard to tell."

"Sh-h-h. Don't ruin the moment."

He grabbed her around the waist, picked her up off her feet, and swung her around several times.

"How was that?" he asked, setting her down.

"Much better. Thank you!" She turned and glanced around the yard, looking for Brody. Finally, she spotted him. He was lying on the grass near the rose garden, his head on the Colonel's shoulder. Both were sound asleep, obviously exhausted from the day's activities.

She started to cry again. She couldn't help it. Her heart was overflowing with happiness, and it was streaming from her eyes. Looking up at Dirk she said, "Then we can really keep him? At least for a while?"

"I asked about that. The CPS gal told me that his mom wants nothing to do with him, said it's his fault that she got nabbed leaving the drug house, and if it wasn't for him, she wouldn't've been charged with felony child abuse."

"What? I guess he whipped himself with that belt and burned his own butt with her cigarettes."

"Believe it or not, that's her defense."

"She's mean *and* crazy. She'll be going away for a long, long time."

"No kidding. So, I asked the CPS woman if she thought there was a chance, even a small chance in hell, that we might be able to actually adopt him."

"Adopt?" The very word sent a thrill through her that

nearly caused her knees to buckle again. "*Adopt* him? Like *forever* adopt?"

"I know, I know. I should have asked you first, but when she told me about his mother I got all excited and thought, maybe we could. Maybe we had a chance. Then I asked her, and she said we had an excellent chance! *Excellent,* Van!"

He paused for a moment to catch his breath, and Savannah saw that he, too, had tears in his eyes. He sniffed, then continued, "But only if you really, really want to. It's a super big deal, I know, and you shouldn't do it just for me. I wouldn't want that. It's gotta be something that you want as bad as I do because—"

He couldn't say any more because she was kissing him, crying, and kissing him again.

"You *are happy*, right?" he managed to gasp when they finally came up for air.

"Ye-e-e-e-s! Ye-e-e-e-s! I'm so dadgum happy I can't stand it!"

"Oh. Good! Then me too!"

Stella "Granny" Reid's youth wasn't the only thing changed by time in tiny, nondescript McGill, Georgia. Except even back in the 1980s, the Southern town still had a way of attracting downright dubious characters—some with a talent for murder.

As quirky as McGill's residents can be, they usually welcome society's oddballs and outcasts into the community with open arms. But the three members of the Lone White Wolf Pack are a different story. Townsfolk aren't feeling the least bit neighborly toward the ignorant gang widely believed to have orchestrated several hate crimes in the area . . .

When the small group's irredeemable leader, Billy Ray Sonner, is found dead in an abandoned motel, most assume it was the result of an accidental overdose. An unfortunate yet predictable end for a man who lived the way Billy did. Only Stella and the sheriff have witnessed the crime scene in person, and the smell of cyanide means something more disturbing happened in that ramshackle room. Something like homicide . . .

While Stella wades through a flood of suspects, uncovered secrets link both Billy's closest allies and respected locals to the incident. One thing is certain—this wasn't an impulsive act of revenge. There's a sophisticated killer on the loose, and Stella must expose deep-rooted fears and dark pasts if she wants to crack a carefully planned murder and stop McGill from descending into chaos.

**Please turn the page for an exciting sneak peek of
G.A. McKevett's
MURDER AT MABEL'S MOTEL
now on sale wherever print and e-books are sold!**

Chapter 1

"Woo hoo! Git a load of Granny!"

"She's got lipstick on!"

"*Red* lipstick! Looks like she's been suckin' on a red lollipop!"

"That's 'cause she's goin' on a date!"

"Granny and the sheriff, sittin' in a tree. K-i-s-s-i-n-g!"

"Yeah, she's gonna get red lipstick all-l-l over his face!"

"Hush up, the lot of you! That'll be quite enough!" As Stella Reid looked around her kitchen table at her snickering grand-angels, she tried her best to fake a frown to go with the command. But, in spite of her best efforts, a grin slipped through.

For a moment, she locked eyes with her oldest, Savannah, and saw the knowing smirk on the child's pretty face. Much to Stella's sorrow, Savannah was mature, far beyond her thirteen years. The residue of having lived her formative years in the household of a mother who made poor choices. Usually, right in front of her children.

The result of those foolish decisions was Shirley paying her debt to society in a Georgia penitentiary and her brood eating all of their meals and sleeping every night in the custody of their grandmother.

Raising seven children was a mighty task that didn't leave a lot of free time for outings of any sort. Let alone of the romantic type.

So, tonight was special. Very special. In fact, it scared Stella to even think what Sheriff Manny Gilford's invitation to dinner and a walk by the river might mean.

"Gran and the sheriff aren't going on a date," Savannah was telling her siblings in a tone that sounded as insincere as that of any grown-up trying to convince children of some falsehood. For their own good, of course. "They're just going to the Burger Igloo for a hamburger, so they can have some peace and quiet to discuss business."

"*Monkey* business!" squealed Marietta, the second oldest. Like her sister, the girl knew far more about activities between the sexes than Stella would have liked, but Miss Mari had none of her big sister's common sense or respect for privacy.

Marietta was, as Pastor O'Reilly would say, Stella's "thorn in the flesh." But being considerably less spiritually minded than the good reverend, Stella simply called Marietta a "pain in the hindquarters." But never to her face.

Like her brother and the rest of her sisters, Mari had been called far too many names, much worse ones than that, by her own mother. Often while dancing at the end of Shirley's belt.

Stella was determined to not repeat her daughter-in-law's mistakes. The children deserved a peaceful, steadfast, loving hand to guide them for the remainder of their childhoods, and she was determined to supply that.

But looking down at her sometimes thorny, pretty much always butt-pain granddaughter, Stella could see the child's mental wheels turning as she considered her next comment. The mischievous sparkle in her eyes warned Stella it would be a doozy.

"I heard what you said to Savannah when the two of you was sittin' out there in the porch swing on her thirteenth birthday." Marietta looked around the table, making sure everyone within earshot was listening. "You told her she was a lady now and had to watch out for boys."

"Marietta, you stop right there, gal. That was a private conversation, and you shouldn't't've been sneakin' around, listenin' with your ears out on stems—"

"Hey, you hear all sorts of good stuff that way!" Marietta shoved a spoonful of carrot slices into her mouth, pushed them to the side of her mouth, like a squirrel filling up its cheek pockets, and continued to talk around them. "You told her they're only interested in one thing and—"

"Don't you say another word, Marietta, or I swear I'll stick you in your bedroom till you're thirty-eight."

"Good idea. Then you won't have to worry about her, and boys, and what it is they're so interested in," Savannah mumbled, buttering her bread.

"What they're so interested in," Marietta continued unsubdued, "is suckin' on your face, then gettin' your clothes offa ya and wrasslin' you onto a bed so they can—"

"Marietta Reid!" Stella was around the table and had a firm hold on Granddaughter #2, thankfully, before she could finish her sentence.

As Stella pulled the girl from her chair and onto her feet, she glanced around the table and saw the startled, wide-eyed expressions on the faces of her four younger grandgirls: Vidalia, Cordele, Jesup, and Alma. She could tell that they sensed they had been about to hear something their grandmother didn't want them to, which, of course, made the missing information fascinating, even unheard.

Savannah, who was seldom rattled by anything or anyone, even Miss Contrary Mari, looked mortified. In Stella's home, such intimate conversations about delicate topics were limited to the front porch swing and only with the older siblings. Stella figured such information was to be disclosed strictly on a "need-to-know" basis.

Her hand tightened around Marietta's arm as she felt the girl trying to pull away from her. Even the pertinacious Marietta knew when she'd gone too far and was about to "get her comeuppance."

Stella led her away from the table and through the humble, shotgun house to the girls' bedroom with its three sets of bunk beds. Turning on a plug-in nightlight, Stella waved a hand toward the top bunk on the far side of the room. Mari's bed.

"Yank off them shoes of yours and crawl up there onto that bed, young lady."

"I ain't tired!"

"Well, I am. I'm plum wore out with your shenanigans. I'm in desperate need of a time-out, so you're fixin' to take one."

Stella gave her a less than graceful boost up onto the bunk, where the girl sat, huffing and puffing like a river toad with a chest cold.

"I didn't finish my supper! I'm still hungry!"

For a moment, Stella considered telling the child she was going to bed without eating the rest of her meal. But Stella couldn't bring herself to exact that particular punishment. She knew far too well how many times her daughter-in-law had sent the children to bed hungry, and it had nothing to do with misbehavior . . . except Shirley's.

In the little town of McGill, Shirley Reid was famous for three things: having more children than she knew what to do with; her addiction issues; and being unfaithful to her long-distance trucker husband when he was out of town, being unfaithful to her.

On rare occasions, when Shirley Reid managed to get her hand on some money, she seldom bought food for her children. Most of her cash was spent on mood enhancers, bought from local dealers on the streets. Her purchases found their way into Shirley's lungs, down her throat, up her nose, and occasionally, in her veins.

No. While Stella's grandchildren had to be disciplined from time to time, she couldn't, wouldn't, deprive them of food.

"I'll stick your plate in the oven and keep it warm till you've had a good, long think about what you said in there and how unsuitin' it was for you to utter such things in front of the little 'uns."

"They're gonna know about it sooner or later," Marietta protested as Stella turned to leave the room.

"Yes, they will. But later's better than sooner, when it comes to matters like that. Let 'em be young'uns as long as they can. They'll have plenty of time once they're grown to fret about grown-up stuff."

"Like whether or not, after y'all get your hamburgers ate, Sheriff Gilford's gonna ask you to go to the motel and do nasty stuff with him?"

Stella caught her breath and whirled back around to face her granddaughter.

In the next few seconds, she prayed the fastest prayer she'd ever offered up to heaven, asking for the fruits of the spirit: love, wisdom, patience . . . and the strength not to jerk a knot in the kid's tail then and there.

She walked over to the bed, reached up, and took her grandchild's hand in hers. Looking deeply into the girl's eyes, Stella could see a bit of fear and was grateful for it. A child who harbored absolutely no fear at all in their hearts was in for a lifetime of troubles and woes. A little old-fashioned trepidation made a body more careful. She was relieved to see Mari had a tad.

Not enough.

But a little.

"My darlin' girl," she said, keeping her voice softer than the feelings coursing through her. "I love you to pieces. You know that I do. You are one of the seven bright stars in my crown and always will be—in this life and when I'm walkin' the streets of heaven, good Lord willin' and I make it there. But when you just said what you did, my heart hurt somethin' fierce. I'd a'thought you'd have more respect for me and for Sheriff Gilford, too, for that matter, to say such a thing. Neither one of us has ever given you any reason to think we'd behave in such a way. It was most unkind of you to suggest that we would, child."

To Stella's surprise, Marietta didn't reply with one of

her ever-ready smart-aleck retorts. Instead, she stared down at her own hand and her grandmother's that was closed tightly around it.

When she didn't answer, Stella added gently, "I do believe that if you apologize to me, you and me both'll feel a heap better."

Marietta drew a deep breath, then looked up at her grandmother. When their eyes met, Stella saw the girl's tears of remorse.

Marietta Reid was feeling remorse! Enough of it to actually make her cry. A little.

Stella's heart soared, borne on the wings of hope for the future! Miracles *did* happen, after all!

"I'm sorry, Granny," she said. "I didn't really think much about what I was gonna say before I spit it out. I was just tryin' to make a funny. I didn't mean to hurt your feelings or make you think I thought you was a wanton woman."

Stella suppressed a chuckle. "*Wanton woman?* Where did you hear the likes of that?"

"Savannah."

"Savannah?"

Marietta shrugged. "She reads too many blamed books."

Laughing, Stella reached up, pulled her granddaughter down from the bunk, gave her a hug and a kiss on the top of her head. "I reckon you've demonstrated genuine repentance for your transgressions. All's forgiven. Just don't do it again."

"I won't." Marietta grinned up at her, the same mischievous smirk that had gotten her in trouble before. "But you talk funny, too, like Savannah. I reckon it's from readin' the Bible too much."

As Marietta stepped in front of her, Stella reached down and gave her a swat on her rear. "You better be glad I do, turkey butt. Sometimes, that's all that keeps me from cleanin' your plow!"

"What's cleanin' my plow mean?"

"Let's just say—you aggravate me like you did, before I've done my daily readin', and you might find out, sweet-cheeks."

Chapter 2

Not for the first time, when eating at McGill's premier dining establishment, it occurred to Stella that the tables in the Burger Igloo were pretty much the same as the one in her own kitchen. But the café's red and chrome, mother-of-pearl "retro" furnishings had been purchased new only a few years ago. They were far less scratched and scuffed than hers, which had been bought shortly after she and Art had been married, back in the fifties, when the dining set had been her pride and joy, the latest in fashionable breakfast sets.

The Burger Igloo's chairs were boring, lacking the character of hers. They weren't split, faded, and stained.

They were "less loved."

Sadly, the restaurant's tables lacked the one unique feature that greatly enhanced the appearance of her "worn to a frazzle" table—the raw plywood extender leaf that enabled a passel of kids to dine at one setting without anybody having to stand at the counter to eat.

Stella had learned that children take a dim view of kitchen counter dining. Any suggestion they should do so produced grumblings of discontent, even among the most well-behaved young'uns.

Yes, the Burger Igloo's tables and chairs were boring, compared to Stella's. But otherwise, the restaurant was nicely furnished with charming décor that was reminiscent of the 1950s: old movie posters on the walls, black-and-white tiles on the floor, the jukebox near the window which, these days, played mostly music by Michael Jackson, Bruce Springsteen, Whitney Houston, and Madonna.

But tonight, Stella was hardly aware of the ambiance of the charming burger joint. She had scarcely even tasted her deluxe burger.

All she could think about was the fellow sitting across from her in the booth.

Although neither Stella nor the sheriff could be considered "youthful" these days, Manny Gilford was a "fine specimen of a man," as Stella's best friend, Elsie, often observed.

"Mighty easy on the eyes, that fella . . . even when he's walkin' away from ya," her neighbor, Florence, had said more than once.

Elsie and Flo weren't the only ones.

Long ago, Stella had noticed that when the sheriff entered a room, every citizen of McGill took notice. Mostly, women gazed longingly at him, taking in his thick silver hair and powerful physique, which was complemented by his freshly pressed uniform, and his face, still as handsome as when he had been in his teens, twenties, thirties, and forties. The women of McGill, Georgia, might have grown up with him, but Manny had always maintained a certain mystique, which garnered adoration from females, appreciation from law-abiding citizens, and grudging respect from lawbreakers.

Stella was proud to be seen with him under any circumstances, let alone one that might, or might not, be considered semi-romantic.

Like the children in her home, Stella wasn't quite sure about the significance of this invitation. Often, he would ask her to accompany him while he was on duty and performing some task for McGillians. But when he had phoned the day before and invited her to have dinner with him, she'd heard a more serious tone in his voice. Maybe even a bit of nervousness, which was completely out of character for an otherwise self-confident man.

Even more confusing was the fact that they had been served ten minutes before, and Manny hadn't eaten more than a bite of his food yet.

Stella was starting to think that, for a man with a ravenous appetite, this was a possible cause for alarm.

As he stared down at his plate, she cleared her throat and said, "Manny, you feelin' all right tonight? You seem like you might be a bit off your feed there."

He looked up at her, his pale gray eyes filled with a level of concern that upset her even further. "No, Stella," he said. "Thank you for asking, but I'm not exactly all right."

Stella's mind raced. So many possibilities occurred to her. With a sheriff, his problem could be almost anything. Heaven only knew what evil might be afoot in the town. Over the years, she'd learned that living in a small town didn't guarantee that everyone inside its borders lived safe, peaceful lives.

He could be troubled about anything from an unpatched pothole to skullduggery of a serious nature.

Maybe somebody had said or done something disrespectful to him. Representing truth, justice, and the American way, as he did, he was often the target of mischief and sometimes genuinely foul play.

Only one week ago, she'd seen him scrubbing the remains of some rotten eggs off the hood of his cruiser.

Or maybe it was she who had done something to offend him. She certainly hoped not.

Sheriff Manny Gilford and his wife, Lucy, had always been close friends of Stella's and her late husband, Arthur. The four of them had made many lovely memories together, having attended high school together and later, as married couples, swimming, boating, and fishing at the Gilfords' lakeside cottage in the summers.

Come winter, they had enjoyed many gentle evenings, playing Monopoly or sitting on the couch, watching the fire blaze, their laps covered with cozy afghans Lucy had crocheted, and listening to oldies from the fifties and the newer hits from the Beatles, Elton John, and Creedence Clearwater Revival on Manny's enormous stereo system.

But all good things come to an end. Manny had lost his beloved Lucy. Then, six years ago, Art had been taken in an accident, working their small farm.

Both widower and widow grieved their losses together, bonding even more closely as friends.

But no more than friends.

Stella knew that Manny wanted to make it more. He had always been so kind to her and hers. He had even been instrumental in helping her gain custody of her grandchildren, when her daughter-in-law had gone to jail on drunk driving and child endangerment charges.

From that moment on, Stella's life was no longer her

own. Taking care of seven kids was a twenty-four-hour-a-day job with no weekends off or vacation time.

Certainly, there was no time for something as distracting and time-consuming as a new man in her life.

Manny understood.

That's why Stella was confused when he asked if he could take her out for dinner. But she had heard a note of urgency in his voice, and she couldn't refuse. He'd sounded strange, like he had something important on his mind.

"Can you share what it is that's botherin' you?" she asked. "If it ain't a private matter of a confidential nature, of course."

He hesitated, and the silence was long and awkward. Finally, he said, still staring down at his plate, "I just can't figure out exactly what this is."

Stella studied the pile of food for quite a while, then shrugged and said, "As I recall, you ordered the meat loaf special." She glanced over at Jean Marie, the short-skirted, big-haired waitress, who was keeping a close and jealous eye on them.

As were most of the ladies in the establishment at that moment.

The townsfolk weren't accustomed to seeing their sheriff engaging in what might be a genuine social interaction with an unattached female. Stella was sure everyone in McGill would be discussing this highly suspicious "tryst" over breakfast tomorrow and expounding an opinion on it.

She returned her attention to Manny and his mystery plate. "I think you got the meat loaf you asked for," she said, "though Jean Marie pert near drowned the poor thing in gravy. Probably meant to impress you. She's carried a torch for you since she was eleven, you know."

Manny didn't seem impressed to hear he was the object of Jean Marie's or anyone else's affections. He looked up at her, and she was concerned to see the worried expression on his face.

"I wasn't talking about the meat loaf, Stella May," he said softly. "I'm talking about this. . . ."

"This *what*?" She tried to understand but had no idea what he meant. "I'm sorry, Manny, but—"

"This, Stella. This . . . us . . . going out to dinner together. Alone."

Stella swallowed, took a quick glance around the room at all the eavesdroppers, and whispered, "Alone, except for the quarter of the town's population that's eatin' in here with us tonight?"

He paused, perused the room, then shrugged. "I don't give a hoot about them right now, and I don't care what's on my plate. I just wish I could figure out. . . . Is this a real 'date' we're on now? Or is this just two old friends having a meal together?"

She sat, flabbergasted and unable to formulate one solitary sentence in her head to answer him.

Finally, she just started to giggle. Far too hard. Much too loudly.

She was further mortified when she realized that she sounded like Marietta after a knuckleheaded boy in her class had asked if he could kiss her behind the bookshelves at recess.

Manny wasn't helping, sitting there, studying her with his gray, piercing policeman's eyes. He missed nothing, and she was wondering what her ridiculous reaction was telling him.

At last, she gained control of herself, other than the occasional, nervous hiccup. "I'm sorry, Manny," she said. "I'm not laughing at you. Truly. It's just that my grandkids were bickering about the same thing as I was going out the door today. Some said I was leaving to have a date with you and others said it wasn't no big deal. Just a burger."

Again, his gaze never wavered as he said, "Well? What did you tell them?"

"I don't recall for sure, but I think I mentioned that Miss Marietta should mind her own business."

"That sounds like your Mari."

She laughed. He chuckled.

Both sounded tense, and Stella didn't like it that they were uneasy in each other's presence. That was unusual for them and most unpleasant.

She decided to be honest with him. Maybe even admit that, although the thought scared her, she had been hoping, deep inside, that it was more than just friends getting together for a burger.

She took a deep breath, and in as soft a voice as she could manage, she said, "To be honest, Manny, I was sorta wonderin' myself. I'm not sure, because I don't know exactly what you had in mind when you asked me."

She watched him start to answer, swallow his words, and then try them once again.

"Since you put it that way," he began, "I'll confess. I was thinking it was more of a date than just a burger between friends. But I wasn't assuming anything. I would've been happy with either—as long as I was with you."

She gave him a shy smile and ducked her head. "I reckon I might as well admit it. I was hopin' you'd say that."

"You were?"

She nodded.

He laughed, loudly enough for the deep sound of it to fill the room and draw even more attention to their table.

"Really?" He leaned closer to her.

"Yes. I think the world of Elsie but . . ." She pointed to her mouth. ". . . I wouldn't wear red lipstick just to eat a hamburger with her."

"I was thinking that!" he said. "When I picked you up, that was the first thing I noticed. I was hoping it was a sign."

She nudged him gently under the table with the pointed toe of her high heel. Actually, Flo's high heels, as she didn't personally own a pair of fancy shoes, high heeled or otherwise.

She continued, "I sure as shootin' wouldn't've borrowed these dadgum shoes that pinch my toes and make my back ache somethin' fierce, just to have breakfast pancakes with Flo."

"Oh, I noticed those, too. Believe me."

"And, hopefully, appreciated them, considering my sacrifice."

"I assure you, they *and you* are much appreciated."

She saw a glimmer in his eye that she had seen before, but not quite so pronounced. She glanced down at her burger to avoid the intensity of his gaze, as well as the way it made her feel.

"Thank you, Manny," she said softly. "I appreciate you, too."

To her surprise, he reached across the table and patted the back of her hand. Just lightly. Only for a second. But it was enough to cause her to draw a quick, sharp breath and feel her knees turn the consistency of a gelatin salad that had been left out on a picnic table, one hot, sunny Fourth of July.

She snuck a quick glance around the restaurant and saw at least ten of her fellow diners suddenly pretend to be fascinated by their dinners instead of their sheriff and whose hand he was patting.

"I'll tell you what," he said. "Since I saw those fancy high heels tonight and how nice you look in them, I'll just hold that memory in my mind, and you don't need to wear them ever again. You don't need to be in pain or even uncomfortable to impress me, Stella May."

"I appreciate that," she said, slipping the heels off under the table. "You have no idea how much. They just ain't me."

She looked up at him and saw he was staring at her lips.

"Wearing lipstick isn't uncomfortable though, is it?" he asked with a grin.

"No. Not a bit."

"Then if you don't mind, and it isn't too much trouble, maybe you could keep wearing that. I must admit, I find it most . . . um . . . appealing."

Despite her best efforts not to, Stella couldn't help recalling what Marietta had said about her getting that red lipstick all over the sheriff's face, and she blushed. Hopefully, not as scarlet as Revlon's shade of Fireball Red on her mouth.

"It's a new stick," she said, when she'd somewhat recovered herself. "I'll only wear it for you, and it'll last forever."

"Maybe not forever," he quickly added.

"We'll see." She nodded toward his plate. "You better eat your supper 'fore it gets cold."

He laughed and picked up his fork, but no sooner had he and she dug into their meals than the bell on the front door rang and an elderly woman rushed in.

"Oh, no," Manny groaned when he saw her. "I already had one run-in with her this morning. I'd hoped I'd be off the hook for a day or two, at least."

As the woman entered the dining area, she looked around the room, her eyes wide with excitement that bordered on hysteria, until she saw Manny.

"It appears Miss Dolly Browning's got herself another emergency of some sort," Stella said under her breath as the woman scurried over to them.

"What else is new? One of those imaginary enemies of hers probably stole her car keys again or got into her refrigerator and drank the last of her milk or cracked one of her eggs."

Stella watched Dolly navigate a crooked path between the tables to get to them. Although Stella had heard she was in her late seventies, she couldn't help thinking Miss Browning appeared older. There was just something about her that suggested she had a lot of mileage on her, more than her years warranted.

Stella could tell that Manny was pretending to be totally focused on his dinner plate, but the newcomer wasn't to be deterred by common courtesy. In her haste to reach him, Dolly lost her balance and stumbled.

No doubt, she would have fallen to the floor if Manny hadn't jumped out of his seat and grabbed her in midtumble.

Stella rose, too, snatched an empty chair from a table nearby, and together, she and Manny eased the woman onto it.

Dropping to one knee beside her, Manny put his hand on the older woman's shoulder. "You gotta settle down there, Miss Dolly," he said, patting her. "Whatever's the matter this time, it's not worth taking a bad fall."

"It's bad, Sheriff," she said, panting. "Very bad, and it took me a long time to find you. I went to your office first, but—"

"That's okay. You found me now," he said. "Just take a deep breath and then you can tell me all about it."

As Dolly struggled to do as he'd suggested and collect herself, Stella looked her over and was surprised to see her so disheveled. Usually, in spite of her infirmities, Dolly Browning was impeccably groomed. But not at the moment. Stella couldn't recall ever seeing her silver hair mussed, her fair complexion so ghastly pale, or her eyes so wild with fear.

Yes, Dolly was prone to having paranoid fantasies, imagining all sorts of persecutions—usually of a minor sort—by unseen ruffians. These "enemies" of hers liked to torment her by moving items in her house around and leaving them in unexpected and inconvenient spots. Sometimes they caused her kitchen sink to leak and her toilet to run. On windy nights, they would bang tree limbs against her windows to frighten her. Worst of all, they frequently stole envelopes containing large sums of money out of her mailbox—cash sent to her from wealthy relatives living abroad.

Or so Dolly believed.

With all her heart.

Every "crime" she promptly reported to the sheriff and heartily expressed her determination that he would find these heinous criminals, arrest them, bring them to justice, and administer a punishment commensurate with their misdeeds.

They deserved capital punishment, she insisted, because who but the worst of the worst would do such things to a poor old woman living alone?

"What's the matter now, darlin'?" Manny asked. "Did they change the channels on your television again?"

"No! No! No!" she shouted. Instantly, the conversation in the restaurant stopped. The room was silent, as everyone turned to stare at her.

But she seemed unaware of them as she grabbed Manny's sleeve and shook his arm. "You have to listen to me, Sheriff," she said. "This is important. Something awful has happened. Not to me. To someone else!"

Stella knew Dolly Browning and her usual rants. This wasn't one of them. Kneeling beside Manny, Stella reached for Dolly's hand and pressed it between her own. It was shaking. Badly. And terribly cold.

"What is it, Dolly?" Manny asked. "Who's in trouble?"

"At the service station."

"Which one?" Stella asked, fearing it was the larger of the two in town, the one belonging to her neighbor. Florence wasn't good at handling bad news.

"The little station at the end of town," Dolly said. "Something terrible happened there. An attack. On Ortez."

"Raul Ortez?" Manny looked surprised.

So did Stella.

Raul was one of the more popular, easygoing citizens of McGill. A gentle, hardworking farmer with a failing farm on the outskirts of town, who managed to keep his head high in spite of his bent back. She couldn't imagine anyone wanting to harm him.

"Someone attacked Raul there at the service station?" Manny asked Dolly again, a bit louder and more insistent than before.

"No!" Dolly said. "Not Raul. His daughter. I can't remember her first name, but—"

"Yolanda?" Stella said, her heart sinking.

"Yes. That's it. The friendly, pretty one with the long black hair."

As industrious as her father, Yolanda Ortez had managed the garage for its absentee owner for the past three years, since she had turned sixteen. She had done a good job of it, too, considering how little she'd had to work with.

Manny looked at Stella, a sick expression on his face. "Long black hair. That's Yolanda all right." Turning back to Dolly, he said, "What's happened to Yolanda?"

"I don't know for sure. But I stopped at the gas station to ask that nitwit who works there with that girl—can't remember his name either, but I hate him—if he'd put some air in my tires for me. But I didn't see him anywhere. So, I walked around to the back, where they work on cars, thinking they might be back there. . . ."

"Yes," Manny prompted her, "and what did you see?"

Dolly shuddered and closed her eyes. "At first I heard them. Shouting. And then their footsteps when they were running away. Then I saw her, that sweet girl, lying on the ground back there, between one of those broken-down cars and a pile of tires. She's hurt, Sheriff. Badly hurt. She isn't dead. I know, because I checked. She has a pulse, and she's breathing. But she has a bad head injury, and I think someone . . . hurt her . . . or tried to. You must go help her! Now!"

But Manny needed no prompting. He had already grabbed Stella's hand, and they were racing toward the door.

Meat loaf specials and burgers deluxe, date or dinner with a friend . . . completely forgotten.